A Fortress Among My People

J.Francis Hudson

A Fortress Among My People

© J.Francis Hudson 2018

Published by
Lighthouse Christian Publishing
SAN 257-4330
5531 Dufferin Drive
Savage, Minnesota, 55378
United States of America

lighthousechristianpublishing.com

In memory of the girl who danced with angels

*With special thanks to Keith, for all your time, patience,
encouragement and computing expertise.*

A FORTRESS AMONG MY PEOPLE

Prologue: The Redactor

PART ONE: WITH THE SONS OF ANATHOTH

Chapter 1	Jeremiah
Chapter 2	Josiah
Chapter 3	Jeremiah
Chapter 4	Ruth
Chapter 5	Jeremiah
Chapter 6	Zephaniah
Chapter 7	Jeremiah

PART TWO: AT THE COURT OF KING JOSIAH

Chapter 8:1	Josiah
Chapter 8:2	Josiah
Chapter 9:1	Jeremiah
Chapter 9:2	Jeremiah
Chapter 10	Huldah
Chapter 11:1	Jeremiah
Chapter 11:2	Jeremiah

PART THREE: IN THE DAYS OF KING JEHOIAKIM

Chapter 12	Jeremiah
Chapter 13	Hilkiah
Chapter 14:1	Jeremiah
Chapter 14:2	Jeremiah
Chapter 15:1	Berechiah
Chapter 15:2	Berechiah
Chapter 16	Jeremiah
Chapter 17	Elnathan
Chapter 18:1	Jeremiah
Chapter 18:2	Jeremiah

PART FOUR: IN THE DAYS OF KING ZEDEKIAH

Chapter 19   Jeremiah
Chapter 20   Zedekiah
Chapter 21   Jeremiah
Chapter 22   Berechiah
Chapter 23:1   Jeremiah
Chapter 23:2   Jeremiah

PART FIVE: IN THE DAYS OF THE GOVERNOR GEDALIAH

Chapter 24   Jeremiah
Chapter 25   Berechiah
Chapter 26   Jeremiah
Chapter 27   Berechiah

Historical Note

PROLOGUE: THE REDACTOR

Night after night I had lain awake brooding over how I might gain entry to the broken city. Now I wanted only to shake its dust from my feet.

The sun had already set; it was the hour when women had gathered on doorsteps to gossip while the men sat beneath their vines and children ran down the streets with sandals flapping. Now the thresholds were empty, the doors hanging off their hinges. Only the ghosts of the unburied dead walked the streets, their chill fingers brushing against my skin, their sightless eyes reproaching me. Even the birds sensed their presence and were silent. When a lone raven took flight at my passing, its sudden noisy indignation scared me half out of my wits.

I had known the living streets like the back of my hand, but now everything looked so different. How would I ever find the house I was searching for? To the north of me the newest, richest quarter of the city was reduced to charred rubble. On Temple Mount, where once the Temple of Solomon and the royal palace had stood, nothing remained but tumbled columns, shattered lintels and ash. Clutching my donkey's halter with taut knuckles I started to walk more quickly.

As the dusk thickened, I was losing my fight against fear. Yet I couldn't have got into the city any earlier in the day. As the scribes have written: a bribe works wonders, and there is little which cannot be accomplished if you know whose palm to grease. Nevertheless, only at twilight, with their bellies full of supper, were the Babylonian sentries ever susceptible.

I knew I should have thought twice before accepting my long-lost cousin's commission, to search out the house he had shared with his master, and from it to rescue the record of the Prophet's extraordinary ministry. It was a hopeless task; looters had removed everything of value before the city was sealed off by order of Nebuchadrezzar the Babylonian king.

Those of Jerusalem's inhabitants who had neither been killed nor taken into exile now eked out a forlorn existence in shanties outside the walls, myself among them. The dregs of society we were, those too poor, too weak or too stupid to be worthy of the conqueror's attention. Certainly *I* was stupid, or I wouldn't have embarked on a wild goose chase like this one.

Then all at once I stumbled upon an imposing residence which matched my cousin's description exactly. Miraculously, the building was almost intact, from its whitewashed walls to the great cedarwood gate which swung open obligingly as soon as I lifted the latch. Marvelling at my unexpected stroke of good fortune, I went through into the courtyard, tied up my donkey, and began to explore.

At first I found everything just as the residents had left it. There were crumpled sleeping-pallets on the bedroom floors, and on a table the remains of a meal which had never been cleared away.

The room which contained the documents, however, had been ransacked. Considerable damage had been done there, either by looters or by the Prophet's personal enemies. But they must have been caught in the act, for although the scroll-chest had been wrenched open, there were still many scrolls inside.

There were also scrolls all over the floor. And tablets. And ostraca. And flakes of papyrus strewn like petals on top of everything. I sat in the midst of the chaos with my head in my hands and despaired.

I should *never* be able to establish what was important and what was not. Son and grandson of scribes as I was, I myself could barely read; I'd rejected the family calling as soon as I could and gone my own rebellious way. Had I not been a feckless waster all my life, I should have been forced into exile along with my relations. As it was, I'd been left behind on Judean soil: I, Joseph, bane of my father's life, left all alone in an altered world... alone, that is, except for my crazy cousin Berechiah, who had walked away from his work in the palace library to follow the Prophet, who was crazier still.

For a long time I'd assumed that the pair of them must have been killed or hived off to Babylon with all the others, since anyone who was anyone had been taken. When at last I had learned that they were still in Judah, the exiles had been gone for many months. Judah no longer had a king, and the man whom the Babylonians had set over us as governor lay dead in a stinking pit. His murderers had vanished; the survivors of the massacre which they had perpetrated were intent on fleeing to Egypt for refuge and I was told that Berechiah and the Prophet were with them.

Lonely and lost as I was, I'd immediately been consumed by an overpowering desire to be reunited with someone, anyone, who was flesh of my flesh, blood of my blood. Yes, Berechiah was crazy and I hadn't seen him for years, but he was alive and I could reach him. So I'd left my squalid shanty and set out in pursuit of the refugees.

I'd caught them up in Bethlehem. They were camped in the wreckage of the town while their leaders suffered a crisis of conscience over taking God's Chosen People back to the land of slavery whence Moses had led their ancestors. I'd entered the camp hoping to persuade my cousin and his master to return with me to what remained of Jerusalem.

But this had proved impossible, because they were being held captive and taken with the refugees against their will. Since the Prophet had come through so much, it was clear that he was under divine protection. Adonai, the Lord our God whose true name is too sacred to be spoken, was looking after his own, and whoever kept close to him would reap the benefits.

I'd managed to see Berechiah briefly - at serious risk to both of us. He'd been shut in a tiny gutted room with his master, who was raving like a drunkard, or so it sounded to me. Berechiah and I had spoken by means of a high window, and through it he'd thrust a parcel of cloth with tablets folded inside. The tablets were covered in minute script, and after filling them, he had written on the cloth itself. These were his notes on the Governor's murder and what had followed; he'd begged me to have them copied for publication so that the truth about these events might become known.

But then he'd gone on to explain to me where the earlier part of his work could be found: the record of his master's ministry in Jerusalem. The whole collection lay rotting in the house which he, Berechiah, had shared with the Prophet during the many years he had served him as secretary. Berechiah had implored me to find some way of entering the city, rescuing his books, and having these read, corrected and published as well.

Me? I'd repeated, incredulous. You imagine that *I* can do that? But he'd only implored me more desperately, kissing my fingers as I'd reached through the little window to grasp his own hand in farewell. So I'd vowed to myself that I *would* do as he'd asked me, since I'd never yet done anything worth while in the whole of my aimless existence.

Now here I was, with my cousin's life's work scattered all about me like so much detritus; and it was nearly dark. Where was I to start? Were the scrolls in the chest the important ones, or might some of those which lay strewn on the ground belong with them? There was nothing I could do but gather the whole lot up and take it back to my shanty... always assuming that the guards would let me out of the city without confiscating my cargo or something worse.

I fetched my donkey's panniers inside the house, and into one of them I put all the scrolls which had been in the chest. Next I spread a blanket on the ground and heaped everything else onto this; I lifted it up by its corners, and into the second pannier I dumped the lot. Then I groped my way through the gloom to the gate by which I'd entered the city.

At one time I would have been praying for all I was worth at a time like this. I would have prayed for Adonai to influence the minds of the guards so that they would let me pass without incident. But no longer. Perhaps it was true that Adonai still cared for the Prophet, I thought, but he certainly cared nothing for the rest of us; either that, or else he had grown weak, and was no match for Marduk god of Babylon who exulted over us.

Yet the guards waved me past, prayers or no, and by the time it was fully dark I was back in my hovel, my donkey tethered outside, and its panniers with their precious contents propped up against one another beside my mattress. I lay down at once and slept until dawn.

I rose with the sun, and applied myself to sorting through the treasure trove of which I was now guardian. But in spite of my sound night's sleep, despair settled upon me again almost straight away. I struggled over the simplest of sentences, and by the end of the day, all I had established was that the collection of scrolls which had been stored in the chest was more or less complete. It seemed that this was the material which Berechiah had been especially anxious for me to make public: the record of his master's prophetic oracles, how, when and why they had been delivered, and how they had been received. But I should never be able to edit it in a thousand years, and as for having it copied and published, there was no one left alive in Judah who would know where to begin.

Then there was all the rest: the nightmare of torn papyri and parchments, broken tablets and potshards which had been thrown around the room. Were these rough notes, which my cousin had meant to discard? Or might they contain valuable information not recorded elsewhere?

The only men capable of helping me decide were languishing in exile half a world away. Exhausted I lay down once more on my mattress and thought of my parents, and my brothers, everyone and everything that I had lost. As the tears ran into my hair and beard I realized that a single course of action lay open to me. Somehow I should have to go and join the exiles.

The next morning I applied to the Commander of the Babylonian garrison for leave to meet up with my relatives abroad, even though I knew that such requests were invariably dismissed out of hand. But fortune continued to favour me, and after several days spent waiting for bureaucracy's wheels to grind, the permit I needed came through. The only proviso I had to accept was that once I had quit my homeland and thrown in my lot with the deportees, I should become as one of them. I should not be allowed to return.

Full of apprehension I packed up my meagre personal possessions, strapped them to my back, and loaded the treasure-filled panniers onto my donkey once again.

The journey was horrendous and I have no wish to describe it here. But it's just as well that I'd misspent my youth, because I had to beg, steal and fight my way through Syria's mountains and forests, and the deserts beyond, until I reached my destination a weary and broken man. Only the welcome I received from my family restored me; when I found my parents and told them that I wished to be a scribe after all, they flung their arms about me and ordered a party to be thrown in my honour, because in the dark night of their banishment a single ray of hope had begun to shine.

Not that life among the exiles was as bleak as I might have supposed. My fellow countrymen weren't being kept in prison, nor even in penury. They had roofs over their heads, and were allowed to use whatever skills they possessed to make a living for themselves. Nebuchadrezzar's policy of deporting the prominent members of subject societies which had rebelled against his rule was designed to prevent further insurrection, not as punishment.

And Babylon is a such a beautiful city, with its crenellated walls, its canals which shine like silver ribbons in the sunlight, its long straight streets lined with palm trees and four-storeyed houses. It has a towering ziggurat and magnificent temples, gleaming tiled gateways, and the palace with its fabulous hanging gardens, designed by Nebuchadrezzar himself. The majestic Euphrates flows right through the city, and the plain on which it is built has the richest soil on earth; *anything* will grow in it, which is why the Babylonians have always sown corn but harvested gold.

The deportees from Judah could have been living prosperously and even happily if they had set their minds to it. But instead they passed their days in futile mourning for what they had lost. Those who were scribes continued to keep their records and edit their documents, but mostly because they had always done so, and didn't know how to stop. There were some who wrote in order to try to reach an understanding of what they had suffered, but the vast majority had lost all sense of direction. Their purpose and meaning were gone.

I, on the other hand, had acquired a sense of purpose for the first time. I apprenticed myself to the Guild of Jerusalem Scholars in Exile, and gave my tutors no peace until I could read and write fluently in both Hebrew and Aramaic, and until I had inveigled half a dozen of the younger and broader-minded among them into helping me edit my cousin's work. Their senior, more conservative colleagues - like my uncle, Berechiah's father - had little time for collections of prophecy. In their opinion prophets were undisciplined, wild-eyed maniacs who cared nothing for tradition or respect. I congratulate myself that I was instrumental in changing their minds.

However, organizing Berechiah's output proved to be no straightforward task even for the men who agreed to work with me. Even the scrolls which had been in the chest were difficult to put into sequence, because we couldn't be sure of what system of arrangement their author had intended.

Yet the oracles themselves had me spellbound. It wasn't so much the beauty of the poetry which impressed me. It was more the message of redemption which pervaded it. According to the Prophet, Adonai was neither weak nor unmoved by his people's plight. On the contrary: he himself had fought against us and led us back into the wilderness deliberately, so that he might woo us there with words of love.

Eventually, once my companions and I had done with these scrolls what we could, we passed on the entire collection to the principal of the Guild himself, for by now I had managed to interest him in what we were doing. I'd shown him the places in the scrolls where the Prophet had spoken of restoration, of a triumphant return to the Promised Land once the lessons which Adonai wanted to teach us had been learned. It is the Principal therefore who has now assumed responsibility for that collection, to restructure it as he thinks fit, and to insert whatever he deems necessary by way of commentary.

But what was I to do with the *rest* of Berechiah's scribblings, the jumble of wax tablets and notes? When I dared at last to wade in to this literary ocean, it emerged that alongside the accounts my cousin had compiled of his master's public ministry, he'd also kept copious records of things which the Prophet had said or done in private. He had chronicled intimate conversations and arguments. He had taken down the words of the laments which the Prophet had sung to himself as he grieved over our ruined world. He'd even found and copied out things which the Prophet must have written down secretly for reasons of his own.

In addition to all of this, there was a wealth of personal detail which my cousin had got by divers means from all manner of other individuals, from highest to humblest: those who had known the Prophet before Berechiah had met him, or who had come across him in different contexts; those who'd served the kings to whom he had ministered, and even some of the kings themselves.

What could Berechiah have been intending to do with all this? Whatever had it all been for? Berechiah had been quite obsessed with his eccentric master, that much at least was clear. And after reading what I've read about the Prophet, I am not surprised. Perhaps Berechiah had been compiling this second account simply for himself, in an effort to understand the man for whom he had sacrificed his career, his family, his inheritance and his very self?

Whether he had or not, I found that I could not simply set this hoard aside. The Lamentations I've had my colleagues compile; as for the remainder, its presentation has been left entirely to me.

I do not know if I am doing right by my cousin, foisting upon the world his private thoughts and those of his master and others. I cannot ask him now; reason tells me that he and the Prophet are both long since dead in the Egyptian desert.

Yet I do know that Berechiah wanted to leave his mark upon this earth. He attached himself to the Prophet as his scribe because this was how he felt he could best make his life count for something. Neither Berechiah nor his master had sons through whom their names might live on.

I don't know if this is the *way* in which my cousin would have liked the material to be presented, either, letting the folk he questioned or to whose diaries he had access speak for themselves. But I wanted to alter as little as possible. This is Berechiah's book, not mine, and the one voice which should not be heard speaking through it is my own. I present it here in my cousin's memory, and in memory of the great man he loved.

PART ONE

WITH THE SONS OF ANATHOTH

Foetid and foul are the sins of Jerusalem;

> *Feculent wickedness makes her unclean.*

With her own filth she has soiled her garments,

> *Heedless of where her excesses might lead.*

Now, dressed in rags, Zion begs by the roadside,

> *But no one is there to allay her distress.*

Adonai is righteous, his statutes unchangeable.

> *Yet we rebel, and suppose ourselves free.*

Lamentations 1:8, 9, 17,18

CHAPTER 1: JEREMIAH

It was midday, midsummer, and the sultry air hung heavy as a cloak over the jumbled peasant dwellings of Anathoth. Inside the mudbrick houses, or in the makeshift shelters on the rooftops, men and women slept and sweated. Among the dusty tamarisk trees even the cicadas were drowsing. In a patch of shade a knot of small boys squatted at play, too engrossed in their game to think of sleep. A couple of goats nuzzled at their necks, not wanting to feel left out.

I was left out, however. I was always left out. I hovered at a distance, watching them through the curtain of my hair. They were playing Dice and Dare, their favourite; I'd watched often enough to know the rules. Each boy throws a pair of dice, and if any throws a double six he sets a dare for the one who has thrown the lowest. Each challenger seeks to outdo the last in the wittiness or originality of the dare he invents.

Today, one boy had been made to recite a prayer to the goddess Anat while standing on his head. Another had had to crawl around the outside of the circle of players braying like a donkey. Most of their games of dare began like this, harmless enough, and noisy with laughter. Usually they got nastier the longer they lasted.

Then one of the players noticed me.

'Hey, Samuel, what are you staring at?' he called out, so that his companions looked up together, and sniggered, some more nervously than others. 'Go away, before you bring us bad luck.'

'Yes, Samuel, go and play with your demons!' jeered a second; and the rest joined in, bleating like so many sheep: Samuel, Samuel, Samuel, get lost.

I took a step backwards, wanting with all my heart to shout: my name *isn't* Samuel. But I didn't have the courage. I didn't even know why that was the nickname they had picked for me. If only I could have found it within myself to say: I just want to be one of you, to *belong*. Why don't you ever invite me?

Yet I knew full well why they didn't. Though time and again I had sought to win them with figs or dates or honey cakes from my lunch, they wouldn't even take my gifts. They were as scared of me as I was of them.

Then one voice rose above the bleating of the rest, as the calling of a shepherd is heard above the flock. It belonged to Hanamel my cousin, son of my father's brother Shallum. 'Perhaps our shy little friend would like to play with us?' he suggested, but my heart didn't leap because there was something horrid in the way that he said it. All of his sheep looked from me to him, for whenever he spoke his playmates listened, and hung on his every word.

However, none of them approached to draw me in. They shuffled uncomfortably, and shuddered if their eyes chanced to lock with mine. Eventually one of the braver ones said, 'Han, he won't play properly. I never even saw him steal a sparrow's egg.'

'Yes, Hanamel,' piped another, emboldened by the first. 'He's a coward, and he has a devil in him. Make him go away.'

But Hanamel waved his hand for silence, and beckoned me closer. I began to wish that I'd run away when they'd told me to, or that my fringe might veil my whole body.

'Come on, then,' he barked impatiently. 'If you want to join in, join in.' And the others moved apart reluctantly to let me sit down, squirming still further away when I'd taken my place. Two of those present were my own younger brothers, yet not even they would meet my gaze. They were six and five years old respectively, and already bigger than me although I was seven. But if I looked at them they would wince as though death itself had stared them in the face.

The game recommenced; the dice came to me, and I threw a three and a four. I bit my lip in relief, for I should neither have to dare nor be dared. The boy next in line threw double one, and blamed it on me; he forced one of the youngest children to change places with him. The next half dozen rounds saw me safe just like the first.

But as ever, the dares began to get tougher. Run to the market and steal a piece of fruit before the stall-holder wakes; climb up the steps to someone's roof and put dung on a blanket laid out to air; snatch the flagon of wine from the dissolute priest in the square who will tan your hide if he catches you.

When this latter prize had been won, the boys swiftly poured its contents down their own throats. Those who got the most wound up drunk; the others pretended that they were. Hence the dares grew crueller still. Throw stones through an old widow's window. Catch a mouse, or even a snake, and squash its head in your hand.

Then Hanamel threw double six, to my double one. At once the boys were laughing and shouting, jumping up and recommending the direst forfeits they could think of, all at the tops of their voices. I cringed, and crouched with my hands to my ears, while they mocked me and crowed that I wouldn't even pull one leg off a spider.

Hanamel simply waited until the well of their vicious ideas had run dry. Finally he said, 'Samuel, you must go to the edge of the village, to the place by the road where the old blind woman sits with her granddaughter to beg. Sneak up and grab what she has in her bowl, and bring it to me.'

A cloudburst of disappointment rained down on him. What a wasted opportunity! *Anyone* could do that; the tiniest tot of three could do it. Since I had a demon to help me, I should be made to jump from a high roof into the street at very least - wasn't it true that devils could fly?

Yet Hanamel was no fool. He was well aware that the boys' taunting might prompt me to risk my own neck to prove myself brave as the best of them. But the old blind woman and her granddaughter were all alone in the world, and if they could not get enough to eat by begging, the little girl would have to be sold to the sanctuary. *Everyone* knew what *that* meant.

Everyone except for me, that is. I knew there were

shrine-girls, and shrine-boys too, who slept by day and worked at night. But I didn't know what their work was.

I stood up, my throat dry as a locust's corpse, and began to walk in the direction the boys were pointing. I meant to keep going until they were out of sight, then slip away home. But Hanamel called after me, 'Wait for *us*, Samuel! Surely you want your *friends* to go with you? I'm sure you'll be braver if we are there too.' He came up behind me and took hold of my right elbow, motioning one of the others to take my left. But in this alone they were unwilling to obey him. My devils might be catching.

Still, Hanamel by himself would have been strong enough to wrestle me to the ground if I'd tried to make a run for it. Nauseous with heat and dread, I walked beside him until we stood before our victim; she sensed our presence and held up her bowl expectantly. But the mat-haired and flea-ridden little girl, who was of an age with the younger of my brothers, saw what we were about. She backed away, tugging at her grandmother's rags.

More than anything else I wanted to steal the few copper pieces and grains of corn in the bottom of that bowl, so the gaggle of watching boys would accept me. Only I knew that the voice that spoke inside my head wouldn't allow it. It wasn't speaking yet, but I felt its presence like a bird on my shoulder. The longer I stood, the worse the conflict inside me grew, until I could stand it no longer.

Reaching into the pouch at my waist, I pulled out my uneaten lunch and threw it in the blind woman's lap. Sick with self-loathing I tore away up the street, running as though a bull were after me.

'Coward! Yellow-belly! Lily-liver!' the boys shouted from behind, and a well-aimed pebble grazed my leg as it shot past. But I heard no pounding feet; what with the heat and the wine, they couldn't be bothered to give chase.

Their taunts still ringing in my ears, I ran home with tears pouring down my cheeks. It hurt so much when they laughed at me; I could never ignore them, whatever anyone said.

My mother was asleep by her quern in the yard; she woke at my mewling but offered no comfort. 'So my firstborn son is weeping like a girl again,' she rebuked me. 'When are you going to grow up, Jeremiah? When are you going to make your poor parents proud of you? Your little brothers don't carry on like this, do they? Have you no shame?'

She didn't expect me to answer her questions, so I didn't. I knew she was cross at being woken, but she wouldn't have dried my tears had she been wide awake already. I'd overheard her so many times haranguing my father about me. 'What hope is there for that boy?' she would demand, throwing up her hands. 'What good will he ever be? Hilkiah, I can't believe he's ours sometimes. And that voice he hears. I wish to God he wouldn't talk about it. I once knew a girl who heard voices; they told her to go and drown herself, and she did.'

'Give him time, my dear, give him time,' my father would respond placidly. Then she would storm away and pound up some herbs to vent her frustration. If truth be told, I knew *she* was frightened of me, too. I could read it written in her eyes, just as I'd read Hanamel's hate. I used to think that everyone could read the feelings of those they looked at.

So I ran back out of the yard and into the street once more. I decided that I would go up from the village to the high place where the sanctuary was, where my father served as a priest. Our village was full of priests; although it was in the territory of the tribe of Benjamin, it had been set aside in the beginning to be occupied solely by the tribe from which priests were drawn. This was the tribe to which my own family belonged: the descendants of Levi.

I was hoping that my father would be at the sanctuary now, but knew that I wouldn't much mind if he wasn't. I loved the place for itself; it was quiet, hallowed by centuries of ritual, and you could sense the other world there, the world of gods and spirits. I often explored the lonely ridges round about, walking among the olive groves and the sparse woodlands, gazing down into the haze of the Judean desert beyond. Anathoth perched on the very boundary between all that was green and alive, and everything arid, barren, red as blood; it existed on the brink of a hungry abyss and sometimes I felt that I did too. When the expanses of rock and sky were too much for me, I would go inside, creeping through the caves and the ancient buildings of the holy precinct. I'd found a chamber so obscure, so dark and dusty, I called it my secret room. It was half under ground, and you had to crawl on your hands and knees to get in. Today, if I couldn't find my father, I would go there, where no one could poke fun at me.

But to reach the sanctuary I should have to pass through the village. I chose the remotest way, keeping to the shadows round the backs of the houses, praying that Hanamel and his boys wouldn't spot me. And my voice said: *Don't be afraid, Jeremiah. I shall not let them harm you. You are set apart. You are mine.*

'I don't *want* to be set apart!' I retorted, still in tears. 'I want to be like *them!*'

No you don't, said the voice. *They are mean, callous and spiteful. You will never be like that.* So angry did this make me that I ran right into a toddler grubbing in the dirt by the road; his sister who was minding him made a sign against the evil eye before scooping him up in her arms.

Once I'd arrived at the high place I began to feel better. Its tranquillity reached out to me; the swaying olive trees whispered the consolation denied me by my own mother, and the standing stones spoke of permanence, eternity, imperturbable strength. On the platform, open to the dome of the heavens, where offerings were made, a thin wisp of smoke still spiralled skywards from the altar where some small creature had forfeited its life. To either side stood an Asherah pole, the sign of the Mother, and a shrine to Adonai.

I found my father in one of the storerooms, polishing bronze libation vessels. He saw I'd been crying, but simply shook his head, and gave me a job to do trimming lampwicks. I was grateful, and settled to my work; I enjoyed helping out, it made me feel grown up. One day I would serve as a priest as well. Then everyone would have to respect me.

Most of the older priests treated me kindly already, and had grown quite used to my visits. A few had tried to befriend me; one in particular I had begun to trust, though he was long dead now. Once upon a time he'd dried my eyes when some other boys had made me cry, and he'd whispered to me that in days gone by, *all* men had heard voices, and only begrudged me mine out of jealousy because the gods no longer spoke to them. As for my having a demon, the word had only come into our language since we'd started to consort with Assyria and Babylon.

The younger priests had little time for me, however. It was they who had to conduct the routine rituals, whilst the young prophets burned herbs to enable them to leave their bodies and search for lost objects or go spying on behalf of their clients. There was never any shortage of the latter; Anathoth was famous for its sacred history. Its name in full was Beth Anathoth, House of Anat, for the place had once belonged to Anat the goddess of love and war. By my time you could pray there to Anat or Astarte or Asherah or Adonai as you thought fit. One or two of the strictest priests harped on the good old days when righteous King Hezekiah ruled, and all cults were banned except Adonai's. But few people took any notice.

As for my father, I knew he was happy with things as they were. Live and let live was his motto: Adonai is the god of our ancestors, but the Baals and their consorts were blessing the harvests of the Canaanite Earth Folk long before Moses brought us here out of Egypt. And why shouldn't women have a goddess to turn to, as we men have a god? Asherah, Astarte, Anat... her name matters not. Nor does it make sense to insult foreign deities when Judah is vassal to a foreign power, the mighty Empire of Assyria, rendering our god subservient to theirs. Even in Jerusalem the gods of Emperor Ashurbanipal must be recognized.

Not that we talked about Jerusalem very much. Some of the priests' hackles would rise at the mere mention of the city's name. For the forefathers of the Anathoth priests had served there in Adonai's Tabernacle before King Solomon had built his great Temple, until one of them, Abiathar, had backed a rival of Solomon for Judah's throne. Abiathar had been High

Priest, but Solomon banished him and his kinsfolk to Anathoth and appointed one Zadok as High Priest in his place.

Once the vessels were polished and the lampwicks trimmed, my father bade me help him carry what was needed to the shrine. Here, a grouchy-looking middle-aged man was waiting to consult him; Father showed me where to position each item while he enquired of the surly stranger what he wanted. It emerged that the fellow's wife was infertile, and innumerable prayers and sacrifices had achieved nothing. Forgetting that I was there going about my task in the shadows, Father began to talk to him about the shrine-girls; perhaps a night spent with one of them might encourage the Baals to make his marriage fruitful? There were several girls whose attributes he wouldn't hesitate to recommend...

And as he proceeded to describe them I left off what I was supposed to be doing and listened, open-mouthed. Creeping closer so that I might not miss any of Father's words, I knocked over a pottery lamp. It smashed in pieces, its oil running over the floor, and Father started as he was abruptly reminded of my presence.

'You clumsy boy!' he barked, taking out on me the anger he felt at himself for allowing me to hear such talk. 'Go outside! Go home! No, don't try to clear up your mess, you'll only make it worse. You aren't fit to handle holy things.'

I gulped, and nodded, and ran out into the sunshine; it hurt my eyes because the shrine had been so dark. It wasn't like my father to be sharp with me; it occurred to me to wonder briefly if he suddenly felt ashamed of some of the things that went on at his sanctuary in the name of religion.

But I didn't want to go home. So I slipped back inside the sanctuary buildings, feeling my way down rough-hewn steps and along darkened passageways between wine-cellars and storerooms, making for my secret place. However, as I approached, the tunnels got lighter instead of darker, and I heard talking. Flattening myself against a wall, I picked out two voices, the first being that of one of the oldest priests, and the other belonging to a young woman.

'Are you *sure* he will be safe here?' she was asking, in

a fearful half-whisper.

'Yes, quite sure. No one uses these rooms. You may stay here with him if you so desire, my lady. You are most welcome. Most welcome indeed.'

'How I wish I could, Simeon. But it is impossible. As for the boy, I shall tell his father that he has run away. There is nothing else I *can* say. My husband's soldiers will look everywhere for him nevertheless. People may die. But what else is to be done?' Her voice wavered; she was near to tears.

'Please, you need not be afraid, my lady,' the old priest reassured her. 'No one will think to search for him in this place. Of those few men who have been told that the boy is here, I alone know who he is. I shall say nothing; I would die first. I despise the Ammonites and their gods. Molech is an abomination. Now, let us go.'

'You aren't going to leave him *alone* down here?'

'I shall visit him frequently but I cannot stay with him, my lady. You must understand: I should be missed. Suspicion would be aroused. He will be well fed, and a guard will be posted at the entrance to these cellars. I'll see to it at once.'

Then the woman said to someone else, 'Be brave, my darling. This will all be over soon. Just a few days, I am sure. Then your father will be missing you so dreadfully he'll put this terrible idea out of his mind. Remember: I love you.'

The light they'd brought with them flared up; their torch had been lifted from its bracket. I held my breath as the wall opposite changed from uniform black to a patchwork of light and shade, cracks, knobbles and flaking plaster... they were coming my way! I was standing in a narrow side-passage, however, and they went past without seeing me.

I saw them, though. I even felt the current made by the swish of the young woman's skirts, and glimpsed gold beneath the plain black robe swathed about her. I waited until the sound of their footfalls had ceased and their light gone, then crept out of my side-passage and turned in the direction they had come from.

The closer I came to my secret room, the more light there was again. Two small oil lamps gleamed beside the very entrance. I hesitated outside, but only for a moment. Then holding my breath again I dropped to my knees and crawled through the hole which served as a doorway. Shaking my fringe from my eyes, I gasped in astonishment.

My room had been sumptuously furnished, complete with a padded mattress spread with furs, tapestries on the floor and walls, and a table with a silver water jug and food bowl. There were so many lamps cheerfully burning that I saw niches in the walls and carvings on the rough ceiling which I'd never seen before. And sitting cross-legged on the bed, looking as astonished as I felt, was a boy the same age as me, holding a very sharp knife trained on the tip of my nose.

He lowered his weapon uncertainly upon realizing that the intruder was a mere boy like himself. Then for some while we stared at one another without speaking. He was solidly built like Hanamel, but his features were fine and his expression guileless and fresh. He didn't seem in the least frightened of me, neither on the other hand did he seem to find my appearance repugnant. It was so extraordinarily thrilling for me to be able to hold any boy's gaze for longer than a second, that I didn't at first take in how richly dressed he was, nor did I notice the gem-encrusted rings on his fingers or the great golden medallion about his neck.

Eventually he asked me who I was, and what business I had in the sanctuary cellars. I told him that I was Jeremiah ben Hilkiah, son of one of the priests. Then I added, 'You need not tell me your name, because I know it's meant to be a secret. You're being hidden here because your father wants to punish you. Well, you needn't fear anything from me. I won't give you away, though what you've done must be very dreadful.'

'I have done *nothing* dreadful, and I'm *afraid* of nothing!' he snapped at me, eyes flashing; I saw their candour and through them his pride, and decided at once that he spoke truly. Then he must have repented of his outburst, for he continued more evenly, 'It's my mother who's afraid - of everything. She exhorts me to have faith in Adonai, yet she will scarcely let me out of her sight even within our own palace!

She sees kidnappers behind every pillar, and demons inside every statue, all because my father's father was King Manasseh, and... Jeremiah? What is the matter?'

My jaw must have dropped so far, I could have swallowed a frog. When I'd told him that he need not give me his name, he must have assumed that I knew it already. So I croaked with the little voice I could muster, 'You are Prince Josiah ben Amon, son of His Majesty the King and the Lady Jedidah? Oh my lord, Your Highness, forgive me...' I could not fall to me knees since I was already on them, so I pressed myself to the floor in a full prostration.

My grovelling prompted a peal of royal laughter, which Josiah quickly stifled as he remembered he was supposed to be in hiding. 'Get up, Jeremiah. There are neither princes nor paupers down in these dungeons. Probably just rats, and lots of them.' I felt his hand on my arm, and raised my head to assess the expression on his face. It was still lit by laughter, but a kindly laughter, nothing like that of Hanamel or those who copied him. He kept pulling at my arm until I got to my feet and brushed down my tunic nervously.

I said, 'I'll go now, my lord. On my father's honour, I won't breathe a word about you, to anyone.'

'Oh, please don't go. I shall be so lonely in this horrible place. Since you already know I'm here, it can do no harm for you to stay and talk with me a little longer. Come, sit beside me.'

I thought I must be dreaming. No other boy had ever wanted to talk to me, and here was the heir to the throne of Judah bidding me sit on his bed. Still, he didn't yet know that I was mad. I wondered how long I could keep him from finding out.

Gingerly I lowered myself onto the mattress. 'That's better,' he announced with satisfaction. 'Now, tell me all about yourself, and where you live. I get so tired of fawning noblemen and their pampered sons. It must be good to live out here in the country and have the freedom of all these hills and valleys to explore. I can't go *anywhere* on my own.'

'I suppose so.' I shrugged my shoulders. I *did* love the

hills and valleys, but thought I would be happy if I never had to spend another moment alone in my entire life.

'Come on, now. You needn't be shy,' he encouraged me. 'What *do* you do with your days? Do you help on your father's farm?'

'My father doesn't have a farm. He's a priest here at the high place. We earn our living from the offerings made by pilgrims, and those due to us as Levites.'

'So no one here grows crops at all? I thought everyone outside of Jerusalem was a farmer.'

'Levites aren't allowed to work the soil. We can keep sheep and goats; my father has some, but his brother Shallum takes care of them.'

'I thought it was the boys who took care of the flocks. Like my ancestor King David did, when he was a boy.'

'Sometimes they do... I mean, *we* do.' I didn't want him to know that my uncle wouldn't let me anywhere near his precious animals.

'Will you be a priest too, when you grow up?'

I smiled a half smile, embarrassed. 'I hope so. But there is so much to learn. I must know how to read and write as well as how to offer sacrifices at the right time and in the right way.'

'You should come and study in Jerusalem. The priests at the Temple know *everything*.'

'Oh no, my lord. I couldn't. The priests here won't even speak to the ones in Jerusalem. In Jerusalem they don't approve of our standing stones or our Asherah pole.'

Josiah laughed out loud again. 'Then you have never been to Jerusalem, have you? My grandfather Manasseh put idols in the very Temple, *and* an Asherah pole. My father himself worships foreign gods. That's why I'm here. He doesn't want to punish me. He wants to sacrifice me.'

'Sacrifice you?' I gaped at him, uncomprehending. 'What do you mean, my lord?'

'Exactly what I say. And stop calling me your lord. My friends call me Josiah. Go on. Say it.'

'Yes, my... I mean...' But I *couldn't* say it. I hung my

head and looked at my hands, which were fidgeting in my lap of their own accord.

Spontaneously he threw an arm about my shoulders. 'Don't worry, Jeremiah. I won't be killed; I'll be safe down here with you. Cheer up. Smile again, like you did before.'

Mortified, I attempted to oblige him. I wondered what it must be like, to assume that everyone liked you and was concerned about you, when for me it was the opposite. Perhaps it *made* people like you. Certainly I liked Josiah.

'You see,' Josiah prattled on, 'Everyone thinks that my father worships Egyptian gods, because Amon is an Egyptian name. But it was given to him after the Assyrians conquered Thebes, the Egyptian city where Amon is chief god. Manasseh called him Amon because he wanted to show the Assyrians that Judah was happy to be in submission to Assyria just like Thebes was, so that he could keep Judah prosperous. My father himself prefers to worship Molech, the god of the *Ammonites*, another people altogether. He's a very powerful god, they say, if you can gain his favour. But the only way to do that is to have your firstborn son pass through the fire at the Tophet. You have to give him to the god.'

Josiah paused, peering at me to see if I knew what he meant. I whispered, 'Your father wants to *kill* you? As a burnt offering to Molech?'

'He doesn't *want* to. He believes he has no choice. He has many enemies. He needs a powerful god on his side.'

'But - you are a descendant of David. Surely you belong to Adonai.' I think this was the first time it seriously occurred to me that perhaps it *did* matter which god you worshipped. The notion was profoundly unsettling, for like all children I'd assumed that my father was always right.

'I know. I don't really understand it either. My mother worships Adonai; she even keeps her own prophet at court, who will have nothing to do with other gods. He's called Zephaniah, and is himself of royal blood. That's the only reason my father allows him to stay.'

'Doesn't your father love you at all?' My pity for Josiah was making me bolder; but I'd asked the wrong question.

Josiah jerked his arm away.

'Of course he loves me!' he lashed out. 'And I love him! He's tall, and proud, and strong. He's the best father in the world!' Then he swallowed very hard and mumbled, 'But he has a bad temper, Jeremiah. Just like I have. He decides things when he's in a bad mood, and then he's too proud to go back on his word. And he *does* have dangerous enemies... *Now* what's the matter?'

'I - I'm sorry, my lord. I didn't mean to insult your father. I don't know why I said such a stupid thing.' I clasped my hands together in anguish. 'Can you forgive me?'

His anger passed as swiftly as it had come. 'I know,' he said. 'I know you didn't mean it. But I'll only forgive you if you call me Josiah. Say: please forgive me *Josiah.*'

'Please forgive me Josiah,' I repeated obediently, as if chanting my part in a litany; then both of us laughed as one. I suppose it came naturally to him, to have people obey him. When we'd grown serious again I said, 'I really should go now. *My* father may start to search for *me*, and your secret could get out.'

'Will you come again tomorrow?'

'I'm - not sure.' I still couldn't believe he would want me to.

'I won't let you go unless you promise me,' he said, but added at once, 'No, that isn't fair. You have friends of your own. You'll be wanting to play with them.'

'No, I won't,' I began, then checked myself because I didn't want him to think I had no friends, lest he discover *my* secret and all would be ruined.

'Sometimes I'd love to be able to play in the street like ordinary boys do,' he said wistfully. 'Tell me about the games you play, before you go, Jeremiah. Tell me the names of your friends, and those of their brothers and sisters.'

I really wanted to lie to him, to make up names and describe imaginary adventures I'd had with their fictitious owners. But I couldn't, any more than I'd been able to empty that pathetic begging-bowl.

So I looked at my hands again and muttered in spite of

myself, 'I don't have any friends, Josiah.'

'I don't believe it. Why ever not?'

And when I didn't reply, he tilted my chin up to make sure I wasn't crying. He looked so mystified, so uncondemning, that I blurted, 'Oh Josiah, if I can keep a secret about you, can you keep one about me?'

'Of course.'

'That's to say... it isn't really a secret, because it's something everyone knows. Only I try not to talk about it any more, so that one day they may forget...'

'Just tell me, Jeremiah.' He grasped my hands. 'I promise I won't say anything, and I won't hate you, whatever it is.'

'I have a demon,' I whispered, feeling the blood rushing to my face. I tried to turn away. But he wouldn't let me.

'A demon? Whatever do you mean?' He hadn't even flinched!

'It lives inside me.' I was speaking so quietly, so hoarsely now that I could barely hear myself above the tumult in my head and the pumping in my veins. Forcing myself to go on, I stammered, 'It - shows me things. Like what is going on in other people's minds. And it talks to me when I'm on my own. I can hear its voice out loud.'

'Really? What does it say?'

His question floored me. No one had ever reacted like this, with interest, not fear, as though I'd said I had a pet snail or something else unusual but harmless. I answered less cautiously, 'It says I'm special. Kind of - chosen.' But I didn't know how to explain any more.

'What do you suppose it means?' Josiah pressed me. 'Chosen for what?'

'I don't know. But it won't let me do things other boys do.'

'What sort of things?'

'Horrid things. Robbing birds' nests, or hitting girls, or calling out names when they see a bald man or someone crippled...'

'*That's* the sort of game they play in your village?' exclaimed Josiah, and he sounded so shocked that all at once I decided I should never again want to do such things as long as I lived. 'It's a funny kind of demon if it won't let you do *bad* things, Jeremiah. A proper demon wouldn't let you do *good* things.'

There was no reply I could make to this; I'd simply never thought of it before. So Josiah enquired, 'Do the village boys do horrid things to *you* because of it?'

'Sometimes. They call me names whenever they see me.'

'What do they call you?'

'Samuel mostly, though I don't know why.' I shivered as I spoke, because the name was hateful to me, and I felt I'd stained my own lips by using it.

Josiah laughed. 'You must know why! You're the son of a priest, and you don't know the story of Samuel?'

It was my turn now to grow angry, because he seemed to be mocking me just like everyone else did. What a fool I'd been, to let him find out about my madness after all, and so quickly too. I hissed in my fury, 'I *don't* know the story. I don't know *anything!*'

'Oh Jeremiah, I'm sorry. I didn't mean it like that.' My hands were still held in his; he squeezed them briefly and it was so, so wonderful to receive even the slightest token of affection from anyone that my anger melted like snow in springtime. He explained patiently, 'Samuel was a boy who lived long ago, before my ancestor David was king; before there even *were* kings in Judah. He served at the chief sanctuary of Adonai, and once he heard Adonai's voice speaking to him in the middle of the night. Perhaps it's a *god* you are hearing. It could even be Adonai himself, my mother's god, the god of our forefathers Abraham and Moses.'

All of a sudden I began to feel giddy and peculiar, unbearably light-headed. From an enormous distance Prince Josiah's voice was asking anxiously, 'Jeremiah, are you all right? Are you going to faint?'

He pushed my head between my knees, but even so, it

was a very long time before I felt anything like myself again. Contrary to all my inclinations I had conceived a desperate need to be on my own, but even when I stood up to leave, my legs were like a new-born foal's. Josiah begged me not to go lest I collapse somewhere in the maze of corridors and never be found, but I promised him faithfully that I would return the following day, and crawled on all fours out of the chamber. Staggering down the passageways, I noticed at the last moment the guard posted at the entrance to the cellars, and managed to find my way to the outside world by a route I don't think anyone else knew. To my amazement I discovered it was dusk already.

I stumbled home in a daze. So many things, both terrible and wonderful, had happened to me in one day. My mother scolded me when I got in, demanding to be told where I'd been all this time, but I let her curses wash over me and went straight to bed without supper. I wanted the night to be over as quickly as possible, so that I might return to the sanctuary and visit my royal friend. It was the first time I ever remember looking forward eagerly to the coming of a new day.

At first light I grabbed some small loaves of bread and a handful of roasted grain, since I must have something to offer Josiah as a present. Then I ran to the high place before anyone was awake enough to stop me.

But when I arrived, Josiah was gone. The lamps were gone, the furniture was gone, everything was as though yesterday had never happened. I stood a moment, bewildered, then flung myself on the ground in despair, the loaves rolling away out of their pouch into the empty darkness. So mad had I become, that I must have imagined the entire episode.

I curled up on the hard stone floor where the tapestries and mattress and cushions had been, and cried my heart out.

CHAPTER 2: JOSIAH

When I was seven years old, my father the King tried to have me killed. Before I was nine it was he who was dead, and I was king in his place.

Naturally I had always known that one day the throne of Judah would belong to me. I'd been brought up from babyhood to be worthy of it; at three years old I could stand or half a morning without fidgeting or scratching or soiling myself. I was firstborn son of a firstborn son - or so I thought - and my grandfather had been none other than Manasseh, the longest-reigning monarch Judah had ever known.

However, I'd never dreamt I would become king in the way that I did. I'd imagined for myself a glorious public coronation with choirs singing, and thousands of my subjects acclaiming me. Not blood and confusion, figures rushing at me from the dark, scooping me up half asleep and depositing me on David's seat, ramming his crown on my head, shoving his sceptre into my hands and breaking the flask of balsam oil over my brow before anyone else could get there first.

Nor had I any idea it would happen so soon. My father was young, healthy and virile. He had ascended Judah's throne at the age of twenty two, and when I'd listened to the courtiers at his coronation blessing him with the traditional benediction, 'May my lord the King live for ever,' I had truly believed that he might.

At first I didn't realize that he was dead. No one had thought to tell me. I suppose they'd assumed that I *would* realize, from the very fact of my being huddled there, rubbing sleep from my eyes, on the throne where he had so recently sat. But I didn't understand. I watched bewildered while people came and went in the shadows, addressing each other in hoarse whispers.

'What is happening? Tell me! Tell me!' I called out, twisting about on the seat where they'd dumped me and trying to snatch at the clothing of those who brushed past. But nobody took any notice; I might as well not have been there.

In the end I climbed down from the throne and marched across the room to where a bunch of ruffians had formed themselves into a makeshift guard. I homed in on the nearest of them, tugged on his tunic and said in my most imperious voice, 'If I am king, I want to be told what is happening. I *order* you to tell me. Where is my father? Where's my mother?'

But no one seemed to know what to say; all at once they must have appreciated how young I was, and how unprepared.

Someone fetched Zephaniah, the prophet my mother kept at court to instruct herself and me in the ways of Adonai. He was barely ten years my senior, but he came and held my hand like an elderly uncle, and did his best to calm me.

'Your mother is quite safe, my little lord,' he assured me. 'You must not be afraid.'

'But what of my father? Zephaniah, where is Father? Why isn't he here, sitting on his throne?'

Zephaniah held my head between his hands and said quietly, 'Your father is dead. But do not fear, for his murderers are dead too. His blood is avenged.' Then the young prophet knelt at my feet and said, 'Hail to Your Majesty, King Josiah of Judah. May my lord the King live for ever.'

For the first time since being weaned, I burst into tears. I didn't want to be king. My beloved father, handsome, proud King Amon was dead, he whose very shadow I had worshipped. When he'd snapped his fingers, men had come running; women had swooned for his beauty. He'd had formidable enemies, I knew that; this was why he'd felt it necessary to present me to Molech. Now I was distraught, because it was *my* fault that he was dead. I ought not to have let Mother hide me. I ought to have gone bravely to the altar, as Isaac had been prepared to do for his father Abraham.

I whispered to Zephaniah when I was able, 'How? How did they kill him?'

He said there was no need for me to know, but I asked the question over again, insisting that I would not be treated like a baby. Then I demanded to be taken to see the body.

Zephaniah didn't get angry; that wasn't his way. He

merely cautioned me that I had better learn some manners if I didn't want to go the way my father had gone. Nevertheless, he took me to see him.

They'd laid him out so neatly. Women were washing him and anointing him, and there was nothing bad to be seen because his wounds were underneath, in his back. While I stood there gazing down at him, Zephaniah described to me as gently as possible what had happened. Some of the King's own officers had done the bloody deed; they'd had their fill of his arrogance. Probably one of them had intended to take his place - this was the method by which kings had been made, as often as not, in our sister kingdom Israel, before she had disappeared between Assyria's ravening jaws. But supporters of David's line had fallen upon the murderers almost at once. The avengers belonged to the party of the People of the Land, the Assembly of Judah's landowners. Next they had come to look for me, and thanks to them I'd been installed on the throne which was mine by right. Now I should get back to bed, Zephaniah advised me. Even a king needed his sleep.

They placed me upon my mattress, but sleep would not come. Inside my head I could hear my parents arguing about the sacrifice Father was intending to make to gain Molech's favour.

'You cannot mean to do such a dreadful thing!' Mother had shrieked at him. 'How can you bring yourself to kill your own son? Don't you love the boy at all?'

'Of course I love him, woman. Can you not see? If I did not, this would be no sacrifice. It would count for nothing.'

'But he is my son too! For nine months I carried him; in pain I gave him birth, all because he was sprung of your seed and I loved you! What you mean to do is wicked beyond belief. It is a disgrace in the sight of God.'

'In the sight of which god in particular, may I ask? Not *Zephaniah's* god, by any chance?'

'Yes, Zephaniah's God, if you must call him that. But he's my God too, and he ought to be yours, since you are the ruler of his people. His laws are wise and good, and Judah would fare better if you followed them.'

'But did not Zephaniah's hero Abraham offer *his* son upon the altar, to propitiate Adonai?'

'How dare you compare yourself with the founding father of our nation! Have you forgotten that Abraham *didn't* have to kill Isaac in the end? But no ram was miraculously provided to take the place of *your* brother, was it, when your heathen father Manasseh took it upon himself to sacrifice *his* firstborn. And shall I tell you why? It's because Molech is an abomination! Adonai is the one true God, and he sent no ram to save your brother because your father was not acting in accordance with his will.'

My father had slapped her cheek then to silence her. But I wasn't shocked, because I was still struggling to take in something far more astonishing which my mother had just said. Never before had I suspected that Amon *hadn't* been a firstborn son. Were it not for what my grandfather Manasseh had done, neither my father nor I would ever have been kings.

I thought about Manasseh too, as I lay there on the night of my father's murder, unable to sleep. Father's father had been dead for two years, but I remembered him well, for I'd loved him almost as much as I'd loved his son. Manasseh had had a reputation for ruthlessness, because he had removed many men of influence from Judah's court in order to secure his own position. But I'd been told that you *had* to be ruthless to be an effective monarch. Besides, he was never cruel to *me.*

He'd done his subjects a great deal of good, too, in successfully keeping the peace with that towering giant Assyria, Israel's destroyer. Long ago in the Golden Age of King David, Israel and Judah had been united under a single sovereign. Later, greed, strife and rebellion had split the nation in two, each with a king of its own. The northern kingdom, Israel, had been much the bigger and stronger, but this had rendered her more attractive to aggressors, and Assyria had swallowed her whole. No one could understand how this had been allowed to happen. Hadn't David's god Adonai promised to protect his people, and preserve us in the land to which his servant Moses had restored us? What then could have caused such an unthinkable disaster to occur? Had Adonai deserted us? Or was he too weak to stand up to Assyria's gods? And if sturdy Israel had fallen, what would then become of her frail little sister Judah?

But my grandfather had gone on to snatch victory from Adonai's defeat - at least, this was how it appeared to many. He'd made a treaty with the Assyrian Emperor: so long as Judah paid an annual tribute, Manasseh would be left in peace upon his throne, and Judah would continue to exist as a nation in her own right rather than as a province in a foreign tyrant's empire. The tribute demanded had been substantial, but a price worth paying, because under Assyrian protection Judah's economy had blossomed. Manasseh had beautified Jerusalem with fine new buildings, and had even been permitted to improve her fortifications. True, we had to pay homage to Assyrian gods as well as to the Assyrian king, but this was acceptable enough to most of Manasseh's subjects. They'd been worshipping Canaanite deities alongside Adonai since the day they'd set foot in the Promised Land; a few additions to our pantheon would make little difference.

My grandfather had ruled for a very long time, however: fifty five years, to be precise. So what had begun as lip-service to the gods of our pagan overlords had become a way of life for many. Young men of Judah, apeing Assyrian fashions in their speech and dress, had also begun to indulge in Assyrian occult practices. Manasseh had personally encouraged their idolatry, building sanctuaries to the Assyrian moon god Sin and the sun god Shamash, and to the goddess Ishtar of the eight-pointed star. He himself had sponsored mediums and necromancers, and practised divination. He'd persecuted anyone who dared to oppose him; it was said that he'd had the prophet Isaiah sawn in half while still alive, but I've never been able to persuade myself of the truth of this. My mother was already maintaining Zephaniah under his very roof, when all is said and done, and *he* outlived Manasseh.

Indeed, in his latter years my grandfather had removed some of his idols from the Temple precincts. He'd once sat me on his knee when I was very small, and winked at me, and told me that he'd removed them because he'd been dragged off in chains to Assyria after foolishly contemplating rebellion. The experience of wearing manacles rather than a crown had humbled him and reminded him that one day we must all come face to face with Adonai, Creator of the Universe.

But my mother said this was all so much stuff and nonsense; no such thing had ever happened to him. The truth was that Assyria's sun was beginning to set, and by removing his idols a few at a time, Manasseh had been testing the ground to see what would happen if he began to withhold his tribute too. When he died, he was buried in his own garden, not in the tombs of his godly predecessors.

I didn't often think about religion as a child, except when Zephaniah made me. But as I lay grieving for my father, the realm of the gods seemed very close. And it was then that I remembered the strange boy I'd met at Anathoth, who seemed to hear the voice of some god or spirit as clearly as I might hear the voices of my playmates. I'd been looking forward so much to seeing him again the next morning. The sons of noblemen with whom I was expected to play could become so tiresome, always fawning over me and competing for my attention because they knew that one day I would be king.

But Jeremiah had been different. There had been something about his face which I had never seen in another's. It wasn't that he was a pretty child, in the way my mother might have meant it. But there had been a *look* about him, a wild yet lonely look; and there had been those startling eyes, hidden half the time behind a curtain of thick black hair. It was probably just as well that they *were* often hidden. I don't think anyone could have endured looking straight into them for very long.

I'd wanted so much to talk to him further, to find out more about that mysterious voice and how he'd first heard it, and to prove to myself and to him that he didn't scare *me.* But someone had spotted a boy creeping away from my hiding place and I'd been hustled off forthwith, because there had clearly been a breach in security.

Messengers had caught up with my mother as she was returning to the palace, and the old priest Simeon had found us somewhere else to hide. We'd stayed there a week; Mother had refused to leave my side again, whatever anyone said. Then we'd returned to the palace, for she was sure that by this time my father would have changed his mind about my fate, having been driven out of his wits by worry over the pair of us.

This proved to be true. The political crisis had passed, and the hapless band of conspirators had been executed. In the excitement of our homecoming I forgot Jeremiah entirely, and soon my old friends were claiming all my attention. Years later I learned that he had sent me letters, but they were intercepted before they reached me. It wouldn't do at all for the heir to the throne to have a commoner as a friend, especially a commoner from Anathoth.

If I'd imagined that my becoming king meant that henceforth I could throw my weight about and bully my elders to my heart's content, I rapidly learned that I had another think coming. I had to learn it the hard way, of course, by means of more than one clip about my right royal ears. But the People of the Land who had put me on the throne had done so for their own reasons: they wanted me as a figurehead while they ruled Judah themselves.

I hadn't previously paid much attention to their faction, or indeed to any other - I'd let politics, just like religion, go over my head. However, I soon realized that I should ignore the People of the Land at my peril. They had property, wealth and influence in abundance, and intended things to stay that way. They were fiercely patriotic, wanting Judah to be strong and independent, for they resented paying heavy taxes so that a foreign suzerain's pockets could be lined with the fruits of their labours. While Assyria had been strong, they had reluctantly accepted Judah's vassal status, but now that this unwieldy empire was beginning to totter they were keen to throw off its yoke. They were resolutely anti-Egyptian also, since they no more wanted to pay tribute to Pharaoh than to anyone else. This was why they had murdered my father's assassins; they believed that these men looked to Egypt for backing.

This was probably true, for it appeared very likely that Egypt would quickly puff herself up to fill any void left by the waning of Assyria. Pharaoh Psamtik was new to the throne as I was, but he was in the prime of his manhood and had already freed his own country from Assyrian domination.

So a council of the People of the Land ruled Judah in all but name, with the support of my mother and of her prophet Zephaniah. These two were happy to support them because in their patriotism the Landowners venerated no god but Adonai. Zephaniah meanwhile undertook to educate me in Adonai's laws, in the history of my people, and in the craft of kingship after the pattern of his own ancestor Hezekiah. He intended to equip me to take over the reins of government for myself at the earliest opportunity, and to rule God's people as Adonai himself would have them ruled.

I didn't much enjoy these lessons. I longed to be outside in the sunshine, riding, or practising with my spear or my bow.

'Why should I have to listen to all this?' I demanded once of Zephaniah, yawning and stretching and examining the doodles I'd scratched on my wax tablet with the point of my stylus. The prophet had been cataloguing for me yet again the names and attributes and histories of the other peoples besides Egypt who were likely to lay claim to slices of the Assyrian cake. There were Medes and Persians, Babylonians and Scythians, and I cared not a jot about any of them. I was even less interested in writing down the names and titles of their rulers and taking care to spell them correctly.

'Because when you are older, you will have to receive their ambassadors, and perchance entertain their princes, and you must deal wisely with all of them,' Zephaniah explained. 'You must be able to understand the implications of everything they say - and of everything they *don't* say.'

'That's not what *real* kings do. Real kings lead armies into battle and win victories which bards will sing about for all time to come.'

'The wise king goes to war only as a last resort,' Zephaniah informed me. 'Do you truly want to see the flower of Judah's youth trampled by the boots of pagan idolaters, the blood of your own subjects mingled with the dust of the ground? Do you want that blood to be upon your own head?'

I shrugged my shoulders, because to me war was all about fanfares and banners, parades and pageants, proud stallions tossing their braided manes and tails, and burnished armour shining in the sun.

'Well,' sighed Zephaniah, 'I fear you may find out about some of our foreign neighbours at first hand all too soon. The Medes and Persians are already nursing ambitions high above their station, and the Babylonians search constantly for a way to assert their independence from Assyria as the Egyptians have done. Were these three peoples to unite in purpose, they would truly constitute a force to be reckoned with. As for the Scythians, so ferocious are their horsemen that I've heard it said they are not men at all, but monsters: human from the head to the waist, and horse from waist to their hooves and their tails. They swoop upon cities from the desert like a plague of locusts, and depart as swiftly as they came, leaving nothing in their wake but headless corpses, for each of their warriors must carry the head of a vanquished opponent back to his sovereign. They have no homes, no land, no crops, and no man can predict where they will strike next.'

I yawned again. 'I wish *I* could be a Scythian horseman. My ancestor King David lived wild in the desert like that. He lived the life of an outlaw, with an army of brigands to cheer him and to pledge him their very lives. That's real kingship. Real *life,* Zephaniah! When David ruled, our nation was great; if he were alive now, *we* would be the ones seeking to take over from Assyria.'

'Yes, under David we were great indeed,' Zephaniah conceded, refraining from reminding me that David was his ancestor too. 'But have you never considered *why* this should have been so? It was because in those days Israel and Judah were one, with one king, and one *God*. The people were faithful to Adonai, so he blessed them and extended their boundaries. Today, Adonai can no longer commend what we do. He is angry with us, because of the idolatry of your father and your grandfather. Mark my words, little King. Unless Judah mends her ways, she will be destroyed just as Israel was destroyed. Adonai himself will bring calamity upon Judah, and upon Jerusalem his own holy city, because of her sins. The Day of Adonai, the great day of reckoning to which the prophets of old looked forward, will be a day of doom, not of triumph, unless we repent while we can.'

'Nonsense!' I retaliated. 'Our God isn't angry with us. Judah is prosperous. Rain falls in abundance in winter, and the sun shines all summer long. Our harvests are plentiful, we produce more corn than we can eat, more olives than we can press, and more wine than a race of giants could drink. If Adonai were angry with us, he would have destroyed Judah when he destroyed Israel - *if* it's true that Israel fell because Adonai willed it. The only reason Judah is no longer powerful is that she has no army any more. But she *shall* have one. When I am older, I shall establish one and command it myself.'

Zephaniah shook his head, throwing up his palms as though he despaired of me. Most probably he did, some of the time at least. 'Judah escaped Israel's fate because at the time her ruler was our ancestor Hezekiah, who followed Adonai faithfully as David had done,' he said. 'Hezekiah prayed for deliverance, and was granted a miracle. We cannot count on the same thing happening again. And what if Heaven were to withhold the rains from our sprouting corn, or the sun from our ripening grapes, or to send frost upon the valleys to kill our olive trees? We depend on Adonai for the very air we breathe, Josiah. He could snuff out our nation's light like a candle's.'

'Adonai would *never* snuff us out! We are his people! He made a covenant with David that Jerusalem would *never* be destroyed! He saved Hezekiah from his enemies, so he will save us from ours; all the prophets say so. And if he does not, he is not worthy of our worship.'

At that, Zephaniah snatched up a tablet and rapped my knuckles with it. 'You may be the anointed king of Judah,' he said sternly, 'But you are also my pupil, and you will not utter such blasphemies in my hearing. Besides, the prophets have *not* all said that Jerusalem is inviolable. The disciples of Isaiah say so, yes, because they suppose that every syllable of their dead master's message is valid in every circumstance, and will remain so for all time to come. But this is not so. Each generation must seek Adonai's *living* word for *itself*, else it will never interpret aright what was said or written in the past. The great prophet Hosea pointed *behind* Adonai's covenant with David, to the one he made with Moses hundreds of years before. In that covenant it was made quite plain that the future of the Chosen People depended upon their *obedience*, to Adonai and his Law.'

But I paid no heed to his warnings, laughing them off as I always did, and quoting by heart the promises Adonai had made to King David: to preserve his dynasty and prosper his kingdom for ever. Zephaniah sighed again, closed up the tablets we'd been using for our lesson, and rose to his feet.

'We have studied long enough for today, Your Majesty,' he announced, and I smiled to myself because I'd exasperated my tutor yet again. But then I flung my arms about him, because he was my mother's friend and in truth I was fond of him and respected him despite our frequent arguments. Unlike so many of the grown-ups I knew, he was always fair, and he practised what he preached. He'd been unafraid to speak home truths to my father Amon, and would say precisely what he thought to me as well. Part of me hoped that I would be a little like him when I was a man, as well as a little like David.

In return, Zephaniah squeezed my shoulders and ruffled my hair. 'Come,' he said kindly. 'Let us go and see your mother, and show her the work you have done today.' And we went off hand in hand, knowing that she would ply us with cakes and sweetmeats, for she took delight in each of us.

CHAPTER 3: JEREMIAH

When I left home at the age of thirteen, I thought I had escaped the unwelcome attentions of my cousin Hanamel and his companions for good. How wrong I was.

I hadn't moved far - only up to the high place to begin my training as a priest. But Hanamel and his cronies had always kept away from it. I think they disliked the place for the very reasons I loved it. You could almost see the ghosts that lingered there, almost hear the prayers of the people who had worshipped there in ages past. The sacred atmosphere seemed thick enough to touch, and the scent of ancient incense wafted down the centuries. Only when I drank deeply of the ambient holiness did I ever dare to hope that I might be something other than insane.

Yet I wasn't exactly enjoying my life at the sanctuary, even before Hanamel poisoned it. There was too much confusion inside my head. I was struggling to sort out what I believed, and no one seemed able to help me. I was striving to distinguish the good things which went on in the holy precincts from the bad, to understand why innocent girls and boys, many of them younger than I, were made to prostitute their bodies night after night in the name of God or the gods. But no one wanted to explain. Even the aged priests who harped on the bygone days of righteous King Hezekiah seemed unable to recall them very clearly. Meanwhile, shivers went up and down my spine every time I chanced to cross the path of one of the polluted adolescents. Their sultry painted faces turned my stomach.

And of course, there was the voice. Just about all it ever said was: *I have chosen you. You are mine.* Yet it said it so often, sometimes waking me at midnight to whisper it in my ear, that it came to dominate my cloistered little world.

I seldom slept right through from bedtime to morning. Sometimes it was the voice, sometimes sickness. I had always been a sickly child. And my health was worst, oddly enough, whenever the voice let me alone for a while. I could ask it to be quiet and it would obey me, but then within a day or two I would find that I couldn't face my food, and anything I did eat came straight back up.

And whenever I relented and invited it to come and speak to me again, such a glow would spread throughout my body that I would weep with the joy of it, until the joy turned to misery and I wept in self-pity because I *was* mad after all. For who but a lunatic was unable to live without some other person sharing his mind?

Although I was quite convinced now that my meeting with Josiah had occurred in a dream, I still wondered from time to time if he'd been right in suggesting that the voice belonged to Adonai. I did ask it, once, outright, on one of the occasions when it woke me in the night. I shouted into the darkness: 'Who are you? Why won't you tell me your name?' All I got in reply was: *I am ... I am... who I am... who I am...* like an echo bouncing from the walls. In spite of the priestly education I was supposed to be receiving, this meant nothing to me. I shouted again, '*Am* I hearing the voice of Adonai? Why don't other people hear what I hear? What do you want of me? See: I am to be your priest; what more can you ask me to do? Why won't you leave me alone?'

Alone... alone... alone... said the echo, and I railed and cursed because I didn't want to be alone and sick, but alone and at peace with myself and the world.

Then it said something new, and said it quite distinctly. It said, *I want nothing more, not yet. I didn't even ask for your dedication to the priesthood. All I want is for you to wait, and learn. Learn of me. Seek me. Know me.*

'How?' I yelled in excitement. 'Where am I to look, if you will not tell me who you are?'

But there was no reply, and then one of the priests who slept at the sanctuary came in to see what was the matter. It was one of the very oldest ones; his junior colleagues mostly spent their nights in the village with their families. Only the widowers and the few novices who hadn't yet married lived full time at the high place, along with the young prostitutes, and the fearsome Canaanite wise-woman who minded them.

'I'm all right,' I tried to assure him. 'Please. Go back to bed.' But the words came out all jumbled and slurred, and the priest wouldn't go away until I'd rolled myself in my blanket and pretended to be asleep for a very long time.

After that, I took to spending many hours walking in the olive groves or along the rocky ridges surrounding the sanctuary. If the voice said anything new to me, I wanted to be able to respond without anyone interfering.

As things turned out, it said nothing that I hadn't already heard, but my love of the rugged landscape deepened and held me in willing thrall. The strength of the stately trees with their twisted trunks and dancing silver leaves, the redness of the earth between them and the flurries of blossom that drifted across it in springtime, the misty blue of the hills beyond the Jordan - I loved them all.

Then one day, when I'd been at the sanctuary a little more than a year, Hanamel and three of his cronies came up from the village. Fortunately I saw them before they saw me, and was able to hide and listen to what they said to the priest who received them.

Each of them wanted a night with a shrine-girl.

I should have guessed; nothing else could have induced them to overcome their aversion to all things sacred. Hanamel was sixteen years old now. Soon enough he would be betrothed and married, but he wasn't prepared to wait until then to prove himself a man. He'd brought the necessary offerings and presented them with an impressive show of gravity; the priest invited him and his companions to enter one of the reception rooms and refresh themselves before undergoing ritual purification.

Once they were out of sight I crept away. But I was so shaken that I didn't look where I was going, and collided with a fat elderly acolyte who'd been sent to fetch food and wine for our guests.

'Jeremiah ben Hilkiah!' he exclaimed, recovering himself. 'Well, if anyone had to knock me off my feet, it couldn't have been a more useful person under the circumstances. There are some nervous young fellows here not much older than you are; who better than you to take them something to eat and make them feel at home? Come with me, now.'

Stricken, I couldn't even protest. I followed him meekly on quaking legs, and held out my hands to receive the tray of victuals thrust at me. I shall never know how I managed to carry it all the way back without dropping anything.

Thankfully, the priest who had received my cousin and his friends was still with them, explaining the various rites they would each have to undergo before being allowed to perform the one for which they had come. So there was no opportunity for the boys to say or do anything to offend me when I laid the tray down in front of them.

In any case, except for Hanamel they were too cowed by their alien surroundings to take much notice of me. But Hanamel curled his lip into a sneer the moment his eyes met mine. I felt my insides shrivel, and got out of his presence as fast as my trembling legs would carry me.

The night's entertainment must have lived up to their expectations, because they returned to the sanctuary again and again, and with other boys too. I scarcely got a wink of sleep on the nights they were there; the thought of them profaning the sanctity of my special place with their primitive lusts drove me to distraction. I found that if I drank enough wine before going to bed, things improved, but then in the middle of the night I would have to get up to relieve myself.

I suppose it was about the same time each night that I had to obey nature's call. Thus I myself provided Hanamel with the opportunity to add a new dimension to his entertainment.

There was a good moon the night it happened. I needed no lamp to guide me as I slipped outside, passed through the olive grove, and went to the edge of the scrubby woodlands beyond to do what I had to do. If I'd gone to the proper place night after night I should have attracted attention and been questioned about the bad habit I'd got myself into.

Just as I was loosening my loincloth, a smack between

the shoulder blades knocked me to the ground. Wine and sleep had fuddled my wits; I offered no resistance to the heavy blows which rained down upon me. One moment I was sprawling in the spiny embrace of a thornbush; the next I was hanging suspended from my armpits and panting for breath, with Hanamel's face pressed against mine.

Bringing his knee up into my groin, he hissed between gritted teeth, 'Think yourself better than the rest of us, do you, Samuel? Fancy yourself as holy, because you wear the robes of a priestling? You'll never exorcize your devils by sucking up to snivelling clerics. You yellow-bellied toad, you'll never even become a *man* without help from those who understand such mysteries. Come along, shrine-boy. It's time for your initiation.'

He snapped his fingers in the air, and his minions began dragging me back through the moonlit olive grove towards the sanctuary. When I tried to scream they stuffed a rag in my mouth, and when I struggled and kicked, Hanamel himself upturned me by the ankles and I was carted convulsing and spluttering into the holy place. Lamplight flickered along the walls; the archaic, blackened image of a mother goddess glowered at me from the shadows.

It was only when they stood me upright, with my back against a wall and my arms pinned out to either side, that I realized I was not their only prisoner. One of the girl prostitutes cowered wide-eyed in front of me, the remainder of her face and body shrouded in her flame-red veil. Next, Hanamel started to lecture me about fertility and progeny, and my duty as a priest to secure plenty of both for my people. Slowly it dawned on me what he was going to force me to do.

I shook my head wildly as the girl was pushed towards me. 'She's been saved for you specially, Samuel,' my cousin jeered. 'She was brought here only yesterday. A virgin as lovely as this would have tempted your namesake the prophet Samuel himself. Unless of course you'd prefer a boy? Let's see if you've learnt to tell the difference.'

So saying, he grasped the red veil between his fingers and yanked it away. The shrine-girl's face was fully exposed, along with most of the rest of her, and I almost choked on the rag in my mouth as I saw that she was the same girl whose old blind grandmother I'd once been dared to rob.

She'd grown up straight and slim, her hair had been washed and combed, but there was no mistaking that frightened face. Hanamel's boys were dancing around her, guffawing lewdly, cupping her breasts in their hands and pinching her naked buttocks. Tears spilled from her closed eyelids; she hadn't recognized me, because she was forlornly trying to convince herself that none of this was happening.

'Not getting excited yet, Samuel?' Hanamel taunted me. 'Or should we see for ourselves?' He took hold of the neckband of my tunic and tore the garment from top to bottom; my loincloth was already half off, and he pulled it the rest of the way. 'Because you see, Samuel, I could certainly fancy this tasty little apple for myself. If you don't take her, I shall. And when I've finished with her, my good friends here will queue up for turns. If you don't want her to suffer *that,* you'll have to make sure they don't get a chance.'

Then he clamped his hand behind the girl's head and kissed her so viciously that she cried out in terror. My own terror was abruptly transformed into a blind red rage; unable to believe what I was doing, I wrenched my arms free, spat out my gag, and took hold of Hanamel by the hair, pulling as hard as I could so that his greedy mouth was parted from the lips of his victim.

He'd got himself so aroused that at first he paid me no attention. However, when I pulled harder and made him stagger, he couldn't ignore me any longer. He twisted about, astounded to see his timorous cousin's features contorted with fury. Before he could collect himself sufficiently to thump me, *I* had thumped *him,* full in his podgy belly.

With an outraged grunt he fell backwards onto the floor. None of his companions lifted a finger to help him. They stood and stared at me as though I were some feral creature come up from the desert. Eventually Hanamel struggled to his feet, and an ugly brawl ensued, the two of us rolling over and over on the consecrated ground.

Fortunately for me, the fight was as noisy as it was

violent, and pretty soon several of the priests who slept at the sanctuary arrived to investigate. Hanamel let me alone at once, darting away with his friends into the night. But he called over his shoulder as he left, 'You'll be sorry you hit me, Samuel. You'll pay for this.' And he was gone.

Nauseous and retching, I lay for a while where I'd landed, sprawled in a corner surrounded by a jumble of broken vessels. I could see two of the girl I'd rescued; both of them were grovelling on the floor to retrieve their veils and hide their pubescent nakedness. Two of the Canaanite wise-woman who supervised the prostitutes made a bee-line for them, squealing about the disgrace which this despicable scene had brought upon the holy place, and declaring that all those involved should be soundly whipped. So I hauled myself to my feet and made a lunge at the girl who appeared the more substantial of the two.

'Run!' I hissed, with such conviction that she obeyed me. I seized her by the hand, and we got out as fast as we could.

The moment we were outdoors, however, she began struggling to make me let go. I held on, still running, determined that the wise-woman should not catch her, and at a loss to see why she would rather face a whipping than seize the chance to escape.

I was in too crazed a state to think where we should go, but my feet took us back to the woods, which I regarded as my domain. There the trees drew their familiar cloak around us, shielding us from the moonlight. Convinced that if I sat down to recover my breath I should never be able to get up again, I plunged further and further into the gloom, stopping only when I tripped on a fallen branch and went headlong down a steep slope. The girl fell with me, and when I chanced to land right on top of her she flung her face to one side and waited for the inevitable.

I didn't at first realize that she expected me to rape her after all. Quite suddenly I was aware of nothing except my own pain; excitement had kept it at bay until now, but as I lay panting I began to appreciate what damage Hanamel had done to me.

I reckoned he'd already paid me back in full for the blow I'd dealt him in the stomach. My own hurt like hell; I rolled over into the prickly undergrowth and knelt there doubled up. There were cuts and bruises all down my legs, and my cheeks were swelling like wineskins. When I put one hand to my face to make sure that my nose was still attached, my fingers came away wet. I promptly threw up all over my bruised and bloody thighs.

I don't know how much time passed by before I felt an arm go about my shoulders and heard a nervous voice whisper, 'I - think your nose is still bleeding. Please. Let me help you.' Tentatively she reached out with her veil, pinching the end of my nose and dabbing at the trickle beneath it. But as I put up my hand again to help her, my fingers touched hers. She recoiled from me like a bow when the arrow has been fired.

'I'm not going to hurt you,' I said, then added, 'On my honour, I swear it,' when she came no closer; perhaps my tongue was so swollen that she hadn't understood what I said?

She condescended to glance at me sideways, but I don't think she would have trusted me if my nose hadn't started to bleed all over again. Again she used her veil to stem the flow, but once she was sure I wasn't going to faint she drew back and sat watching me, the way a gazelle might watch the lion which is poised to devour it. At least she was no longer minded to run away.

'Please, don't be frightened,' I implored her. It had felt so strange to have her arm about my neck, but so, so wonderful. Not since Josiah in my dream had anyone ever touched me except to communicate reproof. 'Surely you don't think I could... I mean...' But I didn't have it in me to express a thing I found so shocking, and I was grateful that the night would hide my blushes. Still she didn't answer, but she continued to look at me now, even when our eyes met. I said, 'You know who I am, don't you?'

She nodded, but when I stretched out one hand towards her she shrank from it as though from a poisoned barb.

I said, 'My name is Jeremiah ben Hilkiah. Aren't you going to tell me yours?'

At first she shook her head. But I waited, and eventually she uttered a single syllable: Ruth.

'And is it true that you came to the sanctuary only yesterday?' I asked her.

She nodded again, clutching her veil more tightly around her, and I saw that she was shivering. Since I was naked as the day I was born, there was nothing I could give her for warmth but the heat of my own body, and I knew that I must not do that.

'Tell me why you came here,' I encouraged her, to distract us both. 'It's not a good place for a girl, nor for a boy unless he's going to be a priest.' She offered nothing, just stared at me expectantly, so I went on, 'That's why *I'm* here. I came to serve Adonai.' Then I felt ashamed, because I was telling her a half truth, so I confessed: 'Actually I came to get away from my brothers, and from my cousin. It didn't work. He was the one who tried to... who nearly... oh, I hate him so much, Ruth. Sometimes I even wish him dead.'

Although until now our conversation had been almost entirely one way, this was the first time I'd ever admitted to anyone how I felt about Hanamel; the misery he'd made of my life came gushing all at once to the surface and I couldn't go on. I crouched with my head between my punctured knees, hating myself as much as I hated Hanamel, because I couldn't master myself and was making such a mess of consoling Ruth, just as I made a mess of everything else.

So I didn't sense her creeping closer to me until she ventured to stroke my knee with the tips of her fingers. I raised my head and she whispered, 'Jeremiah, I don't blame you. I've watched what they do to you. I've watched for years. But I thought you... I mean, everyone said you ...'

Her eyes were full of fear again, yet there was another emotion revealed in them too, one that I found so disconcerting that now it was *I* who couldn't look at *her*. I bowed my head once more and spoke her words for her. 'They said I was mad. And you believed them.'

'Oh Jeremiah, I didn't *want* to believe them!' she blurted. 'Not after you were so kind to me and to my grandmother. I never forgot that; never! But they said you talked to yourself; and you were always on your own; and I used to see tiny children running away from you in the street... How could I *not* believe them? But I didn't believe it when they said you had an evil spirit. I could *never* believe that. No one possessed by evil would have stood up to those horrid boys when they wanted you to steal from us. And no one possessed by evil would have stood up to them tonight. Thank you, Jeremiah. I don't know how else to say it.'

I responded at once, 'Say it by going home, Ruth. Don't stay at the sanctuary. I won't be able to save you from a beating if you go back to that dreadful old woman, nor from what must happen to you night after night if you stay with the shrine-girls. You should never have come here.'

'Do you think I came by choice? My grandmother was starving to death, in her own village, in the house where she was born! We have *never* had enough to eat; not since I was a baby. It wouldn't be so bad if the farmers left us anything to glean when they harvested their crops, as Moses' law says they should. But they pick every last grain of corn, Jeremiah, they shake every shrivelled little olive from their trees because they too are in need. When I was a child, my grandmother would eat nothing until I'd had my fill. Now I'm grown up. I'm twelve years old. It's time for *me* to give something for *her.*'

'Give *something?* I repeated. 'But you'll be giving your whole self, everything you are.'

'I am nothing, Jeremiah,' she said simply. 'So I have nothing to lose. They say you get good food and to spare if you offer yourself to the sanctuary gods - and gifts, too, from satisfied suppliants. I'll be able to feed both of us now, and I'll get used to what happens to my kind in the holy place.'

'But there must be other relatives you could turn to? Ruth - what happened to your parents?'

She shrugged her shoulders, as if to convince me - or herself - that the loss of them no longer upset her. She answered, 'My mother died giving birth to my brother, and he died too. My father was a farmer from the tribe of Benjamin; he was killed by King Manasseh's soldiers during a riot in Jerusalem. It was when the peasants rose up against the taxes they had to pay so that the King could buy off the Assyrians with tribute. Manasseh bought his power and wealth with my father's *blood,* Jeremiah! While the King and his nobles got richer, the poor were losing their own land because of debt. Well, my father paid his debts with his life. But I don't remember him. I was two years old.' She shrugged again. 'My grandmother brought me with her to Anathoth, the village of her birth. Begging is the only life I've known. And I don't want to go back to it, any more than you want to go back to your brothers' bullying.'

There was nothing I could say to that. I'd never thought of my own family as rich; since we were Levites we owned no land at all. But we made a good living from the tithes and offerings presented to us, mostly by the sort of men who could well afford them. I felt suddenly and powerfully ashamed of my father and his peers for allowing others to go hungry in the midst of their plenty. Eventually I mumbled, 'How stupid I've been. I should never have believed what Josiah said. He told me that Manasseh made Judah rich for *all* his subjects.'

My confession met with nothing but stunned silence. Then Ruth murmured in awe, 'You've met Josiah? *King* Josiah?'

I felt myself blush once more, right down to my throat. I was about to admit that I hadn't, that my madness had caused me to dream a dream so vivid I'd confused it with reality. Yet all at once, for the first time in half my life, I was sure that we *had* met, that our meeting had felt every bit as real as the encounter with Ruth which I was having now. And if this latter turned out to be a dream as well, what harm could it do for me to tell one figment of my imagination about another?

'Yes,' I answered her firmly. 'Yes, I have met Josiah, and I do mean the King. But he wasn't King then. He was seven years old, and so was I. We met only once, but we could have become friends, I know it. For a long time afterwards I used to write him letters, and pray that one day he would come back and teach Hanamel a lesson. He looked so brave and strong. And he's the only person who never laughed at my voice.'

'Your voice? What's wrong with your voice?' she asked, and only then did I grasp that incredibly, impossibly, she hadn't known anything about it. She'd thought that I talked to *myself*, and that this was all that my madness amounted to. No wonder she hadn't believed I had a demon.

'Jeremiah? What's the matter?' she demanded. 'Are you going to be sick again?'

'No,' I replied. 'I'm all right. Just cold.' And so I was; I was shivering all over. But I was aching all over too, and my own vomit was congealing on my legs.

Yet it was so thrilling to be sitting there in the moonlight, talking to this girl who didn't hate me, that I never wanted it to end. I looked at her suddenly and saw that Hanamel had been right: she *was* lovely. Though I'd never thought anything like this about any girl before, there was no denying I was thinking it now. Her glossy hair spilled out upon delicate, bird-boned shoulders like water tumbling over rocks when the rains come, and her face was pale and tender as the moon.

Before I could check myself, I found that I was telling her everything I had told Josiah, because somehow it seemed so much better to speak than to be silent.

I told her lots more besides: about the years which had passed since Josiah had come to Anathoth and first put it into my mind that I might be hearing the voice of Adonai as the young Samuel had done in days gone by. I told her how I'd plagued the priests to tell me more about this long-dead prophet whose name had been linked to mine, and how I'd imagined sometimes that Samuel's spirit was watching over me; I'd thought of him as a lonely, crazy little boy just like me. I told her how I'd learnt that my own family was descended, through Abiathar, from the old priest Eli who had ministered in the Shiloh sanctuary where Samuel grew up, and where the

Ark of the Covenant was kept, the symbol of Adonai's presence among his people. Later Shiloh had been destroyed, and the Ark had wound up in Jerusalem, in the Temple built for it by Solomon and tended by the Zadokites, hated rivals of the Anathoth priests. I told her how I'd made up my mind to become a priest too, and how, like Samuel, I'd decided to say to my voice, 'Speak, Lord, for your servant is listening.' Yet all I'd been instructed to do was wait, seek, learn; and the waiting was starting to tear me apart. By the time I'd got all this off my chest I was crying like a baby, and Ruth was cradling me in her arms, bloody and filthy as I was.

'You see,' I said, when I could speak again, 'I *am* mad. I can't control what happens inside my own head. I don't know what's going to become of me.'

'Is that where you hear your voice?' she probed gently. 'Inside your head? Is it part of you?'

I pressed the heels of my hands against my temples to lessen the pounding, and the confusion. 'Yes,' I answered, then, 'No. I don't know. It feels like someone else in the room with me. Or maybe it's like someone else in my *brain* with me. I can't explain.'

'Have you ever seen this person?'

'Seen him? You mean: like a vision?'

'I suppose so.'

'No. I've never seen anything like that. Perhaps it would be better if I did, then I would know for certain that there *is* someone there.' I put my head on her shoulder because it felt so heavy, so full of strife. I said into her hair, 'You know, I thought that if I trained to be a priest I might be taught things which would help me understand what is happening to me. But the more I learn, the worse it gets. I think the priests themselves are confused, because they have no Torah books and have to rely on old memories - so many precious scrolls of Adonai's laws were lost or hidden in Manasseh's reign. One day I'm taught that Adonai alone is God, the next that there are gods and spirits in every river, every tree, every stone. One priest tells me it's wrong to work magic, whilst another has me mixing vile potions to call up the dead. The ten commandments themselves instruct us not to commit murder, yet there are men serving at this sanctuary who have offered up their own sons to Molech. We are told not to commit adultery, but every night married men here at Anathoth are induced to join themselves to harlots, or else you wouldn't be here.' I lifted my head and presumed to stroke back the shining hair from her brow. 'Go home, Ruth. Please. Before you lose your maidenhead and your very self.'

'And have nothing to look forward to but starvation? Is that what you'd wish upon me?'

'You could marry, and have children.' I bit my lip, mustering what little courage I had, and said, 'You are very beautiful, Ruth. Surely you must know it?'

She laughed bitterly. 'What good is beauty without reputation? Who would marry me, when he's passed me begging in the gutter, and when I've worn the scarlet veil of a shrine-girl?'

I responded without even thinking what I said: 'I would.' Then as soon as I'd spoken I was overwhelmed by embarrassment, because of course no girl as pretty as Ruth would want anything to do with a boy who was friendless and spineless and possessed by a devil, however lowly her circumstances.

But to my astonishment she held me closer than before, and there were tears dewing her long lashes as she brought her lips near to mine.

Timidly, then fervently, I folded my arms around her back and kissed her.

CHAPTER 4: RUTH

I rose early, before the birds; preparations for the ceremony were due to begin at dawn. The first of the womenfolk arrived with the merest hint of daylight, and soon our cramped little cottage was thronged with them, from toothless crones to girls my own age. They chattered like so many sparrows, while I smiled and laughed and welcomed each one, whether I knew who they were or not.

Never in my life before had such a multitude of people wanted to know me. The inhabitants of Anathoth had quietly despised my poverty and looked the other way. But everyone loves a wedding, and my bridegroom's father had paid a good price for me, being heartily glad to have found a match for his difficult son. I don't think he even minded that his eldest boy was marrying so far beneath him, for it is a lighter curse to marry down than to remain unmarried altogether.

So I was bathed in an earthenware tub, and my hair was washed and combed; henna was painted for luck on my hands and my feet, then the women dressed me in the robe I'd been sewing for a year. Every inch of fabric was covered in my own embroidery; now half a dozen gossiping girls were stitching on jewels and bright beads of glass which their mothers had loaned me. Others ran up with necklets, bracelets or anklets and fastened them into place; still others began to braid and scent my hair, and adorn it with flowers. My eyelids and lips were painted, my eyebrows stained, my cheekbones powdered, then a chain hung with silver charms was clipped from my nose to one ear.

I was happier than I had ever dreamed I could be. I didn't care at all that the girls who crowded around me had only been my friends since the wedding day was announced, nor did it really concern me that in private they sneered at the one to whom I was betrothed, though I knew it was true. They had whispered and pointed, and pretended to be shocked when they'd seen us together, but none was so proud as to stay away from our wedding. There would be music and food, dancing and wine, and those who were not betrothed or married already could sigh and make eyes at the boys they fancied.

'At least she's being *allowed* to marry a boy of her own choosing,' remarked one of the girls to the others. A few of them exchanged conniving glances, implying: even though *we* wouldn't choose him. '*My* father won't listen to a word I say on the matter. All he cares about is how much property a man has. He'll get me betrothed to some fat old baldhead, you just wait and see.'

'Well, there's nothing to be gained from marrying a pauper, even if he's as beautiful as Tammuz,' another girl observed. 'It's no good having pretty children together if you cannot afford to feed them.'

Children... A warm thrill went through me as I yearned for the day when I would present my husband with his firstborn son. How beautiful the boy would be, if he looked anything like his father. Others might say that Jeremiah was too thin, his shoulders too narrow, his face too pinched. But to me he was bewitching, with his shy solemn smile and the crown of wild black hair that fell in his eyes whenever he turned his head. What eyes they were, too! So intense, so deep, so lonely.

I'd admired him from afar ever since his cousin Hanamel had unintentionally introduced us as children in the dust by the roadside. Jeremiah, frightened though he was, had refused to do the monster's bidding, and in that instant he became my hero. Every morning when I awoke I would pray that I might catch a glimpse of him before sundown; whenever I saw a crowd of boys playing, I would look and look in case he was among them. Yet he never was. On the few occasions I did chance to see him, he was alone, or else being tormented by his peers.

I wondered why this was, and asked my grandmother why some horrid children had friends whilst nice ones were shunned or bullied. But she couldn't explain. When her sight had begun to fail, she had sunk within herself and lost all interest in people and their unfathomable ways.

Because we were beggars, the other village girls wouldn't talk to me, any more than their brothers would play with my little champion. But sometimes I would hide myself and listen in to their conversations. It was from them that I learned not only the name of my beloved, but also that he was mad and possessed by a devil. From then on, I feared Jeremiah as much as I'd loved him, and although I couldn't stop myself gazing after him whenever he went by, my fascination was like that of a person who stares at a cripple without any legs.

So when Hanamel brought me face to face with him once more, seven years later at the sanctuary, I was afraid that my last hour had arrived. Hanamel and his comrades didn't scare me half as much as Jeremiah in his own rabid terror. I'd convinced myself that he couldn't possibly be evil, but one look into his tortured eyes told me he was as mad as a man with a worm in his brain. It was only when he wept in the woods that my love for him bubbled up again in spite of myself and would not be suppressed; but this time it was different, stronger, stranger, as though some dormant seed had germinated in my heart, and would not stop growing until it filled the whole of me. I could have flung my arms around Hanamel himself and thanked him; when Jeremiah kissed me, I was no longer in the woods, but in the Garden of Eden.

After that, I went back home as he'd told me to, because he said he would make sure henceforth that my grandmother and I had food on our table every day. He was true to his word; whether he asked the sanctuary cooks for bread or simply stole it, I never asked. But whenever I went up to see him, I came away with a basketful.

And I took to going there as often as I could. I would meet him in secret, and we would walk in the woods or on the stony red hills, and he would pick flowers and bind them in my hair. We talked and we kissed, but never anything more. He said we should wait until we were married, and by and by he spoke to his father and my grandmother and we were betrothed. I was thirteen years old, and he fifteen.

There were days when he was moody, but I loved him enough to forgive him anything. It happened when he hadn't slept, because of sickness or the voice, though we didn't talk very much about the latter because he thought it upset me. So it did, but I could mostly forget that he heard it, because it never troubled him when I was there. Perhaps that's why he was happy to spend so many hours and days with me.

In time, of course, people found out that we saw each other unchaperoned, and there was disapproval and worse. But Jeremiah said we should try to take no notice; it was nothing new for him to be gossiped about or slandered to his face. Besides, he asked, what could be wrong with his being in love with the girl to whom he was betrothed, when a sordid physical dalliance with a shrine prostitute would have been regarded as perfectly acceptable? But I knew that the things people said about us hurt him deep down. So many things hurt him.

I have to admit that as the day set aside for our marriage approached, he became moodier than before. But I supposed that he was merely apprehensive, afraid he might not be equal to the demands which marriage would make of him. He was barely sixteen years old, after all - not unusually young to be wed or get children, yet little more than a child himself in so many ways. Like a child he still had a secret place, a little den to which he would retreat whenever things got too much. He took me there once, down in the cellars under the sanctuary. But the musty darkness unnerved me, and we didn't go there together again.

'There won't be any more whispering and kissing in the bushes for *you*, young lady, once you're respectably married,' one of the girls announced, as though she'd been scrutinizing my daydreams while sewing her baubles to my dress. 'You'll have to stay at home and grind corn and weave cloth and do whatever *he* tells you to do.'

'No more whispering and kissing *and* who knows what else,' quipped the girl beside her, but it was left to a cattier third to say: 'I hope there *will* be some blood for us all to witness when they hang out your wedding sheet, my dear. And that the first little ben Jeremiah isn't brought into the world before nine moons have waxed.'

They giggled and twittered into one another's ears for a while after that, no doubt debating whether the effete Jeremiah would ever have it in him to father a child. Then a band of musicians arrived and struck up with their flutes and drums, and the girls left off with their teasing and started to dance, laughing and hooting and trilling their tongues. They held out the crooks of their arms to me as though they'd meant me no offence all along, and obligingly I joined in. Even my grandmother, squatting on her haunches in the corner, hummed tunelessly, and clapped, out of time with the music.

Once the sun had set, the high spirits gave way to expectancy. At any time after nightfall the groom was permitted by custom to come out from his house with his male companions, to claim his bride for his own. Jeremiah wouldn't be bringing his brothers or his cousins, but a handful of priests from the sanctuary. His father had added an extra room to his house for us to live in; outside it, the wedding canopy would have been set up and festooned with flowers. The girls would light their lamps and keep me company all the way there; already the streets and rooftops were lined with village folk waving lighted torches. When Jeremiah appeared, men and boys among the crowd would shout out the conventional ribaldries; indeed, many were doing so already, because they had drunk a good deal and were getting into practice. Someone pulled a heavy veil down over my face, for my husband was not to look upon my features until our hands were joined beneath the canopy and the blessings had been said.

However, hours went by, and Jeremiah did not come. Most of the men outside were too drunk to care, but inside our cottage the women fidgeted, and the girls went back to bartering their knowing glances. A few of the kinder ones turned back my veil and exhorted me not to fret: he must be concerned to look his best before showing himself to the crowds or to me. But when midnight came and still he hadn't appeared, some of the younger girls had gone to sleep with their garlanded heads in one another's laps.

At length there was a scuffling of feet and rustling of robes outside the door, but no music or drums. The multitudes who had sung and danced all day and evening fell quiet, and over the threshold stepped Jeremiah's father, Hilkiah the priest, quite alone. He took in the scene with a single glance - a glance at once furtive, wrathful and wretched. He said, 'My son has disappeared.'

Consternation broke out. Those who had been asleep scrambled up in confusion, as their more vigilant elders pelted Hilkiah with questions and recriminations. *When* had Jeremiah disappeared? Why had he been allowed to go off alone on his wedding day? Could Hilkiah not enforce discipline in his own household?

'Would you have me keep the boy chained like a dog?' Hilkiah snapped back, as bewildered and angry as they were. I was becoming hysterical, convinced that some dreadful accident must have happened; Jeremiah had been attacked by wild animals, or even by his cousin, and was lying somewhere unconscious.

'Sir, we must all go out and look for him,' I urged his father. 'We must start out at once!'

'Do you think I have not looked, child? My brothers and I have done nothing else but search for him since noon. Shallum has been to every house in the village, and I have questioned everyone at the sanctuary from highest to least. Jeremiah has made his mother and me look like fools, and when I do find him I shall tan his ungrateful hide.'

'He's been missing since *noon*?' I cried. 'Aren't you concerned he may be hurt? Is it *his* fault if he's had an accident?'

Hilkiah took hold of my wrists; I was making a spectacle of myself, and he was suffering enough humiliation already. At length I stood chastened with my head on his breast, while he explained to me that Jeremiah had gone out arrayed in his bridal garments shortly after sunrise, saying merely that he needed to be alone for a while, and that he would soon be back. All we could do was wait, because he'd had time to walk half way to Galilee by now. The wedding must be postponed.

So saying, Jeremiah's father began to shoo the women and girls out of the cottage, while I knelt on the dirt floor with my grandmother, rocking her in my arms until she permitted me to lay her on her mattress and cover her with blankets. The women shuffled away; even the girls were subdued, walking hand in hand with eyes to the ground. Last of all, Hilkiah himself took his leave, stooping to kiss my brow as though the day had gone as it should have done, and he was now my father too.

I sat by the door, and through the cracks between its boards I watched the crowds disperse, taking their torchlight with them, until the last of the stragglers was out of sight and I was sure that my grandmother was asleep. Then I slipped outside and began searching for Jeremiah myself.

It was early spring, and the cloud still lingered over the village, but not thickly enough to block out the moonlight entirely. I could see quite well where I was going, and now and again the cloud rolled back and the moon shone clearly, bathing the landscape in its pallid glow.

I was now quietly confident that I would succeed where the others who'd sought him had failed, because I alone knew the place to which he would have gone. Nevertheless, it wasn't without trepidation that I followed him to it, and not only because I disliked the place itself.

The closer I came to the sanctuary, the worse I felt. I began to wonder if the village girls were right: I'd been imprudent from the beginning to get involved with such a one as Jeremiah, and had deluded myself into thinking that I loved him, because deep in my heart I knew that no other man would ever want me. It would be best to give him up now, because marriage to his kind brought only misery; his moods would grow blacker as the years went by, and his voice would drive him, and then me, to distraction. I recalled as I climbed among the flowers and the thorns that he had even said as much to me, not three days before: you cannot really want me, Ruth; you should find yourself another, one who can truly make you happy.

But I'd planted kisses on his closed eyelids and whispered: don't be so silly, Jeremiah. I could never love anyone but you.

No one saw me enter the sanctuary buildings. I suppose they were all in a huddle somewhere, discussing the bizarre turn which the day's events had taken. I lifted a lighted lamp from a bracket on the wall and crept down the steps into the cellars, desperately hoping I should be able to remember the way and not wander lost in the winding passageways for ever.

But presently I came to the hidden entrance, and pushing the lamp through in front of me I crawled into the secret room. And there he was, stretched in a full prostration on the ground, with his hands pressed against his ears.

He must have fallen asleep like that, because he didn't hear me enter or notice that my smoky little flame had mellowed the inky blackness in which he was lying. When I crept towards him and put my hand on his shoulder, he started like a thief caught red-handed in someone's jewel-box. Scrambling onto hands and knees he backed away from me, eyes huge and mad in the wavering lamplight.

'Jeremiah,' I whispered, 'It's me, Ruth. Don't be scared. I'm on my own.'

But this only made things worse. He cowered against the wall and stared at me; there were black bags as big as pomegranates under his lower lids, and his lips were white as death. His wedding garments hung in tatters where he'd set about them with his nails.

'Tell me what is the matter,' I pleaded. 'Has someone upset you? Have *I* upset you? If I have, just tell me what I've done.'

He looked so appalling, I didn't expect a coherent response. But he said quite lucidly, 'Don't come near me, Ruth. Don't touch me. I told you I couldn't marry you, but you wouldn't listen.'

'Jeremiah, please...' Heartened because he sounded almost like himself, I approached him in spite of his warning, convinced that if I could reason with him, or - better still - if I could press my lips to his, he would repent of this insanity and come home with me, and everything would be as it had been.

But when my fingers touched his cheek he jumped a cubit in the air and shrieked, 'Get away from me! Leave me alone!' and if I hadn't drawn back my hand quite so quickly, I dare say he would have bitten it.

So there we sat facing one another in desperate silence, two human beings who had been closer than brother and sister, each now afraid of the other and wholly unable to do anything to put things right. Eventually I said, 'I don't care what you say, Jeremiah. I'm not leaving you. I still love you.' I wanted to add: I don't even care that you are mad, that you let me down on my special day. For I was young, naive; I thought that if my love were strong enough, it could triumph over anything.

'But you *do* care that I am mad,' Jeremiah murmured, and now it was my turn to jump, because all of a sudden he sounded perfectly sane; and what was more, he had read my mind. 'You've always cared, and that's why you pretended it wasn't true, that no demon had ever spoken to me. Well it has, Ruth. It spoke to me this morning, and all last night before that, so I got no sleep. It said what it's been saying to me for weeks.'

'What?' I asked, but no sound came from my mouth, so I had to ask again, 'What did it say?' though part of me knew already.

'That I cannot marry you! How many times must I say it before you will believe me?'

'But Jeremiah, why not?' I wrung my hands together in frustration. 'Don't you love me after all?'

'Of course I love you. By every god and goddess in Heaven, Ruth, I love you so much I think I shall die if I never see you again. But it's no good. My demon won't *let* me marry you. And don't try to tell me it isn't a demon. I know it must be, because who but a demon would want me so miserable?

Who but a demon would snatch away happiness every time it comes within my grasp?'

'I don't know, Jeremiah,' I muttered, eyes averted, because anger was rising inside me. Then I blurted, 'You should have told me earlier what the voice was saying to you. I just thought you meant you were *scared* to get married, because everyone would be looking at you, and - '

'And you would have listened to me? I think not, Ruth. I think you would have said I was making excuses for myself, because I'm a coward.'

'I've *never* said you were a coward! I've never even thought it!'

'But it's true nonetheless. If I weren't a coward, I'd tell my demon to go away and never come back, and it would obey me. Instead of that, *it* tells *me* what to do, and *I* obey *it.*'

'Then *don't* obey it! Why on earth should you? Anyhow, since when has it been giving you orders? I think you've been lying to me, Jeremiah. You told me it just said seek, wait, learn.'

'That's what it always *has* said, up until now! Now it says: *you must not marry, or have sons and daughters in this place!* Would any but a demon say *that* to me, Ruth? When Adonai has commanded us to go forth and multiply and fill the earth with our descendants? And the gods of Canaan bid us join our bodies with harlots so that our children may be as numerous as the grains of sand in the desert?'

Our voices had been rising as we quarrelled; now Jeremiah's whole body juddered with emotion and the madness seemed to be claiming him once more. His eyes were shot through with blood, and tears poured down his face in torrents, but I had no more pity left for him. While he began to accuse me of being just like everyone else, of not understanding what he'd suffered, of being unable to comprehend the agonies he'd endured as he'd pleaded and argued and fought with whoever - or whatever - was threatening to steal his very life from him, I was glowering at him with teeth gritted and fists clenched. So when he finished up by screaming, '*Everyone* hates me! Even the people who didn't hate me before will hate me now. Even *you* hate me,' I yelled back, 'Perhaps I do, Jeremiah ben Hilkiah! Perhaps I do hate you!'

And snatching up my lamp I crawled furiously out of the room, no longer having any idea what it was that I felt for him, or what I ought to feel. I was sure only of this: that our betrothal was ended, our marriage over for good before it had begun. Hilkiah would reclaim his bride-gold, and my grandmother and I would slowly starve to death. God alone knew what would become of Jeremiah.

CHAPTER 5: JEREMIAH

I remained a whole week in my secret den, slipping out only once each night to take food and water from the priests' kitchens and to pour away my filth. No one thought to look for me again at the sanctuary; scarcely anyone knew that my underground chamber existed.

I had no idea what to do next. I didn't dare give myself up to the sanctuary staff; I was convinced that the Anathoth folk would tear me limb from limb for what I'd done to Ruth, even though they had treated her and her grandmother like scum for years.

But I couldn't live for ever in this dismal little prison. I decided it would be better to starve myself and die in it, but my voice kept saying: *You must eat, or you will have visions, and they won't be visions sent from me. I have not chosen you so that you can throw your life away in a dungeon.* And it said this so clearly that I asked out loud, 'Then why *have* you chosen me? When will you tell me?'

Tell me, tell me, tell me, echoed the rough-hewn walls, and the very stones seemed to be mocking me. But then the voice spoke again, more clearly than before. *I shall tell you when you have learned to obey me and not to fight.*

'I'm *not* fighting, not any more!' I shouted. 'I even gave up my *bride* for you!'

Then how is it that I hear nothing from you but complaints? How is it that I still hear you saying, 'Why me? I didn't ask to be set apart. Choose someone else'? You cannot lie to me, Jeremiah. I know you. I know everything about you. And I want your obedience, not your sacrifices.

'But what if I *don't* want to be chosen? Why don't *I* get to choose what happens to me?'

You do get to choose, Jeremiah. You have always had a choice, and you always will. You know very well that whenever you ask me not to speak to you, I respect your request.'

'Yes, but you make me ill until I change my mind.'

You bring sickness upon yourself, by denying who you are. I chose you because I foreknew you, Jeremiah ben Hilkiah. I knew your character, your essence, your destiny, from the very beginning, before you took your first breath. I knew that only in serving me would you find your fulfilment. When you reject me, you reject yourself. You know who you are, just as you know who I am.

I am... who I am... who I am.., the walls reminded me; I smashed my fists against them, then winced and sucked on my bleeding knuckles. And the voice said: *Leave this place and return to your father's house. There you will find what your heart longs for.*

I forced a laugh. 'You mean I'll find Ruth prepared to kiss and make up? *That's* what my heart longs for; and whoever you are, you can't tell me otherwise!'

Oh, but I can, said the voice, albeit ever so tenderly because I'd flung myself face down on the floor, felled by a great wave of grief for my lost love. *I know you better than you know yourself. You are so stubborn, so wilful. Yet if only you would trust me, I would lead you as a shepherd leads his sheep. When will you learn to cast your cares upon me?*

Never, I thought fiercely; and that evening I did without food, and in the night that followed I neither went for provisions nor emptied my pail. I lay on the ground in torment, with hunger gnawing at my stomach and madness devouring my soul. When morning came my head and eyes ached like fury, every muscle in my body was stiff, and the room stank of sweat and ordure. But the urge to return to my father's house had grown so strong that at length I had to give in.

I came up from the cellars in broad daylight, and marched through the sanctuary in full sight of everyone there. No one approached me, which was scarcely surprising considering what I must have looked like, my hair all tangled up with the dead flowers which had formed my wedding garland, and my bridal robes filthy and torn. Perhaps they thought I'd returned from the world of the dead, expelled because even the shades in Sheol would have nothing to do with me.

My mother and brothers were all at home, but would not speak to me. My father was there also, but he looked so haggard I would scarcely have known him. I went and knelt at his feet without a word, and laid my ravaged head in his lap. When at length I looked up, I could see the conflict raging inside his own mind as he tried to decide if an embrace was in order, or a flogging. Finally he rose to his feet and announced, 'I am going outside to prepare the offerings I vowed to lay upon the altar at the sanctuary if you returned to us unharmed. It may be that I shall talk to you later. Meanwhile, this was left for you.'

He walked across the room and took a scroll from a niche in the wall. When he placed it in my hands, I saw that it was stamped with the royal seal of Josiah.

'When did this arrive?' I gasped. 'Who brought it?'

'A palace courier came with it yesterday,' my father replied, registering no surprise; I think he had lost the capacity for shock. I glanced at my mother; her face was full of hate, perhaps merely for the kings of Judah, but more probably for me. As for my brothers, they were unable to disguise their awe. Aware that they ought to be disgusted at my receiving anything at all from the palace, they couldn't help but be impressed that I'd somehow attracted the attention of Josiah himself - for good or for ill.

I wasn't going to give any of them the satisfaction of watching me roll out the scroll and read it. I took it to the room which my father had built for me to share with Ruth, and I bolted the door. Then I sat down on the pallet which should have been our bridal bed. As my sweating fingers fumbled to break the scroll's seal, I worried that Ruth might have appealed to the King concerning the injustice of her treatment at my hands. After all, I hadn't even had the decency to go to her grandmother and dissolve our engagement legally. I didn't yet know that my father had been there in my stead - and for the sake of his own honour had bidden them keep the gold he'd paid in brideprice.

But the writing on the scroll said nothing about my marriage. It was a personal message, possibly in Josiah's own hand, commencing with an apology for his not having written to me before, and trusting that I might find it within myself to forgive him. He went on to say that he was writing to me now in particular because something marvellous had happened to him: he had been granted a personal revelation of Adonai. After years of instruction from his tutor the prophet Zephaniah he had at last seen for himself what the faith of his earliest forefathers had meant, and how for generations its purity had been perverted by Assyrian influence. Now the scales had fallen from his eyes, and he could see that there was one God only: Adonai whose name is too holy to be uttered. Therefore the trappings of Assyrian idolatry must be eradicated from his realm, so that Judah could once again hold her head up high among the kingdoms of the world. He himself had repented of his arrogance and given himself wholly to Adonai, as a result of which he'd begun to see the prayers of his heart being answered and to hear his God speaking to him through the words of the holy Torah.

'Not that I hear him in quite the way that you once did,' Josiah's message continued. 'I have only convictions and realizations; I hear no voice. But Jeremiah: *Zephaniah* hears, in exactly the way you did. I've talked to him about you, and now I'm *convinced* it was Adonai's voice you were hearing, and that if you hear it still, you may have the gift of prophecy just as Zephaniah has; and just as Moses had, and Hosea, and Isaiah! Oh, how I wish you could come to Jerusalem and we could talk about this face to face, and you could help me in the task God has entrusted to me. There is so much to be done, and so much wisdom will be required of me. The Emperor of Assyria is still our master, and if we offend him he may strike at us the more viciously now that his power is weaker, just as the lion can be more dangerous once he is wounded.

'Still, Zephaniah says that I must not summon you; that life here at court would destroy what you are to become, even if your gifting is true, until your calling is made plain and you are sure that you want to accept it. But know this, Jeremiah: I have not forgotten you, and I long for the day

when we can renew our friendship. Adonai bless you for ever. -
Josiah.'

When I reached the end of the letter, a euphoria
consumed me the like of which I'd never experienced. I knew
not whether to dance in ecstasy or pass out upon the bed; it
was as though everything at once made sense; even I made
sense, with all my misery and my madness. I felt that if I were
to leap from a tower I could fly like an eagle; if I plunged in
the sea I could dive with the dolphins and come to no harm.
Once upon a time, Josiah had told me that I might be hearing
the voice of his mother's God, and the notion had turned me
faint; now he was suggesting that this God might have
designed me for greatness, and I found that I was laughing
myself to tears. I wasn't laughing at the absurdity of it all, nor
was I laughing because Josiah truly had come to Anathoth,
and still wanted to be my friend. I laughed because there were
angels dancing with my spirit and making me alive.

I didn't care that my parents and brothers would be
able to hear me. I didn't even care when they started banging
on my door and shaking it for all they were worth, or when my
father's voice called, 'Jeremiah? Jeremiah! What the hell is the
matter with you? What is going on in there?' Then he kicked
the door off its hinges, and ran and dragged me from the bed.
I just hung there in his arms, sobbing with laughter. He
slapped my face, and momentarily I sobered up sufficiently to
see how frankly frightened he was. Then the euphoria claimed
me again, and he tossed me back on my bed in disgust.

Never had I sensed the presence of the Divine quite
like this, nor known that anyone could. I felt like a bird soaring
on the wind, or a cloud floating, floating... and I heard Adonai
say: *This is what it can be like for the rest of your life if you
don't fight me. I can be closer to you than any friend, any
brother, any wife. I can be all these things and more to you, as
I was to Moses himself: don't you know that when his wife
Zipporah died, my presence took her place for him, filling the
void which her passing had left? I knew you in the womb,
Jeremiah; I formed you there; I am within you, and you are in*

me. If you unite your spirit with mine, nothing else will ever matter to you, compared with this.

After that I must have slipped from ecstasy directly into sleep, for the next I knew, the sun had sunk low enough to be coming straight in at my window and I lay flat on my back in its softening light, too shattered to move. I thought: I'll leave the priesthood at once. I'll seek out the sons of the prophets, I'll join the disciples of Isaiah.

But though the elation was gone, Adonai's spirit hadn't left me. He said: *You'll do no such thing, Jeremiah. The sons of the prophets may teach you knowledge of dreams, the interpretation of oracles, the use of music for inducement of trances, and how to speak words of power in such a way as to make your wishes come true. But I have more cult seers and court augurs than I know what to do with, and I no more want that for you than I wanted you to be a priest. You are not to learn techniques, but learn to know me.*

'This is the only ministry to which you have called me: to know you? I thought that prophets preached to the people, and saw into the future, and had their oracles recorded for posterity?'

The word prophet is Josiah's, not mine. You must not be hasty to define yourself, for in so doing you will create boundaries for yourself which are not of me. Moses was my prophet, but he was so much more besides; and as for you, I have called you to nothing as yet. What you experienced today was not my calling, but my love.

'I don't understand. Was Isaiah himself not of you? He saw himself as a prophet. Are his words not binding for all eternity? Is this not why they were written in scrolls, not just spoken into thin air?'

My word is alive, Jeremiah. It does not repeat what was said in the past. I am who I am, the same for ever. But you must be possessed of my spirit to interpret my word for your own generation.

I am who I am... now that haunting phrase made sense to me too.

Presently I decided that before the sun went down altogether I must find a tablet and compose a reply to Josiah. I began and began again three or four times, unsure whether to write as to a friend, or to Judah's king. Somehow I found a way in the end to tell him how happy his letter had made me, in spite of the tragedy of my ruined marriage. As an afterthought I bade him send any future correspondence to the sanctuary and not to my father's house. And I called him 'Josiah', not 'Your Majesty' or 'my lord'.

I had no idea how to get my letter to the palace. As a little boy I'd been in the habit of giving such letters to an old man whose brother was a palace servant, but he was long dead. He had a grandson, I knew, but the latter was a of Hanamel's flock and would scarcely be eager to do me a favour.

Anyhow, it was too late in the day to go and see him now. So I spent the night on the bed where I ought to have lain with Ruth, and in the loneliness and the sleeplessness the conflict in my head began all over again. It isn't *fair*, I complained to Adonai; why can't I have Ruth *and* you? It's all very well for you to pour your spirit upon me till I'm drunk as a Philistine, but what about her? She has lost me, together with her only hope of marriage and of bearing her own children. What will you give *her* which can make up for what you've taken?

But Adonai said only: *You're fighting me again, Jeremiah. I shall provide for Ruth, and for her grandmother, just as I shall provide for you. It isn't for you to know how I shall do it.*

I rose at dawn and went directly to the house of Hanamel's boy before my nerve could fail me. Anyone I passed on the way crossed the street to avoid me; girls veiled their faces and more than one spat at my feet. The boy wouldn't speak to me - not until I offered him gold, and that did the trick. I told him there would be a reply in time, and that if there were not, I would know that he'd betrayed me.

Then I returned to the sanctuary, and the priests wouldn't speak to me either, even those who had once been kind to me. I took up my old duties without a word; at least no one hindered me. I was given food and water, but only because I was a human being. They would have done the same and more for a total stranger.

Days went by, and I began to fear that my courier had indeed let me down. No letter came from Josiah, no word.

Just when I was starting to think I should never again hold conversation with anyone, a softly-spoken young traveller appeared at the high place seeking lodgings, and it was I whom he chanced to accost. He was poorly clad and dusty from the road, his skin was as dark as tanned leather, and when he turned back the hood of his cloak I saw that his hair was as curly as a lamb's wool. He told me he was a pilgrim under oath to his god to journey to Anathoth and discharge a sacred duty; could he stay until it was accomplished?

But of course, I replied, you are most welcome; and I set about readying a room for him, and fetched a pitcher of water to wash his feet. I wondered what god he served, for I was sure that he had come a long way, and it struck me as odd that he hadn't gone on to Jerusalem instead; by reputation Anathoth was more a place for goddesses than for gods. I didn't ask, since it would have been the height of insolence. But I blushed scarlet when the young man remarked, 'You think it strange that I should choose to come here? Well, it may be that I shall explain my purpose to you, if Adonai permits it.'

To cover my embarrassment I asked, as was proper, 'Would you like me to arrange an interview for you with one of the priests, sir? They are happy to give counsel as well as to make offerings on a visitor's behalf. I can arrange it when I fetch you something to eat.'

But the pilgrim chuckled quietly and waved a dismissive hand. 'I'm not hungry at present, thank you. And as for arranging an interview, I hardly see the need. *You* are a priest, are you not?'

Taken further aback, I muttered something about barely having started out upon my training. The man said, 'Does training matter so very much? I thought that the job of a priest was to mediate between a worshipper and his god? Surely all that is required is a personal knowledge of both, and I'll warrant you know your god a good deal better already than most of your colleagues ever will.'

I gave up trying to disguise my astonishment, and knelt open-mouthed with his foot in my lap. My guest chuckled again; he was manifestly enjoying my discomfiture, though I couldn't be angry because there wasn't a trace of malice in his amusement.

If I hadn't assumed from his exotic colouring and dusty garments that he'd travelled a great distance, I might have put two and two together and worked out who he was. As it was, I did not.

When I'd got him installed in his quarters, I left him to settle in, and went about my customary tasks. But shortly before I retired to bed he sent me a message, asking that in the morning he might be granted an interview after all, but with me.

That night I had more trouble sleeping even than usual. This dark-skinned stranger somehow expected me to give him spiritual counsel, and I was ignorant and unworthy. It was almost dawn when I thought to call upon Adonai and ask him the obvious questions: 'Who is this man? What is this sacred duty he has come to discharge?'

But Adonai said only: *The traveller is my servant. Do not be afraid to speak with him; I have brought him here so that you may learn and be fitted to serve me also.*

In the morning therefore I took the man his breakfast, and he bade me sit down with him and share it. Then, reading me just like a rolled-out parchment, he suggested that we go and do our talking in the hills.

I quickly discovered that the stranger was in no need of any kind of counsel for himself. Although he asked me many questions about God and the gods, he already knew the answers. It seemed that he was testing me, and I had to confess how little I really understood about the things that mattered. I'd been tutored by priests who were hardly less ignorant than I was, and all I could hope to do was answer from my heart. Yet these answers appeared to please my mysterious examiner more than if I had read all the books in the world.

And gently he started to teach me, as we walked side by side among the olive trees or along the arid ridgeways, gazing down together into the desert valleys or toward the green terraced hills upon which the city of David was built. Sensitively he explained to me that the priests who had been my mentors were hopelessly compromised, and when I said that somehow I'd always known this to be true, he began to list for me the things they did which were evil: bowing to idols and offering unclean flesh upon their altars; working magic; cutting their own flesh to induce their gods to respond to them; inveigling neighbours' sons and daughters into sordid prostitution in the name of religion. Even worse, they condoned the worship of the Mother alongside that of Adonai; they let their wives bake bread for the Queen of Heaven and weep for Tammuz, the young god who dies each year, just as they do in Babylon; and they turned blind eyes to the roasting of innocent children in the fires of the Tophet.

All of these things my father did regularly with no qualms at all, yet I just kept nodding and saying, 'I know. You don't need to tell me that these practices are wrong. I have been confused, but now it has all come clear for me. There are true and false priests, as surely as there are true and false prophets. Adonai alone is God, and him alone am I to serve.'

I surprised even myself with my sudden certainty; as for the pilgrim, he embraced me as though I were his long-lost brother. 'Peace be upon you, and a thousand blessings, Jeremiah ben Hilkiah,' he said. 'My name is Zephaniah ben Cushi, ben Gedaliah, ben Amariah, ben Hezekiah who once ruled over Judah. I am chaplain to the Lady Jedidah, Mother of the King, and to His Majesty King Josiah himself, may he live for ever. And you are the one I was commanded to find. There's no mistaking it.'

'Josiah sent you here, to find me?' I exclaimed, veritably shaking with excitement.

'Not exactly. It was Adonai who sent me. But it was because of what Josiah told me about you that I first suspected you might be the object of my search. Since your letter came, the King has talked of little else but seeing you again. Now I understand why.'

I flung my arms about this man I barely knew and said, 'I so much want to see him, too! Take me now; I cannot wait.'

'I'm afraid that you must.' The prophet smiled, and stroked my hair as though I were a little boy. 'Josiah will send for you, once your calling has been confirmed.'

'What more confirmation do I need? I have been hearing Adonai's voice all my life; I've been filled with his spirit, and told by Josiah and by you that I have the gifting! What else can I possibly need?'

Zephaniah sighed, and held me away at arms' length. 'You need patience, my ardent young friend, and a large portion of wisdom. You are eager to be reunited with the King, but not for this alone must you go to Jerusalem. It is best that you do not go there at all until you have entered into the divine riches which are held in trust for you, and of these as yet you understand nothing.

'Like you I heard God's voice as a child; like you I experienced ecstasy in the presence of his love. But many have known such blessing and imagined that this was sufficient; they have styled themselves prophets and deceived both themselves and the people. When at last my *calling* came, it was something different altogether. I *knew* what it was, and you will know too. Adonai has breathed his sweet breath over you, but you have not felt his hand come upon you, or his power take control of you.

'Your emotions are strong, but they are *your* emotions; when your calling comes, Adonai's spirit and yours will be inextricably entwined, and after that you will feel the very feelings of God. Not merely his joy, but his compassion too, and his pain, and you will think that all this must destroy you. You will be frightened; you'll be broken. Yet this is only the beginning.

'Next will come the knowledge: knowledge of things you could not possibly have known had Adonai not chosen to reveal them to you, and the desire to speak this knowledge aloud will be like a fire in your mouth. You'll feel the weight of God's judgment upon the world, as though it were crushing you alone; you'll be taken over, Jeremiah, until when you are old there will be nothing of you remaining. Ready as you may be for a reunion with Josiah, you are nowhere near ready for what must come with it.'

He was right, of course. So I whispered, 'Zephaniah, what if I'm *never* ready?'

'You won't ever think that you are; but Adonai will know. He will never send you joy or agony more than you can bear. But you must trust him and not rush ahead, nor linger behind. Adonai's timing is perfect. He will reveal to you no more than he needs to reveal, and for that you should be grateful. The venerable Moses himself could stand only to see the hindparts of his God as he passed by; and even for that he had to be hidden in the cleft of a rock.'

'You mean - I'll *see* things, I won't just hear them? I'll have visions?'

'When Isaiah was called, he watched the glory of Adonai filling the holy Temple. He was so afraid, he thought he must die on the spot. Others have fallen into trances and observed things happening far, far away, so vividly that they knew not what they had seen in their spirit and what with their own two eyes. Such blurring of distinctions can turn a man's head; it can make him mad, like someone who sits in the noonday sun and fries his brains. Even if you do trust fully in Adonai, you may find yourself doubting your sanity.'

I said nothing to that, but Zephaniah continued, 'I know: you have had such doubts already. Don't be alarmed; I had those too.'

He was looking straight into my eyes as he spoke these last words, and in that single instant I could see all the pain he had suffered as a child - the same pain *I* had suffered - and the constant misunderstanding he'd encountered from infancy, which I myself had encountered too. In that moment it seemed that our two bruised souls were welded together, just as my spirit was destined to be fused with Adonai's, and I laid my pounding head on Zephaniah's shoulder as once I'd lain it on Ruth's. Zephaniah made no attempt to rouse me, simply waiting, supporting my wilting body in his arms, because all my physical strength was somehow being sapped by what was growing in my spirit. But when finally I stirred myself to look at him again, I saw that he too was deeply moved.

I said when I was able: 'Zephaniah, tell me what *your* calling was like. Did *you* see visions?'

I was well aware that I'd asked him the most personal of questions, and had only dared because of the bond which I felt was now established between us. He said quietly, 'No, there were no visions for me. There have never been visions, as such... not yet.

'But the calling isn't so much in what you see, or what you hear. You are *seized* by Adonai; he takes possession of you, body, soul and spirit. He seized my limbs and made them move as though of their own accord; he seized my tongue and burned it, and all the organs inside me, and my mind itself, and scoured them out. It was as though I were a dry wadi where rubbish has been thrown, and a flash flood comes and carries off the dross without even knowing that it does so. The water gives life to the desert, but anything that was living in the filth of the wadi itself is swept away to destruction.'

A shudder passed through him at the mere recollection of it. 'I sincerely believed that my end had come; I thought I was dying. And in a way I was, because that is precisely what the calling means. You *are* dying, to yourself, and being reborn as the vessel of Adonai, to use as he wills - yet only if you will it too. It is a mystery; I cannot pretend otherwise.'

I swallowed hard, because my throat had gone dry as the wadi whose picture he'd painted with his words. When I could find my voice I asked, 'And what next? What were you called to do?'

'I was called to *be,* Jeremiah, not to do, as indeed are all those whom Adonai touches. The doing grows out of the being, and out of the things which are revealed to us. It is in how the revelations come that each of us differs, one from another. One may fall into a trance and become quite insensible of the world around him. Another may be walking to market in full possession of his faculties, and suddenly the spectacle of the laden stalls, and the noise, and the smells of the fruit and the meat and the animals will all become charged with spiritual meaning and may speak to him of greed or exploitation or the futility of a life lived by bread alone. Or the same man may hear a voice one day and see a vision the next. It matters not which; Adonai's spirit will not be constrained.'

'But for you there has only been the voice?'

'The voice and the... the seeing of things in a different way.' He'd been casting about for a phrase to sum up the experience more succinctly, yet couldn't find one. Although he had delivered Adonai's message many times to kings and to multitudes, he'd never needed to explain just how it had come to him.

'One evening,' he said, 'I walked through an ancient village abandoned and lying in ruins. Owls were hooting from its windows and trees grew up from the fallen walls. There were sheep and goats grazing inside the houses, and all that had once made them homes had been stripped away. Then Adonai spoke to me so clearly that I thought one inhabitant must have remained behind to recite for me a lament he'd composed in his desolation:

'Thus one day soon will great Nineveh be;
Thus will her glory be turned all to dust.
For the hand of the Lord has Assyria smitten;
The city which crowned her, his wrath will devour.'

I stifled an involuntary laugh. 'Adonai spoke like that to you, in rhythm, like a poem?'

'It is not unusual. How do you think the oracles of Isaiah came to be in poetic form? You don't imagine he sat down quietly somewhere when he had time on his hands, and redrafted them that way for his own amusement?'

I shrugged my shoulders. 'I don't know, Zephaniah. There's still so much I don't know.'

'And so much time to learn it,' Zephaniah reassured me with a smile.

'Is it true that Nineveh will soon be destroyed? Assyria's capital city? I cannot believe it.'

'Neither could the people of Jerusalem to whom my oracle was delivered. But their unbelief will not prevent it from happening, any more than yours will; and neither would my own, for that matter. But as it happens I do believe it, because I have been told other things equally unlikely, and watched

them being fulfilled before my very eyes. I was told that His Majesty King Josiah would open his heart to Adonai, and anything more unlikely than that I could not have imagined.'

'Tell me more about him, please,' I begged. 'Is he still handsome, and proud, and brave?'

'Handsome as his late lamented father, yes indeed, and almost as tall. As for pride - until his recent enlightenment he had a great deal too much of it. He is Amon's son and Manasseh's grandson, after all. It has been my task to channel his intelligence and his ardour fitly - a weighty burden if ever there was one, and I shall be glad to hand it on to you one day. Becoming king so young was not good for him, Jeremiah, and would that his father's sins had not made it necessary. You may even have disliked His Gracious Majesty had you met him again but a year ago.'

I laughed without restraint at this; how could I ever have disliked Josiah? Then I asked, 'But how has he changed? What's different about him today?'

'Well, you might say that he has begun to display those qualities which one hopes may make him a great king. He has the rare ability to discern the spiritual potential of those who serve him, just as he discerned your own, thus ensuring that he appoints the right individuals to the right offices. And he is more compassionate now, more thoughtful.' Zephaniah smiled again, and his teeth showed very white against the uncommon darkness of his skin. 'For example, he thought about you for the first time in years, and was profoundly sorry that he must have made you so unhappy when he was forced to leave Anathoth without saying goodbye.

'I just wish he had spoken to me sooner about you, then I might have spared you years of misery. But not even prophets see *everything* in advance. Like anyone else, we have to trust Adonai for our futures; and you and I must trust that he had his reasons for deferring our meeting until now. Certainly the sadness you have endured, and the doubts with which you have struggled, will make you stronger in days to come.'

'What *did* Josiah say about me?'

'He told me about the voice you'd heard, and about the way you'd befriended him with no thought of gain for yourself. He told me about the power he believed he'd seen locked up inside you, and about the intensity he saw in your eyes. And my spirit quickened, because suddenly I started to wonder if you might be the one who would one day receive my mantle, as it were, as Elisha received Elijah's.'

The analogy was lost on me, because at the time the names of these two most famous of Israelite prophets meant nothing to me. Zephaniah continued: 'But Josiah had had other things on his mind, what with having two sons to bring up already, and the elder being so sickly, and his beloved Zebidah almost losing her own life giving birth to the younger. She'll have no more children now, the physicians say, and much as Josiah adores her, he may have no choice but to marry again. It is not good for a king to have so few heirs... Jeremiah? Whatever is the matter?'

I'd let him go on talking about the King's responsibilities without interruption, but I'd been sitting there devastated, swamped by alternate waves of jealousy and guilt. No matter what had happened to me, I knew it was mean of me to begrudge Josiah the joys of wife and family, yet I did, dreadfully, and despised myself for it. He ought to have told me in his letter that he was married, I thought fiercely, though there was no real reason why he should have done so.

'Come, Jeremiah,' Zephaniah chided me gently. 'Your soul is in turmoil. Tell me the cause.'

At first I refused, turning my head away from him before passing the back of one hand across my eyes. Then I found myself blurting, 'It's not fair!' and the whole sorry tale of my wrecked marriage came flooding out on a tide of grief. Zephaniah waited patiently while I got it all said, then held me close and assured me it was quite all right to weep, because the heart of a servant of God must never grow hard, but be sensitive as a maiden's. However, when he said that he knew exactly how I was feeling, I shouted, 'You don't! I'll warrant that *you* have a wife and family waiting for you in Jerusalem .'

'That is where you are wrong, Jeremiah.'

I sniffed, and searched his face with brimming eyes.

'I never believed that it was right for me to marry. A prophet must suffer much, and his family with him. I should not have wished this upon any woman who might have been fool enough to love me.'

'You mean... I'll never marry? No prophet can marry or beget his own sons?'

'It is as I said: each one of us is different, and our ministries are different too. Isaiah married and had many children, to whom he gave prophetic names. Hosea did the same; in fact he was commanded specifically to marry a woman who would break his heart with her infidelities. Perhaps one day Adonai will want you to marry too; perhaps he'll even want the same for me. But until such time, he has chosen to protect us both from the sorrow and distraction which a mistaken marriage can bring.'

Unconvinced, I hung my head and muttered through my tumbling hair, 'Then you have never been in love, Zephaniah.'

'That is where you are wrong again,' he replied, with such unexpected fervour that I shook aside my fringe and looked at him, just in time to glimpse the fleeting wistfulness in his eyes. 'Boys of your age imagine that you alone have hearts of flesh whilst those of your elders are made of stone, when in truth you have not lived long enough to know the first thing about love as it really is.'

Then his countenance altered again as he saw that he was hurting me. 'I'm sorry, Jeremiah. Only do not presume to interpret the feelings of another unless Adonai has spoken to you first. I have suffered what you suffer in this respect as in so many others, and at least you are not reminded constantly of what you cannot possess by being compelled to look upon the object of your desire each and every day of your life.' He paused, needing to master his own feelings before going on. 'You see how hard is the lot of a man of God. Our hearts must be tender so that they can feel with the feelings of Adonai, yet because of that tenderness we yearn for affection and so often are tempted to seek it in all the wrong ways, and in the wrong places, and from the wrong people. Even when we do remain within the will of God, our hearts can be bruised and broken as Hosea's was.'

'I don't believe that Adonai would order a man to marry a woman who was going to be unfaithful. This Hosea must have heard wrongly. He must have followed his own desires and paid the penalty.'

'No, Jeremiah. He was one of the greatest prophets there has ever been. His whole life was Adonai's message. I am fortunate enough to own the scroll on which his oracles were recorded; it came down through my family from King Hezekiah who acquired it when the northern kingdom of Israel fell. I shall lend it you to read, for I have it with me. I like to read a portion of it each night before I sleep.'

But I had no wish to learn about a man who gave his heart to Adonai only to have it broken. It made me very afraid.

Nevertheless, as I was readying myself for bed that night, Zephaniah came to the room where I slept and handed me the scroll. 'Read from it before you lie down,' he bade me. 'I shall miss it tonight, but your need is greater.'

'I'll read it in the morning,' I said. 'I'm too tired now.' And so I was; I felt utterly drained, for not only had so much been said which was still rumbling around in my head like thunder, but also I'd never in my life spent so many hours at a stretch in the company of another human being.

But when I fell upon my mattress and sought refuge in oblivion, the scroll would not allow it. There it lay on my table, and its very presence in the room made the air heavy as camelskin. In the end I had to give in; I unfastened the leather thong which kept Hosea's words bound up, and sat cross-legged on my pallet with a lamp at my side and the parchment unrolled across my knees.

Then an ecstasy transported me; reading the words of this great man of God I felt exactly as I had upon reading my letter from Josiah.

When I found and chose Israel - thus says the Lord –
It was like finding grapes where no vines had been sown.
When first my eyes fell on my people, your fathers,
It was like seeing figs plump and ripe on the bough.

It wasn't so much the choice of words or images that moved me. The work as a whole seemed imbued with the spirit of Adonai; it somehow leached out from the parchment itself and began to upset the balance in my head so I could barely sit upright. That was when I realized that there is ecstasy of pain as well as of joy; yes, I was becoming part of something beautiful, something transcendent, something that made ultimate sense of everything. Yet it was also something awesome and awful, too awful to contemplate.

And as I ploughed on and on into what Hosea had written about his wretched marriage, I felt that I knew him, that I felt with him, and through him I began to sense the earliest inklings of the feelings of the Divine.

How can I leave you, my bride, my own people?
Israel, how can I let you be lost?
My heart will not let me consign you to ruin;
The love that I bear you is simply too strong.
And so I shall lead you once more through the wilderness,
Wooing you back with love's whispers and sighs;
You shall return, as it were, into Egypt;
Assyria's Emperor shall make you his slaves.

It mattered not that I didn't yet understand how the words applied to Judah or to me - or even to Israel for whose people they had been composed. It was enough that when I tasted Hosea's sorrow, tears started in my eyes; and when I tasted the merest hint of the grief that assails Adonai himself on account of the adultery of his own fickle bride, the tears spilled over and poured down my cheeks like Noah's flood.

While I sat there sobbing all over Zephaniah's priceless heirloom and hardly knowing where or who I was, Hosea's words imprinted themselves indelibly upon my quickened soul so that for the remainder of my days I would be able to recall them, syllable for syllable. Accelerated thoughts and amplified emotions made a wreck of me, as though some long-forgotten chamber had come unlocked inside my head and unleashed holy desolation all through me.

Lastly came the fear. It wasn't a fear for myself; I was too far gone for that, trembling and moaning and driven half out of my wits. It was a fear for Judah, for God's people who were my people also, and for the world itself. Hosea had foreseen the horrendous judgment which would fall upon Israel, Judah's sister to the north, and it had fallen just as he'd said.

These fools sow the wind, and so harvest the whirlwind;
*   Their stalk has no head, and produces no flour.*
Hence they will vanish, like chaff from the threshing,
*   Like smoke from a hearth which escapes through a door;*
Like mist in the morning which hangs in the valleys,
*   Like dew after dawn, they will no more be seen.*
Like twigs which are carried away upon water,
*   Israel, her king, and her pride will be gone.*

In Hosea's day Judah had been spared, but I knew that it would not always be so. Hosea had condemned the northern kingdom for the same sins I saw committed all around me every day: idolatry, sorcery, the condoning of pagan forms of worship, ritual prostitution, exploitation of the defenceless. Josiah had expressed a desire to deal with the idolatry and pagan practices, but had said nothing whatever about social injustice, and would he be able to achieve even that which he desired? No doubt there had been plenty of good intentions among the rulers of Israel too, but good intentions are no substitute for righteous actions. Therefore Israel had forfeited her king, her walled cities, her high places; the very fabric of her national existence had been shredded by the talons of Adonai himself. Israel's destruction had been no luckless tragedy which her God had found himself powerless to prevent. On the contrary, Adonai himself had declared war upon his own people, much as it had broken his heart to do so.

And what he had done to Israel, he could do to Judah as well.

CHAPTER 6: ZEPHANIAH

I retired to bed that night with an odd sense of dislocation, as though I'd drunk too much, but not enough to be merry.

I had never sought disciples, although I'd long been convinced that eventually I should meet and recognize the man who would take over where I was destined to leave off. But I hadn't looked to meet him so soon. I'd expected this to happen when I was well on in years, a venerable sage handing on a lifetime's experience to a grown man whose shoulders were broad enough to assume the heavy load of responsibility.

Yet here I was, not thirty years old, becoming more and more sure that an effete and diffident youth of sixteen whom I'd only just met was to become my successor. Years of listening for the voice of Adonai had attuned my inner ear finely, and the faintest whisper within my spirit had been enough to despatch me to Anathoth to see if this boy of whom Josiah had spoken could be the one. And now, having spent but the briefest interval in his company, I should have been surprised if I'd learned that he was not.

For never in my life had I met another like him. There was such a gravity about him, such a charged space all around him which you invaded at your peril. His eyes were so full of loss and of liquid eloquence that they could have belonged to an old, old man, and the thick black fringe behind which he hid them seemed designed as much for your protection as for his.

I have to confess that I was strangely stirred by him in a way I couldn't have predicted, notwithstanding my prophetic gifting. He had already broken one girl's heart, and would doubtless break more before he was through. It was his shyness perhaps, his sensitivity... but what if he were *too* shy, *too* sensitive? He seemed so starved of affection, and he wept so easily... where would it all lead? *Would* he be able to bear the burden which Adonai was going to place upon him? I'd always believed that our God makes no mistakes, yet occasionally one cannot help but wonder.

In the morning I had to rouse him myself, because he had been awake half the night. Once he'd rubbed the sleep from his eyes, he cowered from me in dread and wouldn't speak; eventually he waved one hand at Hosea's scroll, and I discerned the cause of his alarm. His tears had wrought havoc, but when I didn't scold him, because I understood, he poured out to me the whole story of his night's experience. He finished up by asking me plaintively, 'Is disaster going to come upon Judah too, Zephaniah? You said that Nineveh would be destroyed... but what of Jerusalem? Please tell me that our nation will survive.'

I fear that I cannot, because I do indeed sense that Judah's days are numbered.'

'But didn't Adonai promise your ancestor King David that he would preserve his dynasty and its inheritance for ever?'

'Adonai's covenant with David does not override the one he made with Moses. If God's people do not keep their part of *that* agreement, rejecting idolatry and everything connected with it, then all subsequent agreements become void. And so many sacred documents were lost in the reign of Manasseh that I'm not sure anyone today understands fully what the Law of Moses demands of us. Some ancient texts survive, but no one can be sure that they are complete, or how they fit together.'

'But if Nineveh falls, and Assyria with it, surely Judah will be safe? For what nation but Assyria is mighty enough to destroy us?'

'Adonai could summon armies of warriors from lands of which we've never heard. Or he could call up the winds from their lairs at the four corners of the world and blow away our fortified cities without a sword being raised. Judgment must begin with the people of God; but it may go on from there until the foundations of the earth itself are split apart.'

Jeremiah pulled the blanket in which he'd slept tight about his slender frame. He said, 'I wish you wouldn't talk like that. Words have power, do they not? Especially the words of a prophet. Surely now that Josiah has turned to Adonai, disaster can be averted.'

'Perhaps, if the personal repentance of a king can always purchase redemption for his realm. But things may have gone too far wrong for that.'

'Adonai could reject his own people entirely? For ever? I don't believe it.'

'No, not entirely. A remnant might somehow be preserved; indeed, I am sure that it will be. But it may be smaller even than the remnant which escaped the Flood.'

'Perhaps there will be another flood, just like the first one.'

'No, that isn't possible. Adonai made a covenant with Noah even before the one he made with Moses; he promised there would never be a flood of that magnitude again. We simply do not know the form which the next judgment will take. For myself, I don't care to speculate.'

Nor, I think, did Jeremiah. He let the blanket fall from his back and wandered out into the morning sunshine without another word. Through the doorway I watched him bend and smile faintly as he examined a clump of bright spring flowers growing up through a crack in the sanctuary pavement. I suppose it reassured him to contemplate the beauty and constancy of nature, but such reassurance is false because life itself is as vulnerable as a single petal drifting on the breeze.

At least I may not live to see all that I have loved come to ruin, I thought; but that was no consolation either, because it only made me think that perhaps I was fated not to live very long at all. I wasn't afraid to die, but that is not to say that I was ready. There was so much in life which I hadn't yet done, because Adonai hadn't allowed me to do it. Surely he would grant me time enough to arrange my own wedding, to enjoy but one night in the arms of the woman I loved? The Lady Jedidah was still so beautiful, and I firmly believed she wanted me as much as I wanted her. I'm of royal blood, after all.

Jeremiah sat with me while I breakfasted, but he ate nothing. When I'd finished, I told him that I should have to stay for some weeks, if it were permitted; I showed him my pouch full of royal gold and insisted on paying my way. There was so much for him to learn - and to unlearn.

Not that this went down well with his colleagues at the sanctuary. When he'd returned to them in disgrace with his betrothal dissolved, they'd wanted nothing more to do with him. Now that he had a rich guest from the palace, there were suddenly all kinds of chores they expected him to assist with. A group of so-called prophets came to us one day and reproached us for spending so much time conversing in private; when I told them that Jeremiah and I were serving Adonai more faithfully than they were, a torrent of verbal abuse rained down on us.

Jeremiah winced visibly under its stinging spray, but when they had gone I said, 'Let them talk. It's not uncommon for their kind to be more bitter in their condemnation of God's servants than anyone else. But we must not let them silence his voice.'

The boy made no response, and again I thought: he will never cope; he's been criticized all his life simply for being himself. Then I scolded myself for my gloomy thoughts and tried to block them out, because I feared he would read them.

To distract him I resumed a discourse I'd begun earlier that day concerning the history of our people, and the role within it which the genuine prophets had played. Jeremiah went back to being ashamed of his ignorance, and indeed for the son of a priest it was quite appalling. He knew something of Moses, and how he'd freed our forebears from slavery in Egypt and led them back to the Promised Land, parting the Red Sea and receiving the Ten Commandments as he went. Curiously, he knew all about Eli and Samuel and the destruction of Shiloh where the Ark of the Covenant had been kept. But of the period in between when our land had been governed by the Judges, he knew only names like Gideon's and Samson's, and the sorts of stories told to children at bedtime. Of the united kingdom under Saul, David and Solomon, he knew a little; of the divided kingdom and its kings he knew only names once again. I had to recount for him the miracles performed by the prophets Elijah and Elisha, and to describe to him the visions of Amos and Micaiah, the admonitions of Micah, the predictions of Isaiah. These men and others had brought Adonai's word to the people of their respective generations, and each time the message had been the same: *Repent of your wickedness and renounce your evil ways, or the Day of Adonai will mean your destruction and not your vindication.*

Jeremiah took it all in with scant comment, except that he interrupted me sullenly now and again with the same objection each time. 'It isn't right that the people of Judah should be damned for doing things which go on everywhere else as well. Every nation has its idols and its iniquitous customs.'

'And who are you to tell the Creator of the Universe what is right and wrong for him to do?' I countered gently. 'Surely you must know that much more will be expected of those to whom much has been given? It does not do for the man of God to have opinions, Jeremiah; nor can any of God's creatures presume to make pronouncements about justice based upon their own feelings. There can be no place in God's kingdom for the prophet who tells men the things they want to hear.'

'I know,' he sighed, and I was confident that in his head he believed me, but in his heart he pitied the aged priests and prophets of Anathoth who had once been kind to him and to those who consulted them, comforting them with words of peace when in truth the very hosts of Heaven were ranged against them. And so I had to tell him there is a cruelty in misplaced kindness, just as surely as there is kindness which has to be cruel. He said, 'I've known enough cruelty to last me all my days. Don't you be cruel to me too, Zephaniah.'

'What do you mean?' I asked him, but he gave me no answer, turning instead to watch a pair of butterflies dancing patterns together in the still summer air. And as I watched them too, I knew precisely what he meant: don't teach me too much too quickly, Zephaniah, because then you will have no more reason to stay here, and I don't want to be left once again without a friend.

If my life had been my own, he needn't have worried on this account. Much as I missed Jerusalem and those there whom I loved, with each day that passed I loved Jeremiah more. Whereas teaching Josiah had been a battle every step of the way, teaching Jeremiah was pure delight. Perhaps it was because of what he would become; perhaps it had been like this for Elijah with Elisha, I don't know.

What I do know is that I began to tell him all kinds of things which there was no real need for him to hear. I told him all about myself, and my parents, and my own miserable childhood; about the mockery I'd endured because of the swarthiness of my skin and the curls in my hair. Cushi my father had earned his name because he was half Cushite, his mother having been from Ethiopia, but I'd always looked more like her than he did. It was scarcely any wonder that my playmates refused to believe that King Hezekiah had been among my ancestors.

As if all this hadn't been enough, I'd been mocked because of my family's piety, too; my name Zephaniah means 'God has hidden', because I was born in the reign of Manasseh when all that was of God had to be hidden, and we'd tried to practise our faith in Adonai in secret.

And all the while I was persuading myself that the things I was saying to him needed to be said, and that the time we were sharing needed to be shared, and that the long walks we took together on the sun-baked hills all needed to be taken, to prepare Jeremiah for what lay ahead of him.

Eventually I could delude myself no longer. Adonai's admonishment had grown from a whisper in my ear to a griping in my bowels more painful than I could bear in silence. At least Jeremiah could sense the struggling inside me; he knew I wasn't about to abandon him simply through wanting to be elsewhere.

So when he found me packing up my few belongings early one morning some seven weeks after I'd arrived, he made no attempt to deter me. He just sat and watched, and listened when I said that the longer I stayed, the harder it would get; that we could not expect Adonai to go on blessing our friendship when we were rebelling against his will for our lives.

When I'd come to the end of all I could think of to say, he shook his fringe into his eyes and said with disarming candour, 'There's no need for you to explain, Zephaniah. You have made me happy, and so you must leave. I understand. I remember my lessons. I yearn for affection and so I am tempted to seek it in all the wrong ways, and in the wrong places, and from the wrong people.' And he rose to his feet, and turned to walk out of the room.

'Please, Jeremiah! Wait. Don't make this harder than it is.' Hearing him repeat my own words like that was as though he'd made a stake out of one of my bones, driven it into my flesh, then twisted it round in my heart.

'It is you who make it hard by calling me back,' he replied, and I cringed, because he spoke truly.

'I called you back because I wanted to give you this,' I told him; and there was no truth in my words whatsoever, except that once I'd uttered them I discovered I meant them after all. I took the scroll of Hosea from my bag and pressed it into his hands.

He'd no idea what to say. He knew full well it was the single most valuable treasure I possessed. He pushed back his hair and stared at me.

'Only until you receive your call from Adonai,' I explained. 'Then you will send to Josiah and tell him, and he will summon you to his court and we shall all be together. Until then you must read it, and meditate day and night upon its meaning. Will you do that for me?'

'Perhaps,' was all he would say. Then he turned away from me once more, and walked from the room without a backward glance.

CHAPTER 7: JEREMIAH

I remember the day of my calling more vividly than I remember yesterday. Looking back upon it now is like gazing straight at the sun, and being unable to see anything else; even when you close your eyes, its fire is imprinted on your eyelids.

Not that the sun was even visible at the time. I'd spent most of the morning and half the afternoon sheltering in the mouth of a cave, watching drizzle seep remorselessly from a leaden sky. It was late winter, and the muddy grass provided rich pasture for the sheep and goats I had with me. I was twenty one years old, still unwed, and minding someone else's flock. Sitting there with nothing to do but stare at the wet world, I found myself thinking back across the five empty years since I'd heard from Josiah, and the gentle prophet Zephaniah had come to Anathoth.

For the first two or three months I'd been full of nervous anticipation. I'd read from Hosea's scroll night and morning, and prayed fervently that my call might come soon.

But nothing happened. By night my prayers bounced from the walls of my room, by day they would dissipate on the lightest breeze. I became frustrated, then miserable, then depressed. I stopped reading the scroll, and no longer bothered to pray. Nor did the voice of Adonai offer me any comfort or explanation; indeed, it rarely spoke at all.

More months went by, and years, and eventually the depression passed also, leaving a numb kind of exhaustion in its place. I was listless, lethargic, carrying out my duties at the high place like a man entranced, barely aware of what I was doing. It seemed that my voice had abandoned me entirely; I never heard a whisper of it from one week to the next.

My heart was no longer in my training for the priesthood; that much was obvious to everyone. Crisis came one evening when I was assisting my father to make a sacrifice on behalf of a much venerated but somewhat decrepit elder from the village. Not looking where I was going, I tripped and spilled sacrificial blood all down my clothes and over the elder's slave-boy. The poor lad went into a frenzy at the inauspicious omen and made a frightful scene. It took two full-grown men to carry him out, and then the venerable elder swooned in shame and had to be carried out too. My father thought the frail old gentleman's heart had stopped, and he turned on me, hissing venom.

'Now look what you've done, you blundering blockhead! As Heaven is my witness, your mother was right: you'll never be good for anything! You'll certainly never make a priest.'

'Thank God for that!' I yelled back, 'Because I don't want to be one!' I flung the cup with what little remained of its contents at the holy altar, and fled.

After that, I could no longer live at the sanctuary or at home. As I bundled up my things and prepared to depart - for where, I hadn't a clue - I must have been weeping more obviously than I thought I was, for the aged priest Simeon who had once harboured Josiah in my secret room came hobbling up on his staff. He knew I had nowhere to go, and offered to let me stay with him and Hannah his wife in their cottage in the woods half way to Jerusalem. They had a small flock of sheep and goats which they were both too old to tend, and they couldn't afford to pay a hired lad or buy a slave. If I would pasture their animals in return for board and lodging, I was welcome to join their modest household.

So that was what I did. I felt like the young Moses in exile after killing an Egyptian; he too had heard God's voice and tried to obey it, yet wound up an outcast minding herds he didn't own. The only difference between us was that Moses had then seen a burning bush; I saw nothing but rain and brambles.

I'd heard from my family once since moving to Simeon's cottage. A letter came from my father, in which he apologized with convincing contrition for losing his temper with me, and claimed that he wanted to make amends. He begged me not to turn my back on all my training; there might be hope for me yet as a priest. I sent a reply after many days, to say that perhaps I might return at some time in the future; but not yet. It all depended on where Adonai chose to lead me, and for the present I was having some trouble discerning his will.

But if truth be told, I wasn't particularly discontented any more. Simeon and his wife were kind to me and devoted to each other, and they tried to honour Adonai in so far as they could. In the evenings they would sit by their smoky hearth mostly in silence, happy enough with each other after so many years to have no need to make small talk. Hannah would spin or weave, and Simeon would whittle olive-wood toys for a neighbour's children. Occasionally he strummed his home-made lyre and sang the old songs of his clan.

He'd been quite an entertainer in his day - or so Hannah told me - and folk had been surprised when he'd gone to be a priest instead of a bard. So I asked him to teach me to play too, so that when he was whittling and Hannah was weaving I could practise to pass the time. He agreed readily enough, and soon my evenings were flying by like so many birds.

I learned easily, and took to inventing melancholy songs of my own as well as getting Simeon's by heart. Sometimes Simeon would put down his work and listen, astonished at my ability to make poetry and melodies so lovely. His compliments took me aback, for the words just came when I let my mind drift, and the melodies rose like bubbles from the well of my soul. I found myself wishing that he and Hannah had been my parents, and sometimes I pretended that they were. They in turn took to treating me as the son they'd never had.

I still thought now and again about the call which was supposed to be coming for me, but so much time had gone by, it was getting hard to believe in. I wasn't sure I even wanted to go to Jerusalem any more; I was happy for life to carry on quietly as it was, and I reasoned that if I minded my manners I might one day inherit Simeon's little flock.

All this would have been much nicer if I'd had a wife to share it with, of course. Sometimes I wondered if I should creep back to Ruth with my tail between my legs and try again, having acknowledged that fear alone had prevented me from marrying her in the first place. She was almost nineteen years old now, and still not betrothed to anyone else.

A chill wind had got up while I sat in idle contemplation, and I wrapped my cloak tighter about me. Outside, the grazing flock had moved closer to the cave as though hankering after its protection. It wasn't long after noon, but the sky was louring, and perhaps it would thunder; my head started to ache in a dull sort of way, as it often did when the air was close.

Sure enough, the drizzle turned presently to heavy rain, and I glimpsed the first hint of lightning flicking along the horizon. There was no point in my attempting to rush home ahead of the storm; I would have to sit it out where I was and hope it abated in time for supper. I hadn't brought any food with me, and felt very hungry already. Perhaps it was hunger that was making my head, and indeed my whole body, feel empty and peculiar too.

Because of the gusty wind, the rain had begun to wet me where I sat, so I made to stand up and move further back inside the cave. But as soon as I got to my feet I felt as though all the blood had drained from my head to make room for the pain which was expanding to fill it. My legs were quaking, so that I was compelled to sit down once more before I keeled over.

I pressed my fingertips to my temples. Was it possible I could be ill from the damp and the cold? But I didn't feel cold. On the contrary, I felt strangely hot all of a sudden, as though some dark secret fire had begun to smoulder inside me. Invisible flames consumed me, causing my organs to melt and mingle together; nausea forced its way up from them into my throat so that I retched and would have vomited if I'd had anything in my belly to bring up. My heart was pounding, all wild and irregular; without any doubt I was sick unto death and would spew up my soul here alone, with no one to keep the jackals from my flesh or lead Simeon's poor beasts to safety.

The storm had come so close now that the lightning and thunder struck together. And it seemed that every burst of this celestial energy seared right through me, sending my limbs into spasm each time the earth was smitten, and causing me to scream aloud through the choking froth on my tongue. Horizontal rain pelted my face, and it felt like arrows piercing my skin.

Next came a flash of lightning and clap of thunder so intense that I was thrown to the ground. Spread-eagled and gasping while the world spun around me, I dug my nails into the damp earthen floor. Then everything lurched to a standstill, and a voice at once sweetly familiar yet formidable as death began to speak directly into one of my ears. So near me was the mouth from which it issued that I felt warm breath on my cheek and the kiss of lips upon my neck, and simultaneously a cool hand seemed to touch my brow and brush away the pain as it might have brushed away my hair. And the voice said: *Don't be afraid, Jeremiah my son. You are not about to die. Today you shall learn what it is to be truly alive.*

I knew full well that if I looked around there would be no one and nothing to see, but I looked nonetheless. Then the voice spoke again, from the other side of my head: *My son, surely you haven't forgotten me? Be assured that I have not forgotten you. Now stand up, and take off your shoes, for this place has become hallowed ground.*

I did try to stand up. But my muscles had turned to liquid and my bones to blubber, and I was as feeble as a doll made of dough.

Then it seemed that gentle arms went around my waist and lifted me effortlessly to my feet, from which my sandal straps fell away like salt dissolving in water. Still there was no one and nothing to see, except for tiny pinpricks of black that stabbed at my eyes and started to spread as though I were passing out, so that I didn't know if I was actually standing, or lying in a faint on the floor.

What I did know was that I was no longer scared. In fact a kind of heady buoyancy was taking possession of me, and I let myself be caught up in that divine ecstasy which I had tasted twice before. Only this time the waves of rapture were stronger, more overwhelming than I thought I could survive. I felt like a woman in labour racked by contractions each more powerful than the last, causing her to cry out loud as she strives to thrust new life into the world. I was intoxicated with celestial wine, yet could not stagger because of the loving arms which held me aloft, as the woman once her child is born holds it to her breast in pure joy.

And the voice said: *You are my child. I chose you even before I gave you life. Before you were conceived I marked you out as a holy vessel into which I would pour my love, a consecrated instrument on which I would play the music of Heaven. Your time has come, Jeremiah. You will speak for me; you will live for me; you will be my mouthpiece unto the nations. You will summon my rebellious people to repentance, you will stand on the corners of streets and cry out to call them back from the brink of catastrophe, and when they do not listen you will pronounce my judgment upon them. Men and women may ignore you, but the earth itself will hear your words and tremble. I have made you a fortress among my people, which will stand no matter what force comes against it. Kings, officials, priests and peasants will oppose you, but they will never prevail, for I am with you, Jeremiah. I am beside you, above you, below you, within you. I am who I am; and you and I shall be as one.*

Unseen arms were still supporting me, but no longer was I content to let them hold me up. I was struggling against them, begging to be released because I couldn't endure the ecstasy any longer. I had never felt less like a fortress in my life. 'Not now, Sovereign Lord,' I was pleading, my speech all slurred. 'Not now, I implore you. I don't want to go back where the people despise me. I'm too young, I'm too timid. I could never speak to crowds in the streets.'

But even as I poured out my objections, I knew that what I was in my own strength was unimportant.

So it came as no surprise when the voice replied: *Do not say you are too young, too timid, too weak. Put your trust in me, and you will be invincible. Go to those to whom I send you, speak the words which I give you, and don't be afraid. Remember: when they do not listen, I am the one they reject, not you. And I shall deliver you out of their hands. I the Lord of Hosts have spoken.*

I might have protested further except that suddenly the divine conflagration had broken out afresh, upon my tongue. Convinced that I was vomiting fire, I screamed until the cave screamed with me, and the voice said: *Behold, I stretch out my hand and touch your lips. Today I give you authority over kingdoms and nations, to uproot and pull down, to build and to plant. Today your spirit is fused with mine, Jeremiah; this is what you have wanted all your life. From this moment, you will never be the same again.*

A final burst of lightning seared through the cave, and a mighty clap of thunder rent the air. At once the pain and the ecstasy and the arms of God were gone, and I collapsed in a heap on the ground.

I remember nothing after that, until I was awakened by one of Simeon's goats nuzzling my cheek. I opened my eyes and strove to sit up; it was pitch dark all around me, and freezing cold, and there was a wind on my face which meant I was still in the mouth of the cave in precisely the spot where I'd been sitting before all this had happened. But when I tried to rub some feeling back into my feet I saw that my sandals were gone.

I shivered myself to sleep again for a while, too shattered to do otherwise, and when I awoke for the second time the storm clouds had cleared and a low full moon shone wanly into my cave. I was no longer shivering because the sheep and goats had gathered all around me to share with me their warmth. When I counted them, every one was present.

Still, I didn't feel equal to leading them home by moonlight, so I began to hunt around for moss and sticks to light a fire. The snuggling of the animals might be protecting me from the cold, but could offer no defence against wolves, or against dark spirits of the night.

The small effort of collecting kindling and getting it alight made me so tired that I knew I'd been right not to start out for home. Simeon and Hannah would worry, though; guilt pricked me like needles and I half-prayed, half-aloud: why now, Lord, why here?

I scarcely expected an answer, but Adonai's voice said quite audibly: *I have called you now, because Ashurbanipal the Emperor of Assyria is dead, and the whole world is changing; and here, because I needed you to be alone. Fret not for Simeon or for Hannah. I have sent my servant Simeon a dream, and he knows that you are safe.*

So stunned was I by this reply that I almost fell in my own fire. Never before had my voice tried to tell me anything the like of this. Ashurbanipal, dead? Could it be true? And if it were, why should Adonai choose to impart this revelation to me now?

Again I was blessed with an immediate response to my half-articulated questions. *Yes, Jeremiah. Things* are *different now, between you and me. I shall share with you secrets I have shared with no other. You will have no use for dreams or visions; you will simply talk with me as though I had walked into the room in which you were sitting. And* you *will enter* my *chambers, too; you will be present at sessions of my celestial council, and hear heavenly secrets which no other human being has heard. I shall come alongside you when you are eating or travelling or taking a bath; things around you which you see every day, you will see with my eyes so that their very essence is transformed, and they will speak to you of things eternal. Unless, of course, you choose to turn back, and close the gate on the path I have prepared for you to tread.*

'I still have that choice?' I called into the darkness. 'Even now?'

Yes, and you always will. Every step you take, every day of your life, will bring you to a crossroads. But if you walk away from me, you will be for ever alone and without protection in a world which already hates you.

No sooner had these words been spoken than a sharp gust of wind stole the flames from my fire. I shuddered, and cried, 'Don't leave me, Adonai my Lord,' and once more the flames burned strongly.

Then you must promise to obey me, Adonai said. *You must go wherever I tell you to go, do whatever I tell you to do, say whatever I tell you to say. Will you do it?*

I shuddered again, and said more quietly, 'If I am able.'

Remain close to me, and you will always be able. But it will not be easy. That is why I have prepared you, just as I have prepared the path which I want you to take. I have taught you to cope with loneliness, rejection, frustration and despair. But you will know joy, too, joy beyond your wildest imaginings, if you cease to fight me. I love you, Jeremiah.

One of the lambs lying close by my side stirred and awoke and pushed its head into my hands, which lay palms up in my lap. I pressed my face into its soft damp wool and put my arms about its neck, having no other outlet for the answering love gushing up within my soul. To be chosen and loved by the Lord of Heaven, King of the Universe, and to know it... surely there could be no more marvellous thing.

Now, said Adonai, *you must gather your flock and get ready to make your way home, for it is almost dawn. I shall speak with you again upon the way, and yet again when you arrive, so you will know that this was no dream.*

Almost dawn? I was thrown into confusion, not knowing where the time had gone. I felt no more ready for the long walk back than I had when I'd lit my fire. But Adonai rebuked me: *You promised to obey me in everything, yet you cannot even go home when I ask you?*

'Very well,' I agreed, somewhat ruefully, and began to put out the fire and assemble the sheep and goats; it was true that a thin red band of light was already showing where the earth met the sky. Providentially the flock was uncommonly biddable, for I was tired as an ox after ploughing, and moved instinctively, my wits elsewhere. As I set out, the sky grew lighter, and the air was fresh with the promise of sunshine. But the kiss of dawn did little to revive me. It was as though I were watching myself from somewhere high above my own head.

Half way home I flung myself down to rest beneath a tree. It was an almond, the first tree to come into flower as winter surrenders to spring. Already the buds were bursting; I lay on my back looking up at the brightening sky where it peeped through the canopy of blossom and tried to lose myself in my love of nature's beauty, allowing myself to pretend that the storms and the madness of yesterday had never been. I began to doze.

But a voice in my ear said: *Tell me what you see, Jeremiah.*

'The branch of an almond, the sentinel of spring,' I murmured, my happy pretence shattered.

Yes, and I too am a sentinel, on watch to see my words blossom forth into reality. Stand up, Jeremiah. Go home.

I staggered to my feet and forged on, little caring now if the flock followed me or not, yet somehow aware that it did. I thought: perhaps when I reach the cottage and Simeon and Hannah bring me food, I shall stop feeling so strange; then I can sleep; then I can forget.

At length I fell across the threshold and the old priest caught me in his arms, as Adonai himself had done. His voice thick with emotion, he called: 'Hannah, Jeremiah is home! I told you he was safe.'

Hannah arose to welcome me, and in her relief tipped up the pot of soup she'd had simmering on the hearth against my return. Simeon rushed to help her while I sank to my knees on the ground, and Adonai said again: *Jeremiah, my beloved, tell me now what you see.*

I moaned, 'A boiling pot, fallen this way,' and my knees subsided beneath me.

Yes, my son, and destruction is coming this way too, a seething cauldron of violence overflowing from the north and unleashed upon Judah and all her rebellious offspring. The rulers of northern nations will set up their thrones around the walls of Judah's cities and at the very gates of Jerusalem. Jeremiah, you must not shrink back from proclaiming the dire punishment which is to come. If you are frightened now, I shall make you still more afraid when you face those to whom you must speak: the kings, the officials, the priests and the people, all of whom will turn against you. But you must claim my strength to resist them.

'No, no,' I was whining, and, 'Stop, please, I beg you.' I was beside myself with renewed terror, partly at what I was hearing - would Josiah himself turn against me too? - but mostly because Adonai had seen fit to speak like this to me in the presence of people who cared for me deeply and whose affection I desperately longed to retain.

The next thing I remember is lying in bed, with Hannah's hand behind my head as she sought to revive me with what was left of her soup. Far in the distance I could hear her saying in a tremulous voice: 'Simeon, what is he talking about? What can be the matter with him? Where can he have been all night?'

Then Simeon's voice came instead. Calm, reassuring, he bade his wife withdraw, and he took the cup from my lips, laying my head on a cushion. 'I have told you, my dear, we need have no fear on Jeremiah's account. I have seen this before in my time, though once or twice only, and many long years ago.' I opened my eyes with a start at that, and saw that his were moist with tears. 'The voice of God is not silenced at Anathoth after all. No more shall the false prophets have us believe that their meaningless babbling and self-induced frenzies are God-inspired. This is the thing as it should be; Adonai has not forsaken us. Jeremiah must rest now. He will tell us in his own good time what befell him last night.'

I think I may have managed a grateful smile before sleep engulfed me.

When I woke again it was almost dusk; Hannah was watching by my bed, but her head was nodding on her chest. I asked her for something to eat, and it made her jump. 'Have I slept through lunch?' I enquired, attempting a grin, but she exclaimed, 'Jeremiah, my love, you have slept since yesterday!' Then she placed a palm on my brow and said, 'Thanks be to God; the fever is gone.'

'Fever?' I stammered.

'Your head has been burning like the Tophet; it's no wonder you were raving. Simeon, Come quickly!'

The old priest came, and helped me sit up. He smiled, and shook his head, and said, 'I told her she need not worry. But would she listen?' He tutted fondly. 'Women are all the same.' Yet despite his efforts to act as though everything were normal, I saw that he looked at me in a wholly new way.

I said, 'I know you had a dream about me from Adonai. And I know that Ashurbanipal is dead. Both these things are true, Simeon, aren't they?'

I watched them exchanging glances; I read their relief, their awe, and fresh anxiety mingled together. Simeon replied, 'It's true that I had a dream, Jeremiah. But whether Assyria's Emperor is dead... of that we've heard nothing. If he is, we shall know it soon enough. Now drink, and eat; you must recover your strength.'

I didn't get up that evening, because as soon as I'd eaten and begun to feel like myself again, I fell once more to doubting the truth of what had been revealed to me. The Emperor was not dead; I'd been delirious with fever for more than a day and had never spent the night in that cave at all.

But even as these thoughts took shape in my mind, Adonai's voice came clearer than if he were lying in the bed beside me. It said: *Tomorrow you will rise with the sun, pack your belongings, and go to Jerusalem. You will thank Simeon and Hannah for caring for you, and you will tell them where you are going; you will call at your father's house and tell him too. You will cry out the words which I give you, in the streets and the courtyards of my holy city, and return no more to Anathoth until the work to which I have called you has been completed.*

'Already? I must go already, and speak in public, in Jerusalem, to people who don't even know my name? I, a native of Anathoth? Please, Lord, no...'

You will commence your work at the palace, Jeremiah; you will present yourself to the King, who knows your name very well. He will be awaiting you; you will receive confirmation before the door of this house is barred tonight that this is my will for your life.

When it was almost too dark for a man to see the road at his feet, a courier came from Josiah, looking for me. He had brought no letter, merely a message by word of mouth, to be delivered to no one but Jeremiah, son of Hilkiah the priest.

'Come to Jerusalem at once,' I was instructed. 'Ashurbanipal is dead; Zephaniah is sick; and the King needs you.'

PART TWO

AT THE COURT OF KING JOSIAH

Let us examine our ways, let us test them;

> *Let us repent, let us turn back to God;*

Lift up our hands and our hearts to the Heavens,

> *Each of us call on Adonai and say:*

We have failed, we have sinned, we have all

> *nursed rebellion;*

You have not pardoned us; we are undone.

Lamentations 3:40-42.

CHAPTER 8: JOSIAH

I

At noon the next day, I was waiting for him still.

I couldn't comprehend it. A man can walk from Jerusalem to Anathoth and back again more than once before siesta, yet my courier had been gone since the early hours of the previous day, and still Jeremiah did not come.

I was installed in state upon Judah's throne, where I spent my mornings receiving reports from my ministers or entertaining foreign envoys. Today I had turned away all of them and sat alone with Asaiah, the well-born youth who attended to my personal needs, and the strong, silent men of my guard. I brooded, and drummed my fingers on the stone heads of the lions which flanked my seat.

Not that I would have admitted even to myself that I was worried. I was Sovereign King of Judah, scion of the House of David, heir to his everlasting covenant with Adonai Ruler of the Universe; my very person was sacred, and it does not become such a being to countenance even uncertainty, let alone fear. Yet I knew that I stood - or rather sat - on the brink of a new and daunting phase in my life, and in that of my kingdom. Not only this, but the man whose wisdom and spirituality I'd relied upon since childhood had suddenly been struck down.

My servant Asaiah had woken me before dawn the previous morning, his face pinched with anxiety. I'd flung my arms across my eyes to blot out the light of the lamp he held over me, and warned him that whatever was wrong, it had better be important. 'Oh it is, Your Majesty,' the boy had assured me. 'The Emperor of Assyria is dead.'

As I sought to cast the cloak of sleep from about me, asking Asaiah all kinds of questions none of which he could answer - when did it happen? from what source have we learnt this? - I began to take in the significance of the bald fact I'd just been told. Ashurbanipal had barely succeeded in holding his nation's crumbling empire together despite the formidable strength of his own personality. There had been costly border wars with the Scythians, and mounting internal unrest. The acknowledged heir to the imperial throne - Ashurbanipal's son, one Ashuretililani - was not known to have inherited any of his father's statesmanlike qualities. If I was ever to regain independence for Judah, or win back any of the additional territories which my renowned ancestor David had conquered and the kings in between us had lost, the time to do it had come.

I said to Asaiah: 'Fetch Zephaniah the prophet here at once. I need to consult with him. Now.' It would have done no harm to have waited till sunrise, but a sense of urgency had gripped me; it was as though I imagined that if I hadn't rid Judah of every vestige of Assyrian domination by breakfast time, it would be too late.

Of course, I'd already taken certain steps in that direction. Since the age of sixteen when I'd surrendered my soul and will to Adonai, I'd been slowly but systematically removing foreign idols from the land. But I'd had to tread carefully; that had been only prudent. From now on, I should have no excuse when Adonai called me to account for the heathen practices still condoned within my borders.

However, Asaiah returned more distressed than before, and cried, 'Oh my lord, Your Majesty... Zephaniah cannot come. He is sick.'

'Sick?' I repeated angrily, then admonished myself for speaking so sharply to the son of a noble house who was my servant but not my slave. 'I am sorry, Asaiah. But what do you mean, he is sick?'

Asaiah's reply was barely coherent, yet I gleaned enough to appreciate that it was no mere chill from which the prophet was suffering. Too impatient to send messengers for more detailed information, I leaped from my bed, threw a blanket on top of the garment I'd slept in, and rushed to Zephaniah's chambers myself.

He was sprawled on the floor where he had collapsed, his shawl wrapped about his head as he wore it to pray, though the dawn prayer-time was still far off. When I pulled the cloth away from his face, his eyes were open but staring, and spittle drooled from one side of his mouth. Slaves arrived at that moment to get him to bed, and then my mother came running, her lips white with shock. Zephaniah was trying to speak as they lifted him up, but once he was lying on his back I could see that the right hand side of his face was slack as a corpse's. Whilst he reached out and tried to gesture with his left arm, the other lay limp and useless by his side.

Oh God, a stroke, I breathed, and put my head in my hands, at the same time thinking: but surely, only old men suffer strokes? Zephaniah is hale and strong, in the prime of life...

By this time my mother was kneeling in anguish at his bedside. Though she'd never deemed it fitting to declare herself, I knew that she loved the gentle prophet to distraction. I calmed myself by offering her comfort, whilst inside I felt terribly alone. At last Judah's moment had come, but the man who had taught me everything I knew had been felled like a cedar. And no number of political advisers can take the place of one man who hears the voice of God.

Of course, I had other so-called prophets at court, but they were little better than toadies. I had a prophetess too, by the name of Huldah, to whom I had turned in more than one personal crisis and would have trusted with my life, yet to involve a woman in affairs of state was unthinkable.

Then in a moment of inspiration I remembered Jeremiah. And the more I thought about him, the more sure I was that the right time had come for me to send for him. So at first light I despatched a royal courier; and now at noon the following day, I was still waiting.

Some of my apprehension was caused simply by the prospect of seeing the shy son of Anathoth again after so long. It was five years since Zephaniah had been there and returned to me singing his praises, but fully fourteen since I'd seen Jeremiah face to face.

Half way through the afternoon my courier at last reappeared, and threw himself at my feet. 'Your pardon, Your Majesty... I could not find him yesterday until it was too late to return. No one could give me clear directions to the place where he's been living...'

'Where is he, then? Didn't you fetch him with you?'

The courier, still prostrate on the floor, raised his head and looked round in some surprise. He must have assumed that Jeremiah had followed him the length of the throneroom.

But he was standing far off in the doorway, and he looked so lost that I thought: Adonai have mercy, I ought never to have brought him here. When will I learn not to be so impetuous? Zephaniah himself had cautioned me to let the boy be until I'd been told for certain that the hand of the Lord had come upon him, confirming his calling; how could I have forgotten?

I dismissed the courier and bade Asaiah fetch my guest and present him to me. As the two approached me together I saw that Jeremiah was no taller or broader across the shoulders than Asaiah, though my attendant was barely sixteen. Slung over his back Jeremiah carried all that he owned - a small bundle of personal effects and a home-made lyre - and he still had that curtain of black hair which hid half of his face; what I could see of the rest of it was pasty with awe. I found myself looking at the throneroom through a newcomer's eyes, with its great wooden columns, its beams and panelling; not for nothing was it known as the House of the Forest of the Cedars of Lebanon. Little wonder that Jeremiah was overfaced, coming as he did from a mudbrick village most of whose rooftops were scarcely higher than a man's head.

He put his lyre on the floor and prostrated himself as the courier had done. Spontaneously I stepped down from the throne and raised him to his feet with my own royal hands, clasping him close and saying, 'Welcome, Jeremiah, my friend. It's been a long time.'

He didn't know how to respond; nervously he embraced me in return, and I thought: I ought to have received him in my private chambers man to man, not here where he can be nothing but my humble subject. I held him away at arms' length to study his face, but he kept his eyes averted. When I ventured to scrape back the hair from his brow, I saw that the flesh above his cheekbones was blue and swollen, and there was an ugly cut on the bridge of his nose.

'Dear God!' I exclaimed. 'What happened to you?'

'Nothing,' he lied, and turned away once more; I sighed, and motioning Asaiah to follow, I led him away to my chambers after all. I posted my guards where they wouldn't be visible, and had Asaiah pour us both wine. Nevertheless, it took two or three cups, unwatered, before Jeremiah relaxed enough to tell me what had happened. The hand of Adonai had seized him indeed, away in the lonely hills, and he'd already been ordered to come to Jerusalem while my courier was still searching vainly for Simeon's cottage. (Praise be to God, I thought with relief, I should never have doubted you were guiding me.) But when he'd gone to his father to tell him the news, there had been a bitter quarrel.

'So this is it, Jeremiah. You are turning your back for ever on your priestly training; on the kindness of those who took time to teach you; on the village of your birth and on your own clan and family... all to go and serve a man you have never met, whose wicked ancestor robbed us of our status and reputation.'

'It isn't like that, Father. I'm not ungrateful.'

'You expect me to believe that? You have always been ungrateful. Your ridiculous fantasies have always meant more to you than your own flesh and blood. One word from Solomon's whelp and you're licking his sandals; one from me, and you do as you want.'

'But Father, this isn't what I want. It's what Adonai wants.'

'You know *nothing* about what Adonai wants! You are turning your back on him just as you've turned your back on everyone else who has ever cared for you. Did Adonai not say through Isaiah that the Gentiles would come to worship him too? That is what you see happening here at Anathoth: Gentiles as well as Judeans, praising God in their own traditional ways! We at the sanctuaries have built something beautiful in our generation: a bridge between the Sons of Moses and the Children of Canaan, yet neither you nor your naive little kingling can see it. The bigotry of our days in the wilderness was fading, yet Josiah would seek to bring it back! Today we have freedom and tolerance at our high places; there is enlightenment. At Anathoth men and women can search for God and find him, whatever their race, whatever their needs...'

'No, Father. At Anathoth there is confusion and error. There are priests perverting the Law of God and promoting immorality. Truth matters more than tolerance, even when that truth is painful.'

'How dare you say such things to your own father! I should have you stoned for insolence! You spout rebellion, only now you call it prophecy; you abandon all you've been brought up to value and call it obeying Adonai; you scoff at the wisdom of your elders and profane the sanctity of a holy place with your spiteful blasphemies; now you will take yourself off to Jerusalem, the capital city of everything iniquitous in this poor benighted world, and rave in public on the corners of its filthy streets rather than minister to others' needs within a community where order and harmony prevail. Well rave on, Jeremiah, rave on! If you rave for long enough, the jeers of your audience may succeed in convincing you that you are mad after all! But remember this when they do: I gave you chance after chance to prove yourself a worthy son to me; *I* was tolerant with *you* when you were clumsy and inept and the dupe of every bully under the sun. If I am angry with you now, it is you who have brought down my wrath upon yourself. You have changed me, Jeremiah, and not for the better!'

'And if I am ungrateful and insolent and rebellious and spiteful - yes, and mad! - if I am any or all of those things, you and my mother and my kinsmen have made *me* what *I* am, too!'

That was when his father had struck him, as hard as he could with a fist between the eyes, and declared that from this time forth his eldest son was dead. Jeremiah had not wept, but he wept bitterly now as he told me the tale, and this time when I embraced him the ice was broken between us, the more so when I wept too, because of Zephaniah.

Of course, this was the first Jeremiah had heard of the stroke which had felled my mentor, and he was shaken to the core; in my grief I'd somehow forgotten that for a time Zephaniah had been his mentor too. Perhaps, also, Jeremiah had imagined that now his prophetic gifting had been confirmed, nothing would ever come as a surprise to him again.

He asked to be taken to see him; I was hesitant but agreed in the end and took him myself. He sat by the sick man's side without a word, but held both his hands, the good and the bad, so tenderly that I felt ashamed to be hanging back. Then he fumbled in his pack of belongings and drew out a scroll which he tried to make Zephaniah accept, but the latter would not. He was attempting to speak, though nothing much but saliva came out. Yet Jeremiah seemed to understand, for he took the scroll and kissed it and put it back with his things. Then I too understood: the scroll was Hosea's, but between Zephaniah and his disciple it was like Elijah's cloak.

After that Jeremiah let me lead him back to my apartment, though for a while he was distant and distracted, scarcely seeming to hear the questions I asked him, like a diner at a banquet who loses track of the conversation he is part of through trying to listen in on someone else's further up the table.

Deciding that food might restore him, I ordered the evening meal to be brought to us early, and as we ate we began to talk of the paths our lives had taken since the first and last time we'd met. Yet even this he appeared to find difficult, and he was quite unable to describe to me in any detail how his calling from Adonai had come.

'You had a vision?' I prompted him, not liking to let him struggle.

'No, my lord. Not exactly. There was no vision. In fact, I wish there had been. Then perhaps my father might have believed I'd received a vocation.'

'He'll believe soon enough when he hears that Ashurbanipal is dead, exactly as Adonai told you.'

'I doubt it, my lord. He'll think I was told by someone else.'

'And you're calling me your lord again, Jeremiah. Are we not to be friends any more?'

I was grinning as I spoke, but had to shake my head and turn away when he fixed me with that gaze he'd had at seven years old and said, 'Oh my lord - I mean, Josiah - there's nothing I'd like better. No boy ever wanted to be my friend, except you.' And I thought: little wonder, if that's how you looked at them.

Then I started to tell him what the death of Assyria's Emperor could mean for Judah. I said, '*I* need a friend who can speak with divine authority on my behalf - someone the people themselves can recognize as an anointed mouthpiece of God. Then they will be less afraid to unite behind me in defying our oppressors, and our nation's freedom may be won. Do you think you can help me?'

I asked the question because a sceptical inner part of me was still doubting whether he had it in him to become any kind of speaker at all. But he didn't take me quite that way. Hesitantly he answered, 'I don't know, Josiah. I can only speak on Adonai's behalf, not on yours. Unless he commissions me and gives me the words to say, I shall do no more than stammer. He has said nothing to me about freedom; merely about a foe from the north which will sweep down upon us unleashing destruction.'

I have to confess that his reply made me angry, though I did my best not to show it. He knew all the same, and whispered, 'I'm sorry, my lord. I meant no disrespect. But if I speak for you and not for God I'll be no better than the prophets you already have.'

He was right, of course. I conceded his point, saying: 'Zephaniah taught you well, I see. Fear not; you'll have ample time here at court to seek out God for yourself.' Nevertheless, I was left with a bitter taste in my mouth, which no amount of the best Syrian wine over our dinner was quite enough to wash away.

When we'd finished our meal I had him shown to the rooms which had been prepared for him, and my servants explained to him that he would have all of his needs provided for, plus a regular allowance from the Treasury. They told me afterwards that he'd been reluctant to agree to the latter; it seemed like receiving payment for services rendered, and he'd made it clear already that he could work for no earthly employer. I felt like responding: so you'll eat no earthly food and wear no earthly clothes, either? But instead I had them tell him: your allowance comes as my gift to a friend, not as my payment to an employee. If you must see it as payment, it's for being a teacher, not a prophet. I have three sons, and I want them brought up to honour God, just as I was brought up by Zephaniah.

So the following morning I recalled Jeremiah to my chambers and had my wives and children fetched to meet him. As they entered, his nervousness was palpable, and I can't say I wasn't gratified. There is little point in having two ravishingly beautiful wives and three handsome sons if other men are not impressed.

Zebidah came forward first, for she was the first woman I had taken as bride. When Jeremiah dropped to one knee to do her honour she inclined her head demurely. Her eyes connected with Jeremiah's when he arose, only for a second before each of them looked away, but there was no doubting that something in him had impressed her too.

Then came Hamutal, my second wife; by no means second to Zebidah in beauty, yet holding second place in my heart because I hadn't married her for love. There was nothing demure about Hamutal, either in attire or in manner. Because of the guilt I felt for not loving her enough, I was frequently giving her jewels - all of which she liked to wear at once - and instead of inclining her head she bestowed upon Jeremiah one of her most disarming smiles. He blushed scarlet, and I was left wondering somewhat irritably: what could a woman possibly see in him?

Yet I suppose this only shows how little I understand women, even those I married.

My sons were brought to him next, led by their nurses: Zebidah's two boys first, Johanan and Eliakim, of whom the former was six years old and the latter five. Johanan stepped forward and bowed as he was told to, if rather timidly. He was a timid sort of boy altogether, excessively thin and often sickly, which was something of a worry to me. I think Jeremiah saw himself in him, and smiled; Johanan smiled too, and I decided they would get on well.

Eliakim's reaction could not have been more different. He must have discerned whatever it is in Jeremiah which has confounded many grown men, myself included. He clutched at his nurse's skirts and wouldn't let go; when Zebidah knelt down beside him and tried to prize his fingers away, he threw a tantrum. Shelemaiah, Hamutal's son, who must have been three or four, copied Eliakim in this as he copied him in everything else, and might have brought the roof down with his screaming if his nurse hadn't put him over her shoulder and taken him out.

When the others had gone out too, I made my apologies for the boys' behaviour. I said, 'Don't worry about Eliakim, Jeremiah. I'm sure you'll succeed in taming him. Zephaniah tamed me somehow.'

Jeremiah looked panic-stricken. 'Oh, Josiah, surely you want a trained scribe to teach your children, someone who's been through the wisdom schools himself, who can - '

'Who can split hairs and argue that black is white?' I finished off for him. 'No, thank you all the same. The boys have had too much of that kind of teaching already. It produces nothing in the pupil but disrespect for his elders. From today I'm placing my sons' education in your hands, my friend, along with everything I own. You shall have free access to my presence and to my private quarters and to all that is mine - excepting my wives, of course.'

He'd no idea how I'd meant my last remark to be taken, and neither really had I. He said, 'They are both very beautiful, my lord. You've been richly blessed.'

I laughed, with little humour. 'You really think so? When the two of them would scratch each other's eyes out like cats, given half a chance? And there's enough hatred among their sons already to start a civil war. Johanan is spoilt because he's so frail; Eliakim demands attention all the time because Johanan gets too much. Shelemaiah does nothing but whine and follow Eliakim like a shadow. Take my advice, Jeremiah: never get married. Or if you must, do it only once.'

He was shocked; indeed, I was somewhat shocked myself because his wistful jealousy had caused me to say much more than I'd meant to. But that's how it was destined to be all the time with Jeremiah; I could hide nothing from him, and if I made the mistake of trying to impress him I always wound up feeling foolish.

I waited until the next day before confronting him with the officials of my court. They were many, and I knew that their names and functions would bewilder him. Nevertheless, he would have to become used to moving among them as an equal, and sooner rather than later.

I assembled them all in the throne-room and presented them one by one, beginning with Hilkiah the High Priest. He had the same name as Jeremiah's father and was probably of similar age; he was a man of unassuming piety whom I much respected. He was assisted in his duties by a deputy, the Chief Officer of the Temple, who was responsible for the maintenance of law and order within the holy precincts.

The highest ranking of my secular ministers was Shaphan, Secretary of State, chief of the Jerusalem scribes. With his snow white hair, he was as full of wisdom as he was of years - a genuine, godly wisdom, not merely a scholarly cleverness such as that possessed by most of his profession. But his membership of the Governing Council went back only as far as the early years of my own reign. He and his colleagues had each been appointed either by Zephaniah and my mother during the years of my minority, or by me. The idolaters who had served my father had gradually been removed.

Shaphan's eldest son Ahikam served as Royal Steward, and was already one of my most valuable counsellors: godly, shrewd and earnest like his father. Shaphan's three other sons - Gemariah, Elasah and Jaazaniah - were too young as yet to hold office, but had received the finest education in scribal wisdom and statecraft which their father's money could buy, and all showed considerable promise. Ahikam in turn had a son of his own, Gedaliah, an endearingly solid and sensible little boy; not at all like any of mine, I regret to say.

Next came Joah the Royal Recorder; Maaseiah the Governor of the City of Jerusalem; Akbor son of Micaiah, a veteran even older than Shaphan but an equally worthy counsellor; and Elnathan his son, a man of middle years who had an uncommonly pretty daughter called Nehushta.

Last in line stood Shallum, Keeper of the Royal Wardrobe. I could have left him out of the presentations without causing offence because his duties were ceremonial rather than influential, and because by nature he was content to remain in the background. He it was who ensured that I appeared correctly garbed for state occasions; in addition, he kept the moths from devouring the antique robes of the previous kings of Judah. Shallum was balding, plump and placid, a creature of habit who took a quiet pride in his work, and in his young wife Huldah who at twenty five was fifteen years his junior.

It was Huldah whom I was anxious for Jeremiah to meet, but I couldn't very well have sent for her without inviting Shallum also. Huldah was my prophetess; it was I who had discerned her gifting and encouraged her to develop it, woman or no. With Zephaniah sick, I knew there was no one else to whom Jeremiah would be able to turn for help. Besides, some mischievous part of me was intrigued to see how my two prophetic proteges would react to one another.

She stood in the shadows at her husband's shoulder, darkly veiled, until I called upon her by name. I think she, like Jeremiah, felt out of place in this gathering of dignitaries, and was surprised to have been summoned here with them. She was more surprised still when I beckoned her forward; but not so surprised as Jeremiah when he saw that she was no middle-aged matron running resignedly to seed like her husband.

I launched into my explanation of who she was and why I'd deemed it desirable that they should meet, but recognized at once that there was no need. I'd swear that Jeremiah could literally see the divine spirit at work within her, feel the heat of the celestial fire which burned behind her candidly intelligent eyes. Huldah wasn't conventionally beautiful, any more than Jeremiah was handsome, but there was a vivacity and a radiance about her always, and as their eyes met and held I began again to wonder if I'd made a mistake. Anxious to lighten the air, I said to Jeremiah, 'If Huldah had been a man, I might never have needed you to come here at all,' and presumed to pat him on the back to show I meant no harm by my teasing. But he jumped at my touch as though the finger of death itself had been laid upon him. I found myself having to apologize: once again he had made me feel foolish.

Over the next few days, I spent as many hours with Jeremiah as I could afford. I needed to get him settled and ready to work for me at the earliest opportunity - not so much in the teaching of my sons (there would be ample time for that in the weeks to come), but in the backing of my reforms. Admittedly, he'd claimed that things weren't as simple as this. But he'd seemed so unsure of himself in everything else, I naively imagined I would bend him to my will.

I soon learned, however, that I could bend him scarcely at all, even in matters more trivial, once his mind was made up.

'There's no need for you to dress like a shepherd-boy now,' I scolded him gently, noting his simple woollen robe and plain leather belt. 'Didn't I tell you that Asaiah would place you an order with the palace tailors if you asked him? He has such good taste. And have him find you some servants of your own while you're about it. The kitchens are over-staffed; the cooks would gladly spare you some willing slave-boys to run your errands.'

He looked nonplussed. 'But I *did* ask Asaiah to order me some clothes. These are what I chose. And what would I do with slaves? If you've amassed too many bondsmen you should free them, Josiah, especially if they are Judeans. Have none of them served you seven years?'

'I haven't the slightest idea how long any of them have been here. Their fathers and grandfathers were probably here before them.'

'Then you are breaking Adonai's law, my lord, are you not? A Judean slave must be freed after seven years. Besides, there *is* a slave-boy from the kitchens who comes to see me; he brings me food three times each day, for which service I'm deeply grateful. He's most polite and I like him very much.' Jeremiah smiled ingenuously. 'You should take some time to talk with him yourself. Such a sad life he's led, for one so young, yet he harbours no bitterness. They made him a eunuch before he was old enough to know what it meant, and he hasn't seen his parents or his homeland since he was six. He told me his Cushite name today, though I cannot pronounce it. That's why everyone calls him Ebed-Melech, slave of the King.'

I shook my head in mounting exasperation. Here we were with our nation's future at stake, and Jeremiah could think of nothing better to do with his days than to waste them in idle chatter with a Gentile gelding.

So I decided the time had come to speak at length to him of the work I'd already done in ridding Judah of foreign influences and restoring the worship of the one true God, and to inspire him with my vision for its completion. I set about it in earnest one evening when we had taken supper together in the privacy of his chambers, and were lingering over our wine.

'I began with the Temple,' I explained, depositing my cup on the table. 'Since it is the house of Adonai himself, I thought it only right to make its purification my priority. I had my grandfather Manasseh's pagan altars removed from its courts and broken into pieces. I removed his Asherah pole and burned it; I ground the ashes to powder and had them scattered on idolaters' graves.

'Then I destroyed the quarters of the Temple prostitutes; I banished the mediums and necromancers from their practices; I set the pagan priests to manual labour. I forbade the worship of Adonai in the guise of the sun; I disposed of the horses dedicated by my predecessors to the sun's worship, and I outlawed the procession in which they were used.

'After the Temple, I turned to the palace - not that I'm wholly satisfied with things in the Temple, you understand; I should like to see it completely refurbished when resources become available. I removed the pagan altars from the palace roof, and destroyed the idolatrous shrines set up by Solomon when his foreign wives led him astray.

'Finally I pulled down the altar to the goat-demons by Joshua's Gate. And the light which I have caused to shine here in Jerusalem, I shall shed throughout my kingdom, with your assistance, of course, Jeremiah... Jeremiah? Are you all right?'

He was staring right into my eyes, his cup held in mid air as though he'd forgotten what it was for when it was half way to his mouth. Then echoing the first thing I'd said, he whispered: 'I hope you began with your *heart*, Josiah. That is where the letter you sent me implied that you had begun, and I trust that it was true, because the heart is the only place where a worthwhile beginning can be made. Don't allow the fire of your faith to be eclipsed by worthy deeds.'

He spoke with such gravity that I could do nothing but stare back at him open-mouthed. He continued: 'And do not imagine that Adonai dwells in your Temple made with hands. Did not Solomon himself declare at its consecration that not even Heaven could contain the One in whose honour it had been built?'

I picked up my goblet once more and took a nervous draught. Jeremiah continued to stare at me, or rather into me; I felt myself shrinking, deflated and humbled. It was fully five years since I'd pledged my life in Adonai's cause. Perhaps in the meantime I had lost sight of what really mattered; perhaps I *had* squandered the excitement which first thrilled my soul.

Then he smiled, quite unexpectedly, and said, 'Don't let your heart be troubled, Josiah. Rest in Adonai's arms. He has been since the beginning of time, and always will be. Nothing is urgent in his kingdom; nothing needs to be rushed.'

So saying, he took up his lyre and began to play, and to sing a psalm of peace in his low lilting voice. I sighed and lay back on my couch, and allowed the beauty of the music to soothe me. When the final cadence died away I murmured, 'That song was truly lovely, Jeremiah. Was it one of David's? And yet I don't know it.'

He smiled again, shaking back his hair as he raised his head and silenced the humming strings with the palms of his hands. 'It was for you, Josiah. It was what you needed to hear.'

'You mean you just invented it as you went along? I don't believe it. I have never heard words more carefully chosen.'

He shrugged his narrow shoulders. 'I sing, and the words and the music come. I only open my mouth.'

And then, while I was still entranced, he ventured to sit next to me, and simultaneously bold yet timid, asked me to let him pray for me. The reversal of our roles was complete: he whom I had set out to inspire had become the channel of the Divine. He placed his hands upon my head, and peace spread downward through my body. My love for God was renewed, and with it my love for his chosen vessel.

After that he did me the courtesy of listening attentively while I outlined for him my achievements in the military, social and judicial fields, though I have to confess I had done much more in the first of these than in the other two. I'd refounded Judah's professional army which had ceased to exist because of foreign domination. I had strengthened Judah's defences, building forts along the coastal plain to prevent foreign armies from taking its use for granted as a highway for their troops. In short, I had laid the foundations necessary for the reconquest of what had once been David's empire.

With regard to social reform, I had standardized Judah's system of weights and measures, in order to lessen corruption. As for legal procedures, I'd taken to hearing a good many court cases myself, and when I could not, I made sure they were heard by judges whose integrity was above reproach.

All in all I was pleased with what I'd accomplished, just as God was pleased after the six long days of creation - though in my case I knew there could be no restful sabbath ahead. I saw myself as a man of action, a man cast in David's mould. David was my hero, the greatest king my people had known.

'But what of the Tophet?' enquired Jeremiah quietly. 'I notice that you have made no mention of that. Is Molech's shrine still standing? Are innocent children still surrendering their souls to his flames?'

He might as well have thrust a knife between my ribs. I drained my wine and poured myself more. Ignoring his question, I asked him my own. 'What do you think of my work, then, my friend? Shall I not go down in the annals of history as Judah's most righteous and energetic king after David himself?'

'That depends upon who writes the history,' he said, with the faintest hint of a smile; but then it was gone, and he was looking at me very hard once again, as a diviner might study his sticks or the flight of birds. He said, 'What you have done is undoubtedly good, Josiah. Perhaps it is even great. But can anything which you or I do or say change the hearts of the people and bring *them* to repentance? It may be that nothing in earth or heaven can stave off the invasion of the foe from the north any longer.'

'The foe from the north,' I sighed, with deep resignation. But I made up my mind I would not be offended; perhaps he was simply jealous of what I'd achieved in the name of Adonai. Prophets are human beings, after all.

II

The next morning I invited Jeremiah to be present when my ministers met to bring me their reports and discuss the business of the day. Spring was coming, and with it, New Year: the time when the rulers of Assyria's vassal kingdoms had to go up to their overlord's capital to renew their allegiance and present their annual tribute. Soon the critical decision would have to be taken: did I go this year as usual and bow the knee to Ashurbanipal's son, or did I remain at home and risk bloody confrontation?

My sources told me that other vassal kings were debating the same question; and the more who refused to go, the less our fledgling Emperor would be able to do to punish them. Perhaps I should make enquiries among my neighbours with a view to our working together? Naturally this in itself entailed an enormous risk. Those I approached might well choose to betray me.

My counsellors gave this dilemma their most scrupulous consideration. In their verbal balances they weighed up the likelihood of my being sold down the river if I sought to negotiate with others in my position, and whether it would be safer or more precarious for me to act alone. They assessed the potential of Assyria to respond swiftly in strength and anger as she would have done when her star was in the ascendant. Their predictions were based on carefully screened intelligence reports, and upon prodigious political experience.

But Zephaniah had cautioned me a hundred times: never take an important decision without seeking counsel directly from Adonai, because no amount of human reasoning can predict what will happen if God sees fit to intervene. The wisest of mortal wisdom can be exposed as foolishness by a single syllable from the lips of one who speaks for the Divine.

Yet Jeremiah sat in silence, contributing nothing, as though the entire proceedings were being conducted in a language he didn't understand. I wanted to shake him, to force the word of God up from his throat as you might force out a mis-swallowed morsel from the gullet of a friend who is choking.

When the same thing happened on the following morning, and again on a third, I came to the conclusion that he must still be intimidated by my ministers' pedigree and rank. However, I soon learned that this was not the case. Ahikam the Royal Steward had already gone out of his way to offer friendship to Jeremiah, which the latter had seized upon with alacrity. He was still so unaccustomed to affection or even acceptance that he clung like a vine on a trellis to anyone who showed him either.

Ahikam wisely drew his three brothers into the friendship, along with Shaphan their father, else our young guest's dependency might have bled him dry; in addition, Ahikam's little son Gedaliah included the newcomer in his solemn confidences. At least there was no longer a need for me to devote so many hours of each day to Jeremiah's entertainment. His intensity was frankly exhausting, but fortunately little Gedaliah was oblivious to this, or else perhaps he found in his unlikely friend a kindred spirit.

This was unquestionably true of Johanan, my own eldest son. For although Jeremiah had shown no sign of wanting to enter into his prophetic ministry, he had nevertheless commenced his duties as tutor to my children. He and Johanan got at least as well as I'd decided they would; Jeremiah even coined a pet name for him, Hanan, which the boy would let no one but Jeremiah use. Encouraged by this modest success, Jeremiah invented shortened forms of the other boys' names too: Eliakim he called Eli, and Shelemaiah, Shallum. But all in vain: Eliakim answered him back, and smashed up the tablets he was meant to write on; Shelemaiah copied him in this, as he did in everything.

Jeremiah made no complaint to me. But Zebidah came and tactfully suggested that it was my duty as father of her son to instill some discipline into the diminutive rebel before it was too late; and then Hamutal came too, and complained that Eliakim's bad behaviour was having an injurious influence on her own Shelemaiah.

With Zebidah I sympathized. But Hamutal's accusations annoyed me, because I knew that she was really saying what she said all too frequently: *my* son would make a far better king than the peaky Johanan or the naughty Eliakim. In my own opinion, Shelemaiah seemed to have very little about him at all, but the ferocity of his mother's ambition for him sometimes alarmed me.

Nevertheless, I agreed to speak to the wayward lad, and when he stood before me, stunningly handsome, haughty and defiant at such a tender age, I was suddenly struck by the disconcerting thought that probably Absalom had once stood thus before David. When Absalom grew up, his rebellion had torn his father's heart to ribbons, along with his kingdom - and why? Because David, champion of righteousness though he was, had neglected his children. Even I, who worshipped his memory almost as fervently as I worshipped Adonai, had to admit it; and now I myself was falling into his error. I hadn't spoken more than two words to any of the boys in months. There were so few hours in a day.

'I don't *want* Jeremiah to teach me,' Eliakim retorted when I asked him the reason for his conduct. 'I want my other teacher back. He let me argue. He said it was good for me. Jeremiah just says: "It's a foolish person who disagrees with God." He's horrible to me, and to Shelemaiah; he only likes Johanan. Well *I* don't like *Jeremiah*. He's *weird*.'

I said, 'I'm sorry, Eliakim. Your other teacher isn't coming back. The sooner you get used to your new one, the better it will be for everyone.'

'I'll never get used to him! I hate him!' shrieked Eliakim, stamping his feet; recalling Absalom again, I decided that things had gone far enough. I put my son across my knees and thrashed him.

'I shall do this with a strap if I hear that you've been insolent again,' I warned him, and meant it. When he strutted out of my presence without a word I thought, no doubt he hates *me* now, too. Well, it was better for him to hate me than to despise me.

At any rate, after that he argued no more with Jeremiah, though I'm not sure that the sullenness which he cultivated instead was preferable.

Meanwhile, the resentment which I myself was nursing against Jeremiah was silently growing. I was desperate not to let him see it, because I knew it was unfair of me to bear a grudge against him when it was I who had summoned him to Jerusalem.

So I diverted my anger into hunting in the Jordan wilderness with Asaiah and the young noblemen who had been my companions from boyhood. The fierce heat of the desert sun matched the heat of my wrath, and I brought down one wild creature after another: deer, ibex, even lions. My companions were jubilant, paying lavish tribute to my prowess. Only Asaiah, who was more like a brother to me than a servant, discerned the rancour which drove me.

'You should go to Jeremiah and talk to him, my lord,' he advised me while he gave me my bath one evening and sought to massage the tension from my back with practised hands. 'It would be better to have the thing in the open than growing like a thorn-hedge between you. I thought he was your friend?'

'He was. He *is*. Oh, I don't know.' I pushed Asaiah aside and sprang irritably out of the bathtub, spraying droplets of water over the rugs on the floor. I threw a cloak around my bare shoulders and sat brooding; Asaiah fetched me wine and began to dry my hair but again I rebuffed him.

Much later, at an hour when I should normally have been in bed, I accepted that Asaiah was right, and went to Jeremiah's rooms. When I knocked on the door, there was no response; after trying again I walked in, thinking: if I disturb him, it serves him right for having no slave to see that he's left alone.

But the apartment was empty, the bedroll stacked neatly against the wall. I kicked a doorpost to relieve my fury; I'd made up my mind to confront him, and he had no business to be absent. I betook myself to Ahikam's apartment instead, banking on finding my quarry there, but Ahikam had seen nothing of him since the Council meeting that morning. Nor had any member of his family.

I had no choice but to wait till the following day, and most of that was taken up with affairs of state, though my mind was hardly on them. (Where on earth could the wretch have been? What could he have been doing?) At length late in the evening I went again, and as before there was no answer to my knocking. I barged in a second time - and found him prostrate on the floor.

The shock of Zephaniah's stroke was still fresh, and I rushed to rouse him. But quickly I realized that he was not sprawled, but rigidly prone, his limbs composed, his head straight down upon his folded arms. Could this be how he normally prayed when alone, I wondered, or was he begging pardon for some secret sin? What sin could such a one as he have committed? Despite my eagerness to confront him, I left him a while to his silent communion, then I spoke his name into his ear.

He gave no sign of having heard me, and when I ventured to touch his shoulder there was still no response. I marvelled at the depth of his trance, if trance it was, and saw there was nothing I could do but wait for him to come out of it.

After a time he started to mumble, and his head moved from side to side, the unkempt hair falling in his face. Then all of a sudden he looked right at me where I knelt transfixed. The trance was over; though he did his best to recover himself and greet me in seemly fashion, he was too disoriented to stand, and I had to help him to a chair myself.

Having seen him at his most vulnerable, I hadn't the heart to tell him the truth when he asked me what had drawn me to his chambers so late at night. But as always he saw through my dissemblings. He said, 'I understand. You ponder in your heart how it can be that I enjoy such an intimacy with the Divine, and yet it leads nowhere and yields no fruit.'

I looked away from him, ashamed, but to my surprise he offered no explanation. Instead, he threw himself hard against the back of the chair, with his arms across his face, and blurted: 'I don't know! I ask myself the same question,

Josiah! What am I doing, here in this place where I don't belong? Was it truly Adonai who brought me? You are tired of waiting for the word to come to me, but I have been waiting all my life! When my calling came, I thought it was over; yet still Adonai keeps me in suspense, and with every day that passes I grow more frightened of what I shall have to do. He forbids me to go back home until my duty is discharged; even so I might defy him, if there were anything or anyone for me to go back to. Oh Josiah, I'm so unhappy.'

So rather than quarrelling, we finished up embracing while he wept, and I thought: such melancholy confounds me, yet perhaps it is true that a broken spirit alone is genuinely sensitive to God. As for me, a loyal devotee of Adonai I may be, but I could never entirely relinquish control of my mind or my feelings - or my will. I suppose that is why I shall never hear God speaking clearly within my soul, nor shall I ever be quite the man he would like me to be. The price I should have to pay is too high.

The weeks slipped by, and still no word came from Adonai regarding the question of taking tribute to Assyria. I made up my mind to postpone the decision as long as I could; though New Year had now passed, it would still be possible for me to go to the Emperor and claim that unavoidable circumstances had delayed me.

But spring matured into summer, and ultimately the decision made itself, because it was far too late for me to go to my overlord now with lame excuses. All of Judah held its breath to see what would happen; and nothing did. Ashurbanipal's son was proving himself as weak as his father had been strong, and one by one his vassals let their treaties lapse.

I did consider it odd that Adonai had kept his silence on the matter, however. One day when Jeremiah was in a more even mood, I bade him suggest a reason.

Jeremiah replied, 'It may have been of no concern to him whether you took your tribute or not. Maybe there are other issues which concern him more profoundly.'

I was astonished, and demanded to know what could possibly be more important than Judah's sovereignty.

He said simply, 'Judah's sin, Josiah. Judah's sin,' and I pursued the subject no further because the last thing I wanted to hear was him harping once more on the foe from the north.

Summer mellowed into autumn, and with the cooling of the weather Zephaniah's condition seemed to improve. I began to wonder if one day he might be able to return to my service, and Jeremiah might go home after all.

But out of the blue came another stroke worse than the first. From that time on, Zephaniah was like an old, old man, unable even to hold his water or to recognize the faces of those he had loved. Yet still the stricken prophet did not die.

Winter came, and spring once again, but it was a spring like none I could recall. Instead of rain there was scorching heat; the hillsides which should have been carpeted with flowers languished barren and thirsting beneath a merciless sun. Muddy cisterns were jealously guarded; a flask of clean water sold for as much as a flagon of wine, and the babies of the poorest folk were put out to die.

Amid the misery and fear, Maaseiah the Governor of Jerusalem came to me at noon one day to say that Jeremiah was preaching in the Temple courtyard and stirring the populace into frenzy.

'*Jeremiah*?' I repeated, astounded. 'Preaching, in public? And without my permission? You must be mistaken.'

'Oh, but I am not, Your Majesty. It is Jeremiah without a doubt, but I don't know what has happened to him. I never heard *anyone* speak like that before.'

'What in the name of God was he saying, Maaseiah?'

'I couldn't hope to put it over like he did, my lord. But he said he had stood in Adonai's court, and now he himself was acting as prosecuting counsel on his Lord's behalf. He started accusing Judah of infidelity; in bowing down to idols and lying with prostitutes at the high places we'd polluted our land and this was why the rains hadn't come. He said that creation itself would bear witness against us that we'd rejected God's living water and sought refuge in leaking reservoirs, and that priests, prophets and rulers were all to blame. Those who administer justice don't know Adonai in their hearts, and evil is everywhere, and unless we reform ourselves and not just our laws, Adonai will divorce us for our adulteries, the natural order of things will break down, the rains will never come and the land will no longer support us. But... he said it much more poetically than me, Your Majesty.'

'I don't care how he said it! He had no business to say it!' I shouted, thumping my fists on the heads of the stone lions by my throne; but I didn't lose my temper completely until Maaseiah added that Jeremiah had foretold an invasion by a foe from the north.

'Have him brought here this minute!' I yelled, ready to tear the miscreant limb from limb.

'Your Majesty... you want me to arrest him? While he's preaching in Adonai's name?'

'You mean he's still there raving? Good God, Maaseiah, all the more reason to bring him here now, before he does any more damage. Stop arguing with me and do as I tell you.'

Maaseiah bowed himself out; he'd never seen me so incensed. I was beside myself. Who did Jeremiah think he was, making an exhibition of himself in a public place like a common teller of fortunes, ranting about some celestial courtroom when he hadn't had the decency to offer the slightest contribution to *my* Court's discussions? What right had he to stir up panic at a time like this by predicting doom and destruction, and especially when I was doing my level best to right the wrongs I saw around me? In any case, Adonai had promised my glorious ancestor David that his dynasty and city would last for ever, so what harm could possibly come to us above which we could not rise?

Presently messengers came to tell me that the unlikely rabble-rouser was on his way. He'd submitted to my guards without demur, though there had been scuffling among the crowds because feelings were running so high, both for him and against him.

However, as soon as they brought him in, I saw there was nothing to be gained from attempting to rebuke him straight away. He was like a drunkard, flushed of face, pupils dilated; he was laughing and staggering, lurching against the men who held him. When his rolling eyes alighted on me, he stretched out his arms as though to embrace me; he who had discerned my most secret thoughts more times than enough now failed utterly to detect the stench of my blatant anger. Slurring his speech he cried, 'Josiah, it has happened! I am commissioned! Laugh with me, Josiah! Dance with me! What we longed for, what we prayed for... the word of Adonai... his power... oh God, the fire of his coal on my lips...'

The more he said, the less he made sense; none of his sentences were finished, as though his mind were spinning round in his head, and too fast for his tongue to keep up. Then he began to repeat for me, word for word, the message he'd given in the Temple Court - it must have become a part of him - and suddenly *every* sentence was complete, and every syllable made total and terrible sense. But when I asked Maaseiah if this had been the manner of his public delivery too, the Governor of Jerusalem shook his head dumbly, his eyes glued to the prophet's ravaged face. He was frightened, and soon, so was I; sweat poured down Jeremiah's cheeks and neck until all his hair was lank with it and his garments were soaked through. He flung off his cloak and then his woollen robe, and raved on wearing only his loincloth, beating the air with his fists. I ordered the guards to restrain him but he hurled them aside as though something superhuman possessed not merely his soul but his body too.

All I could think of to do was to send for Huldah. She was the only person I knew who might understand what was happening to Jeremiah, and be able to calm him before he injured himself or someone else. She herself had once tried to explain to me how laying yourself open as the channel for Adonai's spirit could send you higher than the strongest wine.

She came at once and held out her arms to him as he'd held his own out to me. For a while he seemed not to see her, and went on ranting. Then gradually the torrent of his words slowed down, became a trickle, and dried up altogether. His eyes ceased rolling, and swam into a dazed kind of focus on her tranquil face; then he laid his hands in hers before collapsing abruptly against her. Fortuitously she had her back to one of the pillars, which prevented the pair of them from falling. I had Asaiah fetch up a couch and there they sat down - at least, Huldah sat down. Jeremiah sagged with his head pressed into her lap, and shook like a wounded bird.

It was when she began to stroke his straggling hair and murmur reassurances into his ear that I realized the two were much better acquainted with one another than I'd previously imagined. A shiver ran up my spine, and the beginnings of speculation, but I was given no time to pursue it because quite without warning Jeremiah sat up. He gazed at me with red-rimmed eyes and a strange washed-out smile and said pleadingly, 'Don't be angry with me, Josiah. Did I not tell you? I was called to go to the people, to stand in their courtyards and on the corners of their streets and cry out to bring them back from the edge of the pit. I have found myself, Josiah. I am in Heaven.' Then his eyes glazed over and he fell sideways onto Huldah's shoulder in a dead faint.

I waited until the following day to vent my wrath upon Jeremiah, once he was more himself again. But even so it left me dissatisfied, because now that the euphoria had left him he would say nothing in his own defence. When I chastised him for flouting my authority he said, 'I know, Josiah. I'm sorry. I wish I'd come to you first.' When I demanded to be told whether I was included in his denouncement of Judah's rulers he whispered, 'I hope not,' and when I bade him reveal the identity of his confounded foe from the north, he cried, 'Oh Josiah, I would have told you already if I knew.' When I railed at him for fuelling the panic in our drought-stricken community - didn't he know that words had creative power, and a prophet's more than any? - he hid his face, and moaned, 'No man's words have power unless they are spoken in accordance with God's will. And I'm sure that mine were not. I don't know what came over me; it can't have been Adonai at all.'

So I was the one who wound up feeling guilty. His confidence in himself and in his God was so low in his weaker moments. The last thing he needed was my crushing it further.

Huldah said to me, 'Don't let this business trouble you unduly, my lord. Jeremiah's gifting is true. You and I both know it, and so does he, deep in his soul. Your displeasure will not have silenced him for ever. It is only because he loves you that your anger hurts him so much. But it's the smile of Adonai that he'll remember, not your frowns. No one can forget the joy which comes from fulfilling God's perfect will.'

'Hmmph,' I snorted, and brooded, and frowned some more. Had I wanted to ruin his ministry? Did I want him silenced, when for so long I'd been desperate for him to speak? Ought I not to be glad that he'd spoken so powerfully for Adonai, and begun to melt the hardened hearts of my people - the very thing I'd fetched him to Jerusalem to do?

Yet I found I could not discuss these things with Huldah, though I'd shared my darkest thoughts with her countless times before. Too many other questions were getting in the way, questions which gnawed like maggots in a wound because I dared not put them to her. Then I felt guilty all over again, because it was I who had brought Huldah and Jeremiah together in the first place.

In the week that followed, Jeremiah rarely ventured from his rooms. The strain of his public appearance had left him exhausted and ill; it seemed that his possession by Adonai's spirit had wrung him out like a rag.

But the impact of his message was still being felt in Jerusalem, and the shockwaves spread to the countryside beyond. There was anger, yes, at the insults he'd levelled against those in authority, yet there was sincere repentance also. The common people, dressed in sackcloth and heaping ashes on their heads, flocked in their thousands to the Temple. They handed over their idols and fetishes to be burnt, confessed that Adonai, not the Baals, was responsible for the fertility of the land, and fervently prayed and sacrificed for the end of the drought. They hailed me as Righteous King Josiah,

Servant of God and Protector of His Holy Prophets. So I had no choice but to smile and acknowledge their adulation, because support for my reforms waxed stronger than it ever had before.

In the end I swallowed the last of my pride, and went to Jeremiah of my own accord to apologize for my anger against him. I, the anointed Sovereign of Judah, went on my knees before a son of Anathoth to crave his pardon, and to recognize that he served a king far greater than I. Jeremiah drew me to my feet, as I'd once drawn him to his, and in that very moment the first spots of rain were heard plashing on the balcony outside.

CHAPTER 9: JEREMIAH

I

The next four years were the happiest I had ever known. I had found friendship and purpose, I was living in comfort in Adonai's holy city, and I was passing on my knowledge and my joy to young Johanan who adored me, and to Ahikam's son Gedaliah, who had become Johanan's bosom friend. I gave my support to Josiah in all that he sought to achieve, and his every enterprise prospered. Week by week I drew closer to Adonai and he to me; whole days were swallowed up in glorious contemplation and abandonment. I prayed with Josiah, too, and with Ahikam and his brothers - excepting Jaazaniah, who was wary of the dizzy spiritual heights we scaled.

From time to time I prophesied again in the Temple Court, reminding the people of the loyalty they had pledged to their God and their King, and inspiring them to maintain it. On occasions I was moved to speak out against the evil ways of our ancestral enemies, the heathen nations which surrounded us - Philistia, Moab, Ammon, Edom, Syria - and for this at least all Judah praised me. Only later did I learn of the opposition mounting against me at the high places; at the time I was blissfully unaware.

Each time I spoke for Adonai in public, I wound up shattered and drained and iller than the time before. Yet this was a tiny price to pay for the exhilaration I felt when my lips were touched by the celestial fire and the whole of my body trembled with the energy of the Divine.

Excited by what they saw in me, droves of eager youths beat a path to my door seeking to become my disciples. All of them I turned away. If they wished to serve God, I told them, they should work hard and do well for themselves and their families, and tender their surplus to the fund for refurbishing the Temple.

Soon, sufficient gold had been amassed for this project to begin. Josiah was ecstatic. Manasseh's abominations would be forgotten, and the Temple would be more beautiful even than Solomon had made it. The threat of the foe from the north was forgotten too.

Only the surliness of Eliakim took the edge off my contentment. As he grew taller and more handsome, his hatred of me grew in parallel. The stronger the bond being forged between myself and Johanan, the more his brother resented it, and the blacker the looks he gave me. He no longer threw tantrums; but he stowed his anger inside, and kept it warm and well fed.

Eventually my close involvement with the royal family forced me to acknowledge what I was missing in having no wife or sons of my own. I caught myself longing for the tender love of a woman, the joys of the marriage bed, the satisfaction of watching my own children grow and flourish. I started to dream about Ruth, and I pictured myself returning to Anathoth now that I had respectability and even fame behind me, and asking her to be my bride after all. Perhaps my parents would welcome me home, now that I'd proved I could be someone? Part of me still yearned for them to accept me. Adonai had said I should not go back, nor marry, until my work in Jerusalem was finished... perhaps now I had done all that was required of me?

However, this wasn't quite the whole story. I had a more pressing reason for wanting to leave Jerusalem and start my own family.

I'd begun seeing Huldah fairly frequently from the day we were introduced, first in the company of others at the palace, later at her home in the new north western quarter of Jerusalem where she and her husband Shallum would invite me for meals. We had so much in common, she and I, and at first it was just so very wonderful to talk once more with someone who knew what it was to fall into the hands of God; never again would I enjoy such conversations with Zephaniah.

And Huldah understood so much. Like the old priest at Anathoth who'd once dried my eyes when the boys had called me names, she believed that once upon a time all of humanity had been able to hear the voice of its Creator, and that we two were among the last of a kind. It was inevitable that we and those like us would be feared by all and reckoned mad by many; each generation would deem us madder than the last as the memory of God's voice faded. In the future, others such as we might even be locked away, condemned to deliver God's message to the walls of their cells. In the past, when the word had come to all, there had been no need for the calling, the seizure, the pain.

'When I was little, I heard without pain,' I said, thinking back for the first time in months to my childhood, before I had known who the voice belonged to. I glanced across the table at Shallum, but his mind was on his food; he wasn't even following what we said.

'You heard Adonai's voice before you were called?' asked Huldah in surprise.

'Of course - though it didn't say very much. Just the same things, over and over again. Why? Didn't you?'

'Never. Perhaps it happens to the greatest only - to those most like the men of former times.'

'Then how did you recover from the shock of your calling, if you'd had no warning about what was going to happen to you?'

'There are callings and callings, Jeremiah. Perhaps their violence is in proportion to the scale of the demands they place upon us. In any case, I did have warning.' Huldah smiled her radiant smile, then turned to gaze upon Shallum, still eating in silence. 'Josiah saw what was latent in me, and he told me; don't ask me how he knew. If anyone else had said such a thing, I shouldn't have believed it. Certainly Shallum didn't believe it, did you, my love?'

Her gaze had become mischievous; Shallum started at the mention of his name, then returned a benign smile. It was plain to me - and to Huldah - that he loved her fondly, but scarcely knew her at all.

So as time went on, Huldah and I had begun to see one another alone, though initially only when I lay sick after giving the word of Adonai. She would come to visit, bringing me grapes, and gossip from the Court; the touch of her hands would restore me to strength, and with her gentle humour she dispelled the doubts which crowded in to assail me after each of my triumphs.

But recently she had been to my rooms when I wasn't ill; and I had been to her home when Shallum was elsewhere. Quite suddenly her being a prophetess had become less important than her being a woman; in fact not until now had I truly noticed the brightness of her eyes, the fullness of her lips, the glossy curls that tumbled out from under her veil when she bowed her head to pray or threw it back to laugh. These days I could think of little else, and found myself bewitched by her every movement, my eyes held captive by the slight swaying of her hips as she walked, by the rise and fall of her breasts when she sat by my side, her own eyes closed in meditation, her breathing deep with the heaviness of Adonai. She was a married woman, thirty years old; I was twenty six and a virgin, acutely aware of my need - and I was frightened. Had I myself not raged with Adonai's wrath against the lusts of the flesh, and harangued his wayward people over their sexual sins? I must find a wife before my illicit attraction to Huldah turned to obsession, and led us where we knew we should not go.

Therefore early in the spring exactly five years after I had come to the city, I asked Josiah for permission to leave.

He was astounded; was I still so unhappy? Was Eliakim's intransigence still grinding me down? If nothing else would solve the problem, the boy could be found another teacher after all.

'No, Josiah,' I said, wishing I might tell him the truth, yet knowing it could do only harm. 'My work here is complete. I want to see my parents and my brothers again.'

'Are you sure they'll want to see *you?* I should think your activities here will have caused them to detest you more than ever.'

He was right, though just then I would not see it; my lack of awareness of the antagonism which my prophecies had stirred up in the towns of Judah had been due in no small part to Josiah's protecting me from it. So I persisted, 'I need to go home. I need to marry, Josiah. I want to marry Ruth.'

He stared at me in disbelief. Then looking almost relieved, he threw his arms around me, thumping my back and laughing. 'So I still haven't managed to persuade you that marriage is a fool's game? Then you're as much a fool as the rest of humanity, though I must confess it's good to know that you *are* human! Go with my blessing, Jeremiah; and you'll have gold and presents as well. But you must promise to return, and bring your blushing bride with you.'

'I can't promise anything like that; you know I can't. I must go where Adonai leads me.'

He held me away from him, saw I was in earnest, and he grew earnest too. 'I shall miss you, my friend,' he said. I don't know how I shall manage.'

'You'll manage perfectly well. You have Shaphan and his sons to advise you. Your reform programme is progressing apace, as is your work on the Temple. You don't need my ranting and raving any more.'

'I need *you*, Jeremiah.' He held me close again. 'But I shall not ask you to act against your will; I know it would be useless.' (All the same, I was surprised he didn't try.) He concluded, 'Promise me only that you'll keep on praying for me and for my work.'

I gave him my word, and the following morning I left.

I refused the carriage and horses which were offered me, not wanting the inhabitants of Anathoth to imagine me grown high and mighty. I went on foot, with a single donkey to carry my things, and it was scarcely worth taking even that, since I owned so little. I had my lyre, Hosea's scroll, a change of clothes, and just enough food for the journey - but a small fortune in gold at my belt. It was my wedding present, Josiah said, and if I refused that, all it would prove was that I was proud and pig-headed.

The closer I came to Anathoth, the more convinced I was that I'd made the right decision in returning. Excitement welled up inside me as Jerusalem's green and gold gave way to Anathoth's red. Yes, David's city was beautiful, with its yellow stone and its terraced vineyards, its fragrant breezes which took the sting from the heat even in high summer. But I had missed the rugged ridges, the hazy views of hills, the hamlets of mudbrick houses clinging for dear life to the steep slopes which plunged into the desert. To this place I'd been born: this dour, dusty outpost of civilization perched on the edge of the abyss.

However, when I entered the village I might as well have been invisible. It wasn't that folk didn't recognize me; they knew who I was well enough. But I'd compounded the sins of my youth with serving a son of Solomon, and with preaching against the practices from which Anathoth's livelihood derived. My father had once pronounced me dead. Now it appeared that everyone was minded to believe it.

So I walked the narrow streets like a disembodied spirit, and my soul withered inside me because I'd become so unused to the rejection I'd grown up with. I went to the house where I'd been born, and my own mother spat on the ground at my feet. 'Please, let me speak just once with my father,' I begged her, but she snapped, 'Hilkiah was never your father. You were born of the devil, so let the devil take you.' Then she closed the door in my face.

For a while I just stood there blinking in the sunshine. I dared not go to the sanctuary; so I went to Ruth's.

The old blind grandmother sat in the doorway, shrivelled and wrinkled as an old carob pod, and quite without teeth. Having learned who I was, she made a sign against evil with her gnarled fingers and rasped, 'Go away! How dare you come here! How dare you!'

'I need to see Ruth, just for a moment - '

'You cannot! She is betrothed.'

The bottom fell out of my world. 'Betrothed?' I whispered. 'To whom?'

'To Hanamel ben Shallum, your cousin. Now be gone! Leave us in peace.'

Hanamel? I could not believe it. I leaned on my donkey's neck, gripping its halter with quaking hands. Then in a moment of madness I strode past the old woman and forced my way into the cottage.

Ruth was there, as I'd known she would be. She gasped, pulled her veil tight around her head, and backed away into a corner so that a table stood between us. Neither of us spoke; she closed her eyes, and the lids were quivering.

At last I stammered, 'Say it isn't true, Ruth. Tell me I'm dreaming.'

'It *is* true. I am to marry him a week from today.'

'But you don't love him. You *cannot* love him.'

'I shall learn to. And at least he loves me. He's been asking for my hand in marriage ever since you left this village.'

'In spite of the way he treated you at the sanctuary?' I expostulated, my voice rising, and breaking; she opened her eyes just wide enough for them to flash fire at me, and she hissed at me to be quiet.

'You will not mention that! My grandmother knows nothing of it, and she must never find out! Hanamel is of good family; he has sheep and goats and will be able to support us. Nothing else need matter to her.'

'To *her?* But what about *you,* for God's sake? Have you forgotten what he tried to do to you?'

She didn't reply; her eyes were closed again and her chest heaving. I smashed both my fists down on the table and blurted, 'Anyone else, and I could have believed it. I might even have wished you happiness. But Hanamel..!'

'There *was* no one else!' she retorted, her veil slipping down onto her shoulders, her bright black hair flying free. 'And you must have known it, or you would never have come here today! There has been no one else in all these years - who would want to sire his sons on a whore whom every man in Anathoth might have lain with, or spat upon as she begged in the gutter?'

'No one at that shrine touched you! You came away as chaste as you went there.'

'You and Hanamel believe that. But who else? Would you condemn me to grow old here all alone? When my grandmother is gone, I shall have no one in the world! At least Hanamel wants me. He's obsessed with me, Jeremiah. Ever since he... ever since you...'

I leaned across the table, my face right up to hers, and said, '*I* want you, Ruth. *I* love you. *You* must have known *that,* or you would have married him already.'

Again she made no reply. Her eyes were averted, though we stood close enough for me to feel her rapid breath on my cheeks.

'You knew I would come back,' I said. 'You waited for me. Didn't you.' And when still she refused to speak, I insisted, 'Look at me, Ruth. Please. Just look at me.'

She shook her head, putting one hand in front of her eyes. But then she jerked it abruptly aside, crying, 'How can *you* bring yourself to look at *me?* It was you who walked away! I loved you, but you threw that love back in my face!'

'It broke my heart when I had to leave you! Oh Ruth, forget about Hanamel now. He doesn't even know what love means.'

Her lashes were dewed with tears; impulsively I swung myself onto the table, then slid off the other side and took her in my arms. But she murmured, 'I've pledged him my troth, Jeremiah, and I shall not revoke it. I shall never do to anyone what you did to me.'

'I was sixteen years old! A man can change.'

'If he can change once, he can change again. You'll leave me like you did before, and then I'll have lost you and Hanamel too; *he* won't come back a second time. He's jealous enough of you as it is.'

'Hanamel, jealous of me?' I made a sour sound in my throat, meant to express contempt, but it came out more like a sob. 'Why ever *should* he be.'

'Because he thinks that I still love you.' She sniffed, and wiped her nose with a fold of her veil, her brimming eyes fixed helplessly on my face. 'He thinks I love you more than I'll ever love him.'

'Perhaps he is right.'

For a very long time she gazed at me. A single tear escaped down one cheek. Then she said, 'Get out, Jeremiah.' And when I would not, she shrieked, 'Get out! Get out!' until I feared all the neighbourhood would come running with sticks and stones.

I stumbled from the house barely able to see where I was going. I seized my donkey's halter and dragged the beast erratically about the hostile streets until more by luck than any sort of judgment we found our way out of the village. In my mind I had no idea where to go next, but my feet took me to old Simeon's cottage. Surely he and Hannah wouldn't shun me?

When I got there, however, the place was deserted. The door hung away from its hinges and the little yard was choked with thornbushes. I left the donkey outside, untethered and still loaded, and flung myself face down on the floor where my bed had once been. The only two people in Anathoth who might have welcomed me were dead and buried; I wanted nothing other than death for myself.

The rest of that day I lay prostrate, oblivious even to the braying of the donkey which hadn't been watered since dawn. I don't know why it didn't wander off, except that like me it had nowhere to go. Just as night began to fall I relented, lifted its burden from its back and gave it a drink. Then I took my things inside and spent a sleepless night on the bare ground.

All the next day I lay there and neither ate nor drank. This time I knew the donkey had wandered off, because I could no longer hear its complaints. I didn't care.

By the third morning my tongue had furred up from lack of water and I was dreaming when awake. Then my voice whispered: *Jeremiah, go back.*

I didn't listen. I didn't even believe it was Adonai any more. It was only my hunger speaking.

But all day and half into the night it kept on at me: *Go back, go back, go back,* till I could ignore it no longer. I sat up and shouted hoarsely, 'Why should I? They will only snub me again. They might even stone me.'

Not back to Anathoth. Back to Jerusalem.

'Jerusalem?' I laughed, an uncertain, cynical laugh, and shook my head into the eloquent darkness. 'You brought me home, and now you want me to go back there? Well I shall not do it. I couldn't face Josiah.'

Jeremiah, Josiah needs you now more than he ever has before. Anathoth is not your home, nor was it I who brought you here.

'What about Huldah, then? Would you have her life ruined, just like Ruth's, because of me?'

I most certainly would not. She is my beloved child, just as you are. And just as Ruth is.

'Then you must change me. You must make me like a eunuch, with no needs, no desires, no manhood at all - '

No, my son. You must learn to master yourself, or you will be of no use to me. Your ministry has barely begun, and in the very hour when Josiah and I needed you in Jerusalem, you were languishing here in a place where you should not have been. Get up, and go back where you belong.

So at first light I did as I was bidden, having strapped my belongings to my own back. My body was weak and my mind a blur, but I made my way back to Jerusalem, needing badly to talk to Josiah, or Ahikam, or even Huldah, or anyone.

Yet none of them was to be found, and the palace was in such a state of consternation that my return was scarcely remarked upon. I went to my old quarters, and discovered there the black eunuch Ebed-Melech who'd been accustomed to bring my food, sitting disconsolate and anxious.

When he saw me he got up and ran, throwing himself on the floor before me, clasping my knees and covering my fingers in kisses. 'Oh master, I have prayed so hard to the god you worship that he would bring you back,' he cried, and I pressed his head against me, being too fatigued and too confused to speak. Then he fetched water to wash the dust from my feet, and brought me food and wine which I was in no mood to enjoy, but eventually I managed to ask him where everyone else was, and what had gone wrong.

'A book of the Law has been found, master. Since you were not here and Zephaniah is so ill, His Majesty consulted the prophetess Huldah about it, and she pronounced it the true word of Adonai your god, a genuine collection of the sayings and doings of Moses himself! They say that as soon as His Majesty learned what was in it, he put on sackcloth and ashes and shut himself up in his throne-room.'

'Why? What did it say?'

'Oh master, I hardly know anything! All I've heard is that His Majesty is in despair, saying you were right all along: he has fallen so far short of what God demands that all his life's work has been useless.'

I was alarmed. 'Who found this book? Where was it?'

'It was hidden in the Temple, in the holiest place where only the High Priest is allowed to go. It was Hilkiah himself who found it. It may have been there for centuries.'

I said, 'Stay here if you wish, and finish this food. It was kind of you to bring it, but I must see the King.'

I went directly to the throne-room and was admitted straight away, because I wasn't alone in being worried for Josiah. He sat on his throne surrounded by white-faced courtiers, Huldah among them. Her eyes met mine only briefly, but long enough for me to tell that she read the pain in them and recognized that Josiah was not its sole cause. But for the moment our own troubles had to wait.

For Josiah was distraught. He'd ripped his royal robes into tatters, and shorn his hair. His head was fallen forward on his breast; Asaiah and Huldah held his hands and sought to bring him comfort.

It was Ahikam who drew me to one side and explained to me exactly what had happened. His father Shaphan had been sent with Joah the Recorder and Maaseiah Jerusalem's Governor to consult with Hilkiah on the progress of the Temple restorations. Shaphan had originally been charged with commissioning the work and obtaining materials, and he was responsible for paying the craftsmen.

However, when they arrived, all work had stopped because of Hilkiah's discovery. Under normal circumstances, the High Priest entered the Holy of Holies just once a year on the Day of Atonement, and on that most solemn of occasions his every action was prescribed by ritual so there was no opportunity for examining the contents of the sacred chamber. But today, special rites had been performed so that he might go in and assess what work must be done there in readiness for the Ark's return; though few people knew it, orthodox priests had ordered its removal during the reign of Manasseh because they could not sanction its sharing space with the apostate's Asherah pole. In inspecting the dais where the Ark would stand, an innocuous-looking earthenware jar had been found; when this was carried outside and opened, there was the scroll, which purported to be an ancient and authoritative record of the words and deeds of Moses. Shaphan had taken it straight to Josiah. Thereupon Shaphan had been sent, with Hilkiah, Asaiah, Akbor and Ahikam himself, to the prophetess Huldah. She had declared it authentic.

At that moment our whispering must have reached the ears of the King. He gave a great groan and ordered everyone to leave; at first no one moved, but he leaped from his throne and roared that he must be alone with his God. Meekly I allowed Ahikam to lead me away, and gazing backwards over my shoulder, the last thing I saw was Josiah face down on the ground in abject repentance.

Once outside, I leaned dizzily against a pillar; I ought to have made more effort to eat. There was an exchange of hushed voices close by my side, and the next thing I knew, Ahikam was gone and Huldah had taken my arm.

I wanted to tell her to leave me be, since I'd made up my mind on the way back to Jerusalem that never again would I meet with her alone. But I couldn't find the strength, and together we made for my chambers. I hoped Ebed-Melech might still be there, but he'd cleared up the dishes and gone. Huldah closed the door behind us.

Against my better judgment I bared my soul before her. Yet she needed to talk to me as much as I did to her, because of what she'd been called upon to do in my absence. 'I'm sorry,' I said, my head in my hands. 'I should never have left the palace.'

'Don't blame yourself, Jeremiah.' She covered my hands with her own. 'Perhaps it has been for the best. Josiah will never again be able to say that a woman cannot be consulted in public affairs.' I couldn't see her face, but she had forced a hint of her mischievous smile into her voice.

Then a fresh wave of grief broke upon me and I blurted, 'I don't blame myself. I blame Adonai! Am I *never* to marry? Am I *never* to father sons of my own, or raise them in the place where I was born? Will Adonai never let me go and live like other men?'

'I think you should ask *him* those questions,' she answered softly, and instinctively put one arm around me. But almost at once she withdrew it, catching her breath, and said, 'I ought to go now.'

However, I restrained her and made her sit down on the couch beside me. Then she started to tell me her own side of the scroll's remarkable story: how when Josiah's delegation had approached her with it, Adonai's spirit had overwhelmed her, and his words had poured from her mouth without her mind being involved. Yet she could recall them now, syllable for syllable, just as I could have done had I been in her place - which was precisely where I should have been. Adonai's wrath was aroused against Judah and Jerusalem, and judgment was coming in accordance with the curses written in the scroll. Yet because the King had personally sought to humble himself to avert disaster, it would not come during his lifetime. He would be permitted to die in peace in the City of David, and be buried there with his fathers.

'Not that this has afforded him any solace,' Huldah finished up with a sigh. 'Josiah is King of Judah through and through. If his nation is destined for ruin, his whole life will have been a failure; at least, that is how he thinks.'

'And what *are* the curses written in the scroll? What does the blessed thing *say*, for God's sake?'

'I don't know. I never got to read it.'

'But you are convinced it contains the true words of Moses?'

'That I never said. I said only that it contains the words of Adonai.'

I slumped back wearily on my couch, fingertips pressed to my temples. So my own predictions of doom were to be proven right after all; ought I to be glad? Or ought I to be relieved that disaster lay so far in the future? For if Josiah were to die a peaceful death, it might not be for fifty years. God willing, I might not live to see the day of judgment either.

When I came alone in prayer before Adonai in my room that night, it was still my own troubles which beset me rather than Josiah's or Judah's. As Huldah had suggested, I put to him the questions which gnawed at my soul. Almost at once I was wishing I had not.

The air grew so heavy with Adonai's presence that I fell to the floor. He said, *Not only must you never marry, my son, but from this day forward you must attend no other wedding, nor any domestic celebration, nor even the funerals of those you love. The time is coming when no man will lead a normal life, and you will be the sign that prefigures it. Did I not tell you that your very existence would become a vehicle for my message? In loneliness and rejection you grew up, to prepare you for loneliness and rejection as a man. You will know intimacy, but only with me.*

I cried aloud in anguish, thinking: this is it, I have had enough. I shall cast off his yoke and every convention that binds me. I shall take Huldah to my bed, and together we'll show the world that we care nothing for Adonai or his callous commandments.

But when immediately the heaviness departed, and the room was empty except for me, I found myself sobbing and begging the celestial presence to return, as I always had and always would. Life at the mercy of Adonai might seem intolerable; but life without it was unthinkable. I might have been tempted to swallow poison before morning, had I not suspected that death wasn't the end.

So Adonai returned, gently this time, granting me pardon for my rebellion and drying my tears. He said: *Remember, my son, it is I to whom you must turn for understanding and affection, not Huldah, not Ruth, not even Josiah. It is for your own good that I command you not to marry, because in the days which are coming, brides will be snatched from their husbands' arms and children's throats will be slit in front of their parents' eyes. Your heart is too tender to bear such agony, yet I cannot make it hard, any more than I can make you less than a man. You will struggle with loneliness and carnal temptation all your life; yet only turn to me, and I shall be more to you than any wife or son could be.*

So I lay basking for a while in the warmth of his love, drifting on a tide of serenity. Then the questions started rising again in my mind. Am I to prophesy till I am old, of an enemy invasion far in the future? Who will believe me when I speak and speak and nothing happens?

It is not for you to know times and places, was all that Adonai would say in reply; and this alarmed me, because of what it might mean for Josiah. He was to be *permitted* to die in peace... but was that what he would choose to do?

Come now, my son, Adonai admonished me, not unkindly. *Lay aside these anxieties. Ask me the question which really matters. Ask me what is written on Hilkiah's scroll.*

But I wasn't sure that I wanted to know this, either. So Adonai said: *Very well, then, I shall not tell you. I shall say only that the curses in the scroll point to exile. It is into a long and galling exile that Judah's sins are leading her, just as the sins of her sister kingdom Israel led* her *away a hundred years ago.*

I was shaken to the core. 'You would banish *all* of your people from the Promised Land? From the land you said would belong to Abraham and his seed for ever? Does your covenant mean nothing?

Did Hosea not say that my people must return to Egypt, that I might woo them again in the desert? Life in this land has grown too easy for them. Their faith is dead, Jeremiah. They have forgotten the drought of four years ago already. They worship me in form, because Josiah compels them, but their hearts are far away. So I shall take the covenant which they have trampled in the dust and establish a new one in its place.

'Egypt? You would send us back there, and undo all that Moses did? I can't believe it.'

What Moses achieved is already overthrown; my people are slaves to their own transgressions. But I shall not take them back to the land of the Pharaohs. Hosea used the name Egypt as a symbol only. Most of my people will go north, to the land whence the foe will come.

'To Assyria? Judah will join her sister Israel in Assyria?'

Assyria is as dead as Judah's faith, and Israel with her.

'Then where? *Where* are we to be sent?'

Again you ask questions which do not concern you. Why don't you sleep, Jeremiah. Then in the morning you can eat a proper breakfast, go to Josiah, and discover for yourself what the Law Book says.

I went at first light, taking with me the gold he'd given me to set up home with Ruth in Anathoth. But I was told he was at prayer and receiving no one. However, there was to be a great gathering at noon in the Temple Court, where the King himself would read aloud the contents of the scroll to his assembled subjects.

'And this gold?' I asked, showing the purse with its fortune to old Shaphan, who had turned me away from Josiah's chambers. 'It was his wedding present to me, but now I am not to marry.'

'You must keep it nonetheless,' Shaphan answered. 'What His Majesty has given cannot be returned without offending against propriety. Invest it in your future, as he meant you to do.'

So I repaired to my apartment and stashed the gold away at the bottom of a chest where I could forget about it.

Shortly before midday I set out with the members of Josiah's Governing Council, and in the Temple Court we took the places which had been reserved for us. I was relieved not to be amongst the multitude of common people, crammed shoulder to shoulder in escalating heat. The story of the finding of the book had gone through the city and its surroundings like fire through a woodpile, and there was a thrill in the air such as comes before an almighty storm.

Presently heralds sounded their trumpets and the noise of the crowd died away. Josiah appeared on the Temple steps, and after appropriate formalities, the recitation started.

His voice was strong and clear at the outset, soaring over the assembly as he read of the might of Adonai and catalogued the many good things which our God had done for his people. It resembled the opening of one of the treaties which emperors make with the vassal kings who rule on their behalf - which is indeed what it was. Josiah was no longer Assyria's vassal; he was Adonai's.

Then, still echoing the style of a treaty, he began to list the requirements which Adonai placed upon his Chosen People. And now Josiah's voice began to waver, in recognition of his own shortcomings and those of his subjects. Not only must idolatry be eradicated from the high places, but the high places themselves must be destroyed lest heresy spring up at them once again. All cultic worship should be conducted at the central sanctuary - in Jerusalem - and the three major festivals - Passover, Pentecost and Tabernacles - should be held there too. Any town where idolatry was found to be rife must be torched as a burnt offering to Adonai, along with its inhabitants and even its animals. False prophets were to be put to death for leading simpler folk astray, and could readily be identified because they were the ones whose predictions did not come true.

There was much else too, the like of which his audience had heard many times before, though without putting it into practice. But the insistence on centralized worship was entirely new to us, and its implications were lost on no one, myself least of all. The sanctuary at Anathoth would have to be levelled along with the rest; what would become of the priests and prophets who earned their daily bread there? What would become of their families? I found that I didn't much care if my parents or my brothers or my cousins starved to death; but what of Ruth?

I was even a little afraid for myself. If the judgment were postponed until Josiah died of old age, might not *I* be taken and stoned for leading men astray? I shuddered, and made myself listen to what Josiah said next.

He'd paused for some time before saying it, because it concerned the conduct of the King himself. For he was not to rely upon the strength of his army, but solely on his God; he was not to heap up riches, nor maintain great stables full of horses. In particular, he must be content with only one wife.

It was when he reached the part of the treaty stipulating the curses which disobedience would unleash upon us that his voice failed him and he could not go on. The people stood aghast, appalled by the spectacle of their young King stricken and swaying where he stood.

Asaiah fetched a chair and Josiah sat down; someone else brought him water, and after drinking deeply he managed to rise and continue to read. He read of drought, disease, destruction... the land of milk and honey would no longer be able to support its population because their depravity had made nature itself their enemy. We who had worshipped foreign gods would end our days on foreign soil, serving foreign masters. The fortunate among us would be those who died before they got there.

A long silence ensued. Josiah stood with bowed head, and Hilkiah prized the scroll from his trembling fingers lest the holy object fall on the ground. Then someone called out from the crowd, 'Your Majesty, what must we do?' And someone else cried, 'Can you offer your subjects no hope?'

At length the King looked up, and held out his arms in appeal. 'There is but one hope of salvation remaining!' he cried. 'It is no longer enough that we are circumcized in the flesh. We must circumcize our *hearts!*'

My own heart leaped as he said this, because it seemed to accord so well with what Adonai had said to me about the coming of a new kind of covenant. But when Josiah began inciting the people there and then to pledge their loyalty to Adonai afresh, I thought: this is merely the old covenant served up with a dressing of desperation. A man can circumcize only his own heart, in the quietness, when Adonai's wings overshadow him. Promises made out loud in the company of a yelling crowd mean nothing.

For the crowd *was* yelling, now, all those present acclaiming Josiah as their saviour and declaring their willingness to swear any oath he chose to demand of them. So he led them in an elaborate avowal of allegiance to their God, after which he was escorted swiftly back to the palace.

Nauseous from the heat, I too returned to my quarters. But scarcely had I sat down when a messenger came and summoned me to the royal presence.

I rather expected Josiah to be jubilant now, elated by his subjects' approbation. However, when I entered his chambers he was lying supine on a couch, head thrown back, one arm across his eyes and the other clasping the stem of a goblet which was balanced on his chest. Its contents were half drunk, and half spilled over the ceremonial robes of which he hadn't bothered to divest himself. I knelt on the floor by his side; he rolled over, spilling what remained of his wine, and pressed his face into my neck. I was deeply shocked, and didn't move, though his nails dug into my flesh like those of a man who is having an arrowhead removed from a wound.

He began mumbling through my hair, confessing to me over and over again how inadequate his work of reform had proven to be; how he had barely scratched the surface of what was needful. 'I've been living in a fool's paradise, Jeremiah. We all have. Now it's too late; we are too far gone in corruption. And to think: I imagined that my being a descendant of David was enough, that his city would stand inviolable and his dynasty never end!'

I whispered, 'Josiah, Adonai forgives you! He sees into your heart and knows you are striving to serve him to the best of your ability; Huldah told you so. And it must be possible for Judah to repent and be saved, or the Book of the Law would not have been found.'

'But my best hasn't been good enough, has it? And it never will be! Adonai knows that my people will never repent in their hearts; that is why he has spoken so much about judgment, through you and now through Huldah. It *can* be averted; but he knows that it won't be.'

I couldn't contradict him, for he spoke the truth. So I said, 'It does no good to torture yourself, Josiah. You must take your stand and continue to do what you can, to keep your own conscience clear.'

'But *I* cannot live up to what the Law Book demands! Yes, I can put idolaters to death if I have to; I can execute pagan priests and prophets. But am I to sell all my possessions and disband my army, when on each of my borders foreign kings wait to pounce and seize my inheritance? And am I to turn one of my own wives out of my house? Perhaps I could do without gold dishes on my table and jewels in my crown, but I could not send an innocent woman back to her father! Yet from my own lips my people have heard what is required of me, so how am I to live with their contempt if I do not do it? How am I to exhort *them* to obey Adonai when I myself am living in rebellion?'

'Certainly you must take no *more* wives. But divorce is hateful to Adonai just as surely as greed is. You cannot know that he requires you to divorce, unless you ask him.'

'I *dare* not ask him! Zebidah and Hamutal are both the mothers of my sons!' Great sobs racked Josiah's body as he tried to put his worst fear into words: that it was his beloved Zebidah, the wife of his youth, who would have to go.

'But why Zebidah? Surely it is Hamutal who should never have become your wife.'

'Because Zebidah can have no more children! A king must have heirs, for God's sake!'

'You have three heirs already. You must pray that they will live, and that one of them will grow up fit to succeed you. If it is right for you to divorce Hamutal, your prayers will be answered.'

'And if it is *not* right..?' Josiah's nails bit harder into my skin; I was sure they must be drawing blood. 'I dare not take the risk of being wrong, Jeremiah! Johanan is sick more often than he's well; Eliakim gets more intractable every day, and Shelemaiah would slit his own throat if Eliakim told him to do it. None of them will be fit to sit on my throne, and that is mostly my own fault too. My sons will undo all that I have done - not that it counts for anything anyway - and judgment will strike. You have said so; Huldah has said so; the Book of the Law itself has said so.'

'Let's pray together,' I implored him. 'I can stand this no longer.'

But Josiah refused; he sprang from his couch lest I start to pray in defiance of him, and shouted, '*You* cannot stand it? What about me? It is only because you can't marry at all that you want *my* married life to be ruined.'

I was appalled. Josiah saw at once how sorely he'd hurt me, and apologized profusely, calling himself every bad name under the sun and begging me to pardon his unbridled tongue. I told him that I did, but when I left him and returned to my rooms, the echo of his accusation still lingered in my ears.

I don't think Josiah went to bed that night. He spent it working like a driven slave, covering sheaves of parchment in tiny writing as he revised his programme of reform and drew up plans for an enormous Passover festival to mark the launching of his fresh campaign. It was as though he believed that a rabid zeal for national revival could atone for his personal failures, when the truth of the matter was exactly the opposite: Adonai had found no fault with our King himself, but with his recalcitrant people. I became very afraid, but wouldn't venture to rebuke him. It would merely afford him the chance to repeat the spiteful accusation he'd levelled at me before.

Josiah's Passover was duly proclaimed, the first ever to be celebrated on such a lavish scale and exclusively within the walls of Jerusalem. Pilgrims flocked to the city, bringing their lambs to the Temple for slaughter; the refurbishment of Adonai's house had been completed, and orders had been given for the Ark to be restored to its rightful place, symbolizing God's presence among his people.

Herein there lay a problem, however. With only three days to go before the festival began, the Holy of Holies was still empty of its most sacred object. In secret Josiah confessed to me his fear that the Jerusalem clergy no longer possessed it. During Manasseh's evil reign, a group of priests had fled to Elephantine, an island in the River Nile, and had begun to build a temple of their own, identical to Solomon's in every respect. Had they taken the Ark with them?

I shrugged my shoulders. 'Send ambassadors to Egypt to find out. If the Ark is there, have it brought back at once, and the priests with it.'

'I *have* sent ambassadors. The Egyptians deny everything and will not give permission for any extraditions. But why build a temple if you have nothing to put inside it?' Josiah banged his fist against the nearest wall. 'Worship will never be as Adonai wants it while that abominable structure exists. Don't you know, they worship Adonai and Anat there as husband and wife? How am I to enforce orthodoxy here, while heresy abounds where I have no jurisdiction?'

'You cannot be held responsible for what happens beyond the boundaries of your kingdom,' I pointed out; then Adonai's spirit seized hold of me even as I sat there, with no warning at all. It was like being suddenly and violently sick, without any feeling of nausea to serve as preparation. *The days are coming*, Adonai said through me, *when the Ark will no longer be missed, because I shall dwell inside every heart.* Then he released me as swiftly as he'd taken me, and I sat there in shock, realizing gradually that the absence of the Ark was actually an integral feature of the great divine plan. But Josiah shook his head: the emptiness of Adonai's shrine was a bad omen, not a good one.

At any rate, the Passover had to go ahead without the problem being solved. Not that many people *knew* there was a problem; since only Hilkiah ever entered the holiest place, no one else could be sure of what was inside and what was not. Meanwhile the Temple Court was filled with the bleating of lambs until its gutters ran with their blood, and I prayed that Adonai might accept it instead of ours.

II

When the festival was over, the latest phase of Josiah's campaign began. Throughout Judah the sanctuaries were closed, their buildings demolished, their holy objects smashed and altars profaned. Since it lay so close to Jerusalem, the high place at Anathoth was among the first to go. Its priests and prophets fled like mice from a blazing barn; I don't think many fell into the hands of the King's executioners. But with its heart torn out, the village itself sank into decline. Josiah paid it a personal visit while touring the land to assess the effects of his new policies; I wondered if he had forgotten how a kindly priest there had once saved his life.

Any opposition to the closures was dealt with speedily and harshly, but there were surprisingly few violent incidents. Most folk were so fearful of the prospect of famine or invasion that they poured from their homes cheering and throwing flowers for the pious young King who had undertaken to save them from Heaven's wrath. Subsequently I myself was commanded by Adonai to join Josiah's retinue when he travelled; together with Shaphan's sons and the other royal counsellors, I basked in my lord's reflected glory, and wore garlands woven from the blossoms which landed at my feet. But I was glad that Anathoth's demise had come before my own travels began, and I studiously avoided going near it.

Two years after the finding of the scroll, Assyria relinquished its hold completely, not only over Judah but also over the territories which had once belonged to her sister Israel. Josiah was exultant, and at once set about extending his influence northwards. He refortified derelict strongholds, in particular that of Megiddo, which was to serve as his northern headquarters.

But I was anxious, not only because Josiah was adding to his wealth and military capabilities rather than reining them in, but also because there was an arrogance about him such as I hadn't seen before. Although Zephaniah had warned me of this aspect of his pupil's nature, personally I'd witnessed no evidence of it. Josiah and I had lived apart throughout the years before he consecrated his life to Adonai. Was it possible that my friend was now taking back what he had given?

Not that I spoke of this to anyone, because on the face of things the notion seemed ludicrous. Josiah's zeal for his God burned hotter than it had ever done.

Yet the more effective his policies proved to be, the more serious were some of the consequences. Jerusalem was too far away for many people to worship there regularly, so they ceased to make offerings or seek religious counsel altogether. Despite my reminding them that Adonai was present everywhere, they were like children playing blindfold games, unable to relate to their God without the familiar images to help them. Josiah seemed oblivious; it was almost as if he preferred his subjects to have no religion at all than one practised outside his own control.

Meanwhile, bands of displaced clerics who claimed that they had never paid homage to idols converged on the capital city. Josiah had encouraged men such as these to offer their services at the Temple; but he'd reckoned without the resentment of those who had served there all their lives. The latter already ministered by turns, and had no desire to share their ministries or their income with refugees from country backwaters who spoke with uncouth accents and had but the scantiest understanding of Temple ritual. Men who had once worn priestly vestments and offered libations in golden chalices could now be seen dressed in rags and shaking beggars' bowls at those who passed by.

And for all the thoroughness of Josiah's religious reforms, many social evils still went unaddressed. There were Hebrews who had been in slavery for seventeen years, or even seventy. There were rapacious individuals who had taken over for themselves enough land to support a small tribe, whilst poor men who had lost their family plots through debt were deprived of any means of making repayments without selling their children or themselves to their creditors.

It was obvious to me why Josiah made no attempt to rectify the situation: he was afraid of losing the support of the People of the Land who had put him on Judah's throne. But little by little his zeal for enforcing religious orthodoxy became more rabid than resolute. Investigators roamed the countryside, sniffing out the slightest whiff of idolatry or heresy and pouncing like mad dogs wherever they found it. Men, women and even children were put to death on the slenderest of evidence. Gangs of hired men who were little better than thugs broke into houses and ransacked everything in sight as they hunted out effigies and fetishes; precious family heirlooms and little girls' dolls alike were thrown into the streets and set on fire.

When these methods began to be employed not only in Judah but in the northern territories too, violent opposition did flare up. Even in David's day the northerners had objected to the pre-eminence of Jerusalem, and when the kingdom was divided, Jeroboam the first northern king had established a rival sanctuary at Bethel. After Israel's inhabitants had gone into exile, deportees from elsewhere in the Assyrian empire had come to Bethel and brought their own gods with them. Now the native Israelites were drifting back, and Adonai was worshipped at Bethel once more - along with a whole host of exotic deities served by gelded foreign priests.

'If we raze Bethel to the ground,' Josiah declared, 'we shall have no more trouble in the north. Bethel is the cradle of its wickedness and apostasy. We shall take soldiers with us and reduce the place to rubble.'

He even managed to dredge up a prophecy given by some obscure holy man in the reign of Jeroboam to the effect that a scion of the House of David would arise and sacrifice Bethel's priests on their own altars, which would be defiled with human bones. There was such a gleam in his eyes when he repeated the oracle to me that I was nearly sick.

'What ails you, Jeremiah?' he exclaimed, smiling broadly. 'Are you not happy to see Adonai's work being done and his kingdom extended?'

I didn't reply. I didn't know if Josiah was doing Adonai's work or not; I hadn't dared raise the question in my prayers. The last thing I wanted was to upset our fragile friendship by provoking a confrontation. We were already drifting apart like ships on a stormy sea, but I wasn't willing to admit it.

So when he asked if I was coming to Bethel to assist him, I said I would.

I shall never forget the horror of what took place there. Bethel was as beautiful as Eden, the sanctuary a numinous jewel clasped in a setting of verdant pine-clad hills. Yet I stood by and watched while Josiah's troops surrounded the sacred precinct by night and threw flaming torches over its walls.

The buildings' wooden rafters and the rushes spread on the rooftops went up like so much tinder; priests and prophets, geldings and acolytes ran about shouting and waving their arms, vainly seeking to drag the sick and the aged from their beds before the conflagration reached them. Terrified youths and girls issued from collapsing doorways with their clothes on fire; these were the shrine prostitutes, whose gaolers had kept them locked up until it was too late. They collided with one another in their panic, and rolled howling in the dust trying to extinguish the flames. Every girl in her burning red robes reminded me of Ruth.

When the fire died down, soldiers were sent inside the precinct to massacre anyone left alive. They seized the young by their hair and old men by their beards, and slit their throats like harvesters scything corn. To most of their victims the stroke of the blade came as a mercy; some grabbed the soldiers' ankles with blistered hands and begged them to be quick.

The sun rose on a scene so revolting that the guiltiest criminal in the world should not have been forced to look upon it. But Josiah strode through the smouldering ruins nodding approval as though inspecting a construction site. Nor was he content to go his way after that and leave the folk who lived nearby to bury the dead and meditate upon the devastation. He wanted the ancient prophecy fulfilled to the letter.

So the bodies of those who had been slaughtered in the night, and the remains of their idols, were heaped up together and torched. Soldiers tore open tombs in the hillside opposite; the bones were brought out and burned on the broken altars. The only burial left undisturbed was that of the holy man whose frightful vision had now been realized. Then all of a sudden it wasn't Bethel that I saw laid waste before my eyes, but Anathoth; the charred corpses and jumbled bones were not those of strangers, but my own parents' and brothers'. Now I *was* sick, violently and abundantly on the desecrated ground.

But while I was standing there retching, the spirit fell upon me. I found myself yelling above the noise of the flames and the wailing of the crowd which had gathered that the day was approaching when every one of Judah's cities, towns and villages would lie in smoking ruins just like this sanctuary, for Adonai's wrath waxed great against his people, and the havoc which had been wrought here in his name had done nothing to placate him.

Almost at once Shaphan's sons had gathered around me. Gemariah and Elasah took me by the arms to restrain me, for I'd begun to pace up and down in my frenzy, and then to run stumbling among the fallen walls and smouldering timbers. Ahikam held my head between his hands; from a long way away I could hear him repeating my name and imploring me to bridle my tongue - Josiah was in no mood for having his actions undermined by those very persons who were supposed to be backing him. But Adonai's voice was much clearer than Ahikam's.

Sound the trumpet in Judah, in Zion;
Raise the signal and cry out aloud!
Run for your lives to the fortified strongholds;
Bar all your gates, and wait for the end!
The despoiler of nations comes forth like a lion,
Springs from his lair to ravage your land.
Weep for yourselves, for your homes left abandoned;
Weep for your kings, whose courage will fail.

A blow to the cheek and another in my stomach put a swift end to my declamation. I staggered, gasping for breath; Josiah caught me before I fell, with his hand around my throat.

'What in all of Sheol can you be thinking of, you stupid fool?' he hissed at me; I blinked and swallowed, endeavouring to focus on my friend's familiar features, but all I saw was a stranger wearing a mask of fury. Behind him black smoke billowed, and I retched again as my nostrils filled with the stench of burning carrion. 'I thought you wanted to see the high places laid low?' he demanded, with each stressed syllable shaking me as a child might shake an offending toy. 'I thought you wanted to see Adonai's power acknowledged, and those who despise him brought to their knees?'

I do, I do, I was trying to say - but he was making it hard enough for me to breathe, let alone speak.

'You do? Then why do I find you blocking my way at every turn? Do you want me to think you insane after all, since you obstruct the very things which you approve? What the hell do you *want* to see me do?'

I shook my head, wishing only that he would release me so I could crawl away into a corner somewhere and die without getting in anyone's way. Eventually he thrust me aside in disgust; as I subsided in a heap on the ground, Ahikam was saying, 'For God's sake, Josiah, he doesn't want to see you *enjoying* all this! None of us do. Perhaps things do have to happen this way, but if Adonai weeps when his people must be punished, shouldn't we do the same?'

So surprised and relieved was I to hear him interceding with the King on my behalf that I raised my head and offered him my own support in return. I said, 'Josiah, there are so many *other* injunctions on Hilkiah's scroll which would be a joy for us to obey, yet we neglect them! Would it not give you pleasure to see slaves redeemed and debtors pardoned? Would it not be wonderful to give back land to the landless and hope to the hopeless, and to see that widows and orphans are treated justly? How can we claim to love God when the poor and defenceless are oppressed?'

'One thing alone would give me real pleasure,' answered Josiah. He spoke very quietly now, and looked out way over my head into the northern hills beyond. 'To see Judah and Israel reunited, with myself as their ruler. Then I should truly be the greatest king since David. And I could do it, Jeremiah! I have so nearly done it already.'

I said, 'Oh yes, my lord. A day is coming when *all* God's people will be united: Judah and Israel and the righteous Gentiles too, and all of them will worship Adonai with a single voice on Zion his holy mountain. But it won't happen in your lifetime, or in mine. It may not happen for a thousand years.'

That evening, back in my quarters at the palace, I summoned all my courage and put to Adonai the question I hadn't dared ask. In the time since the Book of the Law had been found, had Josiah departed from the path prepared for him? Could it be that while he'd had to grope around in the dark he had just and so managed to find his way, whereas now that the light shone brightly he had gone astray?

Ask him again about the Tophet, came Adonai's response.

'The Tophet?' I repeated, taken aback. 'Surely it is no more.'

It was standing when you came to Jerusalem, and it stands today. Ask him why, Jeremiah. You'll be shining my light into a corner of his heart which has never yet been illumined.

So I went before my courage failed me, and asked to speak with him alone. I was admitted to his private chambers - in fact, to his bedroom, whither he had already retired. Having made his master comfortable, the dutiful Asaiah left us together; Josiah sat propped up on pillows, arms behind his head, and yawned prodigiously.

'Aha, Jeremiah, my friend! Your guilt pricks you so acutely that you cannot sleep without disturbing *my* slumbers with your apologies? Please, don't trouble yourself on my account. Your conduct at Bethel is forgiven.' He yawned again, and indicated that I should be seated on the chair next to his bed.

Remaining stolidly on my feet I ventured: 'Your pardon, Josiah... my lord. I didn't come here to apologize. I came to ask you a question.'

'One which couldn't wait until morning?' He tried, unsuccessfully, to keep the annoyance out of his voice.

'Well,' I said, 'it has waited five years since last being asked, but that is no reason to defer it any longer. Is it true that the Tophet has so far escaped destruction?'

He didn't answer, which was answer enough.

'And parents still go there to feed their own children to Molech, whose appetite can never be never sated?'

Again he made no reply.

'Why, Josiah, why? When you have harried all of Judah and half of Israel too, why have you condoned the existence of the vilest abomination there has ever been, right here in Jerusalem?'

He couldn't keep silent any longer, yet wasn't ready to give me an answer. He muttered a string of excuses while I stood with folded arms and waited until they ran out. Eventually he leaned back against his pillows and said, 'You're the prophet. Perhaps you ought to tell me.'

So I did, because even as I'd been standing there listening to his lies, the truth had been revealed to me. I said, 'The Tophet stands because you are the one with the guilty conscience. The child who lives inside you still believes it should have perished in Molech's flames; it still blames itself for its father's death. Your idol was your own father, himself an idolater, yet you never confessed it, so you are terrified of idols wherever you see them. You punish others for the thing you fear most in yourself, and until you deal with that fear you will never again enjoy Adonai's approval.'

He turned so pale that I knew I was right. Yet he didn't break down and beg me to absolve him. Instead he said hoarsely, 'So Adonai is no longer pleased with me? What nonsense is this? Surely I have enacted his will more perfectly since the finding of the Book of the Law than I did before? At least now I know what I'm required to do.'

'That is precisely the point, Josiah. As long as you remained in ignorance, your faults could be excused; your unqualified zeal to see righteousness prevail was enough to please him, even though you barely understood what righteousness was. But your zeal is no longer unqualified.'

'Then why did Adonai allow the Book of the Law to be found? If he was satisfied with my life as it was, he should never have permitted Hilkiah's discovery. All it has done is spoil what was good.'

'I never said that Adonai was satisfied. Only that he was pleased.'

'So now you seek refuge in riddles? It's too late at night to engage in the chopping of logic, my friend. And you know full well that I dislike it at the best of times.'

At last I saw fit to sit down beside him, though by now he probably considered his offer withdrawn. I said, 'If you are not able to hear what I am saying, then I'm sorry. But it's only because you don't *want* to hear! Maturity is not a destination we reach, but a direction in which we travel. Our way is revealed one step at a time, but God is pleased so long as we are treading his path and not going backwards or off into the wastelands to left and right. He will never be *satisfied* until we are perfect, a pinnacle no man can reach this side of the grave. But the man who is content to stand still will be robbed by bandits and left for dead.'

'You're saying that Adonai has abandoned me? That while I've been working my fingers to the bone for him, he has quietly turned his back on me, as he once turned from King Saul?'

'I'm telling you nothing of the kind. I'm saying only that our souls are like fields full of stones; the farmer clears the stones away, but when the soil is ploughed, more will rise to the surface and he must clear those as well. Adonai loves you, Josiah; he doesn't want your soul full of things which shouldn't be there. If you will hand them over to him, he will grant you the greatness to which you aspire, but it will cost you everything you have. Everything you are.'

'And if I'm not prepared to pay the price? Shall I be judged no better than my idolatrous father, whose sins you are so eager to condemn?'

'It is not my place to judge or to condemn. All I know is that if you hold things back from Adonai, he will hold things back from you. Circumcize your heart, Josiah! That's what the Law Book is saying, is it not? Let Adonai shine his light in your darkest places, and then your life will reflect his glory to your people.'

For a few precious moments I believed I'd won him. But then he said slowly, 'Perhaps it's time your *own* heart was circumcized, Jeremiah ben Hilkiah. Perhaps it is time for Adonai's light to shine in *your* dark places. Somehow I suspect that your heart has its secret corners too.'

Thrown, I found myself mumbling, repeating what I'd said about no one being perfect this side of death. But the blood was already rushing to my face when Josiah leaned forward incisively and rammed his point home. 'What about the corner where you keep your image of Huldah, Jeremiah? How often does Adonai get to look in there?'

My mouth fell open, but no words came. Then with both my hands clasped across it, I bolted from the room.

The following morning I would not leave my bed. When the eunuch Ebed-Melech brought me my breakfast, I told him to go away, and to sit outside my door to keep anyone else from visiting.

But he loved me too much to obey me. At noon he entered with a bowl of warmed milk, and wouldn't leave my side until I'd drunk it. Then he remarked - since he thought it would cheer me up, I suppose - 'Master, His Majesty the King has burnt down the Tophet and decreed that the Valley of Hinnom where it stood shall become a place for rubbish to be thrown. If you'd only get up and come to the window, you might see the smoke.'

I groaned, and pulled the blankets over my head. But the stench of burning rubbish had reached me already.

The next day I felt no more inclined to get up, and again told Ebed-Melech I wanted no one to come near. He, however, showed a healthy contempt for my orders, and presently Ahikam arrived at my door with a basket of fruit and a flagon of wine. Like the eunuch, he wasn't content till he'd seen me take nourishment. Then he asked me what was wrong between myself and the King.

I pretended not to understand what he meant, but Ahikam fixed me with his keenest gaze and said, 'Come, Jeremiah. You languish here in misery, while Josiah rampages like a wounded bull. You cannot tell me that the two things are unconnected.'

I thought: much has been wrong between the King and myself for a very long time. But aloud I asked weakly: 'He has burnt the Tophet in anger, then? Not in repentance?'

'He has burnt the Tophet in a frenzy. Now, are you going to tell me what has passed between you, or not?'

'No, Ahikam, I'm not. I'm sorry,' I said; for how *could* I tell him? Loyal friend as he was, I dared not let him find out how I felt about Huldah. I'd been determined that no one should ever find out, and couldn't for the life of me imagine how Josiah had done so, when I hadn't even wanted to admit to myself the potency of the attraction I felt towards her.

But I couldn't do other than acknowledge it now. As I wallowed in the mire of depression, I could think of no one and nothing but Huldah and the hopeless love I'd conceived for her. When I closed my eyes I could see her smile; when I pressed my hands to my ears to shut out Adonai's still small voice, I could hear her laughter; I could smell the perfume she used on her hair, and feel the warmth of her breath upon my cheek. What was more, these sensations disturbed me less than they aroused me. I gave my imagination its head, and took exquisite pleasure in following where it led me.

Never before had Josiah and I been simultaneously so far from where we ought to have been. Although we had counselled one another to surrender all that we had and were to Adonai, neither of us was willing to let go. And when his children have strayed so far, God must needs take drastic steps to pull them back into line, lest they be lost to him and to themselves for ever.

So it should have come as no surprise to me when Ebed-Melech ran into my room that evening and begged me to get up at once; His Highness Prince Johanan had fallen desperately sick, and had been asking for me.

Little else but this could have induced me to rise from my pit. As it was, I threw on my clothes and ran.

As soon as I saw him, I knew that this illness would be his last. He was blue in the face and fighting for breath; his mother Zebidah sat by his bedside, but he was far beyond the reach of her comfort. The royal physicians stood helplessly by, and even as I went to take the boy's hand, his father arrived with Asaiah, both of them pale and fearful. Johanan's eyes found my face and he tried to say my name; Josiah elbowed me aside and laid a palm on his eldest son's brow, whispering, 'It's all right now, Johanan. Your father is here; you're going to be all right.'

But he wasn't, and he knew it. Enervated by a lifetime of illness, the prince's frail body could endure no more. All of a sudden his limbs went into spasm, then the whole thing was over. Josiah uttered a great cry and gathered in his arms the body of the child he'd so rarely embraced when alive; I, who had loved the boy as my own flesh was left to nurse my grief alone in the background, acknowledging at last how futile it is to keep anything from Adonai. He can take whatever he wants, and when we leave him no alternative, he will take what we treasure the most.

The news was carried at once through the palace, and its halls and corridors soon echoed with wailing. Slaves came to wash the prince's body - though fourteen years old, he looked so slight and thin lying there dead, he could have been taken for ten or eleven.

'It's all my fault,' his father was repeating over and over, while Asaiah strove to reassure him. A king has many duties, Asaiah reminded him; he cannot be expected to devote long hours to his children.

'No, no,' Josiah moaned, tearing at the roots of his hair. 'You don't understand.' He had lapsed into incoherence, so it was quite some time before I grasped that he was talking about the Tophet. 'I ought never to have ordered its destruction. Molech has taken my firstborn.'

My God, I thought, things are even worse with him than I'd imagined.

They got worse still when one of the physicians who had pronounced Johanan dead picked up an empty goblet from the floor beside the prince's bed and began examining it closely and sniffing around its rim. 'Poison!' hissed someone, and thereupon the general wailing grew more frantic, and the distraught Zebidah was screaming: 'Hamutal has poisoned my son!'

The physician maintained that he had merely been checking, and had detected nothing untoward in the lees of the cup. But Zebidah wouldn't be told; she called upon all who were present to witness how savagely her rival hated her, and how desperate Hamutal was that her own son Shelemaiah should inherit his father's throne. Then, 'Where is Eliakim?' Zebidah shrieked, tearing herself from the arms of her maidservants. 'Fetch him to me, or the witch will kill him too!'

Someone did as she asked; she clasped her younger son to her breast in a paroxysm of weeping. I noted that the brat himself shed not a single tear for his hapless brother, but rather stared wide-eyed at the corpse in ghoulish fascination. If any one could have poisoned poor Hanan without a second thought, it was Eliakim, beautiful though he was, and barely twelve years old.

Then while the small body was still being washed, a messenger burst into the room and fell at the bereaved King's feet. The prophet Zephaniah had lapsed into unconsciousness and couldn't be roused; his pulse so weak that the physician in attendance reckoned him unlikely to survive the night.

Neither Josiah nor I knew which way to turn. In the end we made the same choice and went to Zephaniah, since there was nothing more we could do for Johanan. Josiah's son would not wake again, but it was possible that the man who had been to both of us a father might open his eyes and know us.

So we knelt at either side of his bed, for once united in purpose and in perfect understanding, and waited for any change which might take place. No doubt we should have prayed, but neither of us could bring ourselves to do so. Josiah's mother, the Lady Jedidah, came in and joined our sad little vigil; her eyes were dry, for she had already cried every tear she possessed for the godly man who might one day have become her husband.

Unlike Johanan's, Zephaniah's end came so softly, so imperceptibly, that we didn't even recognize it. So much of him had died already, and the night too was so far gone that those of us who kept watch were half asleep in our quiet shared misery. I revived with a start when the physician leaned in front of me to cover the prophet's face, and only then did I discover that the feeble pulse had stopped, and that the hand in mine was cold.

CHAPTER 10: HULDAH

I'd always known that my marriage to Shallum had been a mistake. Not until I met Jeremiah ben Hilkiah did I truly know why.

I'd been a mere eleven years old when my parents arranged my betrothal. But I was slender and shapely as a cypress, wilful as an unbroken horse, and too much in love with the world and with life to hide modestly behind my veil if some well-favoured youth chanced to smile at me. It could only be a matter of time before I dragged my father's good name through the mud, and wound up having to marry all too hurriedly - and probably sadly beneath my station.

If there was one fear which kept my father awake at night, it was that his noble blood should somehow become contaminated by the thin, blighted ichor of the common people. He could name every one of his ancestors right back to the time of the Conquest, when Moses' successor Joshua had allotted lands to the men who had helped him win possession of Canaan. From that day forth, our family's estates had prospered, and my father himself was a prominent member of the Council of the People of the Land. Had it not been for him and his peers, Josiah would never have sat upon David's throne. So it was simplicity itself for my parents to ensure that I married an official from the royal court.

If only it hadn't had to be Shallum...

I wouldn't have minded so much if a handsome lawyer had been chosen for me, or a captain in His Majesty's personal guard. But the Keeper of the Royal Wardrobe..! He was more than three times my age, and fat, fastidious and effeminate to boot.

I was still trying to object when my mother was fitting my bridal gown.

'You'll get used to him soon enough,' she said through the pins in her mouth - brusque and blunt as was her wont, but not intentionally callous. 'If you're lucky and you make some effort, you might even get to love him.'

'Like you got to love Father?' I asked sweetly, knowing full well that she never had. She slapped me hard across the face.

'If you weren't so insolent, my girl, you might have earned yourself a little more say in the matter. With a tongue like yours, you should be thankful that *anyone* wants to marry you. And at least Shallum won't beat you. If we hadn't picked someone so placid, you'd be black and blue inside a month.'

I sighed, and endured the rest of her pinning in silence. It was true that Shallum had a genial and generous nature; I'd known him since I was a baby, but as an affectionate honorary uncle, never as a potential husband. As an uncle I liked him well enough, but the thought of his podgy, clammy little hands fondling my flesh in the dark turned my stomach. I'd have run away before the wedding if any of my friends had agreed to go with me. I was quite intrepid enough to contemplate hiding out in someone's barn and stealing food to stay alive, but far too gregarious to want to do it alone.

I did try to love him once we were wed, for I knew there was nothing to be gained from making both of our lives a misery. I ran his household to the best of my ability - in addition to an apartment at the palace, Shallum owned a house in the Mishneh, the new north-western suburb of Jerusalem, where its wealthiest citizens lived. I helped him with sewing by day; I attempted to make pleasant conversation with him in the evenings; and I bit my lower lip till I tasted blood to prevent myself from shuddering when he paid me his fumbling attentions by night.

His desire was seldom strong enough for him to have much success in this regard. So it wasn't surprising that we'd been married seven years before he got me pregnant. My parents' relief was indescribable when finally it happened, and I knew I ought to have felt the same way. But my relief came only when the child miscarried, for the thought of Shallum's ugly seed growing like a canker inside me was worse than that of his fingers on my flesh.

Shallum of course was distraught; all the pains he'd gone to in order to get himself a son had been wasted in a welter of blood and mess in his bed.

To be fair, he was upset and anxious for me as well as for himself. Much as he found it a trial to mount me, he loved me besottedly in his mild-mannered way, and longed to give me a child because he thought it would make me happy. Though I sometimes despaired of his intelligence, he did at least know that I was quietly losing my sanity. I yearned to talk for just one evening with someone whose banalities didn't send me to sleep. And I ached with every nerve in my body to give myself to a man who could excite me. I longed to go to sleep sated with love, instead of crying silent tears of disillusionment.

Yet I had to accept that my wishes could never be granted. Marriage was for life, and by the time Shallum died, my beauty and my energy and probably my wits would be gone.

For it was after I lost the baby that my strange experiences started in earnest. Funny turns, this was what Shallum called them, because so far as he was concerned I simply felt giddy or faint, or sat a few moments oblivious of everything around me. I never dared tell him what was truly going on.

I'd had the occasional hint of what was to come since being a child. Dreams I had in the night would come true the next day, or I would go somewhere I'd never visited before, yet be convinced that once long ago I had been there.

But after the baby, things like that began to happen all the time. I could watch events unfolding in another quarter of the city as though the action were taking place right in front of me, and I could predict what would happen a day or a week in the future. I would fall into trances - only brief ones, but long enough for me to forget where I was or how I had come to be there. One day without warning I fainted on the floor, and while I was out of myself I saw my mother's sister waving me goodbye from the flat roof of her house. The following morning we heard that my aunt was dead; the parapet against which she'd been leaning had collapsed, and she'd fallen from her roof into the street.

Oddly enough, such experiences never scared me. But I knew they would scare other people, so I didn't tell anyone what was happening inside my head. I don't quite know how Josiah found out; only that one day when I'd gone to him with Shallum to assist with the fitting of some new garment, His Majesty looked at me intently and then sent my husband away on some specious errand.

Part of me was hoping he'd got me on my own for the reason that his hero King David had once met alone with Bathsheba. Josiah was young - younger than me - and undeniably handsome. But all he said when Shallum had gone was, 'Don't bury your talent in the ground, Lady Huldah. Present it to Adonai, and he'll transform it, and use it powerfully for good.'

I said, 'Your Majesty, I don't even *know* Adonai.' So Josiah himself prayed with me there and then, and laid his anointed hands on my head, and I was reborn as a prophetess in the service of my God and my King.

For a while after that, I thought I was in love with Josiah. I used to see him frequently in my dreams, and sometimes I'd be given messages which Adonai wanted him to hear yet hadn't succeeded in communicating to him by other means. So apposite did these messages turn out to be that His Majesty took to summoning me to give him counsel when his spirits were low or some domestic crisis had arisen, and soon all Jerusalem was saying that Shallum's wife had the second sight and was a personal friend of the King.

As things transpired, however, it was someone else with whom I was destined to fall in love. The strength of my feelings toward Josiah derived rather from the part he'd played in my calling, for when Adonai's hand comes upon you it's often hard to distinguish what you feel from arousal of an altogether different kind.

Nor was it strictly true that I was gifted with second sight - not any more. The nature of my talent had indeed been transformed, and seldom these days was I aware of events taking place far away, or of what was to happen in the future, unless there was some special reason for Adonai to want me to know these things. I still fell into trances, and now and again I saw visions while I was in them: visions of judgment and redemption, destruction and restoration, death and deliverance. But I was glad they came only rarely.

What I did begin to do quite regularly as a result of Josiah's prayer was to hear Adonai's voice, as clearly as I heard the voices of the people around me. And I was unafraid to pass on his words when this was what he asked of me.

But the moment I was introduced to Jeremiah of Anathoth, I was undone. All thoughts of Adonai were wiped clean from my mind, and never again would I mistake affection or friendship or even spiritual ecstasy for what I felt when the young prophet's eyes met mine.

In those days I was in the habit of spending what free time Shallum allowed me in the company of the wives of other palace officials. We would meet in one another's homes and while away sunny afternoons in gossip and laughter; those who had children let them play together outside, and babies slept contentedly in their mothers' arms. Because our husbands kept so many secrets from us concerning state affairs, we took great pleasure in sharing amongst ourselves the trivial secrets *we* kept from *them*. So when I told my companions that I was in love, I knew there was little danger of my confidence being betrayed.

'Shame on you!' cried one of those present, professing shock but evincing delight. She was the wife of Maaseiah, Governor of Jerusalem and vigorous supporter of Josiah's reforms. She wore the yoke of her husband's respectability with ill-disguised reluctance.

'Shame on *you*,' her neighbour rebuked her. This was the wife of Ahikam the Royal Steward; she partook of his good reputation, and deserved to. 'Can't you see that Huldah is upset? She's a married woman just as we are, and a servant of Adonai. She doesn't want to be in love with another man. She's asking for our help, not our condemnation. *Or* our encouragement.'

I smiled at her gratefully, hoping it was true that the only reason I'd divulged my guilty feelings to my friends was so that they could talk me out of them.

'Oh come now, both of you!' exclaimed one of the younger girls, wife of Joah the Royal Recorder. She was starry-eyed, romantic and naive. 'Huldah is only dreaming, aren't you, Huldah? It does no harm to dream when real life brings us no joy. Tell us who he is, this wonderful man who has captured your heart.'

I demurred, already wishing I had kept my dream to myself. But Joah's wife enthused: 'Let me guess, then! Or at least let me guess what he's *like..!*' She took a deep breath and closed her eyes, clasping her hands around drawn-up knees and tilting her innocent face to the ceiling as if in rapture. 'Yes, the picture's coming clear; I see him quite distinctly! He has wine-dark eyes like limpid pools, and flowing locks like a stallion's mane. His smile would melt the snow on Mount Hermon in winter, but he's shy, and ever so mysterious. A bard, perhaps, or a priest, or a teller of dreams, who walks with his head in the clouds, and visits in his spirit the courts of celestial palaces where angels live, the misty towers of which we lesser mortals can only gaze upon from afar.' She sighed, enchanted by her own florid description, then opened her eyes very suddenly, leaning forward and demanding in great excitement, 'Am I right, then, Huldah? Am I right?'

I stared at her and blushed as red as a desert sunset, because of course she was right. To me, Jeremiah was all these things and so much more; and the more extravagant her flight of fancy had become, the more my heart ached, and the more unlikely it became that I would ever be talked out of my infatuation.

'You *must* be right!' another girl declared. 'Just look at her face! Do *you* know who he is? Can *you* tell us his name, even if *she* won't?'

'Oh no,' answered Joah's wife, waving one hand dismissively. '*I* don't know who he is. I just think that that's the type of man Huldah would take a fancy to.'

After that, there was no diverting them; excepting the wives of Ahikam and Shaphan, they all chimed in with their guesses. None of them hit upon the truth, however, and in the end I was constrained to disclose it myself.

When I did, they were bemused to say the least. A few had never even heard of Jeremiah of Anathoth, and asked if he was rich, who his parents were, and how I had come to meet him. While I struggled with myself and wondered how to answer, someone else answered for me.

'Jeremiah is a peasant.'

So vehemently was this verdict delivered, that everyone turned to gape at the girl who had uttered it; she preened her braided hair and shook her earrings, basking in the attention. Her husband was Jaazaniah, the youngest of Shaphan's sons and the black sheep among them; whereas his brothers' names were bywords for devotion to Adonai, he himself had been accused of idolatry more than once, though nothing had ever been proven. His wife was a girl of fourteen: haughty, affected and vain.

'A peasant?' came a chorus of voices. 'Whatever do you mean?'

'I mean that he's a worthless nobody, with no wealth and no breeding. In fact, peasant is too good a word for him, because he has no land either. He's a common herdsman, and has spent the past five years of his life minding someone else's flocks.'

'Moses once minded someone else's flocks!' I retorted. 'And Jeremiah has no land because he's a Levite!' Then I caught my breath, remembering that I wasn't supposed to want to be in love.

I felt even worse when Ahikam's wife patted my hand again and said, 'Do be careful, Huldah. You have a kind and generous husband who thinks the world of you. Surely you wouldn't want to hurt him?' And her mother-in-law, the wife of Shaphan, added gravely, 'A great *deal* of harm can be done by dreaming. Dreams lead to actions, young lady, and you have Adonai's reputation to think of as well as your own. You may be assured that he never allows his servants to besmirch his holy name without ruining their own lives into the bargain.'

'Take my advice, Huldah dear,' said Jaazaniah's wife, as though she were twice my age rather than just over half. 'Forget Jeremiah; he's a baseborn dog, no more a man than your Shallum is. If you must risk your pretty white neck by embarking on a perilous affair, choose a lover who would stand some chance of vanquishing Shallum in a fight. Or better still, one who wouldn't baulk at slipping some poison in his cup. Mark my words: Josiah's seeress or no, they'll stone you to death if you're found in another man's arms while your wedded lord and master treads this earth.'

I tried to make them all understand that I had no intention whatever of starting an affair with anyone; the thought had never occurred to me.

'Of course it has,' snapped the wife of Akbor, who until now had held aloof from our conversation. Just as her husband was the oldest of Josiah's counsellors, so she was the oldest of the wives, and also the sourest. 'There isn't one woman here who hasn't thought of cheating on her husband; and if any of us had been married to Shallum, we would have *done* it, too, a long time ago.'

'Oh, well said, Grandmother!' cried Jaazaniah's child bride, and she let out a peal of brittle laughter. One or two of the others joined in, and the very air around me tinkled and splintered like breaking glass. I could take no more, and holding my veil to my face I bolted from their midst.

Ahikam's wife came after me, but I shooed her away. I stood in the middle of an empty courtyard, not knowing where to go or what to do, or even what I felt. Was I angry because of some of the things that had been said about Shallum? Yes, he was effeminate and slow, but his heart was in the right place, and he didn't deserve to be despised. Yet I myself was despising him in my head, by filling it with thoughts of another man. Perhaps I was merely angry with myself.

So I tried my best to forget Jeremiah, as all of my companions advised; different as they were from one another, this was the one thing upon which they were all agreed. But the harder I tried to forget, the more obsessed I became, and there was no getting away from him in the day-to-day bustle of palace life. When I went to the throneroom he was there; when I went with Shallum to the apartment of some courtier, he was there; when I saw the King in his private quarters, Jeremiah would be there too. And whenever he saw me, he would venture a smile before he looked away. Within a matter of weeks I knew that, for all my purported devotion to Adonai, if Jeremiah had sent for me at night I would have gone to him.

Yet he didn't; and surely he never would, for I was convinced that his own principles were immutable.

In fact, so far above reproach did he turn out to be that he was quite oblivious to rumour. I suppose because he hadn't grown up in palace circles, he didn't really know how a minor indiscretion can set every tongue in Jerusalem wagging. Thus he made no objection to my offering to visit him when he was ill. He let me sit by his bedside and talk, and I let myself believe that I was only fulfilling a charitable duty. Are we not exhorted to take care of the sick, and succour the afflicted in their distress?

But he was sick so often: whenever he had prophesied in public, and at other times as well. When I listened to his oracular utterances, the fire within him melted my every reservation; when afterwards he wilted and the melancholy overwhelmed him, unintentionally he rendered himself irresistible. That glorious amalgam of intensity and vulnerability disarmed me - a curious thing, when Shallum's effeminacy disgusted me so thoroughly.

Whatever was feminine in Jeremiah was so in a radically different way, however, and perhaps he could not have been a prophet without it, since a prophet must submit to possession by his God just as a woman must submit to her husband. And whatever the cause of my infatuation, I spent so many blissful hours talking him through his doubts and despondencies that I found it impossible to believe he wasn't attracted to me in the same way as I was to him.

I'd taken to inviting him for meals with Shallum and myself; so simple-minded and trusting was my poor blind husband that he even went out and left us alone if duty called him elsewhere. But still Jeremiah did nothing but talk, or play the lyre to me now and again when the mood took him. This went on even after I started to call on him when he wasn't ill, and Shallum believed I was visiting my mother or a cousin or an aunt. How greedily I devoured every word Jeremiah said to me; how avidly I listened when he stroked the music from his lyre, and the poetry fell from his lips like golden rain. And how I longed to kiss those lips, just once, to see where it might lead.

But I didn't dare, for fear that all might be lost. Instead I had to content myself with conversation, patiently steering it on to ever more intimate topics: our bitterest memories of childhood; the aspirations and disappointments of our teenage years; the joy and the pain we had each experienced at the time of our respective callings, and the inner turmoil which had followed.

It was only when he asked the King for leave to return to Anathoth that I knew for certain he felt the way I did. I knew, because when he did the rounds of his friends to bid them goodbye, Shallum and I were left out.

I was temporarily confused when I learned he'd gone in order to get married, but when he came back alone I would have sung for joy, except that Adonai had seized me and used me in a manner altogether different from anything I'd experienced before. At last I understood for myself what Jeremiah went through each time it happened to him.

So powerfully did this seizure affect me, that for a while the fog of my obsession cleared. I was Adonai's vessel, to fill or empty as he willed, and must keep myself pure for his use. No more would I search out excuses to be alone with the enigmatic prophet of Anathoth; rather, I would avoid him, for his own sake as much as for mine.

But I couldn't keep it up. In a while it was forgotten by everyone that *I* had been the one to proclaim Hilkiah's scroll the true word of Adonai. I was nothing but Shallum's wife; Jeremiah himself was the one from whom Josiah sought inspiration these days, if ever he felt that he needed it. Often enough, he followed the promptings of his own soul.

Once again I allowed myself to dream of Jeremiah by day, and I dreamed of him at night whether I wanted to or not. Once again we started to meet in private and to talk, yet even now that I knew the true nature of his feelings for me, I held back from revealing my own. However strong his emotions were, his inhibitions, his integrity, and his sense of duty to Shallum would never let them rule him. And what we had together already was far too precious to risk.

Thus I resigned myself to living out the rest of my life with a slowly breaking heart; but as time went on, it began to be broken along a different plane. For Jeremiah was losing the very quality which had drawn me to him in the first place - the aura about him which caught and reflected the light of the Divine like a mirror - and I was convinced that it must be my fault.

Of course, the deaths of Johanan and Zephaniah must have shaken him badly, just as they'd shaken Josiah, but surely a faith such as he'd once had would have sustained him through the shock and guided him through the grieving? Things were little better with Josiah himself, it was true; the God he served had robbed him of his past and his future simultaneously, and although his reform programme went on, driven by its own momentum, he had taken his hands from the reins. Perhaps he was waiting for Jeremiah to stir him from his apathy, but if so, I thought, he would likely wait for ever. The mirror was clouded, and I was the one to blame; Jeremiah's love for Adonai had become obscured by his desire for me, and the voice of his God was being drowned by the clamouring of temptation.

Things came to a head one day in high summer, a little over three years after Johanan and Zephaniah died. The weather was sultry; Shallum and I had gone to spend a week at our house in the suburbs because I'd been feeling unwell. That particular afternoon, Shallum himself had returned briefly to Court to attend to some business which couldn't wait; though siesta time was over, I was still dozing on my bed when our housemaid ran in and announced that Jeremiah was asking to see me. 'I think you should go quickly, mistress,' the girl added as I eased myself upright. 'He seems a little distressed.'

Indeed he did. When I entered the reception room he was pacing back and forth, dripping with sweat and wringing his hands. As soon as he saw me he fell at my feet like a servant afraid of the strap and gasped, 'Oh Huldah, I'm so sorry to come here uninvited like this. But I couldn't think of anyone else to turn to. Is Shallum at home?'

'No. He went out some while ago.'

'Oh God.' Jeremiah pushed his head against my hands. 'It's just that... today I got this.'

He fumbled inside his tunic and brought out a tablet, which he handed to me with trembling fingers. Looking down, I saw that I was holding a letter from his father.

It said: 'No doubt you recall my once telling you that I intended to live from that time forth as though my eldest son were dead. Soon I shall have no further need for pretence. Unless you resign forthwith from Josiah's service, your life will be forfeit. Woe betide you if ever you set foot in this village again; but do not imagine that you will be safe elsewhere. Hanamel has resolved that the time has come to make you pay for all the harm you have done to us, and every man in the village has declared himself ready to kill you on sight. Perhaps you think that after what happened at Bethel, we should be grateful that any of us are still alive. But do not wonder that we can hate you so much. You have drunk the lifeblood of your own birthplace; now we shall drink yours.'

I said, 'He cannot mean this threat to be taken seriously. If he had, he would have sent you no warning of what was to come.'

'Of course he means it seriously! And of course he wants me to know - and to fear - what is coming to me! A sudden attack and rapid death would be too good for me.'

'Then take this tablet to Josiah. He could have every man in Anathoth arrested. What is contained in this letter would constitute sufficient evidence in itself to condemn them all.'

'My father would deny having written it, and who could prove otherwise? It has no seal impression, nor any other mark to attest its origins. Huldah, I'm so afraid. I'm not ready to die.'

I tried to coax him to his feet; when he would not stand I had little choice but to kneel down beside him. He put his head on my shoulder, and his arms went around my back; I could not prevent them.

'But why all this now?' I asked shakily, deeming it best to keep him talking. 'The Anathoth sanctuary was demolished years ago. If the villagers had wanted you dead, surely they would have killed you then.'

'There has been an incident.' He raised his head a little, but spoke his words into my hair. 'Some pilgrims who had gone there to worship... there were votive figurines in their sacks when they were searched. Josiah's men butchered them on the spot.'

'Gone where to worship? I don't understand.'

'To Anathoth; to the sanctuary! A place doesn't stop being holy just because someone pulls down the buildings which stand there! Pilgrims were journeying to Anathoth when our ancestors were still slaves to the Pharaohs in Egypt.'

'You mean - closing the high places has achieved nothing?'

'What can *anything* achieve unless the heart of man is changed?' He clenched his fists and pressed them hard against my spine. 'Oh, of course *something* has been achieved. The pilgrims have been fewer because they are afraid to be seen on any road which doesn't lead to Jerusalem. Anathoth has been dying for years. But now... oh God,' he said again, and broke down, sobbing and groaning and repeating over and over that he himself was going to die, slowly and painfully, and that he'd never been so frightened in his entire existence.

He wasn't alone in his fear. Not only was I frightened lest Shallum should choose this moment to return, but I was very much more afraid that I lacked the resources to cope with Jeremiah's anguish. Of course I'd seen him distressed more times than enough; his moods could change with the moon or with the wind, for such sensitivity is part of what our gifting is about. But abject despair was something I'd never seen in him, and I'd never heard any grown man cry with such abandon. If only Adonai didn't feel so far away...

'You're not going to die,' I murmured, without convincing even myself. 'Adonai will protect you.'

'No he won't. He didn't protect Zephaniah, did he? He didn't protect Johanan.'

'You can't say that, Jeremiah. There may have been reasons. We don't understand everything.' At one time I would have believed what I was telling him. 'Anyhow,' I added. 'Josiah will arrange special protection for you. He won't let you get hurt.'

'Josiah? He's thought of no one and nothing but himself and his precious dynasty since Hanan died. Oh *God*, how I loved that boy! I can't bear to think of Eli sitting on his father's throne. He's so arrogant, and he hates me so much. If he comes to power he will *pay* the men of Anathoth to kill me.'

'Jeremiah, Eliakim is just a child. Surely you're not frightened of a child?'

'Children grow up, Huldah. Princes become kings.' He put his hands to his face, and his shoulders were juddering. 'I so much wanted to be to Josiah's sons what Zephaniah was to him. I couldn't even go to Hanan's funeral, did you know that? Or to Zephaniah's. Adonai has forbidden me: funerals, family gatherings, weddings - I'm to go to none of them. I tried to disobey, I needed so badly to say goodbye, to each of them, but I was sick as a dog the moment I stepped outside my door. I haven't forgiven Adonai for that, and I never will. Why did he have to take Hanan away from me? And Zephaniah... He was such a godly man. It doesn't make sense. Nothing makes any sense.'

I tried to reply, but found that I was crying too, and no words would come. So we clung to each other and wept, while between bouts of incoherence he complained that nothing had ever gone right for him, every one of his thirty one years had ended in unmitigated failure; he never *had* heard the voice of

186

God. He'd been mad since early childhood, and every prophetic oracle he'd uttered had been the spillage from his own unhinged mind.

'Jeremiah, please. Don't talk like this. Of course your gifting is genuine. How else would you have known of Ashurbanipal's death?'

He made a bitter choking sound in his throat. 'One true piece of knowledge in ten years, Huldah! Can't you see? It was a coincidence, a lucky guess, nothing more. Even you dream dreams, and you needn't try to tell me you don't. You see visions too. Don't you. Don't you!'

He had his hands on my shoulders now, and was shaking them violently; I could see his face at last through his straggling hair, and his swollen eyes were so glassy and wild, I wondered if I myself were in danger. I told him yes - he was always so hard to lie to - but what were visions and dreams compared with direct communication with the Divine?

'I have communed with no one but myself. I talk to myself. I delude myself. I make myself ill. I'm not fit to live, Huldah. But I don't dare slit my wrists because I'm scared there may be more life on the other side. I'm scared I'll have to face Adonai and pay some dire penalty for spouting nonsense in his name. He'll torture me, and the pain will be so bad... I can't stand pain, Huldah. I can't stand it.'

I stammered, 'Please, Jeremiah. I think we should pray together. Adonai *loves* us; surely he'll pity us and listen, even though... even if...'

But even though what? Even if what? The battle inside me was raging worse than ever; part of me could think of nothing for it but to cast ourselves on the mercy of God, but another part was goading me: kiss him, Huldah. Kiss him now. His defences are down; just now he doesn't care a jot about his reputation or his principles, and he'd like nothing better than to pay Adonai back for everything he's had to suffer. You can make him forget his troubles; for this fleeting hour at least, the pair of you can taste true happiness.

'No!' I said, out loud, and I prized his hands from my shoulders and laid them palms up in his lap. When I looked at his thin wrists I could picture them slashed and running with his blood, and I thought: I can't cope with him. Not on my own. Adonai alone can save him.

So I started to pray: anxiously, fervently, helplessly. I placed my hands on Jeremiah's head, and he was too disconsolate and too exhausted to fight me.

For a long long time nothing happened. I grew desperate, and feared that I too would drop from exhaustion before the spirit took him. Then I saw it come; his closed eyelids were throbbing and his lips began to move. Thank God, I thought: now he'll find peace.

My relief was shortlived. Jeremiah might have lacked the will to fight me, but he was fighting Adonai. He looked like a sleeping child who is having a nightmare; he began to jerk his head from side to side, then to wail: a soft, strained, strangulated wail, as though he needed to scream but could not. Alarmed at what I'd begun, I backed away from him and crouched on the floor beyond his reach, watching appalled as he started to tear at his hair, his features contorted like those of a man who is bound and awaiting the surgeon's knife.

Suddenly he found his voice and began to cry out aloud; I couldn't make out the half of what he said, but he was cursing Adonai, accusing him of deceiving his own people, of allowing cultic prophets and Isaiah's disciples to promise them peace when there was to be no peace, of letting Judah grow fat and prosperous now when only horror and torment lay ahead. He charged Adonai with deceiving him personally as well: where was *his* peace? where was *his* joy? *his* benediction, *his* reward? Even his life was now under threat; where was his guarantee of protection? And if he were truly a prophet, where were his dreams and his visions? Where was his vindication, the sealing of his ministry by evidence of his predictions being fulfilled? 'I *hate* this miserable world I exist in!' he yelled in conclusion. 'I hate what you've done to me; I hate what I've become! By all that I've ever called holy - I swear I hate *you!*'

He'd gone beyond the limits Adonai had set for him. I held my breath as he fell to the floor in convulsions. Spittle frothed between his lips; he thrashed and writhed, then a final paroxysm more violent than any before it left him limp and gasping like a fish thrown up on a beach. Still scarcely daring to breathe, I crawled towards him and ventured to push him onto his side lest he swallow his tongue.

However, whilst the convulsions were over, the trance was not. His eyes were glazed and his lips still moved involuntarily, so I sat with his head in my lap, and waited.

I waited a very long time, in dread of Shallum returning and at last accusing me in my innocence of the thing I'd so often longed to be guilty of. I watched the progress of Jeremiah's rapture, as he passed from misery through repentance and consolation to eventual euphoria. After that I think he slept, before stirring and moaning and blinking his eyes in bewilderment. He tried to sit up, but was like someone drunk, and obeyed without demur when I advised him to lie still until he felt better.

Next he tried to apologize for whatever it was that had come over him; he had no idea of what he'd been saying or doing since the moment the spirit had seized him, nor did he know how he'd come to be lying on the floor with his head pillowed in my skirts. All he remembered was what he'd been told in his trance: that the reason why he wasn't sent visions was because Adonai knew that he wouldn't be able to endure the horror of what he might see; but that his life would be preserved, and that the evil men of Anathoth would be paid back in full for their wickedness. What they had suffered so far would seem like a splinter in the finger in comparison with what was coming their way. And the foe from the north was Babylon.

'You mean - he told you, just like that? After all these years of speculation, Adonai simply said: the foe is Babylon?' I shook my head in amazement, striving to take in the enormity of what Jeremiah was saying to me. 'Why has he let you into this secret now?'

'Because he wants to convince me that my gifting is true. He decided to tell me something I wouldn't have been likely to guess for myself.'

'*No* one could have guessed that your foe from the north would be Babylon! The time of her greatness was centuries ago; she's a mere province of Assyria.'

'No, Huldah, not any more. Southern Babylonia declared her independence from Assyria in the year that Ashurbanipal died. She found herself a king, Nabopolassar - I think he may have been some sort of governor under the Assyrians - and he's been consolidating his position ever since. Now he controls northern Babylonia as well, just as Josiah now claims to be sovereign over the whole of what was once David's kingdom.' He renewed his efforts to sit, and this time succeeded, declaring as he did so: 'I must go to him, Huldah. I must go to Josiah at once and warn him.'

'You're going nowhere,' I told him firmly, for the very act of sitting up had sent him dizzy, and he slumped with his head between his knees.

I went and fetched him wine; as I pressed the goblet into his hands I thought for a moment that he'd drifted away once more, for his expression was clouded and distant and his voice when he thanked me was strange. But then he said, 'Huldah, I don't know what would become of me if it weren't for you.'

I laughed a little, averting my gaze, but he said, 'I mean it,' and ventured to raise my chin with the tips of his fingers.

For an imprudently long time we looked into one another's eyes, and I thought: oh God, oh God, this is it, please help me, what shall I do?'

The very moment that his lips touched mine, I heard voices coming from the yard. Springing from his arms like a shot from a sling, I sat down hard on the nearest couch with my hands clasped between my knees. For his part, Jeremiah could think of nothing else but to lay his head on his drawn-up legs with his arms wrapped about it, as though he might render himself invisible.

This was the scene which greeted Shallum when he walked in, with some young friend from the palace in tow. Any other man would have guessed at once what had so nearly taken place.

Shallum merely looked a little inquisitively from me to Jeremiah and back to me again, and when I neither spoke nor moved, he said, 'Huldah? Jeremiah? This is Melchior; he will share our evening meal with us if you have no objection. Will you not bid him welcome?'

Then he poured his guest some wine, and the pair of them chatted on as if nothing were amiss.

CHAPTER 11: JEREMIAH

I

For three whole years after Huldah prayed for me, I kept my peace with Adonai.

I felt closer to him than I had done since my calling. I confidently believed his assurances that I was in no danger from my kinsmen at Anathoth. In fact their incessant threats - for I received many more like the first - served only to make me feel better about myself than I ever had. After all, no one bothers to threaten a man who is no threat to him.

Indeed, I began to accompany Josiah once more when he toured his realm, to demonstrate my fearlessness and to voice my support for his continuing programme of reform. This too I felt happier about than I had in the past; Josiah no longer spoke about Molech having stolen his son, and I took this to mean that his own relationship with Adonai was restored.

In my day to day life at the palace I knew more peace too. I wasn't having to contend any longer with the surliness of Prince Eliakim. A year or so after Johanan's death Eli had turned thirteen, the age of his legal majority. At once he'd informed me that he no longer required my services as tutor, and thenceforward I taught Shelemaiah alone. With Eli's influence removed, Shallum (as I called him) quickly became more docile, and lessons began to be almost pleasant. In the meantime, the King had had another son by his second wife Hamutal; the boy's name was Mattaniah, and he was as sweet-natured and even-tempered as Eli was the reverse.

Even regarding Huldah herself, things had become more straight-forward. On the sultry summer afternoon when I so nearly kissed her, both of us were forced to acknowledge how powerful were our feelings for one another, and how irresistible temptation can be, once we allow it a foothold. So our resolve to stop meeting in private became much easier to keep. Huldah sent me a letter the day after I'd shown her my father's; hers said that the path we were treading could lead nowhere except to disaster. She loved me passionately, and therefore could not bring herself to destroy me or the work I'd been called to do. This state of affairs rendered me oddly content. It was so good to know that a woman like Huldah could find me attractive, yet such a relief not to have to cheat on her poor gullible husband any longer.

On the political front, Judah continued to extend her borders; in addition to maintaining his influence over what had once been the northern kingdom of Israel, Josiah had acquired new territory to the south, in the Negev. Eliakim was smugly looking forward to inheriting a minor empire; my predictions of doom meant as little to him as my lessons had.

Indeed, he was already taking his own steps to guarantee the survival of his father's dynasty. At sixteen years old he married Nehushta, daughter of the Counsellor Elnathan. Lovely to look upon, she was lovely by temperament too: generous, gentle and eager to please, and I felt very sorry for her until I discovered that the couple were besotted with one another, and that he'd got her with child before they were wed. It wasn't so hard to fathom what she saw in him: he was as handsome and charming as Absalom. But he was also insufferably arrogant, vain and selfish, and I wondered how long their love would last once the initial bloom of infatuation had faded.

Gradually, however, the international situation began to change. For Judah wasn't the only kingdom which had been enabled to expand as a result of Assyria's collapse. After several years spent quietly building their power-bases, a number of rival monarchs were flexing their muscles to fight over prizes which the Emperor had left for them. Among these prizes was Josiah's realm; much as he might fancy himself as an inheritor of David's greatness, to many of his fellow rulers he was merely a ripe fig, to be plucked at their convenience.

Egypt, after decades of stagnation, was regaining her former glory. The energetic Pharaoh Psamtik had dealt thoroughly with internal unrest, and had rebuilt the Egyptian army. He'd rebuilt the economy too, encouraging trade with the up-and-coming city states of Greece, and now he was seeking to reassert his nation's authority in the Levant. Josiah's spies informed him that at one time Psamtik had been seeking alliance with Media, a nation which seemed to have grown very rapidly from nothing into a serious force to be reckoned with. Lately, however, the Pharaoh had been intriguing with what remained of Assyria, Egypt's ancestral enemy, because he wanted a buffer between his own arena of influence and the one rival he truly feared: Babylon.

Josiah had done little more than humour me when he'd received my revelation as to the identity of the foe from the north. Unlike Huldah, he'd known of Nabopolassar's ambitions, and that he'd lately begun to oust the Assyrian governors of the provinces bordering his. But Nabopolassar was a self-proclaimed sovereign, quite without pedigree; it was impossible for Josiah, whose ancestors had been kings for almost four hundred years, to take him seriously. To the King of Judah, Nabopolassar was an opportunistic crank with risible delusions of grandeur.

However, in recent months, the crank had begun to turn his delusions into reality. He had faced Assyrian troops in open battle, and won. He had taken on the hordes of Scythians who continued to sweep along the Fertile Crescent in search of fresh pastures, and had successfully halted their progress.

Furthermore, Babylon had succeeded in forging an alliance with Media, whose friendship Egypt had ceased to court. In my thirty fourth year, Media under its king Huvakshatra - Cyaxares as he's known in the west - took possession of Ashur, Assyria's sacred city. The Median princess Amuhea was betrothed to Nabopolassar's eldest son.

It seemed painfully obvious to me, and to most of Josiah's advisers, that Babylon and Media acting in co-operation constituted a menace at least as grave as that of Egypt, and considerably graver than that of Assyria, a nation in its death throes. Yet Josiah would not see it. He'd grown up hating the Assyrians and everything about them; and as for

Egypt, it was the fiercely anti-Egyptian People of the Land who had put him - and kept him - on his throne.

So he focussed all his attention on the strengthening of his fortresses along the coastal plain, to impede communications between the waxing Egypt and the waning Assyria. Not that he could be as thorough about this as he would have liked; up and down the coastline there were still Philistine cities to which Josiah's authority did not extend. All he could do was ensure that the Philistines remained confined to their own territories and did not interfere with his plans.

Then an incident occurred which overturned everything and wiped all interest in state affairs from my mind.

Josiah had gone north to Megiddo; meanwhile I was making a journey south to Arad, whence there had come reports of unauthorized worship taking place at the ruined sanctuary. I never got there, because on a lonely road my party was attacked.

Our assailants sprang from nowhere; trees were few, and the only cover was provided by boulders and thornbushes. Yet all at once we were surrounded by thugs brandishing knives and clubs. Their faces were swathed in scarves, so that at first I took them for common bandits out to strip us of our gold.

'Take it! Take it and leave us alone!' I cried, for one of their number had Ebed-Melech by the throat.

'We don't want your money, fool,' the brute snarled. 'We want you,' and to his fellows he shouted, 'This is him. This is Hilkiah's whelp.' And he might have slain me on the spot had not Hanamel's voice barked out, 'Take him alive. He's mine.'

At once Ebed-Melech was tossed aside. The thugs seized my arms, then whipped my legs from under me and pinned me down. 'Excellent,' came Hanamel's voice again, as he elbowed his way through the rabble.

But while my cousin stood over me relishing his moment of triumph, the soldiers in my party had drawn their swords and gone to work.

Rigid with shock I could do nothing but listen to the noise of the fight and watch men scattering or falling around me. I found that I was no longer pinioned, but I all the same I couldn't get up. Then one of the thugs sprawled across me as he fell, hands clutching at his ruptured belly and its spilling contents. His scarf dropped away and I saw that he was a boy not twelve years old.

'My son! My son!' someone screamed, as I fought to heave the dying boy off my chest; the blood that poured from his stomach was running down my neck and I feared I would choke on my own vomit. At last I succeeded in rolling him away, and saw that the someone who had screamed was Hanamel.

He struggled and threshed in the arms of the men who held him - men not from my party, but from his own, who were striving to drag him away before he got himself captured. He was still shouting, 'My son, oh God, my only son!' and ordering him not to die, though anyone could see it was all over for the poor lad already. He'd been slit up the middle like a fish for the gutting, and more of his innards were in his hands than inside his body. His eyes were wide open, and that was when it hit me that they were Ruth's eyes, and that this was Ruth's son.

After that I was good for nothing. I clung to Ebed-Melech, hearing from an enormous distance Hanamel heaping every curse under the sun upon my head as though the loss of his son were my fault. Perhaps it *was* my fault. Perhaps *everything* was my fault.

I was taken directly back to Jerusalem - by litter, because I was no more fit to walk than I was to bring the word of Adonai to the renegade inhabitants of Arad. As for Hanamel, he and some of his men had escaped; too many of my own party had been killed or wounded for the rest to go in pursuit. Through the closed curtains of my litter I heard the survivors asking one another who could have betrayed us; someone who knew the time of our departure and the details of our route must have conveyed the information to my kinsmen at Anathoth. But who? and why? My companions were mystified.

For myself, I neither knew nor cared. I wanted nothing more than to sleep, to make the world and its violence disappear. But whenever I closed my eyes I saw that poor butchered child with Ruth's face, and his guts spilt all over the road.

Weeks went by after that before I would get out of bed, and I hardly ate. Once in the middle of an interminable night I cut my own flesh with a knife in some half-baked attempt to bleed myself of my wickedness. After that, Ebed-Melech attended me constantly, and a stream of visitors arrived intent on stirring me from my torpor. None of them succeeded. Adonai had promised to protect me; he'd let me down, therefore neither he nor anyone else was to be trusted ever again.

'But your God *did* protect you, master,' Ebed-Melech pointed out cautiously. 'You are still alive. You weren't even injured.'

'But *other* men died! They died protecting me; they died in my place, and they were *good* men, with parents, and wives, and children.' I buried my face in my hands, suddenly reminded yet again of Ruth and Hanamel's son, and picturing Ruth red-eyed from weeping.

'Adonai should have warned me,' I wailed. 'He should have told me what was going to happen, and I would never have set out.' Then I wrapped my arms about my head, because suddenly I knew that I *had* been warned. A matter of days before the attack, a letter had come for me more malicious in tone than any of the others, scorning my ministry as false because none of my prophecies ever came true, I had seen no visions, and had worked no miracles.

The next time Ebed-Melech coaxed me to eat, I gave in to him. I could no longer pretend that Adonai had failed me. I had failed myself, through not thinking, not praying, through taking God's protection for granted. Ruefully I repented, as I'd done so often before, of nursing hatred toward the One who had chosen me and cared for me as my own parents never had. But I still had good reasons for hating myself.

The following day I quitted my bed at last. Ebed-Melech begged me not to overtax myself; I assured him that there was no danger of this because I'd made up my mind never to leave the palace again while Hanamel lived. Yes I *know* I'm a coward, I told Adonai; I always have been. So next time you want me to proclaim your word in the streets, you'll have to deal with Hanamel first.

However, because I had shut myself off from everyone and everything for so many weeks, I wasn't aware that in the meantime another prophet had appeared in Jerusalem. His name was Nahum, from the village of Elkosh, and I learned of his existence from Ahikam who had come directly to me after hearing him speak.

'He has such authority, such charisma, Jeremiah!' Ahikam enthused. 'You should go and hear him. He has predicted that Nineveh will soon fall to her enemies; the people are singing in the streets and declaring that the whole world is destined be ruled from David's city.'

'So this Nahum says nothing about the judgment which is due to fall upon *us?* I challenged him. 'He has not spoken of the righteous anger of Adonai against his people?'

'Not so far as I have heard. He speaks of comfort and consolation; even his name means 'consolation' - if Nahum is his real name at all.'

'What of the heart, then? Does he speak of that? Of its need to be circumcized along with the flesh?'

'He says nothing about such things. He commends Josiah and his programme of reform; I suppose he thinks that is enough.'

'Then his message is false, and the man is a liar.'

'But that's why I want you to hear him, Jeremiah. He recounts visions so strange and so compelling, he cannot possibly have conjured them up by himself.'

'Not all visions come from Adonai. There are other forces at work in the world, Ahikam. Unseen forces, who would seek to delude us and use us for their own evil ends.'

'There is nothing evil about Nahum of Elkosh. I haven't heard tell of a single sin which the man has committed. Even the priesthood applauds him.' And when I no longer argued, he said, 'Well, Jeremiah? Will you come with me to hear him next time he preaches in the Temple, and make up your mind about him then?'

'No, Ahikam,' I replied, and added, 'I think you should go now. You know I haven't been well.'

I don't suppose he'd meant to drag me down. He'd probably thought I would rejoice to learn that Adonai's word was still being published abroad in spite of my own indisposition. Instead, I was consumed by a new deluge of despair. I had no visions. I performed no miracles, my predictions didn't come true. Zephaniah himself had foretold the destruction of Nineveh, long ago; now he and this Nahum would be vindicated, whilst I would be known for the impostor I was.

On the next day there was a riot in the Temple Court. When first I heard of it, I assumed - and rather hoped - that Nahum had provoked it and thus brought his blissful relationship with the priestly authorities to an end. But I soon discovered that Nahum had had nothing to do with it.

It had been started by men who had once been priests themselves. Those who had once served Adonai at the high places had never been accepted by their peers already ministering in Solomon's Temple. Without shelter or income in a teeming city, some had gone back home, but others remained, and were still to be seen with their destitute wives and children, begging for alms.

Now they had invaded the Temple Court as a mob, demanding the rights which Josiah had promised them. Hilkiah the High Priest had appeared in person to appease them, but someone had thrown a stone which had struck him on the forehead. When finally the mob was expelled, several protesters lay unconscious; one at least was dead.

It was reported afterwards that Hilkiah had wanted to issue a public apology for the way things had gone. But his colleagues claimed that the agitators had got no more than they deserved.

That night the spirit came on me powerfully; I woke from a dreamless sleep with sweat running off me, and Adonai said: *The Jerusalem priesthood is corrupt, Jeremiah. Those who make offerings have soiled hands. They imagine that correctness in ritual practice can make atonement for their guilt; they are no less deluded than men who say that David's city can never be destroyed. I shall demolish their precious Temple; I shall smash their altars; and their vessels of gold, silver and bronze will be carried off and placed in the temples of the heathen.*

I said, 'You cannot tell me that Hilkiah is corrupt. I do not believe it.'

Hilkiah is a man of principle, but he is old and weak. Evil men have sprung up around him like weeds around a shoot of corn, and in time their growth will choke him. Go to Josiah at dawn, Jeremiah. Warn him that my patience is running out.

The audience ended as abruptly as it had begun. I slept again at once, and in the morning when I woke I felt fit and bold as a warrior. I dressed and took breakfast and went to Josiah in the throne-room. But I was told to wait outside: the King was conducting an interview with Nahum of Elkosh.

My boldness evaporated. Nahum held no position at Court, and had never been entertained by His Majesty before. While I was wondering what to do next, I was ordered to enter after all; Josiah had declared that this would be an excellent opportunity for the city's two most distinguished seers to be introduced.

Uncertainly I walked between the cedar columns. Josiah sat with his ministers about him, and standing before him was the stranger.

Even from behind, his easy confidence was manifest. He was uncommonly tall, his hair was scrupulously groomed, and he wore his cloak thrown jauntily across one shoulder. As I drew closer I heard his voice, resonant and authoritative even in private conversation.

Josiah leaped from the throne with his huntsman's grace, and held out his hands to me in welcome. At the same time, Nahum turned to face me, and I beheld his features: smiling, genial and fresh. He must have been about ten years my junior.

I returned Josiah's embrace, then Nahum knelt at my feet and said, 'So you are the great Jeremiah. I am honoured indeed. I have long been eager to meet you.'

I didn't reply. I was searching for sarcasm in his tone or his manner, yet found it in neither. Josiah had begun to catalogue for me the admirable qualities he'd observed in Nahum during their brief acquaintance; I merely nodded and made faint sounds in my throat and pondered how soon I could respectably take my leave. When Josiah eventually got around to asking me why I had come, I told him it wasn't important.

'Come come, my inscrutable friend,' His Majesty prompted me. 'You interrupt my morning's business requesting an audience, and now you have nothing to say for yourself?'

'Very well,' I responded, gritting my teeth and beginning to sweat as I had in the night. 'I have nothing to say for myself, but I have something to say for Adonai. The day is coming when Nineveh's fate will be of no concern to you or to your subjects. The fate of Jerusalem is what matters, and that is bleak indeed. There is rot at her very centre; her priests are like maggots which turn an apple bad from the inside out. God's patience with our sin is exhausted.'

A tortured silence ensued. Nahum's smile had dried on his lips and Josiah was enraged. I announced my intention to leave them forthwith, but Josiah barked, 'You will do no such thing! If you imagine that you can come marching into my throne-room, insult my guest and march right out again, you had better think again.'

I said nothing. I simply bowed my head and waited, which only angered Josiah the more. Then Nahum himself addressed me, with bridled hostility. 'Are you implying that my oracles are not of Adonai? Are you accusing me of blasphemy?'

'I make no implications, about your oracles or about your integrity, sir. All I do is repeat what my God has said to me.'

My words were brave enough, but I was shaking as I spoke them. Even Nahum was provoked to fury, and like everything else about him, his wrath seemed larger than life.

As he harangued me he seemed to grow, whilst I shrank like a scolded slave before him. When he'd run out of verbal brickbats with which to belabour me, Josiah interjected, more mildly now: 'Jeremiah, don't you think it is time that our people heard a little about God's love for them and hatred for their enemies? I remember the days when you used to cheer your hearers' hearts by encouraging them to look forward to the downfall of those nations which would seek to oppress them.'

'It's time that our people heard the truth and faced it!' I blurted; then I fled, the pounding of my footfalls and the echo of my words bouncing back and forth among the lofty pillars.

I ran to my apartment and locked myself in it. I was wheezing like a consumptive; it was as though some implacable fiend gripped me round the neck. A plaintive voice was saying in my ear: calm yourself, please, for pity's sake, calm down. I couldn't work out if it was my own or Adonai's, but when at last I was breathing more normally, I found that it had been Ebed-Melech's. He'd forced the door and broken in.

He asked me what was the matter, but I didn't know how to tell him. I was frightened, despairing, and fiercely jealous all at the same time. I was terrified that Nahum had been shown the truth, and I had been misguided all along; despairing because my whole life was a waste and a travesty; jealous, because Josiah had now found in Nahum what he'd once sought in me. Prostrate on the floor, I mourned our ruined friendship, and rejected all consolation. Adonai cared nothing for me, and never had. The voice I was accustomed to hear sprang from some other source, and unseen forces more malevolent than any human being were bent on my destruction.

In the afternoon Josiah himself came to see me, but I wouldn't admit him; he was Nahum's intimate now. Ahikam came, but I despatched him too. Even Shelemaiah appeared, to see if we would have a lesson that day. He had Ahikam's son in tow: the solemn Gedaliah, with whom I had got on so well when his friend Johanan had been alive. Now I couldn't bear to see even him. Reluctantly I permitted Ebed-Melech to stay. His quiet and dogged devotion I could just about tolerate.

At the hour when I should have been sitting down to my evening meal, there came a final knock at my door. Ebed-Melech went to answer it, and standing outside was the prophetess Huldah.

I ordered him to dismiss her, but too late. She had entered the apartment behind him and stood gazing down at me as I lay like a paralytic on my couch. I hid my eyes.

'I'm sorry, Jeremiah,' she said. 'But I didn't come here of my own volition. Josiah sent me. He says that no one else understands you.'

'*No* one understands me,' I corrected her. 'I don't even understand myself.'

'Adonai understands you.' Impulsively she started forward and fell to her knees by my side. 'Adonai *loves* you. Why can't you accept that?'

'Adonai loves Nahum. He sends him visions. He tells him things which the people want to hear. He tells me nothing.'

'So all the oracles you have ever delivered have been the product of your own genius? David himself could not have composed such poetry.'

'I don't know *where* they came from. I don't *want* to know.'

'Because they came from Heaven itself, you obstinate fool!'

'Then Nahum is a liar? Nineveh is not destined to fall? Watch what you are saying, Huldah, else you discredit Zephaniah also.'

'Oh Jeremiah, can you not see? You and Nahum are like the reflection of one truth in two mirrors. Nineveh will fall; Jerusalem will fall. Judgment will come; and consolation. God is just; and God is merciful. And at this very moment his mercy is what you need. Reach out for it. Accept it. You are harder on yourself than Adonai would ever be.'

No, I thought, I am not. Because I would not deny myself a woman's love. So I asked her, 'What about *you,* then, Huldah? Tell me how things are with you.'

'I am in good health. I have good food to eat, fine clothes to wear. I must be content.'

'But you are not.' I stretched out my hand and grasped hers; she withdrew it at once and got up, smoothing her garments with quaking fingers.

'Goodbye, Jeremiah. Please think on what I said,' she whispered; and was gone.

I sighed, and rolled over, with my face turned away from the door.

This time I wished I had kissed her. I wished I had pulled her down on the couch beside me and given her what she would never get from Shallum in a hundred years; except that I wasn't sure I would know where to start. I was hopeless: good at nothing, and good for nothing. If I weren't such a coward, I would have ended my pathetic existence a long time before.

II

Two years went by before Nineveh fell. They felt like twenty to me. I kept to my rooms and grew pale as a shade; I ate like a sparrow but drank like a fish, and set about my flesh with broken pottery, since Ebed-Melech would let me nowhere near a sharpened blade.

I did have other visitors: Shaphan and Ahikam when I could bring myself to receive them; and Shelemaiah who at sixteen years old had ceased wanting tuition but bore me a vague kind of affection, which seemed to be the strongest feeling he could muster for anyone. But his bland and affable nature caused children to love him. Often he would appear on my doorstep with his diminutive admirers: Mattaniah his younger brother - whose sixth birthday coincided with Nineveh's wake - or Jeconiah, rising four, the son of Eliakim and Nehushta. Josiah's grandson had inherited beauty from each of his parents, but, thankfully, his nature from Nehushta alone. Thus I, who had once found children a trial, now took solace from their company. Mattani and Coniah were engaging, generous, innocent; and together with Ebed-Melech should be given the credit for preserving what sanity I possessed.

It was high summer when Nineveh capitulated, brought down by the Medes and Babylonians together. As soon as the news reached us, Jerusalem's streets became thronged with jubilant crowds, and there was dancing on the rooftops. Nahum was everyone's darling, and Josiah their hero, even though Judah's army had played no part in the exploit. For the amount of help which Judah could have given, it would not have been worth Babylon's while negotiating terms of alliance. Besides, it is very bad manners to overrun an ally; and Nabopolassar was a far-sighted ruler whose manners were impeccable. Meanwhile, Assyria's capital was transferred to the city of Harran.

It seemed that in all Jerusalem only I held aloof from the festivities - excepting Ebed-Melech, who chose to keep me company. For once I found it no hardship that I was forbidden by my God to participate in the celebrations of men; what was there for me to celebrate? My rival's vindication and my own humiliation? Or - if by any remote chance I *had* heard God aright - a fleeting triumph which could only end in tragedy? I lay on my couch and drank, until the noise of the crowds abated.

In the months that followed, Josiah consolidated his gains to north and south of the kingdom he'd inherited. He now controlled the former Assyrian provinces of Samaria and Megiddo, in addition to a portion of Gilead. From time to time I was moved to remind him of Babylon's inexorable rising, but I would not confront him face to face, lest Nahum be with him. Instead, I sent him messages scrawled on tablets or potshards, and he sent me messages back, saying: you're very sick, Jeremiah. You should set your mind upon your own recovery rather than worrying yourself unnecessarily on my account. Please get well; I do so much miss you the way you used to be.

Very soon after this, a young man named Habbakuk presented himself at my door. Never having heard of him, I ordered Ebed-Melech to send him packing. But the eunuch protested, 'Master, he has made a long journey to get here. He says he has a special word for you from Adonai.'

'All the more reason to be rid of him,' I groaned. The last thing I wanted was a lecture from some rustic sooth-sayer. 'Send him back where he came from.'

Ebed-Melech bowed and went to do my bidding, but presently returned and said, 'I'm sorry, master, but he will not leave. He has provisions with him, and a blanket, and he says he will spend the night on your doorstep unless you invite him inside.'

I thought about sending for a detachment of the royal guard to come and evict the importunate fellow; yet the notion of someone prepared to sleep across my threshold like a love-sick suitor intrigued me. So I had the eunuch show him in.

He was indeed young, and as nervous as a gazelle. He grovelled beside the couch where I lay half-sozzled, and called me the great Jeremiah, as Nahum had done; I gave a bitter laugh, which made him more nervous than ever. He stammered an apology for his presumption, coming here like this with a word from the Lord when I was so distinguished in Adonai's service, and he no more worthy than a dog. Eventually I took pity on him and told him to pass on his message if it would make him feel better.

He thanked me profusely and tottered to his feet, wiping his palms down the front of his tunic. He said, 'My lord, Adonai has commanded me to tell you that what you prophesied concerning the fate of God's people will indeed come to pass. Babylon will crush us as grapes are crushed in a winepress, until Judah's lifeblood flows like wine in the gutters.'

'Thank you,' I responded, and resisted the temptation to mock the flamboyance of his language. I was thinking: he has heard me speak, and is dressing up my poetry with embellishments of his own, because for some unfathomable reason he wants to flatter me.

'Lord Jeremiah - that isn't all,' he continued. 'When Adonai gave me this word, I wasn't prepared to accept it. I argued. I accused him of injustice, of permitting heathen to treat his chosen people like so many fish, dragging them away in nets and gloating over the catch. I told him that the only conclusion men would draw was that military might alone ensures success in this wicked world; godliness is a useless burden. I said it wasn't right that Judah should be punished for her sins by a nation which terrorizes its neighbours and is more evil than Judah herself has ever been.'

Interested now in spite of myself, I levered myself upward by my elbows until I was sitting rather than lying. I said, 'Well, young man, it seems that you are less afraid of God than you are of me. What answer did he give you?'

'None at first.' Habbakuk blushed, and I thought: poor boy, you have the prophetic personality indeed. Sensitive, delicate, easily bruised; you will wind up a wreck just as I have. Then he went on: 'So - I said I would wait, my lord, like a watchman on a tower. I climbed on the roof of my parents' house, and swore I would not come down until I got an answer.'

'I take it that you got one, then?'

'Yes, my lord, I did; but when it came, I wished it had not.' He lowered his eyes and whispered, 'He sent me a vision and told me to write it down against the time of its fulfilment. But for forty days and nights I couldn't hold a pen. I saw the end of the world, and I swear that in the very hour of my death I shall not be more afraid.'

'Sit beside me,' I said, for at the mere recollection of what he had seen he was swaying where he stood. Once he was seated, I urged him to tell me more.

'A fearful storm split the skies, my lord, and hurled the very stars into the sea. Bolts of thunder pounded the earth and its crust broke apart like stale bread. Disease and death consumed every nation which had dared raise its sword against the consecrated people of Adonai. Mountains collapsed into their roots, then the sun and moon stood still as the omnipotent Creator of the Universe rode forth from Heaven in his flaming chariot to secure the salvation of his chosen ones; I saw the oceans turn to steam as his horses' hooves smote them. And my lord, I collapsed like a dead man when the vision faded. Not until I ascribed to Adonai the unconditional praise he deserves did my limbs cease to tremble. Now I see the error of my ways; Adonai is sovereign, my lord, and his justice beyond the fathoming of mortal man.'

I gasped, 'You saw Adonai himself, and you have lived to tell of it?'

'I saw him in my spirit, my lord, not with my eyes. But I wonder sometimes if I *am* alive any more. Certainly I'm not the same person I was.'

Suddenly in a moment of inspired boldness he seized hold of both my hands. 'Don't ask to see what I have seen, my lord Jeremiah. I would not want my deadliest enemy to be left as weak and wasted as I have become. If God is merciful to me, I shall go from here and never have to serve him in this way again.

'But you, my lord, must serve him all your life, that is your destiny. Adonai has told me of the questions you ponder in your mind, and the longings you have in your heart, and he wants me to say that he has wisdom and grace and love for you sufficient meet all your needs. But none of us will ever comprehend his thoughts with our minds or plumb the depths of his love in our hearts, so it is fruitless for us to fight him. Would that I hadn't fought; would that I had never stood on my watchtower and defied him to answer my accusations. Please, my lord, I beg you, don't be foolish as I was foolish. Be the man you were meant to be.'

Every word he had spoken came straight from the lips of Adonai. Of this I was in no doubt, not only because Habbakuk knew so much, but because the spirit of God welled up inside me as witness, and began to raise me from the mire of my depression into the clear blue sky of ecstasy.

When I came to myself, Habbakuk was gone. The record of his vision he deposited in the Temple, and I never heard of him again. But his ministry had been as vital as it had been brief. From that day forth I was seen once more about the palace, and I resumed my place among the counsellors and courtiers who surrounded Josiah's throne.

Like Habbakuk, Nahum of Elkosh had now retired to the town of his birth. His prophetic word had been fulfilled and nothing more was required of him. Yet Josiah and I, for all our good intentions, were unable to rebuild our friendship. Though we ate together sometimes, and lingered over our wine as we had in the good old days, our conversation was polite and guarded. Too many topics were taboo.

In the spring of my thirty ninth year, Josiah received in my presence an embassy from the Pharaoh. His name was Necho, and he had occupied the throne of Egypt for just a year, his father Psamtik having died at a ripe old age. Thus Necho was no callow youth, but a man of middle age who had been brought up to rule, and was equipped and eager to do so.

The purpose of his embassy was to seek Josiah's permission for Egyptian troops to pass through Judean territory on their way to lend assistance to Ashur-uballit, the latest of Assyria's struggling emperors. The Medes and Babylonians, not content with destroying his former capital at Nineveh, had now seized possession of Harran, whither his seat of government had been transferred.

Josiah's reply was predictable and prompt. Without so much as a glance at his assembled advisers, he gave the ambassadors a curt refusal and swept out of the hall.

While Shaphan strove to assure the ambassadors that His Majesty had meant them no insult, Ahikam and I pursued Josiah to his private apartment. Once inside with the door shut, the King gave vent to his fury.

'How dare that asp Necho suggest such a thing! Why does he think I have spent half my life building forts the entire length of my country? Does he imagine I have made the roads safe simply for *his* convenience? God in Heaven! I have acted specifically to prevent the armies of the Nile from using the coastal route ever again, but he expects me to shake his hand and grant him safe passage, of my own volition... who the hell does he think I am?'

No doubt the answer to this was that Necho took Josiah for exactly what he was, politically speaking at least: a kingling of minor importance who ought to be grateful that the mighty Pharaoh had deigned to treat him with respect. But Josiah thundered on: 'I shall show him who I am; and I shall show him the power of the God I worship! The next thing which Necho begs from me will be his own worthless life.'

I tried to ask him how he could be so sure that he was acting in accordance with Adonai's will. But Josiah would have none of it. 'Necho wants my very kingdom, not my blessing,' he roared. 'Once I grant him access to my domains I shall never get him out again. He wants Megiddo; he wants Beth Shan; he wants every confounded city in Judah and Israel which his predecessors controlled when my forefathers were still their slaves! Does he not remember that the Emperor of Assyria many generations ago sacked *his* capital, at Thebes? How can he contemplate alliance with his ancestors' oppressor? Perhaps I need to remind him of Egypt's history. Indeed I *shall* remind him.'

Ahikam and I exchanged leaden glances and took our leave; the envoys returned to Necho, and we awaited the Pharaoh's inevitable declaration of war. Yet it did not come. The envoys reappeared instead, and claimed that the Pharaoh was frankly puzzled at His Judean Majesty's attitude. Egypt had no quarrel with Judah, but with Babylon and her allies the Medes; once it had been settled, Necho would return to Egypt, and Josiah would be left in peace.

'Please, Josiah,' I implored him when we were alone, his temper mellowed by wine after supper. 'Give Necho what he wants before he takes it by force, along with your subjects' respect for you.'

'And what of my respect for myself? I cannot allow him to march unopposed through David's kingdom. It would be like letting heathen tramp through the Temple.'

'Then at least let us pray together, the way we once used to do. Let us seek Adonai's guidance. Let's do it now, in each other's presence, so that there can be no misunderstanding.'

'Adonai has more important concerns than the answering of obvious questions, Jeremiah. Do we ask him every morning whether we should rise from our beds, or put on our clothes? Do we seek his guidance every time we are tempted to lie with a prostitute or steal another man's wife, or murder our parents? It's perfectly clear to all of us that some things are right and some are wrong. And it's perfectly clear to me that the boots of Pharaoh's soldiers are not meant to desecrate Judah's holy soil.'

So I sighed, and went off to seek Adonai for myself. And in a voice which was clearer than crystal he said to me: *Josiah must comply with Necho's request. I am giving Judah this final chance; if Harran is recaptured and Babylon's pride is dinted, her advancing armies may yet be halted. But should the Pharaoh be hindered in his undertaking, no power on earth or in Heaven will stay the catastrophe which is to come. The ambition of Nabopolassar will become the channel of my wrath, and he and his son will be the instruments of my judgment.*

I went back to Josiah in haste, and gained admission to his apartment. But he wasn't alone; Hamutal his second wife was with him. Neither of them heard me enter, so intent were they upon their conversation, and I wondered why the doormen had let me in. But when I heard what was being said, I understood: Adonai has friends in lowly places as well as in high ones.

'My lord husband, it is not enough to refuse the Pharaoh safe passage,' Hamutal was maintaining, her voice low and insistent. 'You must tell him that if he attempts to cross our borders, he will be attacked. Did not Isaiah the prophet instruct us to make no deals with foreigners? Fight him, Josiah! Fight him and win; it will be a holy war, just like the campaigns of Joshua! Joshua fought to win this land after Moses led our forefathers out of slavery in Egypt; we must fight to keep it, lest Pharaoh enslave us all over again. Think of the glory you will win for Adonai and yourself when Necho is defeated. The People of the Land will stand by you for ever, all the kings of

the world will do you homage, and your praises will be sung in
the Temple for all time to come.'

I was beside myself. What could the crazy woman be
thinking of? Did she wish her own husband dead? How I
longed to rush forward and beseech him not to listen. But I
restrained myself until she departed. Then I went and fell at
Josiah's feet.

'My lord, forgive me, but you must pay no heed to
anyone who urges you to offer resistance to Necho. Please,
accede to his request. Adonai is speaking to you through it.'

Josiah threw back his head and laughed. 'Now I have
heard it all. Adonai speaks with an Egyptian accent.'

'Adonai speaks however and through whomever he
chooses, Josiah! Please, please don't cross swords with Necho.
You'll be killed; all your work will be undone, and that of Moses
too.'

'Is that so? Then perhaps *you* need reminding of
something, Jeremiah of Anathoth. I am to die in peace in
Jerusalem, and be laid to rest with my fathers, don't you
remember? There is little point in your being able to forecast
the future if you have no recollection of what was said in the
past. And I thought it was the duty of a prophet to stir up zeal
for a holy war? I thought you were meant to say, "Stand up for
your God, and he will lead you to victory," and thus the
creative power of your words would bring that victory about?'
Then all of a sudden his face turned from red to white and he
whispered, 'You overheard my private conversation! You
listened to an intimate discussion between your King and his
own wife! Great God in Heaven, Jeremiah, if you hadn't once
been my friend, I would have had your head for this.'

I could take no more, and left forthwith. Night had
fallen; I went to bed, but lay awake until dawn going over and
over what the Lady Hamutal had said to her husband, and
asking myself what could possibly have prompted her to adopt
this insane position. In the end I thought to ask Adonai, and he
answered: *Why don't you ask* her? *Go to her in the morning.
Learn the truth for yourself.*

I didn't want to. I was so unused to women, and all of them but Huldah scared me so badly; with Huldah I was simply scared of myself. I lay in bed half way to noon, trying to pretend that morning hadn't yet come, though I knew full well that Adonai would grant me no peace until I had obeyed him.

So when Ebed-Melech appeared as usual to see if there was anything I needed, I had him visit the women's quarters to request that the Lady Hamutal meet me in private.

I arrived at the appointed place well before her: a secluded courtyard of dappled sunshine, ablaze with spring flowers and dancing with butterflies. I sat beneath a willow tree by the pool in the centre, studying the lazy flicking of the fish, and marvelled that Josiah could want to exchange the tranquil beauty of his palace for the noise and terror of war. So I was startled when Hamutal herself sat down by my side as though we were wont to make a tryst like this every day.

'Well,' she began, in a warm, mellifluous voice, 'And to what do I owe the honour of a rendezvous with the silver-tongued spokesman of Adonai?'

Cringing with embarrassment, I dropped to my knees to do her obeisance, but she merely laughed: lightly, easily, like a girl. 'Get up, Jeremiah,' she said. 'There are no queens in Judah, only wives and mothers of kings.' And when she had made me sit down once again she continued, 'Do you know, in all the eighteen years you have lived here in the city, you and I have not exchanged more than the same number of words?'

Would that we didn't have to add to them now, I was thinking, and determined to have the interview over swiftly I gabbled, 'My lady, I'm afraid for His Majesty, your husband. He must not impede the Pharaoh's progress. Certainly he must not attack him. It would be madness.'

I wasn't looking at her as I spoke; I didn't dare. My mouth was dry as ash, and the apple in my throat felt so big I feared I might choke. Yet Hamutal simply laughed once again, as though it were the arrangements for some courtly entertainment we were discussing, not the prospect of a bloodbath in which her own husband might lose his life. 'Thus spake the prophet,' she taunted me softly; and what meagre courage I'd mustered shrivelled to the size of a poppy seed inside me. In a kinder tone she asked me, 'Where is your faith, Jeremiah? Surely as a man of God you know that if Adonai fights for us, the strongest army on earth cannot prevail against us. The Lord and his anointed together are invincible.'

'*If* Adonai fights for us,' I blurted, and at last I found myself meeting her gaze. It was steady, quizzical, even bemused. 'But my lady, he will not. He has told me quite clearly. He has spoken through the very mouth of Necho - '

A third peal of her melodious laughter stopped me short. 'Surely to God you are jesting?' she exclaimed. 'And yet, I should never have taken you for a tease. Egypt has been the enemy of all that is good since the beginning of time; the fathers of our nation taught their sons to curse the Pharaohs with the first words they uttered. It is better to die a glorious death fighting the forces of evil than to die in your bed for nothing.'

I stared at her, too appalled to respond. And she stared back, haughty and beautiful, yet quite suddenly neither her haughtiness nor her beauty intimidated me. When I was able, I said, 'You know that Josiah may die, but still you encourage him to fight? My lady, death in battle is no more glorious than death in the filthiest gutter. King Saul died in battle; was his a glorious end? His headless body was hung from the walls of Beth Shan; is that what you want for your husband?'

'And the great King David died in his bed, too old to govern his kingdom, to old to foil the scheming of Bathsheba and Solomon her son - too old even to enjoy the warmth of the woman who lay beside him.'

It was when she mentioned Bathsheba and Solomon that the shocking revelation came to me. Hamutal cared no more for Josiah than Bathsheba had cared for her husband David. All that either of them had ever wanted was that their sons should reign when their husbands were gone. Goaded by Adonai, I said so, in so many words.

She didn't flare up at me in anger. Nor did she baulk at the accuracy of my assertion. Instead, she laughed yet again.

'You imagine that *Shelemaiah* could rule over Judah? I thought you knew him, Jeremiah. You tried to teach him for long enough.'

'Perhaps he could not, my lady. But he could sit on a throne; and it is as you said: there are no queens in Judah, just wives and mothers of kings.'

I had bettered her; though the Lord knows, it was he and not I who had done it. I was shaking now like the willow leaves above me, unable to believe what I'd heard myself saying. For an excruciating interval, neither of us spoke. Then she said, 'I can see I have made a mistake, Jeremiah, in thinking of you merely as a paragon of piety and not as a man of uncommon intelligence and perspicacity. I realize now that I shall underestimate you at my peril.'

She had moved a little closer to me as she spoke; involuntarily I edged away. She asked me what was wrong, and in a hoarse and broken voice I answered, 'Your husband was once my friend, my lady. He's as brave and as noble as he is reckless, but you don't love him. He's going to throw himself into the jaws of death, and you do not care.'

'It is not easy to care for a man who cares nothing for you,' she said, with such vehemence that for the first time since she'd taken her seat beside me, I knew she was telling me the truth. 'Josiah has never loved me. Zebidah was his first love, and she will be his last. I am a widow already in all but name. Perhaps when I do have the name, I shall at last be permitted to marry a man who will give me his heart instead of his jewels.'

The sadness in her voice disarmed me, reminding me so poignantly of my own chronic loneliness. I risked an upward glance, and found that she was looking right into my eyes. Then she seized my hand as it gripped the poolside wall, and covered my fingers with her own.

'Surely you don't want to see Eliakim ensconced on Josiah's throne?' she demanded. 'He's more spoilt than Pharaoh's cat, and more vain, and a lover of all things Egyptian besides. He would let Necho share his own bath; he would scrub the monster's back for him if he thought it would guarantee his succession. And he wouldn't turn a single hair if Necho filled Solomon's Temple with statues of his beast-headed gods, or daubed impious hieroglyphs all over its walls. At least Shelemaiah is neither arrogant nor avaricious; and he isn't stubborn. He'll do as he's told. He will honour Adonai, too, as faithfully as his father does - if we tell him that this is what he must do.'

We? In God's name, what on earth was the woman implying? I stared at her gem-encrusted fingers still clasping mine; then looked up in confusion, my eyes meeting hers again and finding themselves held captive just like my hand. 'Come now, Jeremiah,' she said, her voice so soft and so low that I began to feel sick. 'You are a handsome man. You know very well how profound was the impression you made upon me the moment we were introduced. It isn't good for you to sleep alone, with only your worries to keep you warm. We should make a formidable partnership, you and I.'

I tried to snatch my hand away, but she wouldn't release it. I tore my eyes away instead, looking anywhere except at her face, and in place of it glimpsing my own reflected in the water: haunted eyes as deep and dark as wine in a goblet, cheek-bones as pronounced as a youth's, heavy black hair falling almost to my shoulders like a veil. 'Let me go, my lady,' I pleaded, not wanting to look any longer, and in the end she let me. I fled from the courtyard like a thief.

I'd meant to go straight to Josiah, yet could not bring myself. The King's own wife had propositioned me, and been rejected - she whose semi-rejection at the hands of her husband had led her to wish him dead. What therefore would she wish for me? Would she have the palace cooks poison my food? Would she send some eunuch to stab me in my bed? Or would she run to Josiah and claim it was *I* who had propositioned *her*, as Potiphar's wife had once denounced Joseph in days long gone by?

Ebed-Melech plied me with wine, and at length my fears subsided. Like as not, Hamutal would do nothing, save permitting her handmaids a quiet snigger at my expense. She'd been winding me up, like a priest of the Nile winding bandages round a mummy; having rendered me helplessly bound, she would rest content.

Yet was *I* to rest content, convinced that the King's second wife would rather see him dead than happy in the arms of her rival?

For the fourth time and the last I went to Josiah and sought to persuade him to let Necho have his way. But even as we talked - and then argued - and each of us became angrier and more entrenched in our positions, I knew that all was lost. I felt like a man who watches a boulder plunging down a hillside towards his unwary brother. Josiah meant more to me than any man of my own flesh and blood for it was he who had first shown me friendship as a boy, and brought me out of the prison of my solitude. How I longed to dive in the path of that boulder and snatch him to safety; but I was too far away.

So I had to stand and listen while he boasted of his army's strength and the brilliance of the tactics he intended to adopt against the Pharaoh. He had cast himself in the role of David, and would smite the Goliath of Egypt in Adonai's strength; nothing I said could convince him that Adonai might choose to side with Judah's adversary. In desperation I grabbed him by the shoulders and shouted, 'Are you blind, Josiah? Hamutal cares not a jot whether you live or you die! She's in league with the People of the Land, for Heaven's sake; their hatred of Egypt and Assyria has so clouded their vision that they cannot see the truth that stares them in the face, and neither can you! *Babylon* is the foe to be feared.'

'Babylon, Babylon, Babylon!' Josiah shoved me backwards so roughly that I stumbled and fell, puncturing my lip on the corner of a chest as I went down. 'I'm sick of hearing you say that name, do you hear me? You're a fraud, Jeremiah, a damnable insult to our nation and to our God! Nothing you predicted has ever come to pass; now you stoop to the basest slander, accusing my own wife of luring me deliberately into the clutches of death! Oh, why did I not have you silenced before all this happened? Assyria is Judah's enemy, and has been since both of us were babes in arms and before. If Necho helps Assyria regain what she has lost, every last one of us will die!'

No, no, I was mumbling, the blood pouring down my chin. I tried to explain to him that Necho alone could achieve what was necessary: Necho alone was capable of capping Babylon's rise before it was too late. But I was faint at the sight of my own blood, and knew that I wasn't making sense.

The following morning I sat through the session of His Majesty's Court where he outlined his strategy to the assembled ministers of his Government. A table had been brought, for the spreading out of his maps; I sat with my head on my arms upon it throughout, and no one asked me what was wrong, because they knew. Almost every one of them had striven to plead my case before the King, but by now a thunderbolt from Heaven could not have daunted him. 'Does not the Book of the Law itself exhort us to boldness in battle?' he demanded, thumping his fist on the table right next to my head. '"When you go out to war and see chariots and horses and a host that outnumbers you, don't be afraid of them,"' he quoted. '"The Lord your God who rescued you from Egypt in the days of Moses will do so again. Adonai himself marches with us, and he will give us victory."'

So confident did he sound, and so resplendent did he look, kitted out for war already in crimson tunic and bronze breastplate, with his crested helmet set down on the table in front of him, that perhaps the less experienced of his counsellors were tempted to believe him.

Then he turned his attention to the details, waving his hand above the maps laid out before us. 'I have devoted a great deal of thought to our campaign,' he announced, 'and I have decided that it would not be wise to attack the Pharaoh the moment he crosses from Egypt into Judah. The terrain in that region is not favourable to us; his superior numbers would give him undue advantage, and it would be too simple a matter for him to send across the border for reinforcements. No, we shall let him march up the coastal plain as he desires, until the road meets the Carmel Mountains, and we shall await him in secret at the exit from the Iyron Pass by Megiddo in the

Vale of Jezreel. When his troops emerge from the pass we shall fall upon them and vanquish them before they can form up for battle. Then the world will know that David's spirit lives on in the hearts of his descendants.'

'And if Necho should bypass Megiddo? If he should take an alternative route?' enquired Ahikam.

'When the other passes have no roads, and are choked with bushes, and the mountains stretch almost to the sea? I think not; but if he does, we shall know it in good time, and we shall meet him there instead. As his chariots spill out onto the plain we shall drive them back, and smash them against the mountains.'

'*We?* repeated Shaphan. 'You intend to be present at this engagement in person, my lord?'

'Of course. I would have it no other way. When Joshua won possession of the Promised Land, did he himself shrink back like a woman and watch while his warriors marched into the fray on his behalf? I shall mount my chariot and lead my men as an anointed leader should.'

'And if you are killed?' enquired Ahikam with daring directness, causing Asaiah the King's attendant to shudder involuntarily. Josiah was his life.

'Adonai will shield his anointed from harm,' replied Josiah, and now it was my turn to shudder, for his religious fervour was so tragically misplaced.

Early in the summer, word reached us that Pharaoh's army was approaching our borders. Perhaps he expected Josiah's forces to be ranged there to meet him; Josiah however was marching north through the hills on Jordan's western bank. Therefore Necho proceeded northward also, along the coast as Josiah had assumed that he would. My boyhood friend had left without bidding me goodbye; no doubt he knew that even at this late hour I would endeavour to change his mind.

Each day of his absence was worse for me than the last, especially once enough time had elapsed for him and for Pharaoh to have reached the mountains at Megiddo. Har-Mageddon, so close to Gilboa, the mountain where Saul himself, the first of our nation's kings, had lost his life... The very name filled me with dread.

A hundred times a day I saw him fall: slashed with a sword, transfixed by a spear, sliced in two by an axe. I tried very hard to take comfort from the promise on which Josiah himself relied: that Adonai would allow him to die in peace in the City of David and be laid to rest there with his fathers. Yet I had always known that what Adonai would allow and what Josiah would choose might not be the same thing. I tried very hard to pray for him, too, but somehow the words wouldn't form in my mind, and even my wordless cries seemed to echo from the ceiling and rise no higher.

It was midnight when news of his defeat reached the palace. Relays of horsemen had brought it, riding by day and by night, lest rumours should get to us before the official word. Ebed-Melech rushed to my chambers to rouse me, but I wasn't asleep.

The palace was in uproar. Torches converged upon the throne-room, where the last in the chain of riders had delivered his message to the venerable Shaphan, Secretary of State. The old man's face was as white as his beard in the torchlight, his shoulders were bowed, and he seemed to have aged ten more years since I'd seen him at sundown. 'What of the King himself?' hushed voices were asking. 'His Majesty King Josiah; does he live?'

The rider thought yes, though he gave little more; exhausted, he could tell us nothing else but that the battle had been lost and the carnage indescribable, before toppling to the floor insensible. Slaves rushed to fetch him water; palace women whose husbands and fathers and sons had marched with the host clung to one another and wept. In time the messenger revived, to inform us that the Judean survivors were on their way home, and that Necho's army had forged on northwards into Syria. But Necho too had suffered heavy losses. It was unlikely now that he would reach Assyria with the time or forces necessary to achieve his objective. The Medes and Babylonians would be so well established in Harran by the time Necho got there that it would take an earthquake to dislodge them.

It was morning before we learned any more of Josiah. Another courier arrived at dawn to apprise us of the facts, such as they were: His Majesty had survived the battle, but was grievously wounded, and the physicians knew not whether he was destined for life or for death. He was being carried back to Jerusalem in his ceremonial chariot, and his progress could not be hurried. Really he ought not to be travelling anywhere, but he had insisted on returning home with the remnant of his army.

A whole week it took them to fetch him. In the meantime we learned bit by bit what had happened. Pharaoh Necho had indeed selected the Iyron Pass as his route through the mountains of Carmel; Josiah had deployed his troops exactly as he'd planned, on elevated ground across from the pass's opening. These troops had charged when the first of the Egyptians emerged - and been subjected to a barrage of arrows raining down on them from the hills on either side of the defile. Informed of Josiah's presence by spies or by traitors, Necho had sent his archers to run up the hillsides and spread themselves out along the ridge-tops. Firing on our men from above, they'd brought them down in heaps till the rest had turned and fled. Josiah himself, riding out with his captains in front, had been one of the first to fall. Though he had worn no regalia, his bearing and everything about him would have marked him out as the King.

But when they brought him in through the palace gates, I saw at once that he was marked out now for nothing but death. Indeed, rumours were rife throughout the city that he was dead already, and rising above the clustered rooftops the keening of women went up like a cry of reproach to the heavens.

An arrow had pierced his lung; every breath that he took was shallow and rattling. Asaiah, walking beside the stretcher to which he'd been transferred, was weeping shamelessly; the crowd of courtiers and guards who followed in its wake had rubbed dust in their hair and on their faces, and the dust on their cheeks was streaked with tears. One of Josiah's hands hung limply down; I reached out and touched his fingers but he didn't know me. I fell in with the crowd of followers and found myself propelled along with them to the threshold of his private quarters, where physicians turned most of them back. Asaiah himself, whose task this should have been, no longer cared who did what.

I was with those few who were granted permission to enter. Zebidah was awaiting us, as pale and haggard as the patient himself; Hamutal her inveterate rival made an impressive display of solicitude. Standing with their mother were Josiah's younger sons. Shelemaiah, slow of wit and shallow of feeling, seemed bewildered; Mattaniah his brother, just nine years old, was more aware than he of the significance of the scene being played out before him. As for Josiah's counsellors and friends, they huddled in miserable little groups, rendered as helpless as their king himself. Old Shaphan stood with his arms about his sons, and even the sober Ahikam had lost the fight against tears.

I caught myself looking for Huldah, but she wasn't there. For three whole years she had succeeded in avoiding me, ever since we had quarrelled over Nahum and my gifting. She knew the depths to which I'd sunk that day, and to what temptation I could so easily have succumbed.

Eliakim alone of those present was composed, impassive, heedless of his kinsfolk's distress. The reward for which he had waited since the death of Johanan was about to fall into his hands, or so he imagined. Somehow he kept the gleam of greed from showing in his smouldering eyes.

One of the physicians undertook to explain to me the patient's condition. The barb had gone deep in Josiah's side and between his ribs; they'd had to cut away flesh to draw it out, and he'd lost a great deal of blood. Each day on the road from Megiddo he had worsened, and gradually all hope for him had been abandoned. Ironic it was, the physician remarked, that this man who had sought to live like David, Judah's finest king, was going to die like Ahab, Israel's wickedest. Ahab too had been hit by an arrow in battle and been carried from the field in his chariot to die.

At this point I bade the physician be silent lest I strike him. The friend I'd loved as half my own soul was dying in front of my eyes, with our bitterest quarrel unresolved, and this incompetent doctor could offer nothing but a commentary on the sacred history. 'Can't *you* do anything?' someone at my shoulder was asking, but not until they pushed me forward did I grasp that they were talking to me. Then I felt worse than before. The prophet Elijah had healed the sick; he had even stretched himself out upon the corpse of a boy and restored him to life. Could I not perform a miracle now?

I fell on my knees by the bed where they had lain him, and grasped the hand which I'd touched when they'd carried him by. But all I could do was murmur, 'I'm sorry, Josiah, I'm sorry,' and wish with all my heart that he might know me and pronounce me forgiven. Yet he did not. Just once I fancied that his fingers squeezed mine; I bent forward, but his breath was so rank that I had to retreat. I crouched on the floor with my arms wrapped about me, and remained there rocking back and forth like a madman until eventually someone took me out. They must have feared that grief had driven me insane - if indeed I wasn't already.

So I was not there to see Adonai's promise to Josiah fulfilled: he died in peace in the City of David, and all too soon he would be laid to rest with his fathers. He'd been spared from witnessing Adonai's judgment on Judah, but now that he was gone, nothing was left to postpone its coming.

PART THREE

IN THE DAYS OF KING JEHOIAKIM

God in his fury shrouds Zion in darkness,

Her glorious splendour he dashes to dust;

On the day of his wrath he withdraws from his Temple.

He smites us with arrows, he shatters our strength;

Slaughters our loved ones, our joy and delight;

Vents holy wrath on his Daughter Jerusalem.

Weeping prostrates me, my soul is in torment;

My heart is poured out like spilt wine on the ground;

Grief has exhausted me; I am undone.

Lamentations 2:1,4,11.

CHAPTER 12: JEREMIAH

Jerusalem was plunged into mourning. Every corridor in the palace and every street outside resounded with keening. Men tore their garments and heaped dust upon their heads; women beat their breasts and bewailed the fallen King as they would have done their own sons. Everywhere the despair was mingled with disbelief: how was it that Josiah their hero could have been struck down so swiftly? He was young, he was strong, he was valiant in the service of Adonai. It was impossible that he could be gone.

Not everyone had approved of his policies. But there was no one who hadn't been glad of the freedom he'd won them from Assyria and her taxes, and there were few who hadn't relished the glimpse he had given them of the glory which Judah had known under David. For one brief moment it had seemed conceivable that David and Solomon's empire might be regained. Now all was lost. Despite the ridicule with which my prophecies of doom had been received when I'd pronounced them, the unspoken consensus now was that Judah's hopes had died with Josiah.

Not that I derived any comfort from this. Adonai had stolen my friend, without allowing us to patch up our quarrel, without even letting us say goodbye. No doubt he would stop me attending the funeral. I hated Adonai, and I hated myself.

So I stayed in my chambers and mourned and fasted and abused myself there while the rest of Jerusalem's inhabitants cried on one another's shoulders. All excepting Eliakim of course. I knew that his eyes would still be dry. He would intone the Kaddish by his father's bier, and deliver a eulogy in praise of the latter's achievements. Then with flaming torch he would light the great fire to be made in honour of the dead. After that he would be king, and God only knew what was to become of us all.

For Judah's pursuit of independence had been successful until now, with Assyria being so weak, and Egypt fully engaged in shoring her up. But Babylon was sprouting like a weed through stubble, and soon her green shoots would be sturdy trunks and branches, casting long shadows across the lands of the Levant.

Josiah couldn't be buried until the second day after his death. He had died in the afternoon, a matter of hours before Sabbath began, and there was insufficient time for the preparations to be made before sunset. So his body lay in state throughout the day of rest, candles burning by his head, with those who had loved him filing past to pay their respects. I, however, was not among them.

All through the Sabbath I stayed in my bedchamber. Josiah's ministers came to me one after another, urging me to compose a lament for my fallen friend, to be sung by the Temple choir at my direction. But I knew that if I tried to attend the service Adonai would assail me, and I should bring disgrace upon myself and upon Josiah by collapsing in convulsions down the Temple steps. As for composing the lament, there was as much music in my soul just then as water in a ruptured cistern.

Never in my life had I loathed myself so thoroughly. I blamed myself for not opposing Josiah more vigorously when he'd determined to march against Necho; then I changed my mind and blamed myself for opposing him at all. I blamed myself for not having preached more forcefully about the Babylonian threat; then I blamed myself for having broached the subject in the first place. Lastly and most savagely, I blamed myself because Josiah had lain alive beneath my consecrated hands, and I hadn't even tried to bring him healing.

Then, in the middle of the night after Sabbath had ended, I awoke with a start from the first real sleep I'd had in weeks. I had dreamt that Josiah was buried already, and that my spirit had hovered above the crowds at the funeral while my body languished on my bed. I'd listened to the Temple choir sing their lament in his honour: the most exquisite, the most excruciatingly beautiful thing I had ever heard. And wide awake, I could remember it, word for word, note for note. Adonai was saying to me: *You have turned your back on me again, my son, yet still I have not rejected you. Nor did I reject Josiah. He was foolish sometimes, and impetuous always. But he loved me, and I have forgiven him.*

I leaped from my bed and took a tablet and pen to the window, where the moon shone bright as day. I wrote down the words of the song, and the signs for the singers and the players of the pipes and lyres. I made up my mind that if any of Josiah's ministers came to see me the next day, I would present the tablet to them, and bid them pass it on to the High Priest. I would not take it myself, however; still less would I direct the work's performance. Whatever anyone might say, Josiah's funeral was out of bounds for me, like any other.

I ought to have guessed that the only person who would come in the morning was Huldah. Everyone else had come already, and been rebuffed; once again Huldah had been summoned as a last resort. For never before had I acted the part of a madman so convincingly, and never had Judah herself been more in need of me sane.

However, when Huldah arrived, and found me washed and clothed and in my right mind, she was scarcely reassured. She had come by herself, knowing that only on her own could she hope to restore me. Now I stood before her, neither raving nor drooling, and all the more dangerous as a result.

She mumbled her way through some platitudes, saying how pleased she was to see me recovered. Then she drew her veil close about her head and prepared to go. For regardless of what Josiah's counsellors had tried to persuade her to ask of me, Huldah knew that I would not be prevailed upon to show my face at the rites.

But I caught her by the wrist and bade her stay. 'I won't harm you,' I promised her. 'I won't do anything to make you afraid. Don't leave me, Huldah. I'm in hell, and no one but you can understand.'

I don't quite know what caused her to give in to me: guilt, compassion, or her own need to be loved for what she was, and not for the dutiful housewife her husband wanted her to be.

Whatever the reason, she stayed. And I poured out the anguish of my soul to her as I'd done so many times in the past.

'How can you blame yourself for Josiah's death?' she implored me. 'Has healing *ever* been a part of your gifting? Have you any reason for supposing it has become so now?' Nor was there the slightest extra thing I could have done to prevent Josiah from clashing with Necho, she pointed out. The choice had been his, and he'd made it alone.

By the time I'd come to the end of my self-recriminations I was cradled in her arms, not knowing how I'd come to be there. But she murmured, 'It's all right, Jeremiah. It's all right.' Then it was Huldah's turn to give voice to her anguish.

For three long years she had slept alone, at her own request. She had made up her mind that I was the only man she would ever want, and she could never love Shallum however hard she tried. If she couldn't be mine, she would live for herself alone, or rather for Adonai; she and her husband had gone on sharing one house, and one apartment at the palace, but precious little else.

'My God,' I whispered. 'You didn't tell him *why* you wanted to sleep on your own? My name wasn't mentioned..?'

'Of course not. I didn't want to hurt him, honestly I didn't. And truly, I think he was more relieved than upset. He doesn't have to make the effort any more. We live as brother and sister - or as uncle and niece, which is the way I always used to think of us. It's better this way for us both, I know it. Or it was, until Josiah...'

She broke down then, and I could barely make out the words that followed. But her meaning was clear enough. With her patron and friend the King snatched away, any sense of purpose she'd had left was gone. Josiah hadn't consulted her often in his latter years, but the rare occasions when he did so had allowed her to believe that her life was more than pots and dishes, needles and pins. 'Adonai needs me no more than Shallum does,' she wept. 'I dedicated my love to him, and he's thrown it back in my face. To whom shall I give it now? There will be no place for me at the court of Eliakim; and none for you either.'

You could give your love to me, I was thinking, but didn't dare say - not yet. This time, I thought, I'll get it right; this time I shall not frighten her away. Adonai has robbed us of the friend we both served; we owe him nothing.

So I made very certain that when our lips brushed together, it was not I who had first brought them near. Mine were not the eyes which closed first, mine were not the eyelids which first quivered with expectancy. Not until Huldah had wrapped her arms tight around my back did I venture to touch her tear-stained face with the tips of my fingers, then cup her head in my hands and cover her mouth with my own.

I was thirty nine years old, and callow as a youth, yet I burned with the passion of a warrior in his prime. And oh, by every god and goddess who has ever been worshipped, it felt so wonderful when she kissed me in return, when she melted against my chest, when she whispered my name in her bliss as though it were a prayer. Such desire rose up within me that I thought I would die there and then, overwhelmed by the strength of my need before I could fulfil it. Her breasts were heaving, her breath was hot on my cheeks; her dextrous seamstress's hands found a way inside my tunic and moved across my virgin skin like the spirit of God on the surface of the waters when the pristine earth was formed.

I should never have allowed that image to enter my mind. Because even as I held her, even as I pressed myself against her and felt the throbbing in my loins, the hardening, the aching, the imminent approach of release, it was no longer Huldah who murmured my name in my ear. Adonai, so tender, so compelling, so disarming... and all at once the fire went out, the bubble within me burst, the climax came to nothing. Limp as a rag I slumped against Huldah's shoulder and panted out my impotence as though I'd performed the very act for which my body had been preparing me.

'I'm sorry, I'm sorry,' I moaned, begging God to let me die after all since I'd proven myself a failure even in being a man. But Huldah was soothing me, stroking my sweatdraggled hair and swearing to me that it didn't matter, it was all for the best; Adonai loved us both in spite of everything and was not going to let us blight our lives with sin. 'Perhaps one day, my love,' she whispered, and I thought: one day what? One day adultery will not be sin? One day Shallum will die? Perhaps he will, but even then we shall not be free to follow where our hearts are leading us, because Adonai holds mine in the palms of his hands, and he'll press them together and crush it if I try to evade his will for my life. I am not to marry, and that is that. I asked him to make me as a eunuch; perhaps he has done so.

But even while these thoughts were churning round in my head, Huldah's hands passing over it were no longer comforting but caressing, inviting, as though we were lovers after all.

Bewildered, I looked up into her eyes and she was smiling her sweetest smile; time had not tarnished its radiance. 'Kiss me, Jeremiah,' she said. 'For even little children may kiss without shame; a brother may kiss his sister, and nobody minds. One flesh with Shallum I may be. But my heart, my soul and my spirit are yours. This Adonai knows, and does not begrudge.'

So I kissed her on the lips, and folded her in my arms, and it seemed to me just then that where lust had been expelled, a stronger and purer love had moved in and taken its place. Somehow I'd briefly forgotten that it wasn't merely celibacy which Adonai required of me, but intimacy with him alone.

I can't say for sure how long we remained there. We neither talked nor kissed, once the first kiss was over and its warmth had spread through me like the glow of wine. With our spirits entwined like our bodies we shared an unspoken grief for Josiah, and a deep, mute understanding of each other's anxieties and ecstasies, all of which were mollified for the moment, anointed with the oil of tenderness.

At last we drew apart; Huldah rose from the couch and clasped my hand, and said, 'I shall tell Ahikam that you are yourself once more.'

'No you shall not,' I demurred with a smile; and she knew what I meant, for in being so happy I was hardly myself at all. 'But you may take him this,' I bade her, and handed her the tablet inscribed with Josiah's lament. She stowed it in a fold of her garments, and was gone.

At dawn on the first day of the week Josiah's body, swathed in a cocoon of bandages, was laid on its wooden bier. I watched from a window above the courtyard where the procession formed up to accompany its King on his final journey, to the tombs of the kings of the House of David. On one side stood the menfolk: Josiah's two older sons, his courtiers and counsellors, soldiers who had fought with their King at Megiddo and watched him fall. Among these was the squire who had carried the royal shield into battle, and he carried it now, along with Josiah's spear and his sword, and the crested bronze helmet which gleamed like gold in the morning sun. I looked for Asaiah, but the lifelong servant and friend of my friend was nowhere to be seen.

Standing apart from the men were Josiah's wives and his mother, and Nehushta the wife of Eliakim with little Jeconiah their son. Mattaniah his friend was with him, and a huddle of courtiers' sons and grandsons who weren't yet of age. Of their own volition my eyes searched for Huldah; she was there with the wife of Ahikam, their veiled heads pressed together in mutual solace. Waves of conflicting emotion broke over me; I wished I were still as certain as I'd been the day before that we hadn't stumbled into error. For as long as I'd held her in my arms I'd believed what she had told me. Now I wasn't so sure.

I remained in control until the body was carried from the yard, and the last of the mourners had passed from my sight. Then I subsided on to the floor by the window where I'd stood, and lay there drowning in an ocean of misery and guilt. There was no one on hand to drag me to shore; even Ebed-Melech had gone with the cortege, as every palace servant was obliged to do.

I don't know to this day who took me back to my apartment. I know only this: that I was sick as a man with the plague when I got there. I burned and froze and vomited by turns. When I slept or fainted I dreamed terrifying dreams of destruction, death and decay, but knew not whence they came.

Even when the worst of the fever was past, I couldn't remember if I loved Adonai or hated him. He'd taken the life of my friend, but he'd inspired me with the most beautiful lament ever sung since David composed his elegy for Saul and Jonathan. He'd granted me joy in the arms of a woman, yet denied me its consummation. Should I fight him or repent? Did I *need* to repent? Should I eat to regain my strength, or starve myself in protest, or in remorse, or in despair? In the end I gave up trying to decide. When Ebed-Melech poured soup down my throat, I drank it; when Huldah brought me fruit, I ate it, and when she bent over my bed and kissed me, I followed the promptings of my heart and forgot all else. I slept, I woke, I ate a little and slept again; I dreamed, I sighed, I swooned, I wallowed in a haze of fantasies, and might have gone on living this half-life for ever, had not Ahikam come and dashed water in my face and dragged me from my bed by force. He shook me till my eyes were rattling like dice in a cup and shouted: 'You're the only prophet worthy of the name in this benighted land, God damn you! Wake up, you fool; you must assist the High Priest in anointing the King.'

I began to protest, maintaining that I would have nothing more to do with Eliakim as long as I lived.

'Not Eliakim! In Heaven's name, where have you *been* all this time? It's *Shelemaiah*, for God's sake. *Shelemaiah* is to be king.'

'Shelemaiah?' I repeated muzzily. 'But I don't understand. Eliakim is the older. Eliakim has prepared himself for kingship, and that is what he wants. That's what he expects.'

'And that is precisely what he must not get! We must look to the nation's future and wrest the kingship from him immediately, or it will be too late for us all. The People of the

Land are with us; Shelemaiah's mother Hamutal has seen to that.'

'And Eliakim's mother?' I queried, still half-dazed; Ahikam was passing me my clothes and I donned them mindlessly, inside out as likely as not.

'Zebidah is too distressed to care. Things are changing, Jeremiah, faster than you know, and we must harness these changes before they run us down. Asaiah is dead; the Queen Mother is dying. Necho's name has become a curse on every man's lips; we must channel this resentment and use it while we can. All of Judah knows how Hamutal and her friends among the People of the Land hate the Egyptians, and how Eliakim would court Necho's favour if given half a chance. Eliakim must *not* rule over Judah. His greed and his wickedness know no bounds.'

Once I was clothed, Ahikam propelled me out of my apartment and off in the direction of the throne-room. 'Now?' I was mumbling. 'You want him anointed this very minute?' and I found myself thinking: I don't even know what day it is, nor how many have passed since Josiah was laid in his tomb. Then the other things which Ahikam had said began to come home to me, and I asked him how Asaiah could be dead, and why Jedidah the late King's mother should be dying too.

'Poison,' Ahikam answered. 'Or that's what people are saying. No one can prove it, but I think the two of them arranged it together. Lady Jedidah fell ill when the tomb was closed up; Asaiah was found in her room when they carried her back there. Half of her reason to live was lost with Zephaniah; Josiah took the rest.' And Josiah was all that Asaiah had ever had.

I don't know how I got through the proceedings without collapsing. Someone gave me wine part way through, and I drank it, and felt even worse. The place I was in was thronged with people, but I couldn't focus on their faces, and wasn't sure who they were. The horn of consecrated balsam oil was thrust into my hands at the designated moment, and I emptied it over Shelemaiah's brow - or should I say, that of Jehoahaz, for this was his throne-name. 'Adonai has grasped,' was its meaning, though the lad himself, it seemed, had grasped little; of all those present, he alone appeared more dazed than I felt. I was strongly aware that though the holy oil was running down Shelemaiah's cheeks, it was his mother who would be wielding the sceptre.

I wasn't surprised that Adonai had kept me in the dark as regards the succession. I'd seldom seen things so specific in advance. A shrewd mind sharpened by cynicism was much more useful for making political predictions, or so my experience of life at Court had led me to believe.

Ahikam was shrewd, but he wasn't cynical, and as a result he found himself swiftly and thoroughly outmanoevred. Within a week of Shelemaiah's investiture, the composition of the governing Council had been radically altered, and all those members who might prove difficult to manipulate had been replaced. Among these were the venerable Shaphan, Ahikam's father, who had served as Secretary of State for more than thirty years. He was forced into retirement, along with the aged Akbor; it could have been argued that such elderly men ought to have retired from public life already.

But Ahikam himself, Josiah's Royal Steward, was by no means ready to relinquish his responsibilities. Neither was Joah the Recorder; yet both were summarily dismissed. Ahikam's younger brother Gemariah, co-opted more recently to Josiah's Council, retained his position, since he combined the intelligence of a Shaphanite with a certain tractability. Elnathan too held on to his post, because he deemed it his duty as a Minister of Government to do whatever the King required of him, whoever that King might be.

Of my own role, nothing was said. I received no invitation to appear before the new Sovereign, though I still believed that he bore me some affection. But Hamutal and the People of the Land ruled Judah now. I did wonder occasionally whether Hamutal would renew her advances towards me, but reckoned it unlikely. She had more important things to occupy her mind.

As the summer wore on, the Assyrians and their Egyptian allies made strenuous attempts to wrest Harran from Babylon's grip, but to no avail. Whether they would have succeeded had Josiah not impeded Necho's progress was any man's guess. As it was, ferocious battles were fought, in which the Pharaoh sustained further and heavier losses, but achieved nothing. The People of the Land rubbed their hands together in glee; the more the Egyptians wore themselves down in striving against Nabopolassar, the less damage they would be able to inflict upon Judah should they seek to punish her for Josiah's interference in their affairs.

Meanwhile the Babylonians and Medes were merrily portioning out Assyria's former possessions between themselves. Babylon had gained control of most of the Mesopotamian plain, and Media the hillier lands to the north. Our own northern territories remained untouched, but it could only be a matter of time.

Equally, it was only a matter of time before Josiah's reform programme fell into abeyance. Hamutal and the wealthy landowners who backed her worshipped Adonai in so far as they worshipped anything other than gold and power, but the landowners' professed aversion to Assyria's gods while Josiah had lived had been in reality nothing more than an aversion to Assyrian taxes, whilst Hamutal's abhorrence of the gods of Egypt was simply her hatred of Eliakim wrapped in a respectable guise.

Eliakim himself was keeping a distinctly low profile. I found this disturbing, and said as much to Ahikam. But he was far more concerned that the rural priests were returning to their villages, old sanctuaries were re-opening up and down the country, and once again the trappings of idolatry could be bought in Jerusalem's markets. Yet he was powerless to prevent the decadence from spreading.

Ahikam was a rare and precious jewel in Judah's crown: a polished product of the wisdom schools, but one whose devotion to the God of Moses was sincerely and deeply felt. Thus it was frankly beyond him to comprehend how other men could offer prayers but never truly pray, offer sacrifices yet never repent, and circumcize their sons but bring them up without the slightest notion of what it means to know Adonai.

Hence his dismay at finding idolatry so soon resurgent; he simply couldn't believe that it had never died. 'You only need look at things through the people's eyes, Ahikam,' I pointed out to him. 'Josiah's subjects have seen their righteous young ruler struck down by a pagan archer. If this is how Adonai rewards his servants for their piety, why should anyone bother to honour him? In the Book of the Law which Hilkiah found, it was promised that God would protect the faithful, but he has not kept his word. The people conclude that Adonai lies. Either that, or else he lacks the power to fulfil his obligations.'

'They cannot think such a thing!' objected Ahikam, fierce eyes blazing. 'Have they forgotten the exodus, when Adonai parted the waters to rescue them from slavery in Egypt, and drowned the charioteers who pursued them? What god could be more powerful than that?'

'Moses died long ago, Ahikam; Necho is very much alive. What evidence have those who fought with Josiah at Megiddo seen of Adonai's power? All they know is that things went well for them while they honoured the Baals. Then the sanctuaries closed, and disaster struck; it is the old gods' anger that frightens them.'

So the nation went on drifting back to its traditional ways. Smoke rose up once more from altars on the tops of hills and under spreading trees. Shrines were rebuilt, and a new generation of shrine-boys and girls found employment there. Even the Tophet was restored to its former use.

'Speak out against these things!' Ahikam exhorted me. 'Bring the word of Adonai to his people before it's too late!'

'It is too late already,' I reminded him. 'Besides: I speak to the people at the behest of Adonai alone. And he has spoken scarcely a word to me since the day Josiah died.'

'Then pray and fast until he does,' retorted Ahikam in frustration, but I shook my head, meaning: that's not the way my gifting works. What I ought to have meant was that I was wandering out in the wilderness, holding on for dear life to

Huldah's conviction that our highly unconventional relationship accorded with Adonai's will for our lives.

'Find someone else, Ahikam,' I counselled him wearily. 'Of all the so-called prophets at Court, you can surely find one who will stand up and say what you want him to say. It carries little risk; His Majesty and his mother care nothing about such matters, one way or the other.'

'Yes, there is one,' Ahikam conceded. 'There is one called Uriah who will stand and be counted; he would do so from the best of motives and regardless of the risk, and has done so already. But he's young, Jeremiah. The people do not hear him however loudly he shouts.'

'Exactly as they didn't hear *me* when I was young and impassioned and naive,' I observed with a wry smile; Ahikam sighed, and gave up the unequal struggle.

With midsummer past, attempts to recapture Harran were abandoned; Necho fell back to Riblah in Syria. Thence he proceeded to annex the northern territories of Israel.

And who could have blamed him? He had led the flower of Egypt's manhood far away from their homes, whither many of them would not return. It was imperative for him to salvage some small booty from the wreckage of this disastrous campaign. And what better than to bring Syria and Canaan back under Egyptian control, punishing Josiah posthumously into the bargain?

Amid the fear and despondency abroad in Jerusalem I detected the occasional gibe at my expense. Where is that meddling madman Jeremiah now? folk were asking. Skulking in a corner somewhere with his tail between his legs, perchance, because he bade us beware the foe from the north, when all the time it was our old adversary from the Nile whom we should have been wary of.

And so far from God had I wandered once again that deep down I was agreeing with them. I decided that I had deluded myself as thoroughly as I'd sought to delude my fellow-countrymen; recent events had exposed me for the charlatan I was.

The next time Huldah came to see me, I could keep my anxieties about our liaison a secret no longer. As I lay with my head in her lap she brushed the hair from my eyes and implored me, 'What has happened to you, Jeremiah? You used to tell me everything; we exposed our very souls to one another. But now...'

She broke off, reluctant to put into words what she knew would take an axe to the root of my being. I did nothing to encourage her; I merely flung my head to one side and she finished her sentence before pity got the better of her.

'... Now you're like a broken pot, Jeremiah. Whatever magic was inside has leaked away.'

I didn't respond. It was ending, I knew it; I felt like a boy who wakens from sleep on a beach and watches the approach of the wave that will drown him, yet he cannot escape it for his arms and legs are trapped beneath the sand which his so-called friends have piled upon him while he slept.

'Have you nothing to say even *now?*' she demanded, her voice unsteady because she too knew that we were finished. 'You're not what you were, Jeremiah. There was a fire in you, but it has gone out.' Then she covered her face with her hands because our predicament was hopeless. For as long as we remained together, our love, along with what made us both what we were, was doomed to wither. If we went our separate ways, saved our own souls, and fanned the sputtering flames of Adonai's fire inside us, we should each be irresistibly attracted to the glow of the divine within the other just as we had been in the beginning.

'Tell me that we haven't done wrong,' I beseeched her. 'Tell me that Adonai would welcome me back if I sought him, without things having to change; tell me he would let us go on being friends.' But I was clutching at straws. I knew full well what I had to do, and I had to do it now, before I brought Huldah down with me. If she had truly believed until this day that we'd been doing nothing sinful, then perhaps her conscience at least been clear. But she would be sinning indeed if she let things carry on as they were, now she knew the state of mine. This was what the circumcision of the heart was all about: not what you did, so much as why you did it, acting from pure motives, walking in open communion with God as Adam and Eve had done in the Garden of Eden, naked yet unashamed.

So I sat up straight and prepared to tell her: we could not go on, we must commit each other to Adonai's grace, and never exchange another word as long as we lived.

Would that I had done so. Would that my courage hadn't failed me in the instant of crisis, causing me to hanker after one last kiss, one final moment in the arms of someone who loved me. Would that she had been stronger than I. Instead, when Ahikam walked in, we were locked together in carnal embrace.

I recognized his footsteps at once when he entered, though I hadn't been aware of anyone knocking at the door. Fear turned me to stone in Huldah's arms. It was she who started, sprang back, and fled like a villain from the scene of his crime.

If only Ahikam had flown into a rage, or at least demanded an explanation for what he had witnessed. But he merely stared at me in disbelief, then retreated with his eyes still fixed on my face.

I called his name and begged him not to go away. I couldn't bear the thought of him quitting my presence imagining the worst. I listened to myself making all the pathetic excuses which a hundred thousand men must have made before me. It's not what you're thinking; please, wait, I can explain... Then I took refuge in incoherence, because none of it was true. There are more ways to commit adultery than by crude penetration. Of the latter I was indeed not guilty; of the former I was guilty on every count. Eventually my incoherence evolved into something like repentance. I poured out my confession to Ahikam even as he stood there incredulous, and I pleaded with him to accompany me to the Temple where I might make an offering to atone for my sin.

But he wouldn't listen. He kept saying that there was something he had to tell me.

'You don't need to,' I assured him. 'I know I've been a fool, and a hypocrite too. I know I should have confessed all this to you a long time ago, when you asked what was wrong between Josiah and me. Please; don't make me try to justify myself. I'm guilty, I admit it, I've failed yet again - '

'... Jeremiah? Jeremiah!' he shouted, and at last succeeded in breaking through. 'You don't understand. I can't go *anywhere* with you now - no I'm *not* ashamed to be seen with you! - I'm just trying to tell you why I came here. The Pharaoh has summoned His Majesty to appear before him in Riblah. If Jehoahaz refuses to go, Necho is threatening invasion, and this time he won't be marching *through* our territory. For God's sake, Jeremiah, I came here to ask you to *pray*, to seek guidance as to what the King should do.'

'No, Ahikam. Our day is past, Ahikam. This sort of thing can concern us no longer. You hold no office, and I am nothing; I am less than nothing - '

'And who else but us is going to seek the will of God in all this? Hamutal? The People of the Land? Jehoahaz himself? *Huldah*, perhaps?'

I snapped, 'How about Uriah? That was his name, was it not? Your bold young prophet who would stand and be counted, from the best of motives, and whatever the risk.'

'Is this a fitting time for sarcasm, for twisting my words as a scribe would? God have mercy! Judah's future is at stake.'

'Judah's future is already fixed.'

'But what can Necho want from our King? An oath of vassalage? Are we to become the Pharaoh's lackeys, in exactly the way that we used to be the Emperor's?'

'I neither know nor care. Nor could I find out for you even if I did. Adonai will not answer me now; not until I have made my offering. I have sinned against another human being, so I must confess my guilt, repent of it, and atone for it before men, as well as before God.'

'You have made your confession to me, confound you! Is that not sufficient?'

'Perhaps,' I answered vaguely, but secretly I was thinking: perhaps I haven't repented at all. I spewed out my guilt to you only because you caught me red-handed. Had you not come in when you did, I might have been here with Huldah still.

He left my apartment in disgust, though I was barely conscious of his going, nor was I any longer interested in what he must be thinking of me. I didn't even care if he told the whole world what he'd seen. I cared about nothing and no one but Huldah, who would never hold me in her arms again.

However, before the week was out, I had no alternative but to pay attention to what was going on in the world outside my chambers. I learned from Ebed-Melech that our trusting young King had presented himself to the Pharaoh as requested - and promptly been imprisoned at Riblah. A substantial fine had been imposed upon Judah for obstructing Necho's campaign, and Jehoahaz was being held as guarantee of its payment. No promise had been given as to when, or if, he would be freed; only that he would be put to death without compunction if the fine were not paid within the stipulated time.

And even if he did eventually regain his freedom, it would not be as king that he returned to the land of his fathers. For Eliakim had been invested in his stead at the Pharaoh's behest, the young prophet Uriah having been compelled to perform the anointing. Eliakim had taken the throne-name Jehoiakim: 'Adonai has established'. An irony if ever there was one.

Judah's independence had lasted precisely twenty years. We had indeed gone back to Egypt, undoing what Moses had accomplished, for Jehoiakim was the Pharaoh's lackey and proud of it. Though I hadn't been present in person, I learned that for his coronation he had painted his eyes and shaved his face smooth as a eunuch's, and bound up his hair beneath a great black wig. Yet I didn't grasp the full significance of what had come to pass, nor quite how dangerous my former pupil had become, until Hamutal, the exiled Jehoahaz's mother, materialized distraught upon my threshold.

I let her in, though I knew there would be nothing I could do to help her. She must have known it too, unless she was among those who imagined that I was able to work miracles. From her I learned that Eliakim had been intriguing with Egypt ever since her son had deprived him of his inheritance. If Necho would restore to him his birthright, nothing would please Eliakim more than to swear fealty to his champion, and present him with whatever annual tribute he might request. Necho had been only too happy to oblige; a compliant monarch on Judah's throne must have been one of his dreams come true.

'Surely you cannot condone all this?' Hamutal challenged me. 'Egypt has been the enemy of Adonai's people since time immemorial; there can be no consorting with the nation which made us slaves. Eliakim - Jehoiakim - has sacrificed our liberty to his own ambition.'

I shrugged my shoulders, inclined to suppose that she was right, yet only too aware that this was a crime of which Hamutal herself had been guilty. Still, I was utterly unqualified to speak for Adonai on the subject. Excepting when he'd blessed me with the words and music for Josiah's lament, we had enjoyed no communication for months. On a merely human level I was convinced that Eliakim-Jehoiakim was sailing perilously close to the wind, embroiling himself in a power struggle which was set to shake the foundations of half the world. If we had to ally ourselves with any of the prospective combatants, we should have been wiser to choose Babylon.

'I'll be parted from my son for ever,' Hamutal wailed, wringing her hands. 'What has got into you, Jeremiah? You used to teach him, you know how kind and gentle he is; Eliakim has never cared for anyone but himself. What's to become of us, with a villain for a king? What's to become of *you*, for Heaven's sake? He hates you; had you forgotten? Poor Shelemaiah. Supposing they torture him?'

She burst into tears, lowering herself onto the nearest couch. I just stood there looking on; did she want me to take her in my arms and let her cry on my shoulder? Was that what I ought to do? what I wanted to do? She was a beautiful woman, and unlike Huldah, she no longer had a husband.

But I didn't do it. It was Huldah I loved, Huldah I needed, Huldah's face I saw in my dreams when I managed to sleep. I was nursing a hopeless, twisted fidelity towards a woman who was someone else's wife.

As things turned out, I never had to decide what was to be done about Jehoiakim's accession. This was because he decided, all too swiftly, what was to be done about me.

I suppose I was luckier than some. The leaders of the party of the People of the Land were rounded up by night and put to the sword.

At first I was loath to believe it. These men had been venerable elders: rich, respectable heads of ancient families. But I had not yet sounded the depths to which Jehoiakim would sink in order to render his royal status secure.

Nor was I troubled for long with regard to the intentions of Hamutal. She who had once been suspected of poisoning the unhappy Johanan was found in her room choked to death on her own vomit, with spilled wine spread out around her like a lake of blood on the floor. Poison or surfeit of alcohol? Murder or suicide, or simply a tragic accident? We never found out, but I held myself largely to blame.

To pay the fine which Necho had demanded, crippling taxes were imposed upon the whole population. Objections were raised by certain members of the Governing Council; these men were summarily imprisoned, to be replaced by sycophants on whom Jehoiakim could rely to indulge his every whim without question. Thus the composition of the Council was altered all over again.

Yet contrary to widespread expectation, not every officer of Jehoahaz's was divested of his duties. Jehoiakim was shrewd enough to realize that as well as toadies to do his bidding he needed men of experience to offer him prudent counsel. Thus Gemariah, second son of Shaphan, remained in office, as did Elnathan - this latter, of course, being father-in-law of the King. But the Secretary of State was now an appointee of Jehoiakim, a man of royal blood by the name of Elishama. Delaiah the Steward was newly appointed too, as was Zedekiah ben Hananiah the Recorder. All three favoured Egypt, in dress as well as in political persuasion.

A mere fortnight after ascending the throne, Jehoiakim set about dealing with me.

Perhaps I should have been flattered that he'd singled me out so soon for individual attention, when I hadn't done anything to warrant it. Certainly I'd done nothing to deserve a personal visit from His Majesty himself.

He came at dawn, without warning, an impressive detachment of his bodyguard in tow. They hammered on my door with the butts of their spears; when I didn't come running, they smashed it to pieces and dragged me from my bed. I hardly knew what was being done to me, and tried only feebly to protest. I was promptly kicked in the stomach; gasping and groaning I hung in the arms of my assailants, head fallen forward, eyes seeing nothing but hair and the lurching floor. Then the shaft of some weapon went under my chin and forced it aloft, while brutal hands grabbed my hair from behind. Through watering eyes I found myself beholding the face of my King.

In the alignment of his features Eliakim was unmistakeably Josiah's son. Such strength, such symmetry, such aquiline, blue-blooded beauty... Yet his lovely, kohl-painted eyes were cold as they were compelling, the angle of his close-shaven jawline was arrogant and pitiless, and his heavy Egyptian wig so black, so lustrous, so horribly alien, I couldn't bear to look at him. My vision hazed over, then failed me altogether; half asleep and half fainting I half heard him mocking me, cursing me calmly with exquisitely disdainful wisdom-school eloquence.

'Lo, the arch-ambassador of Adonai!' he was crowing, whilst prodding my belly with the knob of his sceptre. 'See how his God has shielded him from harm!' - and he jerked one knee into my groin - 'See how the hosts of Heaven come swooping down to his aid.' Then he kissed my slackened mouth and whispered, 'Ah, the honeyed lips from which the word of God once dripped like venomous dew. What is your God saying now, O serpent of the silver tongue? Strange, is it not, that the boy who refused to be taught has proven himself cleverest of all, has outlived or outwitted his every rival, and claimed the prize of which he alone has been worthy from the beginning?'

In due course he tired of his play, and began barking orders at his henchmen. My paltry possessions were thrown into my coffer, including my lyre and Hosea's scroll, the only things of value that I owned. The chest was then hauled through the doorway, but just as the guards were making to throw me out as well, Ebed-Melech arrived from the kitchens bringing my breakfast.

He saw at a glance what was happening. Dropping his tray on the floor, he attacked the guards who held me, kicking and punching, telling them to leave me in peace: I'd done no one any harm, I'd been invited to live at the palace and assigned my own apartment there by the blessed Josiah himself.

'Josiah's *son* is king here now,' he was reminded, and when he continued to struggle he was knocked to the ground with a single idle blow.

'Now get back to the cookhouse where you belong, you gelded black bastard,' they ordered him. And they drove him away on all fours, poking their spears between his legs. Then I was thrown out after him.

Ahikam found me some while later, draped across the lid of my coffer. He had me conveyed to his house in the city, of which he promised me sole use for as long as he and his wife and son were permitted to retain their apartment at the palace. He also promised to visit, and to bring me a weekly allowance for my expenses; I barely said thank you, and wished he hadn't bothered.

'Don't you know you'd be *dead* by now if it weren't for Nehushta?' he berated me. 'You should thank the God who loves you that Jehoiakim's wife is not like he is, and that her son Jeconiah remembers you for Shelemaiah's sake, and begged his mother not to let you be harmed.'

I was dimly interested to learn why I wasn't dead. But I didn't thank God, any more than I thanked Ahikam. Adonai had cast me out, leaving me without protection at the mercy of my cousin and my father, whose wrath I feared more than that of the King. And he'd brought me to a place where I should certainly never see Huldah again.

CHAPTER 13: HILKIAH

Many people have asked me how a father could grow to hate his own son enough to want him dead. But when that son has broken his mother's heart, disgraced his family and undermined your whole life's work into the bargain, you become capable of anything. By the time my nephew sought to involve me in the plot he was hatching, I'd written off my firstborn as dead already.

They'd come by night to destroy the holy place which had been my life - a rabble of adolescent soldiers, with a captain who was little more than a boy himself. They cared not a jot about Josiah or his Law Book or reviving the religion of the exodus. They'd come to wreak havoc, and that was what they did, relishing every moment of it. They smashed the sacred images and turned the Asherah pole into a pillar of fire. They scattered the votive offerings placed in the shrine by simple-hearted suppliants, grinding honey cakes and bunches of flowers under their boots. They threw excrement on the altars and helped themselves to the gold and silver in the storerooms. At least they didn't kill anyone, and I've heard men say we should have been thankful. But that is like thanking the thief who stole your ox, because he was kind enough not to steal your ass as well.

In the morning I wept without shame at the scene of desolation which dawn had revealed. It wasn't just that the beauty of the place had been violated, and priceless artefacts stolen or wrecked. Worse by far was what it all symbolized to those who are able to discern the meaning of such things.

For we had witnessed the scorning of the very values which Anathoth stood for: enlightenment, tolerance, mutual understanding. Devotees of Adonai or the Baals, Judeans and Canaanites alike... all of them had been wont to come to us, each individual free to offer up petitions to Heaven in his or her own way. At Anathoth we had freed ourselves from bondage to the past: to bigotry and thou-shalt-nots going back to the time of Moses. There may indeed have been a place for rigid rules and regulations when our forefathers were ignorant nomads wandering in the desert, but now, they had served their purpose.

When I myself entered the priesthood, we'd been living alongside the Earth Folk of Canaan for four hundred years. Those of us who could claim to be civilized had long been saying that the time was ripe for us to put our differences behind us. We had come of age; there was no longer any need for our God to treat us like naughty children, threatening fire and brimstone at the slightest hint of heresy. When your son is an infant, you punish him for going too close to the hearth, but not when he has fathered sons of his own. Only a foolish parent attempts to prevent his offspring from growing up. Nowadays Adonai can afford to loosen our fetters, to reveal to us his mercy and his love instead of chastising us.

Granted, our society still has its faults. There is still injustice, the weak are still exploited by the strong, there are still widows and orphans living in terrible poverty and squalor. But such evils have always existed, and always will. Surely it profits us nothing to coerce people into charity, painting them pictures of their God as a slave-driver cracking a whip? Which is better, to do good deeds out of fear, or out of compassion? Who would praise the goodness of a child who only behaves when his father stands over him with a cane?

Certainly the last thing our nation requires is the resurgence of antiquated, hidebound legalism. But that is what we got, embodied in the person of Josiah - and fostered by one who was flesh of my flesh.

His mother and I had been so happy the day he was born. Our first child, and a boy... our hopes for him couldn't have been higher. Jeremiah, we named him, 'The Lord exalts' and I dreamed that one day he would follow me into the priesthood. My wife looked forward to the day when he himself would take a bride, and beget sons, and rule a household of his own. Later he would support us both when old age thinned our blood; the smiles and laughter of grandchildren would fill our autumn years with mellow sunshine. My wife's dreams and mine could all have come true, and ought to have done so.

But almost as soon as Jeremiah could talk, we began to be anxious. He had the religious instinct right enough, yet it seemed somehow warped inside him, causing him to say peculiar things and ask strange questions, some of which I knew not how to answer. He turned up his infant nose at the customs and beliefs of his elders. He took to dreaming by day as well as by night, losing all touch with the world and the people around him, forgetting what he was supposed to be doing, and dropping holy vessels on the floor. His eyes would drift, or stare like a corpse's; sometimes they looked right through you, other times straight to the innermost depths of your being. Little wonder that other boys shunned him, his own two brothers refused to share his bed, and even the mother who had borne him grew scared of the thing she'd brought forth.

And that voice! Of all his eccentricities, the voice he claimed to hear was the worst. Nonsense, we said, of course there is no one who speaks to you when you stand in an empty room or alone at the shrine, or when you walk on the edge of the desert at sunset. It's the beating of your heart, or the lowing of cattle in the fields, or the soughing of the summer wind. When he insisted on its being a voice, I commanded him never to mention it again, and I thought with grim satisfaction: once he gets no more attention from his endless harping on the subject, whatever it is will quickly let him alone.

Imagine my dismay, therefore, when its babblings prevented him from wedding the girl to whom he had pledged his troth, and then caused him to reject his vocation as a priest. I was beside myself, not least because I found myself morally obliged to provide for Ruth and her grandmother until another husband could be found; Hanamel my nephew did me a great favour by taking them off my hands. When Jeremiah crowned it all by announcing that he intended to go to Jerusalem and offer his services to a snivelling scion of Solomon, I could have strangled him on the spot. Had it not been for Solomon, my own family would still be living in Zion's city, and from our ranks all the senior priests would have been drawn. Ironic it is that the High Priest's mantle is worn today by one Hilkiah, a man with the same name as me. It should have been mine.

My firstborn son had spat upon every last thing he'd been brought up to value, and he'd treated his own parents like the dirt beneath his feet. I could find no other explanation save that Jeremiah was insane, or else possessed by devils, and had been so from birth.

So when Hanamel first disclosed to me that the desire of his heart was to silence Jeremiah for good, I raised no objection. The pernicious turncoat had been roaming the countryside drumming up support for his Sovereign's reactionary reforms - God alone knows who penned that Book of the Law which was 'found' in the Temple: Josiah himself, I shouldn't wonder, so opportune was its discovery - thus it wasn't so very difficult for my nephew to ascertain where and when he would be preaching. When the ambush was being planned, I'm not convinced that Hanamel had resolved upon Jeremiah's death. He might well have been content with cutting out his victim's venomous tongue. But the royal guards were so quick; Hanamel's son had his belly ripped open like a lamb got ready for stuffing, and from that moment on, Hanamel himself had no other goal in life than to tear Jeremiah limb from limb.

Yet even in his frenzy, he knew it would be reckless and fruitless to mount a second attack straight away. For a while he and his comrades had to go into hiding, until we learned of the rift which had opened between Jeremiah and the King. After this they felt safe to come out; but Jeremiah did not. He remained cocooned in the palace, concerned to preserve his own skin. Up to a point, therefore, the ambush had succeeded. Jeremiah was silenced, at least for the present.

There were those who took it upon themselves to point this out to my nephew. He'd done what he'd set out to do; wasn't that enough? But Hanamel wouldn't listen. The way he saw it, he hadn't even got his revenge as yet for what had happened up at the high place when at fourteen years of age Jeremiah had humiliated him in front of his friends. Hanamel had been so angry that night at the way his whole plan had miscarried, and so jealous, because what had come out of it was Jeremiah's betrothal to the very girl he'd been incited to abuse. Hanamel had won her in the end, but he was jealous still, suspecting that Ruth had loved her childhood sweetheart in a way she would never love him, the man she had married.

Hanamel resigned himself to having to wait a very long time to exact his revenge in the way that he wanted to. Then out of the blue came Pharaoh's request to pass through Josiah's domains, and the latter's refusal; and the next thing we knew, the accursed King was dead.

What rejoicing there was in Anathoth on the day the news broke! While Jerusalem mourned, my kinsfolk and I ate and drank and were merry. It could only be a matter of time before the former balance of things was restored, and the damage done by Josiah could be repaired. Jehoahaz came to the throne; and almost at once was replaced by Jehoiakim. Even better, for us and for our cause; now we had only to be patient, and wait for Jeremiah's inevitable expulsion from the palace. Hanamel took to visiting the city almost daily, to find out whether this had yet happened, and, if so, where the outcast was living.

Not very long after Jehoiakim's enthronement, Hanamel came to tell me that the time was ripe. I hadn't spared Jeremiah much thought, of late; I'd been too busy getting things ready for the official reopening of the sanctuary. The new King's reign was already bringing changes. The restoration of the sanctuaries promised a corresponding restoration of prosperity for the towns and villages they served. It was true that Jehoiakim had begun to take back in taxes much of what his father's death had bought for us, but surely it was better to pay Necho's fine than to have him invade, and lay waste our fields and demolish the walls of our cities.

However, it didn't take long for the truth to emerge: only a small percentage of what we were paying was going to placate the Pharaoh. The rest was being funnelled directly into the King's personal treasury, for the embellishment of his palace in the city and the building of two new ones. One of these was to be constructed a little way south, on a low pine-clad hill whither the King could repair whenever the pressures of urban life proved too much for him. The other was planned for Mizpah in the uplands to the north; this would be for summer, when the cooling mountain breezes would bring him relief from the heat.

Work on these projects duly commenced. Peasant farmers would pause from their labours and watch as their taxes were converted into mansions of ashlar masonry, with balustraded windows whose delicate limestone columns had capitals carved into petals, and whose rooms were plastered in vermilion. If Josiah had fancied himself another David, Jehoiakim was a second Solomon, concerned that the degree of luxury in which he lived should adequately reflect his exalted status.

He emulated Solomon in his pursuit of wisdom, also - in the sense that he surrounded himself with a host of expert scribes and teachers from the wisdom schools with whom he could engage in clever debate and the splitting of hairs. Some of these were native to Judah; others were Egyptians, and made no secret of the fact.

Unpopular as all this began to make him, there was something else about Jehoiakim which was still more fiercely resented. Once again taking Solomon as his example, our new king resorted to the employment of forced labour in order to get his architectural ambitions realized. Freeborn sons of Judah were bludgeoned into working for negligible pay, breaking up stones and laying them one upon another as their ancestors had done in Egypt. Meanwhile the lord whom they served strutted about like a peacock, blinking his kohl-lidded eyes down the length of his perfect nose, swirling his cloak and puffing up his chest, which was shaven smooth and usually naked save for a gleaming layer of perfumed oil, and the heavy jewelry he wore around his neck.

Those who knew about such things were saying that he dressed like the Pharaoh himself; I suppose he did it so that Necho would think him cultured and deferential, and the stratagem worked. He was left to rule over his father's kingdom without interference, and his subjects swiftly learned that it wasn't wise to speak out against him.

Even when he started to confiscate land in order that his own estates might be enlarged, few cries of protest were heard. The first farms he took over had belonged to his political opponents, all of whom he had put to death. But when the revenues of these proved insufficient, he appropriated land from men who were still very much alive. Rich or poor, our covetous King didn't care - he robbed all and sundry without discrimination. His victims fell into debt, and their creditors seized the revenue from whatever meagre lands had been left to them.

Yet still his avarice went unchallenged. At the sanctuary I heard folk muttering in ones and twos with those whom they trusted: where is Jeremiah now? Why does he who was once God's mouthpiece not cry out against the injustice we all see around us? In the days of Josiah, when more was right than wrong, the Prophet condemned the least departure from Adonai's narrow way. Nowadays when everything is wrong, he keeps his silence.

When I heard them speak like this, I kept my silence too. I thought: at Jehoiakim's accession you hailed him as your liberator, yet already you pine for his father. Why must Jehoiakim be so greedy? Shall we never be ruled by a man who is neither bigotted nor rapacious? Surely it cannot be true that every man is either in thrall to Adonai, or else a slave to his own conceit?

Then I would scold myself, and remember to be grateful for what was ours once again, instead of wishing for the impossible. Freedom of religion had been restored; once again pilgrims of every persuasion converged upon Anathoth's shrine; Canaanite, Assyrian and now Egyptian beliefs were embraced there. Among the votive figurines and the fetishes which suppliants left behind, we began to find some with animals' heads, or beaks like birds'; we began to hear the Goddess addressed as Isis or Hat-Hor.

Indeed, it was rumoured that even in the Temple in Jerusalem, likenesses of animal-gods had been painted on the walls in secret rooms, for the conduct of Egyptian rituals. Hanamel assured me that this was true; he'd had it from the lips of Jaazaniah ben Shaphan who had worshipped there himself. I couldn't help but smile when he told me; Shaphan had been Court Secretary under Josiah, and the most obdurate of all who supported his reforms. How gratifying it was to discover that one of his own dear sons had burst through the bonds of his fettered and reactionary upbringing.

But I'm rushing ahead. When Hanamel came to tell me that my own son's time had run out, the true character of Jehoiakim's reign was still to be made manifest. Hanamel couldn't have cared less about it, in any case, for the only thing which interested him was the fact that Jeremiah was now at our mercy. He was living alone at a house in the city, with no wife, no servant, no companion.

'This may be our best chance!' Hanamel enthused, eyes ablaze. 'Fate has played into our hands; let us strike now! Will you help us, Uncle? Are you prepared to sanction your son's execution?'

'To *sanction* it? I am prepared to wield the knife that kills him,' I growled; and Hanamel seized me by the hand, then embraced me.

That night we gathered in Hanamel's home: Hanamel and myself, my other two sons and a number of our kinsmen and friends. This time no boys would be involved, only men - men who had trained with weapons and were not afraid to use them.

'I know exactly where the house is,' Hanamel told us. 'I've watched it. He hardly ever goes out, and never after dark. It will be simplicity itself for us to break in at night and cut his throat, and be back home in Anathoth before the crime is even discovered.'

'Shall we not be apprehended and detained the moment we set foot in Jerusalem?' someone asked. 'We may be recognized by the guards at the city gates.'

'And who is going to give orders for our arrest? Not His Majesty, that's for sure. If he found out that we intended to send this resurrected Samuel back to Sheol where he belongs, he would probably pay us to do it. But don't worry; we'll take no chances. He won't find out.'

'How shall we enter the city?' someone else wanted to know. 'The gates are closed at dusk. Are we all to stroll in together in broad daylight, bristling with weapons?'

Hanamel shook his head, gesturing for us to muffle our voices. 'I have it all worked out,' he said. 'We enter the city by day, but not together, and not bearing arms. My friend Jaazaniah has promised us the use of his house, and the loan of as many knives as we need. We'll meet up there, collect the weapons, and wait in the house till it's dark enough to get the deed done. We shan't risk going back to Jaazaniah's afterwards; we'll spend the rest of the night as Ahikam's guests. Once the streets are full of people, we'll leave in ones and twos and mingle with the crowd, then walk out through the city gates the way we came in.'

For several moments we all sat in silence, regarding each other's faces in the lamplight. Then one of the younger men shook his head and said: 'It all sounds too simple. Something is bound to go wrong. This Jaazaniah will betray us.'

'Nothing will go wrong!' Hanamel snapped. 'Why construct something elaborate when simplicity will suffice? Simple solutions are *elegant*, Nathanael, and there is less about them which *can* go wrong.'

The young man sighed despondently. 'I don't know, Hanamel. I don't like the sound of it, or the feeling it gives me in my stomach.'

'Who gives a mouldy husk for what there is in your stomach? Are you with us or are you not? Because if you back out of this now, if *anyone* backs out now...'

'You don't need to threaten us,' I said quietly. 'Every last one of us will stand by you, I'll see to that. Now when do we put this plan into action? Next week, perhaps? Could we be ready that soon?'

Another silence followed; then Hanamel answered evenly, 'Every day that passes involves us in unnecessary risk. One of us will make a mistake. Or the pressure will become too great, and someone will crack.' Casting his eyes in Nathanael's direction, he took an ominous breath and concluded, 'It's all set up for tomorrow. We leave for Jerusalem at dawn.'

Audible gasps arose from around our circle. Then from outside it came an almighty crash as a tray of crockery fell to the ground.

So intent had we been upon our scheming that none of us had been aware of Ruth entering the room. She must have brought us all wine, for it spilled from the broken goblets and ran between us, seeping into the earthen floor and collecting in its cracks so they looked like patterns of veins. Then Ruth herself broke into our ring and knelt at her husband's feet.

She was too distraught for many of her words to be clear, but no one could be in any doubt as to what she meant as she pressed his feet against her cheek, and kissed them, and bathed them in her tears. For as long as Hanamel had railed against Jeremiah in rabid impotence, she had let him rail on, and even echoed the hatred he expressed toward the one who had forsaken her and caused the death of her son. Now her feelings had changed.

Not that she professed any concern for Jeremiah. She said what so many others had said already: 'Don't go to Jerusalem, I beg you. We shall never see you again.' And then: 'Oh, my lord, please stay here with me and help me raise our daughters, and, if Heaven is gracious, give me another son to take the place of the one who was lost.'

But Hanamel must have known well enough what she was really saying. For why else would he have kicked her and sent her sprawling, to lie there mortified while a dozen scandalized men glared down at her in her indignity?

At dawn the following day we readied ourselves to travel, and in ones and twos, some with animals and some without, some with baggage and others with none, we made our way to Jerusalem.

To begin with, things couldn't have gone better. Not one of us was challenged at the city gates. We assembled at the house of Jaazaniah in accordance with Hanamel's directions; Jaazaniah's cooks plied us with food, and Jaazaniah himself divulged to us the pleasure which he personally would derive from the death of my son. 'If Jeremiah's gifting were truly divine,' Jaazaniah said, 'He would know that I am no religious dupe like my brothers, and that my father's pathetic devotion to Adonai makes me sick. The only reason I have to be grateful to the old fool is that he gave me the finest education money can buy. Nor has his investment gone to waste; His Majesty King Jehoiakim has already paid it back to me a hundredfold in recognition of my services to wisdom.' And as if to reinforce his meaning, he began to toy with the golden rings on his fingers so that their great flawless stones caught the light.

At dead of night we received the weapons which Jaazaniah had promised us, and concealed them among our garments. We each took a lighted torch with a pot upturned on top of it and made our way by a variety of different routes to the house where Jeremiah was living.

I was with Hanamel himself, and we were the first pair to arrive. Hanamel climbed the courtyard wall with a burglar's ease , springing lightly down on the other side and drawing back the bolt on the gate. Once our companions were gathered inside, he closed the gate and bolted it as before. We now had all the time we needed in which to find the room where our defenceless victim slept alone, blissfully unaware that whatever dream he was having would be his last. We brought out our torches and slipped our daggers through our belts, whence we could draw them quickly. Then we prepared to search the house.

We scoured the place from top to bottom, checking behind every door and jabbing our knives through every curtain, wrenching the lid from every chest and even tearing the panels from the walls. But Jeremiah was nowhere to be found. We split up into pairs again and searched a second time, and a third - all to no avail. We reconvened in what appeared to be his bedroom and admitted defeat: Jeremiah was not at home.

'I don't believe it!' Hanamel shouted, carving the air with his knife to vent his fury. 'He's *never* away from the house at night, and the confounded gate was bolted. We shall pull this place apart until we find him.' And he threw himself on the ground, hacking at the floor as though he believed that Jeremiah might be lying hidden beneath our very feet.

'Keep your voice down!' I hissed at him. 'Do you want the city watchmen to hear us? He isn't here. We've looked everywhere.'

'Then he must have known we were coming. We have been betrayed. One of you is a traitor!'

He leaped to his feet again and seized hold of Nathanael, locking an arm about his throat. 'You!' he screamed. 'You vermin! You gave us away, and don't pretend you didn't. You'll pay with your last drop of blood for this, I swear it.'

He might very well have done so, had not several of us succeeded in dragging the two of them apart. Even as it was, Nathanael had acquired a deep cut in his cheek joining nose to ear, from which he was bleeding profusely. A couple of his rescuers had also felt the kiss of Hanamel's blade. They staunched one another's wounds as best they could while I saw to Nathanael, who was green with shock. In the meantime Hanamel had thrown down his knife on the floor, where he crouched and carried on like a spoilt child who for once has not got his way.

And indeed, at this point his cherished plan was abandoned, for we had no other choice. We extinguished our torches and returned to the house of Jaazaniah by night, just as we had come. His slaves cleaned us up and dressed our wounds, and the blood was washed away; but the stain of Hanamel's shame was not. Somehow his demonized cousin had made a fool of him yet again.

CHAPTER 14: JEREMIAH

I

I had gone to bed early, as usual. Ever since my expulsion from the palace I'd been retiring early and rising late, though when I did lie down I seldom slept. I seldom ate, either, except when Ahikam visited, and made me. I existed on the wine from his cellars.

That particular night I'd slept like a stone, until the moment when I awoke with a start and sat up, my heart pounding against my ribs. I stared and stared into the thick darkness, but saw nothing; I strained my ears, but heard no sound. Then suddenly my voice spoke through the stillness with perfect clarity. *Get up, Jeremiah. Dress and leave the house. There is no time to lose.*

I tried to ignore it. I'd experienced nothing the like of this since receiving the lament for Josiah, and not for months before that. I was less sure than I'd ever been that the voice was coming from outside of me, that it wasn't the product of my increasingly addled mind.

But when I lay down once again, it became more insistent. *Get up, you stubborn fool, or are you deaf now, as well as disobedient? Get up and go. Do it now.*

'Go?' I repeated. 'Go where? What's wrong? I don't understand.'

No, said the voice, *you rarely do. But if you don't leave now, you'll die.*

For so very long I hadn't cared if I died or lived. I existed in a daze, one day following the last in drunken monotony: loveless, restless, purposeless, endless. Suddenly, when death seemed for some unaccountable reason to be staring me in the face, I found that I badly wanted to live.

So I threw on my clothes, wrapped a blanket about my shoulders - we were well into autumn - and made to do as I'd been bidden. I crossed the moonlit courtyard and started to draw back the bolt of the gate, but my voice said: *No. Climb the wall. Let your enemies think you are here, then they will lose time searching for you.*

I still had no idea where to go. So few of my friends had houses outside of the palace which weren't let to strangers. There was Huldah, of course. But the suburb where she and Shallum lived was a long way off, and even had it been closer, I should not have dared go to her. There was only Jaazaniah, the youngest of Shaphan's sons; I knew him less well than his brothers, but reckoned he wouldn't resent my calling upon him in an hour of need.

So I was surprised when my purpose was thwarted. I couldn't take a single step in the direction of his home without pains shooting up my legs as though I trod on broken glass. So I simply drew my blanket around me and went to the gates of the Temple where the beggars slept. I bedded down amongst them, and some reeking, lousy old starveling snuggled against me for warmth.

At daybreak I extracted myself from his embrace, and picked my way among his twitching fellows, wanting to be back home before it was light enough for anyone to recognize me. I sensed no inner resistance, so I knew that the danger was past.

But danger there had certainly been. On returning to Ahikam's house I discovered the gate to the street wide open. There were splashes of blood in the courtyard, and leading into the house itself. Here, curtains had been pulled down along with their fittings, huge panels of cedar-wood had been torn away from the walls, and cupboard doors hung off their hinges. Upturned chests had spewed their contents across the floor; my possessions were all mixed up with the things which Ahikam and his family kept in storage. Among them was my lyre, which miraculously was undamaged. Hosea's scroll was also intact.

Then I found something which was neither mine nor Ahikam's. Lying in the middle of the floor in my bedroom was a blood-stained Egyptian dagger.

There was no mistaking the place of its origin, so distinctive was the style of its craftsmanship: the slender symmetry of the blade, the hilt with its inlays of enamel and its sleek and deadly beauty.

But what did its presence imply? Had Jehoiakim decided to have me assassinated after all? I went closer to the dagger to examine it; I picked it up and turned it over in my hands. That was when I saw the mark of ownership etched into the blade. The knife belonged to Jaazaniah.

I couldn't believe it. I stood transfixed, my hands trembling so violently that the appalling thing I was holding fell to the ground and embedded itself in the floor. From disbelief I passed through self-pity to fulminating rage. Jaazaniah had known me for years and never uttered a single word against me in my hearing. Suddenly I knew exactly how Hanamel had learnt in advance of my movements and thus planned the ambush on the road to Arad.

The depression from which I'd long been suffering vanished like mist in a gale. I was a cymbal whose damper has been removed; a dreamer awoken from a sleep of a hundred years. I seized the knife in my hands and implored Adonai to grant me revenge upon those who had conspired to seek my life. I'd been like Isaac led to the mountain of sacrifice, utterly unaware that a man whom I'd trusted was preparing to betray me to villains who had loathed me from childhood. For I was certain that the malevolent intruders had been none other than my cousin Hanamel and his boot-licking cronies, and I could well believe that my father might have been with them. I hated them; I hated them all, with a hatred so ferocious I could have snapped every one of their necks with my own bare hands.

Then my rage was engulfed by a tide of contrition. I fell to the floor and sobbed out my thanks to Adonai that he'd seen fit to protect me from harm in spite of my stupidity. I'd purposely shut him out of my life for so long, I had forgotten what it was like to feel myself enfolded in the warmth of his wings, or borne aloft by them and soaring, soaring, never wanting to return to earth again.

But I felt all that now. I lay on my back in the mess of blood which might so easily have been my own, and went into ecstasy, laughing and crying and worshipping all together. And Adonai said to me: *I shall* punish your enemies, Jeremiah. *Anathoth's suffering will be such that what Josiah did there will pale into insignificance. Her young men will be killed in war; her women and children will starve. I have appointed a day of reckoning for all her inhabitants, and none will escape the disaster which awaits them.*

Abruptly I came to myself, as the image of a young child's face swam up before my eyes: a girl, with matted hair and an empty bowl in her outstretched hands. Oh God, I thought, oh God, what have I prayed?

'Is there no justice in this world?' I found myself yelling, hauling myself to my knees and then to my feet. 'Must the innocent always suffer with the guilty? How long must *I* endure humiliation, how long must *I* go in fear for my life?'

Ah, Jeremiah, Jeremiah, Adonai replied, so gently and yet so sadly. *Things must become much worse before they get better. If you stumble and fall in safe country, how will you cope in the thickets by the Jordan?*

'The thickets by the Jordan? What thickets?' I tried to ask, but the voice of God went on regardless: *If you expire in the race against men, how will you race against horses? I shall uproot the wicked, I shall bring to ruin the proud and the violent, and those individuals and nations which persist in doing evil. But I shall draw to salvation all who renounce their Baals and their Ashtoreths and walk in my ways. And you, Jeremiah, you too must put rebelliousness behind you. You must put Ruth behind you. Most of all you must put Huldah behind you.*

Once more contrition felled me. 'I know, I know,' I sobbed, prostrate now on the bloody floor. 'I should have known better than to let her lead us both into sin... Please, let me see her just once, to beg her forgiveness.'

She has forgiven you already, Jeremiah. There is no need for you to see her. I know the weakness of your resolve, and the strength of your feelings, and I know that Huldah

He spoke the truth, of course. I confessed it, and all of the sin I had committed in Huldah's regard; and when it was gone, I fell into ecstasy again. Adonai's love poured into my thirsting spirit like the rain which brings life to the desert - so rare, so precious - making green the dusty trees and swelling the seeds which have patiently waited for its falling. When I came round I thought: if only I could spend all my life on the peak of this mountain, and never again have to grovel in the valley of despair.

Yet I knew now that I was wishing for the moon, because this was part of my nature too: to tread the clouds with winged sandals for a day or a week or a month, then to plunge into the mire. As I grew older, it would only get worse: the peaks would be higher but harder to climb, and the valleys deeper and dark as Sheol. I was a prophet, and more than a prophet, and had been what I was from birth, blessed and cursed both at once, gifted and damaged, knit together in my mother's womb in such a way that some part of me would always be fraying, unravelling here whilst growing there. I was what I was, and would be so for ever, till there was nothing left of me.

When my repentance was done, Adonai began to remind me of the truth about Judah also, namely that the work of Josiah was crumbling. Soon it would subside into its riddled foundations, and Judah would have nothing left with which to protect herself against the consequences of Manasseh's apostasy. The poor and oppressed had no one to plead for them, and listened in vain for the message of their God to console them, because I who should have been their advocate and the scourge of their oppressors had chosen to mope in my room like a jilted suitor.

So I repented of all this too, and as the guilt departed, my every sense became charged with the resentment against Jehoiakim which seethed beneath the surface at every level of

Judean society. I could hear the stifled cries of the suffering, and see their tortured faces in the shadows of the plasterwork on Ahikam's ceiling. In my nostrils their smothered anger smelled acrid, and in my mouth was the salt of their tears. I knew there was only one way to recover my inner peace, and to experience once again the bliss of celestial ecstasy which I had enjoyed only moments before. I must go in person to King Jehoiakim and confront him with the evil of his conduct and the certainty of divine retribution.

But this prospect made me physically sick. I crawled on my hands and knees outside to the courtyard and hung my head above the little pool there, all the while chastising myself for my fear of Josiah's spoilt son. Yet at five or six he'd been the bane of my life, a diminutive tyrant in his own childish world. Now the tyrant had come of age, and extended the scope of his tyranny to encompass the whole of the nation.

Please, *please* don't make me go to him, I was imploring Adonai as I shook my head over the poolside, my hair tumbling in the water. Please send someone else; you know that Eliakim never listened to me, even as an infant. What about this Uriah of whom Ahikam spoke?

Yet even as I pleaded the nausea worsened, and a fire flared up in my mouth which scorched my tongue and seared the insides of my cheeks until I had to scoop the pond water into my hands and lap it like a dog. I knew I should not be delivered from the pain until I'd done what I had to do.

So I went inside and got myself ready: I changed my rumpled clothes for fresh ones, and attempted to tame my hair. Then I walked out through the courtyard gates and into the streets where I hadn't ventured in daylight for as long as I cared to remember. As I walked, I reasoned with myself that the Eli I knew was proud and conceited, but not unintelligent. Surely he had no desire to see his kingdom destroyed, nor could he want to be hated by his own subjects. I had only to open his eyes to reality and he would heed the wisdom of my arguments even if he didn't acknowledge their divine origin.

But then I was recognized. Someone I passed shouted, 'Jeremiah! Look, look: it's Jeremiah, Josiah's prophet.' And all at once there were crowds of men jostling me, grasping my hands and tugging at my garments, begging me to intercede on their behalf with the King, or with Adonai, or with both. They couldn't pay their taxes; their lands and their flocks had been sequestered; their wives and children were hungry, their brothers were working their fingers to the bone embellishing His Majesty's palaces when their own mean dwellings were falling about their ears. Some of them had cursed Josiah in their time, but would that he might come back from the world of the dead and punish the son who had consigned his achievements to ruin.

'Don't grieve for Josiah,' I told them, prizing their fingers from my clothing. 'He died with honour, fighting for the freedom of his people. Weep instead for Shelemaiah his son, because he went where he least wanted to go; and much as he longs to return, he never will.'

The words were Adonai's, not my own, and were directed at me as much as at the multitude surrounding me. The period of mourning for Josiah was past. Now it was time to work.

I was admitted without demur to the palace complex, but on reaching the throne-room I was denied permission to see the King.

Well, I have done my best, I thought. I have tried, and I have failed. And I prepared to leave, but the divine fire which had begun to smoulder under my tongue when I'd quitted Ahikam's house surged up and filled my mouth. I sealed it shut with my hands, convinced that any breath which escaped would be turned to a spear of flame like a seraph's. I staggered and retched, and someone asked if he could bring me water; I nodded, but knew that one thing only would extinguish the conflagration.

More desperate than courageous, I flung myself across the threshold of the throne-room half demented with pain. I fell; at once something cold and hard went under my arms, and I found myself hoisted in the air. The guards at the entrance had raised me up with the shafts of their weapons. but this had got me where I needed to be. I was dragged forward and deposited at the foot of the dais on which His Majesty sat enthroned.

So complete had the King's metamorphosis become that I should never have taken him for a native of Judah at all, let alone the son of my boyhood friend. His heavy black wig was crowned with a headdress of solid gold, from the brow of which a golden cobra reared up, its hood extended in a posture of permanent aggression. A great collar of gold and jewels extended from his neck to his shoulders, and down his chest as far as the nipples; aside from this, and excepting his arm-rings and bracelets, the whole of his upper body was bare, shaven smooth as a child's. Equally smooth was his chin, tilted upward so that the perfect line of his jawbone showed all the way to his gold-ringed ears. His face was as beautiful and frigid as a mummy's mask, the eyes lined with kohl, the lips stained crimson, the aquiline nose upthrust. Never in my life had I seen an image at once so lovely and so dreadful, so artificial, and yet such a true reflection of the character for whom it had been manufactured.

To either side of the throne stood his ministers, and an indecent number of personal attendants. On a stool at his feet sat Prince Jeconiah his son, now six or seven years old. It was hard to believe that this solemn, silent boy, clad as outlandishly as the King himself, was the same little Coniah who had come so often to visit me with Shelemaiah his idol, now languishing in lonely exile as a pointer to his people's fate. In the alignment of their features, father and son were wellnigh identical, but where Jehoiakim's devastating beauty was sharpened by arrogance, Coniah's was pure, guileless, unselfconscious. Momentarily his eyes connected with mine, and he almost smiled.

If my unsolicited intrusion had provoked Jehoiakim to anger, the sorry state in which he now saw me transformed his wrath into amusement. 'Let our guest stand unaided,' he commanded his soldiers, as though he did me a favour by releasing me. But he knew full well that as soon as the guards stood back I would fall to my knees, which was precisely where he wanted me.

       Still, he'd reckoned without the might of Adonai. Whilst the pain which my God had sent me had weakened my limbs so my legs buckled like a baby's, his fire had so inflamed my spirit and quickened my speech that the moment I dared to open my mouth again I was an immaculate channel for the divine. Adonai's words spilled from my lips so fluently that Jehoiakim and every member of his entourage listened awestruck, and I listened too, as the voice of the Holy One thundered through the hall.

Hear the Lord's word, you proud scion of David,
      you with your minions who fawn at your feet.
Administer justice, defend the defenceless.
      redeem the oppressed, shed no innocent blood!

Oh, had you heeded these noble commandments
      and ruled from the first with my laws as your guide,
Then sons of your seed might have reigned here for ever
      and passed through these gateways like heroes acclaimed.

But you set me against you, your palace, your city.
      Jerusalem, proud as an eagle at roost,
You deem yourself sacrosanct, peerless, impregnable,
      safe for all time, your election secure.

But you shall be punished, your wickedness paid for;
      from your great height you'll be flung to the plain.
My wrath is a fire, and no creature can quench it;
      your glorious forests like chaff will be burned.

Your palace, as lovely as Gilead's meadows,
      as Lebanon's mountains, their summits capped white,
Is destined to crumble, its chambers deserted;
      jackals alone will be heard in its halls.

Destroyers will come, and its walls and its towers,
      its pillars and pediments raze to the ground.
Its beams they will break, and its panels of cedar;

all of this splendour my flames will consume.

Then strangers will stop; they will stare at your ruins
and ask why your God turned your glory to ash.
And the answer will come, that you flouted his covenant,
lauding the lifeless, the work of your hands.

Woe to the tyrant who builds in unrighteousness,
forcing his subjects to work for no pay
On his towering mansions, his echoing hallways,
his balustered windows, vermilion walls.

Since when did a king become great through his opulence?
Was not your father content with his lot?
He sought to do right, and had all that he needed;
he walked in my ways and he gave me his heart.

But your heart is set on yourself and your riches,
on what you can win through extortion and greed.
You grovel to Egypt, you flatter the Pharaoh,
as your forefathers once owned Assyria's sway.

Yet you will gain nothing; your allies will fail you,
for they, just like you, are all destined to fall.
Death will devour you; no one will mourn you;
like an ass you'll be flung from the walls with the dung.

I warned you when you were secure, but you scorned me;
such was your way from your earliest years.
The judgment to come, you have wished on your own head.
How you will groan when my axe cleaves your root.

No one was more appalled by the content of my
message than I was. I cowered there willing the earth to
swallow me, yet unable to wrest my gaze from Jehoiakim's
implacable countenance. All at once the royal soul was laid
bare before me in its sheer, unmitigated evil, and for the first

time I understood fully what quality of enemy I was now facing.

Jehoiakim feared neither man nor God; toward prophecy he was utterly indifferent. He cared not a jot for justice, nor for what anyone thought of him. He was king, and therefore entitled to have whatever he wanted; if this required him to rob his own subjects or even to starve them, then so be it. As for idolatry, he hadn't the slightest interest in what gods the people worshipped, so long as they revered him above all of them. Thoroughly vain and perfectly ruthless, he would have wrung the neck of Moses himself if the latter had stood in his way. As for me, I owed my continuing existence solely to the fact that Nehushta his wife and Coniah his son had regard for me.

He ordered the guards to take me away, since without a doubt I was mad, and my ravings merited no response save that of pity. But they were too stricken, either by the substance of my diatribe or by the mode of its delivery, to be capable of obeying him.

'By the snivelling shades of Sheol, has this worthless wretch's madness infected you all?' he berated them. 'Does his way with words so impress you that you fancy it empowers him to make his dreary predictions come true? Shame on every one of you, you gullible fools! If I wanted poets to tickle my ears with their stirring syllables, I should appoint my own, not rely on some rat-headed relic of my father's! Indeed, I shall do so; I shall appoint poets and prophets of my own, to predict for me the future I desire! Elishama?' - and he jabbed his golden sceptre under the nose of his Secretary of State - 'Elishama, attend to it at once. Search the sanctuaries and every sacred precinct in Judah for men who are gifted in pronouncing words of power. Bring me dozens of them, scores of them, so their talents will combine. I shall create the future I want for myself, Jeremiah ben Hilkiah! I shall rule this kingdom until I am old as Methuselah, and my sons and grandsons will do so after me. Jerusalem is inviolable; this is the only valid revelation which Adonai has ever given us. As for you, you miserable meddler, I would have your head detached from your body and displayed on a stake in the Temple Court if I thought you worthy of the attention it would attract. You remind me of that other troublemaker, the obnoxious seer Uriah, of whom I do not recall having heard for quite some while.' He turned once again to his attendants, though Elishama had already gone to carry out his bidding. 'Remind me, my friends,' he instructed those who remained. 'What happened to the impertinent scoundrel? Was he ever accorded an appropriate opportunity to - explain himself?'

They conferred in growls and mutters; when the King demanded they answer him at once, someone stammered: 'Your Majesty, he was summoned to trial for disturbing the peace, but he escaped across the border to Egypt.'

'Egypt, indeed!' Jehoiakim tossed back his head, displaying to maximum effect the flawless line of his jaw, and he laughed down the length of his sublimely sculpted nose. His courtiers laughed too, since this was what was expected of them. 'How singularly imprudent,' he observed. 'We shall send to the Pharaoh and have the fellow extradited without delay. Now which of you shall I charge with this delicate task? Elnathan, of course; you at least I credit with some measure of diplomacy. Set out for Egypt at once, do you hear me? If Uriah is so concerned with the implementation of justice in society at large, surely he must recognize that he cannot continue to evade it in his own case?'

I regarded Jehoiakim aghast. Elnathan was his own father-in-law, a venerable statesman more than twice His Majesty's age; how did the latter dare to address him with such condescension, and in front of the man's grandson? Jeconiah still sat there unmoving, apparently impassive, except that his eyes were wide and haunted.

Elnathan bowed his way out of his son-in-law's presence and scurried off on his errand. Then Jehoiakim had me thrown out after him. Deposited in the corridor, I was pitying Uriah more than I pitied myself. He was going to bear the punishment which should have been mine, perhaps because the King's wife favoured me, but more likely because Jehoiakim suspected I would sooner be tortured myself than have someone else suffer on my account. I wished I could believe this was true. I also wished I believed that Uriah would get the sort of trial he deserved.

I think I was mumbling such thoughts aloud as inarticulate prayers when Ahikam found me. Somehow he succeeded in making out what had happened, and reacted with horror. I had entered the throne-room in defiance of His Majesty's orders? And I had promised him defeat, death and disgrace, refusing him even a decent burial when his city fell to the foreign horde? I must be a madman. The only wonder was that I hadn't been strangled on the spot.

'I - couldn't help it,' I slobbered faintly as Ahikam dragged me away, my speech slurred and spittle dribbling down my chin. 'I don't choose what to say. My words don't make the future. The spirit... I wasn't myself... I didn't know what I was doing...'

'You were sealing the warrant for your own death, that's what you were doing,' Ahikam retorted, catching me as I lurched against a wall. 'Couldn't you have waited until he agreed to admit you? Couldn't you have saved the direst of your threats until you had made more effort to gain his trust?'

'Trust?' I repeated, as though the word were not in my vocabulary. 'What is trust, Ahikam? I trusted you, and your brothers. I trusted Jaazaniah.' And somehow I managed to tell him about the knife I had found, and make him appreciate what its discovery meant.

'My God,' he breathed. 'My dear God.' So he too was stopped in his tracks, and we knelt down in some shadowy passageway, our heads on one another's shoulders, each too broken to weep or to pray.

Ahikam recovered himself before I did, at least enough to get me home. I must have passed out altogether, because the next I remember, I was lying fully clothed on my bed, and it was well after dark. Ahikam saw my eyes open and said, 'I shall stay the night. You must not be left alone.'

'No,' I protested weakly. 'I cannot expect that. You have a wife and children. Go back to them.'

He wouldn't be told. He spread a pallet next to mine, and slept at once, or pretended to. I slept too, until midnight when I woke in a sweat, thinking: I cannot stay in this house any longer. Hanamel will return, or Jaazaniah himself, for unlike Uriah they will never be brought to trial.

But Adonai said to me; *No house in Jerusalem would be any safer for you than this one, Jeremiah, and Jerusalem is where I want you.*

'Then it will have to be guarded,' I replied. 'I shall need slaves to watch over me day and night.'

Slaves are corruptible, my son. Besides, you have me to watch over you. I have protected you until now; shall I not do so again? Hanamel accepts the truth of this even if you don't. You must exercise your faith in me continuously, Jeremiah, or it will never grow healthy and strong.

'Was it not exercised today? I did what was required of me. There is nothing more I can do.'

Ah, but there is, Adonai whispered. *It is not right that Jehoiakim's wickedness should seal the fate of my Chosen People. Just as Josiah's righteousness could not atone for their sins, so Jehoiakim's sin need not cause them all to be lost. You must address the people themselves, Jeremiah, so that they too have one last chance at salvation, because I love them, and I long so much for them to return to me. You must prophesy in the Temple Court as you did in the days of Josiah.*

'No!' I moaned, 'Oh God, please, no, anything but that. I'm not ready. I shall run away like Jonah. I shall cast myself into the sea.'

You will be ready when the time is ripe, Jeremiah. And it will ripen soon, because Babylon grows stronger by the day, like an eaglet spreading its wings and preparing to leave the nest. King Nabopolassar is almost ready to make an end of his rival Necho. If my people do not abandon their idols and beg me for forgiveness, Babylon will tear Judah to shreds in the very act of sharpening her talons.

'They won't listen,' I protested. 'There is nothing I can say which will convince them. They've heard it all before. You know it, I know it. What is the point? Prophets, priests, wealthy landowners, leaders of councils and clans, all of them are utterly depraved, and what hope is there for the common flock if its shepherds are beyond redemption?'

You are right, Jeremiah. They will not hear you, but this does not mean that you are absolved from speaking. Don't concern yourself with what to say; the words will be given you.

After that, I fell asleep again; Ahikam hadn't even wakened, or so I presumed. But in the morning I could tell from the way he looked at me that he'd heard every word of my side of the struggle, and understood in a whole new way what my gifting entailed. He couldn't have begrudged it me less.

II

Each morning after that I awoke convinced that today would be the day when Adonai's latest demand would be made upon me. I was in a state of perpetual ferment, as though someone had decided to boil up a soup with what I had already eaten.

Then came a morning which was different from the rest. I felt calm and rational, and my heart was beating with measured purpose. So I knew that the day had come.

My head enveloped in a heavy cowl lest I be recognized too soon, I walked to the Temple without ceremony. It was neither a sabbath nor a festival, so if I was lucky there wouldn't be too many folk around to hear me speak. A seething mass of humanity would confound me.

But a seething mass was what I found. I stood at the gate of the Temple Court, my heart now sinking like an anchor as I beheld the milling throng: worshippers and suppliants, changers of money, sellers of pigeons for sacrifice, peasants come in from the countryside to buy and sell. Everywhere was noise and bustle; no one spared me a second look, and I thought: I could stand here and shout until the stars fell from Heaven, and no one would hear a word of it. I wanted to grab whoever was within reach and say: don't you recognize me? Were you not among those who accosted me on my way to the palace and begged me to intercede on their behalf? Here I am, ready to bring the word of your God to you: will you not bid your fellows be silent, that his message might be heard?

However, neither my voice nor my limbs would obey me. Nauseous and sweating, with cowl thrown back, I stood rigid as an idol, unable even to blink, and suddenly everything around me seemed very far away. Faces were blurred, like phantoms; mouths were open, talking, talking, but I could no longer hear any sound. I had got the silence I wanted, but only inside my own head.

Appalled at the prospect of spewing up my guts in the holy precinct, I stood on the verge of collapse with both hands clapped to my mouth. Some of the phantom faces swung my way and loomed up closer, no doubt asking if I were all right. I took my hands from my mouth to tell them: no, I am not, please, someone see me home, I'm going to be ill.

But the words which came out were Adonai's. The divine message gushed out of me, the poetry spilling from my lips like foaming blood. Meanwhile my soul hovered somewhere high in the air above me, temporarily freed from my body to gaze down upon the multitude and pray the grace of God into every life.

Yet for all that I was divinely possessed, I knew that this prayer would not be answered. Five hundred years of Heaven's forbearance had served only to convince these people that they could live and believe as they liked because Adonai was powerless to chasten them.

To this day I can recall my every syllable, though not a single one of them was of my own choosing. Impassioned, frenetic, I foretold the destruction of the Temple as I roamed its very Court. I denounced the nation's idolatry, the libations poured to the Baals, the burning of children at the Tophet, a practice so horrible there had been no prohibition in the Torah against it because there shouldn't have been any need for one. Not that its inclusion would have made any difference, for every commandment that *was* in the Torah, God's Chosen People had broken. Murder, adultery, stealing, profanity, the telling of lies under oath... and in all of this, the sinners imagined that they were spiting their Creator, when in truth they were making a wreck of their own inheritance. They imagined themselves so clever, twisting Adonai's laws and slipping through the loopholes between them, but had succeeded only in rendering themselves incapable of distinguishing right from wrong. The fabric of our society was therefore coming unstitched; the bulwarks of our nation were crumbling and no number of sacrificial offerings could shore them up. Obedience was all that Adonai had ever demanded; obedience, not sacrifice, had always been the key.

Look at Shiloh! my voice was crying, while I floated higher and higher, the whole of Jerusalem spread out beneath me. *Shiloh was once my principal sanctuary, the resting place of the ark of my covenant. Yet I razed it to the ground for the sins of your ancestors. How dare you people stand in my Court and defy me; my house is not a refuge for criminals! What I did at Shiloh, I swear I shall repeat in Zion...*

From my vantage point above the city I was perfectly placed to watch the mood of the crowd turn against me. What began as heckling from individuals here and there soon jelled into ubiquitous jeering. Cries of 'Blasphemy! Blasphemy!' rose up to meet me, dragging me down until my soul was bound to my body once again. Adonai hadn't yet finished with me; my voice was describing in gruesome detail what would become of the inhabitants of Judah in the impending judgment. The vicinity of the Tophet would reek with the stench of *their* corpses lying alongside their children's; the bones of kings and officials and priests and prophets would be exposed for the jackals and vultures, and whoever was left alive when the enemy came would soon be envying the dead. Gather up your belongings, Adonai concluded, for those of you who survive are destined for exile! Mourn, wail, sing the dirges you use at your funerals; I the Lord have rejected you.

That was when something struck me on the head. I staggered and fell with my hand to my brow; unconsciousness rescued me from the pain, and from the developing riot.

When I came to myself, a company of angry guards was hauling me onto my feet. Pashhur himself was with them, the newly appointed Chief Officer of the Temple. He was a creature of Jehoiakim's, installed as Hilkiah's deputy ostensibly to preserve decorum in the Temple, but in reality to keep the aged High Priest from stepping too far out of line. Hilkiah had been pitifully frail for years, but Pashhur was physically big, and mentally hard as flint. Whilst a ring of his giants stood shoulder to shoulder around us, it was chiefly the force of Pashhur's personality which kept the mob at bay.

'You have perjured Adonai's name, scum of Anathoth!' a junior priest was yelling. 'How dare you prophesy doom for his holy Temple? You should die for this!' And a peal of voices chimed in agreement.

'Stone him, Pashhur! He has spoken against our city, against Zion, David's holy mountain! He has invoked the forces of chaos and called down calamity upon us!'

'Silence!' Pashhur barked, and obtained it at once, at least from those close by. 'This man must be tried.'

Representatives of Jehoiakim's secular government duly arrived. All exits from the Temple Court were sealed behind them, and every tower and gatehouse along the walls bristled with archers. Pashhur's men forced my hands behind my back and bound them with ropes. I was knocked to my knees, and blinking groggily up through the bloodied mess of my hair, I beheld the Egyptianized faces of Elishama, Delaiah, and Zedekiah ben Hananiah, His Majesty's ministers. Their condemnation was the only trial I was intended to get.

I knelt in a daze as voice after voice was raised against me.

'He has caused a riot in the House of God! He has provoked God's people to violence!'

'Isaiah foretold that Jerusalem would stand firm for ever. Jeremiah preaches its annihilation. He calls God's greatest prophet a liar!'

'He calls Adonai himself a liar! Jeremiah is evil incarnate!'

'He's a demon from the pit. He's unleashed the hosts of hell against us, employing words of power for our harm instead of our good.'

'He is jealous. If he and his spiteful kinsmen cannot administer the Temple cult, he would rather see it brought to an end.'

'Well?' Elishama demanded, at last calling a halt to the barrage of allegations. 'Have you nothing to say in your defence, ben Hilkiah?' He kicked me in the belly and shouted, 'Speak up, you worm. No one can hear you.'

'I *shall* speak!' I blurted, my eyes full of bloody tears but my spirit inflamed. 'Do you think I *chose* to come here today and lay my life on the line? Do you think I *want* to see the city I have made my home reduced to rubble? Every word you have heard me say came straight from the lips of Adonai! And he tells you again: unless each one of you repents in sackcloth and ashes, every threat that was made against you will come true! As for me...' - and I hung my head till my hair brushed my lap - 'As for me, do with me as you will. But know this: if you kill me, innocent blood will be on your heads.'

A desperate silence ensued. Gagging and coughing I waited for the order to be given and the stoning to commence. Then a familiar voice cut through the tension like a knife through curds. 'If you stone this man, you must stone me with him.'

Ahikam. I sobbed with relief and gratitude. His hand went under my chin and lifted it up; I beheld his eyes: steady, courageous, inspiring.

'Get up, Jeremiah,' he said, very gently, and stood me on my feet; and I saw that he hadn't come alone. Behind him were Akbor and Joah, both erstwhile ministers of government, who had lived in retirement since Josiah's death. Also there was Shaphan, Ahikam's aged father, who had been Josiah's Secretary of State. No soldier or priest would have dared lay a finger on him. Nor did anyone dare interrupt when he turned and raised his voice to address the crowd.

'Did not the prophet Micah proclaim in the days of King Hezekiah that Zion would one day be ploughed like a field, and that the Temple Mount would be overgrown with forests? And was he put to death for bringing the true word of God to his people? I tell you, he was not; instead, Hezekiah and his subjects fell down repentant at Adonai's feet. And what happened as a result? Disaster was averted, Jerusalem was spared. Did our fathers save our city simply in order for us to destroy it?'

At first, not a soul contradicted him. They gazed in awe at his noble face and were daunted by the dignity of his bearing. It was only when individuals who shared his sentiments called out to endorse them that his detractors ventured to express their disgust. Moments later, the uproar was louder than before, only now I could hear men shouting for me as well as against. And because opinions were now so sharply divided, brawls were breaking out in every quarter.

Pashhur couldn't afford to let matters get any further out of hand. 'Shall we desecrate this holy place with the blood of our own brothers?' he bellowed. 'We must bring this troublemaker's case before the King. Clear the court. Clear the court, I say!'

His guards began to drive the people out through the several gateways, shoving them with the shafts of their spears if they proved unwilling to move. Gradually the horde dispersed; then suddenly Ahikam and I were dragged apart, and the ropes around my wrists were pulled taut. 'Come,' Pashhur snapped, turning on his heels; he strode away at a fearsome pace, and the two giants who had hold of me hauled me along in pursuit. I think that Ahikam and his father endeavoured to follow, but a barricade of swiftly crossed spears blocked their path.

I wasn't taken to the King straight away. Instead, I was thrown into prison and told I would be summoned in the morning.

Never in my life had I been in a place so appalling. I was flung trussed up in a cell so small that not even a child could have stood or lain down at full stretch. It was damp, it stank of urine, and the only light was what came from the crack around the warped oaken door.

'Don't leave me here! Don't leave me...' I called out, for I should rather have faced Jehoiakim there and then, feeling certain that Adonai would have given me the words he wanted me to say. I wasn't half so sure that he would be able to get me through a night of cramped and foetid isolation.

I tried and failed to pray. I tried and failed to sleep. Then while I was crouched there counting the beats of my heart to remind myself I was alive, the door ground open. A hunk of bread was tossed at my feet, and a saucer of water was shunted in after it.

'Thank you,' I tried to say, while my jailer laboured to get the misshapen door re-closed. This must have been more gratitude than he usually got, because he said gruffly, 'You're welcome. I'd make the most of it if I were you. The last one of your kind in here, my bread was the last thing he ate.' Then he started to heave on the door once more.

'Please,' I croaked, 'Wait. What do you mean? Who was put in here? What had he done?'

There were fumbling noises outside. The jailer had taken a lamp from its bracket, and now he pushed the door open further than before, and poked his head around the edge of it. A dour-faced man he was, with a grizzled beard and crooked black teeth. But the gleam in his eye evinced the perverse pleasure he derived from his occupation.

'Uriah, they called him,' he informed me, and coughed at the smell. 'Not three days ago he was brought here, all the way from Egypt, just to be tried for causing an affray. Strange kind of trial it was too, so I'm told. His Majesty ordered one of his guards to strike the fellow down with a damned great sword, right in front of Prince Jeconiah, and they hadn't exchanged three words. His lordship Elnathan, the poor old relic who'd brought the man in, fainted clean away on the spot. Don't suppose it was the sort of trial he was expecting. Then they threw the body in the Kidron valley... pardon my asking, sir, but are you all right?'

I was far from all right. But I said I was, because suddenly I needed desperately to be alone with Adonai. As the jailer backed his way out of my cell I gasped out, 'Why? Adonai, why?' meaning: *why* did you allow Uriah to be killed? You promised protection to me; did you not do the same for him?

Uriah took the way of a coward, Jeremiah. He fled to Egypt because he knew that Jehoiakim wanted him silenced, when I wanted him here.

'But *I'm* a coward,' I protested. 'I always have been. Are you waiting for the day when you can have *me* martyred in cold blood as well? Or have Jehoiakim's minions torture me? I couldn't take it, you know. I would denounce you. I'd agree to whatever they demanded.'

You are no coward, my son. You have done my bidding in spite of your fear. You are not going to die, nor will you be tortured. I know what you can and cannot endure. You will not be subjected to anything worse than you can stand.

In the morning I was dragged from my cell by Jehoiakim's men before the jailer had brought me my breakfast. He'd been on his way as I stumbled past him, bread and saucer of water in his hands. He gave me a black-toothed grin and called out, 'Remember me to your God when you meet him.'

But I wasn't taken to the King. I learned much later that he hadn't been apprised of my actions at all, still less of my words; and a sizeable sum of money had passed from Ahikam's coffers into Pashhur's. It was Pashhur himself who acquitted me. With Elishama, Delaiah and Zedekiah ben Hananiah looking on, he said, 'We have chosen to set you free, ben Hilkiah, inasmuch as you are woefully deluded. It does not become the Temple authorities to execute lunatics who rave through no fault of their own. I shall have you released at once, provided that you agree not to enter the Temple Court again. Your ban from the holy precincts will remain in force indefinitely. Do you accept my terms?'

'My lord,' I assented meekly, and bowed my head before him. My bonds were removed, and I walked from the room a free man.

I went directly to Ahikam to thank him for all that he had done, and to thank his distinguished father too. But I found Ahikam deep in mourning. My advocate, Shaphan his father, was dead; his aged heart had failed him, and he had collapsed as they carried me away to prison.

CHAPTER 15: BERECHIAH

I

I was working in the royal library as usual when everything came to a head. Morning and afternoon, six days in every seven, writing until my eyes and my fingers ached with the strain of it... this was all that I ever seemed to do, and how I had come to resent squandering so much of my youth upon it! I was almost twenty one years old already.

Not that I laboured alone. I would sit in companionable silence with a dozen or so fellow sufferers, each of us engrossed in our own branch of research. Mine was concerned with money; I was supposed to be compiling a collection of proverbs on the subject, culled from as many sources as I could find: Egyptian, Mesopotamian, Aramaic, Canaanite, as well as Hebrew. I must have read ten thousand tablets, and interviewed a hundred people: other scribes, foreign ambassadors and itinerant merchants, wizened old men and harridan wise-women brought to the city from wilderness caves. But the words I'd recorded were dancing now in front of my weary eyes. The whole enterprise struck me as trivial and pointless.

"The love of money gives birth to a litter of evils" ... "Rejoice not thyself over riches gained by robbery" ... "Better is coarse bread when the heart is happy, than luxurious fare attended by sorrow" ... "A fool and his money are easily parted" ... So many pithy little sayings, so much worldly wit. And the further my interest subsided, the more mistakes I would make on my parchment, until there were more corrections than anything else.

I hadn't always hated what I did. There had been a time when I'd loved it: the joy of acquiring knowledge; the thrill of making an original discovery; the tranquil atmosphere of scholarship in the library; the occasional animated discussion when we scribes arranged to eat together of an evening and debate some contentious issue arising from our studies.

Then a fortnight ago I'd had an experience which had altered everything. Walking home for my siesta one day, I'd resolved upon visiting the Temple to offer a pigeon in thanks for my father's recovery from a fever. I never got round to buying a bird, because just inside the New Gate of the Temple Court stood a prophet haranguing the crowds in the name of Adonai.

I'd been told about Jeremiah many times, but never before had I seen or heard him in person. And I was bewitched. What a face the man had, and what eyes! He was like fire incarnate, his rampant locks like a cloud of smoke about his head. He was so alive somehow, so ravaged and yet so wildly, appallingly beautiful. Never in my sheltered life had I heard a man speak with such passion, torrents of poetry streaming from his lips like the latter rain. And what a message he delivered! Never before had I given any thought to my beliefs, or to the way I lived; I was a scribe and the son of a scribe, brought up to copy text and to interpret it, to argue, to examine the minute details of things, not to lose myself in adoration of the Divine. But all at once, this was what I wanted to do. I wanted to fall on my knees in worship, then to follow Jeremiah to the ends of the earth. I could have dropped my mundane life like a piece of half-finished weaving, and watched it unravel without shedding a tear.

So I wasn't aware that the mood of the crowd had turned against him. The first I knew was when the surging and shoving from behind me almost knocked me over. Then at last I heard the shouting; peasants, pilgrims, even priests and prophets were cursing him and calling for his death. Someone close to me threw something heavy and sharp; I watched it strike Jeremiah on the forehead, and he vanished from my sight.

Consumed by the need to assist him, I started to fight my way forward through the mob, but of course I couldn't get near him, and wound up trampled to the ground myself. Winded, I struggled to my feet, but there was no longer any sign of the stricken Prophet. I knew not whether he was dead or alive, and I thought: if he is dead I shall slit my own wrists, because I haven't the slightest wish to live in a world which would seek to extinguish a fire like that one.

Later in the afternoon I learned that he lived, and was in custody, and while I was supposedly poring over my scholarly work, I was praying with all of my being for his release. I prayed all evening too, and most of the night, and when I discovered the following morning that he was free, I thought: hallelujah, it is true, there is a God in Heaven who listens to the cries of his children.

I began to ask my colleagues what they knew of Jeremiah, and whether any of them had ever heard him speak. Some had, some hadn't, but my harping on the subject was soon driving them to distraction - my elder brother Seraiah in particular. 'This is it, Seraiah!' I told him, grabbing his hands and clapping them together between my own. 'This is what I've been searching for! Don't our scriptures say that it is better to quest for one pearl than be content with a thousand pebbles? I must give up my work in the library and become his disciple. Come with me, we'll follow him together!'

But Seraiah just shook his head and gave me his longest-suffering smile. He'd spent all morning copying the words of Moses and their interpretations - what could be more important than that?

'*Anyone* can copy scrolls!' I yelled in frustration. 'An Indian monkey could be trained to do it.' Seraiah's smile disappeared, but I plunged on regardless. 'Who reads our scrolls anyway? No one obeys the commandments they contain; that's what Jeremiah says. And as for the interpretations we amass and pass on: all are corrupt! We twist the meaning of the texts to suit ourselves, but what about integrity? What about allowing God's spirit to touch our lives? All we do is obscure the truth with our own opinions.'

Seraiah's expression was black with rage, and it was almost like confronting an angry version of myself, since we looked so alike: the same short but ungovernable hair, the same bright eyes, the same high forehead and indoor complexion. 'Berechiah,' he roared, 'If you weren't my brother I should slap your insolent face! How dare you spout such blasphemy? The word of Adonai is treated with reverence by every scholar here. It would be a travesty for anyone but a member of the scribal guild to copy the holy scrolls.'

'Oh Seraiah, Seraiah, it isn't the papyrus and ink which are holy! It's the *message,* for Heaven's sake! And what about all this pagan drivel I'm compelled to wade through, all this dross from Egypt and Babylon? I shouldn't be soiling my pen or my mind with it.'

'Berechiah, you know perfectly well how vital it is that we understand how men of other nations think. Our King and his ministers are constantly dealing with the envoys of foreign states. How can we provide His Majesty with worthwhile advice if we know nothing of the wisdom of our neighbours?'

'"The *fear* of the *Lord* is the beginning of wisdom"!' I quoted, aquiver with exasperation.

'The beginning, maybe, but what of its end?' Seraiah shook his head once more. 'Will you never grow up, Berechiah? Even as a child you were a chaser after delusions, obsessed with the notion of dedicating yourself to some ludicrous cause so that you might somehow change the world and be remembered for it. You flitted from one preposterous project to another like a butterfly in a field of flowers! You're too old for such flights of fancy now. You ought to be settling down.'

'But this is different! No one has ever made such an impression on me before.'

'You're simply infatuated with this rascal, that is all, as a schoolboy is besotted with his teacher. You should get yourself married, as Father is always telling you, then you wouldn't have time to develop these stupid fixations. It's a pity the first girl he betrothed you to turned out to be such a bad lot, or you'd be married already.'

'Oh Seraiah, I'm *trying* to grow up, can't you see? All this copying and conflating... anyone would think I was still at wisdom school. I need to *live,* I need to *do* something! I need to *see* the world I write about, before I ruin my eyesight!'

Seraiah said curtly, 'This crazy Jeremiah doesn't have disciples. He doesn't want any. He doesn't even have servants, or a wife. By all accounts he lives like a hermit.'

'Then I'm just what he needs!' I announced triumphantly; but Seraiah rolled his eyes to Heaven and walked away.

I compelled myself to acknowledge that my brother might be right. I honestly tried to put the whole disconcerting episode out of my mind.

Yet I couldn't. I saw the Prophet's face in my dreams by night, and by day snatches of his poetry came back to haunt me; by force of habit I wrote them down, and soon had several pages of papyrus almost word for word. Transcribing my lists of monetary maxims, Jeremiah's were the couplets which were running through my head. "It is a disgrace to be greedy or dishonest," I was writing. "Poor people are better off than liars. Obey Adonai, and you will live a long life, content and shielded from harm."

Only I got to 'Adonai' and made yet another mistake - and this was the final straw, for the whole of that section of the scroll would have to be rewritten. Of course, we do not write 'Adonai', the Lord. We write the consonants of his true name, the one too sacred to be spoken aloud. But if we write it wrongly, the error cannot be corrected.

I leaped to my feet in annoyance - and knew I would never sit down in that library again. I nearly walked out without taking the tools of my trade, but something told me not to be so short- sighted. So I packed up my inkhorn and knife, put my quills and my reeds in their case, and off I went.

Seraiah had seen me get up. He intercepted me in the doorway and demanded to know where I was going. I told him, straight, and he was horrified; he grasped me by the shoulders and hissed at me, 'Please, Berechiah! Just think what you are doing! You belong to an ancient and distinguished scribal family; you'll bring disgrace upon all of us! Father paid out a fortune for your education. He'll never have you in our house again.'

This extreme prediction came true. Notwithstanding his ferocious opposition to my plan, Seraiah is the only one of my academic kinsmen who will condescend to speak to me any more, and once I'd been home to collect the rest of my things the door was barred for ever against me.

I had no trouble finding out where the Prophet was living. It was common knowledge that he was well regarded by Ahikam ben Shaphan, and I soon discovered that he occupied the latter's house in the city. I simply arrived on his threshold and hammered on the gate - and got no response whatever.

I tried again and again, and shouted his name, and stressed that I was alone and that there was no need for him to be suspicious of me. In the end he appeared, but only because the noise I was making showed no sign of abating.

When I saw him, however, I was shocked to the core. He was dressed in sacking, his feet were bare, and all down his arms were criss-crossing scars where he'd gashed his own flesh. There was dust in his hair, and ash ground into the skin of his face, which was sallow and dry as a corpse's. His cheekbones stood out like the ribs of an ill-used mule, and the bags round his eyes were like sacks of charcoal. The only brightness about him was in his eyes themselves, and this was the glitter of drink.

'I've - come to be your disciple,' I mumbled, sounding stupid even to myself. I couldn't disengage my own eyes from his.

'I don't work with disciples,' he informed me. 'Get out of my sight, confound you.'

'But my lord...' I protested, putting out my hand to deter him from shutting the gate in my face, 'My lord, you *should*. You're so brilliantly gifted. You might foster a similar gifting in someone else.'

'You don't know what you are talking about. If I am so gifted, why does no one listen to a word I am saying? I might as well batter my head on a rock. And if you had listened, you'd be gone by now. Go away. Clear off.'

'My lord, please... I listened to what you said in the Temple Court. I remembered nearly everything; and I wrote it all down on papyrus.'

'Then go and put it into practice. Repent of your sins. Consecrate your life to Adonai. Just don't do any of it here.'

'But I could help you! I can do anything. I can read and write as fast as any man can speak. I could take down all your prophecies! I - could even cook your meals?' I concluded lamely.

'I am perfectly capable of recording my own prophecies, thank you very much - *if* I saw any need for doing so, since I can recall in full every syllable which Adonai ever entrusted to me. And I am perfectly capable of cooking. *Eating* is what I find difficult.'

I threw down my bags in the dust and said, 'My lord, I've given up everything to come here. My position in the palace library, my rooms there, even my family. You can't just turn me out into the street.'

'You're a professional *scribe?* The Lord preserve us! I don't know how you had the effrontery to darken my door. Scribes are worse than whores, worse than dogs! At least most harlots *know* that they are sinners, and even dogs have the decency to recognize their guilt when men catch them fouling their property. It was the incorrigible teachers of wisdom who made Jehoiakim the way he is today. There can be no fellowship between the peddlers of human counsel and the spokesmen of Adonai.'

'My lord, you don't understand. Human counsel is not our sole concern. We document the words of the prophets of old, even those of Moses himself. And even our proverbs encourage men to live honourably with their neighbours, and acknowledge the Lord in their ways. How about this one: "A greedy man stirs up dissension, but he who puts his trust in Adonai will rejoice and prosper"?'

Jeremiah laughed: a hollow laugh loaded with bitterness and scorn, but although I had drawn back my hand from his gate, he didn't close it. 'So you see before you here someone blessed with joy and prosperity?' he challenged me caustically. 'I tell you, young man: putting my trust in Adonai has brought me nothing but misery. I have been attacked on the road, I've been thrown into prison, my home has been wrecked, and I narrowly escaped being murdered in my bed. I've been ignored, ridiculed, cursed all my life, and been told quite regularly that I am out of my mind. I'm denied the solace of the company of men: Adonai has forbidden me to go to weddings or parties or even the funerals of those I have loved, or of those few misguided souls who have loved me in return. The girl to whom I was betrothed was taken from me and given to a man who despises me; my own kinsmen abhor me, and almost all of the people who ever cared for me are dead - or else they have betrayed me to my enemies and their treachery has gone unpunished. It is the wicked and those who hate me who rejoice and prosper; and what would the teachers of wisdom have to say about that?'

"'A wise man's wisdom affords him patience,'" I quoted. "'And it brings him glory to overlook his brother's offence.'"

'You suppose that I care a fig about glory? Justice and revenge are what I seek. But what justice can there be under Heaven, when the friend who betrayed me is honoured by the King, and one who spoke out to defend me is dead?' Then, to my horror, tears welled up in his eyes and spilled down his sunken cheeks, making chalky white tracks through the grime.

I decided that I couldn't possibly leave him alone in this sorry state. I picked up my things and walked past him into the courtyard while he squatted on his wasted haunches inside the gateway and wept like an addle-witted sot - which was what he was fast becoming.

I wandered from room to room in search of a place to unpack, but everywhere was filthy, littered with winecups and buzzing with flies. I knew without doubt that Adonai had sent me, for it was clear that Jeremiah was quite unable to look after himself, though I'd never imagined I would find my destiny in the sweeping of floors and washing of dishes. Presumably Ahikam had been used to keeping an eye on things, but the whole of Jerusalem knew that he was deep in mourning for his father.

In the end I dumped my belongings in the room adjacent to Jeremiah's bedroom - or, I should say, the room he apparently slept in. A threadbare pallet and a single chest with a broken lid were the only furnishings in it, and his clothes were strewn over the floor. Across the doorway there had once been a curtain, but someone had torn down the rail, which lay among the clothes with the ruined curtain still on it, and jagged holes in the plasterwork showed where it had come from. The lower part of each wall had at one time been lined with cedar, but most of the panels hung away from their batons. The damage had been done deliberately, and little attempt had been made to put things right.

While I was sorting out my belongings in the room I had chosen for myself, Jeremiah appeared in the entrance, but he didn't speak or interfere with what I was doing. He simply stood there like a spectre, so that I said matter-of-factly, 'I hope you don't mind my having the room next to yours? It's just that it will be easier for you to call when you need me. It's such a big house; I can't believe you've been living here all on your own. Well, you won't be lonely any more.' I sprang to my feet and went over to where he was standing, or rather leaning, watching me dazedly and making no comment on what I'd said. I dropped to my knees at his feet and declared, 'I've decided to pledge you the rest of my life. Berechiah, son of Neraiah the scribe, at your humble and eternal service.'

Still he said nothing; his tears having washed away his anger, it seemed he had no energy remaining to resist me.

Once I'd found homes for each of my possessions, my thoughts turned to food, one of my fondest preoccupations. I asked Jeremiah where the kitchen was, and what provisions I was likely to find there with which I might make us some dinner. But the cupboards were empty. 'I'll go to the market,' I offered, but he gave me to understand that he didn't feel hungry; besides, there wasn't any money.

'No money?' I exclaimed. 'And no food either? God give me strength! You would have starved to death as surely

as birds lay eggs if I hadn't come here.' So I went to market
and used my own silver, and thought to myself: it's true, a fool
and his money *are* easily parted, and I'm the fool.

Back in the house once more, I set about seasoning
the meat I'd bought and chopping the vegetables. But when
I'd professed my willingness to act as Jeremiah's cook, my
confidence had been rooted entirely in enthusiasm, for I'd had
no experience whatever. Preparing meals was the work of
women; thus I'd assumed it must be a perfectly straight-
forward business. By the time I'd cut three of my fingers,
wound up with far more waste than food, and realized we
hadn't a morsel of bread in the place nor a grain of flour with
which to make any, I was exhausted.

'What *have* you been eating all this time?' I demanded
of Jeremiah; he'd been watching me throughout, too wrapped
up in his own troubles to derive any amusement from my
antics.

He shrugged his shoulders, and I had to ask again
before eliciting the truth from him. He'd hardly had a thing
since Shaphan's death, except for wine, of which he'd had
plenty.

So it was probably just as well that the dinner I
produced was of meagre proportions. He couldn't have eaten
much more and kept it down. As it was, I had to cajole him like
a faddy child's mother before he would have what was given
him, and he ate it in silence, gazing fixedly at some invisible
object hovering just below the ceiling. After he'd finished, he
went to sleep with his head on the table, and I thought:
Adonai have mercy, since Shaphan died, Jeremiah has slept no
more than he has eaten.

Over and over again in the next few days I asked
myself whether I'd made an almighty mistake. Ready as I'd
been to give up writing for ever, I felt very strange for not
doing it, as though a gaping void had opened up inside me. I
got no thanks from Jeremiah for my eager ministrations, no
recompense for the money I spent, and scarcely a grunt in
response when I addressed him. He blamed himself for

Shaphan's death, that much was clear from the raw red scars on his arms, but there was no way he would admit it in so many words to me.

As I slowly discovered how to cook, and he relearned how to eat, he began to look a little healthier in body, but in mind he was sick and unreachable. Time alone would heal his inner wounds, I concluded, and time alone would enable him to accept my presence and share his burdens with me. In the meantime, I should make myself useful restoring order to his house.

I knew little more about decorating than I did about cooking, but I succeeded in hiring plasterers and joiners and weavers of curtains, who soon had the place looking more presentable. Little by little I gleaned from Jeremiah the story of how the damage had occurred and who'd been responsible; I asked why Ahikam himself hadn't had it repaired. 'I said he wasn't to concern himself with it,' Jeremiah informed me with another of his dismissive shrugs. 'I said I would see to it myself soon enough.' But I doubt he would ever have done so.

After the craftsmen I got in cleaners, and was resigned to paying all of them myself. But while I was helping to tidy things up, I emptied the chest which was kept in Jeremiah's bedroom. And stashed away beneath his clothes and a scroll of Hosea's oracles, I found enough gold pieces to keep us both in plenty for the rest of our lives.

'Where in the world did you *get* all this?' I asked him, scooping up handfuls of the things and letting them run between my fingers like sand. He frowned at them, seemingly unable to remember; then vaguely he mumbled, 'Josiah. Josiah. For my wedding...' and turned his face to the wall. He stood there and sobbed, with his head pressed hard against the newly dried plaster. I sighed, and thought: I am wasting my time. He has known so much sadness, he'll never rise above it.

Yet I battled on, for something inside me assured me that what I was doing was right. The conviction which had caused me to leave all I knew and come to the Prophet's house had been so compelling... and now when I'd begun to be afraid that my money would soon run out, and that my master and I would quietly starve together, enough had been provided to banish such fears for ever. I'd believed in God from my boyhood; all at once it seemed that he believed in me.

Certainly he was changing me. I'd been no more accustomed to succouring the sorrowful in their distress than I'd been used to running a home, yet in the days I spent waiting for the Prophet to accept me, I myself was being readied to withstand what was coming. Buoyancy and optimism, these were the qualities I'd praised myself for in the past, and the absence of any inclination to moodiness. Now I would have to cope with the moods of a man who was as different from me as anyone could possibly be. And yet every morning I awoke with hope; notwithstanding how thoroughly Jeremiah ignored me, I'd become convinced that I was where I was meant to be, and so I was content.

I think he'd made up his mind to ignore me for ever, or at least until I'd had enough and left. But he could not do it. I was so scrupulously attentive to his needs, learning exactly what he liked to eat and what he didn't, sensing when he was ready to rise each morning and when he wished to retire at night, when he wanted to bathe, and so on, without his having to utter a single word.

At last came the morning when I won my first small victory. Humming away to myself, then singing unrestrainedly for no particular reason while I sliced some fruit for breakfast, I chanced to glance up and there he was by the door, the faintest hint of a smile twisting one corner of his mouth. "'He who gets up early and blesses his brother with a loud voice shall have his blessing counted as a curse,'" he quoted from Solomon's proverbs; and my jaw dropped open.

In my naivety I imagined that things would get easier from this moment on, but I couldn't have been more mistaken. Jeremiah had made a tentative truce with me, but not with Adonai. Before arriving with my chattels on his doorstep, I hadn't given much thought to how the great man of God would spend his days. If I had, I might have imagined him passing his mornings in prayer and meditation, his afternoons in study, or perhaps in discourse with like-minded friends. How far all this would have been from the truth! Most of the mornings he spent half asleep, because he'd lain awake all night, and most of the afternoons he drank, until I plucked up courage to fit a lock on the door to Ahikam's wine-cellar. After that he just sat, on the pallet in his room, or by the side of the pool in the courtyard. Once he sat there all evening too, in torrential rain, for autumn was turning to winter, and each week was cooler and wetter than the last. Never in all this time did I see or hear him pray; until one chilly night when I awoke to the sound of his screaming the place down.

Terrified, I threw on a cloak, grabbed a lamp, and ran to his room, for I thought he must be ill and calling for my help. I found him maddened, entranced, convulsing stark naked on his pallet having kicked his way out of the bedclothes which lay in a sweat-soddened tangle on the floor. I cried out his name and ventured to approach him, meaning to grab him by the arms and shake him back to himself. But I couldn't get a grip, his skin was so slick, and the mass of his hair was straggling in my face and making me sneeze.

'Leave me alone!' he was howling. 'I hate you! I hate you! Leave me alone,' so I retreated in alarm, supposing that he shouted at me. But he hadn't seen me, hadn't even heard me or felt my breath upon his face. He flung his head from side to side, tearing at his hair and yelling, 'I've had enough of this, do you hear me? You lied to me! You deceived me; you've always deceived me! Everyone I loved you have taken; you've stolen my very soul and left me for dead! I wish I *was* dead, are you listening? I wish I had never been born!'

He writhed some more, then threw himself over and crouched on his elbows and knees, hands plastered to his ears. 'I *know* I am fighting!' he whined. 'And who could blame me?' Then abruptly he collapsed, face down on the pallet, and I thought: my God, his heart has given out, and he is dead.

Then to my astonishment he started to laugh: a sobbing, harrowing laughter at first, belched from his lungs like weed from the lungs of a man half-drowned. But soon it came lighter, rising like water from a spring; he rolled on his back once more, and when I caught a glimpse of his face through his hair it was radiant, just as it had been on the day when he preached in the Temple.

Relieved and shaking, I sat down hard on the bed beside him, and presently he drifted from laughter into something like sleep, a sleep so profound that he scarcely breathed. I threw the bedclothes on top of him, and I think I slept too after that, hunched where I sat, for the next thing I remember is hearing my name being spoken almost timidly in my ear. I opened my eyes and Jeremiah was kneeling there on the floor in front of me, wan and vulnerable. Dawn had broken, and his ecstasy was over.

'Berechiah?' he whispered. 'I'm sorry. Truly I'm sorry. I didn't want to make you leave, not any more. But I understand. Don't feel that you have to explain.'

'Leave?' I repeated, bewildered. 'Why should I leave?'

'Because...' he began, then his voice trailed off and he made some gesture, feeble yet eloquent, meaning: because I am mad; you have seen it for yourself. Now you know the truth about me - the truth I have tried and yet failed to conceal from everyone who has ever dared to love me.

'I told you,' I said simply, 'I'm pledged to you for life. Nothing has changed.'

'No, Berechiah. You must not talk like that. You have to go - before Adonai takes you. Before you get hurt.'

'He isn't going to take me anywhere. I'm sure of it. I know it.'

'No you don't. You don't understand. He will *have* to take you. He knows I shall try to get from you what I should be seeking from him. It's always the way.'

'I won't let that happen, Jeremiah. I swear to God that I won't, and if it is true that he reads what is written on our hearts, then he knows I swear truly. This must be why he has let me come here - no, it's why he's *sent* me here.'

'How can you begin to comprehend the will of God? You're no prophet; you are little more than a boy.'

'A boy and a scribe,' I said resignedly, and I might as well have said: a boy and a worm. But straight away bouncing back as was my wont, I added, 'Say what you like, my lord, but I know that Adonai has drawn me closer to him in these weeks and days than I ever could have imagined.'

I waited for him to argue further, but he did not. Instead, he exhaled the breath from his lungs so sharply that his very chest seemed to deflate. He shrank in upon himself, and murmured, 'Perhaps you do know Adonai somehow. Perhaps he has drawn you closer to himself than I could ever come.'

Whatever was he saying? Was his faith really so flimsy, his experience of his God so nebulous that he could possibly compare it unfavourably with mine? 'I see no visions,' he explained, as if he answered my unvoiced questions. 'I dream no prophetic dreams.'

'Neither did Moses,' I reminded him, and quoted a passage of Torah which my brother had read to me not many days before. '"When a prophet of mine is among you I reveal myself to him in visions, and I whisper my riddles in his dreams. But this is not the case with my servant Moses. With him I converse face to face."'

'Oh, he speaks to me right enough. I hear his voice loud as thunder, when all you have is some hazy sixth sense that his spirit is guiding you. But you do not fight him; you follow where that faint sensation is leading you. I run the opposite way as fast as I can, and look for refuge in the desert places of my soul.'

'Then give up the battle,' I exhorted him, once more quoting to buttress my argument. '"Make your peace with Adonai, and do not treat him as an enemy. Submit your cause to the Lord, and he will prosper you."'

'I've acknowledged defeat in a thousand such battles,' he replied. 'And yet the war goes on, and the list of its innocent casualties grows ever longer.'

'Shaphan was old,' I said gently. 'His time had come. And would he not have preferred to go in the way that he went, a martyr for the truth, rather than dying in his bed in weakness and senility?'

'Perhaps,' Jeremiah admitted.

Then quite suddenly the cloud began to clear from his eyes, and I thought to myself: hard though it is to believe, he has not seen it this way until now.

The cloud which had cleared did not return, and in the cool damp days of winter I watched while Adonai raised him very gradually, very tenderly, from the pit of his despair. Jeremiah took to sleeping in the nights and praying in the mornings as I might have expected; he no longer cared about the lock I'd put on the cellar, and instead of just sitting, he played his lyre, and sang the most exquisite songs I had ever heard.

Once I'd grasped that they were his own, and that he made them up as he went along, I would hide in the shadows with my pens and take them down, striving to find some way of recording the melody as well as the words. Notwithstanding how eager I'd been to leave the palace library, it felt so good somehow to be writing again, and so right.

But it wasn't easy to maintain my concentration. I found myself spellbound by the lilt of Jeremiah's voice, by the rapture I saw on his face, by the gentle drift of his fingers across the strings. A hundred times a day I thanked Adonai for the privilege of sharing Jeremiah's home, and his very life, and I prayed with all my heart that things would *not* go wrong, and that we should not steal from each other the love which was meant for the Divine.

And it would have been so very easy for me at least to have done so, because the Prophet was everything which I was not. So powerful were his emotions that they scaled heights I'd never dreamed of, as well as plunging deep into gorges of despair. There was such a core of spiritual energy inside him, and yet he could be diffident as a maiden, unsure of his every step. I was dependable, Jeremiah unpredictable; I was efficient, he frankly feckless; I was pragmatic and down to earth, whereas he so often floated somewhere in his spirit where my pinioned thoughts were wholly unable to follow. For all my expensive education in the wisdom of the scribes, Jeremiah seemed to me to be brilliant in a way that I never could be; he had such insight into the ways of men and nations, and I was quite sure that he could read my mind. So sometimes I was jealous; but was likewise convinced that his brilliance and his so-called madness were bound inextricably together, and that he couldn't have had the one without the other. For myself, I decided I would rather be as I was; had I been like him, I was sure I would have destroyed myself long ago.

All the same, I did dare to hope that a few stray sparks of his brilliance might chance to land upon me, and that one day I might gain at least a little glory through my association with this man whom posterity would surely come to regard as great.

But was Jeremiah as pleased to be sharing his life with me as I was glad to be with him? If he was, he didn't say; the closest he'd ever come was after I'd seen him in his frenzy, when he'd emerged from it so vulnerable and so ashamed. I think he still believed, deep down inside, that something would take me away from him: disease perhaps, even death, and that the more he grew attached to me, the more likely this was to happen. At least, I hoped that this was the reason why he remained so distant, so self-absorbed, and that it wasn't because he despised me still, or took me for granted already.

I did ask Adonai once, in my evening prayers, to confirm why he was letting me stay when he'd refused to sanction his servant's having any such companion before. I got no response in words, but the moment I'd finished my prayer, my pen-case fell from the shelf where I kept it onto the pallet in front of me, its contents spilling out and rolling in every direction. As I gathered the items together, I knew the answer to my question, and my spirit quickened. In serving Jeremiah as a scribe, I should be fulfilling the ministry I'd been made for; those who came before me had known that their true destinies lay elsewhere. And it was for me to ensure that Jeremiah was not distracted from his, since he knew perfectly well that from one source only could he draw the kind of love he needed.

And indeed, not very long after this, he told me that the time had come for him to take Adonai's word to his people once again.

I exclaimed, 'You'll return to the Temple Court and preach, when Pashhur has forbidden you to go there?'

'No,' said Jeremiah. 'I shall go where the spirit sends me. Each place where I speak will be chosen for a reason; the places will reflect the prophecies, or so Adonai has told me.'

'May I come with you? May I listen? May I take notes?'

'You may do whatever you wish; it is no business of mine.'

My heart sank a little, as it so often did when my eagerness to please was rewarded by mere indifference on his part. But determined not to be daunted, I packed up some tablets and a stylus and readied myself to accompany him.

However, he hadn't meant us to leave straight away. When he'd said that the time had come, he'd been speaking in terms of days rather than minutes. In the meantime he went very strange; he would shut himself in his room from one sunset to the next, and would neither eat, drink nor sleep. Then early one morning, quite suddenly, he burst from his room and strode out into the courtyard, and thence into the street, though he hadn't once left the house since I'd been there.

Not having had time to fetch a single pen, I ran stumbling after him. It had rained in the night, and the alleyways were slippery with mud. As always, there were children and animals under foot, and sheep on their way to market, and crooked old men bowed down with age and with the heavy sacks of grain or bales of cloth which they carried on their shoulders. But Jeremiah strode on as though no one else was there.

The overnight cloud had vanished, and a milky winter sun had risen above the jumble of rooftops. We were heading directly towards it, making, as it transpired, for the eastern gate of the city. Here Jeremiah halted, and taking his stand in the middle of the road leading down to the desert, he began to cry out, to anyone who would listen, that Judah's eastern neighbours were doomed. Both Ammon and Moab, together with all their palaces and cities and all their brash young warriors, would soon be torn to shreds by the talons of the eagle of Babylon.

He didn't seem to care whether anyone was listening or not. Perhaps it didn't matter so long as the proclamation was made, since the heavens would hear it, and the gods of the accursed nations. Just as in the Temple, the poetic oracles flowed from his lips as the rains had flowed from Heaven in the days of Noah. With his eyes ablaze, his head thrown back, and his black hair streaming, I thought: I shall surely die if ever I see a sight more beautiful and terrible than this.

And people *were* listening. An enormous crowd had gathered all about him, though its inner ring dared not come any closer than two spear-lengths away. The more dire Jeremiah's predictions became, the more the crowd approved, for there was nothing which the people of Judah liked more than to contemplate the crushing of their ancestral enemies. 'Amen! So be it!' folk were shouting, urging him on, though I don't suppose for a moment that he could hear them.

When he had finished, it was as though his own breath left him, as well as that of the Divine. He swayed where he stood, blinking at the sea of faces, sensing its presence at last. Then he staggered, and had I not reached him in time he would have fallen to the ground. I pulled his arm across my shoulder and he let me lead him home, so exhausted that he almost slept as he walked. He slept all the rest of the day, except that twice he awoke to be sick, though I couldn't imagine what with. His forehead was burning hot to the touch, and the rest of him clammy; but by sundown the fever was gone. He got up, then, and spent the evening in silent vigil and fasting.

And the following morning was exactly like the last. Just after dawn he arose and went into the city, only this time he went to the Potshard Gate in the south, and delivered a tirade against our southern neighbours in Edom. Again the crowds applauded, and again at the end he collapsed and I had to take him home. This task proved harder than it had been the day before, however, because he was barely conscious. The fever was worse today, too, and the retching; he couldn't be sick, for there really was nothing more in his belly.

But again, the fever abated at sundown. I begged him to eat some supper; he would not, though he drank a whole pitcher of water before commencing his vigil once more. How long is this going to go on? I asked of myself and of Adonai. Jeremiah's health had been so fragile in the first place. Mercifully, the third message he gave was the last, for the time being. At the south-west gate he spoke - against Egypt.

The crowd heard him out in stony silence. Waves of dread broke upon me and I knew not whether to will him to stop or to continue, for the more he said, the more highly charged the atmosphere became, but I was sure that when he left off, the spell would be broken and stones would fly. Among the audience were young men in Egyptian costume, apeing the pretensions of their King, from their thick black wigs and kohl-enhanced features to their swinging kilts and long bare legs. I thought: even as he speaks, reports of this must be reaching the palace, and Jehoiakim's guards will come and take him away.

I started to pray, with all the fervour I could muster; and no one touched him, because as soon as his final word was uttered he fell face down in the dirt, and the shocked spectators allowed me to attend to him unhindered. Someone even helped me carry him home.

All the rest of that day I kept watch at his bedside, and the fever was so bad, he began to shout nonsense: the house was on fire, and the ceiling was caving in above his bed. Certainly his flesh was on fire, and he would throw off his covers the moment I spread them over him. I would have gone for a physician, had I dared to leave him.

Then at sundown, just as before, the fever released him. He didn't get up, however. He slept without stirring for hours, then woke in the middle of the night and asked me for something to eat.

I warmed up some broth and fed him with a spoon like a baby. 'Is it always like this?' I whispered. 'Whenever you prophesy, is this how it ends every time?'

'Not always,' he said, attempting a smile. 'When I spoke in the Temple, this was how it *started;* and you witnessed its ending for yourself.' I smiled too, and he added, 'But yes; there is usually sickness, and always weakness. So much is taken out of me... thank you, Berechiah. Thank you for what you have done for me these last three days. I don't know what would have become of me had it not been for you.'

Such joy welled up in my throat that it almost choked me, and in the low lamplight I was relieved that he wouldn't be able to see how red my face was.

'I don't just mean for your fetching me home and looking after me. I mean for your prayers, especially this morning. You know, I could feel the strength of Adonai flowing into me, through you. So I knew that no one would harm me. You kept me going, Baruch.'

For once in my life I was lost for words, and there wasn't a single scribal quotation which could have come anywhere close to describing how I felt. No one had called me Baruch since I'd grown too big to be dandled on my mother's knee, and to hear it on Jeremiah's hallowed lips was more bliss than I could bear.

II

There was no response from the palace to Jeremiah's denunciation of Egypt. I couldn't believe that His Majesty hadn't come to hear of what had been said, but perhaps he wasn't interested. By all accounts he was living a life of luxury and debauchery with his chosen companions.

Meanwhile, when Jeremiah had got back his strength he delivered his oracles against the nations all over again: to me, in the privacy of our home. Word for word he dictated them, and I took them down, without seeing fit to ask why he'd changed his mind and decided that he wanted them recorded. Knowing my thoughts he told me in any case: the documents would stand as a testimony when Babylon's eagle swept down from the north. No one would be able to say that Adonai had failed to give us sufficient warning of its approach.

One sabbath, a month or so after my record was completed, Jeremiah went out to prophesy in public for the fourth time since I'd been with him. I wasn't apprehensive any more; I was certain now that in bringing us together Adonai had made us invincible. Jeremiah would speak while I sustained him with my prayers, afterwards writing down all that he had said. And I felt so proud to be seen with him, to know that throughout Jerusalem my name would now be mentioned in company with his.

I wasn't even concerned when he took his stand at the so-called People's Gate, the one through which the kings of Judah were accustomed to enter and leave the city, nor when he began to vilify the folk who were coming and going, berating them for pursuing their business as though the seventh day had never been hallowed. I wasn't unduly anxious when he placed himself in the path of a group of farmers and accused them of being exactly like their wicked forefathers, stiff-necked and incapable of responding to discipline.

But then he singled out the toughest-looking individual in the party and physically knocked the pack from his back, declaring that instead of Judah's kings passing in and out of this gate an unquenchable fire would be kindled in its mouth and all of Jerusalem's fortifications would be consumed.

The pack had been filled with salted meat. As the top burst open, scrawny children and dogs came from nowhere and grabbed what they could. Some of the farmers shrank back from the fulminating Prophet; the rest shouldered up beside their comrade, who was trying to get near enough to Jeremiah to deal him a blow in the face. But the latter was like a ball of lightning, white-hot and elusive, still shrieking out imprecations. Unable to pray any longer, I stood and bit on my fingers till the blood came, fervently wishing I'd been brought up a wrestler instead of a scribe.

For the victimized peasant had finally succeeded in getting close enough to strike Jeremiah, if not in the face, at least in the stomach. The hail of prophetic curses ceased abruptly; another blow followed the first, and he fell doubled up, with his hair tumbling in the dirt. Emboldened, the peasants formed a ring around him and started to kick him from every side.

I dare not contemplate what might have ensued, had not a fanfare of trumpets blared out at that moment, and heralds' voices shouted, 'Make way for the King! Hail, Jehoiakim ben Josiah, Anointed Sovereign of Judah!'

The peasants scrambled for cover. I hauled Jeremiah to the side of the street, and waited with gritted teeth for the royal party to halt and a detachment of Jehoiakim's minions to drag the pair of us away to some rat-infested dungeon.

Instead, the cavalcade passed us by without even slowing its pace, no doubt making for the King's rural retreat in the southern hills. Ironically - and quite unintentionally - Jeremiah's foe had become the instrument of his salvation.

For the peasants had vanished, along with the children and the dogs. As I knelt in the gutter with the Prophet's head in my lap, a woman from a nearby cottage approached us, with a jar of water and a wad of cloth, and mutely she helped me get the worst of the grit and grime from his cuts. Then slowly, painfully, we made our way back to Ahikam's house.

It was while I was filling a jug from the pool in the courtyard to bathe his wounds properly that I heard someone calling my name and rattling the gate which gave onto the street.

'Berechiah? Berechiah, I know you're in there. Open the gate, you little idiot. It's your brother.'

I froze, for he sounded so angry. Then because it was such a long time since I'd seen anyone who shared my blood or my past, I put down my jug and ran, flinging back the bolts and clasping Seraiah in my arms. 'What are you *doing* here?' I demanded, dragging him inside and slamming the gate behind him, hardly caring that he was struggling to free himself from my embrace.

'I'm here because *you* should *not* be,' he retorted, pushing me away before I smothered him. 'Where is the lunatic? Will he come out and find me?'

'Jeremiah is in bed,' I assured him. 'He was attacked today at the People's Gate. But he isn't mad, Seraiah. He's - '

'I don't want to know! I don't want to hear you speak his name! And I'm very well aware that he was assaulted. He asked for it; that's why you have to leave him and come home with me before it's too late. The man is a danger to himself and to you. Can you not see it, you gullible jackass? Sooner or later he'll get himself locked away, or exiled, or killed... and you'll go down with him.'

'I can't come home, Seraiah.'

'Of course you can. I know Father says he will never have you back, but he'll change his mind if you tell him you are sorry for being so stupid and ungrateful, and that you'll never do anything so irresponsible again.'

'No, Seraiah. You don't understand... I can't come home because I cannot leave Jeremiah.'

'I never heard such drivel; you have allowed infatuation to curdle your brains! There are even some who claim that it's *you* who should be locked away, because you are the one who goads him into saying what he says and making such a fool of himself in front of common yokels and urchins in the streets! Did he ever haunt gateways and gutters and harangue passers by like a hawker of trinkets before you came to live here? They say it is all *your* fault, that you are manipulating him because you bear some grudge against the King and you want divine sanction for your own subversive opinions.'

'Now that *is* drivel, Seraiah! You can't possibly believe a word of it.'

'Of course *I* don't believe it. Because I know you're too dumb to manipulate *anyone!* But others *will* believe what they hear, if they hear it often enough. And suppose the King himself concludes that the pair of you are plotting against him? You'll be indicted for treason, and then you'll be executed... For God's sake, Berechiah, do you think I could stand by and

watch them drag you away to die, knowing I'd done nothing to
warn you?'

He had me by the arms and was shaking me; I
couldn't look him in the face because there was such concern
mingled with the anger in his eyes. Eventually I swallowed
hard and said, 'Please go now, Seraiah. I must attend to
Jeremiah. He's very sick.'

With a snort of exasperation, Seraiah thrust me aside
and marched off towards the gate. After opening it he paused
momentarily, as if to commence his tirade all over again. But
he must have thought better of it, for all he said was, 'Just be
careful, then, little brother. Promise me this at least, on our
mother's life.'

'I'll be careful,' I whispered; and he was gone.

Winter passed and spring returned, and with it came
news of warfare. Every day we heard tales of the exploits of
Nabopolassar of Babylon and his Median allies. Having stripped
the carcass of Assyria, they were now campaigning farther
afield, subduing settled communities and nomads alike, and
ferocious clansmen in the hills whose forebears had never been
conquered in all the history their bards could relate. Soon the
lords of Babylon and Media would be masters of all the
northern world; their only serious rival would be Pharaoh to
the south, whose realm was shielded at present by the paltry
domains of his vassal, Jehoiakim of Judah.

'Is Jehoiakim not even *worried?* I asked Jeremiah.
'Nabopolassar could turn on us at any time.'

'Our noble King has his court prophets to persuade him
that all will be well,' Jeremiah replied. 'My lone voice would
never be heard above their clamour.'

Nevertheless, he spoke out against them, appearing in
the market place one morning when it was crammed with stalls
and people haggling. He went to a seller of herbs, and bought
the whole of his stock. Then he threw great bunches of
marjoram and mint into the crowd and cried out that Adonai
would give the counterfeit prophets bitter plants to eat and
poison to drink, because they had spread their toxic lies

throughout a nation created to be holy. 'Don't listen to a word they say!' he was shrieking. 'What comes from their mouths is vomit, infected with the plague of their hypocrisy! None of these deceivers has stood in Adonai's Council or been made party to his plans. What good is straw, compared with wheat? Adonai's word is a hammer; it will smash them to pieces.'

And still no reaction came from the palace. I was quite sure now that Jehoiakim was ignoring his former teacher deliberately, convinced that this indifference would erode the Prophet's influence far more effectively than attempting to subdue him.

That night, instead of succumbing to sickness, my master was assailed by a grief so profound that he wept for hours, prostrate on his pallet before Adonai. I kept away at first, seeing that he was lost in the presence of his God, but in the end could stand it no longer, and went and knelt beside him and laid my hand upon his head. He twisted about and clung to me, but when his words became audible through his sobbing they weren't addressed to me.

'Oh *God,* will I never find healing for this sorrow? Why spare my body from sickness, only to smite my soul? Up and down the land your people call out: "Is Adonai no longer Lord in Zion?" Why won't you answer them?' He lapsed into incoherence again; when next I could make out words he was wailing, 'Oh, that my head were a well of water! Then I could weep day and night for those bodies will lie unburied in the fields they farmed.' Another bout of sobbing, and then: 'I know, *know* that the people have sinned. I know I could go through the city from one end to the other and find not a single good man. But their priests and prophets have misled them! Let me make confession for their wickedness, if they can't confess for themselves.'

By and by he returned to himself. He gazed at me with reddened eyes and sighed, 'Oh Baruch, how I wish *I* had a palace in the hills where I could go to escape all this, and not have any part in it! *Everyone* hates me, and sometimes I hate them too. But at other times I love them so much that I could die when I think of what lies in store for them. It's Adonai's love, Baruch, not my own. I know that full well. But it's my heart that breaks, my tears that fall.'

I didn't speak - what was there to say? - but watched over him until he slept. At dawn he arose dry-eyed and said, 'Come, Baruch. There is somewhere Adonai is wanting us to go.' And he took me into the streets of the waking city.

I thought he must be intending to preach once again, but instead, we went to the Street of the Potters; a dozen or so had workshops side by side. It was early yet, and one potter only had taken his place at the wheel. The rest were trampling their clay to make it soft.

'What are we doing here?' I hissed at the Prophet. 'Why would Adonai want us to come to a place like this?'

But Jeremiah took no notice. Picking his way through the yard, with its racks of finished pots for sale, and others waiting to be fired, he halted by the open-fronted shop of the potter already at the wheel, and watched him as though bewitched. So I watched too, as the craftsman's boy spun the wheel on its axle, and the master shaped an elegant wine-jar, working with rock-steady hands.

'You'll distract him with your staring,' I whispered to Jeremiah. 'Are we to buy, or to wait for the end of the world?'

He responded, though it was hardly an answer: 'Don't you wonder sometimes what a marvellous thing it must be to create an object of beauty like that? To be good at what you do, and, when you finish your work in the evening, to be able to see some tangible reward for your labours?'

'No,' I replied readily, 'since I did that kind of work for years, and all I ever thought was: why am I doing this same old thing every day? Isn't life more than scrolls of papyrus which fire may consume - or pots which fall from their shelves?'

Jeremiah smiled. 'You are right, of course. No doubt it is better for us to perform the ministry to which we are called, even if we fail in it, than to succeed in a thing which Adonai has not asked us to do.'

I think he spoke more vehemently than he'd intended. The potter, engrossed until now in his task, was startled; briefly his deft hands faltered, and the jar was spoiled.

'Can I help you, my lords?' asked a voice by my shoulder: the potter's apprentice, wiping the clay from his hands on a well-used apron. I turned to the Prophet, but he was staring entranced at the craftsman once more. The potter had flattened the wine-jar and started from scratch with the same lump of clay, reshaping it in quite a different form.

I turned back to the apprentice and shrugged my shoulders, but already one of his workmates was mouthing at him: 'It's the Prophet! Jeremiah of Anathoth! Let him alone!' By which he meant: for God's sake don't provoke him. We don't want trouble here.

Presently Jeremiah blinked, and looked around, then said to the apprentice as though no time had gone by in between: 'Yes, you can help us. I'd like to buy a lamp.' And the lad scurried off to find one.

'Adonai brought us here to buy a *lamp?* I enquired in a whisper. 'We could have got one from the market.'

'We are buying a lamp out of courtesy, Baruch. Adonai brought us here to teach us a lesson.' And while we were on our way home, he told me what that lesson was. Judah was the clay in Adonai's hands, and as the master craftsman he was entitled to do as he liked with it. If his creation had become lop-sided and spoilt, twisted by sin, he could break it down and start all over again, and there was no sense in our getting upset about it. A misshapen pot is good for nothing, and no one has more right to grieve over it than its maker, who at the outset had such high hopes for it. But if flattened out and remoulded, it can be as lovely as it was always intended to be.

'Then there will be a remoulding? After its destruction, the nation will be remade?'

'If we live to see it,' he said, and all at once stopped dead in the middle of the road and laid his hands on my shoulders, hanging his head between them. When he looked up, his eyes were brimming once again, and he groaned, 'How

I wish I were more like you, Baruch, always finding the hope in things, always expecting the sunshine to burn through the cloud! Yes, there will be restoration, but how can I think about that when I know what must precede it?'

Then out of the blue the spirit fell upon him, striking like wayward lightning on a storm-free day. 'Flee for refuge!' he was yelling, standing in the roadway, arms outstretched. 'Escape while you still have time! People of Judah, people of Benjamin...' and he started to harass whoever came near, grasping at their clothing so they screamed and left cloaks or mantles behind as they tore themselves free. He described for them the hosts which were coming from Babylonia, the havoc they would wreak on their march through our country, the siege-ramps they would raise against the city.

'Who can I warn? Who will listen?' he pleaded. 'I am gorged with the wrath of Adonai; I cannot hold it in!' And that wrath would soon boil over, he told them, engulfing the children playing in the alleyways, the youths as they sported and the maidens as they braided their hair, engulfing bridegrooms and brides in their marriage-beds, their mothers and fathers at work, and bald-headed elders with their white-haired wives. All of their homes would be consumed, and their land and their property handed over to strangers. Could it ever be imagined that snow would fall in the summertime and melt in winter, or that birds would forget to migrate? If all of nature obeyed the laws laid down for it, how was it that Judah had broken the laws laid down for Adonai's Chosen People?

He paused temporarily to recover his breath, for his face was almost blue. But then he ran up the steps to the nearest rooftop, taking them three at a time, like Elijah endowed with godlike strength as he ran before Ahab's chariot. Leaning alarmingly over the parapet he shouted:

Take up a dirge on the heights of the mountains!
  Wail and howl like creatures ensnared!
Adonai renounces this vile generation,
  Withholding his breath and denying us life.
Our pastures lie desolate, barren and poisoned,

He couldn't continue, for it seemed that he himself was choking. He hung across the parapet gasping for air until I was certain he would fall to his death. I sent up a desperate prayer for his protection, along with a question: must he *live* his own prophecies now, as well as speak them?

My prayer was swiftly answered, for his breathing eased almost at once. Feeling his way down the steps, he bade me take him home.

Nor did my question go unanswered for very long. Early in the summer Jeremiah informed me that a new phase in his ministry was beginning. Speaking the word of Adonai wasn't enough any more; folk had grown too used to hearing him deliver his oracles in their streets. From now on, his message would not merely be told, but shown. And the actions he performed would set in motion the events they portended.

I wasn't quite sure what he meant. He wouldn't explain any further, however - perhaps he didn't know himself - but he got very excited about the whole thing, his mood soaring until he was quite beyond my reach. Despite the rebuke he'd once issued to me, he sang in the mornings, and chattered and laughed his way through our meals, and exchanged with me whole rallies of proverbial quips, astounding me with his knowledge of a subject he'd claimed to despise.

But it was all so *unlike* him, and not always even appropriate. He laughed when things weren't funny, and when we talked, his thoughts would go too fast for his mouth and come out jumbled, his sentences never completed because some new idea would rise up and oust the one half spoken. He hardly seemed to need any sleep, and would get out of bed in the middle of the night to pray. His behaviour about the house grew bizarre: on one occasion, way before dawn, he entered my room, took every item of clothing I possessed, and tossed it in the courtyard pool. When I emerged bewildered with a blanket round my waist, he roared with laughter and said it served me right for being so lazy and getting up so late.

'Late?' I spluttered. 'It isn't even daylight yet!'

He only laughed harder, then announced that he was going to market to get some provisions; I would have to stay at home since I'd nothing to wear.

Cursing, I devoted the time he was out to rescuing my garments from the pool and spreading them on the ground to dry. He was away so long, I started to worry; and when he returned, the only thing he had bought was a linen loincloth. This he proceeded to put on; I watched open-mouthed, for he'd stripped himself naked right there in the courtyard.

'Don't you want me to wash that for you first?' I asked him. 'Who knows where it may have been?' I put out a hand to take the cloth from him, but he grabbed my wrist and jerked it out of the way.

'It must not be touched by anyone but me!' he barked. 'And it must not be washed on any account. It must be new, pristine, don't you understand?' Then he turned and stalked off towards the gate, and I thought: Heaven preserve us! He's going to go out dressed like that.

There was nothing I could do to prevent it. The weather was hot, so some of my own clothes were already dry; I threw on a tunic and tied a spare one around me, hoping to persuade the Prophet to don it at the earliest opportunity.

If people had ceased to take notice of my master when he spoke, they certainly noticed him striding half naked through their city. On and on he marched, going north until we reached the Benjamin Gate which led to the lands of the tribe bearing that name. The watchmen stood aside and we went straight through.

'Where are we going?' I asked in dismay. A city boy born and bred, I had seldom been anywhere else, and never into the barren red valley toward which we were heading. Jeremiah neglected to reply, but I knew that Anathoth, the village of his birth, lay that way. Could it be that we were going there?

As we left Jerusalem behind, I began to be frightened. The road was narrow, and littered with sharp little stones. Gravel got inside my indoor sandals and punctured the soles of my feet, making every step more painful than the last. My head was aching, for the breeze which cooled the city was no longer blowing. I'd brought no water, and feared I would shrivel like the carob pods lying in the dust.

I begged Jeremiah to stop and let me rest, but he wouldn't. Again it seemed that he'd been endowed with preternatural stamina. And we weren't bound for Anathoth, either; we took a turning which went right past it and plunged away to the east. 'Where *are* we going?' I repeated. 'Please, just tell me how far it is.'

He stopped in his tracks so abruptly that I almost walked into him. He rounded on me and snapped, 'Did I ask you to come with me? Did I? Did I?'

'No,' I croaked wretchedly, and lowered myself to sit on a boulder by the roadside. 'It's just that you're walking so fast. I need a drink. I need to get this grit out of my sandals. And my skin is burning.'

'Perath,' he announced, in answer to the question I'd put to him first.

'Perath?' I echoed, deciding that I must have misheard. I'd come across the name in my studies, but as one of the many which is given to the River Euphrates, a journey of twenty five days away at least.

'Perath the *village*,' Jeremiah explained, somewhat more patiently. 'But for the purpose of what we must do, the River Euphrates is what it will represent, for it is from the lands of the Euphrates that the judgment is coming.'

He'd condescended to look at me at last, and squatting now on his haunches in front of me he said, 'Baruch, forgive me. I shouldn't have been so thoughtless. But it's not far now, and we'll find water as soon as we arrive.' Then briefly he embraced me, and I rested my throbbing head on his neck. I felt awkward and yet blessed, because for the first time our roles were reversed and he was the one giving comfort to me.

Then it was up and onward, with Jeremiah physically supporting me in exactly the way I'd so often supported him. When we reached the first of the squat little houses it was well past noon, and not a soul was in sight. But there was a well, and the Prophet drew water for me, and made me sit in the shade while he went in search of food.

Once the midday heat had gone out of the sun, we walked the length of the village in full view of its inhabitants. The siesta was over: women were going to the well, children wrestled in the doorways, men sat on benches playing games on boards drawn in the dust. No one approached us, but they all followed our progress with their eyes; they'd no idea who we were, but anyone come from the city was rarity enough. Rarer still to see a wild-eyed, wild-haired holy man wearing only a loincloth, leading a pink-faced youth in a sleeveless tunic and flimsy sandals better suited to attending a rich man's banquet than hiking round the desert.

On the far side of the village we came to an outcrop of jagged fissured rocks. Here Jeremiah halted, then took off his loincloth and stood stark naked in front of me. He stretched out one hand to touch my side; I shrank back, before realizing he wanted my spare tunic. He put it on, taking his loincloth and bundling it into a crevice. Then he said. 'Come. It's time to go home.' And we started out on the long walk back to Jerusalem.

Several days later, Jeremiah announced his intentions of going to Perath again. He advised me not to come, but I wouldn't let him travel alone; besides, this time I would be prepared. I wore a robe with long sleeves, and sturdy shoes, and carried a flagon of water and a bag of roasted grain.

When we got to the place where he'd buried the cloth, he stripped off his garments once more and bade me put them in my pack. Then he cleared the sand from the cleft in the rocks, and lifted the loincloth out.

It was ruined. It must have been lying across the entrance to a sand rat's burrow, for it was frayed and dirty, and smelled of dung. But Jeremiah proceeded to bind it around his waist just as before.

I tried to stop him, but the spirit had overshadowed him and he was oblivious to my presence. Whenever I paused on our journey home to drink from my flagon of water he wouldn't have even a sip. On entering the city he strutted through the streets crying: 'This is how Adonai will destroy the pride of Judah! You stubborn people are like this loincloth: meant to be bound to your God, but destined for ruin by the River Perath.'

I thought it would all be over when we got back to the house. Instead, still gorged with the spirit, he said, 'Unlock the cellars, Baruch, and bring up a dozen jars of wine.'

Knowing better than to argue, I did as he bade me, struggling up with the huge amphorae one at a time. Each of them he placed in the street, until there were twelve in a row. Then he started haranguing the passers by, shouting: 'Every wine-jar should be filled with wine!' And when they tried to ignore him, he yelled: 'Thus will Adonai fill everyone in this land; he'll fill you with his strongest wine till you are drunk: kings, priests, prophets... everyone! Then you will stagger, and he'll smash you into pieces, one against another. No compassion will restrain him!' And he would lift up one of the jars and dash it into the next so that both of them shattered, and wine ran like blood in the gutters.

Adonai kept him awake and transported all night. He sat and sang morbid psalms, yanking on the strings of his lyre as though he meant to destroy it. In the morning he ordered me to go to the Temple Court, where a company of priests and elders of the city would be gathered, and to lead them to the Tophet, whither he was going via the Street of the Potters.

I didn't ask how he knew that the elders and priests would be assembled, nor what to do if they wouldn't come with me; I was sure somehow that all would turn out as he'd said. And indeed it did. I don't know what had occasioned the meeting of these dignitaries, but there they all were: senior priests from the Temple and officials of Jehoiakim's Court, leaders of clans and heads of prominent Jerusalem households. When I bade them accompany me to the Valley of Hinnom where my master the prophet awaited them, they followed like lambs. It was uncanny.

He was there when we arrived, standing in the precinct courtyard. To reach him we had to pass the myriad tiny tombstones of Molech's victims: each stone bore the name of a child who had perished in the sacred flames. Pungent black smoke from the furnace billowed even now above the precinct, and lingered over the courtyard where Jeremiah stood, holding in his arms an amphora twice the size of anything in Ahikam's cellars.

A stiff wind was blowing, and the Prophet's hair streamed black as the furnace smoke. Blacker still was his countenance, and his voice when he spoke was like a quaking of the earth. Judah's leaders had tossed their own sons and daughters into Molech's ravening jaws; therefore they themselves were doomed. Their own blood would go down to that of their murdered children, and the foul place in which they now found themselves would no longer be called the Valley of Hinnom, but the Vale of Slaughter. The city would be besieged by the armies of the Euphrates, and so dreadful would conditions become within Zion's hallowed walls that its inhabitants would devour one another, and there would be no more babies for Molech because their own parents would eat them.

At this point, without any warning, he hurled the wine-jar to the ground. 'Thus shall I break this people, and this city!' Jeremiah screamed on Adonai's behalf, dropping to his knees and gathering shards in his hands, flinging them into the crowd. 'The whole of Jerusalem will be a Tophet, reeking of decay!'

He floundered around in the chaos he had created, pieces of broken pottery grinding themselves into his flesh till his knees and shins were cut to ribbons. No one else moved a muscle, for the Prophet was howling now like a jackal, tearing his hair with gore-spattered hands as he rocked back and forth in the dust. I went to his side and tried to drag him away from the grisly mess, but he kept on picking up the sharpest slivers of earthenware and thrusting them under my chin, wailing,

'Look, Baruch, look! What use are these now? What use?' and then stabbing his thighs or his forearms with them, puncturing the skin as though to release the pressure of celestial fury along with the blood. 'When clay is soft,' he wept, 'the potter can crush it and mould it again. But this... what good is this? It is baked and hardened like Judah's heart, fit for nothing but the pit.' He gathered an armful of shards and held them fiercely to his breast, crying over them like a mother mourning a baby which has died while she was giving it suck.

'Come,' I urged him. 'It's time to go home.' For his audience had overcome its shock and was growing indignant: the Prophet had plainly lost whatever vestige of sanity he'd once possessed, and they were fools to be wasting their time with him. But 'You *will* believe me! You *will!*' he shrieked, and made off at a run for the Temple Court.

The ban against his appearing in the Temple had never been lifted, but he went there and delivered his tirade all over again. Pashhur, however, was waiting for him, having been told I suppose that the majority of his senior staff had hived off down to the Tophet in response to his enemy's summons. They had followed him back from there, too, baying for the blasphemer's blood - or what remained of it.

Pashhur would gladly have given them what they wanted. But he wasn't the only man who had been forewarned of Jeremiah's arrival. Ahikam and two of his brothers were waiting as well, and Pashhur knew that they would have strangled him with their own bare hands had he permitted a stoning.

'Jeremiah ben Hilkiah was barred from this place indefinitely and he knows it full well,' Pashhur declared. 'Whatever the content of his preaching, he has defied my personal injunction. As Chief Officer of the Temple, I rule that he must be flogged, and placed in the stocks overnight. He will be released at dawn.'

Then on every side there was shouting and cursing and jostling, and I watched transfixed as they examined Jeremiah's disfigured body to ascertain how much punishment it could withstand. Then he was bound to a pillar; one of

Pashhur's minions produced a leather whip with multiple thongs and the scourging commenced.

I wanted to look away, yet could not. With every stroke the weals on his back grew uglier, until the skin was ruptured and rivulets of blood ran this way and that, their crosshatched pattern glistening in the cruel summer sun. Only the noise of the multitude spared me from hearing him scream. But the raw blind terror in his eyes was less distressing to me than the blood-lust in the eyes of those who were savouring the loathsome spectacle. I wished he would faint and thus gain remission from the pain; then I hoped he would not, because at least while he was writhing I knew he was alive.

At length the chastisement ceased. The man who had administered the beating stood back panting; others approached and loosed the Prophet's bonds, and he toppled sideways onto the pavement. Then he was hauled to his feet and taken to the northern corner of the precinct, where the stocks stood ready. There they fixed him, his ankles, wrists and neck clamped between heavy oaken beams, with his flayed red back still bleeding.

At this point, Pashhur and his underlings departed, leaving a detachment of guards to ensure that the rabble didn't stone their victim after all.

No one tried. But they threw some fairly unpleasant things instead, and their jeering stung my ears. I fought my way forward through the seething mass of malevolent humanity and begged the guards to allow me to tend my master's injuries. Mercifully, they granted my request, and simultaneously Ahikam invaded the cordon, armed with a flagon of water.

In all the time I'd been living at his house, I'd never once met our landlord in person. Now we laboured side by side, tearing strips from our robes and soaking them and cleaning the Prophet's wounds, united in our common task, comfortable in our mutual silence as though we'd known one another all our lives. Jeremiah himself was unaware of our efforts, but when we were finally through, Ahikam said, 'Thank you, Berechiah. In serving Jeremiah so faithfully these past few weeks you have lifted a weighty burden from my shoulders. Truly you're a gift from God.'

I smiled, embarrassed by his lavish praise. He was of an age with Jeremiah, though he looked older: his close-cut hair was receding from his forehead, and responsibility together with bereavement had so lined his face as to lend it a weary dignity. I said, 'Go home to your family, Lord Ahikam. I'll stay with him here until morning.'

But Shaphan's son wouldn't hear of it. 'The mob hates you too, you know,' he reminded me, and I shuddered, recalling my brother's admonitions.

At daybreak Pashhur released him as promised. Jeremiah revived in time to hiss into the priest's implacable face: 'Adonai has renamed you, Pashhur ben Immer! He's named you Terror on Every Side, because you'll be a terror to yourself and to all who are like you! Your henchmen will be slaughtered, and your kinsmen deported; the treasures of your precious Temple will be plunder for the pagans! You'll die and be buried in Babylon, you and all your house!' Then his eyes rolled backwards inside his head and he passed out.

Ahikam helped me carry him home, and when he revived again late in the afternoon, Adonai had slackened his grip and left him to his own pain and to his ravaged emotions. He lay face down on his pallet for hours, then turned on his side with his forehead pressed to his knees and arms about his head. Then he lay out flat on his lacerated back, aggravating his own suffering while accusing his God of hating him, of deceiving him, of promising him protection whilst providing none.

'But you're still alive,' I said to him. 'You preached in the Temple Court, and lived to tell of it.'

My reasoning could not reach him. As if the weals on his back were not enough, he gouged the flesh on his arms with his own jagged nails, re-opening the wounds he'd made with the pot-shards. He refused to eat or drink, but when I reproached him said only: 'The day is coming when no one will eat or drink. Adonai hates us all, and me the most. *Let* him hate me. *Let* him kill me. I don't care.'

And sure enough, from that day forth we had no rain. Summer ran on into autumn, and the former rains should have arrived to soften the ground for the planting of grain. The sky turned grey and heavy as lead, but not a droplet fell from the pregnant clouds. The following spring brought leaden skies once more, yet they were fruitless as the womb of a crone. Food ran short, cisterns were emptied; a flask of water cost more than a jar of wine. Cattle wasted and died in the fields; infants died at their mothers' empty breasts. I asked Jeremiah why we did not pray for the calamity to end.

'I knew things would come to this,' he answered listlessly. 'I knew things would come to this. The drought we had in the days of Josiah was a warning. Even *this* is a warning, that the land of milk and honey is becoming a wilderness. The Promised Land is lost to us, Baruch. Drought prefigures exile; so it is written in the Law of Moses. The sin of mankind wreaks havoc on Creation itself.'

He even had me write all this down and send the tablet to the palace, for the attention of the King. But nothing changed. Jehoiakim gave no call for repentance, and the clouds gave no rain. Soon there was no water to be bought however much one was willing to pay. Jeremiah and I were kept alive by the dwindling resources of Ahikam's cellars, and by paying exorbitant prices for food which the King imported from Egypt for those who could afford to buy it. I don't suppose His Majesty lost much sleep over the fate of those who couldn't, and I don't doubt for a moment that he made a pretty profit out of the rest of us.

For twelve months after that the drought persisted. A message came from Seraiah my brother: his youngest son had died because his wife had no milk. Still Jeremiah refused to intercede for his hapless people, stating simply that the Lord had forbidden him. He lay on his bed and stared at the ceiling until his muscles began to waste away, and his sunken flesh broke out in sores. I had to make him soup with wine and vegetables, because he could take no solid food, and I had to prop him on cushions and feed it to him myself.

In the following spring, it rained. The clouds rolled in overnight and wept their silent tears until dawn, so that only when Jerusalem awoke to the new day did she learn what had happened.

But that very day we got word of initial clashes between the kings of Babylon and Egypt. These encounters had taken place near Carchemish, the Egyptian bridge-head on the Euphrates in northern Syria, which guarded several important trade-routes. The forces of Nabopolassar had taken over some minor stronghold, and then the Egyptians had taken it back. Insignificant border skirmishes perhaps; and the veteran campaigner Nabopolassar hadn't come out of them too well, as Jeremiah's critics were quick to point out.

Yet from insignificant skirmishes dreadful wars may arise. And rumour had it that Nabopolassar, having aged and grown sick, was in the process of transferring the reins of command into the hands of his eldest son. This latter, the Crown Prince of Babylon, was a mere twenty five years old, but brave as Saul, audacious as David, and shrewd as Solomon, all at once. His name was Nebuchadrezzar.

CHAPTER 16: JEREMIAH

Another year went by between the end of the drought and the night on which Adonai next addressed me - or should I say assaulted me. Throughout this time I had kept to my bed, eating and drinking only when Baruch made me.

Poor, patient Baruch; how little thanks he got for his faithful ministrations. It wasn't that I meant to be ungrateful. I was just so sick of life, so sick of everything. Why should I want to get up and go about in a city where so many had starved? Zion was God-forsaken; Adonai had sent us rain for one reason alone: that some of us might survive to see David's City burnt to the ground.

Baruch was the single ray of light in my melancholy existence. Oh, how intensely I'd hated him when first he'd arrived! How I'd resented him dumping his bags on my doorstep, then installing himself in my home. He was so offensively cheerful, so maddeningly witty, so self-consciously learned whilst at the same time being hopelessly naive. But he loved me unswervingly, and as his venerable teachers of wisdom have said: there is a friend who sticks closer than a brother.

The night before Adonai came, Baruch had slept in my room because I'd been too unwell to be left. And what a solace it had been in my restless hours to trace against the wall the faint silhouette of his slumbering form, to watch his shoulders rising and falling so rhythmically, and to study the progress of the moonlight as it groped its way in at my window and crept across his trusting face. He wasn't handsome, but he was young, so very young, and so incongruously innocent in such a wicked world. My own hair was still black, but I was painfully conscious sometimes of all the years that had gone for me, and the little good I'd done with them.

The following day I'd felt rather better, and when evening came, Baruch had retired to his own room. I'd lain down and drifted into a blissfully dreamless sleep almost at once.

But at midnight I was awoken so violently, I thought that the earth must have moved. I leaped to my feet; the moon was full and shining straight through the window and I could see every object in the room. Nothing had broken or tumbled from its place.

Then I was thrown back savagely onto my pallet, and there was such a heaviness oppressing me that I could have believed the ceiling had collapsed on top of me. I was gasping for air and trembling; my heart was missing beats and my head felt like something being pounded on an anvil. I thought: this is it, I'm dying; and I tried to shout for Baruch to come and be with me when I went, but Adonai's voice said: *Arise, Jeremiah. I need to speak with you.*

The next I knew, I was up on my hands and knees; he must have dragged me there. I tried to ask why, why this sudden violence, but understood without his needing to tell me that there was no other way he could have commanded my attention. Then I saw that between my hands was an enormous bowl brimming with wine, and I'd no idea how it had got there. Adonai said: *This is the cup of my wrath, Jeremiah, and you are to cause the nations to drink it.*

I shook my head, for it was full of hammering and I couldn't think. *Rejoice,* Adonai continued, *for the hour of your vindication is nigh. For twenty three years you have served me well, and the words you have spoken are due to be fulfilled. Then the world will know that you were not insane, but inspired.*

No, no, I was trying to say; there will be no rejoicing in this house when Jerusalem falls. If you want to reward me, stay your hand.

Jerusalem is but one doomed city among many, Jeremiah. What has been spoken in my name cannot be unsaid; what you yourself have foretold is already accomplished in Heaven, and earth cannot do other than reflect it. A mighty battle is to be fought between Babylon and Egypt. Babylon will prevail, and then she will overwhelm every nation whose lands divide hers from the Pharaoh's, Judah included. This is the turning point in your ministry, Jeremiah, and the turning point in the history of your people - my *people. You yourself are to inaugurate the time of reckoning. You are to make the nations drink from the cup which is set before you.*

The pain was receding, but not the confusion. What was I meant to do? Was I to travel the world and offer my wine to its kings and princes?

No, Adonai replied, before the questions had even formed themselves fully in my mind. *You are to stand with the cup in your hands, and speak out the names of the cities and the nations destined for destruction. Then you are to drink its contents on their behalf.*

Suddenly all remaining heaviness was gone, and the slightest effort on my part had me upright with the bowl in my hands. *Begin with Jerusalem,* Adonai instructed me. *Judgment begins at the house of God.*

'Jerusalem,' I whispered, and raised the bowl gingerly to my lips.

No, said Adonai. *Shout it aloud. The gods of the nations must hear you. And do not sip at the wine like a beggar at a banquet. You must drink deeply. You must drink till you are drunk with my anger.*

'I don't want to wake Baruch,' I protested, though in truth it was myself I was afraid for.

Baruch will not be disturbed, Adonai assured me. *Now do as I have commanded you.*

So I did. I called: 'Jerusalem!' at the top of my voice, and took a great mouthful of wine. *Good,* said Adonai, while I spluttered and coughed and my eyes filled up; the wine was the strongest I'd ever tasted, but also the sweetest and the best. *Now,* Adonai resumed, *you must name the other fortified cities of Judah. Lachish, Azekah, Libnah, Beth Shemesh... come, we have much to do.*

So 'Lachish!' I called, and 'Azekah!' and after each name I took another draught. When every city in Judah had been cited, I was told to name the cities of the Philistines, and those of Phoenicia, and Edom, and Moab, and Ammon, then the tribes of Arabia... on and on went the list, yet the cup seemed full as ever. Perhaps I am dreaming all this, I thought; yet the glorious flavour of the wine and my growing intoxication were real enough. When I called out the names Adonai gave to me, my speech was becoming progressively slurred, and the room had started to spin.

But no respite was permitted. *The cities of Zimri and Elam*, Adonai went on, and I drank again; *and those of the tribes in the northern hills...* until I was lurching against the walls, and the wine was running down my face and my clothes because I could no longer find my mouth with the bowl. *No city must escape!* Adonai was insisting. *Is Jerusalem to fall while heathen strongholds go unpunished?*

I began to protest again, to claim that I could drink no more. I was nauseous and retching, simultaneously craving one last draught of the divine elixir and sickened by its cloying sweetness. Soon I was too far gone to know if the mess down my tunic had come from the bowl or back up from my belly. At long last I was ordered to name Babylon herself, for when her work as Adonai's instrument had been completed she too was to be consumed. Thank God, I breathed, it is over; for the bowl was finally empty. But Adonai said: *Now, prophesy against the places you have named. Herald their destruction. Open your mouth, and my word will be accomplished.*

If I open my mouth now, I shall only vomit, I thought; but Adonai said: *That matters not, for the nations too will vomit, and stagger, and fall to rise no more.*

Once again therefore I did as I was bidden. I opened my mouth and was sick; I reached for the wall to support myself, and missed, and keeled over, and all the world was turning black. But my voice was calling down fire from Heaven, while my body knew not if it was crawling, kneeling or lying on the ground. When in the end the thing really was over, I rolled in my filth and slept there. But my dreams were full of joy, because I had done what Adonai had asked of me.

It was dawn when Baruch roused me. I surfaced with the mother of headaches, to find him slapping my face and exclaiming, 'Merciful God in Heaven, Jeremiah! What made you do this? Are you not to be trusted even yet?' - sounding more like my father than my scribe.

I tried to explain what had happened, but as I did so, my joy dissolved into misery. I grieved inconsolably for the fate of our city, for our beautiful country with its meadows, its flowers and its misty mountains, its myriad species of birds and animals, and its unhappy people, especially those rare individuals who had striven so hard to love me. What would become of Ahikam or his son Gedaliah, old enough now to get sons of his own? What of Ebed-Melech, the gentle eunuch who had seen to my needs at the palace? What of Nehushta, the godly wife of our godless king, or Coniah her son, or of Prince Mattani his friend? What would become of Huldah, or of Ruth, my first and my purest love...

Let them go, whispered Adonai. *Don't you remember? This is why I forbade you to marry, and why I have kept you from coming too close to anyone, whether man, woman or child. I watch over everyone who puts his trust in me; but unlike you, I know what is truly good for them.*

'What?' demanded Baruch, shaking me again. 'What are you mumbling about? Are you drunk even now?'

'No,' I replied, then, 'Yes. I don't know,' but could say no more, for already Adonai was laying a fresh burden upon me. *Go into the marketplace at once,* he instructed me. *The traders are setting out their stalls for the business, merchants from Egypt among them. Proclaim to them the imminent defeat of their Pharaoh. Nebuchadrezzar my servant, Crown Prince of Babylon, is poised with sharpened talons to tear Necho's army to shreds. The eagle will bite off the falcon's head.*

Baruch did his best to prevent me from quitting the house. But he left off his efforts when he saw that the spirit was upon me. I stumbled through the market in my nightclothes and fetched up at the display of an Egyptian craftsman who worked in iron and bronze. His table was laden with weapons.

Seizing a dagger in one hand and a sword in the other, I described wild circles in the air, whilst in words describing the impending downfall of the warrior Pharaoh. His men would polish their weapons so they gleamed like the ones I brandished; they would harness their horses and march out in splendour. But in chaos they would retreat; in terror they would be scattered. The Sovereign Lord Almighty would raise his sword against the Pharaoh and allow it to slake its thirst with Egyptian blood. The same would become a libation, poured out to Heaven on a foully polluted earth.

Thankfully, Baruch disarmed me before I harmed myself or anyone else. He led me home still raving; I don't think any of the Egyptians present had been especially offended by my carrying on, for they'd dismissed me as quite demented. In the days that followed I was like a child who plays on sand too hot for his feet as I waited for news of the battle to be brought.

At last the reports came through. At Carchemish on the Euphrates young Prince Nebuchadrezzar had won his first military victory, sending Necho and his army running for their lives. Politically he had triumphed already, by marrying Amuhea, princess of Media, thus cementing Babylon's alliance with the only nation left which might have been capable of squaring up to his own.

Necho led the remnant of his forces in a haphazard retreat through Syria, with Nebuchadrezzar hot on his tail. The Pharaoh holed up at another of his bases, Hamath on the River Orontes; and here his adversary defeated him over again. The same then happened at Riblah. Nebuchadrezzar was resolved upon chasing Necho to the very borders of Egypt. Inevitably, the course of this desperate hunt would pass through Jehoiakim's kingdom.

Jerusalem panicked, and all of Judah with her. One day we were vassals of Egypt, the next, Egypt was nothing, and the redoubtable Pharaoh Necho, falcon-god Horus incarnate, was being hounded like a beast of the field. Terrified peasants from the villages around Jerusalem flocked into the city, craving the security which its fortifications seemed to offer. The streets became gorged with refugees, living rough and begging for food. Some were nomads who had never previously lived within walls in all their lives.

Among these latter were the Rechabites, members of a sect whose founder had believed that the only way to preserve the purity of the Hebrew religion was to live in tents and pasture flocks. The Rechabites grew no food and planted no vineyards, nor did they touch fermented drink, lest they be tempted to revere the Baals. The sight of such outlandish clansmen huddling cowed within our walls brought home to many, at last, that Judah was in dire straits.

Baruch, ever impetuous as he was generous, invited a group of Rechabites to lodge with us. But they preferred to erect their tents across our alleyway, with the result that we could no longer enter or leave our home without invading their camp. Meanwhile the multitudes who had chosen to disregard me for years were suddenly pounding on my gates, demanding to be told what Nebuchadrezzar was going to do when he reached Judah. Some of these unfortunates even had dust and ashes on their heads, as though external tokens of repentance could save their wretched skins. 'What is God saying to us now?' they wailed; and, 'Pray for us, please; we don't want to die.' This, I thought, is a turning point indeed. From scoffing at my every utterance, they have come to regard me as expert on everything. Who *are* these Babylonians? they wanted to know. What do they look like? Who are their gods?

And because I could answer so few of their questions, their swollen imaginations provided answers of their own. The Babylonians were giants, and Nebuchadrezzar himself was indestructible - you could cut out his heart and he would not die, but his foaming blood would corrode your blade.

So I stood on my own rooftop and prophesied to them from there, without even needing to venture outside the gate. But the word I brought them was not what they wanted to hear. 'Since the thirteenth year of Josiah, I have spoken the word of Adonai to you, yet you have not listened. Therefore Adonai will bring his servant Nebuchadrezzar against you. All will be waste and desolation, and Judah will serve the King of Babylon for seventy years!'

No longer did they deny that I spoke the true word of Adonai. They wailed all the louder, and tore their clothing, so that my heart went out to them. I told them that Babylon too would perish once the seventy years were completed, and that a remnant of Judah would return and be restored. But none of this would come about until every individual who grovelled before me was dead.

Though no one contested the truth of what I was saying, there were those who disputed its fairness, just as I myself had once dared to do. Why should the pagan Nebuchadrezzar be granted the satisfaction of crowing over our demise?

'You deny that you deserve your punishment?' I shouted back. 'I'll show you why you deserve it!' My spirit aflame with Adonai's fire, I leaped from the roof down into the street, and entered the Rechabite encampment. 'Come with me,' I enjoined the patriarch of their clan, and he did so, signalling his kinsmen to follow. With the crowd milling in our wake, I led the sons of Rechab to the Temple, since this was the only building they would deign to enter. I marched into the Court, and no one challenged me; temporarily at least, every man in the city, Pashhur included, acknowledged my status before God, and feared me because of it.

The men I had brought, and those who had followed, I took to a room where the junior priests would sit to share their meals. 'Be my guests!' I invited the Rechabites flamboyantly, and spread my arms to encourage them all to recline around the tables. Then I offered them wine of the choicest vintage; I clapped my hands, and swarms of Temple boys came running to serve them. But the Rechabites would not partake.

'There!' I announced to those who had protested their own innocence. 'Surely you understand now? These men remain faithful to their law, though it was given to them by a mortal man like themselves. But the rest of you despise the Law of *God!* Be assured that when Babylon's eagle swoops, the sons of Rechab will evade her claws. But know this too: when Babylon falls, there will be for *her* no revival in seventy years. She will fall to rise no more.'

Presently Nebuchadrezzar swept southward over Judah's border, treating Jehoiakim's little kingdom as though it were already his own. Jerusalem braced herself for a siege, but the Prince of Babylon rode on by, the hooves of his horses kicking dust in her face; it was the Pharaoh he wanted to smite, and Necho's vassal could wait. Then a small squadron of cavalry was detached from the main body of Nebuchadrezzar's army, as though as an afterthought. Having ridden back towards us, its captain requested permission for himself and his colleagues to enter the city as ambassadors.

Permission was refused - a foolish response on Jehoiakim's part, as well as an insolent one, but I think he was afraid to have even one of these Mesopotamian monsters in our midst. I didn't see the ambassadors for myself, nor did Baruch, but we had them described to us by Ahikam. They were men of ordinary stature after all, but they wore great crested helmets, and coats of mail, and carried enormous maces denoting their diplomatic authority. Their mounts were stallions whose manes and tails were braided with gold, and the men themselves wore their hair past their shoulders, elaborately curled like their beards. Suddenly, everything Egyptian seemed homely and familiar.

'Very well,' their captain shouted up at the guards on the walls and to anyone else who could hear him. 'Your king has waived his right to be heard, therefore he shall be hearer only. And let him hear this, you his parasites, cowards cringing behind his battlements: His Highness Prince Nebuchadrezzar of Babylon instructs you to bring out to us treasures from your Temple, as a token of your god's deference to ours. And you must send out hostages, who will accompany us when we return to Nebuchadrezzar. Fifty handsome youths of noble birth and proven intelligence; and your king himself.'

Consternation erupted. 'Hostages? Why hostages?' Jehoiakim's counsellors enquired of one another. 'And how can they expect us to surrender the King?'

'The hostages are a guarantee,' Ahikam explained to me when he came to talk the matter over. 'Nebuchadrezzar intends to ensure that we don't send an army after *him* as he passes through our territory, as Josiah did against Necho. If our King and the cream of our younger generation are in his care, we are hardly likely to attempt anything reckless.'

'What would he do with the fifty youths?' Baruch asked anxiously. 'Does he want eunuchs to serve in his harem?'

'More likely wants dogs, to lick his studded boots,' Ahikam said bitterly. 'He would fill their heads with Mesopotamian magic, subvert their beliefs and turn them into Babel-lovers, then send them back here to govern us.'

'*What* beliefs?' I retorted, and laughed. 'The heads of our young noblemen would be filled all too easily, since there is very little in any of them to be cleared away first. So what will happen, Ahikam? Will hostages be handed over? Will the King himself be surrendered? Will Adonai's holy vessels be carried away and placed in the temples of idols?'

'There are those at the palace who argue that they should be,' Ahikam admitted. 'They say that our only hope is to do whatever the Babylonians require of us.'

'We *have* no hope,' I reminded him. 'Except that when all this is over, Adonai may choose to remember our descendants even though *they* forget *him*.'

'You're saying we should persist in our refusal to co-operate? That we should leave Nebuchadrezzar no choice but to subject us to a demonstration of his power?'

'I'm saying it doesn't matter *what* we do, Ahikam. We provoke him now, or we wait for him to turn against us later on. What difference can it make?'

But this verdict was my own, not Adonai's. Even as I finished speaking, I sensed his overshadowing. He said to me: *It* does *matter, my son. Submission to Nebuchadrezzar is imperative. The Mesopotamian Prince is my instrument; for anyone to stand in his way would be worse than futile. Exile is what I have willed for my people, so that I may woo them back to myself by the waters of Babylon as I wooed their forefathers in the wilderness. There will be destruction and there will be death; but how much of either depends on them - and on you.*

'It depends upon *me?* What would you have me do, then? Go to Jehoiakim and recommend that he place himself at the mercy of a merciless oppressor? After who knows what became of Shelemaiah?'

No. You must seek out those at the palace who favour co-operation with Babylon, and you must encourage them to do as they think fit. Assure them that you and I will lend them our support.

'But I shall be labelled a traitor! A traitor and a coward; and rightly so! No matter how much Jehoiakim loathes me, I cannot do it. I *will* not do it!'

Jeremiah, how very weary you make me. You are forty three years old, but still you play the rebel. Have you not learnt? You may fight, but you can never win. All you get is pain in your head from beating it against the wall of my sovereign will. You cannot be held responsible for betraying your country when she has already betrayed herself.

Pain or no, I would not listen any longer. I plastered my hands to my ears, and Adonai withdrew as swiftly as he had come, for he would not force me when my will was hardened at variance to his. He would simply leave me and wait, and I would get weak and ill, because I was who I was, and I needed the breath of Adonai within me to live, as surely as I needed water and bread.

But when Baruch asked me what Adonai had said, and what it was that I would not do, I couldn't tell him. The mere thought of being branded a traitor to my country was worse than all the taunts I'd endured as a child. Even to whisper to my closest friend the gist of what Adonai had said to me would have polluted my patriotic lips.

The following day, although the standoff between Adonai and myself persisted, I learned that the collaborationists at Court had achieved at least some of their objectives. Fifty well-educated youths of comely appearance and noble birth had been gathered together, and had gone out to meet the Babylonian envoys, carrying artefacts from the Temple treasury with them.

I don't know if the adolescents in question had volunteered or been coerced - except in the case of Gedaliah. The brave and dutiful son of Ahikam had kissed his father goodbye and gone of his own accord, urging us all to be of good cheer: surely it was better for a few young men who were healthy and strong to take a calculated risk, than for every man, woman and child in Judah to be sentenced to death?

With him had gone a friend of his, named Daniel, and Gemariah the youngest son of the aged High Priest Hilkiah. Daniel was the cleverest student in the wisdom school of which Baruch was a graduate; he was also unusually devout and universally popular. 'No one will fill *his* head with pagan superstitions,' Baruch assured me. And to Ahikam he said, 'My lord, you need not fear for your son if he's with Daniel.' As for Jehoiakim himself, we heard rumours that he'd actually been imprisoned by the collaborationists, in preparation for his being delivered into the hands of his enemies. But the rumours were not confirmed.

Then all of a sudden in late summer it was reported that Nebuchadrezzar was making his way back to Babylon. The detachment of his cavalry which had come to Jerusalem as an embassy withdrew to join him, taking their hostages with them.

Apparently Nebuchadrezzar's father, who had been failing for some while, had finally given up the ghost. It was necessary for his son to claim the throne - to 'take the hands of Baal', as the Babylonians say - before rivals arose to contest it.

Presumably Nebuchadrezzar had suspected all along that his father was near to death, and had known that his own campaigns to the south might have to be interrupted. *This* was why he had wanted hostages: to guarantee that the influence he had gained in the Levant would not be lost while he was away.

As soon as the ambassadors and hostages were gone, the ringleaders of the collaborationists were rounded up and killed. If the King had ever been imprisoned, he had managed to get himself freed, and made very sure that his opponents knew it.

Soon after that, in the middle of a sleepless night, Adonai returned to me, his approach as tender as that of a bride who slips into her new husband's bed. I'd fallen ill, as I knew I would, and now too weak to fight on, I gave up and let myself go. He didn't say a word, but there was no need, for I knew what was on his heart as surely as he'd ever shown me the heart of any human being. I'm sorry, I whispered. I ought to have done as you said. Now Jehoiakim has killed the men I should have supported, and their blood is on my head. I have failed you again, and I've failed myself. It is I who should be dead by now, for I don't deserve any better.

Perhaps you don't, murmured Adonai, *and yet I love you all the same, and because you are sorry I forgive you. If only you could know how much you mean to me; yet if I revealed to you the magnitude of my love for you in all its fulness, your heart would burst asunder.*

'I love you too,' I said aloud, as I drifted away into ecstasy, my spirit entwined with Adonai's and rising to float above my bed. I gazed down upon my body, thin and frail beneath the covers, my face still pallid with sickness, but the lines on my brow smoothed out, a smile of rapture on my lips, and my eyes closed in abandonment.

What I'd said was true, just then. I *did* love Adonai - when I didn't hate him - though I don't recall that I'd ever said it in so many words before. Somehow it hadn't seemed fitting, to say to the Maker of the Universe a thing I might once have said to Ruth, or even to Huldah. Yet what other words existed to express the joy I was accustomed to feel when Adonai's spirit embraced my own? What other response was possible, when suddenly I knew that Adonai derived the same joy from our brief moments of intimacy as I did? If only these moments could come more frequently, and last a little longer...

They could, Adonai reminded me. *You need only renounce your rebelliousness once and for all.*

Yet he knew me as well as I knew myself, and that I wasn't able to do it.

In a while the ecstasy passed; I could not have endured much more. Yet something remained for me when it was gone, a heady glow which came from having felt the very feelings of God, and from realizing that whenever I experienced ecstasy in the presence of my Lord, he was somehow ecstatic too. This is a mystery which no mortal man can fathom, and yet it is true; and it is also true is that every one of us was made to experience this ecstasy for himself. Would that Adam and Eve had never eaten of that accursed apple; then each of us might walk with our God in the garden in the cool of evening. As it is, he calls for his people like a lover calling for his sweetheart through the forest, but no answer comes. Sometimes I think that Adonai must be lonelier in our generation than he was before there were people for him to love.

As I lay there sated with bliss, he asked me gently what I would do next time I was commanded to advocate submission to Nebuchadrezzar. 'I'll do as you tell me,' I answered drowsily. 'I shall not care what anyone calls me, so long as I feel in my spirit as I do today.'

Then do something else for me, Jeremiah: something I have never previously asked you to do.

'Anything, Lord. Ask me whatever you will, and I shall do it.'

Have Baruch record every oracle you have ever given, up to this very day.

I was taken aback. I remembered each one of them exactly, so the task would not be difficult; but why should it be necessary? Would it not lead men into error, into applying my words out of context to any and every situation just as they habitually did with Isaiah's?

It is just as you said to Baruch when you had him record your oracles against the nations. The written word will stand as a witness to the many warnings I have sent to my people. When disaster falls upon them, I would not have them say that they received no notice of its coming.

So I rose from my bed at dawn, and called for Baruch to come with his pens and papyrus to Ahikam's study. He was in his element; preparing his reeds and mixing his ink and talking nineteen to the dozen. 'If only we had kept records from the beginning,' he sighed. 'Then nothing would have been forgotten.'

'Nothing *has* been forgotten,' I assured him. 'We must do these things in Adonai's own time.' Yet I had to smile, because Baruch's eagerness brought such brilliance into his eyes, and his enhanced vitality lent him a beauty he didn't normally possess.

Though our assignment was straight-forward, it took us many weeks to complete. There was so very much to be written that Baruch took to sitting at a table instead of on the floor with the scroll on his lap, for his back and arm would ache with the speed of my dictation. But the hours went by so quickly, and such was the energy I drew from Adonai that I kept poor Baruch at his desk until his eyes were strained by the dimness of the lamplight, and his head was thick with the need to sleep. Then he would make mistakes and curse aloud, and gradually the truth emerged that the course upon which he'd embarked was no longer so much to his liking. He set himself such lofty standards, too: any mistake whatever would cause him to lay aside his page and begin it afresh, whether the error had been made when writing the name of God, or anywhere else.

Then came the night when he fell asleep where he sat, and the pen as it rolled from his hand drew a jagged line across the page he'd just completed. He woke with a jolt, and the whole gruelling enterprise was suddenly all too much for him. Hurling the offending pen onto the floor, he swept his inkhorn and the rest of his things off the table after it. A side of his character whose existence I hadn't suspected was thus laid bare before me, and I thought: he isn't selfless after all. He came to my house seeking greatness for himself, and although his ambition has been submerged beneath the love he bears me, in the writing of this scroll it has once again risen to the surface. This is why his part in these proceedings has to be performed to perfection, and this obsessive pursuit of the perfect for himself is what has exhausted him.

I tried to upbraid him in the gentlest way I knew how, and I bent to retrieve the scroll and inkhorn myself. But he wouldn't be told; he would neither get on with the job nor retire to bed to begin refreshed in the morning. At a loss for what to say next, I opened my mouth and Adonai spoke to him through it, the first time he'd ever done so, and he's never done it in quite the same way since. *'Woe to me,' you said, 'for the Lord has added sorrow to my pain. I am worn out with my groaning, and find no rest.' But know only this, Berechiah son of Neraiah. I too have laboured in vain, and must overthrow what I have built, and uproot the things I have planted. Seek not greatness for yourself, therefore, nor special treatment. I bring disaster on all mankind, but you will escape with your life because of the generous love you have shown towards my son Jeremiah. Let that be enough for you.*

When it was over, we simply stared at one another in mutual stupefaction. Eventually I blurted, 'Baruch, I'm sorry. I didn't mean to hurt you. But surely it's better that we don't have secrets. Then we shall have no misunderstandings either.'

He didn't reply. His fists were clenched, and he looked away from me, face thrust over his shoulder, the muscles in his neck stretched taut. I don't know which was worse for him: my having learnt his guilty secret, or his having to admit to himself that what I'd learnt was true. I suppose he thought he'd left behind his childish desire for fame and fortune when he'd resigned himself to being my cook, my cleaner, and all too often my nurse.

'Don't take this so hard,' I said. 'Adonai has promised you your life, just as he promised me mine long ago. That means we need have no fear for one another in the coming tribulation. Adonai loves you, Baruch; that's why he doesn't want you chasing after vain delusions.'

Still he wouldn't look at me, though he did condescend to speak. But all he said was, 'I'm going to bed, Jeremiah. Perhaps I'll feel better in the morning.' He got up wearily and left the room.

CHAPTER 17: ELNATHAN

The winter of my seventieth year was uncommonly cold; far too cold for a tired old man whose blood has turned thin, and who no longer has a wife to share his bed. Snow lay for months on the mountains, and for several days in Jerusalem itself. I thought: nature herself is outraged at our sinfulness, and I am more sinful than anyone.

The city was crowded, because crisis was at hand and a special day of fasting had been proclaimed. Multitudes jostled in the slush of the Temple Court, stamping their feet for warmth, blowing on their hands and watching each other's breath take shape on the air. For myself, I preferred the solitude of my room, and the solace of my brazier heaped with burning wood.

I made the most of my little fire; soon I would have to leave it, in order to attend an extraordinary meeting of Eliakim's Council. I felt much too old to be closely involved in affairs of state, but with things being as they were no man of conscience could bury his head in the sand and hope that the trouble would pass.

For Nebuchadrezzar had captured Ashkelon, the mightiest city in Philistia. Its king had refused to acknowledge the supremacy of Babylon, so the place had been razed to rubble; those among its populace who survived the onslaught had been deported to Babylonia. In the first instance Ashkelon had appealed to Egypt for aid, but to no avail; and if the Philistines were helpless in the face of Nebuchadrezzar's military genius, what chance did poor Judah stand? For the first time in my life I felt some sympathy for Eliakim - or Jehoiakim, as I really ought to call him. He was the husband of my daughter, after all, and primped and pampered as he was, the prospects confronting him were bleak indeed.

After laying claim to the throne of Babylon, Nebuchadrezzar had returned to Syria almost at once. This time he hadn't forged onward to Egypt, choosing instead to consolidate his gains in the lands which lay between; he made his own policy now. He'd accepted tribute from the kings of Tyre, Sidon, Damascus and the like, and made them sign away their independence to him. Against any who showed reluctance to do so, he waged war without mercy or compunction, and invariably won. He hadn't yet repeated his demand for the surrendering of Jehoiakim, but he would come soon enough and enforce it, or punish us into the bargain.

It was all so depressing. Staring into my fire, I thought back wistfully to the days when Josiah had reigned, Judah had stood on the brink of a Golden Age. But now our nation seemed as feeble and decrepit as I felt, and equally oppressed by regrets.

Never had I forgiven myself for allowing Nehushta to marry Eliakim. Nor could I forget that it was I who had brought about the death of Uriah, one of the few who had dared stand up to my arrogant son-in-law and tell him the truth rather than what he wanted to hear. When Eliakim had ordered me to fetch Uriah from Egypt, how could I have been so gullible as to suppose that the prophet would be granted an impartial trial? I'd prevailed upon him to come with me quietly, pointing out that things would surely go better for him if he didn't put up a fight. But Eliakim had had him slaughtered on the spot, right in front of my eyes, and in front of the eyes of his son Jeconiah to boot. I'll never forget the look of reproach on Uriah's face as he fell, holding my gaze until his eyes clouded over in death.

This is why I say that I myself am the worst of sinners. I never intended to be; I have always wanted to do right. But alas, intentions and actions are not the same thing.

The swish of a curtain roused me from my reverie. Nehushta herself had arrived to see me, and Jeconiah my grandson was with her, as troubled and timid a creature as you could ever want to meet. He had his father's good looks, softened by his mother's gentleness of spirit, but the hunted, haunted eyes of a fugitive. Since witnessing the death of Uriah he'd developed a stammer, too, and I almost wished that Nehushta wouldn't bring him to visit me so often, because he was a twitching, tormented reminder of my flawed judgment.

Nehushta bent and kissed me, and asked me if I were warm enough; I told her yes, though my feet were numb and an icy draught blew across the back of my neck. She tutted, and wrapped a shawl about my shoulders. She mothered me now just as my dear late wife had once fussed over both of us. How I missed my Elizabeth; and how I missed Coniah our son, away in service with Judah's army, such as it was. He showed much promise as a soldier, and was moving up quickly through the ranks. Young Jeconiah had been named for him, but the two could not have been less alike. Coniah was frightened of nothing, Jeconiah of everything.

'Does Eliakim keep the fast?' I asked Nehushta; for he was the one who had called it, but I'd never known him deny himself anything at all.

My daughter glanced at me sharply, but gave me no answer, and I let the subject drop. Nehushta knew well what I thought of her royal husband, though I never ceased wishing I'd expressed my opinion more forcefully in the beginning. There was no point in doing so now; she had married the villain, and that was that. Poor Nehushta. She was a good girl, but so pretty. Eliakim simply could not have permitted any other man to gain possession of her, for how could it be fitting for one of his subjects to have a bride more exquisite than he had?

If only she hadn't been equally keen for the match to be made. But she was too much like me, I suppose: too willing to see the good in people even when it wasn't there.

I knew exactly what she'd seen in Eliakim. He was handsome even now, though he was starting to run to fat around his waist with all the rich food and strong drink he considered it his right and duty to consume. His lissom beauty was all that Nehushta had cared about as a girl; that, and the fact that he would make her a queen. It wasn't that she was ambitious, or even stupid - just hopelessly romantic and naive. Her devotion to Eliakim had known no bounds, until the first time she'd made some remark which he chose to take the wrong way, and he'd beaten her senseless with his belt. After that, there would often be bruises on her soft white arms, and even around her eyes, and she would wince if anyone made a sudden movement near her. What never ceased to amaze me was that Nehushta loved her husband still, and maintained that he loved her.

If only Jeconiah had been more like his namesake my son. Then I could have imagined him taking his mother's part when he got older, defending her from the worst excesses of her husband's temper. As it was, she would continue to expend most of her energy shielding him.

Eventually I rose from my chair, to begin getting ready for the meeting. Nehushta brought my cloak; I thanked her and sighed, 'Let's pray that summer comes early this year. Perhaps it will put some warmth into these creaking bones.' Then I thought again: perhaps I won't live to see summer, however soon it comes. Perhaps none of us will.

The meeting was to be held in the apartment of Elishama, the Secretary of State, since the King would not be present. He had directed his Council to discuss the crisis and reach a consensus on what Judah's response to it ought to be, before involving him; he was shrewd enough to realize that his presence might curb his ministers' freedom of speech, preventing the wisest counsel from emerging.

I was one of the last to arrive, and already the discussion was in spate. I settled myself in a corner and let the tide of debate wash over me. No wonder Jehoiakim hadn't wanted to be present. What was to be gained from arguing over our response to a crisis to which no useful response could be made?

Elishama himself said little more than I did. Once a vociferous advocate of co-operation with Egypt, the latter's demise had left him embarrassed and his policies run aground.

Eventually a fist was thumped down on the table round which we reclined. 'Why this wasteful bandying of words?' demanded Gemariah ben Shaphan, the only one of Shaphan's sons to hold office at Jehoiakim's Court. 'If Nebuchadrezzar comes here, he comes, and he will do as he likes with us however we receive him. He defeated the army of Necho, against which Josiah himself could mount no worthy resistance. What can our present generals hope to do? They have but meagre experience of command. Their regiments have been cobbled together from the remnants of those cut to ribbons at Megiddo; their men are decrepit veterans or beardless boys.'

At last, I thought, a man prepared to talk sense; but before the illustrious Council could assimilate what he had said there was a commotion outside the door of the apartment, and a breathless adolescent rushed in amongst us.

It was Micaiah, Gemariah's son. Some of those present clearly wanted Gemariah to rebuke him for his intrusion, but Gemariah knew the boy a good deal better than they did, and asked him what was the matter.

According to Micaiah, he'd been alone in his father's rooms when Berechiah the scribe of the prophet Jeremiah had appeared and asked to come in. Micaiah had of course admitted him, as an esteemed family friend, and the scribe had enquired if Gemariah were at home, for he wanted to ask for a favour. He wanted permission to read aloud from a window of Gemariah's apartment - which overlooked the Temple Court - a scroll containing his master's words. Micaiah had explained that his father was out at a meeting and might not be back for many hours. So Berechiah had said he would read out the scroll in any case and take the consequences, because the reading must be done today while the fast was in progress and the Court thronged with people.

Micaiah had been anxious. He knew that the Prophet was banned from the Temple, and that having Berechiah speak on his behalf could only be construed as a provocative ruse. So he had stood there biting his lip while Berechiah proceeded to read. On and on and on he'd read, until Micaiah had grasped that the scroll the scribe had brought with him incorporated all the oracles the Prophet had ever delivered.

'And Father, the more he read, the more anxious I got. He spoke so much of judgment and destruction... he said that Jerusalem would become like Shiloh... When he'd finished, I was scared he'd be attacked, so I told him to stay in our rooms while I came to fetch you. He's still there - if no one has broken the door down. Did I do the right thing?'

'Of course you did, my son. I am proud of you as always,' said Gemariah, a smile of approval on his lips but dismay in his eyes. With the Babylonians set to arrive at our gates any day, were we now to have bloody riots within our walls as well as enemy forces without?

'As ministers of His Majesty's Government we must hear the words of this scroll for ourselves,' Elishama declared. 'And until we have considered their implications, we must ensure that Berechiah has protection. He must be conducted to us at once by a company of the royal guard.'

Jehudi the Council's messenger was swiftly despatched to bring this about, though what Berechiah must have thought when a squad of Jehoiakim's heavies insisted on escorting him from Gemariah's chambers was only too apparent in his demeanour when he was presented to us. An awkward and bookish young man, twenty five years old at most, he was wholly unused to public exposure except at his mentor's side.

'Sit down, Berechiah,' said Elishama kindly, though certain of his fellows were quietly bristling, disinclined to breathe the same air as the Prophet's accessory let alone accord him hospitality. Berechiah sat, and was invited to recite the contents of the scroll a second time. This he did, though his voice was quaking; he'd no idea what had motivated the Council's request, and was patently afraid that he was reading the warrant for his own execution. Of course, it wasn't only the destruction of our nation that the oracles predicted, but the death of her King, and the ignominious treatment of his body. Dishonoured, unmourned, Jehoiakim's corpse would be lobbed off the walls of Zion's citadel like a dead ass with the dung.

Most of those present had heard this prophecy before, when Jeremiah had pronounced it to Jehoiakim in person in the comparative privacy of his throneroom. But never before had Jehoiakim's ordinary subjects been permitted to learn of its existence.

'His Majesty will be baying for blood when he finds out that this prediction was made in public!' said Delaiah the Royal

Steward, roused from his silent animosity at last. 'And we are the ones he'll blame for allowing it to happen.'

'Perhaps he will *not* find out?' Zedekiah the Recorder suggested. 'I'll wager that he was still lying in bed when the public reading was taking place. He may well be there now.'

'Of course he will find out! We must tell him ourselves before the facts reach him from some other source. If that happens, we shall lose our heads.'

'Shall I go and inform him directly, my lords?' enquired Jehudi, but Elishama told him no; we must all of us approach Jehoiakim together; that way, we shouldn't be played off one against another.

'And you and your master must go into hiding,' Gemariah said to the scribe. 'My brother's house will no longer be safe for you; everyone knows by now that you and the Prophet have been living there. A detachment of the royal guard will accompany you - we can see to that - but once the King is informed of this business, their protection will of course be withdrawn. Go now; inform no one at all where you intend to conceal yourselves.' He looked grimly around the assembled company, meaning: inform no one in this room, especially; I am the only man here whose trust you can count on.

Berechiah departed in nervous haste; the scroll, however, we retained, slipped in among Elishama's personal effects. As a body we went to the King, though I for one would sooner have gone back to my fire. Aged as I was, they might have allowed me; but if anything untoward should happen to Jeremiah, I did not want his blood on my head, as well as Uriah's.

The King was shut up in his private quarters, and the guards at his door refused to admit us. They'd been ordered that no one should disturb him, and no exception could be made. 'Then we shall remain here until he is ready to receive us,' Elishama declared, and bade his colleagues sit down on the ground like nomads outside the royal apartment. Eventually permission was granted us to enter; and on doing so, we discovered that His Majesty already had company.

This was in the form of three of Jehoiakim's blue-blooded cronies: one Jerahmeel of the royal house, and two lesser lords by the names of Seraiah ben Azriel and Shelemaiah ben Abdeel. They lounged on couches about a brazier which was dwindling and smoking for lack of attention. It had been burning something much more redolent than plain wood, for the air in the room was thick with a spicy narcotic fragrance which went straight to my head. Azriel and Abdeel's sons were playing a fuddled game of dice for one another's clothing - the semi-naked ben Abdeel appeared to be losing badly, much to the amusement of the chubby gelded slave-boys who nestled against him - and Jerahmeel was noisily asleep with his head in Jehoiakim's lap.

Jehoiakim alone appeared to have failed to drug his sorrows, though this wasn't for lack of trying. I'd never seen him truly downcast before; I'd imagined it wasn't in his nature. But his hair was uncombed, he hadn't got dressed, and his bloodshot eyes gave away the quantity of wine he'd knocked back to no avail.

We fell on our faces before him, and Elishama ventured to explain why we had deemed it needful to intrude upon his privacy. Our obsequiousness restored his spirits somewhat; he waved a languid hand in the direction of the eunuch slave-boys, and had one of them fetch him a robe to replace the blankets in which he was swathed, and the other comb his hair. Shelemaiah ben Abdeel, robbed of the warmth of the plump little bodies next to his, moaned in drowsy complaint; feigning sympathy, ben Azriel embraced him and their dissolute game continued.

The King heard Elishama out in impassive silence, Jerahmeel snoring all the while; the eunuchs had lifted the latter's head to remove the blankets, and giggled when he hadn't stirred. Finally Jehoiakim instructed Jehudi to fetch the scroll to him. Berechiah, we'd been at pains to point out, was nowhere to be found.

Jehudi wavered, glancing at Elishama for confirmation of his orders. Elishama nodded - we had already admitted that the document was in our possession - and Jehudi made haste to get it.

On his return he cast himself at His Majesty's feet once more, and held the scroll out to him. But the King commanded, 'Read it! I do not have dogs that I might do the barking myself.'

So Jehudi stood up, unfastened the scroll and read. But when he'd completed the opening portion - three or four columns at most, I suppose - Jehoiakim waved his hand once more. Deducing that the King must want silence, Jehudi stopped reading and waited, eyes lowered in deference, or perhaps in disgust. But Jehoiakim said, 'Come closer, my dear,' and he fluttered his manicured fingers in Jehudi's direction as though he might somehow waft the youth to a spot within his reach. Jehudi blanched as if beckoned by a harlot, and took a reluctant step towards him. Then with a studied flick of his wrist, the King motioned Elishama to pass him the scribal knife which he carried at his belt, his badge of graduation from the Jerusalem School of Wisdom. Leaning forward on his couch so that Jerahmeel stirred at last, Jehoiakim sliced away the completed portion of the scroll and tossed it in the fire.

I couldn't believe what I'd seen him do. Nor could Jehudi. Unable to carry on reading despite being told to do so, he simply stared at the violated scroll. 'Well?' snapped the King. 'Don't stand gawping like a fish with your mouth wide open. Read on, I tell you. Read on!'

Jehudi swallowed hard and somehow managed to do as he was bidden. When a second portion was finished, His Majesty leaned forward once again and did exactly as he'd done before.

I was appalled. That any man would so carelessly destroy another's work was a dreadful thing. But this was the work of God, not of man. It was almost as though a scroll of the Torah itself were being defaced. Had Jehoiakim no fear of Heaven whatever?

Clearly his empty-headed eunuchs had not. They clapped their hands and laughed their girlish laughs as hungry tongues of flame began to curl about the strips of papyrus and lick it black. The lascivious dicers, however, were gazing at the King in horrified fascination. Jerahmeel, now sitting up with his head in his hands, stared dazedly into the fire.

But I too was studying the King as he watched the papyrus consumed; and for all his affected nonchalance, his eyes told a different story. Once upon a time he might indeed have possessed no holy fear; now he had it in plenty, but madness entangled with it. He seriously believed that in destroying Jeremiah's scroll he could annul the power of the prophecies it contained.

'What is the matter *now*, you blockhead?' he demanded of Jehudi, suddenly angry at the tension developing around him. 'Is there something wrong with you, that you cannot follow a simple instruction? I told you to read, did I not? So read, God damn you, before I cut out your useless tongue.'

Jehudi struggled on, but what remained of the scroll vibrated in his hands. The flames in the brazier leaped higher, and since the palace hadn't been struck by lightning, Jehoiakim's eyes gleamed, and he cut off every second column instead of every fourth. Then he swept the room with a single sneer, challenging each man present to intervene.

It was when a piece of blazing papyrus fell from the brazier onto the floor that I knew I must respond. It landed by my feet, and as I looked I saw the name 'Judah' devoured before me. All that was left was powdery ash, black and insubstantial against the white marble pavement. Even as I went on looking, a draught caught hold of the powder and blew it away, and Judah was gone without a remnant. If I did not speak out now, I felt that I should have the extinction of my very race on my conscience, as well as that of a courageous man of God.

I fell on my face once more by Jehoiakim's feet, then in the sight of all his Council I took them in my hands and kissed them. 'Please, Your Majesty, husband of my daughter,' I implored him, 'I entreat you, burn no more of Jeremiah's scroll, and repent over what you have burnt already.'

'Repent? You would have me *repent,* old man?' Jehoiakim bellowed. 'You imply that a king can *sin?* I am lord supreme, I *make* the laws of this land, I *define* what is sin and what is not. I should have you flayed alive for your insolence! If it were not for Nehushta, I should flog you myself.'

I let him rail on, without once looking up or ceasing to bathe his feet with my kisses. I passed through dread into resignation; I thought: I am old, it is true, and I have enjoyed a life both prosperous and long; perhaps it would be fitting for me to die defending the word of God, to atone for my causing the death of his faithful prophet. I only hope that the King does not kill me in front of my grandson.

But then I found that I wasn't making a lone protest any longer. The courage I'd displayed had loosened the tongue of Gemariah ben Shaphan, who was giving the King the same advice that I had given; even Delaiah the Steward joined in to plead our cause.

All to no avail - except that I wasn't whipped. Jehoiakim merely kicked me aside, then appealed to his inebriated comrades. 'Jerahmeel? Seraiah? Shelemaiah? The men of my own Council have turned against me, as you yourselves have witnessed. But you I trust; go now, take soldiers, and don't come back here until both Jeremiah and Berechiah are under arrest.'

CHAPTER 18: JEREMIAH

I

For as long as Baruch was away at the Temple I gave myself over to prayer. I was so afraid for him; I never would have sent him to read out that scroll had Adonai not compelled me. I knew that Adonai had promised to guard Baruch's life along with my own, but believing for yourself is somehow easier than believing for someone you love - though Heaven knows, either can be hard enough.

I might not have felt so bad if things had been better between the two of us. But ever since the night when Adonai had revealed to me the secret ambition in Baruch's heart, he'd been as prickly as a desert thorn. I thought: what I dreaded most has come to pass. I have grown attached to Baruch in a way I should not, and now Adonai will take him. He'll have him arrested for reading out my scroll, and that will be that. I shall never see him again.

Instead, in the early afternoon he burst in upon me and told me to pack up my things; we must go into hiding at once.

I didn't ask why, since that was obvious. But where? Where could we go to be safe from the King, and from Pashhur, and from the hosts of Nebuchadrezzar? We should have to remain inside the city, that was for sure - not only on account of the protection it afforded from the armies of Babylon, but because Jerusalem was where Adonai had called me to be.

'We must go to Seraiah, my brother,' Baruch said, already starting to pack our belongings as he spoke. 'Everyone knows what he thinks of my living with you. He won't be suspected.'

'Then why should he help us? Supposing he turns us away?'

'He'll help us because he loves me,' Baruch declared firmly, and I wondered which of us he was trying to convince. 'He has a house built into the city walls, where he lives with his wife and children when he isn't at the palace. But we must not be recognized on our way there. The mob is claiming it's all your fault that Nebuchadrezzar has become so strong. You prophesied his greatness; you are a man of God; therefore what you said has come to pass.'

So I stowed into bags the few things I possessed of any value: my lyre and Hosea's scroll, and what remained of Josiah's gold. Baruch had much more to carry than I did. He insisted on taking an enormous collection of tablets and scrolls which he'd amassed since arriving at my house; I'd very little idea of what they contained. Then we made voluminous turbans out of clothing we hadn't packed, and put on the most nondescript robes we could find.

We were escorted by soldiers to a watchtower set into the city walls on the western side. Perhaps the crowds imagined us under arrest already, and it did occur to me to question whether we were - or at least whether *I* was. Since Baruch and I were still at odds with one another, could I be sure that even *he* was to be trusted? I studied the grim expression on his face as we walked, and wished it might be granted me to know his mind at that very moment. Then I looked at the bristling spears all around us and knew I had no choice but to go where I was being taken.

An underground passageway led from the watchtower to another quite a way north; I learned later that it was part of a network linking all of the city's towers together to facilitate communications between them in time of war. Torches were thrust into our hands, and we were told to follow the passage until we reached an upward flight of steps some five hundred paces further on. These would bring us out in a residential quarter where no one would think to look for us; our disguise should then be sufficient for us to get wherever we wanted to go. After that, the responsibility for our survival would be entirely our own. The very guards who had minded us until now would be ordered all too soon to track us down.

The dank and dingy world below the streets might have unnerved me more than it did, had it not reminded me so powerfully of the warren of neglected corridors in the bowels of the Anathoth sanctuary to which I had often fled for refuge as a boy. Presently the flight of steps came into view, and we made our way up to the level of the street above. The picket on duty in the tower had been warned of our coming, and let us pass without challenge; dazzled by the brightness of the winter sun outside, we stood for a moment while Baruch got his bearings, then he led the way to Seraiah's house. I rebuked myself for doubting his loyalty, and hoped that Seraiah was as worthy of trust as his younger brother.

But Seraiah was out. He'd gone to the Temple early that morning to join with his fellow citizens fasting and praying for Jerusalem's deliverance, and hadn't returned - much to his wife's consternation. Someone else had been and told her what Berechiah her half-baked brother-in-law had done at the Temple, and since then she'd been sure that he must have got himself arrested, and that due to some misunderstanding her husband had been locked up with him.

So when Baruch appeared on her doorstep without Seraiah, she knew not whether to be relieved or dismayed, nor whether to welcome him, and me along with him, or bar the door against us.

'For pity's sake, Naomi, let us in!' Baruch begged her. 'If Seraiah doesn't want us here, he can evict when he returns.'

Once we were indoors Naomi grew calmer. She directed servants to wash our feet, while she herself fetched food and wine and set it before us. A demure and dainty woman, still pretty for all her thirty years and several children, I thought how lucky Seraiah was to have her. How comforting it must be for him, to come home from his place of work each evening and have her wait on him, and love him, and bring his infant sons to play in his lap. To be insulated from the evils of the world outside by a cushion of domestic bliss...

All of a sudden, Naomi's eyes met my own, and in crippling embarrassment I realized that throughout my daydream I'd been following her with my gaze as she went about her chores. I tried to smile, in case my staring had upset her, but this only made things worse. She blushed scarlet before looking away and attending to one of her children, who had started to cry. This was when I remembered that another of Seraiah's little ones had died in the drought three years before, and I thought: Adonai was right to deny me a family after all. When the host of Nebuchadrezzar reaches Jerusalem, *no* one will be cushioned from the horrors to come. Perhaps Baruch and I should go and take our chance elsewhere, for Seraiah will soon have enough to worry about without our adding to his burden.

I whispered as much to Baruch, while Naomi's attention was occupied with the mewling infant. 'What? Are you as insane as men say you are?' he hissed at me; then he noticed the way that my eyes were still drawn by the cosy spectacle of the mother tending her child. He looked at me strangely, but I was granted no opportunity to ponder what his look might mean, for just then Seraiah returned.

'Berechiah? You little idiot!' he exclaimed, but then: 'Thank God you thought to come here.'

'You're not angry with me?' asked Baruch in relief, as the two of them embraced.

'Of course I'm angry! But I've spent the best part of my day searching for you, because if you'd been put in prison or worse I should never have forgiven myself for not having hauled you off by the ears from that crazy man's house when I had the chance.'

They embraced all over again, so that Baruch was almost smothered and his eyes were streaming; I couldn't tell if he was weeping or winded, for Seraiah was pounding his back with such vigour. '"A true friend loveth always,"' Baruch quoted when he was able, '"And a brother is born for adversity."'

'So you haven't forgotten *everything* we taught you,' was Seraiah's response, and he let Baruch go at last. It was then that he first saw me.

I do not care to repeat the words he used to revile me once his shock was overcome. In any case, I didn't wait for him to finish. I rose to my feet, slung my bags over my shoulder, and prepared to leave.

Baruch was beside himself. Our friendship had been sorely tested of late, but he loved me all the same. 'Both of us stay, or both of us go,' he said to Seraiah, and stood with his shoulder to mine.

'Then both of us must go, Baruch,' I told him, and began to walk towards the door.

No one moved to stop me, but the anxious glance which Naomi gave her husband seemed to plead our case. Once Seraiah had grasped that even now his brother would not abandon me, he ceased his tirade, had his servants take our bags, and bade us both be seated.

I slumped on a couch in a corner, allowing myself to be ignored while more fuss was made of Baruch, and each of the children was brought to him that they might renew their acquaintance with their delinquent uncle. I think Naomi might have brought her offspring to me as well, had she not feared her husband's reaction. Then again, perhaps she feared me, too.

Presently Naomi took the children away, and the brothers were left to talk in peace. I didn't really listen to their conversation, since I was growing drowsy, and still fretting quietly over Baruch's disposition towards me. So I was somewhat taken by surprise when his voice was suddenly raised in distress and he said, '*What?* The King did *what?*'

'Surely you must have heard. I thought this was why you had come here. His Majesty had already burned the scroll before putting out the warrant for your arrest.'

'He *burned* it? He burned my work, which cost me days of thankless labour, and sleepless nights, and the very peace of my soul to complete? No; it isn't possible. Please, Seraiah; say that this did not happen.'

'But it *did* happen, I tell you! Come now, Berechiah, don't take this business so badly. Shouldn't you worry more about the threat of arrest in the future, than about a thing which has already taken place? What is done is done, my brother. There are still dozens of your manuscripts in the royal library; your name won't be forgotten.'

'Stop it!' Baruch yelled; he leaped to his feet, and bolted through a door which led out to the central courtyard, shouting, 'Leave me alone!' when Seraiah tried to follow. Seraiah snorted and sat down hard in his chair, flinging me a glance so filthy that if looks could kill, I should not be here today.

When a discreet interval had passed, I went after Baruch myself. He was no longer out in the courtyard. The westering sun had plunged it in shadow, leaving it cheerless. I found some steps which led to the roof, so I climbed them. And there was Baruch, his back to the parapet, head in his hands. He was weeping.

This was a sight I had never seen. I sat down in silence in front of him, having made sure that the place was not overlooked. Then I waited, deeming it useless to speak until he did. He would confide in me if he chose to, when he was ready.

And so he did, not very much later, though scarcely coherently to begin with. He kept repeating how sorry he was; how much he hated himself for being so obsessed with our scroll and its fate. 'How can I care about my confounded hard work and sleepless nights, when Adonai is soon to see the nation he moulded from nothing smitten to dust? How can I care about winning recognition for myself, when thousands of human beings are going to be blotted from the face of the earth while I survive? But I *do* care about those things, Jeremiah! I thought I had put them behind me when I came to be your servant, but I hadn't; I thought I had placed my life at Adonai's disposal, but I find I'm no better than a pagan! I'm frightened of everything: of all the things I knew I would have to face if I threw in my lot with you. I'm frightened of war, of hunger, of arrest and torture, of whether I'll pass the tests I shall be put through... I'm sorry, Jeremiah. I have already failed the first of them. I've already ruined our friendship with my stubbornness.'

'Do you imagine that I love you any the less because you have tasted fear and guilt?' I asked him. 'I love you more, Baruch, because I myself am frightened and guilty; time and time again I have set my will at variance with that of Adonai. I never wanted you to be a better man than I am.'

'You never wanted me at all. As soon as you ever laid eyes on me you told me to go back where I'd come from, but I was too stupid to see that you meant it. And don't try to tell me you didn't.'

'I *did* mean it. I meant it for months. You drove me to distraction. So why should I hate you now because I find that you are growing up at last? Why should I hate you for your failures, when I have failed in everything I've ever undertaken? I failed my parents; I failed the girl I was to marry; I failed Josiah, and I failed to teach his son who is now our enemy. I have failed to wean the people of Judah from their wicked ways, and I have failed Adonai more times than I can count. But he loves me all the same, just as he loves you. And just as I love you, Baruch, and always will.'

He wasn't able to answer me in words. But he laid his head against my neck, and while he cried away his shame and confusion, I prayed Adonai's peace back into his soul.

Seraiah's home was spacious and well appointed, and had we not been in hiding, he could have spared each of us a pleasant room of our own. As it was, we swiftly agreed that our quarters should be in the cellar, since a part of it had long ago been walled off from the rest, and the door which led to it could readily be hidden by sacks of grain. The servants were sworn to secrecy on pain of death, and those of the children who were old enough to have given us away were made to understand exactly what would happen to their parents and to them if they did so.

It was cold in the cellar in winter, and quickly got filled up with smoke if we lit a fire. So we would emerge sometimes after dark, when the house was locked up and no neighbour could call unexpectedly. Then we would spend time with Seraiah's family - though none of them ever spoke to me - and

Baruch would keep in touch through Seraiah with what was going on in the world outside.

For the first ten days or so this didn't amount to much, since Nebuchadrezzar and his men were still enjoying their triumph over Philistia, raping and pillaging to their heathen hearts' content. Meanwhile a reward was being offered to anyone who found either Baruch or me and handed us over to the authorities, and Ahikam's house had been pulled apart at the seams.

But no one came snooping at Seraiah's. It was common knowledge in the city that Baruch's kinsfolk reckoned him as dead, and had drawn up all the necessary documents to deny him his inheritance.

At least we had plenty to keep us occupied during our confinement. Once Baruch felt ready to face the task, the written record of my oracles had to be started all over again. The irony was not lost on me that when Josiah had been confronted with a book containing Adonai's word he had torn his clothes, whereas Jehoiakim had torn up the book itself. But if he thought he could destroy the truth it contained, His Majesty was sadly mistaken. Every one of my oracles existed intact inside my head, burned into my memory like a brand-mark into flesh. Once God's word is spoken, no power on earth can unspeak it, for it has been seared into the very fabric of Creation.

Our daily labour was tiring, especially for Baruch, whose eyes would ache from the strain of writing in semi-darkness. So he was glad enough to spend his evenings talking to Seraiah, or playing with the children. For me, the evenings were harder than the days, since the family liked to pretend I wasn't there. I would sit apart and brood, or sometimes play my lyre to pass the hours. Occasionally I would fall asleep as I played, and once fell into a strange and tranquil ecstasy during which I must have continued playing. When I came to myself, the family had gone to bed and the fire was almost out. Baruch himself was asleep on the couch where he sat, head lolling, and a half-eaten honey cake still in his hand.

Confused, I rubbed my eyes and then my temples, setting my lyre to one side. As I did so, I saw that one member of the household wasn't in bed at all, but crouched in the shadows by the smouldering fire.

The spell was broken for her by my sudden movement, but knowing full well that I'd seen her, she couldn't easily creep away. Hands to her face, she whispered, 'Oh my lord, I'm sorry. I mean... I couldn't sleep. I came to get something to drink, and my lord... the music you were playing was so very lovely. I couldn't stop myself listening.' She shook her head, as though unable to believe she had acted so irresponsibly. 'I'm sorry,' she said again. 'I'm sorry. I shall go now.' Yet she did not.

'I have been playing all this time?' I asked in unfeigned astonishment. 'I thought I had fallen... I mean, I assumed...' Then I laughed, embarrassed, because Naomi herself was embarrassed, wiping her palms nervously down her crumpled robe. 'Don't be afraid,' I entreated her. 'I do just wish sometimes that you weren't so wary of me. Oh, I don't mean only you, my lady, you understand. I speak of your children too. Am I so very frightening?'

She didn't know what to say; but still she didn't leave. She was striving desperately not to meet my gaze, yet part of her wanted so much to look at me, and I scarcely needed my prophetic gifting to know it. I said, 'It's just so lonely for me, my lady, sitting by myself of an evening, when no one speaks to me and I only have my lyre for company. Is it any wonder I don't seem to know any more whether I'm asleep or awake?'

'Seraiah...' she began, yet couldn't finish; of course, she'd been afraid all along that if she talked to me he would be monstrously angry. But here she was talking to me now, and we were as good as alone, for Baruch slept on oblivious.

I ought to have bidden her to leave us then, since it appeared that she lacked the will to do so. Yet it was so refreshing to talk for once, however briefly, however awkwardly, with someone who wasn't Baruch. And Naomi was gentle, and graceful, and a woman. Naomi was beautiful.

So I took up my lyre once again and began to play: softly, wistfully, stroking the strings as lightly as a breeze ruffles grasses in a meadow on a bright spring day. For I was determined neither to wake the sleeping Baruch nor to look directly at Naomi, lest I scare her away after all. But from the corner of my eye I could see her kneeling beside me, the narrow hands which had fidgeted so anxiously now lying quiet on her lap as she fell beneath the spell of my music. I sensed her eyes being drawn back toward my face, and reaching out with my spirit I discerned the awe and the fear and the holy dread with which she regarded me. There were other feelings mixed up with these I'd put names to, but I told myself that I didn't know what they were.

I dare not imagine how long I might have kept her there enthralled, had not one of her little sons wandered through into the room where we were, whining sleepily for his mother. Naomi caught her breath and went to him without a backward glance, purring, 'It's all right, my darling. Mummy only came to get a drink.' And she bustled the boy away.

I sighed, and lay back with my head on the arm of the couch. Then I chanced to look across at the shuttered window, and started, for a faint hint of the coming dawn already showed where the shutter didn't quite fit. I went to wake Baruch, shaking him and pressing my finger to his lips.

'What were you doing, letting me go to sleep up here?' I rebuked him. 'It will be daylight soon!' And he scrambled up, believing I'd been dead to the world all night. We made our way back to our cellar, and if he wondered at my sleeping from then until noon, he didn't see fit to question me. No doubt he was simply grateful for a morning free from eyestrain.

The following night I sat up late on purpose, telling Baruch to retire without me. I would play my lyre a little longer and come down in a while when I was ready.

I stayed there almost till midnight, but Naomi didn't appear. Perhaps she'd been up early with the children, I reasoned, and was tired. Another night she would come.

A few nights later I waited up again; but again Naomi stayed away. I began to wonder if the night I had played my lyre to her had been part of a beautiful dream. But something in the way she stole sidelong glances at me in the evenings convinced me that it hadn't.

Then came the day when Nebuchadrezzar's army arrived at the gates of Jerusalem. Baruch and I were able to witness its approach for ourselves, since Seraiah's home was built into the northern wall of the city and there were places from which one could see without being seen.

From a distance the sight was formidable. Weapons and armour glinted in the sunshine like scales of a golden serpent. At closer quarters the motley nature of the host became apparent, for a veritable ragbag of vassals and mercenaries marched alongside the Babylonian elite. There were round helmets and pointed ones, leather cuirasses and chain mail, tunics and trousers, straight swords and curved, and every conceivable variety of javelin and club. Discipline however was impressive, and maintained by officers mounted on horseback, carrying maces and wearing crested helmets whose scarlet plumes danced like the manes of their steeds. Their armour was made from a thousand metal rings sown onto leather, and their studded boots were laced right up to their calves. Of Nebuchadrezzar himself there was as yet no sign.

A division of Judah's army had formed up to face the approaching column, but a sorry spectacle it presented, being small and ill-equipped, with morale even lower than its numbers. The remainder of our troops had had to be left behind at other Judean strongholds, for no one had been able to guarantee that the enemy would not go for the easier targets first, picking them off a city at a time before homing in on Jerusalem. Then again, the haughty young King of Babylon might make another demand for tribute before declaring open war. If Jehoiakim agreed to surrender without a fight, surely Nebuchadrezzar would see no need to plunder our city or massacre its people?

Yet I couldn't see that Jehoiakim *would* agree to surrender. To be a vassal of the Pharaoh, glorious, glamorous god-king of an ancient and noble civilization was one thing. To grovel on his hands and knees before a man who was younger than he was, and whose father had been little better than a common soldier would be quite another.

As events turned out, Nebuchadrezzar did indeed give Jehoiakim chance to submit before blood was shed. Our king was required, within the space of three days, to walk out through the gates of the city in person and pledge his loyalty to Babylon, laying treasures at the feet of his lord and master. Provided that he did so, he would suffer no further harm, and neither would his subjects, except in so far as regular taxes would be demanded of them. Nothing was said this time about Jehoiakim being taken as a hostage, for the political situation had changed, and this was no longer expedient. I suppose Nebuchadrezzar believed that the people of Judah would trouble him less in the long run if their own king was left to rule over them.

I devoted myself to prayer on His Majesty's behalf, despite my firm conviction that it would serve no purpose since he would take not the slightest heed of Adonai's counsel, whatever it was. I knew in advance what this counsel would amount to, in any case: *Submit to the King of Babylon, for he is the rod of my judgment.* Equally I was certain that my former pupil would refuse, and that Nebuchadrezzar would proceed to treat Jerusalem exactly as he'd treated Ashkelon.

Baruch took down the words of the oracle I received, and we prayed together that a way might be found to convey it to the palace without betraying our whereabouts. But Adonai wouldn't answer me; even the oracle had come as a whisper, so that I couldn't be wholly sure that it wasn't an old one which had lurked at the back of my mind. It was Baruch who broke off praying in the middle of a sentence and announced: 'I have it, Jeremiah! Adonai has shown me what we must do.' And he went on to tell me that when his eyes were closed he had seen the face of one of his brother's household servants; he was convinced that Adonai must want the tablet entrusted to him.

Of course, I ought to have given more thought to the question of why Baruch had received this revelation and not I.

But I was so genuinely pleased for him, because it was rare indeed for Adonai to communicate with him directly, that I assumed this reversal in our roles was designed for his encouragement.

During the evening he looked for an opportunity to catch the servant alone, and when one presented itself almost straight away, I was confident that we were moving within God's will. The servant promised to deposit the tablet secretly with reliable friends who would have it delivered to the palace without delay.

And to my amazement, two days later Jehoiakim did obeisance to Nebuchadrezzar.

I saw it happen with my own eyes, else I might not have believed it. From the place where Seraiah's house looked over the walls, I saw heralds ride out through the gates and request permission to parley with the Babylonian officers, whose army was now encamped to the north of the city. Permission was granted; a formal exchange ensued; then the heralds and the officers took their solemn leave of one another, wheeling about and riding back, the Babylonians to their camp and the Judeans to the city gates. Shortly afterwards, Baruch and I were among the first inhabitants of Jerusalem to see Nebuchadrezzar in the flesh.

He rode out with the minimum of ceremony, accompanied by a modest retinue of his senior officers, most of whom were considerably older than he was. He was dressed little differently from the rest of them, except that a fringed scarlet cloak streamed down the length of his back and draped the flanks of his mount. But in bearing he was wholly regal. When he'd ridden half way across the open ground, he halted, took off his helmet, and handed it to one of his companions. His hair fell in oiled black curls to his shoulders, after the fashion of Assyrian emperors of old.

In contrast to this vision of effortless majesty, Jehoiakim's extravagant entourage seemed faintly ridiculous. Blaring trumpets preceded his appearance, and he was borne in a grandiose curtained litter, surrounded by eunuchs and page boys. The men of his Council followed after: I could pick out the faces of Queen Nehushta's aged father, and Gemariah ben Shaphan. Bringing up the rear were attendants bearing Judah's tribute, ingots of gold upon purple cushions, and surrounding the multitude walked spearmen of Jehoiakim's palace guard. Still, I suppose one should not criticize Jehoiakim too severely for putting on this pompous display. It was the only way he knew how to salvage some vestige of dignity from the predicament in which he found himself.

When the two companies met, Jehoiakim's litter was lowered to the ground and our King emerged, subdued and defeated, for all that he wore David's crown and the richest royal robe which the now retired Shallum's successor had been able to find for him. The ceremony of vassalage took place there and then, conducted in Aramaic and Hebrew so that all who heard could fully understand its significance. A plethora of exotic deities was called upon to witness the treaty being made, among whom Adonai was cited as just one more. The stipulations of the treaty were enumerated in long and humiliating detail, and blessings and curses appended in profusion; the latter would come into gruesome force should Judah ever attempt rebellion. Provision was made for copies of the agreement to be placed in the temple of Marduk in Babylon, and in that of Adonai in Jerusalem.

How chillingly similar to this had been the ceremony conducted not so very long ago by Josiah, when the covenant between Adonai and his Chosen People had been renewed. I was thinking: would that we might once again be vassals only of God.

It was Seraiah who informed us the following day that Jehoiakim's decision to submit to Nebuchadrezzar had had nothing to do with the message I'd sent him. His mind had been made up already; once he'd learnt that Nebuchadrezzar intended to leave him in possession of his throne, he had determined to swallow his pride and do what he had to. It would not be long before he was growing his hair and his beard, and curling them, and oiling them, and wearing a tasselled cloak. And he would screw taxes from his people for Nebuchadrezzar just as he'd done for the Pharaoh. He himself would lie in the lap of luxury as he'd always done, and in time his battered pride would recover.

A week or so later, the army of Babylon packed up its tents and withdrew, though a sizeable garrison was left behind to deter Jehoiakim from breaking his oath. The tension in Jerusalem slowly dissipated; folk began to breathe freely again. And I was left looking foolish, for once more it seemed that my cries of doom had come to nothing.

By day I dictated my oracles to Baruch, oracles which now sounded hollow and empty; by night I railed against Adonai, since he'd promised me categorically that the day of my vindication was nigh. But no matter how savagely I inveighed against my Maker, he would not speak so much as one word to me, until late one evening, alone in Seraiah's cellar, I thought to ask why.

Why? said Adonai. *I shall tell you why.* And immediately Baruch burst in upon me, his face crimson with rage. He was cursing me in the foulest language he knew, and if Adonai had gifted him with the ability to call down fire from Heaven to consume me, I dare say he would have done so.

Eventually I recovered from my astonishment sufficiently to ask him what I had done to deserve an earful of such ripe vocabulary.

'What have you *done?* he repeated, beside himself. 'You know very well what you have done. Oh God, Jeremiah! I cannot believe it. Not of you. Of *all* people, I can't believe it of you.'

'Baruch, I haven't any idea what you are talking about. Calm yourself; then perhaps you'll be able to explain to me why you've turned what little air we have down here such a deep shade of blue.'

He regretted then the words he had used, though not the anger which had spawned them. I watched him fighting with himself, unsure if he ought to beg my forgiveness, or berate me some more.

In the end he did neither. He subsided slowly onto the bed beside me and said, 'My sister-in-law is in love with you, Jeremiah. And it's all your fault.'

There was no conscious pretence in my swift denial. 'Come now, Baruch! You're imagining things. You've been living in this miserable cellar too long.'

'I am imagining nothing!' he retorted, eyes on fire once more. 'I wanted to go to bed early; I hardly got a wink of sleep last night, with all your carrying on. I asked you to be quiet, but you didn't even hear me, so I went back upstairs, to sleep there - and found Naomi alone in the living room.'

He paused; I didn't react, but guilt was stirring within me.

'She almost cried out when she saw me; I supposed that she thought me an intruder. I told her not to be scared, it was only me. But she said she'd been scared it was *you*.'

He paused a second time, but still got no reaction. Whatever I'd eaten for supper was rolling around in my belly like cargo loose on the deck of a ship.

'I told her she needn't be scared of you. I told her you were a man, like any other. But she said that this was the point; she was scared that you had come upstairs to see if she was there, and that this time you hadn't brought your lyre. She was scared you wanted something which would be death for her to give you, but that she might be unable to hold back from giving it none the less.'

'Baruch,' I said. 'This makes no sense. I'm a spent and jaded old man compared with your brother. He's handsome and rich and influential. He's the father of her children, for Heaven's sake.'

'You, an old man? I never heard such nonsense! You haven't one grey hair, you're as lean as a youth... God damn you, Jeremiah, can you not see it? It's not just your looks. It's what you represent, it's what you *are!* Your strangeness, your *otherness*, your access to a world which lesser mortals only dream of...' His voice trailed away, as he realized that it was his own fascination he was describing, as much as that of his brother's wife.

And of course I *could* see what he meant, though until now I'd refused to do so. Just as I'd done with Huldah, I'd managed to convince myself that I'd been doing nothing wrong in playing my lyre for Naomi when clearly it brought her some pleasure in our harsh and uncertain world. So when Baruch concluded lamely, 'I'm only surprised that nothing like this has happened before,' I admitted, 'It has.'

I'd never spoken to him about Huldah. I'd never really spoken about her to anyone, except when I'd made my excuses to Ahikam. Now I found myself confessing everything to this young man half my age: how close I had come to breaking the seventh commandment, and how in my heart I had broken it a hundred times. I'd *wanted* to break it, because it was simply so good to know that a well-born woman could desire me.

'I don't know why I have told you all this,' I finished up, 'except that perhaps now it's no longer secret, its power over me will be broken.'

Baruch made no reply. I couldn't tell if he was disappointed by my carnality or frankly jealous. 'I should have guessed,' he muttered eventually. 'In fact I *did* guess, Jeremiah, but I told myself I must be mistaken. I guessed from the way you looked at her on the first day we came here - and the way she looked at you. But I decided it wasn't possible.'

Not possible that I could be tempted like anyone else, I wondered? Or not possible that I could be drawn to a woman at all? But I didn't ask, for I wasn't sure that I wanted to be told the answer. What I *did* want to know was how many sleepless nights Naomi had spent on my account, and how often she'd sat up alone in the darkness, willing me to come upstairs and yet hoping that I would not. Had she perhaps been hiding in the shadows and watching me, those nights when I'd stayed up late, not trusting herself to come out? Aloud I said, 'It's little wonder that Adonai hasn't been listening to my prayers lately, Baruch, but has spoken to you instead. Perhaps you had better ask him to forgive me.'

'There can be no forgiveness without repentance, Jeremiah. Is not that the essence of your own teaching?' Baruch spoke stiffly, and turned his head away lest I should somehow bewitch him afresh with my gaze. 'You have ruined one marriage already, so it seems. I will not have you ruin Seraiah's.'

'Huldah's marriage was over as soon as it began,' I responded bitterly, and no more was said about his praying for me after that. Baruch reminded me that he was dog-tired, and he went to lie down, for it wasn't yet dawn. I lay down also, falling asleep straight away. And a sickening nightmare assailed me: Naomi and I had been caught in flagrant adultery by Seraiah, and I was compelled to watch as he and his neighbours stoned her to death. Next, the authorities came for me, and as I was hauled away to execution Baruch was yelling, 'Take him! Kill him! See if I care!' I woke up shaking and sweating and calling his name. He was there by my bedside at once, and I wailed, 'I *do* repent, Baruch. Oh God, what a fool I can be.' And he laid his hands on my head, and the ocean of Adonai's blessing engulfed me.

I came to a full understanding then of what harm I had done to myself through my sin. Not only had it kept me from hearing Adonai's voice, but it had caused my vindication to be deferred. Instead of recognition in the eyes of men, I had won for myself another bout of their scorn.

'But good has come out of evil,' I said to Adonai. 'I have saved Jerusalem from devastation.'

No, Adonai replied. *The end I had planned for Judah was swift and conclusive. Now it will be slow, and long drawn out. Your vindication will come, just as I promised. But the process will be painful, protracted, untidy. Judah will die like Josiah, of infected blood from a festering wound.*

I wept in Baruch's arms after that, until the sun must have long since risen in the bright, doomed world above our cellar. I wept for myself, and for the added misery I was to bring upon my wretched people. I wept for Naomi, whose innocence I had corrupted with confusion and misplaced desire, and for Seraiah her husband, and for Baruch, because I was the one he had chosen to serve and to love, and I had wilfully betrayed his trust.

'I must never set eyes on Naomi again, nor she upon me,' I vowed when I'd pulled myself somewhat together. 'I

shall not quit this cellar until I can leave your brother's house
for good. I can only hope you will choose to come with me
when I go, though I shall understand completely if you don't.'

'I shall come,' Baruch assured me. 'But I cannot see
how it will ever be safe for us to leave this place. The reward
for our capture will not be withdrawn as long as Jehoiakim
lives.'

'Perhaps not; but he won't live for ever, Baruch.' And I
thought briefly of timid, traumatized Prince Jeconiah. Did *he*
still remember me with affection? Did he remember me at all?

II

For six years after that I lived in Seraiah's cellar
without once seeing the light of day. My skin grew sallow, my
muscles wasted; I ached with longing for the bright blue skies
beneath which I had wandered in my youth, and for the
saffron-yellow jumble of walls and rooftops of David's city
which I'd made my home. Yet I would not go back on my
resolve. Naomi must forget me totally, and never again must I
place temptation in her path.

Once the record of my prophecies was rewritten, I had
nothing to do but pray and dream. I wouldn't play my lyre,
because it had led me into sin, and the renouncing of it was
my penance.

Baruch was there in the daytime as someone to talk
to, but we had precious little to say to one another. For what
can one find to say, when every day is the same as the last?
Adonai alone sustained me, sending me ecstasies such that
sometimes whole days would fly past without my knowing
where they had gone. But then I would wonder if the ecstasies
themselves would push me further than I was already over the
brink of insanity, no longer able to distinguish fancy from
reality, the world of the spirit from that of the flesh.

From time to time Baruch would ask me to tell him
more about my life before he'd met me; I supposed that he
wished to make sure I had no more guilty secrets which he
considered he ought to be party to. After a while, however, I

decided that Baruch wasn't quizzing me as a friend; he was asking as a scribe.

'You should let me document your *life,* not merely your prophecies,' he exhorted me when I challenged him. 'Would it not help the person who reads your words, to know something of your history too, and something of your character?'

'No,' I answered, without even pausing to think. 'Because that person would be reading the words of man, not those of God.'

'But are not men the *creation* of God? Surely we demean the Creator if we argue that the words of his creatures are of no value. And in any case, the writings ascribed to Moses, from which we derive the holy Torah itself, teach us about the actions of Moses as well as about the laws he brought us from God. Is the very Torah contaminated with the babble of men?'

'Of course it is not. But Moses was called to do mighty deeds as well as speak weighty words. Naturally these deeds were recorded.'

'I thought that a man of God was called to *be,*' Baruch reminded me pointedly, for I had told him more than once about the things I'd learnt from Zephaniah, and about the time we'd spent together in Anathoth. 'Besides,' he continued, 'I wasn't referring so much to Moses' mighty deeds as to his errors and his sins. Is it not a comfort for those who seek to follow Adonai today, to know that the fathers of our nation had their faults? Does it not offer us hope for ourselves, for our own redemption?'

'Perhaps,' I acknowledged noncomittally, then added with rather more feeling: 'But I am no patriarch, Baruch. I have fathered no nation; rather, I have sealed the demise of the one which Abraham went to the trouble of begetting.'

But Baruch only smiled. 'You are one of the greatest men who ever lived,' he assured me extravagantly. 'And I shall see that your greatness is recognized, even by those who are not yet born. I shall pray to Adonai, and I shall add to the scroll of your oracles as much else as he will allow me. What he will not permit me to include, I shall document elsewhere, and decide what to do with it later.' Such fervour enlivened his pale face in the lamplight that I didn't demur.

Nor did I interfere when he spent each day that followed with his head bowed over his scrolls and tablets, both those he'd fetched from Ahikam's and others which he must have got hold of through Seraiah. Let him write, I thought, if that is his way of remaining sane.

Before long I even took to writing down thoughts and reminiscences of my own. I found that writing helped smooth out my tangled emotions and sort out some of the confusion I still felt about the way Adonai had chosen to deal with me and with his people over the years. In these accounts of my own I wrote what I wanted without restraint, for I believed that no one but I would get to see them.

Meanwhile, I had Baruch find out what he could from his brother regarding the kind of man Prince Jeconiah was growing up to be. He couldn't discover much, except that the prince and Nehushta his mother spent so much of their lives closeted away together, it was almost as though *they* were husband and wife, and King Jehoiakim the naughty child who drove them to distraction.

At least this must mean - I presumed and hoped - that the Prince's mother had had more influence in the shaping of the boy's personality than had his father. But his thoughts were seldom voiced, for his stammer was as bad as ever, and he would spend long silent hours gazing listlessly at his own reflection in the pool in his mother's courtyard. Perhaps he found his unsullied beauty an incongruous thing in a world where so much of what he had experienced was ugly and corrupt. Or maybe he saw the ghosts of his illustrious ancestors looking at him reproachfully from the well of Sheol.

Late in the autumn of my third year in hiding, Nebuchadrezzar led his troops to the Egyptian frontier to challenge Pharaoh Necho on his own territory. A vast amount of preparation had gone into this campaign, and Nebuchadrezzar had incurred colossal expense in the process. For Egypt under Necho had polished up her faded glory, and

Necho himself was the only ruler in the world who could consider himself a worthy personal rival to Nebuchadrezzar.

The Pharaoh, being aware of Nebuchadrezzar's intentions well in advance, readied himself to mount a strong resistance. When Nebuchadrezzar reached the frontier, he found it lined wide and deep with Egyptian soldiers, heavily armed and prepared to fight to the death for their independence. Ferocious fighting ensued in which the Egyptians prevailed, and Nebuchadrezzar was forced to return to Babylon licking his wounds. Would that those who gloated over his rebuff had remembered that a wild beast can be much more dangerous when wounded.

For Nebuchadrezzar's defeat gave rise to revolts all over his empire. Vassal after vassal withheld tribute, and Jehoiakim was reputedly giving serious consideration to following their example.

Tell him he must not do so, Adonai instructed me. *The setback which Nebuchadrezzar has suffered will soon be reversed; it is only a reminder to him that he owes his power to me.*

I said, 'Then surely it would be better if Jehoiakim *did* revolt. He might succeed in procuring a swift and decisive end for Judah after all.'

Nebuchadrezzar does not have sufficient resources at his disposal to reduce so many rebel states in his present circumstances. He must needs induce others to do his dirty work for him, and their methods will not be as efficient as his own would have been.

So I bade Baruch write to Jehoiakim advising him as Adonai had directed. I pointed out that he had sworn an oath of loyalty to Nebuchadrezzar in Adonai's name; to break it was tantamount to breaking a covenant made with God. But no response was forthcoming.

Then Baruch learned from Seraiah that I was being denounced in public as a traitor. Jehoiakim must have leaked the contents of my letter deliberately, to discredit me still further in his subjects' eyes, and to persuade whoever was harbouring me to turn me in at last. This opportunity to regain our nation's independence has been given us by Adonai, Jehoiakim's toadies were maintaining, yet that charlatan Jeremiah would have you enslaved to a pagan! Treat him with the contempt he deserves, for he *wants* you to be slaves, in order that the rabid drivel he calls prophecy may be seen to have been fulfilled.

So the price on my head was increased; tribute was withheld, and Judah made fresh overtures for protection to her old friend Pharaoh Necho. No doubt Jehoiakim's thick black wig emerged from its closet, and the tasselled robes went back wherever he had found them. The pro-Egyptians who served on his Council - Elishama, Delaiah, Jaazaniah - found themselves back in favour.

I fell into despair, because what I had dreaded had come to pass. In recommending co-operation with Nebuchadrezzar I'd been branded a traitor; it was like being a bullied, tormented child all over again.

Nor was I alone in deserving pity. My heart went out to the parents and friends of those young men who had gone to Babylon to guarantee Jehoiakim's good behaviour, for it was all too easy to imagine what would happen to them now. The clever Daniel whom everyone had loved, and Gedaliah, Ahikam's son... How I wished Adonai would offer me some assurance concerning the hostages' fate. But I couldn't bring myself to pray for this, nor indeed for anything, because Adonai had failed me once again - or that was how it felt. I who loved my country and its people as I loved my own soul was now despised by everyone as a renegade.

But what Adonai had already told me turned out to be true. Nebuchadrezzar had sustained such losses in his battle with Necho that it took him eighteen months to recover his strength. Yet he couldn't allow his seceding vassals to go unpunished. Therefore he stirred up their ancestral enemies to administer punishment on his behalf, and they were only too happy to oblige.

Unruly hordes of Aramaeans, Moabites and Ammonites rampaged across Judah's borders, setting fire to villages, orchards and vineyards, and trampling the growing corn. They raped and pillaged, and killed when the fancy took them: men, women, children, they didn't care. Jehoiakim appealed to Egypt for help in sending the raiders packing, but Necho was too busy getting his own house back in order, for he too had suffered devastating losses in the battle for possession of his kingdom.

'Egypt is a broken reed,' I said disconsolately to Baruch. 'Why can no one see that it will never be right for Judah to throw in her lot with Necho? When Nebuchadrezzar has rebuilt his army he will come back, and he will keep on coming until he has rendered both Judah and Egypt incapable of opposing him again.'

'They call you Nebuchadrezzar's lover,' commented Baruch, and he spoke as morosely as I. 'They say you used dark Babylonian magic to fly to his bed when he was encamped outside our walls. They say that he gave you gold from Solomon's Temple in return for your favours, and for your faking messages from the Almighty advocating our collaboration with the heathen and his gods.'

I put my head in my hands. If only I didn't care what people thought of me; if only my skin were thick, just like our vainglorious monarch's. Yet it was not, and both Zephaniah and Adonai himself had told me it never would be. Chronic sensitivity was part of what it meant to be a man of God.

During the time when the raiders were harrying our land, Jehoiakim compelled Prince Jeconiah to wed, so that the survival of his illustrious dynasty might be assured. How pointless, I thought, when I have told you already that your house is doomed; why get yourself grandsons only to see them carried off into captivity? But Jehoiakim believed the danger from Babylon to be a thing of the past, and that he should now be making plans for a bright and prosperous future. Doubting only his son's virility, he got him not one wife but two - and probably went each night to check that one of them at least was sharing the prince's bed.

Once the restructuring of his army was completed, Nebuchadrezzar set about dealing systematically with the vassals who had broken their treaties with him. He began with the Arabs in the desert to the east of us, the tribes of Kedar and Hazar and their Bedouin brethren. I'd foreknown that this was where he would start, because Adonai had told me, and given me oracles to declaim against the tribes concerned. Not that I could declaim them out aloud; I had them written on tablets, and Seraiah's manservant undertook to have their contents disseminated by his contacts in the city. When events proved me right, I must have regained at least a little respect from Jerusalem's populace.

It was towards the end of my sixth year in hiding that Nebuchadrezzar arrived in Judah. I was exactly fifty years old, and if I'd not had a single grey hair when first we'd taken refuge with Seraiah, I'd acquired plenty since. Pallid and bent as a seedling beneath a stone, with aching bones and joints, I lay on my pallet all day and all night, sleeping, dreaming, waking, staring, coughing, too feeble to pray or even to curse, and knowing Adonai merely as a remote sustaining presence; if he'd sent me into ecstasy now, the intensity of the experience would have killed me.

So when Baruch came and told me that the Babylonian forces were on their way, I barely reacted. He sighed, and took hold of my hand. He'd begun to think I was dying, though he never said so. For myself, I suspected I might be dead already, for what was Sheol, if not a place of darkness under the earth, where the pale, attenuated wraiths of once vigorous men wafted like wisps of cloud, neither asleep nor awake, looking back on their earthly lives and wishing that things had gone differently?

Nebuchadrezzar was making directly for Jerusalem. He was riding with the main contingent of his army at a dignified yet relentless pace. Ahead of him a squadron of mounted officers sped towards us like the wind, empowered to make demands on his behalf and to accept our unconditional surrender, if we were wise enough to capitulate.

In the meantime, refugees from the countryside converged on the capital once again. Precautions were taken against siege: vast quantities of grain and dried fruit and salted meat were brought within the walls; winter was well advanced, so the cisterns beneath the city were full, and in any case we had the Siloam Pool to which water was brought from outside through an underground tunnel constructed long ago by King Hezekiah.

When the advance squadron arrived, they delivered Nebuchadrezzar's ultimatum straight away. Hand over your King, and all those members of his Council who advocated rebellion; you will be punished, but your city will be spared as a monument to my clemency. Refuse, and I shall leave no stone in Jerusalem upon another.

So events had come full circle. Once more Jehoiakim's Council was faced with deciding whether or not to arrest the King and deliver him up to the enemy, for he certainly wouldn't go of his own accord. But this time, half of the Council members were liable for apprehension too. Savage dissension resulted; within the ranks of the nobility factions and sub-factions mushroomed, some of which favoured acceding without question to the Babylonians' demands, whilst others would accede to none of them, and still others wanted to surrender the King but not his pro-Egyptian advisers, or merely some of them, or to surrender the advisers but not the King. While the parties squabbled, the larger part of Nebuchadrezzar's forces reached Jerusalem and began to encircle its walls. Nebuchadrezzar himself was allegedly held up at Riblah.

For myself, because of my vow not to quit Seraiah's cellar, I wasn't able to see the encirclement taking place, nor to watch the foreign troops digging their siege works in Judah's sacred soil. To those who did witness these things, the spectacle was daunting, and many more voices joined in the clamour for capitulation. A howling mob gathered in the Temple Court demanding that the King be handed over to them at once, for despatch to the Babylonian camp.

Meanwhile a second mob collected and jeered at the first, accusing its members of being traitors just like me. A son of David must never again be delivered into the hands of pagans - for who would ever know what had become of the vanished Jehoahaz? - and Jerusalem could withstand siege for however long it took to make Nebuchadrezzar give up and go away. David's City was all but impregnable; her sole area of natural weakness lay along her northern wall, but here the man-made defences could be strengthened, and all available troops, plus any other citizens capable of bearing arms, could be collected together to concentrate our resistance.

Before the arguments of any one of the factions could prevail over the others, an unexpected development put a new perspective on everything. Baruch and I were languishing in our cellar late one morning when we heard the sacks of grain which disguised our doorway being shifted about outside. We froze - could our hiding place have been so suddenly discovered after all this time? - but when the door was finally opened, the person who burst in upon us was Naomi herself. 'Oh Berechiah, Jeremiah!' she exclaimed, 'Your ordeal is over. The King is dead.'

'Dead? How?' Baruch demanded, while I struggled to sit up, clutching my blankets around me.

But Naomi didn't know how the King had died, nor did anyone. He'd been found at daybreak, dead in his bed, without a mark upon him. Jerusalem had been thrown into fresh turmoil; Seraiah himself had gone to the Temple Court on a quest for further details and to try to find out what would happen next.

Whether or not the pro-Babylonian party had had any part in Jehoiakim's death, they were determined to make the most of it. Seraiah returned around sunset and said that they had surrendered the King's dead body to Nebuchadrezzar's officers. The Babylonians had decreed that since the fellow had perjured himself like a common criminal, honourable burial should be denied him. His body had been stripped and cast naked on the open plateau. Thus another of my predictions had received its fulfilment, and the once handsome and vain Eliakim was even now having his kohl-rimmed eyes pecked out by vultures.

By a bizarre coincidence, it was announced the same day that Jehoahaz had died on Egyptian soil. This also contributed to my quiet and gradual exoneration, for hadn't I bidden my countrymen to weep not for Josiah but for his exiled son who would never return to his native land?

Hence Seraiah was inclined to regard me with a new if grudging respect; I could see it in his eyes whenever he stole a glance at me. As for Naomi, I didn't care any more if she glanced at me or not, for I was certain that she could no longer find me a source of temptation. My hair was grey as ash, my skin like crinkled parchment, my chest hollow and my shoulders bent.

Jehoiakim's death did nothing to end the wranglings of the Royal Council. The Babylonians were still insisting on the surrender of its seditious members, who naturally enough defied all attempts to persuade or force them to comply.

Amid the confusion, arrangements were made for the coronation of Prince Jeconiah. Being Jehoiakim's only son, there could be no other contenders for the throne - and I doubt that any sane man would have wanted to put himself forward, things being as they were. With the throne-name of Jehoiachin - Adonai will establish - he was hurriedly installed; though in name Sovereign Lord of Judah, he would rule over little more than the ground on which his throne was standing. Every day the Babylonians' earthworks which were ranged about Jerusalem grew higher, and longer, until the circle was almost complete.

Seraiah attended the installation. The ceremony was conducted jointly by the High Priest and some self-styled prophet whose name I do not recall. Hilkiah, High Priest since the days of Josiah, was so decrepit by now that he had to be led to the throne by the hand, and he proceeded to spill a good half of the holy oil of anointing down his robes. A bad omen! those present were whispering; and had I not myself predicted that Jehoiakim's dynasty was finished?

Hapless Coniah, however, eighteen years old and still as comely as either of the parents whose physical beauty he'd been born with, sat there unblinking, and any thoughts which he had were very far away.

In the depths of winter, Nebuchadrezzar himself reached Jerusalem. The ramparts and trenches surrounding us were finished, and movement of provisions into the city could be curtailed whenever the invader chose. Impatient with our divided Council and its prevarications, Nebuchadrezzar at once demanded that *all* of its members should surrender themselves to him, along with the new king Jehoiachin and his household. He'd been crowned without his suzerain's approval; as overlord of Babylon's empire it was Nebuchadrezzar alone who had the right to appoint the regents who ruled its vassal kingdoms on his behalf.

When still no response was made, the siege commenced.

For more than two months neither men nor supplies could be got into or out of Jerusalem. But while Jerusalem mourned her freedom lost, for Baruch and me came comparative liberty at last. The king who had wanted us dead was dead himself, and those of his subjects who had deemed me insane or dangerous had begun to suspect that it was they who had been the victims of delusion.

I didn't want to leave, though, not any more. I was weak and sick; the brilliance of daylight would hurt my eyes; the prospect of mixing once more with the suffering people I claimed to love filled me with dread. 'But you *must,* Jeremiah,' Baruch implored me. 'It has caused Ahikam much trouble to have his house cleaned out for us, and the broken things repaired... *please*, Jeremiah. Get up. Do it for me. At least try.'

So I tried, because it was he who asked me; he put his arm about me and supported my weight while we mounted the staircase, pausing on every step. When we got to the top I collapsed, and Baruch had to gather me in his arms and carry me out to the litter which was already waiting.

Back at Ahikam's, I wanted nothing more than to lie on my pallet and accustom myself to the semi-daylight of the bedroom. But Baruch wouldn't have it; his native buoyancy restored, he was like a little child who wakes up one morning to see that it has snowed. He would lie on his back in the courtyard, laughing to feel the winter sun on his face; then he would scramble up and come for me, tugging at my arm until I gave in to him and let him lead me on yet another circuit of the yard.

But he acted rightly. Slowly the strength seeped back into my limbs, and the suppleness into my joints. I began to breathe without wheezing, and to walk without hunching my shoulders. I went on thinking of myself as an old and enfeebled wreck of a man for quite some time - but only until Baruch, exasperated, produced a large bronze mirror and made me look into it. I almost gasped, because for all its pallor and its gauntness, my face was handsome in a way it had never been in my youth. Suffering and spirituality were etched into every line; my eyes were bright and sharp as crystal; and my uncut hair, silver white as the wings of a swan, streamed past my shoulders, a dazzling wind-blown veil in the sunshine. It was as though seclusion and sickness had honed me; I'd emerged from my chrysalis transformed, recast somehow in the mould of Moses or one of the ancient patriarchs after all. Yet there was something fragile, something brittle and transparent about my strange new beauty, as though I'd been remade in glass, or reborn as the kind of butterfly which only lives a day.

As word got out that Baruch and I had taken up residence at Ahikam's once again, a steady stream of suppliants flowed to our door: heads of households worried that the provision they had made for their families might prove inadequate; farmers anxious to get back to their fields; mothers wanting me to lay my hands on their ailing offspring; and men, women and children together concerned for kinsfolk or friends who lived outside the city walls, wanting me to discern by second sight whether their loved ones were dead or alive. I prayed the prayers they asked me to, and bestowed on them the benedictions they craved. But I gave them no answers to their questions, for Adonai had given none to me.

Then out of the blue Baruch and I received a group of visitors considerably more eminent than the rest. Some of them were leaders of the pro-Babylonian faction, sons of ancient and noble Jerusalem families. The others wore heavy hooded cloaks and remained quietly in the background at first, allowing their comrades to do the talking.

Baruch showed the whole company inside. They insisted on the gate being locked behind them, and would not state their business until they were satisfied that there was no one but us in the house. Then the senior among the Jerusalem noblemen bowed low before me and said, 'My lord Jeremiah, may I introduce Commander Nabuzaradan. He is captain of the Emperor's personal guard, and the most highly regarded of all his officers. He has a proposition which he would have us put to you in person.'

So saying, the speaker gave a signal to his cloaked companions, who drew back their hoods and unfastened their cloak-pins. There they stood, four sons of Babel with perfumed hair and beards set in dyed-black curls, and tasselled linen tunics reaching down to their slippered feet. Beneath the heavy cloaks with which they'd been disguised, each one wore a short white cape, tasselled like his tunic, and in his hands he carried a staff with his family device carved on the top: one had an apple, another a rose, another a lily. Nabuzaradan's staff was surmounted by a roosting eagle.

I stood and faced them, rigid with apprehension. Why should such men have sought me out? How had they come to hear my name?

Nabuzaradan bowed graciously, exactly as he'd seen the Judean do. He was tall and dark and fastidiously groomed in the exotic Mesopotamian style, with a gleaming golden band around his brow, but there was something genuinely deferential about his handsome features which I couldn't help admiring. With one of the Judeans acting as interpreter, he apologized sincerely for having no word of Hebrew save for 'shalom' with which to greet me and solicit a few moments of my valuable time. But he wished to speak with me none the less, because he understood that I was an especially holy man, much favoured by the god whom I served. He would not therefore waste any longer in pleasantries, since a man of my stature would not be impressed by empty flattery. In brief, he desired that I should go to King Jehoiachin and prevail upon him to comply with Nebuchadrezzar's demands, for the greater good of us all. For it had come to the Emperor's notice that the wise and pious Jeremiah had several times advised the late Jehoiakim to the same effect.

Thereupon he beckoned to one of his subordinates, who approached and laid a jewelled casket at my feet. The lid of it Nabuzaradan himself stooped to open; inside was a prince's fortune in gold and precious stones.

I was aghast. I drew the leader of the Judean contingent to one side and hissed at him: 'You have come to my house to *bribe* me? Get these uncircumcized heathen out of here at once, and have them take their baubles with them.'

'Oh, but my lord... forgive me, I don't think you quite understand. This is a gift, not a bribe.' The Judean was already speaking in a whisper, but now he lowered his voice still further and went on, 'I knew how this would appear to you, my lord, and I advised the Commander to leave the casket behind. But he esteems you highly, my lord Jeremiah, as a prudent statesman of exemplary courage. He doesn't imagine for a moment that you are susceptible to corruption. The giving of costly gifts is a mark of the utmost respect among his people.'

'I am no statesman, nor am I courageous in the least,' I objected. 'I advised Jehoiakim to surrender because that was precisely what Adonai instructed me to do, not because I have ever had the slightest admiration for Babylon, nor indeed because that course of action was expedient. Have these men removed, I tell you. I will endure their pagan presence not a moment longer.'

'So you will not help us?' The Judean sounded as surprised as he was desperate. 'When lives have been put at risk to enable the Commander to come here? When he has risked his own life, no less, in order that he might honour you with his presence instead of sending an inferior?'

'He does me no honour whatever by coming here and inciting me to betray my country. If you would kindly apprise him of the fact, you might the more easily persuade him and his scented stooges to leave.'

'As you wish, my lord,' the Judean assented. He approached Nabuzaradan with an air of chagrin, and spent some considerable time conferring with him in undertones via the interpreter.

Then Nabuzaradan bowed to me again, and bade the interpreter explain something to me in turn. The latter said, 'My lord Jeremiah, the Commander understands fully the reason for your decision, and he accepts it. He says that it is important for every man to seek the will of his god and then obey it. He commends you for doing exactly that, without fear and without any thought of material reward.'

The leader of the Judeans started visibly. Nabuzaradan's subordinate picked up the casket and closed it, and as the party prepared to leave, the Commander bowed before me a third and final time, his grave, deeply-set eyes unafraid and unashamed to lock with my own. When he had departed, I was left with the disconcerting sensation that this was a man of integrity, with whom, under different circumstances, I could have entered into a mutually satisfying friendship.

Not that I confessed as much to Baruch. When our visitors were gone he stormed about the room like a newly-captured beast about its cage. 'How dare those arrogant aristocrats come here and offer us financial inducements to adopt the foreigners' cause?' he thundered. 'How dare they bring uncircumcized pagans with them to defile our home?'

I didn't respond. I still saw the grave, respectful countenance of Nabuzaradan in front of my eyes when I closed them, and found myself wishing that the man had been a Judean. Not only could we then have arranged to see one another again and converse at greater length, but I should not have had to grapple with the question of how it was possible for a pagan to act more honourably and display greater integrity than the overwhelming majority of the Chosen People.

That night, however, Adonai woke me from a fitful sleep and spoke to me clearly for the first time since my release from Seraiah's cellar.

Go to Jehoiachin, just as Nabuzaradan asked you to do. Persuade the new king to surrender himself and his household and all of his ministers to the Babylonians at the earliest opportunity.

'Oh no, my Lord, I beg you. Do you *want* men to think me corrupt? Suppose the people find out that there were Babylonians here, and that after receiving them in my home I went straight to His Majesty advocating surrender?'

Since when were men's opinions important, Jeremiah? Obedience to my sovereign will is what is important, as you said yourself to the Babylonian - and as he said also to you.

'But my Lord... Coniah is only a child! He doesn't deserve to be exiled, thrown away like a broken pot which no one wants. And his mother has honoured you from being a child herself.'

Jehoiachin is the son of his father, Jeremiah, and were his own sons to be permitted to rule after him, they would be no worthier than he. But you need not be afraid for him, nor for his mother. I shall see that they are treated in a manner appropriate to their station.

I got no more sleep until morning. I tossed and turned and sweated and groaned, and at first light I arose and went to the palace. It was so many years since I had been seen at Court that my sudden appearance caused something of a stir. But I was admitted without question, and bidden to wait until His Majesty had breakfasted and taken his place in the throne-room.

At length they showed me in, and there he was: poor, lost Jeconiah esconced on the throne of David, eyes unblinking, slender fingers spread wide on the heads of the stone lions which flanked his seat. He scarcely seemed to see me, but although I pitied him mightily, my feelings were not shared by Adonai. At once he possessed my tongue, and I heard myself proclaiming that even if Jehoiachin were a signet ring on the Lord's finger, he would tear him off and give him into the hands of his enemies. He and Nehushta his mother were destined for deportation, and would die far away from the land which had given them birth. Better for them if they went of their own accord, and better for their beleaguered people too.

All the while I was thinking: this isn't fair; this docile, damaged boy isn't capable of sinning. But Adonai said: *I have looked into his heart, Jeremiah. I have seen the bitterness he harbours against me. This is the canker which has eaten away his wits.* And suddenly I saw it too, like foul black tendrils creeping over his flesh, and I couldn't hold back my tears, because Jehoiakim's wickedness had ruined what had been created so beautiful.

When I had finished, and the spirit released me, I fell to my knees and awaited His Majesty's response - if not summary eviction by his bodyguard. But neither was forthcoming. Jehoiachin went on staring at spectres, and eventually one of his attendants led me outside. I went back home and said nothing to Baruch of where I had been or why. Folk came for prayer and counsel all that day and the next, as usual, and I thought: Coniah didn't even hear what I said.

The day after this one, which chanced to be Shabbat eve, Baruch and I were invited to share the evening meal with Seraiah and his family, and to stay overnight at their house. I was reluctant to accept, but Baruch insisted: his brother had conquered his prejudice against me, and we must not reward him by refusing his hospitality.

Thus it was that we came to witness Jehoiachin's surrender.

Who or what had persuaded him to do as I'd recommended, I do not know; or perhaps it had simply taken three days for what I'd said to percolate through the fog in his mind. Either way, he walked out through the city gates at dawn on the Sabbath day, his mother and her father walking beside him and his wives behind, carrying infant sons whom they must have hoped would one day be kings. His personal attendants and a handful of courtiers followed after him. Every member of the brave and tragic little procession was clothed in sackcloth, and their foreheads and loosened hair were grey with the ashes of mourning.

Was it courage or sheer vacuousness which caused the young King to appear so calm, so serene and collected? He walked sedately across a carpet of early spring flowers, his head erect, his sceptre held proudly in front of his chest; and his reign had lasted but three months and ten days, during the whole of which his city had been under siege. I remembered the ludicrous pomp and pretension with which his father had made that same short journey to the Babylonian camp not so very long before.

Nebuchadrezzar himself rode out to receive Jehoiachin in submission. His senior officers were with him, the pale morning sunshine glinting on their helmets; the man at his right was Nabuzaradan. Jehoiachin dropped meekly to his knees, and I watched in grim silence as the hands of this blighted son of David were manacled by idolaters, and his ankles placed in chains. Each of his companions was bound in turn, as a sign of their nation's subjugation. Yet I drew some comfort from the knowledge that Nabuzaradan was there at the Emperor's right hand. He, I was convinced, would ensure that the royal captives were not subjected to abuse. The mental torture of losing their freedom, of being cut off from all they had known and loved, would be quite sufficient.

And through the opened gates of David's city Nebuchadrezzar's barbarian soldiers streamed in, their studded boots ringing on the stones, their raucous shouts of victory echoing along the deserted streets. From their upper rooms, Jerusalem's inhabitants looked out in miserable disbelief, for few had ever accepted that their God would see them come to this.

Not that things were as bad as they could have been. The Babylonian officers kept their troops in check, and there was no unauthorized looting, no indiscriminate destruction. So far as I know, no women were raped, no children's throats were cut before their parents' eyes, no old men were dragged from their beds and flayed alive. When the shackled royal party had been shepherded into the Babylonian camp, Nebuchadrezzar and Nabuzaradan and their associates rode into the city themselves and entered the Temple Court. Thence they directed Jerusalem's punishment.

Treasures were removed from the Temple precincts and the Holy Place itself. Silver lampstands and furniture for the altars were broken up for transportation, and ancient sacred vessels were piled into carts to be melted down and recast into trinkets or idols.

The Holy of Holies, however, was left intact. The columns Jachin and Boaz remained in position, as did the great Bronze Sea and the marble stands. Whatever portable items the serving priests managed to hide escaped desecration also, and the fabric of the Temple buildings was not harmed. Doubtless Nebuchadrezzar wanted to leave us with something to lose.

Tribute was re-imposed, far heavier than that which had been demanded before, to offset the cost of the military operations carried out against us. Nebuchadrezzar announced his intention to set over Judah a ruler of his own choosing; the man would be named and invested in due course, when the Emperor had acquired the information necessary to make the best appointment.

Finally, several thousand people were to be deported, mostly from Jerusalem itself, but some from Judah's lesser cities also. It emerged that these cities had not been destroyed by the invader; Nebuchadrezzar had been much more concerned to win the surrender of the capital. Among those destined for deportation were all the most prominent figures in Judean society, along with their families: men who were rich, well-born, intelligent, men who had held high office and who might therefore possess the desire and the ability to foment further rebellion in the future. Their immediate subordinates would be going too, and the senior officers from Judah's army - those who could be found, at any rate, for others had vanished with their men into the wilderness. Then master craftsmen were to be rounded up: expert masons, carpenters and smiths who had perfected their skills in the upkeep of Adonai's Temple would now be required to apply them to the embellishment of Babylon's palaces and shrines.

Thus in a single day Judah was robbed of her brightest and best, and I myself was robbed of my oldest friend. Though Ahikam no longer held office, his name was well known in Babylon through his son who was already there; I found solace in the hope that the two of them might now be reunited. Joah also was taken, he who had once been Josiah's Recorder; every member of Josiah's Council was now either exiled or dead.

Of the existing Royal Council, no member fared any better. Elishama the Secretary of State, Delaiah the Steward, Zedekiah the Recorder, Gemariah Ahikam's brother... all were herded together and shackled. Hilkiah the veteran High Priest was taken, and so was his son, and Pashhur his deputy, who had once had me put in the stocks.

This latter made a vigorous attempt to resist arrest, and his friends rallied to his support. As a result he was forced to watch them skewered before his eyes just as I'd predicted, and those of his kinsmen who might have escaped deportation had their names added to the lists of the proscribed.

Of Shaphan's sons, only Elasah and Jaazaniah remained at large. Shallum and Huldah too were left alone, for they had lived in obscure retirement now for many years.

For myself, I half expected Nebuchadrezzar's soldiers to break down the door at any moment and whisk me away, for the Babylonians certainly knew my name.

But when they came to my house, the Babylonians did not take me. To my dismay, they brought me the very casket of jewels I'd been offered once before, and refused to return to their master until I had accepted it. I had done what he had asked of me, therefore I was to have my reward.

PART FOUR

IN THE DAYS OF KING ZEDEKIAH

I am the man who has witnessed disaster,

> *Walking in darkness, deprived of God's light.*

Adonai has lifted his right hand against me,

> *Compassed me round with affliction and pain.*

Piercing my heart with keen barbs from his quiver,

> *He caused my own people to laugh me to scorn.*

All of my teeth he has broken with grit;

> *In the dust of the ground he has trampled me down.*

Peace and prosperity he has denied to me;

> *All I had hoped from my God is now gone.*

Lamentations 3:1,2,3,5,13,14,16-18.

CHAPTER 19: JEREMIAH

A week after the deportees had been marched away, Nabuzaradan's men came a third time to my house. On this occasion I was required to go with them, but did not know why, for they had brought no interpreter to explain.

I was led directly to the palace, and to the throne-room, whose great white throne with its flanking lions stood empty on its elevated dais. Soldiers of Nebuchadrezzar were everywhere; I felt like a bewildered foreigner, here on Judean soil.

Then came the clatter of hobnailed boots on the marble pavement; I turned, and saw an ashen-faced young man being driven towards me. It was so very long since I'd seen him, and he and I were both so afraid, that it was a few moments before I realized who he was.

For not every member of the royal family had been taken into exile. Mattaniah, Josiah's youngest son, uncle and boyhood companion of the deported Jeconiah, remained at the palace. A mere twenty one years old, and little more likely ever to be king than I was myself, he had played no part in affairs of state, preferring to devote his time to his wife and his four small children.

Now he looked as if he believed he would never set eyes on them again, and I suspected that he might be right. If Nabuzaradan had been present I might have felt better, but the officer in charge of whatever proceedings these were was a much older man, with sharp little eyes and a twisted mouth, and hair which would long have been grey had it not been dyed the customary Babylonian black.

A third prisoner was brought in, quite close in age to Mattaniah, though I had no idea who he was. Then others were brought, in a group: the lesser prophets from the Court, their more senior brethren having gone with the exiles. I thought: we are all to be executed, there can be no other explanation. This sharp-eyed character is Nabuzaradan's personal enemy, and he means to have his wicked way while his adversary is otherwise engaged.

But even as this thought was taking shape in my mind, there was a blaring of trumpets and Nabuzaradan walked in, followed by Nebuchadrezzar himself. The Babylonians present threw themselves on the ground or came sharply to attention as appropriate. 'As you were,' is what the Emperor must have said to them; then he snapped his fingers at the soldiers guarding Mattaniah. They took him by the elbows and deposited him on David's throne.

Now I understood, and was appalled. So was Mattaniah. He tried to protest, and even to rise from his seat, but spears were abruptly crossed in front of him. He looked on helplessly as the young man I couldn't identify was stripped of his outer clothing and made to don the robes, the ephod and the decorations of the High Priest, wrested from Hilkiah before he'd been taken away. I realized then who he was: Hilkiah's grandson Seraiah, and he was no readier to be High Priest than the diffident Mattaniah was to be King.

A horn of oil was thrust into Seraiah's hands, and I waited to see which of the court prophets would be selected to join him in performing the ritual. It was clear that the Babylonians had taken the trouble to learn how our coronations were traditionally conducted, even though this perfunctory and private affair scarcely bore any resemblance to the real thing. For this *wasn't* the real thing; Judah already had a king, Jehoiachin, whose tranquil nobility in surrender had won him the respect and affection of his subjects.

But none of the court prophets was singled out. Nabuzaradan came forward and stood before me, his eyes looking levelly into mine.

There were many things I might have agreed to do for him, but condoning the appointment of a puppet king to govern God's people on a pagan's behalf wasn't one of them. Adonai could rebuke me afterwards if he liked, but I would not stoop to this, and my resolve was hardened when I remembered the incriminating casket of Babylonian treasure I'd hidden in Ahikam's cellar.

Nebuchadrezzar spoke sharply to Nabuzaradan then; I think he wanted me forced to submit to his will. But Nabuzaradan kissed the young Emperor's hand and responded pacifically yet firmly, whereupon Nebuchadrezzar snorted and tossed back his hair, and had the eldest of the court prophets dragged out from among his comrades. Thus the dubious honour which should have been mine was accorded to another.

I say that he was the eldest, and so he was, but still he was no more than thirty five years of age, and plainly unused to being the centre of attention. He was commanded to give his name, which was Hananiah, and to stand beside Seraiah. He was less than eager to co-operate, until the sharp-eyed officer drew a sword and held it to his throat.

And so this travesty of a coronation got under way. The liturgy was spoken in Aramaic and in Hebrew through an interpreter, the celebrant being Nebuchadrezzar himself. But all the conventional elements of a Davidic enthronement were included. 'I shall proclaim the decree of Adonai!' this perfumed pagan declared. '"You are my son; today I have become your father."' And he assigned Mattaniah a throne-name, Zedekiah, 'Adonai is my righteousness'. But then he made the fledgling monarch grovel at his feet and swear allegiance to the Babylonian overlord who had bestowed upon him his kingly authority. He had to promise to administer Judah conscientiously on Nebuchadrezzar's behalf, to make no innovation without his lord's consent, and to have no friendship with Egypt. Then the royal robes of Judah were draped about his narrow shoulders, and there he sat on David's throne, shivering with terror, the sceptre juddering in his hands.

Now that we had a new King, a new Royal Council was required to serve him. This could not be convened straight away, because several of its members were to be brought from Babylon: some of those same young men who had been deported as beardless youths eight years before. They had not been killed as a result of Jehoiakim's revolt after all, being much too valuable. Until they could be returned to Judah, high-ranking Babylonians would oversee her administration in their stead.

Thus it was that the inhabitants of Jerusalem grew used to the sight of Babylonians in their midst. Babylonian soldiers patrolled the streets, while Babylonians clad in civilian garb, with short white capes and tasselled tunics, stalked the corridors of power. But I myself heard no more from Nabuzaradan for a very long time.

Two months or so after the Babylonian occupation of Jerusalem began, the young men destined to be Councillors arrived from Mesopotamia. Daniel wasn't among them; but Gedaliah ben Ahikam was.

Not that I should have known him for Ahikam's son. His dyed, ringleted hair reached the small of his back, and his face was made up like a shrine-boy's. I could only hope now that he and his father had *not* been allowed to renew their acquaintance.

He was appointed to the post of Royal Steward; a certain Jonathan, one of his juvenile companions, was made Secretary of State; a third young man, Zephaniah, youngest son of Maaseiah the erstwhile City Governor, was made Officer of the Temple, answering to Hilkiah's grandson.

The remaining government posts were filled by men who had never been to Babylon in their lives, for the prudent Nebuchadrezzar was concerned to minimize the likelihood of future rebellion. Most of the appointees were of good families, but were younger sons spared from deportation by their previous insignificance in the political field, having been brought up to defer to their elders and betters. Suddenly they *were* the betters, for their elders were gone.

Among them were Elasah and Jaazaniah, the two youngest sons of Shaphan; Elasah I knew to be a good man, though I could hardly say the same for Jaazaniah. Coniah, son of Elnathan and brother of Jehoiakim's Queen Nehushta, was named Supreme Commander of Judah's Armed Forces: a position supreme in name alone, for just like his king he was merely the instrument of Babylon, with responsibility for a demoralized and decimated rabble.

But the most surprising appointment of all, to Baruch and myself at any rate, was that of Baruch's own brother

Seraiah as Royal Recorder. Perhaps we were wrong to be surprised; after all, Seraiah was one of the most learned scribes left in Jerusalem, and the association of his name with my own had perhaps won him favour in Nabuzaradan's eyes.

As time went on, it began to feel as though life had returned to normal. Supplies came and went once more through the gates of Jerusalem. The refugees who had crowded the city went back to their homes. Crops were planted, vineyards and olive groves cleared of thorns, and sheep and goats were seen again on the mountain pastures.

And I was forgiven, so it seemed, for I had foretold the coming of Nebuchadrezzar and I had been right, but because of my intercessions the City of David had escaped destruction, and the farmlands had been reclaimed. Granted, foreigners garrisoned our towns and demanded the firstfruits of our labours, and thousands of our fellow-countrymen languished in some god-forsaken world far away. But the Babylonian garrisons caused us to feel secure against the incursions of Ammonites and Moabites and the like, who had all been our enemies much longer than the people of Mesopotamia. And as for the thousands of exiles... well, out of sight is soon enough out of mind, and besides, their estates had become available for redistribution to those left behind. Those who were gone deserved to be exiled, it was agreed, since they had exploited their poorer and weaker brethren for generations. Justice had apparently been done, for Adonai had punished those who had earnt it, whilst he had spared the lowly and innocent.

As far as I myself was concerned, although I knew this interpretation of events to be fatally flawed, it was good, for a season, not to be maligned. But there was worry at the back of my mind.

'Surely Nebuchadrezzar has no cause to wreak further damage now,' Baruch said to reassure me. 'He has installed a king of his own choosing on Judah's throne, one who is malleable as clay and surrounded by advisers half of whom can scarcely remember their Hebrew. The Emperor takes the best of what we produce, and would have nothing to gain by destroying the source of it.'

'Remember, Baruch, it isn't Nebuchadrezzar whom we should fear. The Emperor of Babylon has received his power from one greater than himself just as surely as our reluctant Zedekiah has done. It is Adonai who has chastened us, to bring about our repentance, but Judah is as godless as ever. For every idolater carried away into exile another ten remain, and every greedy landowner who exploited his workers has been replaced by another greedier than the first.'

Nevertheless, for three whole years it seemed that I was worrying for nothing. David's City and Solomon's Temple continued to exist, a Davidic king was still on the throne, and we had a Zadokite descendant of Aaron ministering as High Priest. Moreover we heard that the exiles in Babylon were being treated humanely. Except for Jehoiachin and his relatives they were not in prison; they had been given tents or huts as dwellings, and work was found for them so that they might make their living. They were permitted to save some of their wages to purchase land and build houses for themselves if they so desired.

Not that many were taking advantage of this opportunity, however, because there had begun to be speculation that leave would soon be granted them to come back home. This speculation was fuelled by the palace prophets. Hananiah, the one who had assisted with Zedekiah's coronation, was apparently of the opinion that the exile would last a couple of years at the most, though whence he had derived this information I couldn't imagine, when I had clearly been told that it would last for seventy years.

It was even believed that Jehoiachin would return in the near future to reclaim his throne. After all, the Babylonians hadn't killed him, nor had they confiscated his estates, which were being administered by a bailiff on his behalf. I wondered how this state of affairs was affecting Zedekiah, and I rather wished that he would send for me, or that Adonai would send me to him, that I might get to know how things stood with him.

But Adonai had sent me no word at all since Jehoiachin and the rest of the exiles had departed. There had been no intimacies, no sudden awakenings late in the night. Before long I lost even the background sense of his presence around and within me; prayer times were dry and empty and short.

'What troubles you?' Baruch enquired one afternoon when he awoke during our siesta to find that I had not slept.

But I could find no words to describe what I was feeling. In times gone by, when Adonai had withdrawn his presence from me, I'd had only myself to blame. This time I knew of no sin I had committed. 'Perhaps he is done with me, Baruch,' I said at last. 'Perhaps the thing is over; he has gone in search of a younger and braver man to take my place.'

Baruch said nothing; I wondered if he hoped deep within that this was true. We lay down once more, and Baruch must have slept again, because a little later he arose and said, 'Jeremiah? I had the strangest of dreams. I dreamed that I was you and you were me, so you were asleep and I was awake. A woman came into this room, with baskets of figs in her hands. And she said: "He *has* left you, but only for a season. He is preparing you, because when he returns, what he says to you will be so new and so unexpected that he wants you to be in no doubt that it comes from him." Then she put down the baskets of figs and vanished.'

I chuckled softly. 'And you woke before you got to eat any of the fruit, Baruch? That's not like you, to miss out on the chance of a good snack when it is staring you in the face.'

'But I was you, remember, and you were me,' said Baruch, then he laughed too. And we talked no more about the dream or its meaning, for it was time to rise and go on with the day.

The following morning I awoke with a curious urge to visit the Temple. I didn't know if my ban from its precincts still held, but the urge persisted. So I made up my mind to do as it bade me.

I never got inside the Temple Court, for by one of its outer gates stood a woman with baskets of figs in her hands.

She was challenging the passers by to come and examine for themselves the quality of what she had for sale.

Not since he'd sent me to the Street of the Potters had Adonai quickened my spirit in such an uncanny way. I stood transfixed, while Adonai asked me: *My son, what do you see?*

'Figs,' I replied, and could say no more, for my throat was too dry and my tongue had swelled like a gag in my mouth. It was like being back in the cottage of Simeon and Hannah at the time of my calling, with the boiling pot tipping its contents on the floor, and me unable to move.

What kind of figs, Jeremiah? Inspect them carefully and tell me.

I looked in the basket in the woman's right hand. 'Good figs,' I answered. 'The kind which ripen early.'

And in the other basket? Are those the same?

I looked in the basket she had on her left, and retched, because even as I watched, the figs shrivelled, and their skins were crawling with maggots. The smell which came up was foetid and rank.

'They are bad,' I responded. 'Fit only for throwing away.'

Listen to the word of Adonai, then, Jeremiah. Just like the good figs, I choose to regard as good the exiles I sent from Judah into the land of Babel. I shall watch over them; I shall nurture them as a gardener nurtures his tenderest plants. As for Zedekiah and those who remain in Jerusalem, them I shall make offensive to all the kingdoms of the earth, an object of ridicule and cursing. Like the bad figs I shall discard them; I shall send the sword, famine and plague against them until they are banished from the land I gave to their fathers.

'No!' I protested. 'Those who were taken away are no better than those who were left.'

They are all of them utterly despicable, Jeremiah. Not one of them deserves any better than my blistering wrath. But I am who I am; I show mercy to those to whom I show mercy. I shall give the men and women in exile a heart to seek me, to know me, that I am the Lord. Do you not recall my telling you, as I told Hosea, that the Children of Israel would have to return to the wilderness for me to court them afresh, as I courted their forefathers in the days of Moses? They will again be my people, and I shall be their God.

'But what of me? What of Baruch? Are *we* to be discarded? Are we to be denied salvation because we are still here in Jerusalem? What of Baruch's brother, who protected us? And Huldah, and Shallum...'

The full number of those to be deported is not yet made up. As for you, Jeremiah, you will go where I send you. It is not for you to question the destiny I have chosen for you. You are mine.

Then Adonai's spirit departed, swiftly as a bird when a child runs to catch it. I collapsed, and blacked out at once. When I recovered, a ring of faces surrounded me, and jabbering voices argued over whether I'd had a stroke, or a fit, or my heart had given out. Someone must have sent for Baruch already, for almost at once he was beside me and lifting me up to carry me home.

For days after that I remained in my room, fasting and fighting Adonai harder than I'd ever fought him before. I stormed and raged and flung things at the walls, smashing my own head against them as if to exorcize Adonai's spirit from it for ever.

'How will you win the exiles to yourself in the land of Marduk when you could not win them here?' I screamed. 'In Babylonia evil gods hold sway; they will imprison your people's souls, and you will never break their power! *This* is your land! Babylon belongs to others.'

I am Lord of every land, Jeremiah. I created the universe. The gods of the nations are nothing, and less than nothing.

'Then there *are* no evil spirits? There was no serpent to tempt Eve in the Garden of Eden? There are no devils to possess us, to wreak havoc in the lives of men?'

There are powers and principalities, but I created them all, and one day I shall destroy those who have led men astray, because they rebelled against me exactly as you and your people have done.

'Is it any wonder we rebel? You tell us one thing one day and another thing the next! You tell us that those who are reckoned the wickedest among us, the political leaders and the corrupt priests and the greedy exploitative misers who have been banished from our borders for their sins... all these are better than the rest of us!'

Not better, Jeremiah. Is the murderer of a hundred men any better than the man who kills a thousand? Or is the one who murders a thousand better than the first, because he is the better murderer? Such questions are meaningless, because each deserves death, and each can die but once for the crimes he has committed. But those in exile will grow teachable. Their despair and their longing for home will draw them inexorably towards me, for they have nowhere else to turn, and no one else to take up their cause. I am just, but I am also compassionate. It is my nature to show mercy - but not to the deserving, since there are none. Look to yourself, Jeremiah: your stubbornness wearies me; you are wilful and stupid as a mule. Yet I have chosen to love you. I love you so much that the skies overflow with the tears I weep for you.

Then guilt overpowered me, and I seemed to find myself in the defendant's place in the Heavenly Court, with the God I had wronged presiding as judge. The faces of those celestial beings who had not rebelled were trained upon me, eloquent with pity and reproof.

'Forgive me,' I wept, down on my knees on the courtroom floor. 'I know that a man's life is not his own. I know it is not for me to direct my own steps. Correct me justly, my Lord, but not in your anger, else you reduce me to nothing.'

And immediately Adonai stepped down from the tribunal, raised me up and breathed his life-giving breath into my nostrils just as he had done into Adam's when he created him: new, unsullied, dependent, perfect. He went on blessing me until ecstasy transported me, carrying me far away on waves of liquid love so wild and so wonderful after so very long that I thought I should never be able to return to dry land again. When ultimately I did so, Baruch was beside me once more, imploring me to speak to him, and then to take some food, because I'd had nothing but water for seven days.

He brought me broth and I ate it, but sent him away when I'd finished, because I ached to be alone again with my God. I stayed in my room for seven more days, though I ate the food which was brought to me, and during that time, between the madness and the laughter and the devastating, ravishing weakness, I learned things which no other man had had revealed to him. Adonai is the same - yesterday, today, tomorrow, for ever - but what he had shown us of himself and his purposes in the past had been incomplete, for we had not been ready for more. Soon we should *have* to be ready, and I was the one who must interpret the fresh revelation to my people. Up until now, Adonai had given me fragments of his truth, unconnected, unexplained. Now I was to comprehend the fullness of the will of God for his chosen ones: namely, that we were to be a nation no more, but his people for ever.

I was confused. A people but not a nation - how could this be?

The old must pass away, and never be rebuilt. The Jerusalem cult is dead, Jeremiah. The Temple, the priesthood, the sacrificial system, the rituals... all of these things must go. A new kind of Israel is being born, a new kind of Kingdom of God, to whom no one can belong unless he seek it for himself. This cannot happen on Judean soil, where there will always be those who would strive to reanimate the corpse of history.

'But how?' I asked in bewilderment. '*How* can a man gain entry to this kingdom for himself?'

This you know already, my son, for you yourself have entered it. Your spirit has been awakened. I speak to you and you hear my voice. Josiah knew it too; the mystery was contained in the Book of the Law which I gave him. The circumcision of the heart, *don't you remember? The statutes of the kingdom which is coming will be inscribed on men's hearts, rendering all books of law and tablets of stone redundant. Each man will be responsible to me for his actions, and must seek atonement for himself; no longer will he be punished for his parents' sins, or be able to blame them or his peers for his own.*

'But Josiah never sought to end the Temple cult. He sought to reform it.'

Because he knew me, but only in part. He heard my voice, but only as a whisper through his pride. No reform could ever go far enough; you saw that for yourself. The world can never change unless the heart of man is changed and his spirit brought alive. The cult has served its purpose, Jeremiah. It was a pattern, nothing more. The Law on Moses' tablets was a pattern for what will be written on the hearts of those who love me.

My head was reeling. God's people could exist without a land of their own to define them? Knowledge of God could exist without a religion? There could be atonement without the priesthood, the scapegoat, the sacrificed animals and blood?

Yes, Jeremiah, for I shall provide the means of atonement myself. And I shall make a fresh covenant, but only with those who are willing to accept its terms. Only by the fruit borne in their lives will they be known as mine, not by the food they eat, by their nationality, or by any faction to which they belong. Temples and rituals, hierarchies, rules and regulations... all must be done away with. Then perhaps mankind can be reborn, recreated as he was always meant to be.

This sounded like blasphemy, yet I knew that it came from the lips of Adonai himself because I could never in a thousand lifetimes have dreamt it up for myself. Yes, he had told me many years before that a new kind of covenant was coming, but its full implications I hadn't grasped. Now I understood, and I understood too why exile was the only way it could be inaugurated. The exiles would have faith alone to fall back on - once it had been conceived in them. To ensure that the old was not rebuilt when the exile was finally over, the Temple and all its environs must be demolished, and the Davidic dynasty must come to an end.

'So Jerusalem will rebel,' I concluded. 'That is why more of us will be taken into captivity to join those already swelling Babylon's rivers with their tears. You will not intervene to save Jerusalem, the Ark of the Covenant will never be found, but you won't shed a single tear over any one of these tragedies, because each accords with your sovereign will.'

You are wrong, my son. I shall weep for Jerusalem, and I shall weep for David's dynasty, just as I have wept over you. You will weep too; you'll weep my tears, that my people may witness my grief for themselves.

'So when Zedekiah rebels, I must not dissuade him? I must encourage him to break his oath to Nebuchadrezzar, an oath he swore in your own name, because his rebellion will serve your ultimate purpose?'

No man must be encouraged to sin. You will dissuade him from rebellion as you dissuaded Jehoiakim and Jehoiachin before him, but he will not listen.

I lay with the heels of my hands pressed to my temples. A tentative knock came at my door, and Baruch entered, my daily bowl of soup steaming in his hands. He set it down as usual, but contrary to his custom he did not slip away. He sat on my bed and blurted, 'Don't shut me out of your life, Jeremiah. Tell me what all this is about. Help me to understand.'

I tried. I said that the Temple system was finished, because it had been meant as a way for us all to express our obedience to God, but that the means had become the end. As for sacrifice, each of us must sacrifice the familiarity of our rituals for a perilous spiritual quest. Religion as we knew it led only to factions, feuding and wars. So religion must die, to make way for the living God.

'A religion without religion?' said Baruch. 'It doesn't make sense. *None* of this makes sense.'

'You think I don't know that? You think I understand it any better than you? That's why I need to be here on my own, Baruch, to think things through, and to pray. But the riddles abound; I discover more and more. Adonai leads no man into sin, yet only through Zedekiah's rebellion can God's will be accomplished. None of us deserves Adonai's mercy, yet some of us will receive it. There is hope for the future, but only if everything we have built is swept away. The nation will die, but the people of God will live on.'

Baruch shook his head, then held it in his hands, and I was undone. 'Don't write me off, Baruch,' I appealed to him. 'Not after all these years. Don't think me mad now, when for the first time in my life I begin to perceive the truth as it really is.'

'How can I *not* think you mad?' he retorted, angry because once again I had seen into his soul. 'You have spent two weeks cooped up like a hermit when at last we are free to go where we want to, and now you spout meaningless contradictions! What am *I* supposed to do, while you and your God whisper sweet nothings like lovers in the dark?'

'You do as you please,' I told him absently: a foolish thing to say, because it must have sounded to him as though we'd come full circle, back to the time before I had welcomed his presence in my home. He swore, and left the room, slamming the door in jealous rage. I longed to go after him, yet too many questions remained to be asked and answered before my solitary vigil could end.

'The heart of every man is sick,' I said to Adonai. 'The heart is the most jealous and deceitful thing in all the world, and none of us can fathom its wickedness. How can the Law of God be written on so stained a surface? Why should a man be capable of obeying what is written there in secret on sinful flesh, when he cannot obey what was emblazoned on Moses' tablets for all to see?'

Man by himself can achieve nothing. Man indwelt by my spirit can heal the sick and even bring back the dead from Sheol. He can outrun chariots, pacify storms, drink poison without being harmed, scale the heights of Heaven and plumb the depths of every mystery. My servants Elijah and Elisha did all those things and more. Man indwelt by my spirit can and will obey me, because in such obedience lies joy, power, and the only true freedom a man can know. If he disobeys, he tears himself apart.

'Then why can't *I* obey you? Why do I struggle and fight, kicking out like a man who is blind, when I am one of the few whose eyes are already open? Why do *I* tear myself apart?'

Because you are afraid to let go of what you were, in order that you may become what you could be.

'So this is why I don't see visions, or perform great miracles? This is why I fail you time and again? This is why I shall never be strong like the prophets of old, or those which are to come?'

A time is coming when there will be no more need for prophets than there will be for priests. Everyone will be able to know me for himself if that is what he desires. I shall quicken the seekers' spirits as I quickened yours; I shall give them new hearts for old. I myself shall make atonement for their sins, and they will inhabit a new Jerusalem which will stand for ever. Its king will be a true Zedekiah, for Adonai will be his righteousness. He will be known as the Messiah, the Anointed One, for he will be my unique representative on earth. His heart will be given in pledge to me, and he will lay down his life for the salvation of my people, and for all the world.

'For *all* the world? For Gentiles too? Even the uncircumcized may come to know you?'

Those who seek will find me, Jeremiah. This has always been so. Israel was charged with revealing my glory to the world, but she has obscured its brightness with the cloak of her iniquities. Nevertheless, there are those who have glimpsed it.

Nabuzaradan? I thought, and before I had even framed his name within a question, it was answered.

Nabuzaradan seeks with diligence. And you will assist him with his search - indeed you have done so already. But there are others with whom you must share the revelation I have given you in these days. You must be ready once more to do as I command you, to be rejected, to be laughed to scorn, and to suffer grievous affliction in the cause of the truth.

'I am ready,' I whispered; and could only hope that I was.

As Zedekiah's reign progressed, I watched the last vestiges of Josiah's influence disappear. Egyptian and Babylonian gods were worshipped in Adonai's very Temple, albeit at first in darkened rooms. Sorcery and divination were practised everywhere; magical amulets were worn; the fires of the Tophet burned ever more ferociously, and the pall of its acrid smoke pervaded the city.

Adonai has been vanquished, the people maintained, so how can we be blamed for invoking other gods? Marduk is lord over Judah now.

How Zedekiah himself felt about these developments, I didn't find out for many months. But shortly after my week of revelation he sent for me.

I was shown to his private apartment in the palace, the same I had visited often when it had belonged to Josiah. I might have been apprehensive, going back there now, yet Zedekiah was plainly so much more nervous than I, that I felt I ought to be confident for both of us.

Before I could do him obeisance of any kind, he fell at my feet, and kissed my fingers, declaring himself deeply honoured to have such a great man of God come into his presence in response to his summons. It was summer, and the humble young King wore a plain linen tunic and sandals; he looked like the Mattani I'd known as a boy, and instinctively I laid my hand briefly upon his head to bless him, for I sensed that this was what he was expecting.

Afterwards he bade me sit down, and he poured me wine from a jug with his own royal hands; all his attendants had been sent away. 'Forgive me, my lord,' he said hoarsely, his eyes fixed on the wine-jug because he was still too nervous to meet my gaze. 'I should like to have invited you here sooner, but I did not dare.'

'*You* did not dare?' I repeated, faintly amused. I raised my goblet to toast his health, and smiled at him over the rim. 'But Your Majesty, you are Sovereign King of Judah. Surely you do as you please.'

He suspected that I was baiting him, and perhaps I was. Perhaps he longed to rise to it, too, to take down his defences and admit to me that he would gladly give up everything to go back to the wife and children he scarcely saw any more. But he ventured instead, 'My lord Jeremiah, it is Nebuchadrezzar who sits on Judah's throne and does as he pleases. He has assigned me advisers who work for him, not for me. Some of them I grew up with, but even they have changed out of all recognition, and are much to be feared. I shouldn't have dared send for you at all, except that Adonai's wrath frightens me more than they do.'

'Then you are wiser than the two men who ruled before you,' I said, and thought: is it not possible that we could make a worthy king out of this man in spite of everything?

Next he proceeded to tell me many things I knew already: that idolatry and superstition were rife in his kingdom; yet how was he to go about removing Marduk's image from the Temple, when Babylonian soldiers patrolled its precincts? How could he outlaw the worship of a god in whose name he himself had sworn his oath of allegiance to the Emperor?

'There are those among his entourage who might understand your dilemma, and with whom you might speak,' I suggested, draining my cup to the dregs. But he merely stared at me in shock, and I realized then that he'd sought reassurance from me, not godly counsel. He'd wanted me to say that his position was impossible, that Adonai would smile indulgently upon him just as I had done, in spite of the pagan practices he was condoning.

'But that isn't all,' he said eventually, lowering his voice to a whisper. 'The members of my Council who were *not* trained in Babylon... some of them still look to Egypt. Pelatiah and Jaazaniah especially... they grow weary of submitting to orientals, and of losing half their income in taxes. If revolt broke out again elsewhere in the empire, I know they would want me to support it, and most of the palace prophets would encourage me to do so. My own Council would be riven with dissension, and I should not know what to do.'

'You would know exactly what to do, Your Majesty. You would have to dismiss the secessionists from office straight away, and reaffirm in public your allegiance to Nebuchadrezzar. To do otherwise would be madness.'

'Then we are to serve the Babylonians for ever?'

'Not for ever, Your Majesty. The exiles will be permitted to return in seventy years, and some of them will do so, but what will be built among them will not resemble anything which has existed up till now.'

'You know the future completely, my lord? *All* that is going to happen?' He'd started to pour me more wine, but now his hands trembled as he lifted the jug, and some of its contents splashed like thin blood on the table.

'I know enough. I know that you must not rebel, but that you will, because you will always be persuaded by the man who has most recently bent your ear when any decision needs to be taken.'

Had he been cast in the mould of Jehoiakim his brother, he would have had me ejected from his chambers at that, and probably thrown into prison. But he was Zedekiah - Mattani - a man as conscientious and well-meaning as his brother had been callous and evil, yet also as weak as his brother had been strong, and so much the more dangerous for it.

I excused myself then and went my way, because I felt acutely sorry for the reluctant ruler, and feared that if he begged me to promise him that everything would be all right, I might be tempted to tell him the lies he was longing to hear.

Not many weeks after that, we learned that the province of Elam had risen in revolt. I went out into the city in the morning and strode up and down its crowded streets proclaiming that Elam was doomed, that the four winds of Heaven would blow her to oblivion. It was later reported at the palace that I had wrung the necks of several live birds on sale in the market, to demonstrate what the fate of the Elamite elders would be. Perhaps I did; I really couldn't say. In any case, by nightfall my name was on everyone's lips, and I thought: surely Zedekiah won't rebel after this.

But only a month or so later, revolt broke out in Babylonia itself, and Nebuchadrezzar had to curtail his western campaigns to put it down. There were rumours that Judean exiles had been involved, and that some had been executed as a result; the so-called prophets who had urged them on had gone into hiding. *These rumours are true*, Adonai told me. *You must write a letter to the exiles, and reveal to them the things I revealed to you. They must know that they should seek me and not give up, because I have not given up on them.*

So I summoned Baruch to take dictation, and succumbing to the weight of God's spirit upon me, I fell into a trance and spoke the words of the letter as I would have spoken one of my oracles, directly in the person of Adonai. I commanded the exiles to resign themselves to a settled life where they were, to build themselves houses, plant gardens, get married and have children. I told them to pray for their captors' prosperity, since their own depended upon it. They must never again pay heed to any self-styled prophet who exhorted them to rebel; the rogues who had led them astray on this occasion would swiftly be found and put to death. Every individual in exile must seek the Lord with all his might, for on this quest for spiritual enlightenment depended the future of God's people. The folk who remained in Judah were doomed, and their puppet king with them.

Since Zedekiah had now been king for almost a year, an embassy was due to depart for Babylon, taking Judah's annual tribute to Nebuchadrezzar. Included among the delegates were Elasah, the third of Shaphan's sons, and Gemariah, son of Hilkiah the exiled High Priest. Elasah I trusted, and Gemariah, having been in Babylon himself, was unlikely to object to the content of my epistle. I entrusted it to them, and waited to see what transpired.

In due course a reply was sent back, but not to me. It was addressed to Zephaniah ben Maaseiah, Pashhur's successor as Chief Officer of the Temple - another of the young men who had returned from Babylon with Gedaliah.

And he came at once to my house. Though he wore his blackened hair in ringlets past his shoulders, he greeted me in Adonai's name and placed the open letter in my hands.

'Shemaiah the Nehelamite, to Zephaniah the Priest,' it began. 'The Lord has appointed you to be in charge of his house, and you are beholden to punish any madman who desecrates its holy precincts with blasphemies. Why then have you not punished Jeremiah of Anathoth who poses as a prophet in your midst? He has sent this message to us in Babylon: "It will be a long time. Therefore settle down, build houses, plant gardens, and eat the fruit which they produce." He must be silenced.'

And so on and so forth; reading between the lines it appeared that this Shemaiah, of whom I had never heard, regarded himself as a prophet, and a truer one than I. Strange, then, that he should be implying that I'd preached in the Temple Court.

'Well?' asked Zephaniah. 'Did you send a letter to the exiles in Babylon?'

'Yes,' I answered evenly. 'I can repeat its contents word for word to you if you so desire, my lord, because I remember everything which Adonai tells me.'

'Then the message you sent came from the Lord himself?'

'It did.'

'But you have not sought to prophesy in the Temple Court since I have been in charge there. There are those among the priesthood who maintain that you have the prophetic gifting no longer.'

'I have not prophesied in the Temple because the prohibition against my doing so has never to my knowledge been lifted. I deliver my oracles in the streets.'

Then to my amazement Zephaniah said, 'I shall see that the ban is lifted at the earliest opportunity. In times such as these it is of paramount importance that every man in Jerusalem hears the word of the Lord, and knows that the Temple authorities are not suppressing it. You may write back to Shemaiah as you see fit, and I shall ensure that your letter is safely delivered.' With that, he bade me good day.

For all that Adonai had enlightened me as to his grand design, I could still be surprised by the details of its outworking. Had Zephaniah held on to his faith in Judah's God in spite of the re-education he'd received in Babylon? Or was he simply lending me his support because he knew that I was an advocate of co-operation with the Emperor?

I did write back to Shemaiah. I told him that because he had induced God's people to believe a lie, Adonai would exclude him from the blessings which were to be poured out on his fellow exiles and their offspring. They would all one day become like prophets, hearing from God for themselves, but he would remain cut off, and would die childless, friendless and estranged for ever from the God he'd misrepresented.

I felt better when I'd written it, but not for long. For I learned that the letter received by Zephaniah wasn't the only one which Shemaiah had sent. He'd written also to a number of other priests, public servants and palace prophets, seeking to poison them against me. So I might have won official approval in certain quarters, but likely I'd earnt myself a good deal of hatred in others.

A week or so after my second letter had been despatched, it was announced in Jerusalem that the revolts in Elam and Babylonia had both been crushed.

A week after that, I received another casket of Babylonian gold.

CHAPTER 20: ZEDEKIAH

It was a siesta like so many others: airless, sleepless, fraught with worry. Outside my window a dove cooed softly, and oh, how I wished that I might change places with her, and fly away to a life without care, without complication, without countless decisions to be made.

I couldn't recall sleeping properly since the day they'd thrust me on David's throne. Who would have imagined that I, Mattaniah, Josiah's youngest son, would ever find himself king? With one fell stroke I was severed from all I had known; even my name was taken away and a new one was given me in its place. Zedekiah, Adonai is my righteousness... of course, it isn't true. Adonai has taken no notice of me in all my life; and I don't expect he ever will. After what he has allowed to happen to my nephew Jeconiah, I find it hard to believe that he cares about any of us.

Whenever I did chance to sleep, my dreams were haunted by the spectre of Coniah's face: empty, expressionless, but so very lovely, even in earliest childhood. We had spent those first precious years of our lives together, always together, and were more like brothers than uncle and nephew. We would have taken our lessons together, too, when the time came, had he been capable. But although I was by no means the brightest of students, Jeconiah scarcely seemed able to think at all, and if left alone for more than a few moments would shrink in upon himself, and stare at his hands, or play with his hair, or gaze at his reflection in the polished marble floor of the palace.

Perhaps he'll grow out of this strangeness as he gets older, I hoped; but if anything he got a little worse with each birthday that passed, a little more withdrawn, a little more vulnerable. I took it upon myself to be his protector, and loved him fiercely, because he made me feel important and needed.

But I couldn't do anything to shield him or help him in any way once he was made king. Great men gathered about him, erecting a barrier between us which I couldn't penetrate.

And if I was honest with myself, I had to admit I'd been shut out of his life for some time already, for his self-absorption had become all but complete. When he looked at me with his beautiful, vacuous eyes, I saw in them nothing but my own reflection.

As if this wasn't bad enough, only three months later he was chained hand and foot and carried away to Babylon. There they put him in prison; they couldn't risk a revolutionary movement taking shape around him, with his restoration to the monarchy as its focus. Allegedly he and his mother were being treated quite well in the place they were being held, but in my dreams Coniah would reproach me, rattling his chains, transfixing me with eyes liquid and enormous in a gaunt grey face.

Not that his imprisonment prevented those who favoured him over me from planning his reinstatement. The exile would soon be over, they surmised, so they continued to refer to him as 'King' and me as 'Prince'. Even my own attendants, who called me 'Your Majesty' to my face, behind my back spoke of themselves as servants of King Jehoiachin.

The dove ceased her cooing temporarily, and I put my hands to my ears because the silence unnerved me. Yes, this had become a siesta just like the rest, dominated by memories of him.

And yet in one way it was quite unlike the rest, for there were much more pressing matters which *ought* to have been plaguing my thoughts. But fretting about the past, about things outside my control, was preferable to facing up to the present.

It was three years now since I'd come to the throne, and it was the height of summer, when tempers are at their shortest, and when subjugated nations and tribes decide that they can bear the yoke of oppression no longer. News of fresh dissension within Babylonia itself had fuelled discontent elsewhere in the empire, and now there were envoys from Moab, Edom, Ammon, Tyre and Sidon present in Jerusalem, seeking to entice me to join them in revolt. Some of these countries had been enemies of Israel and Judah since time immemorial, but they were prepared to lay old feuds aside in order to present a common front against the Emperor. If his vassals rebelled one by one, then one by one Nebuchadrezzar would put them down. If they all rebelled together, perhaps he could be beaten.

I'd seen the envoys in secret that morning; the meeting had been set up by those on my Council who had never been in Babylon, and only they and I were present to receive the delegation. I discovered that our visitors didn't want me merely to join them, but to lead them, if I were willing, just as my illustrious ancestor Hezekiah had once led a revolt against Assyria. I have to confess I was flattered that they should have linked my name with a king of Hezekiah's stature. I told them that I would give their proposal my consideration and see them again later in the day, after my siesta.

But by noon the remaining members of my Council had found out what was going on. I shouldn't have been surprised; they ran rings round the rest of us always, their fancy Babylonian education having so greatly enhanced their native cunning. 'Of course they want you to lead them,' Gedaliah ben Shaphan pointed out to me. 'That way, when Nebuchadrezzar defeats your alliance, you'll be the one at whom the imperial finger is pointed.'

While they were still sitting with me rehearsing their arguments, a breathless servant rushed in and told me that the prophet Jeremiah was demanding to see me. Before I could respond, the door burst open, and there was Jeremiah himself, looking for all the world like Baal the harbinger of storms. He brandished a staff in his hand, and his silver hair billowed like the clouds which boil in the blue when thunder is on its way. His eyes were like fire, and when he fixed them on my face they burned right into my soul. 'Ignore these men at your peril, Zedekiah,' he roared. 'For they speak on Adonai's behalf, as do I.' He pointed his staff directly at me; then he was gone.

It was as though God's own wrath had been concentrated within the prophet's body, and then conducted through his staff and into me. Though the day was hot as the

Tophet, I shivered from head to foot, and my teeth chattered so violently that I couldn't speak. Someone fetched wine, and Gedaliah filled put a goblet into my hands. But he had to steady them as I drank, or I should certainly have spilt it all over the both of us.

'Jeremiah means you no harm,' Gedaliah assured me. 'He wants only what is best for you and your people.'

And I nodded, for part of me believed him, and most of the rest of me wanted to. But it was all but impossible to accept that this towering agent of the Almighty could be the same man as the diffident, effete young tutor who had endeavoured to teach my older brothers, and been kind to Coniah and myself as children. Eliakim had made his teacher's life a misery; yet Eliakim had died in exactly the way Jeremiah had predicted, and I was terrified of hearing him predict a similar fate for me.

Yet I was terrified of my own subjects too. They were sick and tired of serving Nebuchadrezzar and paying him exorbitant taxes. Their memories of the short-lived siege of Jerusalem were fading, and Nebuchadrezzar, away in Babylonia struggling to keep his own refractory subjects under control, no longer seemed so invincible. I knew that if the envoys' presence in Jerusalem became public knowledge, I shouldn't be able to resist the general clamour for revolt.

For there were compelling arguments in favour of the would-be rebels' position, just as there were on the other side. 'It is wrong for Adonai's Chosen People to be subject to swine-eating pagans,' they asserted. 'Posterity praises Hezekiah for drawing that conclusion, and although he set his face against the might of Assyria, he won Adonai's favour through his courage, and Adonai sent a plague upon his enemies. He will do the same for us. Did not the prophet Isaiah promise that foreigners would never take Jerusalem?'

'Isaiah said nothing of the kind,' Gedaliah contended, when I repeated the rebels' arguments to him. 'He said that the *Assyrians* would never take Jerusalem, and indeed they did not. But the Babylonians will. The rebels have couched their arguments in pious terms on purpose, Your Majesty, because they trust that you are a God-fearing man, just as your father was.'

I could argue with him no further, because I possessed but hazy recollections of any of the history I'd been taught. And I was somewhat taken aback to think that this kohl-eyed stooge of the Emperor could quote the Hebrew prophets word for word. I had to remind myself that he was a son of the godly Shaphan.

If only I could have had some great statesman like Shaphan on my Council to advise me, instead of men no older and no more experienced in government than I was. Perhaps Jeremiah was right: the good figs had gone to Babylon, and only second rate individuals were left behind.

For my father had known exactly when and how to secede from Assyria's waning empire, and he had enjoyed Jeremiah's favour throughout the process. But what would Father have made of *my* seditious inclinations? Would he have judged me wise to rebel, or a short-sighted fool?

Of course, Jeremiah would have informed me that Josiah owed his wisdom to God, not to man; in fact he had said as much to me already on more than one occasion. He'd also said that I should open my heart to Adonai and have him train my ears to hear his voice, if I wanted to be told what to do. But suppose Adonai told me to do something I wasn't capable of doing? Suppose the fire of his holy spirit burned me to a cinder because of my cowardice and my sin?

And then there was Hananiah, who had been conscripted into anointing me as king. Wasn't Hananiah a prophet too? Didn't Hananiah speak and act as authoritatively as Jeremiah himself when the spirit overshadowed him? Didn't Hananiah preface his every proclamation with the words 'Thus says the Lord'? Yet Hananiah maintained that the exile would soon be over, perhaps in as little as two years. Which of them was I to believe?

I knew that if I'd been a *real* king, born and brought up to rule, I would have made up my own mind about all of these things, and then simply imposed my will upon those around me. That's what Nebuchadrezzar would have done, or

Pharaoh Necho. Yet it hadn't done Necho any good. He'd been dead now for a year, and a new king, Psamtik II, occupied Egypt's throne. No one knew what kind of support he was likely to give to an uprising against Nebuchadrezzar. Besides, there was Jeconiah himself to consider. What would become of him and his mother Nehushta if I were to join the rebels' coalition?   Cursed be every god in Heaven! My thoughts had gone in a circle and come back to Coniah yet again! If only I could have slept, instead of going over and over the same old ground! If only my head didn't ache so much; what with the pressures besetting it on every side, I was sure that one day soon it would burst like an olive under the beam.

In the end I abandoned the unequal struggle with sleeplessness, and got up to prepare myself for my second meeting with the envoys. It was to be held in my private quarters, away from prying eyes and flapping ears, so the wearing of full ceremonial regalia wasn't essential; nevertheless, I should do my best to look like a king even if I didn't feel like one.

So I had my valet comb out my hair and bring me a long-sleeved robe, and presently those on my Council who were calling for revolt arrived with the foreign ambassadors. They began to put their case to me all over again, and I listened, with no more idea of how to respond than I'd had before.

To this day I do not know how Jeremiah learned of the time or place of our meeting. But my father's prophet erupted into our midst just as he'd done in the morning - except that now he was wearing a yoke around his neck.

It was no wonder that my doormen had let him pass; doubtless they'd been stupefied by the sight of him. The yoke was one such as farmers use to attach oxen to the plough; it had wooden crossbars and leather straps, and he had to go sideways to get through the door. 'This is the message to take back to your kings!' he yelled at the astonished ambassadors, thrusting the shaft of the yoke in their faces. 'Thus says Adonai, the omnipotent God of Israel: By my own mighty power I created the earth, together with every creature

416

dwelling upon it, and I bestow that power upon whomever I choose! I am the one who has given all nations into the hand of Nebuchadrezzar, and they will wear his yoke, and that of his son and his grandson after him! If any nation will not submit to his rule, I will punish it with plague and starvation until it is utterly destroyed! Listen to no one who tells you otherwise!'

And so on and so forth, until the ambassadors' heads must have spun; he spewed out oracle after oracle against each of their nations by name, cursing Ammon in particular because its hideous god Molech had caused Adonai's consecrated people to offer up their children in human sacrifice.

Then he turned to me, and I braced myself to withstand a fresh verbal assault. But he didn't harangue me as he'd harangued the others. Instead, he dropped to his knees on the floor by my couch.

'Your Majesty, I beg you, submit to the King of Babylon. Why should you and your subjects die of hunger or plague? There will be no divine intervention to save Jerusalem as there was in the days of Hezekiah; Adonai will unleash plague not upon our assailants but upon *us!* Send these envoys away, and send envoys of your own to Nebuchadrezzar to reassure him of your loyalty, before he learns of the meetings which have taken place in your palace today.'

So intense were his eyes, and so unequivocal was his message, that I said, surprising even myself, 'I shall not merely send ambassadors. I shall go to Babylonia in person, and reaffirm my loyalty to Nebuchadrezzar with my own lips.'

When Jeremiah seized hold of my hands in congratulation, I let my aching head fall forward upon them, and softly he breathed Adonai's blessing upon me as the envoys went away disappointed.

CHAPTER 21: JEREMIAH

Shortly after Zedekiah made his startling decision to travel to Babylon and the rebel coalition collapsed, it was announced that Baruch's brother Seraiah was to be one of the officials who would go with the King on his journey. Seraiah was now Royal Recorder, and would therefore serve as His Majesty's personal scribe.

So I made up my mind to compose another letter to the exiles, and Seraiah was the man I would trust to read it out in their assembly. After all, he claimed to have accepted the integrity of my ministry. Now was his chance to prove it.

I prayed long and hard over what to say, expecting to receive a catalogue of exhortations similar to the last, namely that the exiles should settle down to a protracted stay in the land of their oppressors.

Instead, I was given a host of dire prognostications concerning the ultimate fate of Babylon. The idol Marduk would be shattered, and the great city would become a desert never to be inhabited again. Despite the setbacks Adonai had sent to Nebuchadrezzar by way of warning, he imagined he had won all his victories by the strength of his own right hand. He and his soldiers were accustomed to trample their enemies like cows threshing corn, but they themselves would be trampled in their turn.

Have these things written down on a scroll, Adonai concluded. *Give it to Seraiah as you intended, and he will read it aloud to my people in captivity. Then he will tie the scroll to a stone and cast it in the Euphrates, saying: this is what will happen to Babylon. It will sink, never to rise again.*

I was stunned. How could I ask Baruch to record oracles of this nature when I knew that his own brother would have to repeat them where Babylonian ears would hear them? So I started to write them down in my own inexpert scrawl.

'What do you think you are doing?' Baruch demanded, when inevitably he found me out. 'Have you taken it into that stubborn head of yours to dispense with my services completely, after all these years?' He was attempting to sound amused rather than annoyed.

'Of course not,' I answered him. 'Baruch, please let me be. This really is none of your business.'

'What nonsense is this? Writing is *always* my business.' With that, he sat down beside me and pored over my work, tutting at the clumsy script and already taking his pens from their case. 'We'll begin again,' he declared good-humouredly. 'And perhaps if you say you are sorry, I shall forgive you.'

'As you wish,' I relented, but I knew that his mood would quickly change. Indeed it did; as the substance of the oracles grew more extreme he laid down his pen and asked what all this was for.

I told him, because I couldn't very well do otherwise, and he reacted exactly as I'd anticipated.

'You expect Seraiah to read this aloud, on Babylonian soil? What has got into you? Do you want my brother dead, when he saved our lives?'

'I want nothing of the kind,' I answered resignedly. 'I have done only what Adonai commanded me to do. Seraiah must decide for himself whether to play his part in the undertaking. Our duty is to write; his is to read.'

'But Seraiah has risked enough for us already; you cannot ask him to do this as well. If you do, I shall forbid him to have anything to do with it.'

'You would deliberately prevent him from accomplishing the will of God? If that is your intention, I *shall* dispense with your services. You can pack your bags and leave at once.'

Of course, I didn't mean it. It was my anxiety speaking rather than my conscience. But Baruch took me at my word, and releasing a stream of obscenities he swept up the tools of his trade and went to his room.

None of this can be happening, I told myself as I sat with my head bent low and the unfinished letter spread out before me. Then I followed him to his room and watched dazedly as he stormed about, pulling things out of chests and strewing them over the floor. In the end he sat down in the mess that he'd created and said, 'How can you do this to me? How can you cast me off when I've given you the best years of my life?'

I replied, 'Baruch, that is the last thing I want to do. But it is God whom I serve, not man. If you hinder me in my work instead of helping me, you leave me no alternative. Things are coming to a climax now, I can feel it. Now, do you wish to help me, or not? The choice is yours.'

He made no reply, but sullenly scooped up his things and trailed back to the room I was using as my study. He got out his pens and waited for me to continue with my dictation. His lips were a tautened line across his face.

We got the business done, but not a single friendly word did we exchange until it was finished, and you could have cut the atmosphere between us with one of his scribal knives. It tore at my heart to see him reduced to such wretchedness because of me, but I knew there was nothing I could say which would make him feel any better. Besides, I was wretched in myself because ever since my week of revelation I had felt so close to Adonai and everything had seemed to go so right, even to the point of Zedekiah accepting my counsel.

When the letter was sealed, Baruch took it to his brother. I did think twice about trusting him, but couldn't let him know it, else the attenuated ties which held us so brittly together might have broken.

Meanwhile I myself went to Zedekiah, since I felt I must inform him of what I was asking Seraiah to do. I didn't want the King, whose trust I was slowly gaining, to suspect me of anything underhand.

The nervous yet manifest pleasure with which the young monarch greeted me went some way toward restoring my spirits. It was so very long since Judah had been ruled by a man with whom I could have anything approaching a civil conversation. He received me without hesitation in his private chambers and poured me wine, and I drank of it deeply, for its flavour was rich and full, the very best, as only kings can afford. I said, 'Thank you, Your Majesty. You don't know how welcome this is.'

His eyebrows went up; I suppose he'd assumed that holy men are never anxious, or tired, or discouraged. I added, 'I believe you are as glad to see me as I am to be here, in the presence of a king who it seems neither hates nor strives to ignore me.'

He coloured, and I thought: how young he looks, how ordinary. If only he'd been king in easier days, when he might have had time to come to terms with the responsibilities laid upon him. He said, 'Very little makes me glad any more, my lord Jeremiah. But I would rather see you at my door than any of the members of my Council. At least I know that you will be honest in what you say to me. You will tell me the right thing to do, and help me to do it.'

His frankness surprised me, but he must have grown heartily sick of those who sought only to manipulate him for their own selfish ends. Then again, perhaps he'd already been drinking before I arrived, and it was the wine which had loosened his tongue.

So I told him the cause of my own despondency, because it afforded me a gentle way in to explaining the reason for my visit. I knew that the nature of the mission I was giving Seraiah would scare Zedekiah to death. Had I been in his place, it would have scared me too.

'Oh my lord Jeremiah, do you have to send this letter *now?*' he beseeched me. 'How is Nebuchadrezzar to believe my profession of loyalty when one of my own royal entourage is going about forecasting Babylon's doom?'

'I am sorry, Your Majesty. I am no happier about this unfortunate business than you are. But the reason why I am able to bring you authoritative counsel is because I seek to say and to do what Adonai commands me, however little I like it.'

He couldn't reasonably argue with that, and was humble enough not to try. Instead, he finished his wine and said, 'I wish that I had your faith, sir. Truly I do.'

'Ask and you shall receive, Your Majesty. Faith is a gift from God: one which he longs to bestow upon us all, and upon the occupant of David's throne in particular.'

Zedekiah said nothing more, only stared morosely into the lees of his cup.

So I leaned towards him and offered, 'Your Majesty, permit me to pray for you. Adonai will breathe his spirit into your soul and you will know him thenceforward as I know him, as your father Josiah knew him, and as every man, woman and child must one day come to know him if they wish to be counted among his people. Never again will you want for godly counsel.'

He continued gazing into his cup, but his lower lip was trembling. So I ventured to grasp his hand, and whispered, 'Please, Zedekiah... Mattani. I only want what is best for you. So does Adonai.'

I sincerely thought, as I started to pray, that he would surrender his will and allow the divine to indwell him. Already his eyelids fluttered like those of a man in a dream as the spirit touched him.

But almost at once, fear of the unknown got the better of him. He became unsettled, and shook his head as though struggling to break free of some invisible halter. Finally a bee flew in through the window and filled the room with its buzzing; Zedekiah, now thoroughly distracted, twisted out of my reach and said, 'I'm sorry. This will not work.' I sighed, and lay back on my couch to recover myself, for the spirit had been powerfully present and had succeeded in transporting me if not my diffident sovereign.

I wonder sometimes whether history might have taken a different course, had that bee not intruded upon us when it did. As it was, I went home as despondent as I'd been when I arrived.

So when Adonai commanded me shortly afterwards to enter the Temple Court wearing my yoke, and to repeat in public the message which I'd given to the foreign envoys, I was unwilling to do it. Adonai had let me down yet again, I believed, and still he expected me to jump to attention at the click of his celestial fingers. It was true that he'd had the ban against my entering the Temple lifted; incredibly, both Zephaniah its new Officer and Ahikam's son Gedaliah seemed to have come back from Babylon with their devotion to the God of their fathers intact. But how was I to retain the priests' and people's respect if I made such a ludicrous exhibition of myself?

I grovelled and wept and implored Adonai not to force me to do as he'd asked me. Yet I knew that my breath and my tears were wasted; I was Adonai's servant or I was nothing, and lately I'd grown too used to being honoured instead of reviled. Reluctantly I fastened on the yoke with its leather thongs, Baruch watching without comment; the chariness between us persisted, and indeed had worsened, for Seraiah had accepted the burden laid upon him, and the royal party had set off on its journey a week or so ago.

As I buckled the last of the straps into place, Adonai's spirit descended upon me. His presence was heavier than a hundred yokes, yet it gave me the strength of a hundred men so that I could stand tall beneath it and even exult in its weight. My tears evaporated; I was out of myself and abandoned, an empty vessel suddenly filled, a tool fashioned solely for the use of the master craftsman who owns it.

It was a windless summer day, and the pressure of the beam across my shoulders made me sweat like a pig as I strode along through crowded streets. Flies hovered at my temples and I couldn't brush them aside; children sniggered and pointed, and whilst the parents of some admonished them, others hurled insults. Yet I cared about none of these things. Age had taken its toll on me, but here I was, shouldering the load of a beast of burden, seeing the mocking faces and the wagging fingers but hearing only the music of Heaven.

In the Temple Court I reeled and lurched while Adonai's spirit wrung from my parched lips the words he required me to say. 'Do not let the likes of Hananiah lead you astray with their lies and their blasphemies!' I cried out to those around me, stretching my hands in appeal, though none of them dared come near because my yoke, swinging alarmingly from one side to the other, could have struck someone on the head and killed him.

But my employment of Hananiah's name had worked like an invocation, because all at once he was there before me. And he *did* come up close, his face a scarlet mask of rage. 'How dare you set out to deceive God's people?' he roared. 'Thus says Adonai: I have *broken* the yoke of the King of Babylon! Within two years I shall restore the Temple treasures, and bring back Jehoiachin and the exiles in triumph! I the Lord have spoken.'

'Amen!' I yelled back at him. 'There is nothing which would please me better! But what true prophet ever promised peace and prosperity when God's people were still wallowing in the filth of their sins? Events alone will prove which of us speaks the word of the Lord.'

'And since when have events ever vindicated *you?* You see no visions, and the chastisements Judah has suffered have been but a pale imitation of the horrors you foretold!'

So saying, Hananiah seized both my wrists with one hand in an iron grip, and wrenching the thongs of my yoke undone, he threw it to the ground. Casting me aside, he lifted it and kicked at it until it splintered and came in half - a solid wooden beam so thick and heavy that under normal circumstances I should scarcely have been able to lift it. 'This is how Adonai breaks the yoke which Nebuchadrezzar has put on the neck of all the nations!' he barked. 'And you will see it broken before this year's babes are weaned!'

Mortified, I crouched in the dust incapable of moving. My eyes were shut, but I didn't need to be able to see in order to be starkly aware of the hostility my words and actions had provoked among the multitude. Support for Hananiah was obvious and universal, though no one dared to cheer him. All were standing mute in holy terror. And who could have blamed them? Hananiah was the genuine prophet, not I; where else could he have got the strength to break my yoke, but from Adonai? He was right: I'd never had a vision in my life, and so little of what I'd predicted had ever come true that what paltry success I'd had could easily have been the result of coincidence. I'd deluded myself and the people of God for thirty years, and couldn't begin to imagine what awesome punishment Adonai must have in store for me.

I remained there a very long time, arms wrapped tight about my head, the sun beating on my back and my life once more in ruins. I wasn't accosted, nor did Baruch arrive to rescue me. I think I crawled home on my hands and knees, and there I collapsed on my pallet, pulling a pile of blankets on top of me.

The old pattern was repeating itself. The higher I'd walked in the clouds, the lower the chasm into which I had subsequently plunged. Grovelling in its depths, I couldn't recall being anywhere else. I'd never known ecstasy, only delirium. Never had I stood in the Council of God, but only in the vestibule of Sheol, tormented by its demons.

For days, weeks, months, I lay in a silent stupor. Baruch had to leave his quarrel with me on the shelf, else I would surely have let myself die. He went back to making his soups and dribbling them drop by drop into my mouth.

Summer's heat abated; the rains came, and the wind, and the sleet, and still I lay without speaking, without even thinking, because in order to think, I would have to face up to the enormity of my crimes against God and against humanity.

In early spring Zedekiah returned from Babylon, having spent many weeks as a guest at the Emperor's Court. Knowing nothing of my condition he sent for me at once, and when Baruch informed him that I was confined to my bed, the King came to me.

He arrived without fanfare, conveyed in a sober curtained litter. He left his guards and attendants in the yard and entered my sick-room alone; the first I knew of his coming was when he clasped my hands in his.

I begged him to leave, turning away my face because I couldn't bear to think that I'd led this gentle, well-intentioned young man so badly astray. 'But my lord Jeremiah, I have come to bring you encouragement,' he protested. 'Berechiah your servant has told me the cause of your affliction, and I am here to convince you that your prophetic gifting is genuine.'

'Oh Mattani, Mattani,' I sighed, and though I would not look at him, I saw his face as it had been in his childhood, when he and little Coniah had been accustomed to visit me and strive to lift my spirits even then. 'You are kind, you always have been, but do not fill my ears with hollow blandishments. It will do neither of us any good.' These few words were more than I'd spoken in months.

'But sir, you don't understand. When I was in Babylon I met a holy man who confirmed every prophecy you have ever given. He was young, not much older than me... but the *visions* he's had, and the powers he possesses... there's no doubt he's a man of God.'

Poor Mattani. The more he told me about this extraordinary prophet in exile, the more convinced I became that I'd never experienced anything of God in all my life. The man had seen Heaven opened, and beheld the very chariot of Adonai, surrounded by shining beings with awesome wings. His soul had left his body, and rather than merely floating some little way above him, it had travelled all the way to Jerusalem, and he had witnessed the secret sins of her priests and officials. Whenever the spirit left him alone he was totally dumb, yet when Adonai overshadowed him, the verse which tumbled from his loosened lips was like nothing a man could compose. The prophet's name was Ezekiel, a priest of the house of Zadok.

'But sir, what is the matter?' Zedekiah exclaimed. 'I thought you would be pleased to hear that such a man had endorsed your message. I thought you would be pleased with *me.* The Emperor was gracious towards me; he let me visit Coniah in prison, and...' Embarrassed and confused, Zedekiah found he could not go on. 'I'm sorry,' he muttered. 'I shouldn't be here.' And he departed from my room as though my devils were chasing him.

Anxious at seeing him leave in such a hurry, Baruch came in straight away. He found me lying rigid as an idol on my bed, and on the floor beside me lay an unsealed scroll.

'What is this?' he demanded, snatching it up. 'What did His Majesty say to you?'

I don't suppose he expected an answer, and he didn't get one. So he opened the scroll and examined it, taking portions at random and reading them aloud. They spoke of the tribulations which Judah must suffer, and then of the hope held out by Adonai to his chastened children in exile. In the lands to which his people had been carried, they would remember him, and loathe themselves for having caused him grief. Baruch exclaimed, 'These oracles are so much like things you have said yourself. It seems that Adonai has sent the exiles a true prophet of their own.' He threw down the scroll and said, 'Jeremiah, for God's sake, wake up and read this man's work for yourself.'

He started to shake me vehemently; I was moaning, so he knew I wasn't dead. But I wished I was, and roused myself sufficiently to tell him so.

'Oh Jeremiah, what am I to do with you? How can you possibly doubt yourself, after all that you've said and done? *You* have demonstrated knowledge of things you have not seen, just as this Ezekiel has. You have exhibited impossible strength, just like Hananiah; did you not leave me utterly exhausted once upon a time on the road to Perath? Hananiah got his strength from the demons of his own anger, Jeremiah. Yours came from the living God.'

'Then why have I never seen so much as the hem of Adonai's garment? Where are my *visions,* Baruch?'

'What do visions matter? Who *cares* what you see?'

'*I* care! And if Adonai truly loved me, he would care too!' I clapped my fists to my temples and would argue no more; Baruch walked out and left me alone.

From that moment on, I prayed every waking moment for Adonai to send me a vision. He could whisk me away to Heaven or even to Sheol, or to Babylon itself, so long as he let me come back to Jerusalem afterwards and report what I'd seen.

Don't be a fool, Adonai said. *You are too weak to receive anything of the kind. Look at yourself: you're thin as a bowstring and as highly strung. You're half starved, and the famine hasn't begun.*

'Then I shall eat!' I retorted, and when Baruch brought me my soup, I drained it in a single gulp. 'Bring me proper food!' I instructed him. 'Meat. Bread. Vegetables. Bring some now!'

'Praise the Lord,' said Baruch under his breath; then he saw the madness in my eyes.

I ate enormous meals every day for a week. 'There!' I shouted in triumph to Adonai. 'I'm strong now. Look!' And I leaped from my pallet and strode about my room, stretching to reach the ceiling and bending to touch my toes. 'I've never been stronger in my life.'

Your soul *is not strong. You haven't ventured beyond these four walls in months. If you cannot bring yourself to look upon the faces of your fellow men, how will you dare contemplate those of angels?*

So I threw on my clothes and went out. I went where the crowds were thickest, and glared defiantly into the eyes of the most formidable-looking fellows I could find; most of them backed away, afraid that they were being bewitched. 'There!' I announced to Adonai when I'd got back home. 'I have the heart and soul of a warrior. Deny me my vision now, and I shall reject you for ever, do you hear me? Make me as sick as you like, but I shall swallow poison before I swallow my pride!'

Very well, Adonai consented. *But you have been warned.*

Almost at once it began. One moment I was standing in the courtyard waving my fist at the sky; the next I was flat on the ground. I couldn't breathe; my heart gave irregular thumps like almighty claps of thunder, and my limbs trembled, then went into spasm.

One by one my five senses were taken over. I couldn't feel the ground on which I lay, but seemed instead to be wallowing in mud. Instead of the fragrance of spring I smelled the stench of some dreadful battle, all vomit and blood and burning flesh. My mouth was foul with filth and sick. My ears rang with the din of trumpets and the shrieks of dying men. Lastly a searing brightness struck me blind.

'The pain!' I screamed, or tried to. 'I cannot bear the pain!' But the hand of the Lord had fallen so mightily upon me, there was nothing I could do to evade it now. I closed my eyes against the light which had blinded them, but Adonai wrenched them open, and I could see. What I saw was Jerusalem's end, as though the destruction were already happening; in fact so real did the scene appear to be, that nothing else I'd witnessed in the whole of my life seemed to have been real at all, but the flickering of shadows. All around me lay buildings in smoking ruins and tents reduced to blackened rags. Charred bodies were strewn to my left and my right, some disfigured by plague as well as by fire, others torn apart by starvelings. Fathers squatted in bloody gutters like dogs, gnawing on the bones of the sons their wives had borne them.

'Enough!' I wailed. 'I don't want to see any more!' But Adonai responded: *My poor foolish boy, what is the end of Jerusalem when compared with the end of the world?*

And all of a sudden, Jerusalem had vanished. I stood alone on a desolate plain, where there was nothing but polluted earth and the twisted stumps of shattered trees. Far in the distance the very mountains were shaking, and clouds of acrid smoke blotted out the sun, so that the sky was dark as night. There were no birds, no cattle, no goats, no sheep, no people; all was formless and void, as it had been before creation began. The celestial light had been eclipsed, along with every aspiration, achievement, stratagem and sin of fallen man. For the tiniest fraction of a second I experienced in full the excruciating enormity of Adonai's anguish as he beheld his beautiful universe ravaged and ruined by human greed. Then I looked down, and my own body was nothing but fine white dust, like the pillar of salt into which Lot's wife was turned. When it started to crumble, I blacked out.

I was roused by the sound of keening. My head was hanging backwards and all the blood had rushed there; my limbs were cramped up and I could feel a heavy pressure behind my knees and across my back. I opened my eyes and found myself looking into Baruch's. They were red and swollen, and his cheeks were wet. He'd gathered me up from the ground, and held me like a dead child in his arms.

'Jeremiah? Oh my God, my dear God,' he sobbed, and staggered, and almost dropped me. 'I swear you were not breathing! I swear you were... oh God. Oh my dear God.' He sank to his knees and laid me on the ground once more, before breaking down with his head on my chest. 'I'm so sorry we quarrelled. I'm sorry for everything. I didn't understand. Please say you forgive me.'

But I couldn't say anything, except that I managed to mouth his name in a voiceless whisper. Then I lapsed back into unconsciousness, and did not wake until the following morning.

This time it was Adonai himself who roused me. He folded me in his gentlest embrace and whispered: *Please, never ask a thing like this of me again. I love you, and it breaks my heart to hurt you.*

'Then why did you have to show me what you showed me? Why could I not have been granted a glimpse of your sapphire throne? Why could you not have transported me to Babylon and let me look upon the faces of those who were once my friends?'

I showed you what I myself am compelled to witness every hour of every day, without respite. I shared with you my own anguish, because I longed for another to help me bear the pain of seeing all that I have wrought come to nothing. I showed you my heart, Jeremiah, for what more precious thing can any lover show to the beloved than the heart itself, even if that heart is bruised and bleeding?

Now at last I understood. I understood why the vision I'd had was the only one which Adonai had ever wanted to show me, and I understood why he had withheld it from me for so long. It wasn't that he hadn't loved me enough; rather, he had loved me too much.

So, Adonai said to me, *now that you know in full what it means to be my witness among men, go back to the Temple, to the spot where Hananiah broke your yoke. You will find him there again. Open your mouth, and you will give him a message from me.*

I got up and did as I was bidden, despite being sick with fear. Hananiah was one of the very few men who had ever dared approach me when Adonai's spirit was upon me; and he hadn't merely approached, but confronted me, and accosted me physically, with savage intent.

He was there, strutting up and down like a cockerel, with a gaggle of admirers clucking round about him. I strode in amongst them and opened my mouth, and yelled, 'Thus says the Almighty Lord God of Israel: you have broken a yoke of wood, Hananiah, but in its place you'll receive a yoke of iron! Every nation will submit to the Emperor of Babylon; even the beasts of the field will serve him! I never commissioned you, yet you have caused my people to swallow your lies. Therefore I shall blot you out from the face of the earth. Before this year is over, you will be dead.'

Six months later Hananiah the palace prophet died in his sleep. He was a man in his prime, not yet forty years old.

CHAPTER 22: BERECHIAH

I never wanted to argue with Jeremiah again after we quarrelled over my brother's mission to the exiles. The rift it caused between us made a wreck of me, yet Jeremiah didn't seem to care. I'd given up everything to serve him, yet it seemed that he was prepared to watch me pack my bags and leave, without experiencing the slightest regret.

Surely he must know deep down how badly he needs me? I thought, as I forced myself to write the letter he intended Seraiah to carry and read to our brethren far away. But there wasn't a trace of emotion in his voice as he dictated. When I came back from Seraiah's, having placed the lethal document in my brother's hands, he wasn't even there. He'd gone to see the King: young, naive, Zedekiah, and I thought: Jeremiah *doesn't* need me, after all.

Then came the months of depression, after Hananiah had broken his yoke in the Temple, and again I was indispensable. But never a word of thanks came my way, and his glassy eyes looked right through my head. Enough is enough, I decided, this man has destroyed my life. Where is my sense of humour, where is my buoyancy, my optimism... where are the qualities which made me me? I shall have to leave, or the pair of us will go stark raving mad together.

But as soon as I'd made up my mind to hire him a nursemaid and go, he had his vision - if that is what it was. When I found him his face and lips were blue, and I swear to this day that he wasn't breathing. Consumed with guilt and the bitter memory of a love I would never know again, I lifted his body in my arms; then his eyes came open, and he spoke my name.

So once again I abandoned all thoughts of leaving, knowing that life would be no better than death without him. Surely now, I thought, he will see how much he means to me; and when he had told me about his vision I thought: he will see how much he means to Adonai too, and will cease tormenting himself by comparing himself with those he regards as his rivals. Things can be as they were in the days when our friendship was a source of strength instead of strife.

Yet the vision solved nothing. He rose from his abyss, but went on rising, until he left me down on the ground gazing up while he floated lost in the clouds. Day and night he roamed the city, oracles tumbling thick and fast from foaming lips. Mostly he fulminated against the others of Hananiah's breed, the professional prophets who earned their bread by tickling their clients' ears with the words they were wanting to hear. Their empty ranting had brought divine revelation into disrepute, he claimed, and a time would come when people would search for God and for truth in vain. Adonai would give them up to their own idle thinking: imagining themselves so clever, they would rationalize their world into extinction.

But I knew it would only be a matter of time before he plummeted once again, and although I might stretch out my arm to catch him as he fell, I should be left with nothing but the torn-off corner of his robe in my hand. On the rare occasions our lives made genuine contact, I knew that the arguments would continue, and would become uglier and more distressing as time went by.

At least my brother came to no harm through carrying out Jeremiah's commission. The exiles and the Babylonians alike indulged him as a scholarly eccentric, and the apocalyptic content of the epistle he read them caused little offence. Whether it had any positive effect among them is another question.

Eight years on from the day the exiles had been taken away, another new Pharaoh ascended the Egyptian throne. This man was Hophra, son of Psamtik II, and he was different from his late father in every respect. Psamtik II had been cautious and calculating, but Hophra was more like Necho: ambitious, aggressive, endlessly energetic.

I had no need of Jeremiah's brand of gifting to know that Judah's time had run out. Everything was falling into place: as soon as the Egyptian sympathizers on Zedekiah's Council could make contact with their friends on the Nile they would incite Zedekiah to reconvene the rebel coalition, and once more ambassadors from Moab, Edom, Ammon and elsewhere would converge upon our city. The kings of these nations, Judah included, would each throw in his lot with Hophra, and that would be that.

All of this meant that time had run out not only for Judah but for me and my own life's work. The mass of information I'd garnered from various sources concerning Jeremiah's life before I'd come to know him, and the jottings I had made from my own experience, or from what he or others had told me, still languished uncollated among my possessions. There were several scrolls of his oracles now, and I knew that Jeremiah had kept personal records also. My scribal education made me determined that some of these documents at least must survive our deaths.

So I began the task of assembling my notes into some sort of order. They were all over everywhere: on tablets, scrolls, potshards, even scraps of cloth... whatever I'd had with me when I'd wanted to write something down. I started to sort them into piles by topic, then changed my mind and arranged them by date. At one point I decided to separate the narratives from the oracles completely, but the distinction between the two seemed artificial, so I reinserted just as much narrative as seemed necessary to give the prophecies a context.

I wasn't at all satisfied with the result, but this was less of a worry to me than what I was to do with the information which I had excluded. I realized that I wanted somehow to document Jeremiah's life in a way that an annalist might document the history of a nation, but I was quite at a loss as to the form in which I should present it. And what of the accounts Jeremiah had written himself? I knew that he wouldn't give them to me of his own accord. But I also knew that any record of his life which left out his own observations would not be complete.

Thus I took to working when he wasn't around. I worked when he was high and stalking the streets; I worked when he was low and dead to the world. When the record of his oracles was finished, I put the scrolls comprising it out of the way in a chest; everything else I heaped on the table in my room making little effort to hide it except during the intervals when he was passing from one of his extremes to the other. At times such as those I didn't work at all, because for a few brief and glorious days he would remember that I existed, and we would converse together in a shady corner of our courtyard, or walk on the hills outside the city while we were still free to do so.

Once I'd got my material into some semblance of order, I was able to see where the gaps in my record lay, and I set about filling them in. I interviewed anyone and everyone who might shed light in an obscure corner, and I even got hold of letters and personal journals wherever they existed and their owners would let me look at them. Soon all that I lacked were Jeremiah's own writings.

So I would wait until he'd gone to the palace or to the market, and then I would rake through his belongings until I found a parchment, tablet or shard pertaining to my task. Taking it to my desk, I would copy the essence of its contents before slipping it back whence it had come.

I never expected him to find me out. He showed so little interest in what I did that I thought it would be possible for me to rifle his possessions right in front of him without his noticing. But late one night I rose to trim the lamp by which I was working, and when I made to sit down once more he was seated in my place.

I didn't speak. I couldn't. He sat there and read, his long white hair making mossy smudges in the ink. Then calmly he took my lamp from its bracket and held my parchment over the flame.

'No!' I spluttered. 'No! For God's sake, no!' For already a brown-rimmed hole had appeared in my work, and there was no knowing where he would stop. I swept the rest of my writings out of his reach.

'For God's sake?' he asked, 'Or for yours?' and he fixed me so hard with those incredible eyes that I crumbled to nothing and whispered, 'I'm sorry. Truly I'm sorry. I didn't mean to upset you. It's just that I - '

'Upset me? *Upset* me? You have *deceived* me, you serpent, you venomous toad! You have *betrayed* me!'

'No... Jeremiah... you don't understand. You never have. That's why I couldn't tell you....'

'I understand all too well, Berechiah ben Neraiah. I understand that your father was a scribe, and his father before him, and that you yourself were hammered out on the same twisted anvil as they were! You are arrogant meddlers, the lot of you, imagining that you can make the past your own, that you can reduce the whole range of human experience to a few strokes of your accursed pens, telling things the way you want them told! Damn you, Berechiah, damn you and all your blasphemous breed! You would block up the stream of life itself to create your stagnant pools of imprisoned memory, just so that those who come after you might repeat the hollow syllables of your name in tones of hushed veneration! The past belongs to Adonai alone, do you hear me? Just like the future, *and* the present! How dare you take what belongs to God? How dare you take what belongs to *me?*'

'Because you have taken what was *mine!* My profession, my parents, the chance to have children of my own; you have taken my love, my joy... my very soul! I gave up *everything* for you, I sacrificed my very self, whilst you give back nothing!'

'*You* sacrificed everything? You know *nothing* of sacrifice! You came to live in my house because you wanted to! It is I who have given my very self, in the service of Adonai. It is *my* soul which has been stolen, *my* life which has been torn apart! And you want to tell all and sundry everything there is to know about my ruination; you want to exhibit my vilest faults and my failures for the whole world to see! And you expect me to thank you!'

Throughout his diatribe he'd been holding the burning parchment in his hand. Now the flames were scorching his fingers so he tossed it away, casting it deliberately into the shambles of my writings which lay scattered on the floor. Frantically I stamped out the fire before it spread, but by the time I'd made certain that nothing was smouldering, Jeremiah was gone. I went to his room, and there he was, lying supine on his pallet, eyes fixed on the ceiling as though our altercation had never taken place.

In despair I returned to the scene of his crime and began to gather the battered harvest of my labours into my arms. Perhaps Jeremiah was right. Perhaps I ought to destroy it all myself, for the sake of our ruined friendship. Berechiah, he had called me, just as though these twenty years had never been... absently I took a scroll at random and wafted it over the lamp-flame.

Though I'd worshipped Adonai faithfully for half my life, he had spoken to me directly on two or three occasions at the most. Now he spoke again.

Baruch, your work is precious, however mixed the motives which caused you to undertake it. What you have written must be preserved, and you must continue writing until the record is complete.

'My Lord? Is that you?' I gasped aloud. And from the way that my heart was racing, I knew that it was. So I appealed to him with all the fervour within me: 'Please, my Lord, tell me how I can put right what has gone so wrong. Tell me how I can win back his respect and his love.'

You cannot. Even if you were to consign your entire output to the flames it would accomplish nothing. So do not do it; remember, I never required any man to cast his firstborn into the jaws of Molech.

'My Lord, don't say you can't help me! Surely you can make Jeremiah trust me like he used to?'

I make no man bow to the will of another, or even to my own. Jeremiah could have turned his back on me for good whenever he chose. Just as you *could have turned your back on* him, *yet you have not.*

'But I *shall*. If he will not accept my friendship, I shall go and live with Seraiah. What reason would I have to stay?'

You could stay for my sake, so that you might complete the work I have called you to do. Remember, Baruch, whatever happens, it was I who brought you to this house, and you have served me here very well.

Thus it was that I came to stay with Jeremiah to the bitter end in spite of everything. He was never to confide in me again, because I had abused his trust, and because his lifelong battles with Adonai and with himself had put such a strain on his soul that something had finally snapped inside him. His very sanity, I would guess, for not until after Jerusalem fell would he again see things for himself as they truly were. Even then, he would never accept that my desire to document his life sprang from the fountain of love for him which had welled up in me long ago - a fountain which had now run all but dry.

Nor would he accept that the further he'd driven me away from himself, the closer I'd been coming to Adonai. I was beginning to learn the lesson which Jeremiah had been trying not to learn all his life: that from Adonai alone can we derive the love and esteem which each of us craves.

A month after this I learned from Seraiah that Zedekiah had entered into negotiations with Pharaoh Hophra, requesting support for a revolt.

Not that he'd wanted to at first. Seraiah knew this for a fact, since he himself was one of those who had sought to dissuade the King from this course of action, along with Gedaliah the son of Ahikam, Gemariah ben Hilkiah, and Gedaliah's uncle Elasah. But their colleagues on the Council who were pressing for discussions with Egypt were equally persuasive.

'We know very well that you swore an oath to serve the King of Babylon, and that Jeremiah the Prophet won't let you forget it,' they had said to him. 'But things are different now. When you swore that oath, Egypt was weak; you had no alternative! No man is bound by an oath sworn under duress. Now Egypt has a new master who can supply you with all the resources you need. And Jeremiah is old; what does he know of the modern world? It is time he retired gracefully, to enjoy what he still has left of Nebuchadrezzar's gold.'

'Jeremiah received a bribe from the Emperor?' Zedekiah was mortified.

'More than one,' they assured him. 'Send for him and ask him yourself if you don't believe us. He wouldn't dare deny it, lest his God strike him dead. Act now, Your Majesty! Cast off the burden of foreign oppression; you have borne it long enough. The Tyrians and Ammonites will support you too.'

'But the Edomites will not,' Seraiah pointed out, when Zedekiah put these arguments to their opponents. 'Yes, I know they were involved in the conspiracy five years ago. But now they are wiser. If revolt breaks out, they will assist the Babylonians in quelling it; and when they succeed, their reward will be plunder from Your Majesty's treasury.'

Indecisive as ever, Zedekiah hovered between one opinion and the other, until Jeremiah turned up at Court preaching his familiar sermon: submit to Nebuchadrezzar, for he is the servant of Adonai.

'But whose servant are *you,* Jeremiah?' enquired the pro-Egyptian Council members pertinently. 'Or does Nebuchadrezzar send you presents just because he likes you?'

'I am Adonai's servant, Adonai's alone!' Jeremiah shrieked, working himself into an all but bestial frenzy. Then rather than standing his ground to argue his case and regain Zedekiah's confidence, the Prophet had run headlong from the palace yelling incoherent prognostications of doom at people and walls and palm trees alike.

Perhaps his hearers would have written him off after that, except that fresh reports of Ezekiel's prophecies were reaching us all the time, agreeing in every respect with Jeremiah's. No one could write off a man who was able from afar to give accurate descriptions of idolatrous rituals being conducted in the Temple, and identify the culprits taking part. He had named Jaazaniah, the black sheep among Shaphan's sons, and Pelatiah too; Pelatiah had since dropped dead without warning.

So Jeremiah couldn't be written off either; but he could be hated, and once again I heard talk of plots against his life. Jeremiah himself knew nothing about them; he'd lost the capacity to comprehend anything at all except for what Adonai saw fit to divulge to him directly.

Ezekiel, on the other hand, missed nothing. He knew that Judah, Tyre and Ammon were plotting revolt, and he knew that they would fail. Nebuchadrezzar would come with rams and machines on towers and hem Jerusalem round with massive earthen ramparts. Thousands more Judeans would go into exile, but Zedekiah himself would never see Babylon.

In this alone it seemed that Ezekiel and Jeremiah disagreed, for Jeremiah had declared that Zedekiah would be taken to Babylon in chains. But I could only speculate as to why a discrepancy between his own prediction and one of Ezekiel's wasn't causing Jeremiah to pity himself for once, but Zedekiah.

CHAPTER 23: JEREMIAH

I

For Judah, for her King and for myself, the final nightmare had begun.

For me, it began with madness, because only in flight from reality could I suppress a growing compulsion to do away with myself altogether. I was convinced that death was all I deserved, and that whatever horrors lay in store for me on the other side of it, I'd deserved those as well. Moments of lucidity were rare and appalling, replete with self-recrimination. I'd ruined the lives of everyone I loved, Baruch included, and I'd ruined my own by fighting tooth and nail against the One who loved me more than any human being could ever do. Better to rave than to live with the self inside my skull. Not until Jerusalem fell did I grant myself full access once again to my own thoughts, and even then only briefly, sporadically. Today, writing this, I am in control. Tomorrow I may be foaming at the mouth or unable to recall my own name.

For Judah and for Zedekiah, the nightmare began when Nebuchadrezzar set out from Riblah in central Syria, where he had established his military headquarters for the purpose of crushing the rebel coalition. Don't ask me how he had come to learn of the coalition's existence, since it hadn't so far done anything but mutter and seethe. I was semi-senseless all the while and didn't even know until later that the Emperor was on the move. It was as though I lived in another century; I had no past and no future; I could see, I could hear, but nothing came near me, and it was as though a thick veil altered the look and sound of everything.

It was widely believed, I am told, that Nebuchadrezzar would swoop down upon Jerusalem as he had ten years before, leaving the rest of Judah comparatively untouched. But on that occasion he hadn't wanted to destroy, merely to demonstrate who was master. This time it was different. This time we were to be brought face to face with Nebuchadrezzar the implacable, Nebuchadrezzar the instrument of God's judgment as I'd witnessed it in my vision: definitive, exhaustive, absolute.

Reports came through of one city after another falling to Babylon's armies. From those which surrendered, droves of residents were deported, and the people who were not taken were left with little more than rubble to live in. As for those places whose inhabitants deemed surrender unthinkable, they were obliterated and entire populations were massacred. Few of our so-called strongholds were properly fortified, nor did they have garrisons capable of offering anything but nominal resistance. Yes, Judah had an army of sorts, commanded by Coniah, uncle of the exiled Jehoiachin. But it had fled before the invading horde, scattering into isolated companies holed up now in burnt-out settlements or remote mountain caves.

Soon only Lachish and Azekah remained; as Judah's strongest cities after Jerusalem, the Emperor had left them and ourselves until last.

What had become of the Pharaoh's pledged assistance, no one could say. It seemed that Babylon's eagle had swooped upon us more swiftly than Hophra had anticipated. Promises kept on coming, but nothing else, and all the time Nebuchadrezzar was getting nearer, leaving smoking ruins in his wake. It was said that Coniah had gone in person to the Pharaoh to beg him to hasten his preparations; then it was rumoured that Coniah was a prisoner of the Babylonians. Perhaps the truth was that he had simply vanished, being no longer able to endure the shame of his impotence.

Eventually Lachish and Azekah were encircled and besieged by Nebuchadrezzar's subordinates. Meanwhile the Emperor himself, with the greater part of his army, descended on Jerusalem.

Anathoth, of course, lay in his path, as did Gibeah, the village where Saul the first King of Israel had once held his simple court. Both were set ablaze. Thus the prayers I had prayed long ago against my kinsmen who hated me found their answer; but when Baruch succeeded in communicating to me what had happened, I raved more rabidly than ever.

'Ruth!' I wailed, picturing her as a young girl yet, her legs splayed beneath some grunting heathen's clumsy bulk, his thrusting uncircumcized member pumping its polluting juices into the sacred place where Hanamel had so nearly made me pump mine.

But no one could tell me what had happened to her, or to any of my brothers, or to my parents. No one had waited to see; those who had sense had fled for refuge to Jerusalem before the invaders were even in sight, but none of my kinsfolk were among them. Their hatred of Jerusalem and all that she represented was still so savage that they had preferred to face death than to run and hide in the mother city's skirts.

Better for Jerusalem herself if others had felt as they did. Once again the streets were festooned with tattered tents, and the smallest patch of vacant ground sprouted shanties and rickety shelters built with anything from palm branches to shepherds' crooks and ploughshares. When Nebuchadrezzar and his soldiers arrived, Jerusalem was effectively besieged already.

It was as though time had gone round in a ten-year circle. All that had happened before began to be done again. Earthworks were raised around the city, ramps and watchtowers were erected, forests which had cloaked the Judean hills for centuries were hacked down so that their timber might furnish ever more elaborate implements of war. Late at night the enemy campfires glowed like malevolent stars; by day their helmets and armour flashed in the sunlight: helmets and armour from all across the Empire and beyond. Edomites laboured as dutiful vassals for the Emperor whom they, like us, had once defied; men from faraway Greece served him for oriental gold.

Go to Zedekiah, Adonai commanded me. *Tell him to surrender forthwith.*

And I obeyed, for notwithstanding my worsening madness, Adonai could speak to me as lucidly as ever, and so long as I was actively doing his will the other, derisive, destructive voices within me were unable to make themselves heard.

'I *cannot* surrender, not now!' Zedekiah cried, almost spitting the words in his terror. 'Jeconiah surrendered, and where is he today? Dead in some festering Mesopotamian prison; dead because I have been weak and a fool, because I listened to the counsel of villains! It's too late, Jeremiah. Now I must die too. Ezekiel has said so; or have you not heard?'

Seraiah stood beside him; he turned, and presumed to grasp the young King by the shoulders. 'You don't *know* Jehoiachin is dead, Zedekiah,' he said. 'No one has come here to tell us.'

'He was taken hostage for my good behaviour! How can he not be dead after this?' Zedekiah tore himself away and fell at my feet. 'Jeremiah, my lord, I implore you; if you are truly a prophet, tell me if my nephew lives.'

Ask Ezekiel, I thought bitterly, but the madness was rising and I dared not say anything which was not of Adonai, nor even think it, lest I wind up convulsed and helpless on the floor. So I opened my mouth for Adonai to speak.

> *I, the Lord God, have relinquished this city;*
> *Nebuchadrezzar will burn it to ash.*
> *You, Zedekiah, will be taken and tortured;*
> *In Babylon, broken, you'll spew out your soul.*

Under no other circumstances could Adonai have induced me to say such an appalling thing. Zedekiah was as frightened of physical pain as I was; in so many ways, he reminded me of myself as a very young man. He grovelled shamelessly before me, begging me to prevail upon my God to pity him. Death he would accept, if such was his fate, but let it be merciful, and the sooner the better, before he had to go down in the annals as the King who was on the throne when all that David had won was spectacularly lost.

Did he wish this dubious honour on one of his sons? Perhaps he believed them too young to care; or perhaps his fear had made him forget them altogether. Either way, I said,

'You will not die in disgrace, Zedekiah. As men burned incense when they buried your ancestors, in the same way they will burn incense for you, and bury you as kings should be buried.'

The message was from Adonai, I was sure, though how it tied in with what had gone before, I didn't know. Nor could I begin to work it out, because even as I tried, the clouds of madness rose again. I no longer knew who I was, where I was, or how I had come to be there; and some stranger I didn't recognize was slavering in extravagant gratitude over my feet. Panic engulfed me, and I collapsed on the ground in a swoon.

Aside from the overcrowding, it was to take many months for the impact of the siege to be felt inside the city. Hezekiah's feats of engineering meant that Jerusalem had water all the year round. Fruit trees had been planted in courtyards, and vines had been trained over doorways; cellars were full of grain and dates and salted meat.

The enemy was compelled to concentrate therefore on the breaching of our walls or the forcing of our gates, whilst hoping that one of us would have them opened for his own good reason from inside. Indeed, there were those who might have done so, but they were prevented. And despite the enemy's skill in constructing machines and in tunnelling underground, they could not break in by force. Every citizen fit enough to wield a bow or sling was drafted to defend the battlements - Baruch himself took his turn - and our archers shot flaming arrows at the wooden engines and set them alight. Where the Babylonians sought to build ramps against the walls, counter-ramps were raised to bolster the defences, and the Babylonian builders came under constant fire. Morale in Jerusalem rose; until we learned that Azekah and then Lachish had fallen.

So dense and verdant had been the forests close to Lachish that the enemy had heaped up wood till it stood higher than the city walls. Then they had fired the lot; sheets of flame had lit up the sky day and night, and the very stones in the walls had burst asunder. Nebuchadrezzar made sure that we in Jerusalem heard the news in graphic detail.

I remember hearing it myself, but it failed to move me. My tears were reserved for Ruth alone. By day I would drift from room to room calling her name; but at night in my dreams I saw her raped a thousand times, and her smooth round belly slit open, rupturing the violated womb which ought to have nurtured my sons.

Then Zedekiah sent men to my house, to beg me to pray for the city's deliverance. The priest Zephaniah, Chief Officer of the Temple, was one of those sent, because he was known to have respect for me, and I for him. Pashhur ben Malciah, a member of the Royal Council, came as his colleague.

But I had to tell them what I'd told Zedekiah all along: surrender to Nebuchadrezzar, for God is on his side.

Zephaniah knew full well that this was the verdict of Adonai. But Pashhur was angry, and I saw I had made an enemy of this new Pashhur just as I'd made one of his namesake who had put me in the stocks.

The following day, Adonai took me to the Temple Court. I moved among the crowds crying: 'Give yourselves up! If your King will not capitulate, then let yourselves down on ropes from the walls, and hand yourselves over one by one! Save your own skins, for you cannot save your city.'

And some people heeded my advice. They slipped across the battlements by night and were taken prisoner; none of them died. But those who were left behind despised them, and despised me too. Had Zephaniah not been Officer of the Temple, I should certainly have been arrested.

Zedekiah himself would not be told. He refused to accept that God wouldn't change his mind - I suppose because he himself changed his own more often than he changed his clothes. He suddenly gave out an edict that every Hebrew slave in the city must be freed, in accordance with covenant regulations, a more radical revival of Mosaic Law than even Josiah had attempted. He went to the Temple himself to issue the decree, and a very fine speech he made, at some minister's prompting, stressing how wrong it was for any

Judean to be held in bondage by one of his fellows even for a day, let alone for seven years. A calf was ritually slaughtered and cut in two, and the King and the members of his Council and the priests and the people walked between the halves to render their agreement binding. I wondered what had prompted all this; had Zedekiah been importuned by callous masters who resented having too many mouths to feed?

Three months into the siege, he must have thought that his ploy had worked. For unexpectedly in spring the siege was lifted; Hophra was coming at last, and Nebuchadrezzar had little choice but to march off to meet him.

Jerusalem was jubilant. Parties were held in every street, weeks' worth of food rations were gorged overnight... and almost at once, the freed slaves began to be taken back into captivity.

Zedekiah may not have been aware that this was happening. Certainly he was genuinely concerned to preserve his new-found reputation for piety. Once more he sent men to my home, to request my prayers that the lifting of the siege would be permanent. Again Zephaniah was one of those who came, but he was accompanied by Jehucal, another of Zedekiah's ministers.

I gave them Adonai's response: that our liberation would be temporary, because we'd granted only temporary liberation to our slaves. Impermanence was the mark of Zedekiah's reign - impermanent decisions, impermanent repentance - so how could he expect anything more than impermanent respite from his tribulations?

Zephaniah again accepted my response as being of God, but Jehucal was just as angry as Pashhur had been. I wasn't interested; I'd become obsessed with one thing only, and that was to go to Anathoth while it was possible, and discover what had happened to Ruth.

'You cannot go out there!' Baruch shouted at me, shaking me furiously as though he thought he could shake the clouds of madness clean away. 'Adonai has charged me to serve you, and serve you I shall, though you could rush out and impale yourself on Nebuchadrezzar's own spear for all that

I care any more! Think of the dangers, for God's sake! You don't know that *all* the Babylonians have gone. And what about the starving homeless whose towns and fields have been ruined? They'll kill you for the food you carry and the clothes you stand up in! Even if you *do* get to Anathoth, any survivors will throw you to the jackals if they realize who you are.'

But I took no notice. 'I must claim my inheritance,' I told him, whilst wondering hazily why I was bothering to explain myself to a man whose very name I was struggling to recollect. 'My father owns substantial property. If he is dead, I must lay claim to what is mine before my brothers seize it.'

'Inheritance? Property? There is nothing out there but wreckage! What does it matter which pile of ruins belongs to whom? And stop grinning like that, do you hear me?' He turned his back on me, hiding his face; he couldn't bear to behold the plain evidence of insanity stamped all over mine.

So I stuffed a random assortment of provisions into a bag and left the house, forbidding him to follow me. I got as far as the Benjamin Gate, where I was recognized, apprehended, and dragged into the gatehouse in front of the officer in charge, one Irijah ben Shelemiah. He was a thick-set, coarse old veteran with a grizzled beard, and arms like a stone-cutter's. Brusquely he accused me of deserting to the enemy.

'No. No, no,' was all I could manage to stammer. Irijah's face was blurred and distant, and I could barely understand what he was saying, as though he'd made his accusation in a foreign language.

He repeated it, maintaining that it was blatantly obvious what I was doing, since this was the course of action he'd heard me recommending to others time and again. He had his minions tip out my baggage, and there were pieces of Babylonian gold in amongst it. 'Look at this!' he thundered. 'Is this not proof enough of where your interests lie?'

I was shaking my head, but already I'd forgotten who Irijah was, why I was under arrest, and where I'd been going in the first place. All I knew was that there was an enraged and ugly face glaring into my own, and I started to panic. My heart was missing beats, I was fighting for breath, and there was sweat pouring off me. I closed my eyes to make the dreadful face go away; when I dared to re-open them I gasped in astonishment, for Irijah had become an aged olive tree, twisted and gnarled, and the men he commanded were date palms standing to attention. 'Take him away,' the olive tree snapped impatiently. 'He must go before the Council; he's under His Majesty's protection, though God knows why.'

I didn't object as they hauled me off. The next thing I can recall is standing in some hastily assembled court, with guards to either side of me, holding my elbows to keep me from falling.

I don't think that all the Council members can have been present, or there would have been considerably more disagreement among them as to what should be done with me. No doubt those who hated me had convened the session without informing their detractors that it was happening. Certainly Zedekiah himself hadn't been informed.

Pashhur and Jehucal took turns in accusing me, dredging up long-stale evidence against me, such as Nabuzaradan having been witnessed entering and leaving my house way back in Jehoiachin's reign. When they had finished, it was decided that I should be flogged and then locked up in prison. The flogging would constitute my punishment; the imprisonment would ensure I could not desert to the enemy.

My sentence was carried out forthwith. I was stripped naked and flogged in public in the Temple Court, where I'd been flogged more than twenty years before. But this time I scarcely felt the pain, because when I looked at the scourge it became a bunch of scarlet poppies whose soothing juices numbed my skin. They couldn't stop the blood, but its droplets turned to petals as they landed, and blew away on the light spring breeze. I laughed as I watched them go, until it was decided that I'd had enough, and my bonds were loosed. I subsided limply, dreamily, like a man whose bones have melted into water, and I slipped into a deep black sea of unconsciousness through the film of red petals which drifted on its surface.

They threw me in a vaulted cellar beneath the house of Jonathan, Zedekiah's Secretary of State. Not that I knew until afterwards that this was where I was, nor why I'd been put there: to wit, that my trial, conviction and confinement were all illegal, and I could not be placed in the city prison without the King's sanctioning what had been done to me.

All I knew was that I was somewhere inky black and foul and infested with rats, and spiders which spun their webs around my face and in my hair. My back burned as though stung by hornets, and whenever I moved, the scabs would burst and a fresh flow of blood would thicken the taut brown mat which had grown across the weals.

No one sent for me. No one came to check on me. Only by Adonai's grace did my undressed wounds not turn putrid. Stale bread was thrown down to me from time to time, and water was lowered in a bucket, but I couldn't tell day from night and I still don't know how long they kept me there. I can quite believe that they didn't inform the King of where I was or why for several days, or even weeks, for they had nothing to gain by telling him, and everything to lose.

Gradually the ration of food they allowed me grew smaller, then petered out. The thought occurred to me in a moment of near lucidity that the Babylonians might have returned already and killed everyone who knew where I was. But I hardly cared. My madness had become a blessing, because a good half of the time, I didn't know where I was. I could be walking through Anathoth's olive groves as I'd done in my boyhood, or helping my father polish the sacred vessels at the high place, or laughing and joking over supper with Josiah as a young man. I lay in the arms of Ruth, or Huldah, or even Naomi, basking in their illicit adoration. Can a madman's lustful fantasies be reckoned sinful? If so, then I sinned down there in Jonathan's cellar, all alone and febrile and drooling, floundering about in my mess, and coughing, and starving, and dying.

Then all at once there were men milling around me, hauling me onto my feet and out through the door whilst colourfully cursing their master for having them work in such filthy conditions. They bantered incessantly with one another in the crude language that servants use among themselves, but spared not a word for me. I presumed that Jonathan was sick of my stench pervading his house and had decided to finish me more efficiently.

Outside the cellar there was scarcely any more light than inside, for it was the middle of the night. But even the dim glow of oil lamps hurt my eyes. I was given a bath, and when they had washed me, the slaves rubbed scented oil into my skin, trimmed my nails, dressed me in fine linen garments, and gave me food which I promptly threw up again. Then they took me to Zedekiah.

They had to carry me. Having laid me on a couch in the King's private quarters, they left us alone.

I think Zedekiah was trying to apologize for what had been done to me; he'd been demanding for many days that I be found. But I didn't hear much of what he said. I lay there capable of little but breathing. In the end he knelt down and put his head on my neck. 'Don't die, Jeremiah,' he whispered. 'Don't desert me now. The Egyptians were defeated; the siege has begun again. And a letter has come from Ezekiel... not even he will call me King, did you know that? He addresses it to Prince Mattaniah, and dates it by the reign of Jehoiachin. He says that the citizens of Jerusalem will be eating their own children before this is over. Say it won't happen, Jeremiah. Say he speaks falsely.'

He gripped one of my hands to make me respond; I blinked at him vaguely, wishing I didn't keep forgetting who he was. The panic came back, the sweating and the palpitations, and in my derangement decided that I must have married Ruth after all, and that Zedekiah was my son.

I folded the frightened young man in my arms, but when I tried to speak, I could not. It was only when he pleaded, 'Is there no word from Adonai? No word at all?' that the latter restored my voice and said through me, 'Yes. You are about to be handed over to the King of Babylon.'

Then tears poured down my face, because I'd wanted to bring him reassurance, yet could not. All I could do was rock him against me and murmur, 'My son, my son, my beloved son,' until he must have looked into my eyes and seen the dementia. He backed away, and glanced to either side for his guards to take me back whence I'd come. Then he looked at me again, distraught, as though suddenly he suspected that my descent into madness might actually be his fault, because it was his ministers who had kept me locked up alone in the dark so that my wits had been scared clean away, just like Jehoiachin's.

So I gasped while I could: 'Don't send me back there, I beg you. If you do, I shall die, and you will have killed me.' Then I fell into a fit of coughing and fresh confusion.

He hung there irresolute, while I lay fighting for breath and for reason, the clouds boiling around me. Eventually I abandoned the struggle; they swallowed me up and I drowned in a miasma of oblivion.

When I came round I was no longer in Zedekiah's chambers, nor indeed in Jonathan's cellar. I was penned in some kind of stockade with bars all around it and guards outside. Clearly I wasn't in the city prison, for there were stars overhead in a balmy spring night, and a breeze wafted wisps of my hair across my face.

Had I asked out aloud where I was? I wasn't aware of having done so, but one of the guards turned round with a mirthless laugh. 'Put a traitor like you in the city prison?' he sneered. 'The convicts would tear you apart.' He spat on the ground. 'If I had my way, I'd kill you now.' And he jabbed at my belly with the point of his spear through a gap between the bars of my pen.

Only when the new day dawned did I learn where I was: the courtyard of Zedekiah's palace. True to form, he had compromised, but satisfied no one. He couldn't let me go, since I'd been found with the Emperor's gold about my person; he would not throw me back in Jonathan's cellar because he didn't want my death on his already tortured conscience. So here I was, in a place which my enemies reckoned too good for me, and which my supporters maintained was fit only for the keeping of animals.

I myself expressed no opinion. At least the stockade was light in the daytime and dark at night. Clean water would be given me every day, and a loaf of bread - until supplies ran out. Best of all, I should not be alone; there would always be people about, even if they mocked me, and any who counted themselves my friends might be granted permission to visit me.

Baruch came first; I called him by name - by this name - and he was so much moved in spite of himself that he clasped my two hands between the bars, until the guards beat him off. 'I thought they had killed you,' he whispered, and I smiled, so that perhaps he dared to hope that he'd got me back sane as well as alive, and disposed to forgive him everything. But then I started to question him about my wife and son, and I saw the hope in his eyes fade away.

Zephaniah came also from time to time, and Gedaliah, and Elasah, and sometimes I even knew their names too. But none of them stayed very long. My madness embarrassed them, and so much the more because I was there on show like a trophy of war. Of course, this pleased Pashhur and Jehucal no end: the public humiliation of the so-called prophet who had first humiliated them, now exhibited in his true and livid colours. All could see now for themselves that I was no man of God, just a sadly demented derelict with such a morbid hatred of the society which had spurned him that he'd turned traitor for the price of a few meals and a jug of lousy wine.

Zedekiah would have liked to think that too. He would have liked to think that my prophecies of doom were nothing but the frenzied outpourings of an unhinged mind. He came every day and sat outside my cage, striving to convince himself that this was true.

In the meantime, Adonai continued to use me. Gripping the bars of my cage and rattling them for all I was worth, I commanded the startled attention of all who came within shouting distance. 'You wretches proclaimed freedom for your slaves in a holy covenant with your God!' I yelled. 'But now you have taken them back into bondage! So hear what freedom Adonai proclaims for *you!* He'll give you freedom to *die* - by the sword, by pestilence and by famine! The men who broke his covenant he will treat like the calf they cut in two! Their corpses will be food for the beasts of the field!'

Almost at once these predictions began to be fulfilled. For as summer came upon the overcrowded city, a plague broke out. This was scarcely surprising, since Moses' laws about cleanliness of body were being flagrantly contravened along with those about purity of spirit. And how could they not be, when so many people were living on top of each other like lice, with nowhere to bury their dead except in the midst of the living, nowhere to empty their filth except in open gutters, and everyone was drinking from stagnant cisterns full of flies and detritus because Hezekiah's waterworks could no longer cope with the demand.

In the rarefied atmosphere of the palace we were safe from the pestilence at first. Our water was clean, we had space to breathe, and physicians to check our visitors for signs of fever. Thus it was difficult for anyone within to comprehend the gravity of the situation on the other side of the palace walls, though Baruch tried to paint me pictures in words when he thought I was listening.

It began among the poorest of the poor - the beggars and the refugees - and more especially among their children. First came the headaches, the lethargy, and the inability to face what little food their parents could find for them. Then came fever, nosebleeds, excruciating pains in the stomach and bowels and a livid pink rash on the body. The fever rose higher and higher till at length, a week or even two weeks later, the victims shuddering like demoniacs, death's lightest caress would set them free.

But by then, the mothers who nursed them had fallen sick too, and their elderly grandparents were dead already. Finally, men in their prime succumbed, until whole families lay dead together, with no one to bury them and nowhere to do it. Some of the bodies were tossed over walls into other people's courtyards, or even over the walls of the city, in the hope that the infection would spread through the enemy camp. But it was precisely as I'd predicted: when Hezekiah's Jerusalem had been under siege, Adonai had sent plague against her enemies, but in these latter days he'd sent it upon his own people.

Soon, no one would touch the bodies at all, for those who did were often the next to sicken. Corpses were left to rot in the gutters; insects swarmed above them and the sky turned black with crows and vultures, the beating of their wings like the continuous rolling of thunder.

'It's the end of the world,' Baruch moaned, his forehead pressed against the bars of my cage. 'Every day new cases are reported, and not only amongst the poor. Not that anyone is rich any more. For what is wealth, when a bag of gold won't buy a loaf of bread or a phial of the cheapest scent?' And I noticed then how pitifully thin his arms were, how hollow and grey his cheeks. Forgetting to hate him, I pushed my daily ration of bread towards him, saying, 'No, Baruch, this is not the end of the world. I have seen the end of the world. I have seen it...' Then I fell asleep in the middle of my sentence, for the carrion crows had kept me awake for a week with their exultant cawing.

The following day, Baruch didn't come, nor the day after that, and then I lost count. I was all but insensible with hunger because I'd taken it into my head that I ought to save him my rations, though by the second day I'd already forgotten who I was saving them for. In the end it was Seraiah who came; Baruch and all of Seraiah's family had gone down with the sickness, and Seraiah was desperate. 'Pray for them, Jeremiah,' he begged me. 'You're my only hope. Pray for Baruch at least. You must still care for him a little?'

Pray..? Baruch..? The words meant nothing. I stared at Seraiah, a blurred and broken image, and he yelled at me, 'Jeremiah, God damn you! Baruch is dying! Naomi is dying!' and only anger kept his tears at bay.

But I couldn't do what he wanted, not any more. I hadn't prayed in months; I'd merely been a passive instrument, a human harp upon which Adonai still elected sometimes to play his tune. Naomi... I closed my eyes, and all at once it was I who was playing the harp, with Naomi kneeling entranced on the floor by my feet. On and on I played, and she leaned her head against my couch and went to sleep. When I put down my harp and bent to rouse her, she was dead, with a gentle smile on her foam-flecked lips.

So I knew that when Seraiah got home, it would be too late.

That night I had a vivid dream like none I'd had before. I dreamed that I was sane and young, and that I was strolling through flower-filled meadows with Adonai himself walking by my side. *Look,* said Adonai, directing my gaze toward vineyards and olive groves - and all the vines and all the trees were laden with fruit. Children ran laughing between them, gathering the grapes in buckets and shaking the olives onto cloaks spread out on the ground. Away in the fields, their fathers worked the soil and their brothers watched over thriving flocks; their sisters came back from wells which were brimming with cool clear water, and it splashed like liquid silver in the sun from the jugs balanced on their heads as they laughed and chattered together.

'Why are you showing me what we have lost?' I complained bitterly to my divine companion. 'It's cruel. I don't want to see it.'

This is not the past, answered Adonai. *You are looking into the future, to a time when the judgment is over.* And sure enough, here and there were the ruins of towns which Nebuchadrezzar had destroyed, but they were grown over now with brambles, and birds had made their nests in the tumble-down walls. New towns were springing up, and when I looked toward Jerusalem she was built afresh, larger and lovelier than before.

The time is coming, Adonai said, *when people will no longer swear by the living God who brought them out of Egypt, but by the One who brought them back from Babylon. Did I not tell you that I am going to establish as king a righteous descendant of David, to rule wisely and do what is just throughout the land? A true Zedekiah, one who can say in all sincerity that I the Lord am his righteousness? He will be called the Messiah, my unique representative; when his reign is inaugurated, the world will live in peace.*

'I don't believe you,' I retorted. 'This is only a dream. You never speak to me in dreams.'

I speak to you in whatever way I must, my son, Adonai replied. *By day you have closed your mind to me, just as you have closed it to reason. Remember, Jeremiah, I love you.*

He squeezed my hand, and I turned to look into his face, but in that very moment I awoke.

So it was, that when Jerusalem had sunk to the nadir of despair, I began to preach hope. While starving refugees broke into houses and stole the grain of those still alive with no more compunction than they robbed the dead, I told of a time when men would willingly give to their neighbours from their own superfluity. While mothers ate the plague-riddled bodies of their children, I harped on a time when Zion's streets would be paved with gold. While Judah's cities lay in smouldering ruins, I spoke of restoration: to a generation born for exile I spoke of the remnant's return; to a people saddled with a king who would not rule and who had been foisted upon them by their enemies, I promised a king who would rule so righteously that it would be obvious to all that he'd been appointed by Adonai himself. Finally, to a nation which God had abandoned, I gave assurance that a day was coming when every man, woman and child would be able to know Adonai as intimately as I did, and walk in fellowship with him just as I had in my dream.

Then one day, when the spirit had released me from delivering one of these oracles, and before the madness had claimed me once more, I saw outside my cage a familiar figure seated on the ground with a pen in his hand and a tablet on his knees. He was thin and gaunt and wasted, but there was no mistaking that short ungovernable hair, streaked though it was with grey, that high intellectual forehead, for all its extra lines, or those bright intelligent eyes, notwithstanding how sunken they were in great black sockets over starkly protruding cheekbones. Adonai had kept his word; Baruch's life had been spared. The plague had claimed him, but Adonai had snatched him from its grasp, and he lived.

II

As autumn approached, the virulence of the plague abated. But another scourge took its place. Unless you had stocks of firewood stashed away safely where thieves couldn't find it, there was none to be had for love or money. Men who had once been heads of households fought one another in the street over heaps of dung. Baruch brought me cloaks and blankets and had Seraiah petition the King to take me indoors. But Jehucal and Pashhur argued against him, and another unsatisfactory compromise was reached: I remained in my stockade, but fuel was allowed me from the royal stores to light a fire in the yard.

And still the Babylonians, their allies and their mercenaries encircled our walls. It seemed impossible that Jerusalem in her enfeebled state could have held out for almost a year already. But the strain upon us all was taking its toll, and I wasn't alone in finding insanity a refuge. Perhaps those who had died were the ones to be envied.

Certainly Seraiah thought so. He had lost Naomi and all his children but one. He'd buried their bodies in the courtyard of their house, then shut the place up and taken his surviving son to his apartment at the palace. The boy prayed to God every day that he might be found worthy to join his brothers.

Winter closed in, with angry black clouds scudding above my cage, but they didn't rain except in my dreams. Whenever I slept I dwelt in a paradise of plunging waterfalls, shining rivers, and lakes teeming with fish; and when I awoke, Adonai wove these dreams into oracles of restoration. But then one night came a dream quite different from all of the rest. I was sitting in my cage, calm and in my right mind, when my odious cousin Hanamel appeared. He said, 'Buy my field at Anathoth, Samuel. As my next of kin it's your right and duty to do so.'

'Your field?' I repeated. 'But you're a Levite. You can own no land.'

'I can own whatever anyone chooses to sell me,' he replied with a leer; then he vanished, and I emerged from my dream convinced that what I'd dreamt must be about to happen.

Had I still been right-minded on waking, I should no doubt have concluded that this could not be. Whatever fields Hanamel had come to possess were now in the hands of the enemy. And supposing that Hanamel were alive at all, he would be quite unable to enter Jerusalem even if he wanted to.

This latter conclusion, however, would have been wrong. To worsen the overcrowding and the shortages, the Babylonians were allowing as many Zion-bound refugees through their lines as were prompted to approach them, and there was always someone on the inside who would throw down a rope to hoist his friend or kinsman over the wall.

As it was, I didn't think about such things. All I could think was: if Hanamel is now my next of kin, then his father is dead, and my father and my brothers. And if all of *them* are dead, then Ruth must be dead too.

Three days later, Hanamel came. Had it not been for my dream, I doubt I would have recognized him, with his snow-white hair, and his face deeply scored by grief. But because I'd been expecting him, I knew him at once, and somehow the sanity I'd known in my dream spread a thin film of lucidity on top of my mental ferment.

'So, we have sunk to this,' Hanamel said, referring to my prison and to the sorry state of my clothing, and he tried to leer as he'd done in my dream. Yet he couldn't; too much grief was too close to the surface.

'Then it's true,' I said faintly. 'Your parents and your brothers are dead, and my own also. God have mercy on their souls.'

He was taken aback; how had I known? He opened his mouth to ask, but checked himself before doing so, lest he should be forced to admit the unpalatable truth: that I'd been chosen and gifted by Adonai after all, and that my voice had never been a demon's. So he blurted instead: 'Perhaps you are satisfied now, Samuel? Or will you not rest until I am dead too? All the others who hated you are gone, every man of Anathoth whom you cursed, except for me! And I am subjected to a living death, asking myself every day, every hour, why I alone survived when all who gave my life meaning are no more.'

'So that is true too,' I murmured. 'Ruth also is dead.'

He didn't reply; but he grasped the bars of my cage and pressed his head against his hands.

Perhaps he expected me to weep; and indeed I would have done so, had I not been mourning her loss for three days already. 'Have you no heart at all?' he demanded. 'My firstborn son - my *only* son - died because of you! Now all my daughters are dead, and my wife! My home is gone, my wealth is gone... and meanwhile you harp on joy and peace, restoration, eternal happiness - you, who have lost nothing, because you never had anything to lose! There can *never* be joy or peace for me, Samuel.'

I didn't ask him where *his* heart had been in the days when he had made my own childhood a misery. I didn't ask where it had been when he'd tried to force me into committing rape, nor when he'd attempted more than once to have me killed. I simply waited for him to say what he'd said in the dream; and so he did. 'Put your money where your mouth is,' he challenged me. 'If our land is to be restored, buy my field at Anathoth, so that I may buy a loaf of bread. You're my next of kin now, after all. It's your right and duty.' He managed his leer at last. 'My ruined, salted field, for your Babylonian treasure. *Now* we shall see how strongly you hold your prophetic convictions.'

'Very well,' I responded. 'I shall buy your field. I shall not live to see the restoration take place, but it will happen, and this purchase shall be a sign which points to its coming. Only you must restore to me my father's property too. Had I not been imprisoned, I should have come to Anathoth to claim it.'

'You would have come to Anathoth to *die*,' Hanamel scorned me. 'I should have slit your treacherous throat, and would do so still, were it not for the guards who protect you.'

'So,' I said, 'You didn't come here to sell me your field at all. You came because even now you are bent on exacting your revenge on me for crimes you imagine I committed, when in truth I have never in my life done anything to harm you. Be done with this bitterness; cast it away and be reconciled with the God who has preserved your life as well as mine. Undoubtedly he has kept you safe until now because he still hopes that you may repent of your wickedness and be changed.'

This was the last straw for my tormented cousin. He spat full in my face, but when I continued to stare him out, with his sputum dribbling down my cheeks, he crumpled visibly in the intensity of my gaze. I don't think he really *knew* why he'd come, except that he'd had nowhere else to go, and deriding me in my madness and incarceration had seemed to him the only thing left worth doing.

'Well then,' I said at last, 'If you *do* wish to arrange a sale, you had better tell me your price. Then we must send for my scribe to fetch my money, and a balance to weigh out the silver.'

Hanamel risked a backward glance over his shoulder. By now a modest crowd had gathered behind him, intrigued, I suppose, to hear me talking for all the world as though my sanity had returned.

But I still felt like a man in a dream. Perhaps sane men have dreamt that they are mad, and when they have woken, the madness is still inside them. With me it was the other way around, but I knew that this was only because Adonai had his hand on me.

'Yes,' Hanamel announced eventually. 'Yes, I *do* want you to buy my field. My price is seventeen shekels of silver.' That was what he said. What he meant was: I do want you to demonstrate to all of these people gathered here, once and for all, that you are barking mad. You *deserve* to be a laughing-stock, and that I can arrange.

So I called to one of the guards, and asked that Baruch be summoned, bringing with him the weight of silver which was required, and some scales to check it. He came, and wrote two copies of the contract at my dictation; both were signed and witnessed, then one of them I sealed, whilst the other was left open, in case debate should arise in the future over the terms of the transaction.

The care I took with the details of the documents made the onlookers laugh more than anything else: as if anyone would ever care what land had belonged to whom in a future where everything belonged to the King of Babylon!

'You are wrong!' I harangued them, knowing their thoughts. 'Fields shall again be bought and sold in this land! Fields and orchards, olive groves, vineyards and houses too!'

But by now I had accomplished what the Lord commanded me to do, and as his hand relaxed its grip on my mind, the madness flooded back in. 'Fields and orchards, olive groves, vineyards, houses!' I cried again, no longer remotely aware of what I was saying or why. Before me stood a man I did not recognize, avidly wrapping his cloak around a pile of silver which could never bring him pleasure, and whoever he was, I knew I should never see him again. He went away, and slowly the crowd dispersed. They had seen me rave so often that such antics held no fascination for them any more.

As winter progressed I got colder and colder inside my stockade. The fire could no longer warm me in the marrow of my bones, and soon the fuel ran out. My ration of bread had been halved, and even the palace children were growing thin, their limbs like knobbled sticks, their bellies distended, their eyes like great black caverns. Baruch brought me furs and made me wear them, but still I shivered, and had a cough like the rattle of death. I don't doubt that I *ought* to have been dead; only Adonai's promise was keeping me alive.

Yet I never left off proclaiming my message of hope, nor did I cease to recommend that all who were able should surrender to Nebuchadrezzar.

And they did, in their dozens, their scores, even their hundreds. Soon, perhaps, there would be no defenders left; the Babylonians would march in and find no one there but me, still locked in my cage.

Sometimes envoys of the Emperor would ask to speak with Zedekiah or his representatives, and if permission were given, they would try yet again to persuade us to capitulate. However, the terms they offered were never anything but unconditional surrender.

Zedekiah's ministers grew more and more dismayed by the escalating number of desertions to the enemy, and inevitably I became their scapegoat. Pashhur ben Malciah and Jehucal ben Shelemiah had called for my execution when I'd been arrested at the Benjamin Gate; now their demands were vigorously renewed. When Zedekiah wouldn't dare do what they wanted, they resolved upon doing it themselves.

They came at dead of night, with two of their illustrious colleagues and a handful of attendants. The men appointed to guard me were ordered to open my cage on the King's authority, and when they explained that the key was kept elsewhere, the scoundrels cut their throats, and set about my cage with axes. Too weak and too befuddled to ask what they were doing, I let them drag me out; I let them pummel my face, and kick me in the stomach and groin growling: 'Traitor. Confounded apostate. Your game is over, you cheap clod of Anathoth filth. You must not be left here where all and sundry are subjected to your seditious ravings.'

I tried to gather my wits to protest; I tried to say that I loved only God, and that I wouldn't change so much as my tunic for a bribe. But I couldn't; I couldn't even manage to ask if His Majesty knew what was going on. I managed only to stammer his name, though they knew full well the substance of the question I was struggling to put into words.

'Of course the King is aware of what we are doing,' Pashhur sneered. 'He told us we could do what we liked with you; that it wasn't in his power to stop us.' How sadly typical this was of Zedekiah. He didn't want me harmed, yet cowered before the resolve of those who did.

But they didn't intend to kill me outright. They carted me off to the barracks of the palace guard, below the courtyard of which was a great pear-shaped cistern with a heavy stone lid across the top. I could only watch, as by the light of a single torch my captors' attendants shifted the stone, then approached me with ropes and looped them around my chest. Next they shoved me to the rim of the hole and kicked my legs from under me. The ropes cut into my flesh as they broke my fall, then slowly, inexorably, I was lowered into the abyss.

All the water had long since been drunk. But the bottom of the cistern was thick with mud; though I couldn't see it, I felt it devour my feet, then my calves, then my knees. It reached my thighs and I thought, oh God, I shall go on sinking till it covers my head. This viscous sludge will set hard around my body and become my sarcophagus.

But once I was buried to the waist, I sank no further. I looked up in time to see one final flicker of torchlight far above me, before the lid of the cistern ground into place, and I was alone.

This place was many times worse than Jonathan's cellar. When I brought up my hand to my face to wipe away the blood and the snot, I couldn't see my own fingers. The air was dank and foul. I had cramp in both my legs, yet couldn't move so much as a toe to get any relief. I tried to shout for someone to save me, but was overtaken by a fit of coughing which re-echoed from the invisible walls as though every brick mocked me. I wished I might pass out and never wake, yet it didn't happen.

Once again, it was madness alone that came to my rescue. Even as I strove to cry out to Adonai, the mud became feathers, and the stench was transformed into essence of spikenard. The blood which seeped down my face was scented oil poured lovingly over my brow from tender hands, and the mocking echoes became the voices of ministering angels murmuring my name.

Only after dawn did I regain any sense of where I was. I knew it was after dawn because when I looked up, a crack of light had appeared, and it was getting bigger. Then there were voices which really were calling my name, and loops of rope came swinging towards me, with wads of rag tied onto the ends of them, to pad my armpits while my liberators - whoever they were - tried to pull me out.

Somehow I managed to get the rags and the loops beneath my arms, though my fingers were numb with cold, and there were several men on the lip of the cistern yelling contradictory instructions. Then they pulled for all they were worth, and gradually I started to rise through the mire into which I'd sunk.

When they got me out, I was dizzy and quaking with cold and shock. Blankets were swathed around my stinking body, and someone who wasn't Baruch hugged me against him; I was too far gone to know or to care who it was, but pressed my head into his shoulder regardless, gasping out my gratitude once I could get enough breath to do so. Someone else brought a mug of warmed spiced wine, and when I raised my head to take a sip, I saw who it was that I was embracing.

It was over twenty years since I'd seen that face, exotic and smooth and dark as seasoned wood. But it had scarcely altered - those of eunuchs seldom do, if they keep themselves from running to fat, and no one in Jerusalem was fat any more. 'Ebed-Melech,' I whispered, overcome, and he burst into tears, which his kind do so easily, because he must have known like everyone else that I was mad, and often unable to put names to the faces of folk I'd seen just the day before.

When he recovered himself, Ebed-Melech tried to explain how he'd learnt what had happened to me, and how he had prayed to every god whose name he knew for my safe deliverance. It was while he'd been calling upon Adonai, the God of Abraham and Moses, that he had received his reply.

You are the one who must deliver him, Adonai had said. *You must approach the King directly, and appeal to him on Jeremiah's behalf.* He'd at once done as he was bidden, resolving that if the King agreed to receive a personal petition from a mere cookhouse gelding, it was proof that Adonai was the greatest god in Heaven.

Zedekiah, already stricken with guilt over what he'd allowed to be done to me, had not only heard the eunuch out but commissioned him to bring me to safety. So back I went to my stockade, and Ebed-Melech to his kitchen. But he went with a lightness in his step, and a promise that he would visit me every day; Adonai would make it possible.

However, that same afternoon I was taken out again, bundled into a curtained litter, and whisked away without explanation. When we reached our destination and the bearers set me down, a cloak was thrown over my head; I was put over someone's shoulder and carried bodily up several flights of steps. I heard a door open; I was deposited on a mattress, and the door was closed behind me.

For a while I lay and didn't move. Then feebly I fought myself free of the cloak, and someone I knew I should recognize was gazing down at me.

I asked where I was, or attempted to. 'The third entrance to the Temple,' the someone replied. 'In the guardhouse above the gateway.' And indeed, as I looked about me, I saw weapons stacked against the walls, and the slashes of brightness which were slits whence arrows could be fired. But the face gazing down was not a soldier's, and the mane of tousled brown hair which framed it was too untidy and much too long.

'I'm Mattaniah,' he whispered urgently. 'Mattani. Don't you remember me? *Please* remember. You *must* remember.'

'Mattani,' I repeated, dully, and then suddenly, miraculously, I *did* remember. 'Your Majesty,' I said, and then was racked by a paroxysm of coughing from which I might never have recovered had Zedekiah not given me to drink of the wine he carried hidden beneath his robe; he could no longer be without it.

He launched then into a protracted apology for the way I'd been treated, and for his own very existence. Then he apologized for the secrecy of this meeting - but he was so dreadfully afraid. He was afraid of his own Council, in front of which he had sworn never to have truck with me again, because only two of its members, Elasah ben Shaphan and Gedaliah ben Ahikam, retained the remotest respect for me. He was hopelessly afraid of the Babylonians, because soon there would be no food even for the royal family, and then the siege would be over. But he was almost as afraid of himself, of his own inability to control the mounting panic inside him. This was why he'd dismissed his attendants; the pair of us were quite alone. He wanted no one else to witness his final collapse.

I couldn't think why he should admit all this to me, nor why he seemed not to mind what *I* witnessed, unless it was because I was already swimming in the ocean into which he felt himself falling. Whatever his motivation, he grasped my hands between his own and said, 'I'm going to ask you one last time what I must do, Jeremiah. I want you to answer me honestly, but I want you to consult with Adonai again before you do it.'

I shook my head wearily. I knew that if I brought him Adonai's word, he would not heed it, and would only be more terrified than ever.

'You *must* do as I tell you!' he hissed at me. 'I'm your king. I *order* you to do it.' And in desperation: 'I'll have you put back in that cistern if you don't. I'll have you put to *death.*'

You'll have me put to death if I *do,* I thought, and must have managed to say, because Zedekiah declared: 'I swear to God that I won't. Nor will I hand you back to those who want to.'

He squeezed my hands harder; I could feel his every bone and joint. 'Surrender, Mattani,' I whispered. What was the point of my consulting Adonai again, when his word to Zedekiah had already been spoken a hundred times?

'But there *must* be some other way! It would be worse if I surrendered now than if I'd done so in the beginning! Think of those who have died from pestilence and hunger, whose lives I could have saved! Think of the members of my Council, who have worn themselves out trying to *prevent* folk from surrendering! How can I undermine what they have worked for?'

'Because your life would be spared if you did,' I answered, my voice coming stronger now, and my mind clearer, because the spirit of Adonai was starting to flow. 'The lives of your wife and children and surviving subjects would also be spared, and David's city would not be destroyed.'

'But I should be tortured,' Zedekiah protested, his own voice cracking and wavering even as mine grew steady. 'What would my life be worth then? With my every waking moment full of pain?'

'I have told you before, Mattani. Surrender of your own accord, and the Babylonians will not torture you.'

'It's not just the Babylonians, Jeremiah! It's my own subjects! Those who have surrendered already... when I am taken to Babylon *they* will torture me, because I let their loved ones die. Oh God, what a nightmare this is. I wish I had never been born.'

He was weeping uninhibitedly now, kneeling on the grubby floor, his royal robes spread in the dust. But much as I pitied him, Adonai would not let me bring him words of comfort. When I opened my mouth, I found myself painting a hideous verbal picture of the future the King was creating for himself by his refusal to listen to reason. Jerusalem had become an inferno just like Lachish. Zedekiah stood alone on the battlements, tearing out his hair by the roots, because his own wife was being dragged away naked into the camp of Nebuchadrezzar, her garments claimed as trophies by those who had raped her. Her sons had been slaughtered before her eyes, and as for her daughters, no one even knew where

they were. The other palace women were rounded up together, and as they were led away they sang in melancholy chorus:

> *The trustiest friends of our King have misled him;*
> > *They brought him to ruin because he was weak.*
> *Now they have left him bereft, unprotected.*

He *is the one now cast down in the mire.*

This oblique reference to my own tribulations wasn't lost on the wretch who had condoned them. He crawled about on the floor not knowing where to put himself; finally he threw himself down on top of me and implored me to tell no one at all about this meeting between us. If anyone representing the Council should question me, I was to deny that I'd seen him today at all; if my story wasn't believed, I should say that we had met at my own request.

Only when I had promised to do as he asked did he give the order for me to be removed from his presence. The last I ever saw of him, he had his back towards me as he strove in vain to prevent the guards who came to collect me from seeing what a pathetic state he'd been reduced to. Poor Zedekiah. He wasn't wicked like his brother Jehoiakim, nor feeble-minded like Jehoiachin his nephew. He was honest and kind-hearted and his intentions had always been good. Yet he was to preside over Zion's destruction exactly as he'd dreaded, because weakness of will can do more damage than hardness of heart or inadequate intellect.

From that day forth I was left undisturbed in my stockade until the city fell. Four more months it held out, four more months of privation and misery, four more months during which I could only grow sicker and madder in spite of all that Baruch and Ebed-Melech tried to do for me. The visions I'd once longed for I now had in profusion, but they were not the result of prophetic gifting. I saw roses climbing up the bars of my cage, and a vine cascading from its roof, gravid with fat red grapes. But whenever I reached up to pick them, they turned into droplets of blood, and whenever I coughed, there was blood on my hands when I took them away from my mouth.

Yet even now, Adonai could use me. Even now he cried out through me to his starving people, and offered salvation to those individuals who sought refuge with him. Even for Ebed-Melech a lucid message came through: he would witness Jerusalem's demise, but he himself would escape with his life, and would live it out in freedom, because he, a foreigner, had put his trust in God. He would become a symbol of the riches held in trust for everyone, Gentile as well as Judean, against the time of restoration.

At the height of summer my ration of bread was discontinued, because there was simply no more to be had. Neither Baruch nor Ebed-Melech could bring me a morsel to eat, nor was there any for the guards who remained on duty outside my cage. They didn't desert their posts, because they had nowhere else to go and no strength to go there. They simply crouched in the dust like the rest of us and waited to die.

Just as the food ran out, the Babylonians breached Jerusalem's defences.

This came as no coincidence. For weeks and months they had pounded on our walls and gates with rams, axes and picks; for weeks and months the defenders had plied them with flaming arrows and boiling oil, and with stones or bricks hacked from the walls of unoccupied houses. But now there were no defenders left. Those who hadn't surrendered lay prostrate with hunger or crushed by guilt because they'd eaten the bodies of their comrades. When the Babylonian rams broke through, they encountered only the silent stench of corruption.

Perhaps they were disappointed. Perhaps they'd been looking forward to fighting their way through the city building by building. Or perhaps the silence unnerved them; perhaps they feared the ghosts of those who had starved or died of the plague, whose corpses still festered on their beds. Whether led on by anger or by a fear of the dead, they put the whole of the north west quarter of Jerusalem to the torch. It was the northern wall, west of Temple Mount, which had been breached.

So it was that the newest and finest houses were the first to be destroyed: the elegant homes of the rich, with their several storeys and their private courtyards. A thick black pall billowed up and masked out the sun above my stockade, and flakes of ash like evil black snowflakes settled softly on my clothing and my hair.

So far gone was I in hunger and dementia that although I knew there was someone in the north west quarter I ought to be concerned for, I couldn't work out who it was. Only when I dreamed that I myself was running through the burning streets, my own clothes on fire and my own hair blazing a fiery trail like a comet, did I remember whose house I was running to. Many years before, I had run there in fear for my life; now I feared for hers.

'You *must* find out what has happened to her!' I demanded of Baruch, grasping at his garments through the bars of my cage. But he was as weak and famished as I was, and stared at me blankly, not knowing who I was talking about.

'Huldah!' I barked at him. 'You must go and bring her to safety.'

But Baruch had hardly the strength to prize my fingers from his tunic.

So I waited for Ebed-Melech to come from the kitchens; no matter how hungry and ill he was, he came without fail every day.

'Ebed-Melech, won't *you* find Huldah?' I begged him; and how could he refuse? I gave him precise directions to her house, remembered from my dream, which in turn had been woven from strands of long-buried memory. Off he went; Baruch could do nothing but watch him go.

Sporadically the Babylonian horde found the trouble it had been cheated of. Wretched little gangs of starving patriots held onto a cellar here or a storeroom there, and picked off the careless with slingshot or arrows. The Temple itself held out for almost a week. But at the finish Babylonian boots clattered through its courtyards.

In Jehoiachin's day, Nebuchadrezzar had deterred his men from looting and needless destruction. But not any more. They had served him well; they deserved their reward, and they got it. They helped themselves to whatever they could carry. They defecated on the steps between Jachin and Boaz; they urinated in the great Bronze Sea. They stampeded through the vestibule of the Temple building and entered the

Holy Place, where no one but the priests was meant to go. Here they tore down the panelling, smashed the lampstands, and fought like dogs over the sacred instruments of sacrifice.

Finally they desecrated the Holy of Holies itself. Disappointed to find that it contained neither images nor treasures, they smeared excrement over the walls, and drank wine there, looted from the King's own cellars. They drank it in noisy celebration until they were slewed - native Mesopotamians and mercenaries together, laughing and singing and lurching about. There were even Edomites among them, Edomites whose brothers had once plotted rebellion against Babylon just as we had. When they were through with their belching and gloating, they lobbed their empty goblets at the gilded cherubim flanking the Ark. Of the Ark itself nothing was reported, and to this day I do not know what has become of it.

No one knew what had become of Zedekiah either - at least, not at first. Later we heard that he had tried to flee the city by night, but whether he had got away, no one could say.

Nabuzaradan established his own military council in Jerusalem. Martial law was imposed and enforced from here; Nebuchadrezzar had gone away to his Riblah headquarters in Syria. Perhaps I should have rejoiced at the news, for soon my benefactor would have me freed and honoured. But I was unable to rejoice at all, for Ebed-Melech, the tattered remains of his clothing charred to his flesh, came and informed me that Huldah was dead.

So it was that the third of the three women I had loved departed this life, and took with her the last attraction it held for me. War had snatched away Ruth; plague had taken Naomi; now Huldah had died by fire... three innocent and beautiful women, all of them fallen victims to the implacable forces of Adonai's chastisement.

Such apparent injustice might have challenged the faith and threatened the sanity of the staunchest man of God. But I, who was mad already, was flung headlong onto the road back to reason.

Oh yes; I wept and I howled and I tore my hair. I cursed the day of my birth, and the unlucky man who had come from the midwife bringing my father the news of my safe arrival in this world; I wished he had killed me in the womb where Adonai had first laid his finger on me, and made my mother's belly my grave. But I knew precisely who I was, where and when I'd been born, and where I was now; I remembered everything which had happened to me since the time when I'd quarrelled with Baruch over the records he was keeping of my life and something in my mind had become detached, plunging me into a world of confusion. I was morbidly depressed, but madness was denying me a refuge at last. I would have to begin to face reality again, in all its horror, all its savagery, all its raw repugnance.

More than once I begged Baruch to lend me his scribal knife, that I might slit my wrists and pour out my blood as a libation to Huldah's memory. But when he saw the sober resolve in my eyes, he feared it more than the wild gleam of dementia, and shook his head. He'd grown to appreciate my fear of what might lie in store for us on the other side, whereas I no longer cared.

So I vented my fury on Adonai, praying for the first time in months, if indeed a torrent of abuse can be called a prayer. '*You* should have killed me in my mother's womb!' I berated him, 'if that is truly where I was when you singled me out and consigned me to torment!' And I meant it. I wanted to deny that I'd ever been chosen; I wanted to undo everything I'd ever done for him, since all of it had been a pathetic waste. My entire ministry had been a failure, a consummate disaster. In my direst need, my God had shown himself to be just like a dried-up wadi: from a distance promising streams of living water, but on closer inspection pregnant only with dust. If ever there had been joy, if ever there had been sweetness, if ever there had been ecstasy, it had all been so long ago that the faintest afterglow was gone.

So you would have had me punish my people without any warning? Adonai asked me, causing me to start and look about me, so long had it been since he'd spoken to me, not through me, except in my sleep. *You would have denied them any opportunity to repent, and deprived them of the promise of hope for the future?*

'They didn't listen. They never do,' I argued, but already my resistance was disintegrating; his voice was so soft, his love so strong. 'They no more believe in salvation in the future than they used to believe in the judgment which has even now fallen upon them. And if you were truly concerned to treat your people fairly, Ebed-Melech would have got to Huldah in time. She served you as faithfully as anyone could. Didn't you promise the psalmist and all who come to you for sanctuary: "A thousand may fall dead beside you, ten thousand all around you, but you will not be harmed"?'

You would have had me prolong Huldah's life when her time had come and she was ready to die? When she was lonely and tired, and her kinsfolk and friends were dead already? Don't forget, Jeremiah: she was no longer young. Death comes to all in the end; would you have wanted her to suffer, rather than enter my rest?

I made no reply, for I didn't know *what* I would have wanted, except to have married Ruth in the first place, in some other world untainted by sin, where I should never have had cause to meet either Huldah or Naomi, or endure what I'd had to endure.

PART FIVE

IN THE DAYS OF THE GOVERNOR GEDALIAH

How lonely lies Zion, once crowded and happy!

She who was rich, like a widow now mourns;

The queen among cities is sold as a slave.

Judah's proud people are forced into exile,

Aliens now, with no land of their own;

Encompassed by foes, with no means of escape.

The roads to Jerusalem languish deserted;

Her gateways stand empty, the pilgrims all gone;

Her priests wring their hands; the girls' timbrels are hushed.

Yet this I remember, this one hope I cling to:

Our God loves us still; we shall not be consumed.

As sure as the sunrise his mercy endures.

Lamentations 1:1,3,4;3:22.

CHAPTER 24: JEREMIAH

On the third day after the desecration of the Temple, Babylonian soldiers marched into the courtyard where I was kept. Prominent among them were three senior officers with crested helmets and burnished breastplates; the tallest removed his helmet and bowed before me, his steady, candid eyes engaging my own.

'Forgive me, my lord Jeremiah,' said Nabuzaradan in Hebrew carefully rehearsed. 'I should have come sooner. But I was not told until today that you were in custody.' Then he snapped his fingers at his men, and they set to work on the lock of my cage with saws. It fell away soon enough, but I lacked the strength to stand up, and neither Baruch nor Ebed-Melech could help me. They slumped back to back against the bars.

So Nabuzaradan bade bread and wine be brought to me, and in the meantime introduced to me his two distinguished colleagues. Nergal-Sharezar was Commander of the Emperor's Host; Nebushazbal was an expert in government, appointed to assist in converting Judah from vassal to province.

But I didn't want to know their unpronounceable names, or anything else about these arrogant pagans who were responsible for the subjugation of God's people. I acknowledged Nabuzaradan's courtesy with a joyless smile, and insisted that my bread be shared with my companions, and with those of my guards who weren't too far gone to partake of it.

I wanted to ask what had become of Zedekiah and Judah's royal family. But I couldn't bring myself to enter into conversation with men who caused me to feel like the traitor I was supposed to be. Besides, the bread made me vomit when I'd nothing to eat for days, and the wine went straight to my head. In the end, a detachment of Nabuzaradan's men was sent to fetch litters, and Baruch and I were carried like kings through the ravaged city to Ahikam's house, which had so far survived the burning and looting.

As for Ebed-Melech, he would not come. He was unwilling to intrude upon my friendship with Baruch, loveless though it had become. I have never seen him since, and can only assume that Adonai kept his word to prosper him.

The distance was not great, but the journey seemed the longest I had ever undertaken. Borne aloft on the shoulders of my enemies I beheld the holy city, Adonai's bride, ruined and broken as a discarded whore. Corpses still lay where they'd fallen, and the air thrummed with the droning of the flies which swarmed above them. Great black crows strutted up and down as though they, and not Nebuchadrezzar's host, were the victors; now that they were permitted to feast on human flesh they had lost all fear of men. I watched a gaggle of urchins drive one flock away, only to usurp its place and hack with daggers and flints at what the birds had left behind. I saw young noblemen begging, possessing barely the strength to hold out their hands as we passed by. Some didn't try; when you looked more closely their eyes had turned to glass, or were gone altogether. Here was the body of a pregnant woman, the belly torn open and the baby hewn out; there was a mother giving suck to an infant which had certainly been dead for many days. I watched a flat-chested girl of nine or ten being raped in broad daylight by a squadron of Edomites; I witnessed elders of Judah pawing through refuse for scraps, excavating faeces with their fingernails in search of an undigested seed or husk of corn.

But Baruch and I, when our escort departed, were left with bread and cake and wine, and even fresh fruit. Baruch would have eaten what he could, but after seeing what I'd seen on our journey I knocked the food from his mouth, asking, 'How can you eat when our people are starving? How can you eat the bread of our enemies? How can you drink Zedekiah's wine?' And I sat up all night on my pallet, chanting dirges over Zion and her unhappy King. Baruch sat up with me, and from force of habit took down the words of my elegies. When the sun came up I left off, and fell into febrile prayer; on rousing myself from this, I found Baruch collapsed insensible where he'd sat, the pen still clutched in his hand.

I crawled across to him, coughing; there was blood in my phlegm, and the tiny distance between us seemed many times greater than it was. But I could no longer deny his blistered lips a dribble of wine, nor refuse him bread when he'd revived enough to take some. However, he would not eat or drink now unless I did. So I had to relent.

During the course of the next few days, the Babylonians began feeding everyone. The supply lines which had sustained their victorious army now provided for the vanquished as well; bedraggled, bewildered survivors waited in silent queues to receive provisions from the hands of their conquerors. Gradually the pillaging and raping had ceased, as the common soldiers had had their fill of it; now the officers began to take charge, and soon the fate of our city and its remaining population would be determined.

Then, in the middle of a sleepless siesta, Babylonian thugs broke in and dragged us from our beds.

'What is this? There must have been some mistake!' Baruch protested, struggling to free himself but to no avail. 'We were brought here on the orders of the captain of the Emperor's guard.'

'You are Jeremiah ben Hilkiah and Berechiah ben Neraiah?' demanded one of the intruders, in something resembling Hebrew, and when Baruch nodded, he said, 'Aye, then you're the ones we've come for. And bring your cloaks. You'll not be coming back.'

Baruch was still creating as they bore us away, fearful chiefly for his precious tablets and scrolls. Finally they kicked him hard in the groin, and we were carted back to the palace.

We were taken to the central courtyard, which was crowded with terrified prisoners. The sun beat down from a cloudless sky and there wasn't a sliver of shade. Soldiers were moving among them, herding them into groups and then hauling them away, so that gradually the crush lessened. But the noise-level rose, as friend was parted from friend, and each was made to stand with this huddle or that, while manacles were fastened to his wrists.

Families were being grouped according to the breadwinner's occupation - gold and silver smiths here, cloth makers here, stone masons beyond - and once the business was concluded, we were all to be deported to Babylon. Every individual of influence or means, or skilled in a craft, all those men who had assumed the mantles of those deported a decade before, were now to go with their wives and children - if such they still had - to join their fellows in exile. Only the unskilled and uneducated would be passed over, from whose ranks no leader was likely to arise to mount another rebellion.

Gold and silver smiths here, cloth makers there... and scribes in the opposite corner of the courtyard. Suddenly Baruch and I were forced apart; afraid to be without him in spite of everything, I made a frantic attempt to hold onto him, but my fingers closed around air. He was still shouting my name as they took him away, still maintaining that there must be some misunderstanding; we were entitled to the protection of the Emperor's personal favourite. I cringed and wished he wouldn't say such things, especially here in the midst of this crowd who would gladly have eaten us alive. But there was nothing I could do to silence him or to bring him back. My efforts to reach him served only to rob me of breath; dizzy with the heat, and puking blood, I was thrown in with a motley crowd of fortune-tellers, diviners and professional seers, and my hands were chained to theirs.

It seemed that ours would be the last group to be dealt with. I saw the smiths and the clothiers and the masons led away, and even the scribes. My group alone was left in the searing heat, to fight over flagons of water and chunks of bread which were thrown in amongst us.

I didn't even try to get any of the food or water for myself. But presently somebody recognized me, and either from pity or from awe he gave me a share of what he'd acquired. Better for both of us if he hadn't. As soon as the others learned who I was, they spat in my face and threw gravel in my eyes, thumping and kicking the man who had helped me. I got off lightly in comparison; anyone could see how weak I was, and none of them would risk having the death of Josiah's Prophet on his conscience.

Eventually an officer came and explained to us in halting Hebrew what would happen to us next. Once our number was complete, we would be taken to Ramah, a town a short distance to the north, to await deportation. Jerusalem itself was to be evacuated.

'Why?' 'What about the folk you are leaving behind?' those with me were demanding, jostling and shoving, striving to prevent the officer from walking away before he'd told them everything they wanted to know.

Well, he explained, the hawkers and the litter-bearers and the labourers and the menial servants from the palace would be driven away into the countryside to fend for themselves. After all, the peasants still living there would need plenty of help to restore the farmland to fruitfulness so that the quotas of tribute demanded by the Emperor could be met. The pick of the palace women would be offered to the Babylonian soldiery, as I myself had predicted: relatives of the King would go to the officers, and serving girls to the rank and file. There would be no more need for the maintenance of a royal household, since Judah was no longer to have a king. As a province rather than a vassal, she would have a governor instead, appointed by Nebuchadrezzar.

This governor was to be none other than Gedaliah, son of my exiled friend Ahikam and grandson of Shaphan, who had gone in his youth to Babylon as one of the fifty hostages taken after the Battle of Carchemish. Having returned at the beginning of Zedekiah's reign and served for a while as his steward he'd been back in Jerusalem ten years exactly.

I had clear memories of him as a child: solemn, intelligent, honest. His appointment was a wise one; fluent in the Babylonians' language and fully conversant with their customs and expectations, he also belonged one of the most distinguished Jerusalem families. I had no doubt but that he would discharge his duties conscientiously, though many of those for whom he was responsible would fiercely resent his foreign education. His task would not be an easy one.

His executive council would consist chiefly of native Babylonians, but there would be Judeans as well: men who had been trained in Babylon as he himself had been. They had gazed upon the splendour of Nebuchadrezzar's capital city and would appreciate the futility of any form of resistance.

Gedaliah's administrative headquarters would be at Mizpah which, like Ramah, was a small town in the hill country north of Jerusalem. The palace in Jerusalem was to be burnt to the ground - as was Solomon's Temple - and the city walls were to be demolished. Then the entire area was to be declared out of bounds.

Suitably subdued, the group of which I was a member was marched away to Ramah.

A healthy person could walk from Jerusalem to Ramah and back again twice in the time it took our party to get there, and it was well past dusk when we arrived. We were left in another courtyard, and had to sleep where we dropped. In the morning I saw the masons and the manufacturers, but not the scribes. A soldier gave us food, and I asked him where they'd been put; he must have been heartily sick of such questions, because all I got in response was a clip around the ear.

Presently, however, there were officers searching through the crowd. I watched them come closer, barking at captives and guards alike, until they got within earshot and I learned that they were looking for me.

None of my companions was prepared to point me out to them; they were determined that I should suffer with the rest. So each of us in turn was asked our names, and when I alone declined to reply, they detached my chains from my neighbours' and led me to Nabuzaradan's quarters.

These were located in a private house, one of the few left standing. Nabuzaradan was there, dressed in a simple military tunic, and I thought how drained and worn he looked in spite of his face paint. The sight of me safe afforded him some relief; he rose to greet me, apologizing profusely because once again I'd been subjected to unwarranted humiliation, and I was immediately struck by the radical improvement in his Hebrew even since last we had met. He promised that I would be liberally compensated for this latest indignity, and that those of his men who were to blame for allowing the mistake to be made would be severely punished.

I wanted to say that I'd neither expected nor deserved preferential treatment. But nothing came out except coughing and blood. Nabuzaradan exhaled a voiceless oath, and barked an order which brought a dozen men running. Locksmiths, launderers, physicians and barbers descended upon me like so many bees; my manacles were undone, my ragged clothes were peeled away, and the physicians poked and prodded my chest while the barbers trimmed my hair and beard, seemingly all simultaneously. Finally I was bathed and doused in scent, and dressed in a suit of the finest clothing which the markets of Mesopotamia could afford, all fringes and pleats and intricate embroidery. I emerged from this whirlwind of pampering decked out like Marduk himself. The physicians alone had been unable to do anything to help me, and shook their learned heads in resignation.

Perhaps it was his understanding of their unspoken verdict that led Nabuzaradan to keep me with him longer than he might otherwise have done. Anything he wanted to ask or say to me would have to be asked or said before the door of opportunity was closed for ever. And seemingly there was plenty of it; I could read this so clearly from his forthright gaze that I knew Adonai's spirit was powerfully present. Nabuzaradan bade me recline and eat with him, and how could I not accept, when Adonai was all but forcing me down on the couch in front of me? While I sat there upon it, tensely upright, Nabuzaradan gave a fresh set of orders to another set of servants. And when the food he had asked for arrived, I noted that there was nothing on the table which I as a law-abiding son of the Torah could not eat.

Insisting that I start to eat before he did, Nabuzaradan said, 'You must understand, my lord Jeremiah, that you have earned the gratitude and respect of the Emperor himself for the part you have played in bringing this senseless rebellion to its conclusion. Your advice has been clear and coherent throughout; you have spoken consistently in the best interests of your own nation as well as of ours, in spite of the persecution we know you have had to endure as a result. And now, because things have turned out as you predicted they would, the deportees are proving much more docile than they might have been had you not prepared them in advance to accept their fate.'

'Never once have I spoken or acted with the slightest regard for Babylon's interests,' I responded, heartily wishing I were not wearing this man's clothes or eating from his plate, and wishing even more that I simply didn't find myself liking him so much. 'Nor have I acted in the interests of my own people. I have served Adonai my God, and him alone; and even this I was reluctant to do.' Nor did I want to do it now. I wanted to be gone from this plausible foreigner's sight; I wanted to find Baruch. In spite of all that had gone wrong between us I couldn't imagine myself surviving without him. Why was Adonai detaining me here? Why had he chosen now to lend me the energy to converse at length, and the capacity to do it so rationally?

'It matters not why you did what you did,' the Babylonian explained. 'The result was the same; indeed I am *glad* that you have always regarded yourself as your God's servant and no on else's. If you had simply turned traitor for personal gain, you might have switched your allegiance back again later with equal impunity.' He didn't say: then *I* shouldn't have liked *you* so much, either; but he meant it.

'So your King is well content,' I said. 'But what about ours? What has become of Zedekiah? Or is there no one here who knows?'

'You speak as though you care,' Nabuzaradan observed; and *he* was speaking as though he considered my concern misplaced. 'Zedekiah is naive and foolish. I know exactly what has happened to him, and it's not a jot worse than his actions have merited. As you are no doubt aware, he sought to escape Jerusalem by night, by way of the royal gardens. He succeeded, too, and made it through the desert as far as the Jordan River. I would guess he was heading for Ammon, since the Ammonite King is a seditious fool just like him, and one who has not yet been taught his lesson.'

'And then?' I demanded. 'I take it he got no further?'

'He was pursued at daybreak when his disappearance was discovered, and intercepted not far from the Jericho oasis. All his companions deserted him - evidence, I think, of the low regard in which he was held, and deservedly so. He was taken before the Emperor at Hamath in Syria. His infant sons were found and put to the sword. Their execution was the last thing your wretched King ever saw.'

'He is dead too, then?' I whispered, almost hoping that he was, yet already knowing what Nabuzaradan's reply would be.

'No, he isn't dead; at least, not so far as I'm aware. They blinded him with firebrands and sent him in shackles to Babylon.'

Thus it came about that both Ezekiel's prophecies and mine had found their fulfilment.

I almost went on to ask what had happened to Zedekiah's daughters, but checked myself just in time. No one had mentioned them; was it possible that the Babylonians knew nothing of their existence? Might the little girls have been hidden, or smuggled away to comparative safety? So long as there was the remotest chance of their being alive, I must hold my peace. Instead, therefore, I enquired after individuals who had been exiled ten years before: our rightful king Jehoiachin, his mother Nehushta, my friend Ahikam and other friends too. Had they and the thousands with them been punished for this latest rebellion, which hadn't involved them at all?

'No,' answered my host in some surprise. 'It was Zedekiah who rebelled, and therefore Zedekiah who was punished. Was it not Nebuchadrezzar who put him on the throne in the first place, and gave him all the authority he had?

'You know,' Nabuzaradan went on when I did not speak, 'You are a man very different from all of those we arrested in the palace who call themselves prophets. You are different too from the prophets of Baal Marduk, in the land from which I come.'

'Others may call me a prophet,' I told him. 'I claim no such title for myself. Titles restrict; they limit the ways in which God can use us.'

'Perhaps that is so,' he conceded. 'But you speak in this way precisely because you expect that your god *will* use you. *They* look for nothing of the kind. They look to be reverenced; they hanker after favour from men, and remuneration too. Yet you are content to suffer with the suffering, and to share the fate of the sinners you hold responsible for your god's defeat at the hands of ours.'

'I am a sinner no better than the next man, and worse than many,' I confessed. 'But know this, my lord Nabuzaradan: our God has not been defeated. He is master of the universe, and God of all the gods. He gave your Emperor his authority just as surely as the Emperor gave authority to Zedekiah. And when the time is ripe, Nebuchadrezzar will lose it in just the same way, unless he bows in submission to Adonai.'

Nabuzaradan baulked; then smiled, his dark eyes dancing. 'You do not merely impress me, Jeremiah. Frankly you amaze me. You know that I could have your severed head for a wineskin, but you are not intimidated. There is nothing I could do which would undermine your faith in this god whom your fellow countrymen have manifestly scorned and rejected.'

I averted my gaze, embarrassed by his blatant admiration. 'I'm afraid that my age is more prodigious than my faith,' I said. 'The fear of death by violence recedes, when the only alternative is death by disease and slow decline. But the strength of my faith matters not. It's the strength of my God which is important, and the breadth of his mercy, and the depth of his love.'

'Yet this god has permitted his holy city and his temple to be destroyed. His treasures will be placed in the temple of Marduk in Babylon, alongside those of all the other deities whom Marduk has vanquished.'

'And alongside their idols too, my noble lord. But you will find no idol in the Temple of Adonai, for no earthly shrine can contain him. Marduk's temple and everything in it belongs to Adonai. The past and the present and the future belong to Adonai. My predictions come true because Adonai has control over everything, and knows what will happen henceforth until the end of the world.'

'Even the razing of your temple fails to distress you? The temple which David planned and Solomon built?'

These words caused me to smile at him in my turn. 'I see, my lord, that you have been labouring hard to understand the people you have conquered. Yet they do not even understand themselves. They do not understand that the days of the Temple are over. The rituals, the sacrifices, the offerings and libations, even the priesthood itself... all these things were merely a preparation, the scaffolding round a building which must be dismantled once the building is complete. It is *we* who must be consecrated as temples; it's in the hearts of men and women and even children that our God desires to take up residence. He wants to quicken the spirit of every human being, so that all may commune with him as I do. Until these lessons are learned, it will be better for the people of Judah to worship in the open air and have neither priests, prophets nor teachers, nor any special land to call their own. Nebuchadrezzar has been the agent of our God and the channel of his revelation just as surely as I have been, for he has enabled me to find the road by which God's people must travel.'

I left off, and waited for Nabuzaradan to rebuke me. Instead, he had sunk deep in thought; he was stroking his beard and nodding. As for me, it was such a long time since I'd sought to explain to anyone the details of the astonishing revelation my God had given me, that I felt to be almost in ecstasy. To speak Adonai's word to a man who listened, to a foreigner, an alien, a man who had been born a pagan exactly like his father and grandfather before him... I could almost believe he would have let me place my hands upon his head and pray for the quickening of his spirit there and then.

But this was not to be. For his servants came back just then to remove our dishes and ply us with wine. When they left us again, Nabuzaradan's thoughts had turned back to me.

'Well,' he said, 'I have loosed your chains, which means that you are free. Free to remain in Judah or to come with me to Babylon, if that is truly where you believe your people's future lies. You could travel with my entourage, and I would see to it that you were cared for when you arrived. The choice is yours.'

I didn't know how to respond; I could scarcely recall when I'd last had a choice about anything. Besides, neither of the alternatives with which he presented me held the slightest appeal. I would not go to Babylon and live among men who reckoned me a traitor. But to remain behind in Judah was to identify myself with the land and the community which God had rejected, the bad figs too bad to be eaten. What would the exiles conclude? That I had lied to them after all.

Then again, I owed an incalculable debt to the House of Shaphan. Perhaps I could repay some of it by offering my support and counsel to Gedaliah.

So I said, 'I don't know *what* I want, my lord, except to be reunited with Baruch my scribe. If he must go to Babylon, then so must I.'

'He must be freed at once,' Nabuzaradan declared, and sent a message forthwith that Baruch should be found and escorted into his presence. Then he looked me full in the face and said, 'If the choice were left to me, I should take both of you with me. Then I should never lack for intelligent conversation or someone to answer my questions about the gods. But I cannot keep you from going where yours would have you go. I release you with my blessing, that you may present yourself willingly to Gedaliah.'

I was speechless. Part of me thought: he speaks as a prudent statesman; he knows that I shall be of more use to the Emperor in Mizpah than if I went with him back to the heartland of the empire.

But I knew that this part of me was wrong. I knew that Nabuzaradan liked and respected me enough to covet me as a friend, but too much to court me against my will. And he could *read* that will - in the lines on my brow, the set of my jaw, the mist in my eyes, when I couldn't even be sure of it myself - and he knew that this was Adonai's will too, because Nabuzaradan had the gifting. Adonai had already touched him, and without my mediation his spirit had begun to come alive. This was how it should be. Just like Ebed-Melech, Nabuzaradan was a sign of what the future held in store.

While I was still thinking these thoughts, Baruch was led into the room. His manacles were gone, and even as he entered, a fine new robe was put around his shoulders. But he didn't smile, or throw himself down at my feet. For among the scribes he had found his brother Seraiah, and now he was afraid that he would never see him again.

I questioned Nabuzaradan with the smallest gesture: couldn't Seraiah be freed as well? But he answered no; only Baruch and I were covered by the Emperor's provision; we alone of those destined for exile had won exemption.

'Well,' I said to Baruch, 'You are a free man now just as I am. Go with your brother, if that is your heart's desire.'

But he shook his head, constrained by love, or duty, or habit - I knew not which. And as I looked at him, and then at Nabuzaradan, and tried to reconcile my warring emotions in front of this enemy who wanted to be my friend, Nabuzaradan took off a chain which he wore round his neck, and fastened it round mine.

'Remember me, when I have returned to Babylon,' he said. 'And pray for me sometimes to your all-powerful god.'

'You may pray to him for yourself,' I replied, meaning it in the kindest way; and I believe he understood what I was saying.

Baruch and I departed for Mizpah that same afternoon, escorted by a detachment of Babylonian troopers. Baruch insisted on walking, as a furious and desperate protest, because he was not permitted to return to our house in Jerusalem even for the short time it would take him to pack up his scrolls and tablets. The city had already been sealed off;

soon the palace and Temple would go up in flames, and after that, what was left of the other buildings would belong to the birds and the beasts of the field.

As for me, I travelled by litter. For after I was led from the presence of Nabuzaradan, the strength which Adonai had lent me for the duration of our meeting deserted me as swiftly as it had come.

CHAPTER 25: BERECHIAH

With only two days left before the festival, the little town of Mizpah hummed with activity. In the market square the noise of sawing and hammering was compounded by the shouts of men to one another and to the boys who fetched tools, nails and wood for the makeshift tables. Women called out encouragement to their husbands as they themselves tied flowers and branches of willow to doorposts and lintels. Meanwhile girls practised their dancing, weaving nimbly between the tables, taking care not to tread on stray animals or their own younger brothers and sisters who played in the dust. Sheep and goats bleated, cooking fires crackled, and now and again there was even the sound of laughter or a voice raised in song.

On the outskirts of the town and in its alleyways villages of tents had sprung up, and every street was thronged with crowds. It was almost like looking at Jerusalem under siege, but more like listening to the guests assembling for a wedding. Two months had passed since the fall of the city, but very many more since anyone had had cause for celebration. Passover and the Feast of Weeks had been more like fasts than festivals, but now the governor Gedaliah had proclaimed a festival of his own. He wanted the survivors of Judah's ordeal to come together in gratitude to Adonai for preserving their lives, and because enough of this year's crops had been salvaged for us to have food on our tables, wine in our cups and oil in our jars.

The idea was a good one, and typical of Gedaliah who was proving himself a wise, just and popular ruler. Not many of the peasants whom he governed had seen their kinsfolk exiled or killed in action, but all had suffered hardship, and not only since the coming of the Babylonians. They desperately needed to feel that they belonged to a people with a future as well as a celebrated past. Now, thanks to Gedaliah, hope was being kindled within them.

And as Gedaliah's reputation for wisdom and fairness grew, it was not merely peasants over whom he was presiding. Gradually the remnants of Judah's scattered army, desperate men who had been holed up for months in woods and in wilderness caves, had arrived at Mizpah to throw in their lot with Ahikam's son. No one seemed to know what had become of Coniah their Commander in Chief. But his officers - Azariah ben Hoshaiah, Seraiah ben Tanhumeth, Jezaniah the Maacathite, the sons of Ephai - all of whom had ended up living like bandits with what was left of their troops, had begun to see that there was nothing more to be gained from baiting Babylonian units as they patrolled the recovering countryside. There were always more where they had come from; the war against them could never be won, and the incessant harassment did more damage to the Judean farmers struggling to rebuild their world than it did to Nebuchadrezzar. And those officers who came forward were granted land of their own, along with a share in work of government.

If only I myself could have felt more like celebrating. I had spent half the morning strolling through the crowds, hoping that their cautious optimism might rub off on me. Once upon a time the promise of a good party would have been more than enough to cheer me, but too many things were missing from my life all at once for me to rejoice in the bustle around me. The scrolls and tablets I'd had to leave in Jerusalem, my brother Seraiah carried away with the rest of my kin to a distant land... I still had Jeremiah, of course, but for how much longer I would be needed to take care of him I could not tell.

His health had improved, a little, now that he had food to eat and a roof above his head. But he was still as thin as a beanstalk, and he still had that rattling cough and the unmistakeable shadow of death around his eyes. I wondered if he would stir himself to attend the banquet; before Jerusalem fell Adonai had banned him from all such occasions as a sign of the tribulation to come, but now things might have changed.

Just then I caught sight of the Governor himself, walking with his minders in the square, smiling at the progress being made and exchanging banter with the folk whose paths he crossed. How his appearance had altered in the time since his return from Babylon! Though the foreigners in his retinue wore tasselled capes, and their hair in ringlets, Gedaliah looked like his father Ahikam reborn. It wasn't only in his neatly groomed hair and modest dress that he resembled him, but in the sense of purpose conveyed in his every gesture. He was serving Adonai as a statesman like his father and grandfather before him, and though his charges were mostly peasants today, in years to come who could say what they might accomplish? Jeremiah maintained that the good figs were those in exile, but surely Adonai could not withhold his blessing from what was being grown here in Judah's sacred soil. Idolatry, greed, exploitation... all had been conquered for the moment at least; why should we not build God's kingdom afresh, here in his Promised Land?

Not that Gedaliah's circumstances were in every respect to be envied. Just like mine, all his kinsmen were in exile. And there was still one serious rival with whom he would have to contend.

Everybody knew that Ishmael ben Nethaniah, the last of the wilderness warlords, remained at large, and that he claimed to belong to the Royal House of David. His claim was probably valid, for his grandfather too was said to have been of royal blood. Elishama had been Secretary of State under Jehoiakim; it was in his apartment at the palace that I myself, as a nervous, knock-kneed youngster, had read my first scroll of Jeremiah's oracles to the members of Jehoiakim's Council. Elishama had been as mild-mannered an individual as his grandson was reputedly the opposite, and throughout the reading had looked as though he wished he were somewhere else. Ishmael wished for one thing only: to govern Judah in Gedaliah's place, while wearing David's crown.

But by all accounts Gedaliah only laughed whenever the vagabond's name was mentioned. He would see sense in the end, like all the rest of his kind, Gedaliah maintained. If he himself did not soon grow tired of living in a cave, his supporters would.

As I watched the Governor moving among his people, at peace with himself and his rustic realm, two of the little girls dancing let go the hands of their playmates and dashed towards him. He scooped them up, one in each arm, and hearing them shriek with delight, it was hard to believe what they had lived through. Their father had been blinded and their brothers killed; God alone knew what had become of their mother. They were being brought up with the rest of the Mizpah orphans by widows who had mostly lost children of their own; there were only a handful of people who knew that the girls were Zedekiah's daughters.

Noting that the sun was almost at its highest, I decided I had better go and look in on Jeremiah before taking my siesta. When I'd left him in the morning he had not woken; like as not he would be still be asleep. We had rooms in the Governor's Residence - a grand-sounding name for what would have been regarded as a modest dwelling in days gone by.

But when I opened the door to his bedroom, he was no longer there. For a moment I struggled to believe what my eyes were telling me. Then with my heart already pounding I searched the house. I ran from room to room calling his name, then out into the streets where I asked all and sundry whether they had seen him. He had not been outside since coming to Mizpah; physically he had been too weak, and who could guess what fresh delusions might be clouding his mind? I pictured him lying in some alleyway, having collapsed or been brutally attacked, and I tried not to think about what I would do when eventually, inevitably, my duty to Adonai in taking care of his Prophet had been fully discharged.

Following some hazy leads and one or two hunches of my own, I found myself walking through a garden of olive trees on the edge of the town, and there, gazing out at the vista beyond, I found Jeremiah on his knees.

'Thank God,' I murmured, but he did not hear me; nor did he see me when I knelt before him and ventured to take his hands in mine. His troubled eyes stared straight through my skull, and his matted hair hung like dirty white ropes about his face. His lips were working furiously but no sound came out of them, and unable to penetrate his uneasy trance I was left with no choice but to go back home without him.

As I passed once more through the square I discovered that work had been suspended. All eyes were fixed on a band of newcomers who marched through the midst of the merriment: with their ragged cloaks, wide leather belts, and scarves tied round their heads I took them at first for shepherds arrived for the feast. It was only when I saw their weapons - clumsy staffs and clubs for the most part - that I realized who they were.

'Ishmael ben Nethaniah!' someone whispered, grasping my elbow and pointing; and as word flew round the crowd, folk started to applaud, then even to cheer and throw flowers at the strangers' feet. Ishmael's followers were clearly well pleased with their reception; Ishmael himself looked grim. Though handsome and not much more than twenty years old, his face beneath its twisted headscarf was hard and dark with brooding passion. I wondered if this was what David had looked like in the days before he was king, when he led his desert warriors on the run from Saul.

But Gedaliah gave no sign of having noticed the black expression on his rival's face. He approached the returned prodigal with arms spread wide, and everyone heard him say, 'Come, eat, drink! Welcome to my house!' Ishmael and his men followed the Governor inside, to enjoy his hospitality and swear the oath of fealty which would be required of them.

After my siesta I went again to the garden of olives to persuade Jeremiah to come home. But his trance persisted, the working of his lips more agitated even than before. When he had not moved by sunset I resolved upon dragging him home by force, but he knocked me aside with the merest flick of his finger.

Loath to retire for the night without him, I drifted about doing meaningless chores until well after dark. Then a servant of Gedaliah came to tell me there was someone in the hallway asking to see me.

In the flickering lamplight all I could see of my visitor at first was his headscarf and haunted eyes. I started; but the man was not Ishmael. He introduced himself as Johanan ben Kareah and said, 'Forgive me, my lord, for coming to you at this hour, but I did not know what else to do. You are scribe to the prophet Jeremiah, are you not?'

'Do you have news of him?' I asked impatiently. 'Please, if you have seen him, tell me at once what you know.'

But the man had brought no news of my master; rather he wished to talk about his own.

'My lord, I have served under Ishmael ever since the struggle with Babylon began. He hates the Babylonians with every fibre of his being, and never for a single moment has he approved the appointment of one of their lackeys as ruler of Judah. Again and again I have advised him to offer Gedaliah his support, and I have been called every name under Heaven for my pains. Now he has marched into Gedaliah's home and pledged him his allegiance; my lord, I do not know what to think.'

'Surely you have cause for rejoicing, not for perplexity,' I pointed out, bidding my guest sit down, but he would not. 'You have brought him round to your way of thinking at last.'

'But I cannot believe that I have: Ishmael is not a man to change his mind over something like this. My lord Berechiah, let me tell you frankly: I fear for the Governor's life.'

Shaken, I said, 'Come now, Johanan. Gedaliah owes his office to Nebuchadrezzar, it is true, but by birth he as Judean as you or I, and by inclination a loyal follower of Adonai. What could be gained from removing such a man and bringing the might of Babylon down on us here as it fell in Jerusalem? It would be madness.'

'To a man thinking clearly, indeed it would. But Ishmael does not think at all. Passion is what drives him, my lord, by his determination to see a Davidic king on David's throne once again. He knows the scriptures by heart; he knows that this land was granted to Abraham and his seed as an everlasting inheritance, yet now a pagan emperor treats it as his own, and writes off vast tracts of it to Edomites in return for the help they gave him in bringing Judah back into line.'

I heard what Johanan was saying, though I did not like it. I said, 'You have put your case eloquently, my friend, but why bring it to me? Why not approach Gedaliah himself?'

'I *have* approached Gedaliah,' Johanan replied, and at last consented to take the seat I had offered him. 'But he will not listen. He says that Ishmael has already eaten and drunk with him, and his respect for the laws of hospitality would prevent him from murdering his host in cold blood. Moreover, he has sworn an oath of allegiance, which as a man of honour he must not break.'

'All of which you should find reassuring,' I pointed out. 'If Ishmael is as zealous for the Law as you maintain, then Gedaliah's arguments cannot be refuted.'

'My lord, there are the laws of God and the laws of men; there are oaths sworn to God's creatures and those sworn to the Creator himself. Ishmael has sworn before Adonai in my own hearing not to rest until every inch of the Promised Land is farmed by Judean farmers, and every stooge of Babylon is driven from our domains.'

'But if Ishmael kills Gedaliah he will simply be killed in turn. The Babylonians will hunt him down and put him to death, and the next governor they impose upon us will be no more Judean than Nebuchadrezzar himself.'

'They may hunt for Ishmael but they will not find him. He'll flee across the border; King Baalis of Ammon will harbour him. Baalis may even be paying him already to keep the Babylonians occupied so they cannot punish *him* for his own sedition.' Johanan got up from his seat once more and took to pacing up and down, one hand clenched like a fist inside the other. 'Gedaliah is simply too trusting, my lord Berechiah,' he said. 'He himself is a man of his word and he cannot believe that other men are not as he is. His integrity may have got him where he is today, but I fear it will prove his undoing.'

Reluctantly I had to concede his point. 'But you still have not told me my part in all this,' I reminded him. 'Why have you come to me? What are you asking me to do?'

'I want you to speak to your master the Prophet. If *he* were to approach Gedaliah, the threat which Ishmael poses might be taken more seriously.'

'Johanan,' I told him, 'I could not even persuade Jeremiah to come home to bed. At this very moment he kneels beneath the stars in a trance; I have long since given up trying to bend his will to mine or even fathom what goes on in his head.'

Johanan opened his mouth to protest, then closed it again; I believe he understood from his own experience what it is like to serve a man of vision whose viewpoint you can never share. Finally he said, 'Then come with me yourself, my lord Berechiah. Two can be more persuasive than one.'

'Very well, if you think it will do any good. I will go with you to see him in the morning.'

'With respect, my lord, the morning may be too late.'

I knew we were wasting our time, but I went, because Johanan was desperate, and because I knew I would not sleep in any case. Gedaliah received us politely, though he himself had already retired for the night and had to be woken and dressed by his valet before we were admitted. But there was no disturbing his serenity.

'My friends, your concern for my welfare I value deeply,' he assured us. 'But Ishmael is a patriot who has sacrificed the best years of his life in the cause of resistance. From what you have told me he was already leading men into battle at an age when most of us can barely heft a sword. It will take him some while to adjust to peacetime conditions, but in time he will do so.'

We were making no progress, and Gedaliah knew it even if Johanan did not. 'Since it seems you have no fresh points to make, I would appreciate your leaving,' he told us in the end. 'I am tired, and much remains to be done before the feast.'

I awoke the following morning to find that Jeremiah had returned. He sat on his bed, silent and composed, and this time when I approached him he looked straight at me. But when I told him how relieved I was to see him, he said, 'The time has come to be vigilant, Baruch, not relieved. The war is reaching its climax.' Before I could ask him which war he meant, he had rolled on his side and gone to sleep.

The rest of the day he went on sleeping like the dead, while outside the hammering and shouting continued. Ishmael's men I saw mingling with the crowds and enjoying their favour; Johanan was among them, with a companion I learned was his brother Jonathan. Ishmael himself was nowhere to be seen. Then in the evening Johanan came to me again. This time his eyes were points of black fire and the rest of his face was hidden, for he wore his scarf bound tightly around it.

'Berechiah,' he announced, all deference thrown to the wind, 'I know what I have to do. I have no choice but to kill him myself.'

'Kill Gedaliah? Johanan, what are you talking about?'

'Not Gedaliah. I have to kill Ishmael. And I must do it tonight, before it's too late.'

'A man you have known half your life?' I was incredulous. 'A man under whose command you have served, and beside whom you have marched into battle? How can you live with your captain's blood on your head? Are you out of your mind?'

'Indeed I am not; but he is. Rather one man's blood on my head than hundreds'.'

'You cannot execute a man for a crime not yet committed, and which he may not even be considering. Johanan, let's go to the Governor again. It may be that he will pay heed to us if we speak to him a second time.'

Johanan was all but rabid in his frustration. 'What would be the point? I have thought about this, Berechiah. Even if he does believe us, there is nothing he can do to protect himself.'

'Johanan, that is nonsense. He has bodyguards provided by the Emperor. And he has protected the two royal princesses perfectly adequately until now. Ishmael is not the only carrier of royal blood still residing on Judean soil.'

'Zedekiah's daughters are alive? They have been brought here?'

'They have been here longer than I have, living right under the noses of Nebuchadrezzar's men. Please, Johanan, let's speak with the Governor again.'

'Very well,' said Johanan; but the words he said to Gedaliah were not what I wanted to hear.

'I can do it secretly,' he insisted when Gedaliah reacted exactly as I had done. 'I can make it look like an accident. I can even make it look as though Ishmael has taken his own life; he would have more than enough reason to do so. No one need ever know the truth.'

'You expect me to condone the murder of an innocent man? A man who has committed his cause to me of his own free will?'

'If you do not let me do this you condone the deaths of hundreds, perhaps of thousands, and the end of all you have worked for.' Johanan sprang to his feet; something flashed in the lamplight and I saw he had drawn his knife already. 'Why should he take *your* life, for God's sake? Why should he cause the remnant of God's people to perish?'

'If we *are* the Remnant,' said Gedaliah quietly, looking at me.

'By every god in heaven, Gedaliah, are you as blind as the king whose place you have taken?'

'There is but one God in Heaven, and I would rather that *you* kill me, here and now, than make me a party to the death of an innocent man. What is more, if any harm befall Ishmael while you and he remain at Mizpah, I shall hold you fully accountable.'

Cursing in disgust, Johanan threw down his weapon and swept out of the room, no longer caring whether I came with him or not.

On the day of the festival I woke up late, and found that Jeremiah had gone out once again. I went to his olive grove, swimming against a flood of folk which surged the other way: women and girls with flowers in their hair, boys shouting, men with small children on their shoulders. But when I came to his sacred place, he was not there, and once I had turned and begun to swim with the flow instead of against it, I wasn't able to go anywhere except to the square. And when I arrived, seated in the place next to the one reserved for the Governor was Jeremiah.

Not that he looked anything like I had seen him look before. He wore a sumptuous woollen robe of deepest blue, with sleeves wider than they were long. He wore a wide crimson sash around his waist, and a scarf about his neck. His hair, washed and combed, flowed over his shoulders and down his back like a white Babylonian cape. But every one of his splendid garments had been torn as though in mourning, his forehead was marked with ash, and his eyes were blue wells of tears poised waiting to fall. I faltered, not knowing whether to sit down beside him or not; and as I tried to decide what to do, someone took my arm and steered me away.

'Come, Berechiah, he has no need of you today. Join us,' Johanan invited me, and because he spoke firmly, and had me by the elbow, and because it seemed such a long, long time since I had shared the company of other men, I went with him. Encircled by a throng of Ishmael's rowdies, most of whom had already been drinking, I could not help but accept the goblet of wine pushed into my hands. With Johanan to my left and his brother on my right, it felt so very good to belong to their world even for a single hour that I felt my scruples washing away like mudbricks in a rainstorm. Already the fires were lit for the roasting of kids and lambs; the air was heady with the scent of spices, a reminder of luxuries I had almost forgotten existed. Platters of food and flagons of wine were put down on our table, and filled up when we emptied them, and filled again; Johanan said, 'Drink, Berechiah, for the night is past and Gedaliah lives another day.'

I was already too fuddled to ask him where Ishmael was, and why he wasn't eating and drinking with his men. Perhaps he had been earlier on, and Johanan had not noticed him slipping away. For he and his brother were both well oiled; clashing their cups together with mine they toasted peace, and plenty, and the future. Musicians struck up with pipes and timbrels, and everywhere there were happy voices raised in laughter and song; for the first time since Jerusalem's demise, these things didn't seem out of place. Little boys played games; the girls danced in and out amongst the tables as they had practised, the older ones who led them skipping like shuttles up and down, drawing their human threads behind them, and setting garlands of olive and myrtle on the heads of the guests whom Gedaliah chose to honour. Jeremiah was among them; I watched a child with a dimpled chin place the wreath in his hair then back away in haste, suddenly afraid of what she had done. There was something oddly distasteful in the spectacle of the Prophet, grave and unsmiling, with the tears in his eyes and the garland perched above his ash-stained brow as though to mock him.

All members of the Governor's retinue were honoured too, both Babylonians and Judeans, and it seemed at first very strange, and then somehow very wonderful to see men who had once been deadly enemies now feasting side by side, and, as the wine washed away their remaining reservations, clapping their arms around one another's backs and teaching one another the songs which had taken their armies into battle on opposing sides. Someone produced a lyre and tried to persuade Jeremiah to play it, with conspicuous lack of success.

But it was so very long since any of us had eaten or drunk for pure pleasure. When it was still broad daylight there were young men and old up dancing on the tables, whilst others spewed in corners, and still others lay snoring soundly, heads in their empty bowls. Even Gedaliah was well away, beaming fatuously at all these splendid people to whom he was giving such an uncommonly good time after all their years of deprivation. He waved his goblet above his head in a toast to Heaven, and swarms of giggling children clambered on and off his lap.

I'm not altogether clear as to what happened next up on Gedaliah's table, because suddenly there was a girl on my lap too. A bevy of buxom peasant lasses had attached themselves to our company, attracted it seemed by the glamour which Ishmael's warriors exuded. Johanan and Jonathan were the centre of attention but even I, it appeared, was rendered glamorous by association. Never in my life had a girl so much as held my hand, and now here I was, with this wench's arms about my neck, and the fragrance of her perfume filling my nostrils, filling the whole of my head. She covered my mouth with hers and put her legs about my hips, and there was nothing I could do but close my eyes and kiss her in return. She was laughing at me to begin with; she was pretty and pert and she knew it, whereas I was clumsy and gauche and the drink didn't help.

It was some while later when I chanced to open my eyes and look out through the veil of her hair. And I saw an ugly knot of men clustered around the Governor, the glinting of their knives dulled by the sticky coating of Gedaliah's blood. I caught the odd glimpse of Gedaliah himself, calling for help and clawing at the air, then feebly flailing as the strength went out of him. Finally they flung him forward across the table and there he lay bleeding, his limbs jerking like a speared boar's before a rush of blood from his mouth silenced his futile cries.

Naturally his guards had striven to protect him, but Ishmael and his accomplices had come from nowhere. To my right and left Johanan and his brother were up now and shouting; they had drawn their knives and were forcing their way to the scene of the crime, but much too late. Brawling had broken out between the Governor's retinue and his murderers, then amongst the guests in general. 'Zedekiah's daughters! We have to find them!' Johanan was yelling, as Babylonian went for Judean, official for peasant, vine-dresser for wine-waiter. The spirit of reconciliation which had pervaded the early part of the banquet was extinguished in a welter of gore; fists, clubs and knives were used indiscriminately, and even silver amphorae served as weapons. The women were fighting as ferociously as their men; voices which had blended melodiously in praise to God now shrieked in panic or howled in hate. Everywhere children were crying and babies mewling; many would be orphans before the day was out. And cries for mercy turned to moans as Ishmael's men slit the throats of any man with curls in his hair or tassels on his clothing.

Above the tumult soared a single, bird-shrill voice, screeching its denouncement of Judah's incorrigible wickedness, calling on Heaven's hosts to witness that Adonai had acted with unimpeachable justice in obliterating our once-holy nation from the face of the earth. Just as I realized that the voice was Jeremiah's, it too was cut off in mid-cry.

But I was effectively paralysed. Disabled at first by repletion and then by shock, I had sat and watched the slaughter as though it were part of some children's game, to which a halt would soon be called so that the dead could get up, brush themselves down and walk away. With the girl propped against my shoulder, I'd merely stared in horrified fascination at the spectacle of Johanan's captain now crouched on the table where Gedaliah lay, gloating like a predatory animal over its kill.

To murder one's host, with his food in your belly and the warmth of his wine in one's veins... few more impious crimes can be imagined. And yet Ishmael had planned it to perfection. Even the girls he had sent to distract us had performed their part in proceedings with consummate skill.

But Ishmael's veneration of the sacred hadn't entirely deserted him: when he saw that one of his men held a knife at Jeremiah's throat, he yelled, 'Let him go! He's a man of God, you ignorant fool! Do you want lightning to come from Heaven and strike us down?' The fellow who had hold of the Prophet cast him aside; Jeremiah's head struck the corner of an upturned table as he fell, and he lay without moving, draped across the body of a child. I blinked and looked again; the child was the girl who had crowned him, her dimpled face all bloody and black, her dead eyes staring at the sky.

CHAPTER 26: JEREMIAH

Splashes of wine on my face brought me round. Baruch crouched above me, his clothing spattered with blood.

To begin with, I thought I'd been unconscious for a matter of moments. Only gradually did I realize that the twilight into which I'd woken wasn't the dusk after sunset, but the dusk before morning. Baruch must have spent all night striving to rouse me.

Most of the dead still lay where they had fallen, but not all. A number of bodies had been dragged away - why or by whom I couldn't tell, but there were long bloody smears to show where they had gone, which was out of the market place into the town.

'I saw this,' I whispered, gazing out upon the sea of carnage. 'I saw it all before it happened. If only Gedaliah had listened to me. Why didn't he listen, Baruch? Why did I not try harder to make him hear me? And where is he now?' For the table onto which he'd collapsed was bare.

Baruch shrugged his shoulders and stared at the great brown stain which was Gedaliah's blood.

'We must find him,' I said. 'Ishmael will give his body to the crows. But he must be buried with honour, for the sake of his father. Come, Baruch, you have to help me.' And I started to struggle to my feet.

Baruch tried to deter me, and to say that I must rest. But how was I to rest, with the body of the son of my friend still in the hands of his murderers? With my arm across Baruch's shoulder we followed the bloody trail out of the market place and through the desecrated streets of Mizpah.

We swiftly discovered where the bodies had gone, and who had moved them. There was a huge disused cistern beneath the town, built in the reign of King Asa. Here Ishmael's minions were disposing of the corpses one by one, with no reverence or ceremony, no concern to identify the dead or inform their next of kin as to what had become of them. Some of the dead were Babylonian, of course, but most were Judeans, murdered by other Judeans in the lofty cause of patriotism.

Nevertheless, I would not rest until I'd seen Gedaliah. I made Baruch lead me down into the cellar where the entrance to the cistern was located, and down the slippery steps which spiralled around it. By an act of God or some macabre quirk of fortune, we found him; his belt had caught on the remnants of a wooden handrail, and his body had lodged on the edge of the steps instead of falling in the pit with the rest.

Baruch rolled him over, and I sat there on the steps with him laid across my lap, intoning the prayer for the dead. My voice echoed forlornly from the dank plastered walls; then raucous above the echoes rose the shouts of Ishmael's men ferrying more of their ghastly cargo from the square.

They were drunk as Arabs and I didn't know whether to hope they would see us or hope that they would not. Had we been any further down the steps, we should have been quite invisible. As it was, we were spotted by Ishmael himself.

'Prophet!' he hailed me, drunk as his subordinates. 'Why defile your holy hands by touching the corpse of a traitor?' And descending the steps towards me, he kicked Gedaliah's body over the edge.

I begged him to draw his sword and send me down there too, since *I* was a traitor, and worse, while Baruch was fending him off me and shouting, 'Don't listen to him. He's out of his mind.' But Ishmael laughed, and the walls of the cistern laughed with him.

'Leave the dead to look after themselves,' he admonished us both. 'Come, let us begin the festivities afresh! Eat, drink and be merry, for now we surely *do* have a cause for celebration. I am to be anointed regent of Judah, to reign on Jehoiachin's behalf until his return. Again the House of David will have a man upon David's throne!'

'Are *you* insane *too*?' Baruch harangued him. 'When Nebuchadrezzar finds out what you've done, you'll be as dead as Gedaliah, and Judah will be broken apart like a Passover loaf.'

But Ishmael laughed again, and bounded back up the steps two at a time. Having no longer any reason to remain where we were, Baruch and I made our way slowly up after him. We emerged in the ruined street where many of the kinsfolk of the dead were now gathered.

Most of the rest of that day I stayed there with them, sharing their grief, leading them in songs of lamentation. My voice quavered out of tune, and I couldn't manage half a line without coughing blood, but I had to get the pain out of me somehow. I implored Adonai to make me mad once more, that I might forget everything and be happy. Yet he would not.

Towards evening a large band of men was seen approaching Mizpah from the north. Consternation erupted; were the Babylonians upon us already? But as the company drew closer, it became apparent that it consisted of mourners like ourselves, their clothing torn and ash upon their brows. Also they had shaved off their beards and cut their flesh with knives, extreme tokens of grief frowned upon in Judah but frequently seen in the northern kingdom.

And this was in fact where the party had come from. Knowing nothing of Gedaliah's murder, they were in mourning for the destruction of the Temple and were on their way to pay their respects at the hallowed site.

It was promptly explained to the pilgrims that what remained of the holy city was out of bounds. They were invited to stay in our houses and tents as guests for the night, before returning on the morrow to their own homes.

'Surely not without paying our respects to the Governor and presenting him with the gifts we have brought him?' they protested; so then we braced ourselves to describe to them what had happened.

But at that very moment Ishmael appeared on the scene with a troop of supporters. I suppose that his spies had seen the travellers coming, just as we had, but in spite of the size of Ishmael's retinue, its members appeared to be unarmed and without malicious intent. Its leader, despite his reputation for brutality, was seen to be weeping.

He didn't give any excuse for his sorrow. He merely spread his arms in a tearful welcome, and asked the pilgrims who was their spokesman. An elderly man came forward, and Ishmael embraced him. 'Come with me and see Gedaliah, by all means,' he invited the man and his comrades warmly. 'I assure you that he is most eager to make your acquaintance.'

I did my level best to dissuade the northerners from going with him. 'This man is a butcher!' I cried. 'He has *killed* Gedaliah! Now he will kill you too! He cannot allow you to learn what has been done in this place, then depart from it alive.'

But I might as well have shouted my words into a sandstorm. They were whisked away like chaff by the wind of Ishmael's plausibility; his noble breeding showed in his handsome face, whilst I must have looked like the kind of demoniac who spends his life among tombs. Ishmael made no attempt to have me silenced; it wasn't worth his trouble.

The pilgrims were led to the Governor's Residence, because once they were all inside, the doors could be closed and there would be no escape. 'Don't go in there! Don't go in!' I shrieked, having dragged myself after them all the way. 'He'll kill every last one of you!'

This wasn't *quite* what ensued. He killed them all except ten, hurling the bodies into Asa's cistern with the rest, crowing, 'You wanted to see Gedaliah? Well there he is!' The ten whom he spared won remission by promising to tell him where they knew of stashes of honey, oil and grain hidden in an underground silo; commodities such as these were still in short enough supply to be something to bargain with. But he couldn't afford to let the survivors return to their own towns and report what they had seen, so he kept them as his prisoners.

'Will the savagery never stop?' I asked Baruch. 'Will Ishmael kill or imprison every person who comes here?'

My questions began to be answered the following morning, when the pair of us were hauled onto our feet and taken back to the market place.

Ishmael's men were rounding up everyone left alive in Mizpah, resolved upon fleeing with them eastwards across the border to Ammon, the kingdom of Baalis who had certainly been a party to the Governor's assassination. At last the truth had dawned on the Davidic pretender that if he remained on the Emperor's territory he wouldn't win a throne but a grave.

Like so many sheep we were herded back into the defiled square: men, women, children, the sick and the healthy all thrown together. Certain of those who had once been soldiers in Zedekiah's army were conspicuous by their absence: there was no sign at all of Johanan or his brother, or any of those like them who had dared to offer resistance to Ishmael's butchers at the banquet.

Some of the prisoners wept; most were too far gone in shock. They'd all imagined the nightmare to be over; recently they'd begun, however tentatively, to believe that things might get better. Now the bereaved held out their hands in supplication to their captors, and then to Adonai, crying, 'Why?' and I added my voice to theirs.

You know why, Adonai replied. *I have told you and told you again. In order to grow, a seed must fall to the ground and die. For my spirit to grow in the hearts of my people, Judah must be destroyed.*

'But why Gedaliah? Why did *he* have to die?' I shouted, suddenly excited because I hadn't expected a reply. I was struggling against Adonai once again; I didn't *deserve* a reply.

I reply because I love you, Jeremiah. I loved Gedaliah too, and he loved me. He promised me in Babylon that if I would bring him back to the land of his fathers, he would lay down his life for me, and die a happy man.

'But you didn't have to hold him to that promise!' I argued; and by now a great space had opened up around me, as people shrank away from the madman who was challenging the empty sky and waving his fists at shadows.

You think it would have been kinder of me to allow him to see all he had achieved brought to nothing? Adonai asked, and I don't suppose *he* expected a reply from *me*. Nor did he get one; all I could think of to do was to snatch up handfuls of dirt and hurl them in the air, as though into his celestial face. Honouring my wishes he withdrew, so that soon I truly *was* just railing at the sky. Becoming conscious of the prisoners' staring, I left off my imprecations and crumpled to the ground. Baruch sat down beside me, and I sank into black despair.

Not that Baruch was much less dejected than I was. In many ways he would have been better off if Ishmael had sent me tumbling into Asa's cistern as I'd requested. So far as I could see, only a foretaste of the guilt he would experience afterwards had caused him to interpose himself so vigorously between me and the murderer of Ahikam's son. Jabbed by an isolated pang of sympathy for the plight of this man who had once loved me enough to give up all that he had and all that he was to serve me, I stretched out one hand to lay it in his. And there we sat, with only our mutual distress left to unite us.

Eventually it seemed that the harvest of survivors had all been brought in, though there was still no sign of either Johanan or Jonathan. The exits from the yard were then sealed off, while Ishmael's men moved among us, binding us together with chains, ropes, torn-up awnings and curtains. Despite Ishmael's professed regard for my sacred person, Baruch and I were subjected to the same ignominious treatment as everyone else. Ropes were bound so tightly about our wrists and ankles that the flesh was chafed whenever our neighbours moved a muscle. Those closest to me, who could see the vile stuff I was coughing up, had every reason for pulling as hard away from me as they were able.

Before our latter-day exodus began, Ishmael took it upon himself to address us all, informing us of where we were being taken and why. A precarious platform was rigged up from broken tables so that he might be seen and heard above the crowd. He told us that we'd been trussed up for our own protection because it was crucial to our mutual survival that we went where he wanted us to go without dissension, since speed was imperative. Once we crossed over into Ammon we would not only be free of our bonds, but of Nebuchadrezzar's oppression as well. With him, Ishmael, as our leader - he didn't say king, or even regent now - we could live in genuine liberty as men of Judah, on land which Baalis would willingly make over to us in gratitude for our rising against the Emperor.

There we would settle down and marry and raise new families to replace the ones we had lost; we would increase and multiply while decadent Babylon went into decline, and when the time was ripe we would despatch Nebuchadrezzar to the outer darkness where he belonged.

I listened to Ishmael's courageous words and studied his bold gestures, but heard and saw only his fear. For all his fierce pride, he was very young and very vulnerable, and at last he'd awoken to the awfulness of what he had done in destroying everything he'd wanted to save. Throughout his speech he snatched glances over his shoulder, knowing now that he stood to be hunted down like the beast which has become the scourge of the flock. Far from being our shepherd, he was the wolf which had got into the fold.

At noon or thereabouts, we began to move off. I didn't expect to get to Ammon; there was desert to pass through on the way, and the Jordan to be crossed. I remembered some words which Adonai had spoken to me long ago: *If you stumble and fall in safe country, how will you cope in the thickets by the Jordan?* And I thought: I shall not. I shall fall and never get up, and not before time.

But we got nowhere near the Jordan, neither Ishmael nor I nor any of us. For while we were resting up by the Great Pool at Gibeon, Johanan and his fellow officers appeared, leading a band of men at least as large as Ishmael's, and came to our rescue.

Some of the prisoners saw them approaching, their horses' hooves throwing up dust as a fire throws up smoke. It was astonishing that Johanan had found such a multitude of men to ride or march with him; for there were many on foot in addition to those on horseback. Most of the former set to work removing the prisoners' bonds - every liberated captive could then pit himself against his captors - while those who were mounted went directly into action against the enemy.

The so-called Great Pool was really a rock-hewn cistern not unlike the one which had become Gedaliah's tomb, so the location of the battle in which so many of Ishmael's supporters were killed was singularly appropriate. Being far too frail to join in the fighting on my own account, I searched the field with my eyes until I found Johanan, and then willed him on to victory. I prayed that Adonai would grant him the strength to fight without flagging, and the courage to stand firm against the brigand who had once been his commanding officer. The first of these prayers was spectacularly answered: Johanan fought like a man possessed, despatching scores of souls to queue quaking at Sheol's gates.

But Ishmael himself he never got to face. Somehow in the confusion the patriotic pretender got clean away, to take refuge with Baalis, the pagan king in whom he had placed his trust.

CHAPTER 27: BERECHIAH

We prepared to spend the night sleeping rough in the ruins of Gibeon. Like so many other towns of Judah, the Babylonians had rendered it all but uninhabitable, except by rats, jackals and crows. These we had to chase out before we could tend to the wounded or bury our dead.

Just as I had lain down to sleep, Johanan sent for me. I was reluctant to face him, expecting to find his mood offensive. He would be exultant in his victory, or smug because his suspicions about Ishmael had proven correct, or conceivably depressed at the death of Judah's governor and the loss of his own captain and friend. I did not want to deal with him in any of these humours. But when I was shown into his quarters - one room of a house which was still partially roofed - I found him sober and apprehensive.

'Berechiah? Thank God,' he said, rising from a crooked table to greet me. 'And the Prophet; is he safe too?'

'Yes,' I assured him. 'Though I don't know what is keeping him alive. He's been sick for so long, you would think that the gentlest breeze would fell him. And yet he has lived through all this.'

'I won't waste words, because both of us need to rest,' Johanan said, paying no attention to my wistful observation. 'But I mean to leave for Egypt tomorrow, and to take with me everyone here who is fit enough to go. I want Jeremiah to sanction my intentions, and I want you to persuade him to do it.'

'*Egypt?* I baulked. 'Why Egypt? Ishmael won't come back now. We have no more to fear from him.'

'I know he won't come back.' I was sure that Johanan's voice was tinged with regret as well as with relief. 'But it isn't Ishmael I'm afraid of any longer. It's the Emperor.'

'*You* have done nothing to provoke Nebuchadrezzar. Quite the reverse.'

'Do you think that he and his ministers are going to make detailed investigations into what has gone on here? They will descend like vultures and wreak vengeance on us *all*. We dare not wait for that to happen. And where else but Egypt can we go? Eastwards lies Ammon, south eastwards the desert, westwards the sea, and we have neither ships nor sailors to crew them. To the north, Nebuchadrezzar holds Syria. The south west alone is left, but few of our compatriots will dare head for Egypt unless they have it on good authority that Adonai will let them go back to the land from which Moses delivered their forbears.'

'Then you must petition Jeremiah yourself, Johanan. It may be that he will listen to you. He certainly will not accept such a mandate from me.'

Johanan was growing impatient, though he sought to hide it. He said, 'You persuaded him to speak to Gedaliah in the end, did you not? I heard it from several sources that Jeremiah warned the Governor to be on his guard at the banquet - for all the good that it did him.'

'I heard it from Jeremiah's own lips that he had given such a warning, but it was not I who persuaded him to do it,' I pointed out. 'In any case, as things stand with him at present, he will neither speak *to* Adonai nor *for* him - not unless a thunderbolt strikes him. And if *that* happens, he will speak out *against* your going to Egypt, I know it. Whenever Adonai's spirit has come upon him, he has consistently forbidden the people of Judah to place any trust in the Pharaoh.'

'You are saying that the great prophet Jeremiah rebels against his God like the rest of us?'

'Indeed yes, though his rebellion never brings him anything but despair, of which each bout is worse and longer-lasting than the one before it, just as each ecstasy takes him higher. I don't know which will finish him first. But you would be better advised to do nothing and go nowhere until he is more himself. Then you should ask him to present your predicament to Adonai without attempting to prejudice the outcome.'

Johanan muttered something in consent, but remained patently unconvinced. As for me, my pounding heart belied my apparent impartiality. If I were constrained to go to Egypt, I should have to abandon any hope of retrieving the scrolls and tablets I'd left in Jerusalem. I was still recording all that I could, keeping the documents close about my person even when I slept. But all of those which related to events prior to Jerusalem's fall remained inside - or had been destroyed with - Ahikam's house.

Johanan dismissed me, and for two days he followed my advice, saying nothing more to anyone about quitting Gibeon for Egypt. Meanwhile Jeremiah's depression only deepened; with his clothes torn to ribbons he drifted about the ruined town day and night like his own ghost, scaring away children and grown men alike by intoning his eerie laments over and over again. Even I had them word for word going round in my head.

To my surprise, Johanan bade me share his supper both evenings. I accepted his invitation, glad of any respite from Jeremiah's company. I soon learned why Johanan wanted to spend time with me. Not only did I represent for him the stability of middle age in his volatile world where youth had so far called the tune, but also he knew that I, of all people, might understand the contradictory feelings he bore towards Ishmael ben Nethaniah who had been both his friend and his foe. Only in rescuing Zedekiah's daughters had Johanan been able to salvage any self-respect from the catastrophe which had ended their long association.

'I cannot let Nebuchadrezzar get his hands on those girls, Berechiah,' Johanan said to me during our second supper together. 'If the Emperor learns who they are, he will kill them as he killed their brothers. We *have* to leave this place, and if we must do so without Jeremiah's blessing, then so be it.'

'You would be making a serious mistake,' I warned him. 'At very least seek God for *yourself*. Don't make such a critical decision without reference to the will of Heaven.'

'How can I pray at a time like this? I am exhausted. As soon as I sit still I fall asleep.'

I thought about offering to place my hands on his troubled head and pray on his behalf, as Jeremiah might have done. But I didn't quite dare. I had faith enough left for myself, more or less, but not enough for another man too.

In the morning, Johanan instructed his fellow officers that camp should be struck, and our faces be set towards Egypt.

Remarkably few objections were raised. Most of the folk he had rescued from Ishmael's clutches were simply so grateful that they would have followed him to the moon. I thought: for now I shall go with them, and fetch Jeremiah too; it may be that the Prophet will be roused from his apathy once we are on the move and he realizes where we are headed.

So we gathered ourselves together, and travelled that day as far as Bethlehem. The place was deserted, and again we made our camp amid rubble. We foraged in verminous cellars for food; driving a flock of birds from a dilapidated shanty, I found a handful of grain for roasting, and even a few dried figs. But Jeremiah refused all sustenance. On the road he'd walked in my footsteps without a word. It really was as though he were already dead, and only his ghost remained with us.

'This is the curse I am under,' he said bleakly, when I lost my temper at last. 'Adonai vouchsafed me my life, and so I live on, and shall live on for ever, though the skin fall off my bones, and my body be riddled with poison, and my stomach deprived of all nourishment.'

'What new nonsense is this?' I rebuked him. 'No man can live for ever. No man can live at *all* without food, though Heaven knows, you have tried to disprove it more times than enough.'

'I have brought this fate upon myself,' Jeremiah droned on, as though I hadn't spoken. His eyes stared right through mine and away toward some distant place which no one but he could see. 'I have rebelled all my life against the ministry prepared for me. I have rejected God's love and refused to enjoy the fellowship he offered me. I have spurned his call; I have wished that he might kill me; I have wished that I'd never been born. So now I am compelled to live in futility, to know the desolation of death even in life. My soul must haunt the hallways of Sheol, even while my feet tread the earth. My very life has been a reflection of Judah's rebellion, instead of reflecting Adonai's compassion, and now it is too late.'

'It's never too late,' I admonished him, out of my depth and resorting to platitudes. But before I had to think of anything more to say, there were footsteps approaching. Johanan himself was picking his way through the rubble towards us.

Falling on his knees before the Prophet, who sat cross-legged in the dust, Johanan said, 'My lord, your servant Berechiah speaks truly. I cannot take these people to Egypt unless it is God's will for us to go there. I beg you: pray to him for guidance.'

'Pray to him yourself,' Jeremiah replied. His eyes didn't so much as flicker while his mouth shaped the words. 'Adonai is as likely to listen to you as he is to me.'

'But not so likely to answer,' Johanan countered, his desperation making him bold.

'Adonai does not communicate with any man to order. A prophet waits patiently upon him; he does not demand oracles in the manner of a pagan diviner.'

Johanan, at a loss as to how to proceed, departed as burdened as he'd come, while Jeremiah simply went on staring.

When morning came, Johanan was back, but not on his own. He had his brother Jonathan in tow, and most of the surviving officers of Judah's army. In addition he'd brought representatives from the ranks of the refugees themselves, from brawny peasant farmers to palace servants who had spent their former lives dressing ladies' hair. '*Please* do what we ask of you,' they implored Jeremiah in concert. 'Pray to your God for us, whose lives he has preserved until now. Pray that Adonai will show us where to turn.'

For a long time Jeremiah remained impassive, not even acknowledging their presence. But then his head jerked forward, as though he'd been struck on the back of the neck. His eyes went wide, and fixed on Johanan's face, and he said,

'Very well. It may be that Adonai will agree to give you his counsel. But only if *you* agree to do exactly as he tells you.'

'Of course. Of course!' Johanan was all but tearful in his gratitude. 'We'll go anywhere; may God be witness against us if we don't follow his directions to the letter. Whether we approve them or not, we shall carry them out; we know that all goes well with those who submit to Heaven's will.'

Yet I didn't share his conviction that all would now turn out for the best. Go anywhere, he'd said; in other words, he was still wedded to the assumption that flight was essential.

I asked Jeremiah if he wanted me to send the deputation away while he gave himself to prayer. But it seemed that the Prophet himself was the one who would go away. Bethlehem is situated in the hill country, as far to the south of Jerusalem as Anathoth is to the north, and it was out among the hills that Jeremiah wanted to go, for he knew that he would never see hills like these again if Egypt was his destiny. And since he claimed that he'd been running from salvation all his life, there was no more appropriate place than Egypt for him to end up.

I offered him food for his journey, but he maintained that no morsel should pass his lips until God's word came to him. I asked if he wanted me to accompany him, but he seemed not to care. I thought: this is the war that he spoke of in Mizpah, and its last battle has begun. Jeremiah and his God have been locked in mortal combat since the Creator's fingers shaped him in his mother's womb, and the final engagement of the war has commenced.

I followed him out into the hills, which is not to say that I went with him. He was utterly absorbed in himself. His cloak was wrapped about his body like a shroud, and his mind was wrapped in contemplation. Only his fine white hair, like floating mist about his shoulders, was uncontained. He found a great bare rock perched high as an eagle at roost, and here he sat down to await Adonai's message, or to wrest it from him if need be.

Though the afternoons and evenings might still be warm, the nights were not, for winter was approaching. Yet

Jeremiah sat until dawn on his rock without shifting, without shivering, without even coughing. Each time I awoke with the cold or with cramp, there he was, a motionless outline erect against the moonlight.

When day broke, he hadn't moved. I crept up close, but just as in the olive grove at Mizpah he did not know that I was there. So I went in search of water and filled up a wineskin from a spring among the rocks. I tipped some of its contents into a cup which I set down before him, but it was more like making an offering to an idol than attending to the needs of a man.

The whole of a second day he remained in his place; he took the water, but when I put food beside the cup, he let it go stale. Why does Adonai not answer him? I wondered. Is it really true that we who did not go to Babylon are wholly cut off, Jeremiah included? If that is the case, this battle will end only when Jeremiah's body is as dead as his soul.

After the third day passed without event, I sat down beside the Prophet and blew gently on his face. But he did not blink. I touched his shoulder, and still there was no response. I was scared to touch him again lest somehow he crumble away, like the wife of Lot who became a pillar of salt for the winds and rain to erode.

By the fourth day he was talking nonsense to himself. His waxy skin was sunken between his bones like the membrane of a bat's wing, and his eyes were drifting. By the fifth day he was drooling; by the sixth, his head had fallen forward in his lap, and I couldn't see his face for his tumbling hair. Yet the water I set before him continued to disappear. I never saw him raise the cup to his lips, but I no longer knew when I was awake and when I slept, so I wasn't surprised.

But what was going on inside him? I knew that he was crushed by the weight of the sorrow and persecution he'd had to endure throughout his ministry, which he saw as nothing but a failure. And he was wasting away for lack of fellowship with Adonai as surely as for lack of food. He wasn't going mad - he had already passed through madness - rather, the contents of his mind were somehow draining away, so that when on the seventh day I mustered all my courage and lifted up his head between my hands, his eyes were vacant, and his mouth hung slack like that of a child born simple. Yet there was a pulse in his throat, and although his breathing was shallow, I could feel its feeble warmth, light as a feather's caress upon my brow.

On the eighth day, without any warning, he rolled on his side and lay curled up, as though back in the womb where Adonai had marked him out for greatness. I laid his head on my knees and dribbled water onto his tongue, but when my wineskin was empty, I didn't dare leave him to fetch any more. On the ninth day I myself felt so weak that I couldn't have got to the spring and back if I'd tried. I lay down on the rock beside him, my arms about his waist, and waited to die there with him.

Then on the tenth day, Adonai spoke. Perhaps he'd been striving to speak all along, but could no more penetrate the cloud of Jeremiah's depression than anyone else had been able to do. Only now, when the Prophet's faculties were utterly broken down and there was nothing around which that cloud could gather, could Adonai's light illumine him.

There was no violent seizure, no ecstatic weeping or laughter. Jeremiah's wasted body could no longer have withstood such dramatic manifestations of spiritual power. But with my own body pressed against his, I felt the astonishing heat of the Divine sweep through him, restoring life to his shrivelled flesh and ardour to his soul.

For a while he remained where he was. Then in one fluid movement he slipped from my embrace and was on his knees gazing down at me, with the strangest of smiles playing about his lips, and his eyes like molten glass. For all that he was thin and frail as the stem of a poppy growing up among thorns, he didn't look sick any longer, or even old; the lines on his face which had so eloquently told the story of his life seemed miraculously smoothed away. It was as though the Jeremiah I had known, and loved, and loathed, and execrated, was gone from me completely. The war was over, the rebel had destroyed himself, Adonai had triumphed over him, and it was Adonai's face that I beheld.

'Come, Baruch,' he said warmly, not so much as though I were forgiven, but as though there were nothing to forgive. And although he used the name by which only Jeremiah had ever called me, it was as though some other person were saying it.

I couldn't find it in me to respond. I tried to study his face but the sun was shining from directly behind his head, dazzling me and turning his hair into a halo of brilliant gold.

So he stretched out his hand and caught hold of mine, and the divine heat coursed through me like lightning. No longer weak or thirsty, I roused myself and we stood up together. I thought: I must be dreaming, or else hunger and loneliness are causing my mind and my eyes to play tricks on me. Or perhaps we have both died, and his soul is leading mine to Sheol.

But it was back to the ruins of the town that he led me. Although the going was rough, he didn't once glance down to see where he was putting his feet. We walked among the broken-down walls where Johanan's multitude of dependants was still encamped. They issued like spectres from their hovels and followed us unconsciously with their blank sheepy eyes. But those whose eyes connected with the Prophet's fell on the ground as his shadow passed over them.

We went to the house where Johanan was staying, but instead of addressing him privately, he who had once been Jeremiah climbed up on the half-sound roof and stood on what remained of the parapet. A whole section of it fell away and crashed into the alleyway below, but the part he was standing on stayed where it was, and he kept his balance without effort. From here he called out to the multitude.

Thus says Adonai, the Lord God Almighty:
Abandon your flight and stand firm where you are!
If you are willing to tarry in Judah,
My sword shall defend you and keep you from harm.
Again I shall build you, not bring you to ruin;

Again I shall plant you, and you will grow strong.
The havoc I wrought on you fills me with sorrow;
  The pain you have suffered has wounded my heart.
Cease now to fear Nebuchadrezzar of Babylon;
  I shall redeem you from tyranny's grasp.
Return to your homes, for because I am merciful,
  Him shall I cause to be merciful too.
If you insist on escaping to Egypt,
  The evils you fear will catch up with you there.
War and starvation and terror will follow you,
  Death be your portion, the desert your tomb.

I was dumbfounded. What could this mean? According to Jeremiah, any hope there was had always lain with the exiles. The bad figs, the people whose names had been rejected when the Babylonians had compiled their lists of those to be deported, had been rejected by Adonai too. Had the Almighty now changed his mind on a whim?

While I was struggling to make sense of all this, the Prophet ranted on, reminding his hearers that in the Book of the Law which King Josiah had found in the Temple it was written with reference to Egypt: 'You are not to go that way again.' When Adonai had promised to take his people back into the wilderness and there to woo them once more to himself, he hadn't been speaking of the Valley of the Nile. Moses had brought the Children of Israel in glorious exodus from the Pharaoh's domains; to return there would be to fling back salvation in Adonai's face.

For all that this message jarred so harshly against the many which had preceded it, to me there could be no shadow of a doubt but that it came directly from Heaven. You only had to look at the messenger to know it - to behold the strength concentrated in that emaciated figure, to wonder at the ageless beauty which lit up the ancient face. The loveliness of youth and the serenity of extreme old age combined together in his countenance, and I had to shield my eyes against its radiance. Adonai was indeed a God of mercy, and if he chose to be merciful in spite of everything to this wretched and feckless rabble, then who was I, or anyone else, to complain that things had changed?

But all of this was lost on the dogged Johanan. In spite of the promises he'd made us, he would never question the assumption that he had to take his people somewhere. While the Prophet continued with his tirade, Johanan ran up on the roof behind him, with Azariah ben Hoshaiah his colleague from the days of Zedekiah's army. They seized hold of him from either side and dragged him down inside the house.

'You're lying!' Johanan harangued him. 'Adonai hasn't spoken to you at all. *Berechiah* has stirred you up against us, so that the Babylonians will catch us and kill us or carry us off into exile with the rest.'

I could not credit what I was hearing. Did he seriously imagine that this was why I had refused to put his request to my master in the first place? 'Don't be a fool, Johanan,' I cautioned him. 'Do you think that I am like Ishmael, ready to condemn my fellow Judeans to death for the sake of some warped ambition of my own?'

'How dare you compare yourself with him!' bellowed Johanan, letting go of the Prophet just long enough to strike me in the face and drive his knuckles into my eyes. 'You and your master are both filthy traitors! Ishmael would rather have died than compromise his principles as you have done!'

I didn't respond. It was all I could do to remain on my feet.

'Arrest them both!' he shouted at whoever chanced to be within earshot. 'We *shall* go to Egypt, and these wretches will come with us whether they choose to or not.'

Azariah rounded up some veterans of his unit, who duly bound me with ropes. But they couldn't be induced to lay a finger on the Prophet. He sat on the ground where he'd been deposited: compliant, composed, dispassionate. In the end Johanan and Azariah themselves tied him up, and told us that we should both be kept under guard until dawn, when our journey to Egypt would be resumed.

We were marched to a cottage whose walls and roof were still secure enough for us to be imprisoned there. All the way I was begging Johanan to think again.

'Everyone you rescued from Ishmael will die!' I persisted. 'Have you not learnt yet to heed Adonai's warnings?'

'Jeremiah does not speak for Adonai,' Johanan sneered. 'He's an agent of the Emperor, and that is precisely what he has always been.'

'So why did he not go to Babylon and take refuge with the Emperor when Jerusalem fell and he had the perfect opportunity to do so?'

'How should I know? When has he ever done what appeared to be rational or expedient?'

'A holy man does as God tells him, Johanan, whether expedient or not. You would be wise to do the same, and take us all back to Mizpah.'

'If Jeremiah is as holy as you say, then no harm will come to us wherever we go. Adonai will not wipe us out while his beloved is found among us.'

What more could I say? Furiously resentful, I sat with fists clenched hard above my tightly bound wrists, in the corner of the foul-smelling room where they threw us. Its walls were blackened with soot, and by the light of the one tiny window high up above me I saw heaps of rotting dung all over the floor which feral animals had excreted there. The Prophet was flung in beside me; callous in my bitterness, I told him that I wished I'd gone to Babylon with Seraiah after all.

'Do not give yourself up to sterile anger, Baruch,' he said evenly. 'We shall go to Egypt if that is where Adonai has decided to send us, and we shall work for him there while we wait for the exile to be over and the promised Messiah to come. The night may be dark, but the dawn is approaching.'

'The exile is to last seventy *years*, or had you forgotten? *We* shall never see it end.'

But he only smiled at me indulgently, the epitome of tranquil dignity seated on his cushion of excrement, so that I felt even angrier than before. Had he truly found peace at last?

Had he truly surrendered his stubborn will to that of the Almighty, when it seemed now that the Almighty had misled him all along?

'Adonai misleads no one,' he said, his voice as smooth as a pebble which has lain for a long long time in a stream of living water. 'He is disposed to show mercy to everyone, and will work with whoever trusts in him. It is just that he knows in advance who these people will be; and they happen to be the ones he has sent to Babylon.'

Unwilling to engage him in argument only to have him read my mind, I snorted and turned my back on him. For a while he lapsed into silence once more, but presently fell to chanting rapturous psalms to Adonai. Presumably he invented them as he went along, because I'd never heard any of them before, nor the language in which they were composed.

As night stole upon us, and a pallid moon arose in our window and shone on the Prophet's face, I saw that he'd succumbed to trance once more - if indeed he'd ever come out of it. For although he sang with his lips and voice, his eyes had rolled back and all I could see was the whites. A shudder ran up my spine; he had spoken of the Messiah, the emissary of the divine, the one who will feel the very feelings of Adonai, share in his sufferings and exult in his joy, the one who will represent God to man and man to God, and I thought: Jeremiah is a harbinger, a type prefiguring the one who is to come.

Then all at once, there was something happening outside. There was a crunching of gravel, a brief exchange of voices, and suddenly the light of the moon was eclipsed as a face looked in at our window.

'Berechiah? Is that you?' demanded a voice from far in my past. 'What in Heaven's name is going on in there? Are you all right?'

'Joseph?' I whispered, incredulous. 'Can it be you?' For Joseph was the youngest of my own cousins, albeit one I'd seldom seen. Having abandoned the scribal profession as a boy, the family had all but expelled him, just as it had later expelled me.

Yet now his voice was the sweetest sound I'd ever heard. 'What are you *doing* here?' I demanded, excited as a child lost in a crowd who at last hears his father calling him. 'Have you been with the refugees all this time?'

'No, of course I haven't! I've been traipsing all over Judah, looking for *you.* Since the rest of our kinsmen were deported I've been searching high and low for someone of my own flesh and blood.'

'Then what has taken you so long? You must have been told that Jeremiah and I were at Mizpah.'

'Eventually, yes. But when I got there, Ishmael had... Berechiah, what *is* going on in there? Are you locked up with a lunatic?'

For the Prophet was still crooning his unintelligible psalms, more fervently now than before. I tried to explain to Joseph what had happened to Jeremiah during our ten day retreat in the hills, but couldn't seem to find any words.

'I was going to persuade you both to come back with me to Jerusalem,' Joseph said. 'But now I'm not sure it would have been such a good idea, even if you'd been free to come.'

'Back to *Jerusalem?* You've been allowed inside the city?'

'Not inside, no. But a settlement has grown up at the foot of the northwest wall, or what's left of it. That's where I've been living.'

'Then you *could* get in, if you had to? You could dig through the rubble, or bribe someone..?'

'It's been done; but by men more intrepid - or richer - than I am. It's cost me nearly all the silver I possessed to bribe the guard out here to let me speak to you now.'

'You have to do something for me, Joseph. If it's possible for *anyone* to get into Jerusalem, you must find a way of doing so. You must find the house which belonged to Gedaliah's father. All my scrolls are there, Joseph, all my tablets, all the records I kept of Jeremiah's life and work, of the war, of the siege; and there is a scroll of Hosea's prophecies too. You have to gather them together and get them out before they are lost for good.'

'If they aren't already. Nebuchadrezzar's men have lifted anything of any value for themselves.'

'What value would scrolls have for common soldiers? Oh Joseph, I know it's not too late, or Adonai would never have brought you here tonight! Won't you do this one thing for me, and for Adonai himself, in return for his having led you to me?'

I knew, as he knew, that he couldn't say no. He began to ask all sorts of questions about what he was to do with the documents if he found them, in such a way that I knew he'd made up his mind already.

So I bade him wait only until I'd completed my final record. I had him ask the guard for a torch, and I propped it up between some bricks which were strewn among the dung. Then I drew from my garments the parcel of tablets I still carried with me - even the fabric in which they were wrapped was covered in my own tiny writing.

And here I sit, in the dirt and the debris, scribbling the final words of my life's work which I must entrust to a man I hardly know. Anything which I write in Egypt, Adonai will have to find some other way of saving. Beside me, his face beatific in the glimmering torchlight, the Prophet is singing - in Hebrew now - the psalm with which I shall close. Although I have lived in his shadow half my life, it seems to me now that I really don't know him at all.

Adonai has loved you with love everlasting;
Again he will build you, and you shall stand firm.
Dance with the joyful, O daughter Jerusalem;
Take up your timbrels, your loud tambourines!
You will plant vineyards once more on the hillsides,
Drink wine which Samaria's grapes will provide.

Heralds will cry from the mountains of Ephraim:
Let's go to Zion; come, worship the Lord!
Lift up your voice for the children of Jacob,
For Israel, pride of the nations once more.
Sing to Adonai, sing praise to your Saviour;
The remnant is ransomed; the exiles return.

Home from the plains of the north he will lead them,
Harvesting men from the ends of the earth:
The blind and the lame and the women in labour,
Laughing and weeping will find their way home.
Adonai will guide them by streams of bright water,
By paths which are smooth, where the footing is sure.

'For I am their father, and they are my children:
The nation of Israel, my own firstborn son.
I am their shepherd: I gather and guard them;
I pay their ransom and set them all free.
For joy they will shout on the fair heights of Zion,
Their sorrow forgotten, their pain turned to praise.'

Jeremiah 31:3-13.

HISTORICAL NOTE

'No braver or more tragic figure ever trod the stage of Israel's history than the prophet Jeremiah'. Thus wrote the scholar John Bright about the man who was arguably the greatest of all Jewish prophets.

From the Bible's pages we can learn more about Jeremiah the man than we can about any other canonical prophet: not only about the events of his life, but about his turbulent relationship with his God. Born the son of a priest at the close of the seventh century BC, he came from Anathoth - near the modern village of Anata - and lived through the reigns of the final four kings of Judah. We last hear of him being forcibly taken to Egypt by Jewish refugees, and continuing to rail against idolatry there.

A great deal is known also about the period in which he lived. We have detailed information in the Bible - in the Book of Jeremiah itself, and in Lamentations, 2 Kings, 2 Chronicles and several of the other prophets. Much of this information is corroborated by other ancient literary sources, and by archaeology. Notable among the literary sources are the Babylonian Chronicle, the Lachish Letters, the Egyptian records relating to the Pharaohs of the 26th Dynasty, and the Histories of Herodotus.

The history of the formation of the biblical Book of Jeremiah is extremely complex. The arrangement of the contents seems little short of chaotic, and some sections read like 'variations' on the work of other prophets. This has led some scholars to question the very existence of the man around whom all this material has accumulated. But it is difficult to see why any material should accumulate about a non-existent core, and it would be strange indeed if a prophet were not influenced by those who had gone before (Jeremiah owes much to Hosea in particular). There is in fact no valid reason to doubt that many of the poetic oracles, together with much of the rest of the collection, do date back to Jeremiah himself. Probably this data was then edited by the

'Deuteronomists' - Jewish scholars at work in Babylonia during the Exile.

Some scholars think that the Deuteronomists were responsible not merely for the arrangement of the Book of Jeremiah - which seems to be partly chronological but mostly by topic - but also for generating all the biographical detail about him. Others, however, argue that Jeremiah's secretary Baruch himself recorded this alongside Jeremiah's words, and perhaps compiled two separate accounts, one of each type of material. Only some of the biographical element finished up in the biblical book: namely that which was strictly relevant to Jeremiah's public ministry.

For the purpose of my novel, I have adopted this theory of Baruch's having made two separate collections, one of material which he certainly wished to be made generally available, the other of more personal recollections. I have imagined the Deuteronomistic editors publishing the former as the Book of Jeremiah, and the latter as this novel. (Lest any of my readers be troubled by the notion of prophets or other individuals of this period keeping their own private records, I refer them to 1 Chronicles 29:29-30, where it is claimed that details of David's reign can be found in the records of Samuel, Nathan and Gad.)

Tradition, taking its cue from the Septuagint, Vulgate and Talmud, ascribed the biblical Book of Lamentations to Jeremiah as well. Most scholars now reject this ascription, but the style and subject-matter are strikingly similar to Jeremiah's in many ways, and there are strong linguistic and rhythmic echoes. The author of Lamentations certainly comes across as an eye-witness of the horrors he describes, and it is difficult to imagine who else but Jeremiah could have been moved by them to such eloquence and depth of emotion combined with such profound theological understanding.

The Babylonian Chronicle records the first siege of Jerusalem in 597BC, the deportation of Jehoiachin and his subsequent maintenance, and the appointment of Zedekiah to take his place. (According to Jeremiah chapter 52, Jehoiachin was eventually released from prison and permitted to dine at the Emperor's table for the rest of his life.) Of course, Babylonian documents tell us a great deal about Nebuchadrezzar/ Nebuchadnezzar, in Babylonian Nabu-kudurri-usur ('May the god Nabu protect my succession'). Emperor of Babylonia from 605-562 BC, he was the most distinguished ruler of the Neo-Babylonian (Chaldean) Dynasty founded by his father Nabopolassar in 627. We also possess many inscriptions left behind by Nebuchadrezzar, stressing not so much his remarkable military exploits as his exercise of justice, his moral qualities and religious devotion, and his architectural achievements. His wife was a Median princess, and it is supposedly for her that he built the famous Hanging Gardens, to remind her of the blossom-covered hillsides of her homeland.

Despite the wealth of information we have about the society in which Jeremiah lived, it is not without its puzzles. There are difficulties with chronology, due in part to the differences between Babylonian and Palestinian methods of dating kings' reigns. It is not always easy to establish which system any particular writer, biblical or otherwise, is using at any one time. Confusion is also caused when writers refer to the 'New Year', which may be regarded as having begun either in spring or in autumn. Thus the fall of Jerusalem is variously dated to 587 or 586 BC.

Confusion arises concerning numbers as well as dates. Discrepancies seem to abound regarding the numbers of people taken into exile on the various occasions, and whether they were taken from Jerusalem or from Judah as a whole. It is impossible to tell whether a certain writer is counting only adult males or all individuals regardless of age or sex. I have sought to keep clear of this minefield by avoiding explicit reference to numbers altogether.

There are actually more differences between the various biblical accounts than there are between the Bible record taken as a whole and extra-biblical evidence. For example, in Chronicles, King Manasseh repents spectacularly of his idolatry, whereas in Kings he does not. The two books also seem to disagree about the chronological order of Josiah's reforms. In Chronicles Josiah comes across as very devout from a much earlier age than he does in Kings. But in fact, neither book is primarily interested in chronology. Perhaps the truth is that Josiah did seek to do right from his youth, but was not fully aware of what Adonai required until the Book of the Law was found. This book probably became the core of what is now Deuteronomy. On balance Josiah was certainly one of the 'good kings' of Judah, but 2 Chron. 35:22 shows that he did not always listen to God very closely.

Another puzzle concerns the fate of King Jehoiakim. 2 Kings 24 states that Nebuchadrezzar invaded Judah at some point and that for three years Jehoiakim had to be his vassal, at the end of which time he rebelled. Armed bands from various neighbouring nations were sent against him, but the outcome of their actions is not recorded; of Jehoiakim's death, 24:6 states simply that he died.

In Jeremiah 36:30-31, the prophet predicts that Jehoiakim will be horrifically punished, and that his body will be denied a decent burial.

2 Chron. 36 tells us that Nebuchadrezzar invaded Judah and took Jehoiakim to Babylon in chains, seizing treasures from the Temple at the same time. When Jehoiachin was king, Nebuchadrezzar came again and besieged Jerusalem, and carried Jehoiachin off into exile.

Daniel 1:1 states that in Jehoiakim's third year, Nebuchadrezzar attacked Jerusalem, captured Jehoiakim and some treasure, and took back prisoners including Daniel himself.

I have reconciled these statements as follows.

605BC - After the Battle of Carchemish, Nebuchadrezzar sweeps down through Syria and Palestine into Judah. He attacks Jerusalem and demands the surrender of Jehoiakim, the handing over of Temple treasures, and the tendering of aristocratic youths to act as hostages to ensure Judah's good behaviour. The treasure and hostages are supplied as demanded, but the King is not given up. The pro-Babylonian party ultimately succeed in kidnapping him, and throw him into chains ready for handing over, but

Nebuchadrezzar is unexpectedly recalled to Babylon, to claim the throne upon his father's death. Jehoiakim is released, and his kidnappers are executed.

604BC - Nebuchadrezzar returns to Judah. He demands Judah's formal vassalage. After initial reluctance, Jehoiakim agrees to tender submission, and is therefore left in possession of his throne. The three year period of vassalage begins.

601BC - Jehoiakim rebels, by withholding annual tribute. Nebuchadrezzar does not have the resources to march against him immediately, so he induces neighbouring nations to act on his behalf.

598BC - The Babylonians themselves come and lay siege to Jerusalem. Jehoiakim dies just before they arrive; his body is surrendered to the enemy, who treat it with flagrant disrespect, then Jehoiachin is enthroned. The first phase of the Exile begins, in 597, when Jehoiachin and a number of prominent citizens are deported.

None of the sources tell us in which year Gedaliah, the man appointed to govern Judah after the demise of Zedekiah in 587, met his untimely end. We are only told the month, which was later commemorated in an annual Jewish fast. I have chosen to regard the death as having taken place in the same year as Gedaliah's appointment, on the assumption that the text would make it clearer if this were not the case, and also because it seems that at the time of Gedaliah's death there were still shortages of some types of food, caused by the Babylonian depredations. We do not know who followed Gedaliah in office, or how the province was then governed. Some time after 582 it seems to have been swallowed up in the province of Samaria; Judah as such ceased to exist.

Archaeology has shed plenty of light upon Jeremiah's story, and provided us with some fascinating glimpses into his world[1]. Regarding the siege of Jerusalem, evidence has been found of the fighting and the subsequent destruction of much of the city. Babylonian arrowheads have been recovered from the ruins, and visitors can still see the blackened remains of burnt-out houses, charred beams and furniture. We also have evidence that Lachish was set on fire at this period, and many towns and villages of Judah ceased to be inhabited. Babylonian seals have been found in the vicinity of Mizpah and Gibeon, and there are clear signs of the Edomite occupation of southern Judah after 587. The 'high place' at Arad has supplied ample evidence of the kind of worship which took place outside of Jerusalem during the latter days of the Judean kingdom; the sanctuary seems to have continued in use in defiance of Josiah's demands for centralization.

The famous 'Lachish Letters' constitute a poignant echo from the last days of Judah. Written on ostraca found between the inner and outer gates of the city in a layer of ash created by the burning of the city by the Babylonians, they seem to have come from the commander of a small outpost located between Lachish and Azekah, the last two cities to have held out against the enemy apart from the capital itself. The commander tells his superior at Lachish that he is awaiting a signal from him, because none are now coming from Azekah. Another ostracon complains of low morale among the defenders, exacerbated by defeatist words spoken in influential circles - a reference to the teaching of Jeremiah? The letters also mention one Coniah ben Elnathan, Commander of the Host, who visited Lachish on his way to Egypt to seek military assistance from the Pharaoh.

Interesting personal effects have also been found at Lachish. Most notable is a seal-impression bearing the name of one Berechiah (Berekhyahu), and this Berechiah's father has the same name as the father of Jeremiah's scribe. Another seal-impression says: 'Belonging to Gedaliah who is over the house.' One artefact which has never been found is the Ark of the Covenant. In the Bible it is not listed among the precious objects which the Babylonians stole from the Temple. It has been suggested that it had already been removed, perhaps by devout priests during the idolatrous reign of Manasseh; in 2 Chron. 35:3 Josiah gives instructions that it should be put back, but we are not told whether this order was carried out. It is popularly believed that the Ark was taken, via the Jewish community at Elephantine in Egypt, to Axum in Ethiopia where it now resides[2]. We do not know for sure when the colony at Elephantine was founded, but it was certainly well established by 525BC when Egypt was conquered by the Persians. We do know that the colony had its own temple, built as a replica of Solomon's. Was its purpose to house the Ark? If the Ethiopians do now possess it, their religious authorities are no more willing for ordinary mortals to gaze upon it than were the high priests of old, and so its location can no more be verified than it could in the days of Jeremiah.

To sum up our brief survey of the literary and archaeological evidence relating to Jeremiah's life: there is no reason for us to be any more suspicious of historical information presented in the Bible than we are of material gleaned from other ancient literary sources. Indeed, secular historians seem more willing to trust the Bible as a reliable primary source than theologians are.

So wherein does Jeremiah's greatness lie? Certainly not in his uncompromising dedication to God; the biblical Book of Jeremiah shows him questioning, rebelling, fighting every step of the way. He was introspective, ultra-sensitive, assailed by crippling self-doubt, and subject to violent mood-swings. The passages known as the 'Confessions of Jeremiah' are unique in prophetic literature for the anguish and bitter spiritual struggling which they reveal. These days he would probably have been diagnosed as manic depressive or even schizophrenic; the prophetic personality and that of the madman are very closely related. I recall hearing in a television programme about a girl who 'sang and danced with angels'; she was quite happy with this aspect of her life, and posed no danger to herself or to anyone else, but was diagnosed as delusional and forced to take medication. She claimed that the drugs killed her angels, and in the end she committed suicide, preferring to face death herself than carry on living without them.

Jeremiah does seem to have known himself to be special from an early age, claiming that his relationship with God began even before birth (Jer.1:5)[3]. Although Jeremiah frequently sought to reject his calling (20:9a), he found himself spiritually and even physically unable to do so (20:9b) and wound up wishing he had never been born at all (20:14-18), because the vocation he could not escape was gradually tearing him apart.

His greatness no more lies in his visionary experiences than it does in his commitment to his ministry. There is nothing in Jeremiah to compare with the call vision - or the subsequent visions - of Isaiah, or of Ezekiel, Jeremiah's younger but very different contemporary. Perhaps his lack of such dramatic experiences contributed to his sense of personal inadequacy, of being unfit for the task to which God had assigned him.

Nor does his greatness lie in his capacity to forgive. Like Jesus, he prayed for the wicked, and for his own enemies - but Jeremiah prayed for their destruction, not for their redemption (cf.12:3, 18:23). Being thin-skinned and unsure of himself, criticism and opposition seriously undermined his confidence. He longed for love and affection, yet was shunned and hated; he loved his people, yet was branded a traitor.

So why *is* Jeremiah regarded by many as the greatest of all the prophets?

Partly it is because of his astonishing theological perception. He was very possibly the first person to appreciate that religion must pass away in order to make room for God. There can be no place for empty ritual, hierarchical power struggles, or violence between sects and creeds in the lives of spiritual people. Jeremiah predicted and indeed looked forward to a 'post-Temple' society. During the Exile in Babylon, this was precisely what Judaism was going to have to become.

The significance of the Exile cannot be overestimated in the development of Judaism. The covenant between God and Israel had been tied up, inextricably it seemed, with the Promised Land, the City of Jerusalem, the Temple and the Davidic Dynasty. All these were lost at a stroke, and it was Jeremiah who saw that the Jewish faith and identity could not only survive without them, but would be better served. The reliance on externals would have to give way to true spirituality, an inner experience, a relationship between the individual and God, yet with that individual remaining a member of a distinct covenant community.

However, I am inclined to agree with those who argue that mainstream Judaism ultimately strayed away from this ideal in basing itself exclusively upon codes of law rather than upon genuine spiritual experience. Only in Jesus Christ did Jeremiah's vision come to fruition, because only through Jesus' death and resurrection can hearts truly be changed and the new covenant which Jeremiah predicted be established.

Indeed, Jeremiah has been regarded as prefiguring Jesus himself, for there are many parallels between them. Jeremiah is often called 'The Weeping Prophet' or 'The Prophet of the Broken Heart'; Jesus was the 'Man of Sorrows'. Both condemned social injustice, speaking up for the poor and the oppressed; both wept over the sins of Jerusalem, and foretold its destruction. Both were reviled and misunderstood, incurring the wrath of the civil and religious authorities and undergoing torture at their hands. Herein lies a clue to another aspect of Jeremiah's greatness: his transfigured humanity. He shared all of our faults and weaknesses, yet he succeeded in achieving what God had called him to do, even when that success looked to him like failure. He is someone with whom we can all identify, but by whom we can be inspired to speak out for truth and justice regardless of the consequences, and to live in honest fellowship with our Creator.

Jeremiah has also been hailed as a great poet. Most - if not all - of his oracles seem to have been delivered in poetic form, as were those of the other Hebrew prophets. The consensus among Christian Old Testament scholars is that the canonical prophets, unlike their predecessors, did not deliver their messages 'ecstatically' because the poetry was too well crafted; they may have received their oracles in some trance-like state, but they must then have sat down and recast them in poetic form. However, the American psychologist Julian Jaynes in his book 'The Origin of Consciousness in the Breakdown of the Bicameral Mind'[4] argues that ecstatic utterance, in whatever culture it has appeared, has generally been in metrical poetry. In its early days the Delphic oracle spoke metrically, and when in its later phase priests were employed to translate the Pythia's words into dactylic hexameters, this was due to a nostalgia for the metrical verse which had previously been the norm. The Roman historian Tacitus, describing a visit to the oracle of Apollo at Claros at the end of the first century AD, explains how the entranced priest 'swallows a draught of water from a sacred spring and - though generally illiterate and ignorant of meters - delivers his response in verse'. Even today, in cultures familiar with instances of 'spontaneous possession', the utterances are frequently metrical, and Christian glossolalia is often dactylic in rhythm. These phenomena are perhaps caused by the fact that poetry, music and divine speech are associated with the right hemisphere of the brain, whereas rational speech comes from the left. I would recommend Jaynes' book, startlingly offbeat though it is, to anyone interested in the psychology of prophecy. Equally worth reading on this subject is Gerhard von Rad[5].

Certainly Jeremiah's poetry is extraordinarily powerful. So moving are his verses that we begin to glean some inkling of what it must be like to 'feel the feelings of God', for this is as much a part of the prophet's role as is the speaking of God's words.

But perhaps the greatest thing about Jeremiah's poetry, and about Jeremiah himself, is that his predictions came true; in Deuteronomy, this is the acid test of any prophet's authenticity (Deut.18:21-22). Jerusalem fell, and the people of Judah were taken into exile, precisely as he had foretold.

But we have yet to witness the apocalypse graphically described in Jeremiah 4:23-26. Likewise, we have yet to experience the joyous consummation of God's designs, of which Jeremiah 31 paints a spectacular picture.

---

[1] See Philip J. King: 'Jeremiah - An Archaeological Companion', Westminster/John Knox Press 1993.

[2] See Graham Hancock: 'The Sign and the Seal - A Quest for the Lost Ark of the Covenant', B.C.A. 1992.

[3] To 'know' in this sense means in Hebrew to 'be intimate with'. Regarding this intimacy, there is a rabbinic legend that the 'Shekinah' (glory/presence) of Adonai - which the rabbis saw as the feminine aspect of the Godhead ('ruah'/spirit is also a feminine noun in Hebrew) - became the spouse of Moses in place of Zipporah after her death. It accompanied him and filled him with secret joy. When he died, the Shekinah bent and kissed him, and on this kiss his soul travelled to Heaven. Although the term 'Shekinah' in this sense does not occur in the Jewish Bible, the concept originates there, and is frequently alluded to in the New Testament. Jeremiah was commanded not to marry in the first place and in many ways his ministry reflects that of Moses; eg. his reluctant acceptance of his calling; the ingratitude of the people among whom he ministered; the seeming fruitlessness of his labours. Both are tragic figures, not because God abandons them, as he did with Saul, but precisely because he does not. God seizes them and then pushes them to the uttermost limits of their endurance.

[4] Julian Jaynes: 'The Origin of Consciousness in the Breakdown of the Bicameral Mind' - latest edition published in Great Britain by Penguin, 1993.

[5] Gerhard von Rad: 'The Message of the Prophets', SCM 1968.

DRAMATIS PERSONAE

Jeremiah, son of a priest at the sanctuary of Anathoth.

Hanamel, cousin of Jeremiah, son of Jeremiah's uncle Shallum.

Hilkiah(1), Jeremiah's father, a priest at Anathoth.

Simeon, aged colleague of Hilkiah at the Anathoth sanctuary.

Jedidah, wife of King Amon of Judah.

Josiah, son of Jedidah and Amon; Prince, later King, of Judah.

Zephaniah(1), prophet of Adonai, maintained at the royal court by Jedidah.

Ruth, granddaughter of a blind beggar-woman of Anathoth.

Hannah, wife of Simeon the priest.

Asaiah, personal attendant of Josiah.

Zebidah, Josiah's first wife.

Johanan(1), elder son of Josiah, by Zebidah. Also known as Hanan.

Eliakim, second son of Josiah by Zebidah. Also known as Eli. Throne name Jehoiakim.

Hamutal, Josiah's second wife.

Shelemaiah(1), son of Josiah by Hamutal. Also known as Shallum.

Hilkiah(2), High Priest in Jerusalem, under Josiah.

Shaphan, Secretary of State (Court Secretary/Scribe) under Josiah.

Ahikam, son of Shaphan; Royal Steward and adviser to Josiah.

Gemariah(1), Elasah, Jaazaniah, others sons of Shaphan; brothers to Ahikam.

Gedaliah(1), son of Ahikam, later Zedekiah's Steward, then Governor of Judah.

Joah, Royal Recorder under Josiah.

Maaseiah, Governor ('Mayor') of Jerusalem under Josiah.

Akbor, adviser to Josiah.

Elnathan, son of Akbor, another adviser to Josiah.

Shallum, Keeper of the Royal Wardrobe.

Huldah, wife of Shallum, and a prophetess at Josiah's Court.

Ebed-Melech, eunuch slave at Josiah's palace in Jerusalem.

Mattaniah, second son of Josiah by Hamutal. Throne name Zedekiah(1).

Nahum, a prophet of Judah from Elkosh.

Nehushta, daughter of Elnathan; later, wife of Eliakim.

Jeconiah, son of Eliakim and Nehushta. Also known as Coniah. Throne name Jehoiachin.

Habbakuk, a young visionary.

Necho, Pharaoh of Egypt 610-595 BC.

Elishama, Secretary of State under Jehoiakim. A man of royal blood in his own right; his grandson Ishmael later becomes a pretender to the throne of Judah.

Delaiah, Royal Steward under Jehoiakim.

Zedekiah(2) ben Hananiah, Royal Recorder under Jehoiakim.

Pashhur(1), Deputy High Priest under Jehoiakim, responsible for maintenance of law and order in the Temple precincts. Also known as Chief Officer of the Temple.

Berechiah ben Neraiah (Baruch), scribe who becomes Jeremiah's secretary.

Seraiah(1), Berechiah's brother, also a scribe. Later Royal Recorder under Zedekiah.

Nebuchadrezzar, son of Nabopolassar; Crown Prince, later Emperor, of Babylon.

Micaiah, son of Gemariah(1) and grandson of Shaphan.

Jehudi, messenger to the Royal Council under Jehoiakim.

Jerahmeel, Seraiah(2) ben Azriel, Shelemaiah(2) ben Abdeel, three of Jehoiakim's courtiers.

Naomi, wife of Seraiah(1), and sister-in-law of Berechiah.

Nabuzaradan, Captain of Nebuchadrezzar's personal guard.

Seraiah(3) ben Azariah, High Priest under Zedekiah.

Hananiah, a court prophet under Zedekiah.

Jonathan(1), Secretary of State under Zedekiah.

Zephaniah(2), son of Maaseiah. Deputy High Priest/Chief Officer of the Temple, under Zedekiah.

Gemariah(2) ben Hilkiah, Pelatiah ben Benaiah, Gedaliah(2) ben Pashhur, Pashhur(2) ben Malciah, Jehucal ben Shelemaiah, other members of Zedekiah's Royal Council (which also includes Elasah and Jaazaniah, sons of Shaphan, Gedaliah son of Ahikam, and Seraiah(1)).

Coniah, son of Elnathan, Commander of the Host under Zedekiah.

Psamtik II, Pharaoh of Egypt 595-589 BC.

Hophra, Pharaoh 589-570 BC.

Irijah, Officer of the Guard at the Benjamin Gate of Jerusalem.

Nergal-Sharezar, Commander of Nebuchadrezzar's frontier troops.

Nebushazbal, Chamberlain/Grand Vizier of Nebuchadrezzar.

Johanan(2) ben Kareah, an officer in Coniah's army.

Jonathan(2), brother of Johanan(2).

Ishmael ben Nethaniah, grandson of Elishama. Another officer in Coniah's army, and later pretender to Judah's throne.

Azariah ben Hoshaiah, Seraiah(3) ben Tanhumeth, Jezaniah the Maacathite, the sons of Ephai, other officers in Coniah's army.

Joseph, the Redactor.